The Nāsiketa Story

The Nāsiketa Story

(Nāsiketopākhyāna)

Edited & Translated by

AMOS NEVO

MOTILAL BANARSIDASS PUBLISHERS
PRIVATE LIMITED • DELHI

First Indian Edition: Delhi, ***2010***
Earlier published by Xilbris Corporation, USA, 2009

ISBN: 978-81-208-3483-5

MOTILAL BANARSIDASS
41 U.A. Bungalow Road, Jawahar Nagar, Delhi 110 007
8 Mahalaxmi Chamber, 22 Bhulabhai Desai Road, Mumbai 400 026
203 Royapettah High Road, Mylapore, Chennai 600 004
236, 9th Main III Block, Jayanagar, Bangalore 560 011
Sanas Plaza, 1302 Baji Rao Road, Pune 411 002
8 Camac Street, Kolkata 700 017
Ashok Rajpath, Patna 800 004
Chowk, Varanasi 221 001

Printed in India
By Jainendra Prakash Jain at Shri Jainendra Press,
A-45 Naraina, Phase-I, New Delhi 110 028
and Published by Narendra Prakash Jain for
Motilal Banarsidass Publishers Private Limited,
Bungalow Road, Delhi 110 007

CONTENTS

I dedicate this book to my beloved family –

my wife Nava

and my children – Eran, Yuval and Yael.

Preface

This book is the outcome of my long-term relationship with Naciketas. I first encountered Naciketas in the early 1960's, in Dr. T. Gelblum's course about **Kaṭhopaniṣad**, at the Hebrew University of Jerusalem. I was so intrigued by his story, that over the next 30 years I repeatedly returned to it. In 1994 I decided to write a thesis about the educational implications of **Kaṭhopaniṣad**, and then a Ph.D. dissertation on Naciketas.

Naciketas is the human hero of the **Kaṭhopaniṣad** story. The narrative serves as the framework for presenting a new philosophic message, the idea of "Mokṣa", liberation, achieved by spiritual efforts – by "Knowledge". Naciketas is a very attractive young boy. Seized with a sudden enigmatic spirit of faith – *śraddhā*, he confronts his father, trying to save him from the disastrous results of what he considers an erroneous sacrifice. When his father curses him to death, he obediently goes to meet Yama – the Lord of Death. Naciketas is easily sympathized with, conceived as the innocent victim of his father's excessive rage. He is attractive also because of his strong personality – as a young child he resists Yama's temptations, relinquishing the world's most desirable pleasures, for the sake of spiritual Knowledge – a model for any seeker of absolute Truth.

Naciketas' character has undergone many changes in the various versions of the story, and so has my attitude towards him. While examining all aspects of Naciketas' behaviour in the different scriptures, my initial fascinated attraction to the poor heroic child, has become a more balanced attitude. In the later versions Naciketas is no more a seeker of spiritual Truth, but rather the representative of Dharma, reporting his experiences in Yama's realm. Moreover, in **Varāha Purāṇa**, and even more so in **Nāsiketopākhyāna**, Naciketas' conduct towards his father is portrayed in a way that may arouse a doubt as to his total innocence in the curse scene[1]. Nevertheless, the story remains fantastic and fascinating, attractive to Hindus and non-Hindus alike, to modern scholars[2] and artists[3], as well as to common people.

---

1 Nevo (2005).

2 The most recent study that I have come across is Filippi (2001).

3 The sculptor David Booker, the poet Sehgal, and others.

This presentation of the "**Nāsiketopākhyāna**" is the first academic work dealing comprehensively with all the Sanskrit versions of the Naciketas/Nāsiketa story, and the first translation into English of a critically edited text, based on several manuscripts and printed versions.

Acknowledgements

I am most indebted to two scholars, without whose help I could not have accomplished the task:

Prof. David Shulman, my tutor from the Hebrew University of Jerusalem, guided me all along the process of writing my dissertation. He read and reread the Sanskrit text, helping to emend and reshape it.

Dr. Nirmala Kulkarni, from Pune University, helped me a great deal with the initial deciphering of the text and with forming a primary reasonable version of it. I shall always cherish her kindness and ever readiness to assist, whenever needed.

Despite Prof. Shulman's and Dr. Kulkarni's help, I am fully responsible for any remaining mistakes.

Many more people have helped me, and it is impossible to mention and thank all of them. However, I would like to express my gratitude to a few more people who helped me in different ways, at various stages of my research:

Dr. R. P. Goswami, former librarian of the Pune University Sanskrit library – a true Sanskrit scholar, whose advice and friendship I highly appreciate.

Mrs. Tilaka Joseph, senior library assistant, University of Mumbai library, who was always kind and willing to help with my search in Mumbai.

Dr. R. K. Trivedi, University of Jabalpur Sanskrit department, who accompanied me in my efforts to locate relevant manuscripts in the Jabalpur area.

Mr. D. H. Mishra, in charge of the manuscripts collection at the Sanskrit University of Varanasi, who assisted me in locating the needed manuscripts, and then spent hours with his staff (even after official work-hours), photocopying them.

Prof. S. Y. Wakankar, Research Officer at the Oriental Institute of Vadodara, who kindly helped me locate the manuscripts in the institute collection.

Mr. B. Pandya, manager of the Jamnagar President Hotel, who offered his assistance in various ways, locating people who might have had any information as to the whereabouts of the lost manuscript collection of Suryaśaṅkar Tulyaśaṅkar Śāstri, from Jodhiya.

Mr. David Booker, sculptor, who kindly provided me with photos of his sculpture Naciketas, used for the book cover.

Dr. Itamar Theodor from the Haifa University, who helped me trace the source of the verses extracted from the Bhāgavata Purāṇa, cited in appendix I.

Mrs. Vivienne Burstein, who edited the English text translation.

Last but not least, I am most obliged to my wife, Nava, for her constructive comments on the non-textual parts of the book.

Introduction

The Story Features and Themes

This is the first critical edition of one developmental branch of the Nāsiketa story – **Nāsiketopākhyāna** – based on several manuscripts and printed texts. It is also the first translation of a full Sanskrit version of the story into English[1]. The introduction is a general examination of the Naciketas/Nāsiketa story scriptures[2], leaving a large scope for further detailed analysis of the story, from various different aspects.

Previously, the literary figure of Naciketas has been extensively dealt with in the context of **Kaṭhopaniṣad**, and only a few studies have been dedicated exclusively to the story of Naciketas, focusing on Naciketas' name[3], Naciketas as the seeker of knowledge[4], etc. Most studies deal with one or two scriptural sources, and only a few briefly refer to all the scriptural occurrences of the story[5].

The **Nāsiketopākhyāna** is a late version of the well known Vedic story of Naciketas, partly based on the **Varāha Purāṇa** version. It is more elaborated than its preceding Purāṇic version, with additional fantastic and dramatic elements that render it attractive to listeners and readers. All the previous versions, including **Varāha Purāṇa**, start with the death curse scene. Nāsiketa's history prior to that scene is the most unique additional characteristic feature of the Nāsiketa story. Nāsiketa's father is more elaborately portrayed, and a mother figure – Candravatī – is added, rendering the ancient dyadic myth

---

1 There is a curtailed translation into Italian - Belloni-Filippi (1902-4), and the existing English translations are from other Indian languages: Nāsiket Ākhyan (1892) translated from Hindi, and a translation from Rājasthāni (Krause 1924).

2 It encompasses the Sanskrit versions of the Naciketa story, excluding the Prakrit versions. It also excludes modern works like Naciketasaṁ (Ghimire, 1975), Amṛta Manthanaṁ Mahākāvyaṁ (S.S.P. Sharma), Brahmarishi Nachiketas (V. S. M Iyer, 1981), and others.

3 Wadhawani (1972, 1973).

4 Ramaswami (1966).

5 Belloni-Filippi (1902-4), Upadhyaya (1964), Panda (1998).

into triadic – more compatible with traditional myths[6]. There are other new figures, like Candravatī's father - King Raghu – and his consort, the sages Yājñavalkya and Nārada, etc., all enriching the story with more episodes, and more Dharmic messages.

The myth describes a **fantastic** ancient period when human beings could communicate directly with Gods, like for example, the scene of Uddālaka, Nāsiketa's father, discussing the issue of progeny with Prajāpati[7] (1.43-9). The most legendary fantastic element is no doubt, Nāsiketa's immaculate conception through his mother's nose (2.22a), and then his birth through the nose (3.23a), all following Prajāpati's enigmatic prophecy to Uddālaka – "First will a son arrive, and then there will be a wife"[8]. Other fantastic elements are, for example, Nāsiketa's ability to speak as a newly born baby (3.24-5); when sent away as a baby by his mother, his grass "boat" goes upstream, instead of drifting naturally downstream (3.35); his return alive from the realm of the dead, etc.

Nāsiketa's visit in the realm of the dead and his safe return, are both fantastic and most **dramatic.** There are many other dramatic elements in the story, for example, Candravatī's expulsion from the palace by her father[9], her desertion in a desolate forest (2.43-4), and her rescue by Yājñavalkya; Candravatī's sending Nāsiketa in the river to be found by his father; the meeting between Candravatī and Nāsiketa after years of separation; the meeting of Candravatī and Uddālaka; Candravatī's reconciliation with her father, and her marriage to Uddālaka; etc.

A close examination reveals **ironic** elements too, like Uddālaka's description as – ". . . the master of anger, subjugator of the senses"[10], while losing his control and his great anger towards Nāsiketa are the causes of all the ensuing events.

The ancient Naciketa story has incited the imagination of Hindu writers for many generations, and it serves as means for conveying religious,

---

6 Lévi-Strauss (Chicago, 1983), vol. II, p. 72.

7 Brahma, his own father.

8 *prathamaṁ putrasaṁprāptiḥ paścād bhāryā bhaviṣyati* - 1.46b.

9 Compare to the Greek mythology story of King Acrisius expelling his daughter Danaë and her immaculately born baby Perseus.

10 *jitakrodho jitendriyaḥ* - 1.43b.

philosophical and social ideas. This introduction examines the various versions of the story, referring to their formal and thematic features, offering an integrated perspective of the story as representing basic issues in the Hindu tradition.

A. The Story Patterns

Naciketas is a young boy, who, after being cursed to death by his father, goes to the realm of the dead, meets Yama the God of Death, and returns alive to Earth having acquired new knowledge.

These are the basic features common to all the versions of the story, enabling us to recognize the story in versions remote from the original Vedic story, and to disallow it in others. The story first appears in **Taittirīya Brāhmaṇa** III.11.8, but, following Sāyaṇa, there are commentators[11] who identify a more ancient paragraph in the scriptures—**Ṛgveda** X.135—as the first allusion to the story. The Ṛgvedic story of an anonymous boy conversing with Yama lacks most of the above basic features, and is therefore excluded here from the Naciketa lore.

The next, most important and popular version of the story is **Kaṭhopaniṣad**, where Naciketas is the main human hero. Two other versions are known in the *smṛti* scriptures – **Mahābhārata** XIII.60[12] and **Varāha Purāṇa** II.193-212[13]. Later, the story develops into the Nāsiketa Story – **Nāsiketopākhyāna** – of which most Sanskrit versions are still in manuscript form[14], and only a few have been printed[15].

Scholars have usually dealt disjointedly with **Kaṭhopaniṣad** and other versions, while here, using formal criteria rather than thematic, the whole corpus has been divided into three main story patterns, each having its unique characteristics:

---

11 Oldenberg (1912), p. 351/2; Śarvananda (1962), p. iii/iv; Pelly (1924), p. 5; Coomaraswami (1938), p. 49f; Easwaran (1987), p. 98.

12 SR - Southern recension (1935).

13 S.V. Iyer (1985), or Gupta (1981) - II.191-210.

14 The MSS are registered in the New Catalogus Catalogorum (Raja, 1997/8). See also appendix II.

15 Belloni-filippi (1902-4); Nāsiketagrantha (1930); Nāsiketopākhyāna (1945).

1. The Vedic pattern.
2. The Itihhāsa-Purāṇa pattern.
3. The Nāsiketa Story pattern.

The **Vedic** pattern includes the Brāhmaṇa and Upaniṣad versions. They differ in length, language, rhythm and rhyme, representing different concepts and aiming at different goals. Nevertheless, they pertain to the same story pattern, since the narrative in both texts is similar. In addition to the above basic features, the paternal curse occurs during a sacrificial ritual, and Yama, as a householder, hosts Naciketas at his home and grants him three boons.

The **Itihhāsa-Purāṇa** pattern consists of the **Mahābhārata** and **Varāha Purāṇa** versions. The narratives of both texts, in addition to the basic features, have the following unique characteristics:

1. The Vedic sacrifice scene and the three boons are missing.
2. While the narrator of the Vedic pattern is anonymous, a known narrator is mentioned here – Sūta and Vaiśampāyana in **Varāha Purāṇa**, and a whole chain of delivery in the **Mahābhārata,** ending with Bhīṣma telling the story to Yudhiṣṭhira.
3. Naciketas' father is clearly presented as a sage.
4. Yama hosts Naciketas as king of the dead, rather than as a householder.
5. The main additional characteristic feature of this pattern is the hero's extensive guided tour in Yama's kingdom.

The **Nāsiketa story** pattern is comprised of scores of versions, representing different developmental branches of the story, the vast majority of which are hardly known to the Indological community. It is an extension of the Purāṇic version – the guided tour in Hell generally matches the equivalent parts in the Purāṇic text, Uddālaka is a known sage, and here also the main narrator is Sūta, while Vaiśampāyana is telling the story to King Janamejaya. The main additional unique characteristic is Nāsiketa's fantastic early history, prior to the curse scene. A further unique and important element is the theological debate between Nāsiketa and his father, as the catalyst of the father's rage.

B. Thematic Features

Three main universal components of the mythic narrative may explain why and how it has survived throughout the ages:

1. The character of **Knowledge.**
2. The enigma of **Death.**
3. The **father-son** relations.

The narrators and writers of the story at all times, made use of these basic universal elements as a means for conveying their different, and sometimes contradictory, religious, social and philosophical ideas. The tension between two principal ideas in Hinduism – "Dharma" and "Mokṣa"[16] – can be detected in almost all the story patterns. In most cases it is implicit, but it becomes explicit and reaches its climax in the debate scene of the Nāsiketa story.

1. The Character of Knowledge

The knowledge conveyed by the various versions of the Naciketa story is twofold – both philosophical-theoretical and practical:

A. The **Kaṭhopaniṣad** philosophical "Yama Doctrine" – the identity of Ātman/Brahman (*brahmavidyā*), the realization of which brings Liberation.
B. Sacrificial knowledge in **Taittirīya Brāhmaṇa** (and **Kaṭhopaniṣad**) – mainly the "Naciketa Fire" (*nāciketāgni*[17]).
C. The practice of Dharma, and especially of cow gifts (*godāna*) to the priests, in the **Mahābhārata**.
D. Devotion to Viṣṇu and adhering to the norms of the multifaceted Dharma, in **Varāha Purāṇa** and **Nāsiketopākhyāna**.

A) Philosophical-theoretical Knowledge

Kaṭhopaniṣad promotes "Mokṣa" – liberation – by Knowledge of the Absolute – "knowing"[18] Brahman. It is a relatively new spiritual idea of reality, developed

---

16 Zaehner (1969), pp. 84/5, 126. Biardeau and Malamoud claim that these opposed polar ideas, mutually attracted, have both contributed to the formation of Hinduism, and cannot be conceived separately: "Ces deux aspects, qui ont contribué à former l'hindouisme, sont comme deux pôles qui ont subi une attraction mutuelle et qu'il est impossible de concevoir séparément" (Biardeau et Malamoud (1976), p. 65).

17 See also *trināciketāgni* - KU/1.15.

18 The semantic and epistemological issues at the stage of "Mokṣa" - when the distinction between "knower" and "known" disappears, as well as all other distinctions - are excluded from this study.

in the Upaniṣads[19] in the middle of the first millennium B.C., undermining the monopoly of Brahmins over Knowledge. Naciketas is an archetypal student striving for spiritual knowledge, whom the most tempting material offers of Yama cannot deter from his goal[20]. I consider the philosophical ideas of **Kaṭhopaniṣad**, as the most important knowledge communicated by the Naciketa story. It is quite surprising that there is no known extension of this philosophical trend in later versions of the story, and I assume that such scriptures must have existed and have been lost. My assumption is based on logical conjectures and on a few hints in the scriptures:

- The narrative suggests that Naciketas must have grown up as an important sage. Having been resurrected from death and having learnt directly from the Lord of Death, he must have been more knowledgeable than any other sage.
- The sage Naciketas is a guest at the inauguration of the Sabha – **Mahābhārata**, SR.II.4.23.
- Naciketas is the source of Yama Gitā – **Agni Purāṇa**, 382.1.
- Naciketas is one of the eleven founders of the *puṇyatīrtha* - **Brahma Purāṇa**, 4.1.28.

I have made numerous efforts to find the lost manuscripts of the "Naciketa *Smṛti*", and collected as many manuscripts of the Nāsiketa story as possible[21] Though I ended up with no positive results, I believe that the presumably lost scriptures may still be found.

B) Practical knowledge

All other versions of the story promote practical knowledge, which is here referred to as "Dharma" – sacrificial practice, moral behaviour, devotion to Viṣṇu, etc.

The Naciketa story in **Taittirīya Brāhmaṇa** is an etiological text explaining the origin of the Naciketa Fire sacrifice name – *"nāciketāgni"*. Its context, chapter III of the **Brāhmaṇa,** is dedicated to various sacrificial practices, including the technique of the Naciketa fire[22].

---

19 The first signs of the idea appear earlier in the Ṛgveda.

20 KU/I.2.4.

21 See appendix 2.

22 Elaborated description - Pelly, p. 28, n. 2.

In the **Mahābhārata** version, one of Bhīṣma's answers to Yudhiṣṭhira's question about the best means for liberation is the need of granting gifts – especially cow gifts (*godāna*) – to Brahmin priests, promising purity of mind[23], and eternal good life in Heaven[24].

The principal knowledge that Nāciketa/Nāsiketa brings back from Death in the **Varāha Purāṇa** and the Nāsiketa story versions, is the need for devotion to Viṣṇu, as well as the benefit of behaving according to the rules of Dharma. The hero's experience in the realm of Death, authoritative in and of its own, is enhanced by frightening descriptions of the horrible punishments awaiting the sinners in Hell, and by (fewer) promises of pleasures awaiting the righteous in Heaven.

2. Solutions for the Enigma of Death

The story versions of the premature death of Naciketas, and his fantastic return to Earth, reflect the different attitudes of Hindus towards death, and their different solutions to thanatophobia. The option of resurrection – returning (immediately) to the world in the same material body – suggested by the Naciketa story, is a rare solution in Hinduism[25]. Three other main alternatives for coping with Death are presented by the story:

- The Vedic solution of life after death – the two paths: "the ancestors' way" (*pitṛyāna*) and "the way of the gods" (*devayāna*).
- The Saṁsāra-Karma doctrine.
- The total denial of death.

These characteristic solutions stem from different and contradictory conceptions of reality, yet they are all integrated in the Hindu faith. In the Naciketa story they are sometimes intermingled in the same story pattern, and even in the same text.

The first two solutions represent a **dualistic** conception of the universe, mainly expressed by terms like "body and soul", "this world and the Hereafter", etc. Since Vedic times, it is believed that when a man dies, he

23 For example - SR/13.60.44.

24 For example - SR/13.60.47.

25 Compare with the story of *Sāvitrī* - SR/3.248-254.

leaves behind his material body (*liṅgaśarīra*), and his soul (*preta*) goes on living in a subtle body (*sukṣmaśarīra*), either in Heaven (*svargaloka*)[26] or in Hell (*naraka*)[27]. The dead man's son has a most important role in the *Śrāddha* rites for the deceased, guaranteeing the father's soul future existence in Heaven[28]. Thus, by causing his only son's death, Naciketas' father ruins his own prospects for life after death, as stated by himself in **Varāha Purāṇa** (191.23-4)[29]:

> "*Having thus destroyed the line of my family, I would also perish, censured by everyone as a miscreant wretch. The hell termed as 'Puta' is known to be a painful hell. The man who has a son is exempt from that hell. So do all men desire for a son for their welfare in this world and the next*".

Saṁsāra - transmigration of souls – though mentioned in **Kaṭhopaniṣad**[30] – is not yet developed as a systematic theory in the Vedic pattern. The idea of man's fate, integrating the Saṁsāra and Karma doctrines, combined with man's fate in Heaven and Hell, is fully developed in the Itihhāsa-Purāṇa pattern, as the main solution to the enigma of death. One example from **Varāha Purāṇa** is the following fate of an extreme sinner (200.39-40)[31]:

> "*Let this greedy and extremely roguish one who had indulged in arson, be burnt in firewood (in Hell – A.N.), till his misdeeds are worn away. Thereafter would he be born as blind of one eye. Immediately after being released from that state, he would be born as a worm suffering from intense pain. Thereafter he would be a dog or a beast and then a human being again*".

---

26 "Heaven" - *Svarga loka* (TB/III.11.8.5a, KU/1.12, 1.13, 1.18) - is identical to *pitṛloka* - "the world of manes" (Atharva Veda - 18.4.64) - Filippi (1996), p. 199. See also - KU/6.5.

27 The idea of Hell is mentioned in the Vedic scriptures, but it becomes fully developed in the Itihāsa-Purāṇa literature. See for example, in addition to the descriptions of Hell and its punishments, also the names of the hell-quarters. **Varāha Purāṇa,** 198.1-2, and in our text - 7.44-5.

28 See details - Merh (1996), pp. 129-166.

29 Gupta (1981), p. 860.

30 KU/3.7. See allusions to Karma - KU/1.7, 1.17, 2.6, 4.10-11, 5.7, 6.4.

31 Gupta (1981), p. 905.

The later **Nāsiketopākhyāna** version of the story also conveys the same idea[32].

The **Kaṭhopaniṣad** idea of liberation *(mokṣa)* is the unique solution for the enigma of death in the Naciketa lore, meaning the total denial of death – "Brahman is immortality"[33]. At the liberation stage one transcends all empirical experiences, when the personal Self (*ātman*) recognizes its identity with the universal Self (*brahman*) as infinite Oneness. Having realized his oneness with the Absolute, a man can no longer "die", since all distinctions disappear. The terms "life" and "death" lose their meanings, and language becomes impotent and redundant[34]. This **monistic** conception does not grant death ontological existence, as it denies it for all other empirical distinctions.

There are hints in the text that Naciketas may not be literally dead – for example, Yama's words to Naciketas in the **Mahābhārata**: "You are not dead, O gentle sir"[35]. A doctor writer considers Naciketas alive, describing his condition as similar to coma, but not exactly a coma[36]. Some commentators[37] argue that his death is symbolic, suggesting an initiation theory as a substitute for the ideas of actual killing or sacrificing Naciketas. Most prominent among these is Helfer (1967/8) who reads the Upaniṣadic text as a description of an Adhvaryu priest initiation ceremony. Others consider the story as representing a symbolic initiation, aimed at achieving spiritual knowledge[38]. Naciketas is a literary hero, and I accept his death as literarily real, assuming that it may represent an ancient tradition of human sacrifice[39]. Naciketas' return safely back from the realm of the dead is a

---

32 For example, chapter 18 is entirely dedicated to this solution, counting both the meritorious' and the sinners' fates, in Heaven and Hell, and afterwards their rebirth on Earth, all according to their deeds.

33 *brahma tad evāmṛtam ucyate* - KU/5.8, 6.1.

34 Though this stage cannot be transmitted by words, we have no other alternative but use words to convey the idea.

35 *na mṛto 'si saumya* - Mahābhārata, SR/XIII.60.17. *Saumya* - in vocative - the proper mode of addressing a Brahmin - Manu's law book, II.125 - Monier Williams (1993), p. 1254.

36 Śivaram (1981), p. 23f.

37 Eliade, (1958), p. 118; Eliade, (1977), p. 15; Kaelber, p. 55; Sahi (1980), p. 4.

38 For example - comparing it to the biblical *Aqeda* story - Shulman (1993), p. 125.

39 Rawson (1934), pp. 59f, Nevo (2003), pp. 89f.

miracle, a fantastic feature of the myth, representing a most basic human wish for victory over Death.

3. Father-son relations

The father-son relationship forms one of the main features of the story and plays a crucial role in it[40]. Tradition portrays Naciketas as an obedient and loving son, ready to sacrifice himself in order to save his father from a gloomy fate[41]. Why then does his father curse him to death, making him the innocent victim of his wrath?

The Vedic text is short and vague, leaving the case open to various interpretations. "Anger" is not mentioned in the **Taittirīya Brāhmaṇa,** nor in the **Kaṭhopaniṣad** narrator's words. In the Vedic pattern it is only mentioned in Naciketas' words: ". . . let Gautama's anger towards me be pacified . . ." (KU/1.10a)[42]. The later texts, as well as Śaṅkarācarya[43] and most of the succeeding commentators, claim that the father is angry (*kruddaḥ*). Grinshpon doubts this claim and rejects "anger" as the exclusive explanation for the father's behaviour. He suggests an alternative explanation – "fear and agitation"[44] – resulting from "psychophysical exhaustion"[45], caused by the delicate situation of the sacrifice, where the father's future immortality is at stake.

The Nāsiketa Story is a link in a chain of attempts at solving the riddle of the father's behaviour. On the explicit level of the early story patterns, the father's anger is unaccounted for, but there are implicit allusions to Naciketas not being such an innocent victim. In **Kaṭhopaniṣad** Naciketas' question – "*Father, to whom wilt thou give me?*"[46] – expresses his feeling about the insufficiency of the sacrifice. His doubt is justified by the sudden "faith" (*śraddhā*) that has seized him, but it may also allude to his being condescending[47]. The implicit tension

40 An elaborate discussion - Nevo (2005).

41 Rawson (1934), p. 59; Hiriyanna (1915), P. 6; Vasu (1905), p. 7

42 "*. . . vītamanyu gautamo mābhi.*".

43 Shankaracharya (1927), p.37.

44 Grinshpon (2003), p. 95.

45 Ibid, p. 92.

46 KU/1.4a. Translation - Śarvananda (1962), p. 4.

47 Naciketas' condescension is not dealt with in any previous commentary. However, Grinshpon raises the possibility that "perhaps Naciketas is not such a good boy" - Grinshpon (2003), P. 98.

between Naciketas and his father in the Vedic pattern can also be traced in the later versions of the story. A similar arrogance and condescending attitude is revealed in Nāciketa's lecture about the need of adhering to one's word – to Truth (*satya*) – in **Varāha Purāṇa** (191.33-44) and also in **Nāsiketopākhyāna** (5.45b-49).

The continuous attempts at solving the riddle of the father-son relationship reach their climax in the Nāsiketa story. The implicit allusions to the conflict become clear, as the text explicitly describes an open confrontation between father and son over the issue of sacrifice that culminates in the death curse. Father and son debate over the means for liberation – the advantages and disadvantages of sacrifice as compared to Yoga. Nāsiketa, although young, is described as experienced in Yoga and meditation. He confronts his father and argues with him as an equal adversary, which probably alludes to former conflicting incidents. In the fierce debate, when Uddālaka's reasoning fails, he angrily curses Nāsiketa to death as a last, drastic resort. Nāsiketa is portrayed as an overconfident son, who opposes his father's authority and therefore, from a patriarchal point of view, deserves punishment, and thus becomes partly responsible for his fate.

The father-son conflict reflects the general inter-generation conflict in human society, and symbolically – the conflict between old traditions and new ideas. In the Hindu context it represents the tension between "Dharma" and "Mokṣa" – Uddālaka representing "Dharma" and Naciketas/Nāsiketa representing "Mokṣa". The tension between "Dharma" and "Mokṣa", best demonstrated in the father-son relationship, can also be traced in the other basic elements of the story – in the different and contradictory kinds of Knowledge, and in the diverse solutions for the enigma of Death.

The texts of the Naciketa lore do not have a decisive solution for the "Dharma" and "Mokṣa" conflict. There is no clear winner in the father-son conflict, nor is there a decisive selection between "Dharma" and "Mokṣa". Hinduism has developed and integrated these concepts, and thus, contradictive monistic and dualistic ideas are interwoven also in the Naciketa story versions.

Chapter 1

Uddālaka's Anxiety

śrī gaṇeśāya namaḥ śrī gurubhyo namaḥ[1]
sūta uvāca[2]
gaṅgātīre sukhāsīnaḥ kṛtvā snānam alaṅkṛtaḥ[3]
dānāni sa tato dānaṁ dvijebhyo janamejayaḥ[4] [1]
prāyaścittaviśuddhyarthaṁ dīkṣāṁ dvādaśavārṣikīṁ[5]
pitṛbhir dīkṣitaś caiva ṛṣibhir brāhmaṇaiḥ saha[6] [2]
upāgamyā sa papraccha vaiśaṁpāyanasannidhau[7]

Salutation to śrī Gaṇeśā and to the teachers.
Sūta said
Janamejaya(I) *was sitting comfortably on the riverbank, decorated, after having taken a bath,*
and after having given presents to the twice born (i.e. Brahmins). [1]
He took a vow of penance for 12 years, in order to become totally cleansed(II).
Thus, having taken the vow, he came along with relatives, seers and Brahmins. [2]
He approached Vaiśaṁpāyana's seat (in order) to pose a question,

---

1 N2 - śrī gaṇeśāya namaḥ śrī mahāvīrā namaḥ. In N3, N10 - salutation to gaṇeśa only.

2 N2 - śrī sūta uvāca.

3 N7/1.2a - gaṅgātīre sukhāsīnaṁ kṛtas(ś)nānam alaṅkṛtaṁ.
Bo/1.2a - gaṅgātīre sukhāsīnaḥ kṛtasnāno hy alaṅkṛtaḥ.

4 N2/1.1b, N3/1.1b, N10 - dadāti sma tato dānaṁ dvijebhyo janamejayaḥ.
N7/1.2b - yo dadāti tato dānaṁ dvijebhyas taṁ muniḥ yayau.
Bo/1.2b - dānaṁ datvā ca vidhivad dvijebhyo janamejayaḥ.
Ra/1.1b - dānāni sa tato dānaṁ brahmaṇebhyo mahādānaṁ datvā śri janamejayaḥ.

5 N10, N11 - prāścitraviśuṣyarthaṁ dīkṣāṁ (N7/1.3a - vīkṣya) dvādaśavārṣikīṁ.
Additional half verse: N2/1.2b - cakāra (- - -) rājā tapaḥ śri janamejayaḥ.

6 N3/1.2b - pitṛbhir dīkṣitas tatra (N7/1.3b - dīkṣāṁ caiva pitṛṇāṁ) ṛṣibhir brāhmaṇaiḥ saha.
Ra/1.2b - upadiṣṭo mahābhāgo dvijāṁś ca vṛtavāṁs tathā.

7 N1/1.3a - upagamyāsanaṁ paśyan (N2/1.3b - upāgamyā ca papraccha) vaiśaṁpāyanasannidhau,

pāṇḍuvaṁśasamutpanno janamejayamahīpatiḥ[8] [3]
janamejaya uvāca
pṛcchāmi tvāṁ mahāprājña sarvaśāstraviśārada[9]
vyāsaśiṣyo māhāyogī sarvajño vedapāragaḥ[10] [4]
kathayasva kathāṁ divyāṁ sarvapāpapraṇāśinīṁ[11]
yasyāḥ śravaṇamātreṇa prāyaścittaṁ na vidyate[12] [5]
vaiśaṁpāyana uvāca
śṛṇu rājan kathāṁ divyāṁ sarvapāpapraṇāśinīṁ[13]
yāṁ śrutvā sar vapāpebhyo mucyate nātra saṁśayaḥ[14] [6]

the great king Janamejaya, a descendant of the Pāṇḍu lineage. [3]
Janamejaya said
"I am asking you, O great knowledgeable one, well versed in all branches of knowledge,
the disciple of Vyāsa, great Yogin, all knowing, master of the Vedas[(III)]*. [4]*
(Please) tell the divine story that removes all sins,
which, by just listening to it, all vows become nonexistent". [5]
Vaiśaṁpāyana said
Listen, O king, to the divine story, that removes all sins.
Whoever hears it is liberated from all sins, there is no doubt about it. [6]

---

8 N10 - pāṅḍuvaṁśasamutpannau (N11- [janame]jayamahīpatiḥ) jan[a]mejayamahīpatiḥ.
Using "janmejaya" instead of "janamejaya" is common in N1, N2, N3, N10, N11.
Ra/1.4b - upāgatya mahātejā (N7/1.4a - vaiśaṁpāyanasannidhau) vaiśaṁpāyanam abravīt.

9 N10 - pṛcchāmi tvāṁ mahāprājñam arthaśāstraviśārada.
N7/1.4b, Ra/1.5a - pṛcchāmi tvāṁ (Bo/1.3a - te) mahāprājñasarvaśāstraviśārada.

10 N3/1.4b - vyāsaśiṣy(a)o māhāyogī(n) sarvasya ca viśāradaḥ.
N7/1.5a - vyāsaśiṣyo māhāyogya[ḥ] sarvajño vedapāragaḥ.

11 Bo/1.3b, Ra/1.6a - kathayasva kathāṁ divyāṁ sarvapāpapraṇāśinīṁ.

12 Ra/1.6b - sarvārogyapradā caiva bhuktimukti pradāyinīṁ.

13 N7/1.7a - śrūyatāṁ mahārājan (Bo/1.4a - rājaśārdula) kathāṁ paurāṇikiṁ śubhāṁ.
Ra/1.7a - śṛṇu rājan kathāṁ divyāṁ (BF/1.6a - āgamoktāṁ paurāṇikiṁ) śubhāṁ paurāṇikīm imāṁ.

14 N8/1.6b - yāṁ śrutvā sarvayogebhyo (Bo/1.3c, Ra/1.7b - sarvapāpebhyo) mucyate nātra saṁśayaḥ.

kathayāmi mahādivyāṁ kathāṁ paurāṇakīṁ śubhāṁ[15]
śṛṇvantu ṛṣayaḥ sarve ye cānye 'tra tapasvinaḥ[16] [7]
kaścid āsin mahārāja ṛṣiḥ paramadhārmikaḥ[17]
uddālaka iti khyāto brahmaputraḥ sutāpasaḥ[18] [8]
jvaladagninibhaḥ śrīmāṁś candrasūryasamadyutiḥ[19]
tatkāyakāntyā rājendra dīpyante hi diśo daśa[20] [9]
lakṣaṁ ekaṁ tu varṣāṇāṁ ṣaṣṭyaṣṭādhikasaṅkhyayā[21]
taptam ugraṁ tapas tena ūrdhvapādena tiṣṭhataḥ[22] [10]

I will tell the great divine, auspicious story, told in the Purāṇas.
Hear you seers, and all other Yogins (gathered) here. [7]
Once there was, O great king, a seer, staunchly religious,
a great ascetic, son of Brahmā, known as Uddālaka. [8]
Because of his body luster, O divine king, the ten quarters[IV] were in light. [9]
For 168000 years in number,
he performed fierce penance, standing with his feet upwards. [10]

---

15 N2/1.7a - kathayāmi mahābāho (N3/1.10a, N10, N11 - mahārāja) kathāṁ paurāṇikīṁ śubhāṁ.

16 N2/1.7b - śṛṇvantu ṛṣaya(s)ḥ sarve ye cānye (N7/1.7b - ca tapasvinaḥ, Bo/1.4b, Ra/1.8a - tapasisthitāḥ) 'tra tapasvinaḥ.
Final S before sibilants occurs systematically in N2.
BF/1.7 - śṛṇuṣvā 'vahito bhūtvā kathām etāṁ śubhāvahāṁ
śṛṇvantu ṛṣayaḥ sarve ye cānye tava sevakāḥ.

17 N3/1.8a - kaścid āsit purā rājan ṛṣiḥ (N10 - paramavārmikaḥ) paramadhārmikaḥ.

18 N1/1.8b, N10 - uddālaka iti khyāto brahmaputraḥ sutāpas(m)a[ḥ].
N7/1.8b - uddālaketi viṣyāto (Bo/1.5b - vikhyāto brahmaputras tu tāpasaḥ) brahmaputrasutāpataḥ.
BF/1.8b - uddālaka iti khyāto (Ra/1.9a - brahmaputras tu tāpasaḥ) brahmaputro mahātapāḥ.

19 N3/1.9a - jvaladagninibhaḥ śrīmāṁś candrasūryajyotisamaprabhā (vi).

20 N1/1.9b - tatkāyakāntyā rājendra dīpyate h(v)i diśo da(i)śaḥ.

21 N1/1.10a - lakṣ(jj)am ekaṁ tu varṣāṇāṁ ṣaṣṭhādhikata (N10, N11 - ṣaṣṭyāṣṭādhika) saṅkhyayā.
N2/1.10a - lakṣam ekaṁ tu varṣāṇāṁ ṣaṣṭhāyāndhikaṁ ca saṅkhyayā (vi).

22 N1/1.10b - taptam ugraṁ tapas tena (N3/1.10b - ūrdhvapādena tiṣṭhati) ūrdhveyādita (N10, N11 - tiṣṭhatā) tiṣṭhatāṁ.
N2/1.10b - taptam ugraṁ tatas tena ūrdhvapādena tiṣṭhatā.

gaṅgātīraṁ samāśrityas taptaṁ suduṣkaraṁ tapaḥ[23]
tapasā tasya rājendra amarendram akaṁpayat[24] [11]
brahmalokaṁ gataḥ śakras tato munivaraiḥ saha[25]
dattāsanaḥ kṛtārthaś ca sāṣṭāṅgaṁ praṇipatya taṁ[26] [12]
dīnānano bhayāviṣṭo brahmapādāgratasthitaḥ[27]
tato brahmā sabhāmadhye paprachedaṁ sahetukaṁ[28] [13]
brahmovāca
brūhīndra katham āpannaḥ kūto bhayasamanvitaḥ[29] [14]
śakras tadākhilaṁ tasmai pravaktum upacakrame[30]
indra uvāca

He resorted to the riverbank, practicing that hard penance.
(He was) blazing like a burning fire, brilliant like the moon & sun together.
By his penance, O divine king, even Indra trembled. [11]
Then Śakra (i.e. Indra) went to Brahmā's region, along with the best of sages.
Having been given a seat, he (i.e. Indra) bowed to him eight times. [12]
Frightened, wretched-faced, he stood at Brahmā's feet.
Then Brahmā asked him purposefully, in the midst of the assembly hall. [13]
Brahmā said
"Speak, O Indra, tell me, why have you come and what are you so afraid of?" [14]
Then Śakra planned to tell him everything in detail.
Indra said

---

23 N2/1.11a, N3/1.11a - gaṅgātīraṁ samāśrityas (N10, N11 - tasaṁ suduḥkaraṁ tapa) tapas taptaṁ suduṣkaraṁ.

24 Emendation - DS (Prof. D. Shulman). N1/1.11b - tapasā tasya rājendra (N2/1.11b, N3/1.11b, N10, N11 - padamaindram) am[ar]endram akaṁpayat.

25 N11 - brahmalokaṁ gataḥ śakas tato munivaraiḥ saha.

26 N1/1.12b, N11 - dattāśaneḥ kṛtārthaś ca sāṣṭāṅgaṁ praṇipatya taṁ.
N3/1.12b - dattāsano gṛhītārdyaṁ sāṣṭāṅgaṁ praṇipatya taṁ.

27 N1/1.13a - dīnānano bhayāviṣṭo brahmapādāyatasthitaḥ.
N2/1.13a - dīno bhayāsamāviṣṭo (N3/1.13a - brahmapādāgrasaṁsthitaḥ) brahmapādāgratasthitaḥ.
N10, N11 - dīnānano bhayāviṣṭo brahmapādāgrataḥ sthitaḥ.

28 N2/1.13b, N3/1.13b, N11 - tato brahmā (N10 - sa sābhāṣya) samābhāṣya paprachedaṁ sahetukaṁ.

29 N2/1.14a, N3/1.14a, N11 - brūhīndra katham āyātaḥ kūto bhayasamanvitaḥ.

30 N11 - śakras tadākhilaṁ tasmai pravaktum upa[ca]krame.

śṛṇu brahman jagatkartar vārtām ekāṁ mayoditāṁ[31]
uddālako mahātejās tava putraḥ pitāmaha [15]
martyaloke ciraṁ kālaṁ tena taptaṁ mahat tapaḥ
deveśa tapasoddālakasya hi kaṁpan tiṣṭhāmi[32] [16]
gacchāmi kutra deveśa tad vadasva mahāprabho[33]
śakrasya vacanaṁ śrutvā brahmā vacanam abravīt [17]
brahmovāca
indra jānāmi dharmātman mama putro mahātapāḥ[34]
uddālako nāma sutas tapasā trailokyaviśrutaḥ[35] [18]
vedavedāṅgatatvajñaḥ yaḥ karmakuśalas tathā[36]

"O Brahmā, creator of the universe, listen to the story that I tell.
Uddālaka, your brilliant son, O Grandfather (Brahmā), [15]
has been practicing great penance for a long time in the world of mortals.
Uddālaka's penance makes me tremble so, O Brahmā! [16]
Where should I go, God? Please tell me that, O Great Lord".
Hearing Indra's words, Brahmā said the following words. [17]
Brahmā said
"O Indra, moral soul, I know that my son, Uddālaka, is a great Yogin.
Because of his penance he is known in the three worlds. [18]
He is skillful in ritual and knows the Vedas and what comes after them (Vedāṅga).

---

31 N1/1.15a - śṛṇu brahman jagatkatrī (N2/1.15a, N3/1.15a - jagatkarttā) vārttām ekāṁ mayoditāṁ.

32 N1/1.16b - deveśa tapasoddalakasya hi kaṁpan tiṣṭhasi.
N3/1.16b, N2/1.16b - tapasā tasya deveśa kaṁpate hy āsanaṁ mama.
N10 - tapasoddālakasya hi. Incomplete verse, missing a pāda.
Additional verses N2/1.17-18a:
upāyaṁ vada me deva kutra yāmi (N3/1.17a - bhayākila[ḥ]) bhayākula[ḥ] sthātuṁ mama mahārāja (N3/1.17b - purābrahma) tvayā dattāmāravatīṁ kampa so 'pi (N3/1.18a - kampate deva) deveśa tapasoddālakasya hi.

33 N2/1.18b - kva tiṣṭhāmi kva gacchāmi (N3/1.18b, N10, N11 - kathaṁ tiṣṭhāmi gacchāmi) kutra deveśa tad vada.

34 N3/1.19b - indra jānāmi dharmātmā mama putro mahātapā,

35 N1/1.18b, N11 - uddālakīṁ nāma sutas tapas trailokyaviśrutaḥ.

36 N2/1.20b, N10 - vedavedāṅgatatvajñaḥ (N11 - yat karmakuśalas) ṣaṭkarmakuśalas tathā.
BF/1.9a - vedavedāṅgatatvajñaḥ (N7/1.9a, Bo/1.6, Ra/1.9b - smṛtisiddhāntaparagaḥ) śrutismṛtyarthaparagaḥ.

trikālakuśalo dharmajñaḥ sarvaśāstraviśāradaḥ[37] [19]
smṛtisiddhāntavettā sa matprasādena vāsava[38]
dānto dakṣo mahāprajño muniśreṣṭo mahātapāḥ[39] [20]
mokṣam ākāṅkṣate vidvāṁs tava rājyaṁ na kāṅkṣati[40]
kuru ca nijarājyaṁ tvaṁ svastho· bhava śacīpate[41] [21]
tasyāśramaṁ paraṁ ramyaṁ munibhiḥ parisevitaṁ[42]
nānādrumalatākīrṇaṁ nānāpuṣpopaśobhitaṁ[43] [22]

He masters the knowledge of the three times[(V)]*, knows what is morally right, (and) is well versed in all branches of knowledge. [19]*
By my grace he knows, O Vāsava (i.e. Indra), the theories of Smṛti scriptures.
He is well trained, clever, a great knowledgeable one (and) a great ascetic. [20]
I know that he desires liberation (and) does not desire your kingdom.
Rule your own kingdom (and pay him no heed), be calm, O Lord of Śacī". [21]
His (i.e. Uddālaka's) hermitage was very beautiful, frequented by sages, full of various trees and creepers, and rich with a variety of flowers and beasts. [22]

---

[37] N1/1.19b - trikālakuśalo dharmataḥ (N2/1.21a - dharmasya) sarvaśāstraviśāradaḥ (vi).
N3/1.20c - trikāladarśītatvajñaḥ sarvaśāstraviśāradaḥ.

[38] N1/1.20a - smṛtisiddhāntavedo sa (N3/1.21a - smṛtisiddhāntavettā ca) matprasādena vāsava.

[39] N1/1.20b - dānto danto (N3/1.21b - dajño, N11- dato) mahāprajño muniśreṣṭo mahātapāḥ.
N7/1.9b - dānto dakṣo muniśreṣṭo mahāprajño mahātapāḥ.
BF/1.9b, Ra/1.10a - dātā dayālur dakṣo 'sau muniśreṣṭhas tapodhanaḥ.

[40] N1/1.21a - māṁ janmāṁ (N11 - mī janma) kāṅkṣate vidvāṁs tava rājyaṁ na kāṅkṣati.

[41] N1/1.21b - kvanu (N10, N11 - kuru) cha nijarājyaṁ svaṁ (N2/1.23a - kuruṣva nijarājyaṁ tvaṁ) svastho bhava śacīpate.
N2/1.23a - kuruṣva nijarājyaṁ tvaṁ (N3/1.22b - ca) svastho bhava śacīpate.

[42] N7/1.10a - tasyāśramaṁ paraṁ ramyaṁ ṛṣibhir munisevitaṁ.
Bo/1.7a - tasyāśramapadaṁ ramyaṁ (BF/1.10a - siddharṣimunisevitaṁ, Ra/1.10b - ṛṣibhiś copasevitaṁ) ṛṣibhir munibhiḥ śritaṁ.

[43] N7/1.10b, Bo/1.7b - nānādrumasamākīrṇaṁ nānāpuṣpopaśobhitaṁ.
BF/1.10b - nānādrumalatākīrṇaṁ (Ra/1.11a - nānāpuṣpopaśobhitaṁ) cakravākasamanvitaṁ.

sevyamānaṁ khagānekaiḥ susaraḥ kamalākulaṁ[44] [23]
haṁsakāraṇḍavākīrṇe cakravākopaśobhite[45]
kokilā bahavo yatra mayūrāḥ śukasārikāḥ [24]
ekadā hyāgatas tatra pippalādo mahāmuniḥ[46]
taṁ dṛṣṭvātha tapovane āgataṁ sahasā muniḥ[47]
kṛtāñjalipuṭo bhūtvā svāsanaṁ pradadau tathā[48] [25]
pādārghyeṇa samabhyarcya samutthyāya kṛtāñjaliḥ[49]

It was frequented by many birds, and its beautiful lake was full of lotuses, [23]
spotted by swans and ducks, and adorned by Cakravaka birds.
Many cuckoos were there, peacocks, parrots and Myna birds. [24]
Once, the great sage Pippalāda came there.
Seeing the Yogin coming all of a sudden, the sage (Uddālaka)
with bowl-shaped joined palms, gave him his own seat. [25]
He received him properly with water to wash his feet, (his) palms joined together.

---

44 Emendation - NK (Dr. N. Kulkarni). N1/1.23a, N3/1.24a, N10, N11 - sevyamānaṁ khagānīkaiḥ susaraḥ (N2/1.24b - sasara) kamalākulaṁ. N7/1.11b - sevyamānaṁ khagānīkaiḥ susaraḥ kamalair upaśobhitaṁ. BF/1.10c - sevyamānaṁ munigaṇaiḥ sarasair iva satsaraḥ. Bo/1.8b - sevyamānaṁ khagānīkair mahiṣair gavyair mṛgaiḥ (short).

45 N2/1.25b, N3/1.25a, N7/1.11a - haṁsakāraṇḍavākīrṇaṁ cakravākopaśobhitaṁ. Ra/1.11b - haṁsakāraṇḍavākīracakravākād alaṅkṛtaṁ. Bo/1.8a - haṁsaiḥ kāraṇḍavāiś caiva cakravākaiś ca śobhitaṁ.

46 1.25a = N1/1.23b, N2/1.25a, N3/1.24b. In N10, N11 - 1.25a precedes verse 1.24. N7/1.12a, Bo/1.9a - āgataś cāśrame tasya pippalāyana mahāmuniḥ. BF/1.11a - tasyāśrame samāyātaḥ (Ra/1.12b - āgataḥ kautukāt tatra) pippalādo mahāmuniḥ.

47 Emendation - NK. N1/1.25a - taṁ dṛṣṭotthaya vanayām ārāmya sahasā muniḥ. N2/1.26b - taṁ dṛṣṭvātha tapovane āgataṁ śirasā muni. N3/1.26a, N10, N11 - taṁ dṛṣṭotthāya vinayāt praṇamya sahasā muniḥ. Bo/1.9b - tam āgataṁ tathā dṛṣṭvā atitheyaṁ ca kārasaḥ.

48 N2/1.27a, N3/1.26b, N11 - kṛtāñjalipuṭo bhūtvā hy āsanaṁ pradadau tathā. Bo/1.10a - svāgataṁ muniśārdula viṣṭare copaveṣya taṁ. Ra/1.13a - abhivādya yathānyāyam āsane (N7/1.12b - sopaveṣya saḥ, BF/1.11b - copaveṣya ca) cāpaveṣya taṁ.

49 N1/26a - pādārghyeṇa samabhyarcya samucyapakṛtāñjali. N7/1.13a - pādārghyaṁ ca samabhyarcya mune tiṣṭha tapodhanā.

pippalādaṁ uvācedaṁ kim arthaṁ bhagavān mama[50] [26]
pippalāda uvāca
śrūyatāṁ vacanaṁ brahmann uddālaka mahāmune
yuṣmat pūrve mayā dṛṣṭā bahavaś ca tapodhanāḥ[51] [27]
sapatnīkā mahātmānas tapasyanto mahātapāḥ[52]
pūrvaṁ vaṁśadharāḥ santo yatanti śreyase yataḥ[53] [28]

He then said to Pippalāda "O honourable one, what is the purpose of your coming to me?" [26]
Pippalāda said
"Hear my words, O great Sage, Brahmin Uddālaka,
I have heard of you, many are the treasures of your penance[VI]. [27]
In the past, great souls used to perform hard penance together with their wives, O Great Yogin.
While maintaining a family, they strove, restrained, for the Good. [28]

BF/1.12a - pādārghyeṇa (Ra/1.13b - pādyārghyeṇa) samabhyarcya śuśrūṣam akarot tataḥ.

50 N2/1.28a, N3/1.27b, N10 - pippalādaṁ uvācedaṁ kim arthaṁ bhavadāgamaḥ.
N7/1.13b - uddālako munir vācaṁ kim artham iha cāgataḥ.
Bo/1.10b - yadartham iha cāyatas tad vadasva tapodhana.
Ra/1.14a - apṛcchac (BF/1.12b - papraccha) ca muniḥ prītyā tasyāgamanakāraṇaṁ.
Ra/1.14b - kim artham āgato vipra vedavedāṅgapāragaḥ.

51 N1/1.27b - yuṣmat pūrva (N2/1.28a - viprā sarve) mayā dṛṣṭvā vadayasva tapodhanāḥ.
BF/1.13b - dṛṣṭaṁ caiva mayā sarvaṁ mahāścāryaṁ mahat tapaḥ.
Ra/1.15b - dṛṣṭvā caiva mayā sarve yūyam atra (N7/1.14b - sarvaṁ yūṣmānn uktā) tapodhanāḥ.

52 N2/1.29b - sapatnīkā mahātmānas tapasyānto (N3/1.29a - sudustarā) mahat tapāḥ.
BF/1.14b - sapatnīkā hi munaya āpur siddhiṁ parāṁ mune.
Bo/1.13a - tava pārśve sapatnīkā ṛṣayas tapasisthitāḥ.
Ra/1.16b - ṛṣayaś cāśrame sarve sapatnīkāḥ (N7/1.15b - upasthitāḥ) sadā sthitāḥ.

53 N1/1.28b - pūrvaṁ vaṁśadharāḥ (N2/1.30a - sānto japanti śreyasāṅgatiṁ) santo yatanti śreyasāṅgatiḥ.
BF/1.15a - santatyarthaṁ sadā dārā draṣṭavyā munayo jaguḥ.
Bo/1.13b - saputrāḥ santi bho brahman putrahīnas tvam eva ca.
Ra/1.17a - tapyante ca tapovipra sarve vaṁśadharāḥ (N7/1.16a - vaṁśaparāḥ) smṛtaḥ.

vaṁśe naṣṭe muniśreṣṭha sarvaṁ eva vinaśyati[54]
pitaro devatāś caiva na tuṣyanty asute jane[55] [29]
tasmai kāmān prayacchanti yasya putro 'tidhārmikāḥ[56]
kulāni tārayet tasya suputro vaṁśavardhanaḥ[57] [30]
aputrasya jagac chūnyam aputrasya gṛheṇa kiṁ[58]
aputro vaṁśanāśāya śrutir eṣā sanātanī[59] [31]
tasmāt sarvaprayatnena putrasasyaṁ samārabhet[60]

Without a family, O Great Sage, everything is gone (perished).
Ancestors, and even gods, are not pleased without progeny. [29]
The most religious (say that) whoever has a child, all his wishes come true.
A good son increases the family and helps it traverse beyond, (to Heaven). [30]
Without a son the world is a void, of what use is a house without a son?
Without a son the family vanishes, so state the Śruti (i.e. Holy Scriptures). [31]
Therefore all efforts should be made in order to beget a son crop.

---

54 N1/1.29a - vaṁśe naṣṭe muniśreṣṭho (BF/1.15b, N7/1.16b, Ra/1.17b - muniśreṣṭa) sarvam eva vinaśyati.

55 N1/1.29b - pitaro devatāś caiva (N2/1.31a - ca va) na tuṣyanty akṣate jane.
BF/1.16a - pitaro devatāḥ sarve (N7/1.17a - duṣyanti ca aputriṇaḥ) putrahīnaṁ na tuṣyanti.
Ra/1.18 - pitaro devatāś caiva tasya tuṣṭhā na karhicit
manpante pitaro (N7/1.17b - devā yasya putra susobhataḥ) devair yasya putro 'sti śobhanaḥ.

56 N1/1.30a - tasmai kāmā prayachanti paśyaṁ putreti dhārmikāḥ.

57 N2/1.32a, Ra/1.19a - kulāni tārayet sapta suputro (N3/1.31b - saputro) vaṁśavardhanaḥ.
N7/1.14b - kulaṁ ca tārayet sarvaṁ suputro vaṁśavardhanaḥ.

58 N3/1.32a - aputrasya jaga(t)c ch(ś)ūnyaṁ aputrasya gṛheṇa kiṁ.
N7/1.18a - aputreṇa jaga(t)c ch(ś)ūnyaṁ aputreṇa gṛhaṁ ca kiṁ.
BF/1.18a - aputrasya jagac chūnyam aputrasya gṛhaṁ kutaḥ.
Bo/1.14a - aputrasya gṛhaṁ śūnyaṁ (Ra/1.19b - hy aputreṇa gṛheṇa kiṁ) paraloke gatir na hi.

59 N7/1.19b - aputreṇa vaṁśanāśāḥ śrutir eṣā sanātanī.
BF/1.18b - aputro vaṁśanāśo hi (Ra/1.20a - 'sti) śrutir eṣā sanātanī.

60 N1/1.32a, N11 - tasmāt sarvaprayatnena (N2/1.33b, N4/1.20a, N7/1.14b - putro vaṁśasya kāraṇaṁ, Bo/1.14b - putram utpādayen naraḥ) putrasaṁsyaṁ samārabhet.

dharmikas tanayaḥ proktaḥ paratreha sukhapradaḥ[61] [32]
tasmāt sarvaprayatnena kartavyā santatiḥ dhruvaṁ[62]
uddālaka uvāca
ṣaḍaśītisahasrāṇi varṣāṇi tapasi sthitaḥ[63]
pippalādādhunā so 'haṁ evaṁ varte punaḥ punaḥ [33]
kathaṁ patāmi narake ghore śrutir eṣā sanātanī[64]
upavāsādikaṁ kṛtvā ye vikalpanti te 'dhamāḥ[65] [34]
tapo gṛhītvā viprarṣe kathaṁ tat tyajyate mune[66]
tena hīnaś ca loke 'smin nāpāvādāspado bhavet[67] [35]
pippalāda uvāca
anuktaṁ caiva yuktaṁ ca pippalādo bravīmy ahaṁ[68]

The religious experts say that progeny brings utmost happiness. [32]
Therefore, all efforts should be made for the continuation of the family".
Uddālaka said
"I have spent 86000 years performing penance(VII)*,*
O Pippalāda, and yet I am (born here) now, again and again. [33]
How can I fall into a terrible hell, as stated in the Holy Śruti?
Those who abandon fasting and all the other vows, become the lowest (of people). [34]
O Brahmin seer, holding penance, how can I leave it, (please tell me), O sage.
Does not whoever is without them(VIII) *in this world, become blameworthy?" [35]*
Pippalāda said
"I Pippalāda advise you, what is logical and was not told.

---

61 N1/1.32a - dharmiṣṭhatā tapaḥ proktaṁ paraveha (N2/1.34a - paradeha) sukhapradaḥ.

62 N10 - tasmāt sarvaprayatnena (Ra/1.21b - kartavyā santatiḥ sthirā) kartavyā santi dhruvaṁ.

63 N1/1.33a - ṣaḍaśītisahasrāṇi varṣāṇi yātaya sthitāḥ.

64 N1/1.34a - gaccheti (N2/1.36a - gacchati) narake ghore śrutir eṣā sanātanī. N4/1.22b, Ra/1.23a - sa eva narake ghore (N8/1.20a, N7/1.22a - gaccha(n)ti śrutir eṣā sanātanī) gaccha(n)tīti śrutaṁ mayā.

65 N1/1.34b - upavāsādikaṁ kṛtā ye vikalpanti (N3/1.36a - cādhamāḥ, N2/1.36b - te 'dhamāḥ) vādhamāḥ.

66 Emendation - DS. N13/1.35a, N11 - tapo gṛhītvā viyurṣe kathaṁ (N10 - ta tyajate mune) taptyanya te mune.
N7/1.23a - gṛhītvā tapa viprarṣe katham tasman nivartate.

67 N1/1.35b - te hīnaś ca loke 'smin nāpāvādāspado (N10 - bhava) bhavet.

68 N2/1.38a, N10, N11 - ayuktaṁ caiva yuktaṁ va pippalādo (N3/1.37b - uddālako) bravīmy ahaṁ.

santatiṁ hi vinā mūḍhanṛṇāṁ dharmo na vidyate [36]
ṛṣiḥ pūrvatapas tyaktvā kuryāt kiṁ na śrutaṁ tvayā[69]
ṛtukālābhigamanaṁ sutasantatihetave[70] [37]
evam uktvā tatas taṁ hi pippalādo mahāmuniḥ[71]
uddālakaṁ namaskṛtya tu punaḥ svāśramam āgataḥ[72] [38]
uddāllako 'pi sa muniḥ cintayāmāsa vai hṛdi[73]
vaiśaṁpāyana uvāca
evaṁ hi tapaso rājan purā vighna upasthite[74] [39]

Without progeny, fool-people's Dharma (i.e. righteous act) does not exist. [36]
A sage should abandon the old type of penance – have you not heard? –
(and) indeed should approach his wife in the right time, for the sake of progeny." [37]
The great sage Pippalāda, having said so to him,
and having saluted Uddālaka, returned to his own hermitage. [38]
Sage Uddālaka's heart was perplexed.
Vaiśaṁpāyana said
O king, now that his penance was obstructed, [39]

---

69 Emendation - DS. N1/1.37a - ūciḥ pūrvatapas tyaktvā kurvan kiṁ na śrutaṁ tvayā.
Suggested emendation by NK - ūcuḥ pūrvatapas tyaktvā kṛtaṁ kiṁ na śrutaṁ tvayā.
N3/1.38a - uciḥ pūrvataraspaṣṭau putrān kiṁ na śrutaṁ (N2/1.39a - sutaṁ) tvayā.
N4/1.25a - pūrveṣaṁ tapo bhraṣṭaṁ putrārthe na śrutaṁ mayā.
N8/1.22b - uciḥ pūrvatapo (N7/1.24b - bhṛṣṭa putrārthena svatatva hi) naṣṭaḥ putrārthena śrutaṁ mayā.
Ra/1.26a - pūrveṣaṁ hi tapo bhṛṣṭaṁ putrārthaṁ hi śrutaṁ mayā.

70 N1/1.37b - kiṁ tu kālārtigamanaṁ sutasantatihetave.

71 N3/1.38a - evam uktvā tatas tena hi (N4/1.26b, N8/1.27a - tato rajan) pippalādo mahāmuniḥ.
N7/1.26a - evam uktā tatas tasmin pippalādo munir mahāt.

72 N1/1.38b - praj(t)āpatinamana tu [p]unaḥ svāśrayam āgataḥ.
N2/1.40b, N3/1.39b - praj(t)āpatiṁ namas kṛtya punaḥ svāśramam āgataḥ.
N10 - prajāpatiṁ namaskṛtya tu punaḥ svāśramam āgataḥ.
N4/1.27a, Bo/1.17b - uddālakaṁ namas kṛtya sa (N8/1.24b, Ra/1.28b - cātmīyāśrama gata) muniḥ svāśrama yayau.

73 N1/1.39a, N11 - udd(ll)āll(s)ako 'pi s(v)a muni(ṁ)ḥ svitayāmāsa vai hṛdi.

74 N1/1.39b, N10 - vaiśaṁsyaṁ (N11 - vaiśaṁśvaṁ) hi tapo rājan purā vighna upasthite.
N2/1.41b - evaṁ hi tapaso (N3/1.40b - vighne purā rājan upasthite) rājan purā vighna upāgame.
N4/1.27b, N7/1.27a, N8/1.25a, Ra/1.29a - evaṁ rājan purā vṛtt(aṁ)e tapo vighnam upasthitaḥ.

uddālako 'tiduḥkhārtaḥ kathaṁ vaṁśaṁ karomy ahaṁ
kva yāmi kanyakāṁ kasmāl labhe 'haṁ so 'nvacintayat[75] [40]
kaṁ cāhaṁ abhyarthayiṣyāmi ko me dāsyati kanyakāṁ[76]
punar uktaṁ tu yāsyāmi prajāpatiniveśanaṁ[77] [41]
pradadāti ca me 'bhyarthaṁ śreṣṭhāṁ vaṁśadharāṁ śubhāṁ[78]
prayātaḥ sa ca tatraiva yatra devaḥ prajapatiḥ[79] [42]
brahmovāca
svāgataṁ te dvijaśreṣṭha tapasā vidyayānvitaḥ
vimuktaḥ sarvapāpebhyo jitakrodho jitendriyaḥ[80] [43]

Uddālaka was very miserable – "How shall I establish a family?
Where should I go? From whom shall I get a girl?" so he kept thinking. [40]
"Whose daughter am I going to ask? Who will give me his daughter?"
Then he again said (to himself) "I shall go to Prajāpati's place, [41]
the auspicious one, who will respond to my request and support my lineage, (my) good family".
He set out then to the place where Prajāpati was staying. [42]
Brahmā said
"Welcome, O Brahmin of good family, full of knowledge acquired by penance,
liberated from all sins, the master of anger[(IX)], subjugator of the senses. [43]

---

[75] N1/1.40b - kiñjāmi (N11 - kā jāmi) kanyakāṁ kasmāl labhe 'haṁ so 'nvacintayat.

[76] N2/1.43a - kiṁ cāhaṁ arcayiṣyāmi yo me dāsyati kanyakāṁ.
N3/1.42a - kasmin nabhyarthayiṣyāmi yo me dāsyati kanyakāṁ.

[77] N1/1.41b - punar uktaṁ tu yāsyāmi (N31.42b - prajāpatyaṁ nivedanaṁ) prāptvā (N10, N11 - prāptā) yatpativeśanaṁ.
Ra/1.31a - nidhāya cintaṁ yāsyāmi prajāpati niveśanaṁ.

[78] N2/1.44a, N3/1.43a - sa dāsyati (N3/1.43a - sa dadāti) ca me bhāryyāṁ śreṣṭhavaṁśadharāṁ śubhāṁ.
N10, N11 - sa dadāti ca me bhāryyāṁ śreṣṭhavaṁśadharāṁ śubhā.
Ra/1.31b - dāsyatīti sa me bhāryyaṁ śreṣṭhāṁ vaṁśakarīṁ śubhāṁ.

[79] N1/1.42b - prayātaḥ prāha muninā śreṣṭhaṁ sarvaṁ pitāmāhaḥ.
N10, N11 - prayātaḥ prāha muniśreṣṭaṁ pitāmaha (short).
Additional verse - N2/1.45:
prajāpatiṁ (N3/1.44a - prajāpati) namaskṛtya tad agre prāñjalisthitaḥ
uddālakaṁ tataḥ prāha muniśreṣṭaṁ (N3/1.44b - pitāmaha) pitāmahaṁ.

[80] N1/1.43b, N10, N11 - vimukta(s)ḥ (N3/1.45b - viyuktaḥ) mayayā yebhyo jitakrodho jitendriyaḥ.

kimarthaṁ tvam ihāyātaḥ kāraṇaṁ tad vadasva me
prajāpativacaḥ śrutvā tata uddālako 'bravīt[81] [44]
kṛtāñjalipuṭo bhūtvā atihṛṣṭaḥ pitāmahaṁ[82]
santānārthaṁ samāyāto divyadarśana te namaḥ[83] [45]
brahmovāca
bhaviṣyati ca putras te yo 'sau vaṁśavivardhanaḥ[84]
prathamaṁ putrasaṁprāptiḥ paścād bhāryā bhaviṣyati [46]
sarvalakṣaṇasaṁpūrṇā raghuvaṁśasamudbhavā[85]
vardhayiṣyati sā gotraṁ mama vākyaṁ na cānyathā[86] [47]
svāśramaṁ gaccha bhadraṁ te vaktā taṁ he prajāpatiḥ[87]
acintitaṁ phalaṁ bhāvi mā cintāṁ kuru kām api[88] [48]

What is the purpose of your coming here? Tell me that".
Hearing Prajāpati's words, Uddālaka then said [44]
to the Grandfather, saluting with bowl-shaped joined palms, very happy:
"For the sake of progeny have I come to see you, O God, I bow to you". [45]
Brahmā said
"You will have a son, who will increase your lineage.
First will a son arrive, and then there will be a wife, [46]
endowed with all auspicious marks, born in the lineage of Raghu.
She will increase your family, (that is) my word, and nothing else. [47]
Go to your hermitage, my dear, this is what (I), Prajāpati, am telling you.
The unimaginable fruit that you desire will come true". [48]

---

81 N1/1.44b - prītayeti vacaḥ (N11 - prayātativacaḥ) śrutvā tata uddālako 'bravīt.

82 N2/1.48a, N11 - kṛtāñjalipuṭo bhūtvā cātihṛṣṭaḥ pitāmahaṁ.

83 N2/1.48b, N3/1.47b - santānārthaṁ samāyāto divyadarśana te (N10, N11 - nataḥ) 'grataḥ.

84 N3/1.48a - bhaviṣyati ca putras te yo vau (N11 - so) vaṁśavivardhanaḥ.

85 N3/1.49a - sarvalakṣaṇasaṁpūrṇā raghuvaṁśavivardhinī.

86 N2 - vardhayiṣyati sā gotraṁ mama vākya ca nānyathā.

87 N2/1.51a, N10, N11 - svāśramaṁ gaccha bhadraṁ te vaktā te ha prajāpatiḥ.
N3/1.50a - svāśramaṁ gaccha viprendra vaktāhaṁ te prajāpatiḥ.
N4/1.38a, N8/1.35b - gaccha tvam āśramaṁ vidvān nāhaṁ vaktā prajāpatiḥ.
BF/1.38a, Ra/1.53a - gaccha tvam āśramaṁ puṇyaṁ madvaco nānyathā bhavet
Bo/1.27 - gaccha tvam āśrame vipra uddālaka mahāmune.

88 N1/1.48b, N11 - acintitaṁ phalaṁ bhāvi sācintākulaṁ(nu) t(k)ām api.
N3/1.50b - acintitaphala bhāvi mā cintāṁ kuru kām api.

uddālaka uvāca
vinā bhāryāṁ kutaḥ putraḥ katham evaṁ prajāpate
mahat kautukam etan me mativākyena te vibhau[89] [49]
etac chrutvā muner vākyaṁ kṣaṇenāntaradhīyata[90]
gataṁ prajāpatiṁ dṛṣṭvā nivṛttaḥ sa dvijas tataḥ[91] [50]
mithyāvākyāni kasmāt tu brūte brahmā mayā saha[92]
pūrvaṁ tu syāt kathaṁ putrāḥ paścād bhāryā kathaṁ bhavet[93] [51]

iti śrībrahmāṇḍapurāṇe nāśiketopākhyāne uddālakacintāvarṇanaṁ nāma prathamo 'dhyāyaḥ

Uddālaka said
"Without a wife, from where will a son come? How really, O Prajāpati?
Your words have caused me a great wonder, O Omnipresent One!" [49]
Thus hearing the sage's words, in a moment he (i.e. Prajāpati) disappeared inside.
Having seen Prajāpati going, the Brahmin then returned. [50]
(He wondered) – "Why has Brahmā told me such incorrect things?
How can a son come first, (and) how will a wife be afterwards?" [51]

This is the first chapter of the Nāsiketa story, pertaining to the Brahmāṇḍa Purāṇa, called – the description of Uddālaka's anxiety.

Translation Notes

I – In Varāha Purāṇa (191.1) and the Rajasthāni version (Krause (1924), p. 411), it is Vaiśaṁpāyana who is sitting on the riverbank, and not the king.
II – The sin of killing a Brahmin (Iyer, (1985), VP/191.1, Dowson (1961), p.133), or of killing serpents in his famous Sarpasattra (the serpent sacrifice).

[89] N2/1.52b - mahat kautukam etan me bhavi (N10 - bhāti) vākyena te vibho.
N3/1.51b - mahat kautukam ābhati tvadvākyena ca me vibho.
N11 - mahat kautuka (tan m)etan me mātivākyena te vibhau.

[90] N1/1.50a - tac chrutvā (N3/1.52a - eta(t)c ch(ś)rutvā) munivākyena [kṣ]āṇe(o)nāntaradhīyata.
N10 - sa tac (N11 - etac) chrutvā muner vākyaṁ kṣaṇenāntaradhīyata.

[91] N2/1.53b - gataṁ prajāpatiṁ (N11 - pratāpatiṁ) dṛṣṭvā nivṛttaḥ sa dvijas (N3/1.52b - tathā) tata.

[92] N4/1.39a - mithyā vākyāṁ bhavato nama vediti niścitāṁ saṁśayaṁ.

[93] N3/1.53b - pūrvaṁ me syāt kathaṁ putrāḥ paścād bhāryā kathaṁ bhavet.

III – 0r – gone beyond the Vedas.
IV – The whole universe.
V – Present, past & future.
VI – According to other versions: "terrible are the treasures of your penance".
VII – Compare verse 1.10a – 168000 years of penance.
VIII – Penance and vows.
IX – Notice the author's irony, keeping in mind Uddālaka's future great anger, the cause of Nāsiketa's adventure in Yama's realm.

Chapter 2

Candravatī's Entrance into the Forest

vaiśaṁpāyana uvāca
śṛṇu rājan mahāprājña sarvaśāstraviśārada[1]
uddālaka uttapya tapaḥ punar bhāryābhilāṣayā[2] [1]
prajāpativacas śrutvā vinā bhāryaṁ kutaḥ sutaḥ[3]
uddālakasya satataṁ dhyāyataḥ satataṁ hi tat[4] [2]
ajñātareto viprarṣeś cyutaṁ mohād acetasaḥ[5]
tad vīryaṁ padmamadhye tu palān nikṣipya yatnataḥ[6] [3]

Vaiśaṁpāyana said
Listen, O king, the great knowledgeable one, expert in all branches of knowledge.
Uddālaka performed penance again, desiring a wife. [1]
Having heard Prajāpati's words, (he was wondering) "where should a son come from without a wife?"
Thus Uddālaka kept thinking constantly. [2]
Then the Brahmin seer, having lost control of his mind, unknowingly (his semen) slipped out[(1)].
He put that semen in the midst of a lotus flower (wrapped) with straw. [3]

---

1 N11 - sṛṇu rājan mahāprāj[ñ]a sarvvaśāstra(u)viśārada.

2 N1/2.1b - uddālako ta havyena punar bhāryābh(m)ilakṣayā.
N2/2.1b - uddālako(s) sutas tatra punar bhāryābhilāṣayā.
N10, N11 - uddālako 'tatha(ṁ) tatra punar bhāryābh(m)ilākhāyā.
N7/2.1b - puna(ḥ)s tapatyasau vipras tapakūryābhilakṣaṇaḥ.

3 N1/2.2a - putrāpattivacastaptaṁ (N2/2.2a - prajāpativaca(s)ḥ satyaṁ, N10 - putāpattivacaḥ samaṁ) vinā bhāryaṁ kutaḥ sutaḥ.

4 N1/2.2b - uddālakasya satataṁ dhyāyataḥ (N10 - tatajaṁ hi tat) satataṁ hi kṛt.
N2/2.2b-3a - dhyāyate ca paraṁ jñānaṁ yasyevaṁ ca varaṁ janaṁ tenaivābhvāsa yogenoddālaka pari(r)varttataḥ.
N7/2.2 - dhyāyante ca paraṁ jñānaṁ prajāpat(y)e varaṁ jaraṁ tenaiva vākyasaṁyogeno(e)ddālaka viceṣṭita.

5 N1/2.3a - ajñātareto viprarṣe(ḥ)ś cetamohād acetasaḥ.
N2/2.3b, N3/2.3a - ajñātareto viprarṣeś cyutam (N11 - śvatam) āhlādacetasaḥ.

6 N1/2.3b - tad vīryaṁ yam(s)a madhye tu palā nikṣipya tat kṛtaḥ.
N2/2.4a - tad vīryaṁ padmamadhye tu (N3/2.3b - jalān nikṣipya tat kṛtaṁ) dhṛtaṁ nikṣipya yatnataḥ.

taṁ kuśāgrair veṣṭayitvā gaṅgātīre vyacikṣipat[7]
vāyunā tat tato nītaṁ gaṅgāyām apatan nṛpa[8] [4]
prajāpatyatiyogena kṛtvedaṁ vrajasaṁpuṭaṁ[9]
atha bhāgīrathītīre raghurājñaḥ śubhā purī[10] [5]
tatra rājagṛhe ramye viśāle rājakanyakā[11]

He threw that lotus flower, wrapped in Kuśa grass, at the riverbank.
Fallen into the river, it was then floating, blown by the wind, O king. [4]
Prajāpati's promise was thus fulfilled by Yoga, in that wandering bowl.
There, on the Bhāgīrathī (i.e. Ganges) riverbank was the wonderful city of king Raghu(II)*. [5]*
There, in the beautiful spacious king's palace (lived) the king's daughter,

---

N10 - tad vīryaṁ yama madhye tu palān nivipya (N11 - patnān nikṣipya) tat tataḥ.

Bo/2.4b - tad vīryaṁ padmapuṭake kṣiptaṁ yatnena vai tat.

Ra/2.4b - tad vīryaṁ padmamadhye tu sthāpayitvā prayatnataḥ.

7 Emendation - NK. N1/2.4a - taṁ kuśair thecchayitvā tu gaṅgātīre vyacittayat.

N2/2.4b - taṁ kuśair veṣṭayitvā tu gaṅgātīre (N3/2.4a - sākṣipat, N10 - vyacikṣighama, N11 - vyacikṣi(a)pat) vyacikṣipet.

8 N2/2.3.5a - vāyunā ta(ṁ)t tato nītaṁ gaṅgāyām aparen nṛpa.

N11 - vāyunā tat tato vīry(t)a gaṅgāyām a(u)patan nṛpa.

9 Emendation - DS. N1/2.5a - prajāpatīti yogena kṛtāyaṁ vrajasaṁpuṭaṁ.

N2/2.5b - prajāpatīti yogena tadāmbuja (N3/2.5a - tatrāmb(v)uja) [tu] saṁpuṭaṁ.

N10, N11 - prajāpatīti yogena tatāyaṁ vrajasaṁpuṭaṁ.

10 N1/2.5b - atha bhāgīrathītīre raghunāthaḥ śubhāsu nu.

N2/2.6a, N3/2.5b - atha bhāgīrathītīre raghurājñaḥ śubhā purī.

N10 - atha bhāgīrathītīre raghurājñaḥ (N11 - raghubhāgyaḥ) śubhā surūpātimanoharā (vi).

N7/2.5a - atha gaṅgātaṭe tatra ragurājāpurī gṛhaṁ.

N4/2.6, N8/2.45b-46a, Ra/2.6 - tatra gaṅgātaṭe yatra raghurājapurīvarā tatra saughe mahocchrāye rāja te rājakanyakā.

Bo/2.5b - tatra gaṅgataṭe rājño raghoś ca mahatī purī.

11 Following N2/2.2.6, N3/2.5b-6a. Verse 2.6a-b is missing in N1.

N7/2.5b - tatra pauragṛhe ramye vilāse rājakanyakā.

pravālādhararamyā sā nāmnā candravatī śubhā[12]
taptakāñcānaraktābhā surūpātimanoharā[13]
na devī na ca gandharvī nāsurī nāpsarā kvacit[14]
tādṛg rūpavatī kanyā triṣu lokeṣu kāpi na[15] [6]
yamasatyādikaṁ tasyā adbhutaṁ kim u kathyate[16]
sā tu śṛṅganibhe ucchaprāsādasyopari sthitā[17] [7]
tatra sā ca satī nityaṁ rājakanyā manoramā[18]
kanyā daśasahasreṇa sevyate ca divāniśaṁ [8]
gandharvyo nāgakanyāś ca raṁbhādyāpsarasas tathā
candravatyā mahārāja kalāṁ nārhanti ṣoḍaśīṁ [9]

a young sprout, the image of beauty. Her name was the beautiful Candravatī -
such a beautiful princess, red as polished gold.
No goddess, no Gandharvī, no Asurī, not any Apsarā,
indeed no any other beautiful girl in the three worlds could be compared to her. [6]
How can her wonderful restraint, truthfulness, etc. be described?
She used to stand on a high terrace in the palace, [7]
there she was always, the king's beautiful daughter.
She was attended by 10000 maidservants[IV]*, day and night. [8]*
No Nāga girl, nor a Gandharvī, nor the celestial dancer Rambhā and her like,
were worth (even) the sixteenth part of her beauty, O king. [9]

---

12 N2/2.7a - pravāla ca sā nāmnā śubhā candrāvatī khalu.
N7/2.6a - pravāla sā dharā tatra svapādā dīptatejasā.

13 N2/2.7b - taptakāñcānavarṇābhā surūpātimanoharā.
N4/2.7b, N8/2.47a, Ra/2.7b - taptakāñcanakāntam ābhisurūpā padmalocanā.

14 N1/2.6a - yāti manoharān devī na ga(ā)ndharvī na cāsurī.
N11 - [na] devī [na ca] ga(ā)ndharvī nāsurī nāpsarā kvacit.
2.6b and 2.7a are switched - 2.7a is 2.6b in N1.
N4/2.8a, N8/2.47b, Ra/2.8a - na devī na ca ga(ā)ndharvī na nāgaduhītā kvacit.

15 N1/2.7a - nādṛśyaya cā(a)tī kanyā triṣu lokeṣu kāpi na.

16 N11 - yamasatyādikaṁ tathā adbhutaṁ kim u kathyate.

17 Emendation - NK. N1/2.7b - (ne) sa tu śṛṅganibh(ā)e (ty)u(ś)c[ch]aprāsādas yopari sthitā.
N2/2.9b, N3/2.9c - meruśṛṅganibhātyucchair prāsādasyopari sthitā.
N10 - meruśṛṅganibhātyucca (N11 - meruśṛṅganibhātsucca) prāsādasyopari sthitā.

18 N10 - tatra sā ca vasat(ī)i nityaṁ rājakanyā manorathā (vi).

sakhībhiḥ sā samaṁ tatra krīḍate rājaveśmani[19]
vedavidyādharāḥ viprāḥ satyavrataparāyaṇāḥ [10]
prajāś cātisukhāḥ sarve rājā cātyantadhārmikaḥ[20]
raghur nāmeti vikhyāto vratī tatra narādhipaḥ[21] [11]
tasya rājye prajāvṛddhiḥ subhikṣaṁ ca mahīpate[22]
dīrghāyuṣī prajāḥ sarvā nārujo nirupadravāḥ[23] [12]
dhīrā janāś ca vikrāntā dhārmikāḥ kṣatravaṁśajāḥ
tasya putrī mahārāja vipulāyatalocanā[24] [13]

With her girl-attendants she used to play in the king's palace.
Brahmins there (i.e. in Raghu's kingdom) were well inspired, had all Veda knowledge (and) Truth was their goal in life. [10]
The king was also righteous, (and) the citizens were very happy.
The king was self-controlled, known by the name Raghu. [11]
In his kingdom there was abundance of food, and the number of citizens increased, O great king.
All his people enjoyed longevity – free from disaster and disease. [12]
The men were Kṣatriyas, brave, victorious, (and) righteous.
His daughter, O great king, had elongated eyes, [13]

---

19 Additional half verse: N2/2.12b - tretayuge mahāpuṇye dhartiś ca sarvavarsakāḥ.

20 N1/2.11a, N10, N11 - prajā(s)ś c(t)ātisukhāḥ sarvā rājā cātyantadhārmikaḥ.
N3/2.13a - prajāś cātisukhāṁ sarve yad rājātyantadhārmikaḥ.

21 N2/2.14a, N3/2.13b, N10, N11 - raghur nāmeti vikhyāto hyāsi tatra narādhipaḥ.

22 N1/2.12a - tasya (N10, N11 - rājye) rājya prajāvṛddhiṁ (N3/2.14a - rājño prajāvṛddhiḥ) subhikṣaṁ ca (N2/2.14b - prajāpate) mahīpate.

23 Emendation - DS. N1/2.12b, N11 - dīrghāyuṣaḥ prajāḥ sarvā nārujo (N2/2.15a, N3/2.14b - nirūjo) nirupadravāḥ.
N10 - dī[rghā]yuṣaḥ prajāḥ sarvā (N11 - nārūjo mitūpadravāḥ) nirūjo ni[r]upadravāḥ.

24 N1/2.13b - tasya putrī mahārāja vipulāpattanovamāḥ.
N10, N11 - tasya putrī mahārājñī vipulāyatalocanā.
N4/ 2.15b, N7/2.17a, N8/2.55b, Ra/2.15b - vīrāś ca vikrāntā dhārmikāḥ kṣatravaṁśajāḥ.
N4/2.16b, N8/2.56a, Ra/2.16a - tasya putrī mahārāja (BF/2.18b - padmapatāyatekṣanā) kamalāyatalocanā.

sā sakhībhiḥ paritā sarvābharaṇabhūṣitā[25]
kṛttvā snehanaṁ gaṅgāyāṁ yāti nityaṁ nṛpātmajā[26] [14]
nirgatā saptayānena sā sutā śubhalakṣaṇā[27]
mauktikābharaṇā sā vai kṛtābharaṇakuṇḍalaiḥ[28]
śubhāṅgī turagārūḍhā dhvajacāmaraśobhitāḥ[29]
nirmalāḥ kanyakāḥ sarvā athājagmuḥ yathā narāḥ[30] [15]
mahādundubhinādena gītāvāditraśobhinā[31]
śaṅkhabhir anvitā mārge vṛtā varminaraiḥ saha[32] [16]
gaṅgāyāṁ snātum āyātā raghurājasya kanyakā[33]

surrounded by her girl-attendants, all adorned with ornaments.
The king's daughter, after having anointed herself, always used to go to the river, [14]
by a carriage of seven horses, that daughter of a wonderful figure.
She was adorned with pearl ornaments, and wearing earrings.
She had beautiful limbs, riding on a horse with fine banners and fans.
All pure women, as well as men, came out (to see her). [15]
They were accompanied by singing and the sound of big drums,
along with conches and smaller drums, protected by the best of armoured guards. [16]
King Raghu's daughter, went to the river to take a bath,

---

25 N1/2.14a - sā saṁratībhiḥ (N11 - saṁravībhiḥ) paritā sarvābharaṇabhūṣitā.
N2/2.16b, N10 - sā sakhibhiḥ parivṛttā sarvābharaṇabhūṣitā.
N3/2.16a - sakhībhir anvitā mārge divyābharaṇakāntibhi[ḥ].

26 Emendation - NK. N1/2.14b - kṛttvā snehana gaṅgāyāṁ [yāti] nityaṁ nṛpātmajā.
N2/2.17a - kṛtvā snānaṁ gaṅgāyāṁ [yāti] nityaṁ nṛpātmajā.

27 Emendation - NK. N1/2.15a - nirg(m)atā sapt(v)ayānena sā sutā śubhalakṣaṇā.
N2/2.17b - nirgatā sā svajānena (N10, N11 - sāśvayānena) snātuṁ sā śubhalakṣaṇā.

28 Ra/2.18ab - muktāhārala sat kaṇṭhā hemakuṇḍalam aṇḍitā.

29 N1/2.16a - śubhāṅgī turagārūḍhā dhajayā bharaṇobhitā nirmalā.
N7/2.20a - sarvāstā turaṅgārūḍhā dhvajacāmaraśobhitāḥ.
BF/2.21b - sarvās turaṅgam ārūḍhā dhvajacāmaradharaṇyāḥ.

30 N10 - nirgatāḥ kanyakāḥ sarvā (N11 - sardhā) āpājagmuḥ yatho narāḥ.

31 N1/2.16a, N10, N11 - mahān dundubhinādena gītāvāditvaśobhitā.
N2/2.19a - mahādundubhinādena gītāvādhariśobhitā.

32 Emendation - NK. N1/2.16b - śaṅkhabhir anvitā bhārge vṛtāvarmai varaiḥ saha.
N2/2.20a, N10, N11 - sakhībhir anvitā mārge vṛttā varṣavaraiḥ saha.

33 N10 - gaṅgāyāṁ snāyituṁ yātā (N11 - snātum ātā) raghurājasya kanyakā.
Bo/2.10a - gaṅgāyāṁ snātum āyātā śakhibhiḥ parivāritā.

krīḍati sma taṭe ramye vratasthā brahmacāriṇī[34] [17]
sarvalakṣaṇasampannā rūpeṇodyotakāriṇī[35]
apaśyat tatra sā kanyā durād gāṅgāṁbhasi sthitaṁ[36] [18]
divyaṁ saugandhikaṁ padmaṁ pravāhāntaram āvrajat[37]
na tatra kramate sūryo na ca vai tatra candramāḥ [19]
adṛṣṭaṁ mānuṣair ca tat padmaṁ tat vipulaprabhaṁ[38]
puṭakaṁ veṣṭitaṁ darbhair dṛṣṭvā vismayam āgatā[39] [20]
gatvā tam ānayāmāsa padmaṁ paṅkajaśobhanaṁ[40]

playing always on the pleasant bank, that unmarried girl who kept her vows. [17]
Endowed with all virtues, her beauty was very attractive.
Standing in the water of the river, that princess saw from afar [18]
coming floating in the current, the heavenly fragrant lotus,
(that) neither the sun, nor the moon, could reach. [19]
Such a lotus, with far reaching luster, has never been seen before by men.
Seeing that (lotus) held by bowl-shaped grass, (she) was filled with admiration. [20]
(Strongly desiring it she ordered): "Go bring that shiny beautiful lotus".

---

[34] N1/2.17b - krīḍati sma tare (N2/2.21a - krīḍante (N3/2.17a - krīḍiti) hi, (N7/2.23a - krīḍate ca) taṭe) ramye vratasthā brahmacāriṇī.
N10 - krīḍati sma taṭe ramye taṭasthā brahmacāriṇī.

[35] N10 - sarvalakṣaṇasampūrṇā rūpeṇodyotakāriṇī.
N7/2.(23b) - sarvalakṣaṇasampannā rūp(a)ān lavaṇyasamyutā.
Ra/2.23a - sarvalakṣaṇasampannā krīḍantī cakre sakhīvṛtā.

[36] N1/2.18b, N11 - t(j)y ap(y)aś(s)yat tatra sā kanyā durād gāṅgāṁbhasi [sthitaṁ].
N3/2.18a - apaśyataṁ ca sā kanyā durād gāṅgāṁbhasi sthitaṁ.
N10 - apaśyat tatra sā kanyā (N4/2.21b, N8/2.61b - krīḍantī daivayogataḥ) durād gāṅgāṁbhasi syat taṁ.

[37] N1/2.19a - (na) divyasaugandhikaṁ padmaṁ pravāhāntaram (N11 - āvrajat) āvrajan.
Ra/2.24a - divyaṁ saugandhikaṁ padmaṁ gaṅgāyāṁ samupāgataṁ.

[38] N1/2.20a, N11 - adṛṣṭaṁ mānuṣāṁ ca tat padmaṁ vipulaṁ prabhuṁ (short).
N2/2.23b - adṛṣṭaṁ mānuṣāṁ tu tat padmaṁ tat vipulaṁ prabhuṁ.
N3/2.19b - adṛṣṭaṁ mānuṣāṇāṁ ca tat padma (N10 - padmaṁ) vipulaṁ śubhaṁ.

[39] N1/2.20b - puṭakaṁ veṣṭitaṁ dar(ṛ)bhair dṛṣṭvā vismayaṁ āgatā.
N4/2.23b - puṭikaṁ (Ra/2.25b - puṭi taṁ) veṣṭitaṁ darbhair dṛṣṭvā vismayaṁ āgatā.

[40] Emendation - NK. N1/2.21a - e(i)kām ā(ya)bhāv(y)ayāmāsa ābhapadaṁ (N10 - ānayedaṁ) suśobhanaṁ.

ānīya ca tadā dattaṁ rājaputryai tad aṁbujaṁ[41] [21]
āghrātamatraṁ tad vīryaṁ praviṣṭaṁ nābhimaṇḍale[42]
snātvā ca prasthitā veśma kanyākābhir drutaiva sā[43]
māse tu prathame tasyā abhūd garbhasya saṁbhramaḥ[44]
dvitīye hy abhavat tasyās tiktamiṣṭādike ruciḥ[45] [22]

That "water born"(V) *was brought and given to the king's daughter. [21]*
(Just) by smelling it, the semen entered her body, into the belly.
After having bathed, she set out for the palace, along with her girl-attendants.
In the first month, she became very bewildered by the embryo (in her womb).
In the second, she became fond of bitter and sweet food. [22]

N2/2.23b - ekām ājñāyayāmāsa (N3/2.20b - ānayed akṣu śobhanaṁ) cāna padaṁ suśobhanaṁ.

N4/2.24a - tada sājñapayāmāsa sakhīṁ (Ra/2.26a - catvarayānvitā) caturaveṣṭitaṁ.

41 N2/2.24a - ānīya ca tayā dattaṁ (N10 - tadā datte) rājaputryai (N3/2.21a - rājñaputrī) tad aṁbujaṁ.

42 Following - Bo/2.14b.

N1/2.22a - grāsamātraṁ tu tad (N2/2.25b - grāṇamātraṁ) vīryaṁ praviṣṭaṁ (N10 - nābhimaṇḍale) nābhi (samaṁ) maṇḍalai.

N4/2.25b, Ra/2.27b - tasmād āghrāṇamātrāt tad vīryam atyadbhutaṁ mune.

N4/2.26a - ājñayā nīyatāṁ tayā praviṣṭaṁ nābhimaṇḍale.

BF/2.29b - āghrātamatraṁ nāsāgrāt tad vīryaṁ aviśat tadā.

43 N2/2.25a - snātvā ca prasthitā veśma kanyākābhi(s)ḥ saha saṁvṛtā.

N3/2.22a - snātvā ca prasthitā veśma kanyākābhivṛtaiva (N11 - kanyākādhṛtaiva) sā.

N4/2.27b - śnāsvā ca prasthitā veśma kanyakābhi[ḥ] paritā.

44 N1/2.22d, N11 - māsaṁ prathame tasyā (ra) ca abhūd garbhasya saṁbhramaḥ (vi).

N2/2.25b - māse ca prathame tasyāḥ abhūd garbhasya saṁbhramaḥ.

N10 - māsaṁ prathame tasyā sva abhūd garbhasya saṁbhavaḥ.

N8/2.68b - māse tu prathame tasyāḥ śukraśonitaṁ (Ra/2.29b - saṅkramaḥ) saṅgamaḥ.

N7/2.28a - kanyayā prathame māse vai nivartteta sonitaṁ.

Bo/2.15b - māse tu prathame tasyāḥ militaṁ śukraśonitaṁ.

45 N3/2.22b - dvitīye hy abhavat tasyāḥ tyaktamiṣṭādike (N10 - taktamiṣṭādike) ruciḥ.

N4/2.28a, N8/2.69a - ajāyata dvitīye tu (N7/2.28b - dvitīye anyathā ceṣṭā) śarīraṁ (Ra/2.30a - vipulāyitaṁ) vipulāyataṁ.

N7/2.29a - caturthe caiva saṁprāpte udaraṁ vyaktarūpiṇaṁ.

N7/2.30a - saṁbhūtam udaraṁ dīrghaṁ māse ṣaṣṭe ca saptame.

Ra/2.30b - tṛtīye masi sā kanyā vabhau pāṇḍumukhacchaviḥ.

tataḥ krameṇodaraṁ ca vavardha nṛpanandana[46]
stanau pṛthulatāṁ yātau śyāmau cāsye ca pāṇḍutā[47] [23]
dṛṣṭvā cihnāni sā kanyā bhraṣṭatejā kulekṣanā[48]
udvignamanasātīva patitā śokasāgare [24]
rudantīṁ tāṁ tato 'pṛcchan bhītāḥ kanyāḥ bhṛśaṁ tadā[49]

And thus, successively, her belly grew, O son of a king.
Her breasts grew bigger, (the nipples) blackened and her face grew pale. [23]
Seeing the signs (of pregnancy), that very girl of noble family was alarmed.
She lost her vivaciousness, falling into the ocean of sorrow. [24]
(Seeing her) weeping again and again, her girlfriends then asked her, frightened:

N8/2.69b - caturthe māsi saṁprāpte hy udaraṁ (N4/2.28b, Ra/2.31a - vyaktatāṁ gataṁ) vipulāyataṁ.
Bo/2.17-19a - romarājitaraṅgaś ca dvitīye māsi cābhavat
tṛtīye māsi saṁprāpte śarīraṁ vipulāyate
caturthe ca tato māse stanaṁ kṛṣṇamukhaṁ bhavat
pañcame māsi saṁprā(p)te udaraṁ vyaktimeti va
saṁbhūtam udaraṁ dīrghaṁ māse ṣaṣtame ca saptame.
N4/2.29b-30a, Ra/2.32 - pañcame pṛthulaśroṇiḥ stanabhārālasatī (short) atyantavyaktaṁ udaraṁ māse ṣaṣṭe vabhuvaha.

46 N2/2.26a - tataḥ krameṇa udaraṁ ca vavardha nṛpanandana (vi).
N3/2.23a - tatra krameṇodaraṁ ca vavṛdhe nṛpanadinī.

47 N10, N11 - stanau pṛthulatāṁ yātau ś(s)yāmā cāsye ca pāṇḍutā.
N4/2.29a - romarāji ca (N7/2.29b - romarājitaraṅgāni) śuśume stanau pṛthulatāṁ (Ra/2.31b - vipulatāṁ) gatau.

48 N1/2.24a - dṛṣṭvā cinhāni sā kanyā(s) tuṣṭatejakulekṣanā.
N2/2.27b - dṛṣṭvā cinhāni sā kanyā bhraṣṭatejā(ḥ) (N11 - kulekṣanā) kulakṣanā.
N10 - dadhac cinhāni sā kanyā bhraṣṭatejā kulekṣanā.
N7/2.30b - dṛṣṭvā cāpy udaraṁ kanyā bhraṣṭatejākulekṣanī.
Bo/2.19b - dṛṣṭvā cāpy udaraṁ kanyā bhraṣṭatejās tadābhavat.
Ra/2.33a - dṛṣṭvā tu sodaraṁ kanyā naṣṭejās tu (N8/2.70a - lakṣaṇaṁ) lakṣaṇaiḥ.

49 N2/2.28b, N10 - rudantī tāṁ tato 'pṛccha bhītāḥ kanyāḥ (N11 - 'pṛcchan bhītāḥ kaṁpa) bhṛśaṁ tadā.
N3/2.25b - rudatī ca tato 'pṛcchan dhātrī kanyā[ḥ] pṛcchaṁ tadā.
N4/2.31a, Ra/2.34a - rudantī (Bo/2.20b - rudantīṁ) tāṁ tato bhītāḥ papracchaḥ kanyakāḥ (N8/2.71a - kanyakāṁ) 'kh(k)ilā.
N7/2.(32a) - rudamānā tu sā kanyā bhītā papracchanti kanyakāḥ. (Verse numbers missing).

devī rodiṣi kasmāt tvaṁ kathayasva yathātathaṁ[50] [25]
sakhīnāṁ vacanaṁ śrutvā rodamānā yathā 'bravīt[51]
idam atyadbhutaṁ duḥkhaṁ pravakṣyāmi kathaṁ sakhi[52] [26]
vinā rajas samudbhūtaṁ kulākīrtiṣu dāyakaṁ[53]
māmākīrtikaraṁ bhadre raghuvaṁśasya dūṣaṇaṁ [27]
saṁbhūya tam udaraṁ paśya kiṁ karomīti tad vada[54]
tenāhaṁ duḥkhasantaptā raghuvaṁśasya dūṣaṇāt[55] [28]
na devī na ca gandharvī nāsurī na ca rākṣasī[56]

"O princess, why are you crying so? (Please) tell (us) the truth". [25]
Hearing the friends' words, (still) crying, she said the following:
"How shall I tell my so extraordinary sorrow, O friend(s). [26]
The cessation of my monthly period brings shame upon my family.
My deed, O dear, has defiled the Raghu family. [27]
You see my pregnant belly; just tell me what to do.
I am full of grief because of the defilement I have brought upon the Raghu family. [28]
No goddess, no Gandharvī, no Asurī and no Rakṣasī, (and no woman)

---

50 N1/2.25b - avi rodasi kasmāt tvaṁ kathayasva yathātathaṁ.
N4/2.31b, Ra/2.34b - kim arthaṁ (N7/2.(32b) - rodase devī) rodiṣi (N8/2.71b - rodasi) sakhe (Bo/2.20b - devī) kathayasva yathātathaṁ.

51 N1/2.26a - sakhīnāṁ vacanaṁ śrutvā rodamānā ya kā kvācit.
N3/2.26b - dhā āstu vacanaṁ śrutvā rodamānā ca sā 'bravīt.

52 N1/2.26b - idam atyadbhutaṁ dṛṣṭe saṁpravakṣyāmi kathaṁ sakhi (vi).
N8/2.72b - idaṁ mamādbhutaṁ duḥkhaṁ pravakṣyāmyālayaḥ kathaṁ.
Bo/2.22a - idam apy adbhutaṁ duḥkhaṁ pravakṣyāmi kathaṁ sakhi.

53 N3/2.27b - vinā rajas (N10 - rājaḥ) samudbhūtaṁ kulākīrtipradāyakaṁ.

54 N1/2.28a - saṁbhūyatam (N10, N11 - saṁbhūtam) udaraṁ paśya kiṁ karomīti tad vada.

55 N1/2.28b - tena hy eva (N10, N11 - tenāhaṁ) duḥkhasantaptā raghuvaṁśasya dūṣaṇāt.
Verse 2.28 is missing in N3.
N4/2.34, N8/2.74, Ra/2.37 - idaṁ mamodaraṁ sakhyaḥ (N7/2.34b - saṁbhūyataṁ udaraṁ paśya) kiṁ kariṣyāmi mīhitā
tenāhaṁ duḥkham apannā raghuvaṁśasya kāraṇāt.

56 N3/2.29a - na devī na ca gandharvī nāsurī na ca (Ra/2.38a - pannagī) mānuṣī.
N4/2.35a - na daive na ca gandharve nāsure na ca rākṣase.
N7/2.(35)a - na devā na ca gandharvā nāsurā na ca rākṣasāḥ.

na punar mānuṣī loke mādṛśī duḥkhapīḍitā[57] [29]
mahādbhutaṁ samutpannaṁ triṣu lokeṣu dṛśyate[58]
tasyās tad vacanaṁ śrutvā vihvalā sā bhayānvitā[59] [30]
tadā kaṁpitasarvāṅgā gatā rājñīniveśanaṁ[60]
bhayād vijñāpayāmāsa kṛtāñjalipuṭāsthitā[61] [31]
abhayaṁ dehi me rājñi tadā tat kathayāmy ahaṁ
sakhyā vijñāpitā rājñī bhayavihvalacetasā[62] [32]
rājñy uvāca

in the mortal world, has ever suffered like me. [29]
Something extraordinary has happened in the three worlds".
Hearing her words, trembling, seized with fear, [30]
they went then to the queen's palace, all their limbs trembling.
Fearfully she stood greeting with bowl-shaped joined palms. [31]
"Please permit me to speak freely, Your Highness",
the girlfriend requested from the queen, fearfully confused. [32]
The queen said

---

57 N1/2.29b - mupeyur mānuṣī loke mādṛśī duḥkhapīḍitā.
N4/2.35b - na punar mānuṣe loke yathedaṁ (N8/2.75 - kathedaṁ) samupasthitaṁ.
N7/2.(35)b - na punar mānavā loke akṣagocarasaṁsthitāḥ.

58 Emendation - NK. N1/2.30a - [a]bhy adbhutaṁ samutpannaṁ triṣu lokeṣu dṛśyate.
N2/2.33b - abhutaṁ tat samutpannaṁ triṣu lokeṣv adṛśyata.
N10 - [a]bhy a(u)dbhutaṁ (N11 - h(bh)y a(u)dbhu[ta]ṁ (tat)) samutpann(k)aṁ yan na lokeṣu dṛśyate.
N4/2.36a, N8/2.76a - adbhutaṁ ca samutpannaṁ (N7/2.(36b) - janalokeṣu jāyate) yan na lokeṣu dṛśyate.

59 N3/2.30a, N10 - tasyās tad vacanaṁ śrutvā vihvalā (Bo/2.23b - sā bhavat tadā) sabhayānvitā.
N7/2.(37a) - tasyās tu vacanaṁ śrutvā vihvalās tā (N4/2.36b, N8/2.76b - vihvalāś ca) bhayānvitāḥ.

60 N4/2.37a, N8/2.77a, Ra/2.40a - tadā tu kanyakāḥ śrutrvā gatvā rājñīniveśanaṁ.
N7/2.(37b) - tatas tā[ḥ] kanyakā[ḥ] sarvā gatā rājaniveśanaṁ.
Bo/2.24a - tadā tu kanyakāḥ sarvā gatā rājñīsamīpataḥ.

61 N4/2.37b, N8/2.77b, Ra/2.40b - tatas tā ca namaskṛtya cintayā parayānvitā.
N7/2.(38a) - vijñāpayanti tāṁ kanyāyāṁ kṛtāñjalipuṭā sthitā.
Bo/2.24b - vijñāpayanti kanyāyāḥ kāraṇaṁ mahad adbhutaṁ.

62 N1/2.32a - sakhyā vijñāpitā rājñī 'bhavad vihvalacetasā.

abhayaṁ te mayā dattaṁ brūhi kanye yathāvacaḥ[63]
mahārājñīvacaḥ śrutvā kanyā vacanam abravīt [33]
kanyovāca
avācyam adbhutaṁ devī paramaṁ lomaharṣaṇaṁ[64]
na devā na ca gandharvā nāsurā na ca mānavāḥ[65] [34]
na kinnareṣu lokeṣu vrajanty antaḥpuraṁ janāḥ[66]
tatra sthitāyā daivena duhitur garbhasaṁbhramaḥ[67] [35]

"Have no fear, my permission is given to you, tell all the details, girl".
Having heard the queen's words, the girl said the following words: [33]
"An extraordinary thing has happened, that cannot be explained, causing the hair to bristle.
No god, nor a male celestial being, and no man, [34]
nor a Kinnara – no male has entered the harem.
Staying there, by fate, your daughter became pregnant". [35]

---

63 N3/2.32b - abhayaṁ tu mayā dattaṁ brūhi kanye yathāvacaḥ.
N4/2.38a, N8/2.78a, Ra/2.41b - kiñcid vijñāpayiṣyāmo mātas tvan no 'bhayaṁ yadi.
N7/2(38b) - śṛṇu rājña mahāvṛtam abhayaṁ dīyatāṁ mama.
Bo/2.25 - bho rajñi kathayiṣyāmaḥ kanyāyā vṛttam adbhutaṁ
abhayaṁ cet pradīyeta brūmaḥ sarvaṁ suvismitāḥ.

64 N1/2.34a - avācyam (N3/2.34a - anyac ca) adbhutaṁ devī paramaṁ lokamarṣaṇaṁ.
N10 - avācyaṁ yad bhave devī paramaṁ lomaharṣaṇaṁ.

65 N2/2.38a, N11 - na devā(ḥ) na ca gandharvā nāsurā na ca (N3/2.34b - kinnarāḥ) mānuṣāḥ.
N4/2.40, Ra/2.43 - śṛṇuṣvedaṁ hi mātas tvam adbhutaṁ romaharṣaṇaṁ
dev(ad)ā [na] na va gandharvayakṣarākṣasapannagaiḥ.
Bo/ 2.27a - atyadbhutaṁ mahādevi na bhūtaṁ na śrutaṁ kvacit.
Bo/ 2.28a - na devā na ca gandharvā nāsurā na ca rākṣasāḥ.

66 N2/2.38b - na kinnaro (- - - -) vrajanty antaḥpuraṁ janāḥ.

67 N2/2.39 - tatra sthitāyā daiva tu duhitur garbhasaṁbhavaḥ
kva to rājñi kim adyāhaṁ vadāmi tava ca (-) ke.
N3/2.35 - kiṁ punar mānuṣe vrajaty antaḥpurapure
tatra sthi(e)tāyā daiva tu duhitur garbhasaṁbhramaḥ.
N10 - tatra sthitāyā daivaduhitur garbhasaṁbhramaḥ.
Bo/ 2.28b-29a - tasyā dṛṣṭipathe devi narāṇāṁ caiva kā kathā
tathāpitasyā garbo 'bhūd duhituḥ kuladūṣaṇaṁ.
Ra/2.44a - kiṁ punar mānuṣair anyair agamye puṁvivārjjite.

kanyakā vacanaṁ śrutvā adbhutaṁ lomaharṣaṇaṁ[68]
sā rājñī duḥkhasantaptā patitā dharaṇītale [36]
vikalā naṣṭavijñānā mūrcchitānekavihvalā[69]
labdhasañjñā tato rājñī visasarja sakhījanaṁ [37]
preṣitā svālayaṁ sarvāḥ gatāḥ sakhyo bhayādbhutāḥ[70]
rājñaḥ samīpe sā gatvā vacanaṁ cedam abravīt[71] [38]
avācyam api bhūpāla sarvaśāstraviśārada[72]
abhayaṁ dehi me deva kathayāmi tavādbhutaṁ[73] [39]

Having heard the girl's extraordinary, hair-bristling words,
the queen fell, sorrow-stricken, to the ground. [36]
She was confused, losing rational thinking, and she fainted several times out of distress.
Regaining consciousness, the queen sent the girl-attendants away. [37]
All the girl-attendants returned to their dwellings astonished and frightened.
Approaching the king, she (the queen) said her words: [38]
"O mighty king, master of all branches of knowledge.
Permit me, O king, to tell you an extraordinary (story)". [39]

---

68 N2/2.40a - kanyakā vacanaṁ śrutvā hy adbhutaṁ (N3/2.36a - romaharṣaṇaṁ) lomaharṣaṇaṁ.
N4/2.44a, Ra/2.47a - evaṁ kanyā vacaḥ śrutvā romaharṣaṇam adbhutaṁ.
N7/2.42a - kanyakā vacanaṁ śrutvā adbhutaṁ romaharṣaṇaṁ.

69 N2/2.40a - vihvalā naṣṭavijñānā mūrcchitā śokavihvalā.
N3/2.37a - vikalā naṣṭavijñānā (N10 - mūrcchitāśokavihvalā) mūrcchitā śokasagare.

70 N3/2.38a - preṣitā (N1/2.38a - yoṣitā) svālayaṁ sarvā(ḥ) gatāḥ sakhyo (N11 - bhayādbhutaṁ) bhayā(a)tmakaṁ.

71 N7/2.44 - preṣitā āśrame sarvās tvaritā sa sakhījanaṁ
gatvā rājñaḥ samīpe sā sakhīvacanam abravīt.
Bo/ 2.31a - rājñaḥ samīpaṁ sā gatvā rājñī vacanam abravīt.
Ra/2.50a - rājñī ca rājasadanaṁ gatvā vacanam abravīt.

72 N2/2.44a, N10, N11 - avācyam asti bhūpāla (N3/2.38a - vācyam asti mahārāja) sarvaśāstraviśārada.
N8/2.87b, Ra/2.51a - śṛṇuṣvedaṁ mahābhāga sarvaśāstraviśārada.

73 N2/2.42a - abhayaṁ dehi me rāja kathayāmi tavādbhutaṁ.
N7/2.45b - [a]bhayaṁ dehi asmāsu adbhutaṁ pravadāmi te.
BF/2.46b - tavāgre kathayiṣyāmi lomaharṣaṇam adbhutaṁ.
Bo/ 2.31b - śṛṇuṣvedaṁ (N7/2.45a - śrūyatāṁ ca) mahārāja sarvaśāstraviśārada.
Ra/2.51b - abhayaṁ dehi me deva kathayāmy adbhutaṁ tava.

rājovāca
brūhi bhadre yathātatvaṁ dattaṁ te hi mayābhayaṁ[74]
bhūpates tad vacaḥ śrutvā mahiṣī vākyam abravīt[75] [40]
rājñy uvāca
candravatī nāma sutā atīva kuladūṣiṇī[76]
adbhutaṁ bhūpa sañjātaṁ tasyā garbhasya saṁbhavaḥ[77] [41]
tasyās tad vacanaṁ śrutvā rājā krodhasamanvitaḥ[78]

The king said
"You have my permission my lady, tell then what you have heard".
Having heard the king's words, the queen said the following. [40]
The queen said
"Our daughter, Candravatī, is ruining our family,
(something) extraordinary has happened, O king – she is pregnant!" [41]
Thus hearing her words, the king was filled with anger.

---

74 N1/2.40a - brūhi bhadre yathātatvaṁ dattaṁ te hi (N2/2.45a - mamābhayaṁ) mayā katha[ṁ].
N7/2.45a - brūhi bhadre yathānyāyam abhayaṁ tava vidyate.
Ra/2.51b - brūhi bhadre yathānyāyam abhayaṁ te dadāmy ahaṁ.

75 N1/2.40b, N11 - (ya) bhū[pa]tes (N10 - bhūpates) tu vacaḥ śrutvā mahiṣī vākyam abravīt.
N2/2.45b - bhūpates sa vacaḥ śrutvā rajñy uvācādbhutaṁ vacaṁ.
N7/2.45b - bhūpasya vacanaṁ (Ra/2.52a - iti rāja vacaḥ) śrutvā rajñī vacanam abravīt.

76 N1/2.41a - candravatī nāma sutā atīva (N10, N11 - kulabhūṣiṇī) kulabhūṣaṇī.
N4/2.51b - mahāraṇye candravatīm (Ra/2.56a - enāṁ t[u] kuladūṣiṇīṁ) etāṁ sma kuladūṣinī.
N7/2.47a - duhitāya candravaty atyantakuladūṣiṇī (short).

77 N1/2.41b - adbhutaṁ bhūpa (N3/2.41b - rūpa[ṁ]) sañjātaṁ (N2/2.46b - tasyās tu garbhasaṁbhavaṁ) tasyā garbhasya saṁbhramaḥ.
N11 - adbhutaṁ bhūpa sañjā taptasyā garbhasya saṁbhramaḥ.
N7/2.47b - adbhutaṁ svāmi sañjātaṁ gaccha tatraiva saṁbhramaḥ.
Ra/2.53a - adbhūtaṁ deva sañjātaṁ garbhas tasyā vabhūva ha.

78 Ra/2.54a - evaṁ rajñīvacaḥ śrutvā rājā krodham (N4/2.50b, N8/2.90b - samanvitaḥ) avāpa ha.
BF/2.51a - iti śrutvā sa bhūpalaḥ kopākulitamānasaḥ.
Bo/ 2.32b - raghus tad vacanaṁ śrutvā sakaṁpaś cābhavat kṣanāt.

kurvan he heti pāpiṣṭhe mahānarthaḥ kṛtaḥ tvayā[79] [42]
raktākṣaḥ kopasampannaḥ prāha bhṛtyajanaiḥ saha[80]
ajane tūrṇam ādāya yāta enāṁ mahāvane[81] [43]
tato bhūpavacaḥ śrutvā tathā cakrus tadājñayā[82]
rudantīṁ tāṁ samādāya kṣiptvā nirmanuje vane[83] [44]

Crying, he said with disapprobation: "O most wicked; you have committed a great immoral (sin)!" [42]
Enraged, his eyes reddened with blood, he ordered his servants:
"Take her quickly to that unpopulated big forest". [43]
Having heard the king's order, they (immediately) fulfilled it,
taking her weeping, (and) leaving her in an unpopulated forest. [44]

---

79 Emendation - NK. N1/2.42b - kurvan he heti pāpiṣṭhe ma[h]ānarthaḥ kuto 'patat.
N2/2.47b - uvasva kurvatī kaṣṭaṁ hā pāpo kim idaṁ mahat.
Additional half verse: N2/2.48a - mukha (- - - -)pama lakṣaṇaṁ vaha vistaraṁ.
N3/2.42b - kurvan ha heti pāpiṣṭhe mahānarthaṁ kuto patat.
N11 - kurvan he heti pāpiṣṭo mahānarthaḥ kuto patat.
N7/2.48b - kurute ca mahat kaṣṭaṁ hā pāpaṁ kim idaṁ kṛtaṁ.
N8/2.91a, Ra/2.54b - akaroc ca mahāduḥkhaṁ hā pāpe kim idaṁ kṛtaṁ.
BF/2.51b-52 - duḥkhena dīnahṛdayaḥ kiṁ karomīty acintayat.
raktanetro 'tiśokāntaḥ kiṁ kanyā duḥkhitā nijā
kiṁ vā kulaṁ suvimalaṁ kva śaṅkitam idaṁ mahat.
Bo/ 2.33a - tataḥ kruddho nṛpaḥ (N4/2.51a - duḥkhaṁ) pāpe hā kanye kim idaṁ kṛtaṁ.

80 N1/2.43a - raktā(a)kṣaḥ kopasampannaḥ 'bhyāha bh[ṛ](ya)tyajanaiḥ sa(kṛt)ha.
N2/2.48b - raktākṣaḥ bhogasampannaḥ āha bhṛtyaṁ janā asaḥ.
N3/2.43a - raktākṣaḥ krodhasampannaḥ āha bhṛtyajanaiḥ saha.
N11 - raktājaḥ kopasampannaḥ 'bhyāha bhṛtyajanaiḥ saha.
Ra/2.55b - evaṁ hṛdi samālocya bhṛtyān ājñāpayan nṛpaḥ.

81 N1/2.43b, N10, N11 - [ty]ajadhvaṁ tūrṇam ādāya pāpam enāṁ (N2/2.48b - pāpi tenāṁ, N3/2.42b - pāpam etāṁ) mahāvane.
N4/2.52a, Ra/2.56b - tyajadhvaṁ tvaritaṁ duram avicāryaṁ madājñāya.
N7/2.49b - mahā[ra]ṇye tyajyetāṁ vai rājā vacanam abravīt.

82 N3/2.44a - tato bhūpavacaḥ śrutvā tathā cakrus (N2/2.49a - tathājñaya, N10, N11 - tadājñaya) madojayaḥ.

83 N1/2.44b - rudantīṁ tāṁ samādāya pakṣimā nirmune (N2/2.49b, N11 - kṣipvā nirmanuje) vane.
N4/2.54a, N8/2.94a, Ra/2.58a - rudatīm api tāṁ kanyāṁ ratham āropyati tadā.

samīpam āgatā rājñas tūrṇam ājñākarā narāḥ[84]
tyaktvā tatra mahāraṇye siṁhavyāghraniṣevite[85] [45]
ekākinī dharmaśilā kanyā kamalalocanā[86]
ruroda tāraśabdenā ha vidhe kim idaṁ kṛtaṁ [46]
vīkṣate sma diśaḥ sarvā yūthabhraṣṭā yathā mṛgī[87] [47]

The men arrived quickly before the king, having fulfilled his order,
leaving her there in the big forest, full of tigers and lions. [45]
The beautiful-eyed girl, once the pillar of righteousness,
was now weeping loudly – "O fate, what have I done?" – [46]
looking in all directions, like a female deer, gone astray from her herd. [47]

N4/2.54b, N8/2.94b - vyasṛjan tāṁ mahāraṇye (Ra/2.58b - bhītā bhūpativākyataḥ) rājaśāsanatatparāḥ.
N7/2.50b - rodamānā ca sā kanyā niḥkṣiptā nirjane vane.
BF/2.53b - āhūya kanyakātyāgam ādideśājane vane.
Bo/ 2.34 - rodamānā ca sā kanyā bhṛtyair nītā vanaṁ prati
ratham āropayitvā ca nikṣiptā nirjane vane.

84 N2/2.50b - samīpam āgatā rājñas (N3/2.45a - tūrṇamo - - - - -) tūrṇa[m] (r)ājñākarā narāḥ.

85 N2/2.51a - tyaktvā (N10, N11 - tyaktā) tatra mahāraṇye siṁhavyāghraniṣevite.
N7/2.51a - tya(i)kt(a)ā vai rodamānā sā rājñaḥ ājñākarā gatāḥ.

86 N4/2.56b, N8/2.96, Ra/2.60 - ekākinī vane tasmin siṁhavyāghrasamakule.
BF/2.55b - ekākinīṁ rājñakanyāṁ tyaktvā tūrṇam upāyayuḥ.
Bo/ 2.35a - ekākinī vane tasmin vyāghrasiṁhaniṣevite.

87 N1/2.47 - vīkṣate sma diśaḥ sarvā yūthabhrakṣā yathā mṛgī.
N10 - vīkṣante sya (N11 - bījate sma) diśaḥ sarvā yūthabhraṣṭ(y)ā yathā mṛgī.
N4/2.56b, N8/2.96, Ra/2.60 - bhramantī bhayasantrastā kanyā kamalalocanā.
N8/2.97, Bo/ 2.36, Ra/2.61 - rudanti tāraśabdenā ha vidhe kim idaṁ kṛtaṁ vīkṣantī ca diśaḥ sarvā yūthabhraṣṭā mṛgī yathā.
N4/2.58, N8/2.98, Ra/2.62 - vanād vanāntaraṁ ghoraṁ jagāma (N4/2.58a - nṛpanandinī) nṛpanandanī
na lebhe śarmma kutrāpi kuñjacchāyājalādiṣu.
BF/2.56 - ruroda sā bhṛ(ra)ṣaṁ bālā mṛgayuthaiś ca vīkṣitā
sīteva rāmasaṁtyaktā valmiker āśramāntike.
Bo/ 2.35b - vihvalābhayasaṁpanna kanyā kamalalocanā.

iti śrībrahmāṇḍapurāṇe nāsiketopākhyāne candravatyaraṇyapraveśo dvitīyo 'dhyāyaḥ

This is the second chapter of the Nāsiketa story, pertaining to the Brahmāṇḍa Purāṇa, called – Candravatī's entrance into the forest.

Translation Notes

I – In other versions (BF/2.5a, Bhandarkar No. 377, 2.5a, Göttingen No. 109) Uddālaka is described explicitly as tormented by passion (*kāmapīḍitaḥ*), and this is the cause of the outburst of his semen.
II – Most versions start with the mentioning of Raghu's town, and not with the description of his daughter.
III – According to N8/2.50b and Ra/2.10b – 100000 maid servants.
IV – Lotus.

Chapter 3

The Father and Son Meeting

vaiśaṁpāyana uvāca
tasmin mahāvane ghore paribabhrāma vihvalā[1]
atha kaścid ṛṣiḥ prāptaḥ satyadharmaparāyaṇaḥ[2] [1]
vane kuśapalāśādīn samāditsan paribhraman[3]
gṛhītvā phalapuṣpādīn yayau rājan svam āśramaṁ[4] [2]
gacchan dadarśa tatraiva tāṁ kanyāṁ sa mahāmuniḥ[5]

Vaiśaṁpāyana said
She (i.e. Candravatī) was roaming distressed, in that terrible big forest.
Then a certain very religious sage, adherent of Truth, came along, [1]
wandering in the forest, gathering Kuśa grass, fire sticks, etc.
Holding fruits, flowers etc., he was walking to his hermitage, O king. [2]
That great sage, walking, saw there, that same girl.

---

1 N1, N2, N3, N11 - tasmin mahāvane ghore (N10 - paribhrāmavihv(vh)alā) parivabhrāma vihvalā.

2 N2/3.1b - kaścit (N7/3.1b, Bo/3.1a - kaścic ca) tatra ṛṣiḥ samāyātaḥ satyadharmaparāyaṇaḥ (vi).
N10 - t(m)atra kaścid ṛṣiḥ prāptaḥ satyadharmaparāyaṇaḥ.
N4/3.1, N8/3.98, Ra/3.1 - evaṁ tasyāṁ bhramantyāṁ tu daivayogān mahān ṛṣiḥ kaścit tatra samāyā(p)taḥ satyadharmaparāyaṇaḥ.
N7/3.1a - evaṁ kṣiptvā vane tasmin bhramyamāno mahāṛṣiḥ.

3 N2/3.2 - ṛṣis tasmin vane śākaphalamūlarthikaḥ paraḥ
vane palāśāpatradarbhādī samāditsu[ḥ] paribhraman.
N3/3.2a - vane kuśapalāśādī samāditsu[ḥ] samaṁbhramaṁ.
N10 - vane kuśapalāśādīn samāditsu(ṣ)ḥ (N11 - paribhraman) paribhramat.
N4/3.2a, N8/3.99a, Ra/3.2a - mahāraṇye samitpuṣpaphalamūlakuśecchayā.
N7/3.2a - tasmin vane samedharthe vanamūla phalārthakaḥ.

4 N1/3.2b, N10, N11 - gṛhītvā phalapuṣpādi yayau rājan sv(y)am āśramaṁ.
N2/3.3a, N3/3.3a - gṛhītvā phalapuṣpādīn gacchan rājan svakāśramaṁ.
N4/3.2b, N8/3.99b, Ra/3.2b - tato gṛhītvā darbhādi homasādhanam uttamaṁ.

5 N2/3.3b - tasmin dadarśa tatraiva tāṁ kanyāṁ rodamānāṁ sa muniḥ (vi).
N4/3.3a, N8/3.100a, Ra/3.3a - nivarttamāno dadṛśe rudantīṁ kanyakāṁ muniḥ.

śīlena sā tathā kanyā yathāhalyā ca gautamī[6] [3]
brāhmaṇī girijā lakṣmī sāvitrī reṇukā yathā[7]
śacī citrotpalā durgā tathā rohiṇy arundhatī[8] [4]
āgatā kim araṇye 'smin yat tvayā dyotitā diśaḥ[9]
rodamānātidurvartā dṛśyate kena hetunā[10] [5]
tad ṛṣiś cintayāmāsa kaṁpayā cātirūpiṇīṁ[11]
kinnarī nāgakanyā ca gandharvatanayāthavā[12] [6]

By her conduct, that girl was like Ahalyā[(1)] *and Gautamī, [3]*
Brāhmaṇī (Śaktī), Girijā (Parvatī), Lakṣmī, Sāvitrī, Reṇukā,
Śacī, Citrotpalā, Durgā, Rohiṇī (and) Arundhatī. [4]
"Why have you arrived in this forest, you who illuminate (all) directions?
What calamity has befallen you? Why do I see you so miserably weeping?" [5]
The sage, thinking of that superb beauty (started) trembling with compassion –
"(She is like) a Kinnari girl, a Nāga girl, an offspring of the Gandharvas, [6]

BF/3.2b - śuśrāva ruditaṁ durād dayārdrīkṛtamānasaḥ.
Bo/3.1b - kandamūlaphalākāṅkṣī dadarśa tatra kanyakāṁ.

6 N1/3.3b, N2/3.4a, N11 - śīlena sā tathā kanyā yathāhilyā (N10 - yathādiṣṭyā) ca gautamī.
N4/3.4-5a, N8/3.1-2a, Ra/3.4-5a - kim iyaṁ damayantī kiṁ citralekhā tilottamā
ghṛtācī menākā vā kiṁ kim ahalyā nṛpottama
yakṣiṇī vā kinnarī vā vidyuddāmasamaprabhā.
N7/3.5 - damayantī bhavet kiṁ vā (Bo/3.2b - svic) citralekhā tilottamā
ghṛtārcī menakā raṁbhā ahalyā gomatī hi sā.
BF/3.5 - ahalyā draupadī vā 'sti apsarā vā tilottamā
ratiḥ kiṁ kāmahīneti cintayā vyākulo 'bhavat.
Bo/3.3 - urvaśī menakā vāpi ahalyā rohiṇī bhavet
yakṣiṇī vāpi gandharvī kinnarī nāgakanyakā.

7 N10 - brāhmaṇī girijā lakṣmī sāvirt(a)ī re(i)ṇukā yathā.

8 N1/3.4b, N10, N11 - śacī citrotpalā durgā (N2/3.4a - rohiṇy arundhatī yāthā) tāpārohiṇy arundhatī.

9 Emendation - NK. N1/3.5a - āgatā kim araṇye 'smin yat dṛśyā (N10 - pahayā, N11 - yat dṛyā) dyotitā (N3/3.5a - tad upādyotitā) diśaḥ.
N2/3.5b - āgate kim araṇye 'smin yad upādyotitā diśaḥ.

10 N2/3.6a, N3/3.5b, N10 - rodamānātiduḥkhartā dṛśyate kena hetunā.

11 N2/3.6b - sa ṛṣiś cintayāmāsa kātra ṣā syātirūpiṇī.

12 N3/3.6b-7 - kim eṣā damayantīti citralekhā tilottamā
ghṛtācī menakā cāpi ahalyā gautamī na vā
narī vā nāgakanyavā gandharve tanayā na vā.

rājakanyāthavā vāpi iti vismayam āgamat[13]
yad rajate vane hy eṣā vidyujjyotiḥsamaprabhā[14] [7]
sujātacaraṇāv asyāḥ suṣṭhujaghanastanau[15]
karau ca kamalākārau nayane kamalākṣike[16] [8]
nābhiś ca dakṣiṇāvartā madhye ca trivalī śubhā[17]

or like a princess" he said (to himself) with wonder,
"really lighting this (dark) forest, bringing light to where light is very dull". [7]
That girl of a good family, highly praised, of fine bust and behind, fell to the (sage's) feet,
her pupils like a pair of lotus-ponds in her lotus-shaped eyes. [8]
She had three folds in the midst of her belly, and her navel turned to the right[(II)].

---

13 N3/3.8a - rājakanyāthavā kāpi iti (N10 - jñati) vismayam āgamat.
N2/3.7a - rājakanyāthavā kā svid (Bo/3.4a - rājakanyāthavā śreṣṭhā) iti vismayam āgamat.
N4/3.5b, N8/3.2b, Ra/3.5b - rājakanyāthavā śreṣṭho kācid anyā kim idṛśi.

14 N3/3.8b - yad rājate vane tv eṣā (N7/3.6a - hy evā) vidyu[j]jyotisamaprabhā
N4/3.6a, Ra/3.6a, N8/3.3a - virājate mahāraṇye vidyud dāma samaprabhā.
N7/3.6b - rājate vanamadhye tu vidyu[j]jyotisamaprabhā.
Bo/3.4b - śobhate vanamadhye tu vidyullekhā yathā ghane.

15 N1/3.8a - sujātacaraṇau yat yāḥ suyacche (N11 - sujacche) jaghanastanau.
N2/3.8b - sujātacaraṇau yasyā sujaghe (N10 - sujacche) jaghanastanau.
N3/3.9a - sujātacaraṇau suṣṭhujaghanesaghanastanau.
N7/3.6b - supratiṣṭau ca pādau ca jaghanau sadhanau stanau.

16 N1/3.8b, N2/3.9a, N3/3.9b - karau ca kamalākārau (N10 - kamalākāro) nayane kamalādhike.
N4/3.6b, N8/3.3b, Ra/3.6b - pādau kokanadākārau karau ca kaṭhinau stanau.
N7/3.7a - karau ca kamalākārau nayanau kamalāyakau.
Bo/3.5a - karau rāgeṇa śobhantau vidhātrāracitau śubhau.

17 N4/3.7b, N8/3.4b, Ra/3.7b - nābhiś ca dakṣiṇāvartā (N7/3.7b,Bo/3.5a - trivalīmadhyasaṁsthitā) trivalībhir alaṅkṛtā.
Additional verses:
N2/3.10 - taptahemani bhau kārau stanau pārtha ca sthitābhau saṁpūrṇacandravadanā (N4/3.8a, N8/3.5a, Ra/3.8a - madanājñeva saṁsthitā) ākarṇāyatalocanā.
N3/3.10b-11a - taptahema sa mākrānti kanyā bhavatim arhati saṁpūrṇacandravadanī vā karṇāyatalocanā.
N7/3.8b - saṁpūrṇacandrabadanā ākarṇāyatarlocanā.

devadūtī ha sā kanyā sā pṛṣṭā muninā tadā[18] [9]
kā tvaṁ kanye mahābhadre kimarthaṁ tvam ihāgatā[19]
devagandharvakanyā tvaṁ sutā kasyāsi tad vada[20] [10]
kānyovāca[21]
na devī na ca gandharvī na nāgī na ca kinnarī[22]
raghurājasutāhaṁ tu adbhutād garbhasambhavāt[23] [11]

The sage then asked that god-sent girl: [9]
"Beloved girl, my dearest, for what purpose have you come here?
(Please) tell (me), you are the daughter of what god or Gandharva?" [10]
The girl said
"I am not a goddess, nor a Gandharvī, neither a Nāga girl, nor a Kinnarī.
I am the daughter of king Raghu, and because of the extraordinary case of carrying a baby, [11]

---

18 Emendation - NK. N1/3.9b - devadūtī sa hā (N2/3.10, N3/3.11b N10, N11 - īdṛg rūpavatī) kanyā sā pṛṣṭā muninā tadā.
N4/3.9a, N8/3.6a, Ra/3.9a - pṛcchati sma mahātejāḥ karuṇāyattamanasaḥ.
N7/3.9a - itthaṁ rūpavatīṁ kanyā pṛṣṭā sā ca dvijanmanā.
Bo/3.6a - atyadbhutaṁ ca tad rūpaṁ dṛṣṭvā provāca kanyakāṁ.

19 N3/3.12a - kā tvaṁ kanyā mahābhadre kimarthaṁ tvam ihāgatā.
N4/3.9b, N8/3.6b, Ra/3.9b - kā tvam atyadbhutākārā kiṁ āyātā mahāvane.
N7/3.9b - kā tvaṁ kanye mahābhadre kimarthaṁ iha cāgatā.
Bo/3.6b - kā tvaṁ kasyāsi rambhoru kimarthaṁ vanam āgatā.

20 N1/3.10b - devagandharvakanyānāṁ munyasyāsi ta (N10, N11 - [s]utānyasyāsi) tad vada.
N2/3.12a - devagandharvakanyā tvāṁ sutānyasyāsi (N3/3.12a - marttyānā(m)ṁ [s]utānyasyāsi) tad vada.

21 N2, N7 - candravaty uvāca.

22 N2/3.12b, N3/3.12b, N4/3.14a, N8/3.11a, Ra/3.14a - nāhaṁ devī na gandharvī na nāgī na ca kinnarī.
N10, N11 - nāhaṁ daivī (N7/3.10a - surī) na gandharvī n(t)a nāgī na ca kinnarī.

23 N1/3.11b - raghurājasutāhaṁ t(u)v adbhutād garbha[sam]bhra(u)māt.
N2/3.12b - raghurājasutāhaṁ ca tv adbhutād garbhasambhavāt.
N3/3.13a - raghurājasutā cāhaṁ duḥkhabhāreṇapīḍitā.
N10 - raghurājasutāhaṁ t(u)v adbhutād (ra)[gar]bhasa(e)mbhramā[t].
N7/3.10b - raghoḥ suduhitā cāham adbhutaṁ garbhasambhavāt.
N4/3.14b, N8/3.11b, Ra/3.14b - raghos tu kanyakā rājño mune svakuladūṣaṇī.
Bo/3.8a - raghos tu duhitā cāhaṁ pitā me garbhe dūṣanāt.

tyaktā pitreti kopena nirjīvā nirjane vane[24]
śokaśalyena ārtāhaṁ duḥkhabhāreṇa pīḍitā[25] [12]
evaṁ bruvāṇāṁ tāṁ kānyāṁ rudantīṁ duḥkhakarṣitāṁ[26]
dṛṣṭvā duḥkhena santaptāṁ munir vākyam uvāca ha[27] [13]
yājñavalkya uvāca[28]
adya prabhṛti me devī kanyā tvam asi mā śucaḥ[29]

I have been left lifeless in this unpopulated forest, by (the order of) my enraged father.
I am now distressed, burdened with misery, having been hit by an arrow of grief". [12]
Thus spoke that weeping girl, (deeply) wrinkled with grief.
Seeing her, grief-stricken, the sage said the following words. [13]
Yājñavalkya said
"From this day on you are my divine girl, don't grieve".

---

24 N2/3.13b - tyaktā pitreti kopena (N7/3.11a - pitā me krodhasantapto) nikṣiptā nirjane vane.
Half verse 12a is missing in N3.
N4/3.15b, N8/3.12b, Ra/3.15b - kruddhena ca tadā pitrā nikṣiptā gahane vane.
BF/3.14b - kopākulena tātena tyaktāhaṁ nirjane vane.
Bo/3.8b - tyaktavān nirjane 'raṇye raghur mām atra suvrata.

25 N1/3.12b - śākaśalyena ārtāhaṁ duḥkhabhāreṇa pīḍitā.
N2/3.14a - śokaśalyena vārtāhaṁ (N10 - ārtīhaṁ) duḥkhabhāreṇa pīḍitā.
N4/3.16ab, N8/3.13a, Ra/3.16a - śokaśalyāturā cāhaṁ (N7/3.11a - duḥkhe reṇuvibhaṣitā) bhramāmi bhayapīḍitā.

26 N2/3.14b - evaṁ bruvāntī tāṁ kānyāṁ rudantī[ṁ] duḥkhaduśitāṁ.
N10, N11 - evaṁ bruvāṇā[ṁ] tāṁ kānyāṁ ruda[n]tī[ṁ] duḥkhakarṣitāṁ.
N7/3.12a - evam uktā tu sā kānyā rudantā duḥkhakarṣitāṁ.
N8/3.13b, Ra/3.16b - evam uktā tata[ḥ] kanyā ruroda b(v)ahudhā punaḥ.

27 N3/3.14b - dṛṣṭvā duḥkhena santapto (N11 - svaṁ taptāṁ) munir vākyam uvāca ha.
N2/3.15a - dṛṣṭvā duḥkhena taptāṅgaḥ ṛṣiś ca samupāgataḥ.
Additional half verse: N2/3.15b - uvāca tāṁ tataḥ kanyāṁ bahuduḥkhaprapīḍitāṁ.
N4/3.17a, Ra/3.17a - dṛṣṭvā (N8/3.14a - dṛṣṭāṁ) tāṁ tadṛṣiṁ kānyāṁ ṛṣiḥ kārṇiko 'bravīt.

28 N7/3.13, Bo/3.9 - ṛṣir uvāca.

29 N10 - adya prabhṛtti me devī kanyā tvam asi mā śuca.
N4/3.17b, N8/3.14b, Ra/3.17b - adya prabhṛti me bhadre duhitā tvaṁ na saṁśayaḥ.
N7/13a - adya prabhṛti mā devī duḥkitāś cāśrame mama.
Bo/3.9a - adya prabhṛti me putrī dharmatas tvaṁ śubhānane.

gṛhītvā caiva tāṁ kanyāṁ muniḥ svāśramam āgamat[30] [14]
ihāśramapade ramye mama tiṣṭha nṛpātmaje[31]
dināni tāni garbhasya gamayantī tadāśraye[32] [15]
tasthau kuśādisaṁskāraṁ kurvatī bhūmilepanaṁ[33]
atha prasūtisamayaḥ prāptas tasyās tu duḥkhadaḥ[34] [16]
tataḥ kanyāśramaṁ tyaktvā sajjātinarapīḍitā[35]
gaṅgātīraṁ samaśritya namaskṛtya vaco 'bravīt[36] [17]
baddhvā karāñjalipuṭaṁ dhyātvā nārāyaṇaṁ vibhuṁ[37]

Holding that girl, the sage returned to his hermitage. [14]
"Stay now in my beautiful hermitage, O king's daughter".
Many days did the pregnant girl pass in that haven. [15]
She stayed there sorting Kuśa grass and smearing the floor.
The time of delivery was approaching, giving her pain. [16]
Thus, that girl, distressed by people (company), left the hermitage.
Arriving at the riverbank (and) having saluted, she said her words, [17]
standing there, with bowl-shaped joined palms, meditating on the omnipresent Nārāyaṇa (Viṣṇu).

---

30 N2/3.16b - gṛhītvā caiva tāṁ kanyāṁ (N3/3.16b - ṛṣi) muniḥ (N10 - svāmum upāgamat) svāśramam āgataḥ.
N7/13b - gṛhītvā caiva tāṁ (Bo/3.9b - tāṁ tataḥ) kanyāṁ ṛṣir āśramam āgataḥ.

31 N11 - ihāśramapade ramye mama tiṣṭha nṛpātmane.
N4/3.19a, N8/3.16a, Ra/3.19a - tatrāśrame nṛpasutā piturgṛha ivāvasat.
N7/14a - ihāśramaṁ paraṁ ramyam atra tiṣṭha nṛpātmaje.
Bo/3.10a - asmin mamāśrame ramye sukhaṁ tiṣṭha nṛpātmaje.

32 N3/3.17a - dināni tāni garbhasya gamayantī (N2/3.17a, N10 - tadāśrame) madāśrame.
N4/3.19b, N8/3.16b, Ra/3.19b - dinaiḥ katipayais tasyā garbhaḥ pūrṇo 'bhavan nṛpa.
N7/14b - dinaiḥ katipayais tatra pūrvagarbhā dinakramāt.
Bo/3.10b - udaraṁ vavṛdhe tasya garbho 'sau divasaiḥ kramāt.

33 N3/3.17b - tasthau kuśādisaṁskāraṁ kurvatī bhūmitoyanaṁ.

34 N2/3.18b - atha prasūtisamayaḥ prāptas tasyās tu (N10, N11 - duḥkhadaḥ) susadaḥ.

35 N1/3.17a - tāta kanyā śubhāṁ tyaktā (N10, N11 - tyaktvā) sajjātinarapīḍitā.
N2/3.19a - tataḥ kanyāśramaṁ tyaktvā lajjātibharapīḍitā.

36 N1/3.17b, N11 - gaṅgātīraṁ samaśritya namastutya vaco 'bravīt.

37 N11 - badhvā (N10 - cadhvā) karāñjalipuṭaṁ dhyātvā nārāyaṇaṁ vibhuṁ.

praṇamya gaṅgāṁ sūryaṁ ca tathānyān dharmarakṣiṇaḥ[38] [18]
antaryāmin mahāviṣṇo maheśa girijāpate
aham asmi yadi śuddhā śuddhavaṁśodbhavā tathā[39] [19]
raghuvīryāt samutpannā mātā satyavatī śubhā[40]
saṁbhavo me yadā śuddhaḥ dehena parivarjitaḥ[41] [20]
yathā yenābhavad garbhas tena mokṣaṁ avāpnuyāt[42]
ityuktvā tat kṣaṇād garbha udarād dhṛdayaṁ gataḥ[43] [21]
tataḥ kampas samāyāto nāsāgre samupasthitaḥ[44]
māse tu daśame kanyā prāsūta tanayaṁ satī[45] [22]

"I am saluting the river and the sun, and all the protectors of religious law. [18]
Something entered inside me, O Viṣṇu, O great god, lord of the mountain's daughter[III].
If I am pure, born in a pure family, [19]
of the seed of Raghu, to the wonderful mother Satyavatī,
and if I am pregnant with no bodily intercourse, [20]
then, let my baby be relieved (i.e. born) from the same (organ) by which it has been conceived".
Having said that, the girl's embryo passed from her womb to her heart. [21]
Thus, trembling, he reached the nose and stayed there.
In the tenth month, the girl gave birth to a male boy, while still a virgin. [22]

---

38 N2/3.20b, N10, N11 - praṇamya gaṅgā[ṁ] sūryyaṁ ca tathānyān (N1/3.18b, N3/3.20b - tapānyā) dharmasākṣiṇaḥ.

39 N1/3.18b, N10 - aham asmi yadā (N2/3.21a, N3/3.21a - yadi) ś(s)uddhā śuddhavaṁśodbhavā tatha.

40 N3/3.22a - raghuvīryāt samutpannā mātā satyavati yadā.

41 N1/3.20b - saṁbhavaṁ te śuddhaṁ deyaṁ pavivarjitā (short).
N2/3.22b - sarvabhavena (N3/3.22b - śuddhāhaṁ padāpāparivarjitaḥ) sudhāhaṁ sadā pāpavivarjitā.
N10, N11 - sarva bhave [yadā] ś(m)uddhā d[ehen]a (yadā) pāpa(vi)varjitaḥ.

42 N1/3.21a, N10 - yathā yenābhavad garbhas tena mokṣam avāpnuyāṁ.
N3/3.23a - yathā 'yaṁ me 'bhavad garbhas tena mokṣam avāpnuhi.

43 N1/3.21b - ity uktvā tat [kan]yā[garbha] (ṇā nama bhad) udarā(t)d dh(h)ṛdayaṁ gataḥ.
N3/3.23b - ity uktvā tatkṣaṇād garbhodarā(t)c ch(c)a dūrdhayaṁ gataḥ.

44 N10 - tataḥ kaḥ samāyāto n(m)āsāgre samupasthitāḥ.

45 N7/3.15a - māse tu navame (kanyā) putraṁ [pra]sūta (Ra/3.20a - putraṁ suṣuve) sā nṛpātmajā.
N8/3.17a - māse ca (N4/3.20a - tu) nāvame putraṁ prāsūta sā nṛpātmajā.
BF/3.17b - māse tu navame (Bo/3.11a - tasyāḥ prasūtir abhavan nṛpa) kanyā nāsāmadhyād ajijanat.

nāsāgreṇa tu niryāto nāsiketas tad ucyate[46]
dharaṇyāṁ patito bālo vadati sma vacas tv idaṁ[47] [23]
bāla uvāca[48]
mā śuco janani tvaṁ hi satyavrataparāyaṇā[49]
nāsiketābhidhāno 'haṁ daivāt tvadgarbham āgataḥ[50] [24]
brahmavaṁśe samutpannaḥ pitā coddālako mama
gaṅgātīre tapas tīvraṁ karoti sa mahātapāḥ[51] [25]
bālakasya vacaḥ śrutvā mātā vismayam āgatā[52]
gṛhītvā modam āpannā stanapānam akārayat[53] [26]

Since he came out of the nose, he was called Nāsiketa.
That boy fell to the ground, and then said these words: [23]
"Don't grieve, O mother, you who always adhere to Truth as your final goal.
Nāsiketa is my name, coming from Fate to your womb. [24]
My father is born in the lineage of Brahma, and Uddālaka is his name.
That great sage performed severe penance on the riverbank". [25]
Hearing the boy's words, the mother was seized with wonder.
Holding him, feeling happy, she breast-fed him. [26]

---

46 N1/3.23a, N11 - nāśāgreṇe (N2/3.25a - nāśāgreṇa, N3/3.25a - nāśāgre sa) tu niryāto (N10 - nāsāgreṇa tu niryātau) nāsiketas tad ucyate.
N7/3.15b - nāśāgreṇa t(m)u niry(j)āto nāśiketu tad ucyate.
N4/3.20b, N8/3.17b - nāsāgranirgato yat syāt (Ra/3.20b - nāsāgrān nirgato yasmān nāsiketas) nāśaketas tad ucyate.
BF/3.18 - nāsikāntaḥsamudbhūtaḥ sarvalakṣaṇasaṁyutaḥ
nāsiketur iti khyāto munibhiḥ kṛtamaṅgalaḥ.
Bo/3.11b - nāsāgreṇa tu kanyāyāḥ puruṣaḥ sarvalakṣaṇaḥ.

47 N1/3.23b, N10, N11 - dharaṇyāṁ patito bālo varatisma vacas tv idaṁ.

48 Following N2/3.26.

49 N2/3.26a - mā śocasi (N3/3.26a - śoca) janani tvaṁ satyavrataparāyaṇā.
N10 - mā śuco janani tvaṁ hi satyatrattaparāyaṇā.

50 Emendation - NK. N1/3.24b - nāsiketābhidhāno 'haṁ (N2/3.26b - garbham samāgamaḥ, N3/3.26b - tvadgarbhaṁ yāmy ahaṁ) daivāt yad garbha āgamaḥ.
N10 - nāsiketābhidhāno hi daivāt tvadgarbham āgataḥ.

51 N2/3.27b, N3/3.27b - gaṅgātaṭe tapas tīvraṁ karoti sa mahātapāḥ.

52 N1/3.26a - bālakasya vacaḥ śrutvā mātā vismayagomatā.

53 N2/3.28b - gṛhītvā bālakaṁ ta tu vismitā sā vicārayat.
N3/3.28b - gṛhītvā taṁ sutaṁ tanvi (N10, N11 - moham āpannā) stanapānam akārayat.

tam ādāya ṛṣeḥ pārśve candravaty āgamat tataḥ
tadagre hy avadad vākyaṁ nāsāgreṇa yathā janiḥ[54] [27]
so 'pi nāma tathā cakre bālo 'yaṁ śubhalakṣaṇaḥ[55]
jñānavān buddhimāṁś caiva bhaviṣyati suśobhanaḥ[56] [28]
pālayantī ca duḥkhārtā sasnehā munisadmani[57]
anvahaṁ rodamānaṁ tu dṛṣṭvā sutam uvāca ha[58] [29]
vatsa rodiṣi kasmāt tvaṁ pāpakarma durākṛte[59]
tvadīyakāraṇāt putra avasthā mama cedṛśī[60] [30]

Candravatī thus came, bringing him to the sage.
Then, before him, she said "He has just been born through the nose!" [27]
He (the sage) then gave the boy of most beautiful shape, his name,
(and said): "That wonderful (boy) will also become an intellectual, excellent in knowledge". [28]
She took care of the baby with love, in the sage's house, (and) was distressed, seeing the boy weeping everyday. She said to her son: [29]
"O son, why are you crying, you sin-child of bad character?
You, son, are the cause of my present situation, as it is". [30]

---

54 N3/3.29b - sa cāgre hy avadad vākyaṁ nāśagreṇa yathā janiḥ.

55 N7/3.17a - ṛṣibhir nāmedaṁ cakre puruṣaṁ sarvalakṣaṇaṁ.

56 N2/3.30b - jñānavān buddhivāṁś caiva bhaviṣyati suśobhanaḥ.
N7/3.17b - jñānavān buddhivān bālaḥ svarūpaś cātiśobhanaḥ.
Bo/3.12a - jñānavān buddhisaṁpanno bālo 'sau vinayānvitaḥ.

57 N1/3.29a - pālayantī ca duḥkhārtā sa snehā (N2/3.31a, N3/3.31a, N11 - lajjā) munisadmani.
N10 - pālayatī ca duḥkhārtā saptajāmu 'timanati (samani).
N7/3.17a - pālayantī sa duḥkhārttā lajjāmānā ṛṣīn prati.
Bo/3.12a - etādṛśaṁ pālayantī duḥkhārttā samavartata.

58 N1/3.29b - ahaṁ ca bālako - dṛṣṭvā sutam uvāca ha.
N3/3.31b - anvahaṁ rodamānaṁ tu sutaṁ dṛṣṭvā uvāca ha.
N7/3.17b - atyanta (v)rodamānaṁ tu sutam dṛṣṭvā uvāca sā.
Bo/3.12b - ekadāraṇyamadhye taṁ rudantaṁ sā nṛpātmajā.

59 N10 - vatsa rodiṣi kasmāt tvaṁ (N2/3.32a - pāpakarmapurākṛtaḥ) pāpakarmapurākṛtaṁ.
N7/3.18a - kimarthaṁ rodase vatsa pāpakarmadurātmakaḥ.
Bo/3.13a - kimarthaṁ rodiṣi tvaṁ me pāpasamparkakāraka.

60 Verse 3.30 is missing in N3.
N7/3.18b - tvadīye kāraṇe vipra avasthā cedṛśī mama.
Bo/3.13b - tvadīye kāraṇe putra hyavastheyaṁ mamedṛśī.

vaiśaṁpāyana uvāca
tataḥ saṁvatsare prāpte mañjūṣaṁ samakārayet[61]
tasyābhyantarataḥ kṣiptvā darbheṇa pariveṣṭya ca[62] [31]
samādāya pravāhe tu gaṅgāyāṁ tam acikṣipat[63]
etad vākyaṁ samuccārya putrasyāgre tu kanyakā[64] [32]
na jāne te janitāraṁ kathaṁ garbhasya saṁbhavaḥ[65]
yasya vīryeṇa saṁbhūto vatsaka tvaṁ mamodare[66] [33]

Vaiśaṁpāyana said
Thus, by the end of one year, she made a box and
put her child inside it, having wrapped him with grass. [31]
She reached the river bringing him, intending to throw him in.
The girl then pronounced the following words before her son: [32]
"I don't know your father, O son, (or) how you were conceived.
Dear, from whose seed you were created in my womb, [33]

---

61 N1/3.31a, N10, N11 - tataḥ saṁvatsare prāpte (N2/3.33a, N3/3.32a - pūrṇe mañjūṣaṁ) mapūśaṁ samakārayet.
N4/3.23b, N8/3.21a, Ra/3.23b - putraṁ tyaktuṁ manaś cakre pūrṇe samvatsare nṛpa.
N4/3.24a, N8/3.21b, Ra/3.24a - kārayitvā ca mañjūṣāṁ dṛḍhāṁ vivaravarjitāṁ.
N7/3.19a - tataḥ saṁvatsare pūrṇe mapūśaṁ tatra kārayet.
Bo/3.14 - tayā saṁvatsare pūrṇe mañjūṣaṁ tatra kāritaṁ.

62 N2/3.33b - tasyābhyantarataḥ kṛtvā (N3/3.32b - kṣiptā) darbheṇa pariveṣṭya ca.
N10 - tasyābhyantas tataḥ kṣiptvā darbheṇa pariveṣṭa ca.
N7/3.19b - tasyai cābhyantare kṣiptas tainen(v)a pariveṣṭitaḥ.
Bo/3.15a - tasyābhyantarataḥ putraṁ yatnena pariveṣṭitaṁ.

63 N1/3.32a, N10, N11 - samādāya pra(u)vāhe tu gaṅgāyām tam avikṣipat.
N7/3.20a - gṛhītvā tu pravah(bhāv)eṇa gaṅgāmadhye vinikṣipet.
Bo/3.15b - kṛtvā tatra vanoddeśe gaṅgāmadhye vinikṣipat.

64 Verses 32b-34 are missing in N3.
N10 - etad vākyaṁ samuccāyaṁ putrasyāgre t[u kan]yak(a)ā.
N7/3.20b - tayā vākyaṁ vinikṣiptaṁ putrasyāgre nṛpottamaḥ.
N8/3.23b, Ra/3.27a - śri gaṅgābhimukhī (N4/3.27a - tatra gaṅgā mukhī) bhutvā vākyam evam abhāṣata.
Bo/3.16a - tayā vākyaṁ ca kathitaṁ putrasyāgre tu kanyayā.
BF/3.21a - tadā roṣākulā bhutvā sā 'bravīt bālakaṁ prati.

65 N2/3.35a - na jānī te janetāraṁ kathaṁ garbhasya saṁbhavaṁ.
N10 - na jāte te janetāraṁ katha garbhasya saṁbhavaḥ.

66 N2/3.35b - yasya vīryeṇa saṁbhūto vatsa tvaṁ ca mamodare.

tenaiva saha saṅgaccha yady ahaṁ dharmacāriṇī[67]
tato gaṅgāpravāheṇa jagāmarṣigaṇāśramāt[68] [34]
tato vismayam āpannā jananī valite sute[69]
tataḥ paścād gatā dṛṣṭvā rudatī vaikavihvalā[70] [35]
tataḥ pravāhe gaṅgāyām āgacchat kanyakāsutaḥ[71]
gaṅgātīre maharṣiṇāṁ tapasām āśrame punaḥ[72] [36]
teṣām anyo mahātejā munir uddālako 'bhidhaḥ[73]
āgacchantaṁ ca mañjūṣam apaśyad munisattamaḥ[74] [37]

to him you should go, if I am (really) a pious woman".
Then he was carried by the river current, away from the hermitage of the seer's group. [34]
She (i.e. Candravatī) was filled with wonder when she saw her son turning (upstream).
She then followed him, crying, full of confusion. [35]
The girl's son, in the river current, then arrived again
at the hermitage of the great ascetic sages, on the riverbank. [36]
There was among them, the great brilliant sage Uddālaka.
That excellent sage saw that box arriving, (and) [37]

---

67 N2/3.36a, N10 - tenaiva saha sā gaccha yady ahaṁ dharmacāriṇī.

68 N1/3.34b, N10, N11 - tato gāṅgā pravāheṇa (N2/3.36b - jagāmarṣigaṇāśrayāt) jagāmarṣigaṇā[śr](s)amāt.

69 N10, N11 - tato vismayam āpannā j(t)ananī valite sute.

70 Emendation - DS. N1/3.35b - tata paścadrutāṣṭvā ca rudatī(n) ekavihvalā.
N2/3.37a, N10, N11 - tataḥ (N3/3.36a - tasya) paścād gatā sā ca rudatī(n) ekavihvalā.

71 N2/3.38a - tataḥ pravāhe gaṅgāyā(s)ḥ sāgamat (N11 - gaṅgā āgacchat - short) kanyakā sutaḥ.
N7/3.23a - tataḥ pravāhe gaṅgāyāḥ putram ādāyayau agre.
Bo/3.18a - gato pravāhe gaṅgāyās taṭ(r)a(n)ṁ kanyā sutas tadā.

72 Emendation - NK. N1/3.36b, N11 - gaṅgātīre maharṣiṇāṁ tapasā(s)m (N2/3.38b - tapasā mā āmanyataḥ) āśr(su)ame manaḥ.
N3/3.37b - gaṅgātīre mahārṣiṇāṁ (N10 - tapasā sā śrumātātaḥ) tapatā āśramāgrataḥ.
N7/3.23b - tasya nadītīre [yatra] tapas tapyanti pāṇḍavāḥ.
Bo/3.18b - āgataś ca nadītīre yatra tapyanti vaḍavāḥ.

73 N2/3.39a - teṣāṁ mādhye mahārāja (N10 - mahātejāḥ) munir (N3/3.38a - ṛṣir) uddālakābhidhaḥ.
N7/3.24a - teṣāṁ madhye mahātejar(ṛ)ṣir uddālakaś ca yaḥ.

74 N1/3.37b - āgacchantaṁ mavapuṣaṁ apaśyat munisattamaḥ.
N2/3.39b - āgacchantaṁ ca mañjūṣam apaśyan munipuṅgavaḥ.
N3/3.38b - āgacchantī ca mañjūṣam apaśyan munisattama.

atha tīraṁ samānīya kṛpākautūhalānvitaḥ[75]
samāpya devakarmāṇi pitṛkarmāṇi vai tathā[76] [38]
uddālakas tv unmucya mañjūṣaṁ śubhalakṣaṇaṁ[77]
dṛṣṭvā bālam atiprīto vipro vismayam āgataḥ[78] [39]
vidhivākyaṁ ca sasmāra svavīryatyāgam eva ca[79]
na mṛṣā brahmaṇo vākyaṁ na mṛṣā vīryam asti naḥ [40]
vitarkya tadā vācam uvācātimudānvitaḥ[80]
vatsa tvam āśrame tiṣṭha sukham asmin mamāniśaṁ[81] [41]

filled with wonder and compassion, brought it to the bank.
Having performed the rites to the gods and the ancestors, [38]
Uddālaka freed that most beautiful (baby) from the box, (and)
seeing the child, the sage was very pleased, filled with wonder. [39]
Remembering Brahmā's words and his own burst of semen,
(he thought) – "Brahmā's words are not false, neither is my semen wasted". [40]
Still pondering so, he said his words, filled with great joy:
"O child, stay you in the hermitage (and be) always happy". [41]

N10, N11 - āgacchantaṁ c(gh)a mapūṣam apaśyan munisattamaḥ.
N7/3.24b - āgacchaṁ mañjūṣ(pūkh)aṁ taṁ dṛṣṭvān munisattamaḥ.

75 N3/3.38a - atha tīraṁ samānajya (N10, N11 - samānīya) kṛpākautūhalānvitaḥ.

76 N3/3.38b - samāpya devakarmāṇi pitṛkarmāṇi ce tathā.

77 N1/3.39a, N10 - uddālakas tu unmucya mapūṣaṁ śubhalakṣaṇaṁ.

78 N2/3.41b - dṛṣṭvā bālam atiprīto (N3/3.38b - vismayaṁ paramaṁ gataḥ) muni[r] vismayam āgataḥ.
N4/3.39-40, N8/3.36-7, Ra/3.40-1 - kutūhalāt sa mañjūṣām udghaṭya tam avekṣya ca
bālam udyaddinakaraprabham adbhutadarśanaṁ
sarvalakṣaṇasaṁpannaṁ dhyānayogena saṁsthitaṁ
raktanetraṁ tam atyantaṁ muni[r] vismayam āgataḥ.
N7/3.27b - svarūpaṁ raktanetrāṁ taṁ dhyānayogena saṁsthitaṁ.

79 N2/3.42a - vidhivākyaṁ ca sasmāra svavīryas tyāga eva ca.
N4/3.41a, N8/3.39a, Ra/3.42a - dhyānayogena ca jñatvā taṁ svavīryasamudbhavaṁ.

80 Emendation - DS. N1/3.41a, N10, N11 - vitaṣkoti tadā vācām uvācātimudānvitaḥ.
N2/3.43a - vitarka vācanaṁ ceti prā(- -) munipuṅgavaḥ.
N3/3.38b - vitarketi to vācām uvācātimudānvitaḥ.

81 N1/3.41b, N3/3.40a - vatsa svam āśrame tiṣṭha sukham asmin mamāniśaṁ

sa tatra payasā bālaḥ phalamūlaraseṇa ca
puṣṭo vyavardhat tadā uddālakaniveśane[82] [42]
tatraiva krīḍate nityam āśrame cātiśobhane[83]
sarvoṣadhisamāyukte phalamūlasamanvite[84] [43]

iti śrībrahmāṇḍapurāṇe nāsiketopākhyāne
pitṛputrasaṅgamo nāma tṛtīyo 'dhyāyaḥ

There he was, (nourished) by milk and the best of fruit juices,
growing up and becoming fat, in Uddālaka's house. [42]
He always used to play there, in the so beautiful hermitage,
full of trees and plants, as well as fruits and root vegetables. [43]

This is the third chapter of the Nāsiketa story, pertaining to the Brahmāṇḍa Purāṇa, called – the father and son meeting.

Translation Notes

I – Famous righteous and beautiful women and other female beings.
II – All are signs of beauty and of birth in a good family.
III – The "Mountain Daughter" is Parvatī, Śiva's consort.

N4/3.42b, N8/3.39b, Ra/3.43b - vivasa tvaṁ yathā kāmāṁ ciram asmin mad āśrame.
N7/3.29b - vatsala māśra(s)me tatra saṁtiṣṭha svayayā sukham.
BF/3.28b - vatsa tvam āśrame puṇye tiṣṭha tvaṁ tapasi sthitaḥ.

82 N1/3.42b, N11 - puṣpo (N10 - putro) vyavardhatta tadā uddālakaniveśane.
N2/3.44b - puṣṭo vyavardhata tadā uddālakaniketa(ta)ne.

83 N2/3.44b - tatraiva krīḍate nityam āśrame hy atiśobhane.
N7/3.30b, Bo/3.22b - atraiva ramate nityam āśrame cātiśobhane.

84 N10, N11 - sarvauṣadhisamāyukte phalamūlasamānvite.

Chapter 4

Candravatī's Marriage

vaiśaṁpāyana uvāca
raghuvaṁśodbhavā kanyā rudantī śokavihvalā[1]
putraśokena santaptā gaṅgātīre samāgamat[2] [1]
ānveṣayanti taṁ putraṁ babhrāma parito bhṛśaṁ[3]
munīnām āśramāt puṇyā rājakanyātiduḥkhitā[4] [2]
ekasminn āśrame taṁ ca gaṅgātīre 'tiśobhane[5]
krīḍantam ātmajaṁ dṛṣṭvā putratvāt taṁ uvāca ha[6] [3]

Vaiśaṁpāyana said
The girl born in the Raghu family, was crying then, afflicted with grief.
Heated by the pangs of (longing for) her son, she reached the riverbank. [1]
She was looking for her son, wandering repeatedly around,
that suffering pious princess, away from the sages' hermitage. [2]
On a very beautiful riverbank, in a certain hermitage,
she saw her own son playing. Assuming that he was her son, she spoke to him. [3]

---

1 N4/4.1a, N8/4.42a, Ra/4.1a - raghuvaṁśodbhavā kanyā rudantī tadanantaraṁ.
BF/4.1a - raghuputrī kṛtakrodharahitā putravatsalā.

2 Half verse 4.1b is missing in N3.
N4/4.1b, N8/4.42b, Ra/4.1b - nāsiketaviyogārtā prayātā sā ca tad vanaṁ.
BF/4.1b - śokārtā satī rudatī gaṅgātīraṁ samāyayau.

3 N10 - ānveṣayanti taṁ putraṁ b(v)abhrāma parito bhṛśaṁ.
N4/4.2a, N8/4.43a, Ra/4.2a - kadācid vaiva yogena tayā duḥkhārtayā bhṛśaṁ.

4 N10 - munīn(t)ām āśra[mā]t puṇyā(n) rājakanyātiduḥkhitā.
Verse 4.2 is missing in N2.

5 N2/4.2a - ekasminn āśrame puṇye (N3/4.2b, N10 - tatra) gaṅgātīre 'tiśobhane.
N4/4.2b, N8/4.43b, Ra/4.2b - uddālakāśramaṁ dṛṣṭaṁ (N7/4.3a - dṛṣṭaś caivāśramaṁ ramyaṁ) gaṅgātīre suśobhanaṁ.
Bo/4.3a - dṛṣṭaś caivāśramo ramyo gaṅgātīre suśobhanaḥ.

6 N3/4.3a - krīḍantam ātmajaṁ (N2/4.2b - dṛṣṭā) dṛṣṭvā (N10, N11 - yu hṛṣṭā) prahṛṣṭā (N10 - ta sudhādya ha) tam uvāca ha.
N4/4.3a, N8/4.44a, Ra/4.3a, N7/4.3b - dṛṣṭvā cātmasutaṁ tatra krīḍamānaṁ tad āśrame.
Bo/4.3b - paśyati sma sutaṁ tatra krīḍamanaṁ tam āśrame.

candravaty uvāca
bāla te nāma kiṁ kasya muneś ca tanayo bhavān[7]
tad brūhi tava kutrāsti pitā gehe 'thavā bahiḥ[8] [4]
putra uvāca
uddālakābhidhāno me pitāmātā munīśvaraḥ[9]
tāto 'stī phalamūlārtham agnihotrī svayaṁ vane[10] [5]
atikālo 'bhavat tasmin gate pitari kānane[11]

Candravatī said
"O boy, what is your name? Whose sage's son are you?
Tell me, where is your father? Is he at home or elsewhere?" [4]
The son said
"Uddālaka is his name. This great sage is (both) my father and mother.
My father has gone to the forest for fruits and roots for his Agnihotra. [5]
A long time has passed since he went to the forest, (and he) may return soon.

---

7 N1/4.4a, N10, N11 - bāla te ṇāma kiṁ kasya mune[ś] ca (sve) tanayo bhavān.
N4/4.3b-4a, N8/44b-45a, Ra/4.3b-4a - uvāca vacanaṁ prītā vatsa kasyāyam āśramaḥ
pituś ca tava kiṁ nāma pṛcchāmy etad ahaṁ vada.
N7/4.4a - kiṁ nāma tasya viprasya etat pṛcchāmy ahaṁ tavaḥ.
BF/4.6 - putra kasyāntike tiṣṭasyāśramaṁ kasya vā muneḥ
kena tvam uddhṛtas toyād etan me vaktum arhasi.
Bo/4.5a-b - kas tvadīyaḥ pitā putra kasyāyaṁ cāśramaḥ śubhaḥ
kiṁ nāma tasya viprasya pṛcchāmy etad vadasva me.

8 N2/4.4b - brūhi me putra (N3/4.3c - tad brūhi mama) kutrāsti pitā gehe 'thavā bahiḥ.
Additional half verse: N2/4.5a - harṣitaṁ me manaś cādya tava darśanata(s)ḥ suta.
Bo/4.5c - harṣitaṁ me mano bhūri darśanāt tava putraka.

9 N4/4.6b, N8/4.47b, Ra/4.7a - mama bhadre (N7/4.5a - māta) pitāśreṣṭha uddālaka mahāmunīḥ.
BF/4.7a - mātar me matpitā hy atra tiṣṭhaty uddālako munīḥ.
Bo/4.6a - mama mātāpitā caiva munir uddālako mahān.

10 Emendation - NK. N1/4.5b - tato 's[t]ī (N2/4.5b, N3/4.5a - gato 'sau, N10 - gato 's[t]ī) phalamūlārtham agnihotrī svayaṁ vane.
N4/4.7b, N8/4.48b, Ra/4.8a - phalamūlakuśādyarthaṁ prayātaḥ saṁprataṁ vanaṁ.
N7/4.5a - gataḥ sa phalamūlārtha agnihotraṁ karoti ca.
Bo/4.6b - gato 'sau phalamūlārtham agnihotrasya kāraṇāt.

11 N3/4.5b - atikālo 'bhavat tasmai (N10, N11 - tasmin) gate pitari kānane.

drutaḥ eṣyati tat kurve agniśālānulepanaṁ[12] [6]
putrasya vacanaṁ śrutvā mātā vacanam abravīt
mātovāca
ahaṁ te putra jananī svastho bhava yathāsukhaṁ[13] [7]
agniśālānulepādīn karomy aham anuttamaṁ[14]
evam uktvā samālipya punar gaṅgātaṭe gatā[15] [8]

Meanwhile I am cleaning and anointing the place of the fire-rite".[6]
Having heard her son's words, the mother said the following.
The mother said
"I am your mother, son, be calm and happy. [7]
I shall do the cleaning of the fire-rite place etc. in the best way".
Having thus spoken, she cleaned and anointed all over, then went to the riverbank. [8]

---

12 N1/4.6b, N10 - drut(s)a (s)eṣyati tat kurve (N2/4.5b - kurv(aḥ)o) agniśālānulepanaṁ.
Verse 4.6b-7a is missing in N3.
N4/4.8b, N8/4.49b, Ra/4.9a - ito gatvā kariṣyāmi agniśālānulepanaṁ.
N7/4.6b-7a - āgamiṣya(ām)ti me tāta agniśālānulepanaṁ
upalepaṁ kariṣyāmi kuśān prastārayāmy ahaṁ.
BF/4.9b - yatas tasyāgniśalāyām upalepanaṁ āhare.
Bo/4.7b - devatāpitṛkāryārtham agnisālāvilepanaṁ.

13 N2/4.8a - ahaṁ te putra jananī svastho bhava yathāsuta.
N4/4.10a, N8/4.51a, Ra/4.10a - vatsāsmi tava mātāhaṁ putras tvaṁ ca mamāgrataḥ.
N7/4.8a - ahaṁ te jananī putra svastho bhava [ya]thāsukhaṁ.
Bo/4.8b - viddhi māṁ mātaraṁ putra tvaṁ svastho bhava putraka.

14 N2/4.8b - agniśālānulepaṁ hi (N11 - agniśālāmulepādi) karomy aham anuttamaṁ.
N4/4.10b, N8/4.51b, Ra/4.10b - anulepādi sāmagnīṁ kathaṁ saṁpādayiṣyasi.
N7/4.8b - agniś(s)ālā tv agnihotra upalepaṁ karomy ahaṁ.
BF/4.10 - toyāharaṇam ālepam agniśālāsv ahaṁ suta
karomi tvaṁ sukhaṁ tiṣṭha svatātasyāntike ciraṁ.
Bo/4.9 - śālāyām agnihotrārtham upalepaṁ karomy ahaṁ.

15 N3/4.6b - evam uktā samāliṅg[y]a (Bo/4.10 - ca tat kṛtvā) punar gaṅgātaṭe (N2/4.9a - gaṅgātaṭaṁ) gatā.
N10, N11 - evam uktvā samālipya punar gaṅgātare gatā.
N4/4.11a, N8/4.52a, Ra/4.11a - ity uktvā cāgniśālāyāś cakre 'laṅkāram uttamaṁ.
N7/4.9a - evam uktvā kṛtaṁ samyak yayau paścāt svam āśramaṁ.

etasminn antare prāpte munir uddālako 'nvagāt[16]
dṛṣṭvā saṁmārjitāṁ śālām āśramaṁ sa kalaṁ tathā[17] [9]
putram āhātisaṁhṛṣṭo munir uddālakas tadā[18]
na kadācit kṛtaṁ putra tvayedṛg anulepanaṁ[19] [10]
adya lepena saṁbhāti yathā ca suramandiraṁ
putra uvāca
mayādya na kṛtaṁ tāta yajñaśālānulepanaṁ[20]

By that time, the sage Uddālaka arrived, (returning from the forest).
When he saw the perfectly cleaned hermitage, with soft voice, [9]
the sage Uddālaka, very pleased, said then to his son:
"O son, never before have you done such (a perfect) cleaning. [10]
(Today it) is clean and anointed all over, shining like a temple".
The son said
"I have not done the cleaning and anointing of the place of the sacrifice, father.

---

16 N3/4.7a - etasminn antare prāpte (Bo/4.11a - prāpto) munir uddālako vanāt.
N4/412a, N8/4.53a, Ra/4.12a - etasminn antare rājann uddālaka mahāmuniḥ.
N7/4.9b - etasminn [an](e)tare prāpta uddālako vaco 'bravīt.

17 N1/4.9b, N10, N11 - dṛṣṭvā saṁmārji(a)tāṁ śālā(ṁ)m āśra(u)maṁ s(kṣ)a kalaṁ tatha.

18 N2/4.10b - putraṁ mahāti saṁhṛṣṭaṁ munir uddālakao 'vadat.
N3/4.8a - putro mahānti santuṣṭo munir uddālakas tadā.
N4/4.13b, N8/4.54b, Ra/4.13b - saṁhṛṣṭaḥ putram āliṅgya vacanaṁ cedam abravīt.
Bo/4.11b - vilepitām agniśālāṁ dṛṣṭvā vacanam abravīt.

19 N2/4.11b - na k[ad]ācit kṛtaṁ putra (N3/4.8b - īdṛṣaṁ cānulepanaṁ) tvayedhā anulepanaṁ.
N4/14, N8/4.55, Ra/4.14 - tvayā vatsa kṛtaṁ saṁyag adya saṁmārjjanādikaṁ āśrame cāgniśālāyāṁ tuṣṭo 'haṁ tava bhaktitaḥ.
N7/4.11-12a - puṇya prakaraṇīyāni kṛtāni tava suvrata
tuṣṭo 'haṁ tava bhaktyā hi agniśālāyalepanāt
na hi kvacit tvayā vipra īdṛsaṁ ś(s)obhanaṁ kṛtaṁ.
BF/4.13a - tuṣṭo 'smi parayā bhaktyā varaṁ varaya suvrata.
Bo/4.12b - tuṣṭo 'ham adya me putra hy agnihotrasyalepanāt.

20 N3/4.10a - mayādya na kṛte tāta yajñaśālānulepanaṁ.
N4/4.15b, N8/4.56b, Ra/4.16a - mayā nādya kṛtaṁ tāta sarvaṁ saṁmārjanādikaṁ.
N7/4.12b - vistareṇa mayā tāta karma kiñcit susaubhanaṁ.
BF/4.14a - mayā naitat kṛtaṁ tāta mātā me samupāgatā.
Bo/4.13a - niḥsaṁśayaṁ mayā tāta karma kiñcit kṛtaṁ na hi.

manmātraitat kṛtaṁ tāta śālāśramavilepanaṁ[21] [11]
munir uvāca
kutas te putra jananī prāptā caitat kuto gatā[22]
putra uvāca
na jāne kva gatā tāta dṛṣṭvā neṣyāmi tām ahaṁ[23] [12]
sa hṛṣṭa ṛṣibhiḥ sārddham agnihotram acīkarot[24]
kṛtavān devakāryaṁ ca pitṛkāryam anantaraṁ[25] [13]

My mother has done that, father, cleaning and anointing the hermitage". [11]
The sage said
"From where, son, has your mother arrived, and where has she gone?"
The son said
"I do not know where she went father. Seeing her, I shall fetch her"(I). [12]
(Uddālaka) was pleased (and) performed the Agnihotra along with the sages, performing first the gods' rites, and then the ancestors' rites. [13]

---

21 N1/4.13c, N2/4.12b, N3/4.10b - man mātraitat kṛtaṁ sarvaṁ śālāśramavilepanaṁ.
N4/4.16a, N8/4.57a, Ra/4.16b - man mātrā 'laṅkṛtaṁ saṁyag āśramaṁ cāgnimandiraṁ.
N7/4.13a - mātrā caiva kṛtaṁ karma upalepaṁ tavāśrame.
BF/4.14b - tayāśramaṁ samaṁ tac ca śobhitaṁ racitaṁ bhūtaṁ.
Bo/4.13b - mātrā mama kṛtaṁ sarvam upalepaṁ tavāśrame.

22 N1/4.11a - kutas te putra jananī kṛtvā (N2/4.13a - tad vai kuto 'gamat) caitat (N10, N11 - vaitat) kuto gatā.
N3/4.11a - kutas te putra jananī bhūtā caitat kuto gatā.
N4/4.16b, N8/4.57b, Ra/4.17a - mātā putra kadā prāptā sāṁpratam kutra vā tava.
N7/4.13b - kutas te jananī putra kṛtvā karma kuto gatā(ḥ).
Bo/4.14a - kva cāste putra te mātā kṛtvā karma kathaṁ gatā.
BF/4.15a - putra mātā kva te yātā vihitāśramasatkṛyā.

23 N1/4.11b, N11 - na jāne kva gatā tāta dṛṣṭvā n(t)eṣ(d)yām(p)i tām ahaṁ.
Bo/4.15a - kṛtvā karma tatas tāta gaṅgāsnānārthinī gatā.

24 N1/4.12b - sa dṛṣṭo ṛṣibhiḥ sārdha(ṁ)m (N10 - agnikā[r]yam avīkarot) atikopam acīkarot.
N2/4.14a - sa hṛṣṭa ṛṣibhiḥ sārddham agnikāryam avākarot.
N4/4.18a, N8/4.59a, Ra/4.18b - śrutvaivam atisaṁhṛṣṭo munir uddālakas tadā.
Bo/4.15b - saṁhṛṣṭo 'sau ṛṣis tasminn agnihotraṁ cakāra ha.

25 N4/4.18b, N8/4.59b, Ra/4.19a - agnihotraṁ daivakāryyaṁ pitṛkāryyaṁ tathaiva ca.
Bo/4.16a - sa kṛtvā devakāryaṁ ca pitṛkāryaṁ tathaiva ca.

samāpya nityakarmāṇi dadhyau nārāyaṇaṁ tadā[26]
tataḥ provāca tanayaṁ putrāhūya svamātaraṁ[27] [14]
vinayācārabhāvena putro mātaram abravīt[28]
nāsiketa uvāca
āśrame mātar āgaccha bhuṅkṣva mūlaṁ phalādikaṁ[29]
āgato matpitā gehe kāryaṁ kṛtvā sa tiṣṭhati[30] [15]
mātovāca
ayuktaṁ putra kiṁ brūṣe mamedaṁ lomaharṣaṇaṁ[31]

Having performed the routine rites, he then meditated upon Nārāyaṇa.
Then he said to his son – "O son, (go) speak[(II)] *to your own mother". [14]*
(Coming to her), the son, modestly, said to his mother.
Nāsiketa said
"(Please) mother, come to the hermitage, enjoy root vegetables, fruits etc.
My father has returned home. Having performed the rites, he is (now) waiting". [15]
The mother said
"What you have (just) said is inappropriate, son, causing my hair to bristle.

---

26 N2/4.15a - samāpya nityakarmāṇi dadhyau nārāyaṇaṁ tathā.
N4/4.19a, N8/4.60a, Ra/4.19b - samāpya ca kiyatkālaṁ dhyānayogena saṁsthitaḥ.

27 N4/4.19b, N8/4.60b, Ra/4.20a - tato 'bravīn muniḥ putram ānayasva mātaraṁ.
BF/4.16b - ābhūya tāṁ darśayeti munis taṁ putram abhyadhāt.
Bo/4.16b - uvācainaṁ tataḥ putraṁ mātaraṁ darśayasva māṁ.

28 N2/4.16a, N3/4.14a - vinayācārabhāvena yukto mātaram abravīt.

29 N11 - āśrame mātar āgaccha bhuñjvaṁ mūlaṁ phalādikaṁ.
N4/4.21b, N8/4.62b, Ra/4.22a - mātar āśramam āgaccha mā khedaṁ kuru sāṁprataṁ.
N7/4.18b - āgaccha (Bo/4.17a - svāśramaṁ) āśramaṁ mātar āhāraṁ te dadāmy ahaṁ.
BF/4.18a - āgaccha mātar tato 'yaṁ samāyāto vanāntārāt.

30 N1/4.15b, N3/4.14b - āgato matpitā gehe kālpaṁ kṛtvā sa (N2/4.16b - kāryaṁ kṛtvā ca) tiṣṭhati.
N4/4.22b-23a, N8/4.63b-c, Ra/4.23 - ato matpitur āvāso nikaṭe tava yujyate gaccha tvam āśrame puṇye mayā sākaṁ yathāsukhaṁ.
N7/4.19a - pitā mama āśrame tatra tiṣṭha matar yathechayā.
BF/4.18b - tatrāhārādikaṁ kṛtvā svayaṁ tiṣṭha yathecchayā.
Bo/4.17b - pitā vaivāśramaṁ prāptas tiṣṭha matar yathecchayā.

31 N1/4.16a - ay(m)uktaṁ putra kiṁ brūṣe mamedaṁ lomaharṣaṇaṁ.
BF/4.19a - ayuktam uktaṁ bhavatā vatsa āścaryataraṁ vacaḥ.
Bo/4.18a - ayuktaṁ te vacaḥ putra śrutaṁ vai romaharṣaṇaṁ.

adharmyaṁ dharmaviduṣo na praśaṁsanti te vacaḥ[32] [16]
pitā vāpy athavā bhrātā mātā vāpy atha mātulaḥ[33]
yacchanti kanyakām ete na yacchet mātaraṁ sutaḥ[34] [17]
ity uktaḥ sa pituḥ pārśve gatvā sarvaṁ nyavedayat[35]
putroktaḥ sa punaḥ pṛccha mātaraṁ kasya vaṁśajā[36] [18]

The experts of moral conduct would not praise your words, (but) consider them immoral. [16]
(You want to lead me to your father, as in marriage, but only) a father, a father's brother, or (the girl's) own brother, a mother, or a mother's brother,
may lead a girl (to her promised husband), but a son may not lead his mother". [17]
Having thus been told, he went to his father and informed him of everything.
He said to his son: "Ask your mother again, of what lineage she is. [18]

---

32 N1/4.16b - adharmyaṁ (N2/4.17b, N3/4.16a - adharmaṁ) dharmaviduṣo na praśasyanti (N2/4.17b, N3/4.16a - napraśaṁśanti) te vacaḥ.
N10 - adharmma dharmaviduṣo na praśaṁsati te vacaḥ.
N4/4.23b-24a, N8/4.64, Ra/4.24 - ayuktaṁ bhāṣase putra (N7/4.19b - mama vai romaharṣaṇaṁ) vicitraṁ lomaharṣaṇaṁ
adharmmavacanaṁ cedaṁ tava putra na śobhate.
N7/4.20a - adharma[ṁ] kim idaṁ vākyaṁ na praś(s)aṁsati dharmavit.
Bo/4.18b - adharmayuktaṁ vākyaṁ te na praśaṁsanti dharmavit.

33 N2/4.18a, N3/4.16b - pitā vā athavā bhrātā mātā vāpy atha mātulaḥ.
N4/4.24a, Ra/4.26a - pitāmātā tathā bhrātā mātulo vāpi tām ahaḥ.
N7/4.20b - pitā vāpy athavā bhrātā mātā vā atha (Bo/4.19a - vāpy) atha mātulaḥ.
BF/4.20a - pitā pitāmaho bhrātā sakulyo janaṇī tathā.

34 N3/4.17a - yacchanti kanyakām etāṁ na yacchet mātaraṁ sutaḥ.
N4/4.24b, Ra/4.26b - yacchanti kanyakām ete na putro mātaraṁ dadau.
N7/4.21a - dadate kanyakāṁ sarve (Bo/4.19b - yacchanti kanyakām loke) na putro mātaraṁ dade[t].
BF/4.20b - kanyāpradāne śaktaḥ syān na putraḥ kutracid yataḥ.

35 N2/4.19b, N3/4.17b - ity ukta[ḥ] sa pituḥ(ṣ) pārśve gatvā sarvaṁ nivedayat.

36 N2/4.20a - putrokta sa punaḥ pṛccha (N3/4.18a, N10 - praccha) mātaraṁ kasya vaṁśajā.
N4/4.29, N8/4.69b-70a, Ra/4.29b-30a - iyaṁ tava kathaṁ mātā jātā kasya kule punaḥ
kathaṁ jāto bhavan putraḥ kathaṁ vātra samāgatā.
N7/4.25 - mātaraṁ pṛccha putra tvaṁ kasya vaṁśe 'si tvaṁ bhavā
kathaṁ jāto bhavān putraḥ katham āgamanaṁ kṛtaṁ

abhavat te kathaṁ putraḥ katham āgamanaṁ kṛtaṁ[37]
evaṁ pṛccha yathānyāyaṁ gatvā tāṁ mātaraṁ svakaṁ[38] [19]
putra uvāca
mātaḥ satyāṁ vadasvaitat pitā tvāṁ paripṛcchati[39]
kasya vaṁśe samutpannā abhavat te sutaḥ kathaṁ[40] [20]
kathaṁ cāgamanaṁ tv atra kathaṁ vā garbhasaṁbhavaḥ[41]
vada sarvaṁ susatyaṁ ca kanyake tvaṁ yathāvidhi[42] [21]

What has happened that her son has been born, and how she has come here.
Indeed, ask her properly". Having gone to his own mother, the son said: [19]
"Mother, tell the truth, this is what my father asks you.
In what family were you born? How was your son generated, [20]
and how did it happen to you? How did you get pregnant?
(Please) tell the whole truth, O girl, in the proper order". [21]

BF/4.27b-28 - gatvā svaṁ jananīṁ jātā vaṁśe 'si kasya vā.
kathaṁ vā tava jāto 'haṁ putraḥ kamalalocanaḥ
kathaṁ vā vanavāsas te jāto vayasi madhyame.
Bo/4.23a - mātaraṁ pṛccha putra tvaṁ kasya vaṁśe samudbhavā.

37 N1/4.19a - prābhavat te kathaṁ putraṁ (s)tavehāgamanaṁ (N10, N11 - kathaṁ) kṛyaṁ.

38 N3/4.19a - evaṁ pṛccha bhayānyāyaṁ gatvā tāṁ mātaraṁ svakīṁ.
N4/4.30a, N8/4.70b, Ra/4.30b - sarvam etad aśeṣeṇa pṛcchyatāṁ mad anujñayā.
N7/4.26a - evaṁ vada yathānyāyaṁ pṛccha vai tatra mātaraṁ.
Bo/4.24a - evaṁ vada yathānyāyyaṁ sarvaṁ pṛccha yathārthataḥ.

39 N1/4.20a, N11 - mātaḥ satyāṁ vadasvait(k)at (N2/4.21b - vadasvaiti, N10 - vadasvaikaṁ) pitā tvāṁ paripṛcchati.

40 N1/4.20b, N11 - kasya vaṁśe samutpannā (N2/4.22a - hy) abhavat (N3/4.20a - te kathaṁ sutaḥ) te sutaḥ kathaṁ.
N4/4.30b, N8/4.71b, Ra/4.31b - kasya vaṁśe samutpannā kathaṁ (Bo/4.25b - putro hy ahaṁ tava) cāhaṁ tavātmajaḥ.

41 N1/4.21a, N11 - kathaṁ cāgamanaṁ (N10 - te 'tra) tva ca (N2/4.22b, N3/4.20b - katham āgamanaṁ tatra) kathaṁ vā garbhasaṁbhavaḥ.
N4/4.31a, N8/4.72a, Ra/4.32a - katham atrāgatā bhadre brūhy etat sarvam āditaḥ.
Bo/4.26a - katham āgamanaṁ hy atra satyaṁ brūhi yathāvidhi.

42 Emendation - NK. N1/4.21b - vada sarve susatye (N2/4.23a - na) ca (N10 - vada sarve susatye ke, N11 - vanakanye ke) kanyake tvaṁ yathāvidhi.

mātovāca
śṛṇu putra mahāprājña yan māṁ tvaṁ paripṛcchasi[43]
pūrvakarmavipākena jātam etad viceṣṭitaṁ[44] [22]
anivāryā gatiḥ putra karmaṇāṁ pūrvajanmanaḥ[45]
kathayāmi yathāvṛttaṁ śṛṇuṣvaikāgramānasaḥ[46] [23]
raghur nāmeti vikhyāto rājā dharmaparāyaṇaḥ[47]
tasya vaṁśe samutpannā yathā putras tathā hy ahaṁ[48] [24]
kanyā daśasahasrāṇi mama śuśrūṣaṇe ratāḥ[49]

The mother said
"O son, great knowledgeable one, listen to that which you are asking me.
The ripening of former deeds (karma) occurred, this is what happened. [22]
It is hard to stop the process of former karma taking birth, O son,
I am telling (it) as it happened, listen carefully[(III)]. *[23]*
(There is) a very devout king, known by the name Raghu.
In his family I was born and was like a son to him. [24]
Having ten thousand girls at my service,

---

43 N7/4.28a - śṛṇu putra mahāprājña yan tvām aparipṛcchasi.
Bo/4.26b - satyaṁ śṛṇu mahāprājña yan māṁ tvaṁ paripṛcchasi.

44 N10 - pūrvakarmavipākena jātam etad va ceṣṭitaṁ.
N4/4.32a, N8/4.72a, Ra/4.33a - pūrvakarmānusāreṇa jātam atyadbhutaṁ mama.
Bo/4.27a - pūrvakarmānuyogena yat tu jātaṁ (N7/4.28b - etaj jātaṁ) viceṣṭitaṁ.

45 N1/4.23a, N10 - anivārthā gatiḥ putra karmaṇāṁ pūrvajanmanaḥ.
Verse 4.23 and the first two words of 4.24 are missing in N11.

46 N7/4.29 - apravijñātasaṁyogaṁ dustaraṁ putra karmaṇāṁ
kathayāmi yathā vṛttaṁ śṛṇuṣvaikamanā[ḥ] sutaḥ.

47 N10 - raghur nāmāti vikhyāto rājā dharmaparāyaṇaḥ.
N4/4.32b, N8/4.72b, Ra/4.33b - āste raghur iti khyāto rājā trailokyaviśrutaḥ.
N7/4.30a, Bo/4.28a - raghur nāmeti vikhyāto rājā trailokyaviśrutaḥ.

48 N3/4.23b - tasya vaṁśe samutpannā yathā putras tathā svakaṁ.
N4/4.33a, N8/4.73a, Ra/4.34a - tasyāhaṁ kanyakā śreṣṭā kadācid daivayogataḥ.
N7/4.30b - tasyya vaṁśe ahaṁ putrī samutpannā hi putraka.
Bo/4.28b - tasyya vaṁśe samutpannā putro girisutā iva.

49 N7/4.31b - kanyā daśasahasrāṇi mama śuśrūṣaṇe ratāḥ.
Bo/4.29b - kanyā daśasahasreṇa ramanti sukhasaṁyutā.

sudhādhavalite tatra sthitā rājagṛhopari[50] [25]
vasante mādhave māsi tṛtīyāyāṁ naradhipaṁ[51]
śukle vijñāpya gaṅgāyāṁ gatā snātuṁ sakhīvṛtā[52] [26]
tatrāhaṁ kurvatī snānaṁ kamalaṁ darbhaveṣṭitaṁ[53]
sugandham āgataṁ dṛṣṭvā samānāya kareṇa tat[54] [27]
muktāḥ darbhāḥ mayājñānāt madhumad gandham uttamaṁ[55]
mayāghrātaṁ tu tasmāt tan me iha nābhimadhyagaṁ[56] [28]

I stayed there, in the king's milk-white palace. [25]
On the third day of the bright half of the month Caitra, in springtime, I informed my parents,
that I was going along with my girl-attendants, to bathe in the river. [26]
While I was bathing there, a lotus flower wrapped in grass,
was coming, very fragrant, (and) I ordered to bring it to me. [27]
Freed from the grass, (that) wonderful flower, with an aroma sweet as honey, I, unknowingly,
smelled it, and that is how the semen entered my womb. [28]

---

50 N1/4.25b, N3/4.24b, N10, N11 - sudhā vacati te tatra sthitā rājagṛhopari.
N7/4.31a - dhavalagṛhasaṁsthāhaṁ sakhībhi[ḥ] (Bo/4.29a - pariveṣṭitā) parivaritā.

51 N10, N11 - vaṁśate mādhave māsi tṛtīyāyā (ta) naradhipaṁ.

52 N1/4.26b, N3/4.25b - śukle vijñāpya gaṅgāyāṁ gatā snātuṁ sakhīvṛtā.
N7/4.32b - vijñāpito mayā tato gaṅgās(ś)nānārthinīgatā.
Bo/4.30 - ṛtau vasante saṁprāpte gaṅgātīre s(ṣ)upuṣpite
vijñāpitā sakhībhiś ca gaṅgās(ś)nānārthanir(ī)gatā.

53 N7/4.33a - tatrāhaṁ s(ś)nānaṁ ku[rv]a(v)tī svāgataṁ kamalaṁ śubhaṁ.
Bo/4.31a - tatra snānaṁ prakurvantyā mayā dṛṣṭaṁ jalopari.

54 Emendation - DS. N1/4.27b, N10, N11 - sugandham āgataṁ dṛṣṭvā samāyāṇya (N2/4.29a, N3/4.26b - samādāya) kareṇa tat.
N4/4.34, N8/4.75, Ra/4.35 - tatrāikaṁ kamalaṁ dṛṣṭaṁ gaṅgāmadhye kuśair bṛtaṁ
ānāyi tat tathā sakhyā kautukāc ca kare dhṛtaṁ.
N7/4.33b - puṭake veṣṭitaṁ darbhair gṛhītvā tu mayā kare.
Bo/4.31b - santarad veṣṭitaṁ darbhaiḥ puṭakaṁ kamalasya hi.

55 N11- muktādarbhān mayājñānān manān madhumad gandhasundarāṁ (vi).
N2/4.29b - muktāḥ garbhān mayājñānān madhuvadgandhasundaraṁ.
N3/4.27a - muktāḥ darbhān mayājñānān madhumad gandham uttamaṁ.
N7/4.34a - darbhādau mauktikaṁ padmaṁ sugandhaṁ viditaṁ mayā.

56 Emendation - NK. N1/4.28b - mayā(dhuraṁ)[ghrā]taṁ t(ś)u tasmā(a)t [t]an me [i]ha(n) nābhimadhy(v)agaṁ.

tatas tat daivayogena mama garbhe 'bhavad bhavān[57]
sakhībhir uktaṁ mahiṣyai tayā rājñe niveditaṁ[58] [29]
atīva kupito rājā śrutamātreṇa satvaraṁ[59]
bhṛtyān uvācā kanyaiṣā kānane tyajyatāṁ drutaṁ[60] [30]
nikṣiptā kānane śūnye tadbhayād rājakiṅkaraiḥ[61]

Thus, by fate's Yoga, you became my fetus.
What my girl-attendants had told to the queen, she informed the king. [29]
On hearing what had happened, the king became very angry.
He said to his servants: 'Leave this girl in the empty forest, at once!' [30]
I was thrown in that empty forest by the servants, fearing the king.

N4/4.35, N8/4.76, Ra/4.36 - āghrataṁ ca mayā vatsa kautukāt tat saroruhaṁ tato gaṅgāṁ namaskṛtya samāyātā svamandiraṁ.
N7/4.34b - tasyābhyaṁ tava (-)ore tu nābhy abhyantarato gataṁ.
Bo/4.32 - tad gṛhītvā sakhīhastād āghrātaṁ kamalaṁ mayā tasyābhyantarato vīryaṁ nāsābhyantarato gataṁ.

57 N1/4.29a - tat taṁs taṁ (N2/4.30b, N10 - tas (N11 - taṁs) tu) daivayogena mama garbhe 'bhavad bhavān.
N4/4.36a, N8/4.77a, Ra/4.37a - atīte tu kiyatkāle garbho me vismayāvahaḥ.
N7/4.35a - saṁbhūto hi tataḥ putra mama garbhe na saṁśayaḥ.
Bo/4.33a - saṁbhūtaś ca tato vipra mama garbho na saṁśayaḥ.

58 N1/4.29b - sakhībhir uktaṁ manasās (N3/4.27a, N10, N11 - man mātus) tayā rājñe niveditaṁ.
N4/4.36b-37a, N8/4.77b-78a, Ra/4.37b-38a - vabhūva sa vayasyābhis tadā rājñyai niveditaḥ
rajñī ca raghunāthāya sarvam eva nyavedayat.
N7/4.35b, Bo/4.33b - sakhībhir jñāpito rājā kopāviṣṭas tato raghuḥ.

59 N4/4.37b, N8/4.78b, Ra/4.38b - tataḥ kruddhena raghuṇā samādiṣṭāś ca kiṅkarāḥ.

60 N1/4.30b - bhṛtyān uvācā kanyaiṣā kānane tyaj(bh)yatāṁ drutaṁ.
N4/4.38a, N8/4.79a, Ra/4.39a - satvaraṁ tyajyatāṁ pāpāṁ sutāṁ mama mahāvane.
N7/4.36a - ājñāpitām ahaṁ bhṛtye kānane satvare tyajet.
Bo/4.34a - ājñātagarbhāṁ māṁ tato vane tatyāja nirjane.

61 N1/4.31a - bhijitvā (N2/4.32b, N3/4.30a - nikṣipya, N10 - nikṣ(j)iptā) kānane śūnye tadbhayād rājakiṅkaraiḥ.
N4/4.38b, N8/4.79b, Ra/4.39b - nikṣiptāhaṁ tadāraṇye rājña kruddhena kiṅkaraiḥ.
N7/4.36b - nikṣiptāhaṁ vane ś(s)ūn[y]e rājākruddhena kiṅkaraiḥ.

rudantī tatra māṁ dṛṣṭvā yājñavalkyo munis tadā[62] [31]
kṛpātīva samutpannā tena nītā nijāśramaṁ[63]
tadāśrame ca tiṣṭhantyā prasūtisamaye bhavān[64] [32]
nāsāgreṇa suto jātas tan nāma muninā kṛtaṁ[65]
nāsiketa idaṁ tena varṣānte tan mayā bhavān[66] [33]
mañjūṣopari vinyasya nikṣipto jāhnavījale[67]

The sage Yājñavalkya, seeing me there weeping, [31]
was filled with compassion (and) he led me to his hermitage.
In that hermitage I stayed until the time of your birth came. [32]
From my nose a son was born, who was given a name by that sage.
Nāsiketa is the name he gave (you). After one year, I [33]
put you in a box, wrapped (with grass and) threw the box to drift on the river Ganges (Jāhnu),

---

62 N2/4.33a - rudantīṁ tatra māṁ dṛṣṭvā yājñāvalkyas tadā muniḥ.
N4/4.39a, N8/4.80a, Ra/4.40a - kenacin muninā tatra dṛṣṭā puṣpaphalārthinā.
N7/4.37a - rodamānāpy ahaṁ tatra dṛṣṭā ṛṣiphalārthinā.
Bo/4.34b - rodamānā ty ahaṁ dṛṣṭā muninā tu phalārthinā.

63 N2/4.33b - kṛpayā parayā tena nītāhaṁ ca nijāśramaṁ.
N4/4.39b, N8/4.80b, Ra/4.40b - kṛpālunā ca nītāham āśramaṁ tena duḥkhitā.
N7/4.37b-38a - kṛpā tasya samutpannā ānīta tena cāśrame.
Bo/4.35a - mamopari kṛpāṁ kṛtvā hy ānītā svāśramaṁ prati.

64 N1/4.32b - tadāśrame ca tiṣṭhantyā prasū(a)tisamaye bhavān.
N4/4.40a, N8/4.81a, Ra/4.41a - prasūtā cāśrame tasya (N7/4.38a - mayā jāto 'sya (Bo/4.35b - bhavān jāto 'si) putrakaḥ) vatsa tvām iha niṣcitaṁ.

65 N4/4.40b, N8/4.81b, Ra/4.41b - nāsāgreṇa ca saṁbhūto yato vidhivaś(l)ān muniḥ.
N7/4.38b - nās(ś)āgreṇa saṁbhūta ṛṣir nāma tava dhruvaṁ.
Bo/4.36a - nāsikātaḥ samutpanno yātas tvaṁ mama bālakaḥ.

66 N3/4.32b, N11 - nāsiketa idaṁ tena varṣita tan me bhavān 'bhūt.
Verses from 4.33 to the end of chapter 4, are missing in N10.
N4/4.41a, N8/4.82a, Ra/4.42a - nāsiketa idaṁ nāma tasmād (N7/4.39a - uktaṁ mayā suta) yuktaṁ tadākarot.
Bo/4.36b - nāsiketeti te jñātvā nāma proktaṁ mahātmanā.

67 N1/4.34a, N11 - mañj(pu)ūṣopari vinyasya nikṣipto jāhnuvījale.
N2/4.35a - mañjūṣe ca va vinyasya nikṣiptā jānhuvījale.
N4/4.41b, N8/4.82b, Ra/4.42b - mañjūṣāyāṁ ca saṁsthāpya gaṅgāyāṁ kṣepitas tataḥ.
N7/4.39b - mañj(pu)ūṣaṁ parisaṁsthānaṁ gaṅgā nikṣipya taṁ mayā.
Bo/4.37a - tataḥ saṁsthāpya mañjūṣe nikṣiptas tvaṁ mayā jale.

punaś cānveṣayantī tvāṁ saśokātra samāgatā[68] [34]
putraitat sarvam ākhyātaṁ bhavajjanma yathābhavat[69]
etad eva tvayā vācyam ātmanaḥ pitur agrataḥ[70] [35]
tato gatvā pituḥ pārśve nāsiketas tad abravīt[71]
nāsiketa uvāca
śṛṇu tāta pravakṣyāmi yan mātrābhihitaṁ mama[72]
raghubhūpasya duhitā gaṅgāṁ snānārthinī gatā[73] [36]
āgataṁ padmapuṭakaṁ darbhair vipariveṣṭitaṁ[74]

and afterwards, overwhelmed with grief, I went looking for you again. [34]
O son, I am telling you everything about how your birth took place.
Go and tell your own father all this, indeed". [35]
Going before his father, Nāsiketa said the following.
Nāsiketa said
"Listen O father, I am going to tell what I have been bidden by my mother.
She, the daughter of king Raghu, went to bathe in the river. [36]
A lotus flower arrived there, bowl-shaped, wrapped in grass.

---

68 N3/4.32b - punaś cānveṣayanty ahaṁ caikā samāgatā.
N11 - punaś cānviṣayantī tvāṁ s(ś)aś(s)okātra samāgatā.
N4/4.42a, N8/4.83a, Ra/4.43a - tvaṁ mayā punar eva tvām anveṣyanty āgatāśrame.
N7/4.40a - tava ś(s)okena caivāhaṁ bhramantī ceru cāgatā.
Bo/4.37b - punar viyogaduḥkhārtā vīkṣantī tvāṁ samāgatā.

69 N3/4.33a - putraitat sarvam ākhyātaṁ tava janma yathābhavat.
4.33-38 verse numbers are missing in N3.

70 N2/4.37a - etad eva mama vācyam ātmajo janmavṛttakaṁ.
N3/4.33b - etad eva (N11 - iva) tvayā vācyam ātmātmanaḥ pitur agrataḥ.
N4/4.42b, N8/4.83b, Ra/4.43b - etat sarvaṁ tayā prokto nāsiketo narādhipa.
N7/4.40b, Bo/4.38a - etad eva mayā proktam ātmīyaṁ sthitikāraṇaṁ.

71 N2/4.37a - tato gatvā pituḥ pārśve nāsiketas tato (N11 - tadā) 'bravīt.
N4/4.43a, N8/4.84a, Ra/4.44a - pitro nivedayāmāsa lajjamāno yathā tathā.
Bo/4.38b - tato gatvā pituḥ parśve nāsiketto nyavedayat.

72 N3/4.34b - śṛṇu tāta pravakṣyāmi yan mātrā nihitaṁ mama.
N7/4.41a - śṛṇu tāta yathānyāyaṁ mātrā (Bo/4.39a - tv abhihitaṁ mama) yat kathitaṁ mama.

73 N2/4.38b, N3/4.35a - raghubhūpasya (N7/4.41b, Bo/4.39b - raghurājñāś ca) duhitā gaṅgāsnānārthinī (N11 - gaṅgāsnānārthinā) gatā.
Bo/4.39b - ragho rājñās tu duhitā gaṅgāsnānārtham āgatā.

74 N2/4.39a, N3/4.35b, N11 - āgataṁ padmapuṭakaṁ darbhaiś (ca) vipariveṣṭitaṁ.

padmaṁ tan madhugandhi tu svacchaṁ atyantaśobhanaṁ[75] [37]
ajānantyā mayāghrātaṁ tato garbho mamābhavat[76]
pitrā kopād vane tyaktā ghore siṁhādisevite[77] [38]
sarvaṁ tat pitur ākhyātaṁ vistarādyantayoditaṁ
sutasya vacanaṁ śrutvā munir vismayam āgataḥ [39]
aho prajāpater vākyaṁ anyathā jāyate kathaṁ[78]
putra tiṣṭhāśrame 'smākaṁ jananyā tvaṁ ihaiva hi[79] [40]
tadartham adya gacchāmi raghuvaṁśasya veśmani[80]

'That most wonderful, bright coloured, sweet smelling lotus flower, [37]
unaware, I smelled, and thus became pregnant[(IV)].
By my father's anger, I was left in a horrible forest, where lions and their like, lived'". [38]
He told all this to his father, in detail, from beginning to end.
Hearing his son's words, the sage was filled with wonder. [39]
"Oh, Prajāpati's words, how could they be otherwise, (but true)!
You, my son, stay in our hermitage with your mother, now. [40]
Today I am going for her to the palace of the Raghu family".

---

75 N1/4.37b - padmaṁ tan madhu gatvā (N2/4.39b, N11 - madhumatvā) tu svaccham atyarthaśobhanaṁ.

76 N1/4.38a, N11 - ajānant[y]ā mayāghrātaṁ tato garbho mamābhavat.
N2/4.40a - ajñānān mayāghrātaṁ tato garbhasya saṁbhavaḥ.
N7/4.43a - tan mayā ghrapitaṁ samyak tato garbhasya dharaṇaṁ.

77 N2/4.40b - pitrā kopād vane tyaktā (N7/4.43b - nirjane siṁhasevite) ghore sindyādisevite.

78 N4/4.44a, N8/4.85a, Ra/4.45a - prajāpater vacaḥ satyaṁ tadāsmarad aśeṣataḥ.
Bo/4.44a - aho prajāpateḥ satyaṁ saṁbhūtaṁ vacanaṁ tava.

79 N3/4.40b - putra tiṣṭhāśrame kiñca jāj jananyādya seva hi.
N4/4.44b-45a, N8/4.85b-86a, Ra/4.45b-46a - putram ūce vaco ramyaṁ satyam eva prasūs tava
ato mamāśrame puṇye ciraṁ tiṣṭhatv akalmaṣā.
Bo/4.44b-45a - ity uktvā svāgataṁ vipraḥ punaḥ putraṁ sa cābravīt
tiṣṭha putrātra tvam atraiva mātrā saha tapovane.

80 N2/4.43a - tvadarthaṁ (N7/4.47a - tadartham) adya gacchāmi raghuvaṁśasya veśmani.
N4/4.45b, N8/4.86b, Ra/4.46b - ahaṁ tu raghurājāsya tadarthī yāmi mandiraṁ.
Bo/4.45b - tasyāś cārthī gamiṣyāmi raghorājñaś ca veśmani.

sarvam uktvā tatas tatra kanyārthī munisattamaḥ[81] [41]
jagāma paramaprīto raghurājasya veśmani[82]
taṁ dṛṣṭvā raghurājo 'pi jvalann iva hrutāśanaṁ[83] [42]
muniṁ pradakṣiṇīkṛtyā nanāma bhuvi daṇḍavat[84]
dattāsanam athāgreṇa vidhivac ca apūjayat[85] [43]
praśrayāvanato bhūtvā raghur vacanam abravīt[86]

Having said all this, then and there, the excellent sage, for the sake of marrying the girl, [41]
went smiling and satisfied to the palace of king Raghu, (and)
King Raghu saw him glowing (and radiant) like fire. [42]
Having circumambulated him, right side first, he bowed to the ground, (stretching) like a stick.
He gave him his seat with respect, and reverenced him according to the rule. [43]
Bowing humbly, King Raghu said the following:

---

81 N4/4.46a, N8/4.87a, Ra/4.47a - evam uktvā tato vipro jagāma raghumandiraṁ.
N7/4.47b - evam uktvā tato vipra kanyārthī (Bo/4.46a - samagacchat) so 'pi nirgataḥ.

82 N1/4.42a, N2/4.44a - jagāma parama(yaṁ)prīt(au)o raghurājasya veśmani.
N7/4.48a - karmaṇā tatra saṁprāptaḥ śubhe ca raghumandire.
Bo/4.46b - krameṇaiva tataḥ prāptaḥ śubhaṁ ca raghumandiraṁ.

83 N1/4.42b, N11 - taṁ dṛṣṭvā raghurājibhij jvalann iva hrutāśanaṁ.
N3/4.41b - taṁ dṛṣṭvā raghurājo 'pi jvalantam iva pāvakaṁ.
N4/4.46b-47, N8/4.87b-88, Ra/4.47b-48 - dvāḥstham uddālakaṁ dvārapālo rajñe nyavedayat
tatas satvaram āgatya raghur dvāri dadarśa ha
sthitaṁ munivaraṁ bhūpaj (Bo/4.47a - sa dṛṣṭvā vipram āyāntaṁ) jvalantam iva pāvakaṁ.
N7/4.48b - taṁ dṛṣṭvā raghunātho vai jvalantam iva pāvake.

84 N2/4.45a - pradakṣiṇīkṛtvā sa muniṁ nanāma bhuvi daṇḍavat (vi).

85 Verse 4.43b-44a is missing in N2.
N3/4.42b - datvāsanam athārghyeṇa vidhivat tam apūjayat.
N4/4.48b-49a, N8/4.89b-90a, Ra/4.49b-50a - āsane cottame vipraṁ niveśyārghaṁ nivedya ca
pradakṣiṇaṁ parikramya upaviṣṭas tadājñayā.
N7/4.49b - kṛtā(ṁ) pradakṣi(a)ṇā tena āśane tu niyojitaḥ.
Bo/4.48a - kṛtvā pradakṣiṇaṁ caiva madhuparkeṇa cācaryat.

86 N8/4.90b, Ra/4.50b - munim ūce sukhāsīnaṁ raghuḥ paramapāvanaḥ.
Bo/4.48b - sukhāsīnaṁ ca viprarṣiṁ raghur vacanam abravīt.

adya me saphalaṁ janma adya me saphalāḥ kriyāḥ[87] [44]
adya me saphalaṁ dānaṁ bhavān yad darśanaṁ gataḥ[88]
munir uvāca
deyā sutā svavadhvai rājakanyā pṛthivīpate[89] [45]
na bhavet sadṛśā kvāpi dīrghāyur bhava suvrata[90]
raghur uvāca
gavāṁ śatasahasrāṇi svarṇakoṭiśatāni ca[91]

"Today my birth bears fruit, today my deeds bear fruit, [44]
today my donations bear fruit, by seeing you coming, O venerable one".
The sage said
"I am asking for your daughter, the princess, to be my wife, O lord of the land. [45]
There cannot be anyone like her, may you live long, O benefactor."
Raghu said
"A hundred thousands cows and hundreds of millions of gold (coins),

---

87 N2/4.45b - adya me saphalaṁ janma cādya me saphalāḥ (N3/4.44b, N11, N8/4.91a, Ra/4.51a - adya me saphalā kriyā) kriyāḥ.

88 N2/4.46a - adya me saphalaṁ dānaṁ (N3/4.44c - yad bhavān darśanaṁ kṛtaṁ) bhavad darśanato muneḥ.
BF/4.49b - adya me saphalaṁ rājyaṁ jīvitaṁ ca sujīvitaṁ.

89 Emendation - DS. N1/4.45b - deyā sutā svava(davo)dhvai rāja(ā)ka(ḥ)[nyā] pṛthivīpate.
N3/4.45a - dṛṣṭā sutāś ca vahavo (N11 - dṛṣyaḥ sutā svavadavo) rājānaḥ pṛthivīpate.
BF/4.51b-53a - kuśalaṁ te narapate rājyāṅgeṣv akhileṣv api
tvayaiva dhāritā pṛthivī śauryeṇāpratimena hi
dayayā sarvajantūnāṁ dānena ca guṇena ca
ato 'haṁ kanyakādānaṁ śāstroktavidhinā nṛpa.

90 N2/4.47a, N3/4.45b, N11 - na bhava s(ś)adṛśaḥ ko 'pi dīrghāyur bhava suvrataḥ.
N4/4.51b, N8/4.91c, Ra/4.52b - na tvayā s(ś)adṛśo dṛṣṭo dīrghāyur bhava suprabhuḥ.

91 N3/4.46a - gavāṁ koṭisahasrāṇaṁ svarṇakoṭiśatāni ca.
N4/4.52a - datvā (emended in the text itself from "gatvā") śatasahasrāṇi hemakoṭiśatāni ca.
N8/4.92a-b - d(g)atvā śatasahasrāṇi hemakoṭiśatāni ca gavāṁ koṭisahasrāṇi hemakoṭiśatāni ca.
BF/4.54a - gobhūgajāśvavastrānnahiraṇyādīn samarpitān.
Bo/4.50a - gavāṁ ś(s)atasahasraṁ me hemakoṭiśatāni ca.

turaṅgādir yad iṣṭaṁ te tad vadasva dadāmy ahaṁ[92] [46]
munir uvāca
nāhaṁ gośatasahasraṁ svarṇakoṭiśatāni ca[93]
na yāce 'śvādikaṁ kiṁ ca yad vadasy adya bhūpate[94]
vaṁśasya dhāraṇārthāya bhavatsānnidhyam āgataḥ [47]
tan mahyaṁ nṛpaśārdūla kanyām ekāṁ dadasva hi[95]
rājovāca
rājyaṁ dadāmi te vipra na kanyā mama sadmani[96]

horses etc., as many as you wish, just say and I shall give (all to) you". [46]
The sage said
"I do not desire a hundred thousands cows or hundreds of millions gold (coins),
I do not desire horses etc. that you have just promised, O king,
I have approached you for the sake of forming a family. [47]
(Please), O brave king, give me only that one girl".
The king said
"O sage, I (would) give you (my) kingdom, but there is no daughter in my palace.

---

92 N2/4.48a - turaṅgādisahasrāṇi (N3/4.46b - turaṅgādi(ḥ)r yad iṣṭaṁ [te] tad) yad vadasva dadāmy ahaṁ.
BF/4.54b - gṛhāṇa tūrṇaṁ brahmarṣe yat kiñcin mama vartate.
Bo/4.50b - turaṅgamādi sarvaṁ me rājyaṁ tubhyaṁ niveditaṁ.

93 N2/4.48b - nāhaṁ go śatasahasraṁ svarṇakoṭi samaprabhaṁ.
N7/4.54a - na suvarṇāni koṭi nīyā ca yāminatāni vai.
N4/4.52, Ra/4.53 - na vā śatasahasrāṇi hemakoṭiśatāni ca
gavāṁ koṭisahasrāṇi yācyante (N8/4.92c yāñcyante) bhūpapuṅgava.
Bo/4.51a - nāhaṁ turaṅgamādi ni hemakoṭiśatāni ca.

94 N1/4.47b - ma gnāce 'śvādikaṁ kiṁ ca yad vadasyadya bhūpate.
N2/4.49a - aśvādikaṁ na yāce 'haṁ yad vadāmi ha bhūpate.

95 N4/4.53, N8/4.94, Ra/4.54 - kiṁ tv ahaṁ prārthaye rājan kanyām ekāṁ prayaccha me
yasyāṁ saṁpāḍayiṣyāmi putraṁ paramadhārmikaṁ.
N7/4.54b-c - adyāhaṁ prārtha tāṁ kurve kanyāṁ ekāṁ dadasva me
vaṁśasya karaṇārthī ya[ḥ] kanyārtham iha cāgataḥ.
Bo/4.51b - rājyaṁ necchāmi rājendra kanyām ekām ahaṁ vṛṇe.
N3/4.47b - tvayā ye 'śvādikaṁ kiñci[d] vadānyendra mahīpate.
N11 - ma yāci 'śvādikaṁ kiñcid yad vadasye ha bhūpate.

96 N7/4.55a - rājyaṁ dadāmi te vipra na kanyā caikā (Bo/4.52a - kanyā mama) na vidyate.

ekāsīc ca purā kanyā sā mṛtā dvijasattama[97] [48]
munir uvāca
na mṛtā nṛpa te kanyā sā tiṣṭhati mamāśrame[98]
suśīlā paramā satyā satyadharmaparāyaṇā[99] [49]
purā patigataṁ vākyaṁ prajāpatimukhān nṛpa[100]
tad anyatho bhaved nṛpa na devāsuramanuṣaiḥ[101] [50]
śṛṇu sarvam idaṁ rājan yad vṛttāntām abhūt purā[102]

I once had just one daughter and she is dead, O excellent Brahmin". [48]
The sage said
"Your daughter is not dead, O king, she is staying at my hermitage.
She is of good conduct, very truthful, adhering to Truth and moral law (Dharma). [49]
Once, I went to Prajāpati, for words coming from Prajāpati's mouth, O king,
(since his words) cannot be altered, by gods, by demons, or by men. [50]
Listen to all of it, O king, to what happened to me once.

---

97 N3/4.49a - ekāsīc ca purā kaṇyā sā mṛtā veśmani.
N7/4.55b - kanyā caikā purā āśīt sā mṛtā ṛṣisattama.
N4/4.54a, N8/4.95a, Ra/4.55a - kanyā mama gṛhe nāsti sarvajñas tvaṁ ca yācase.
BF/4.55a - nāsti kanyā gṛhe me sā kṛtāntasya tapodhana.
Bo/4.52b - kanyaikā me purā hy āsīt sā mṛtā munisattama.

98 N7/4.55c - yā kanyā sā tvayā yātā āśrame mama tiṣṭhati.
BF/4.56a - tvadīyā kanyakā rājann āśrame sā 'sti suvratā.
Bo/4.53a - na sā mṛtā tu kanyā te mama tiṣṭhat(c)i cāśrame.

99 N2/4.52a, N3/4.50b - suśīlā paramā stutyā satyadharmaparāyaṇā.
N7/4.55d - na mṛtā cāpi rāj(y)endra satyadharmaparāyaṇ(aḥ)ā.
BF/4.56b - kumarī yauvanākrāntā satyavrataparāyaṇā.
Bo/4.53b - mahyaṁ tāṁ dehi rājendra satyadharmaparāyaṇā.

100 Emendation - NK. N1/4.50a, N10 - purā pati(r)gataṁ vākyaṁ prajāpatimukhād vaca[ḥ].
N2/4.52b - purā pa(n)tigataṁ vākyaṁ prajāpatimukhān nṛpa.
N3/4.51a - purā pat(a)i[r] hi taṁ vākyaṁ prajāpatimukhād vacaḥ.

101 N2/4.53a - tad anyathā bhavej jātu na devāsuramanuṣaiḥ.
N3/4.51b - tad anyathā na bhaved bhūpa na devāsuramanavaiḥ.
N7/4.(56a) - prajāpatikṛtaṁ karma purāvākyaṁ niyojitā.
There are no verse numbers in N7 after 4.55.

102 N1/4.51a - śṛṇu sarvam idaṁ rājan yad vṛttaṁ māṁ abhūt purā.
N4/4.56a, N8/4.97a, Ra/4.57a - śrotavyaṁ sarvam etat te yat purā vṛttam adbhutaṁ.

vaṁśasya dāraṇārthāya gato 'haṁ yatra padmabhūḥ[103] [51]
namaskṛtyopaviṣṭo 'haṁ tadā pṛṣṭaḥ svayambhuvā[104]
uddālaka kimarthaṁ tvam iha vipra samāgataḥ [52]
tan mayā kathitaṁ rājan putrasantānahetave[105]
tena coktam idaṁ rājan pūrvaṁ putro bhaviṣyati[106] [53]
paścād bhāryā ca viprendra raghuvaṁśasamudbhavā[107]
evam uktvā tatas tatra kṣaṇenāntaradhīyata[108] [54]
tato 'ham āśramāyātas tatra cintāsamanvitaḥ[109]

I went there to the lotus-born (i.e. Brahma), for the sake of forming a lineage. [51]
Having bowed, I sat down, and was then asked by Brahma,
'O sage Uddālaka, what is the purpose of your coming here?' [52]
Then I said, O king, 'I have come for the sake of having a male child'.
Then he told me this, O king, 'First you will have a son, [53]
O venerable sage, and afterwards a wife, born in the lineage of Raghu'.
Having thus spoken, he then disappeared in a moment. [54]
Then I returned to my hermitage, full of thoughts –

---

103 N1/4.51b - vaṁśasya dāraṇārthāya gato 'haṁ yatra (N3/4.52a - viśvasṛk, N11 - sagnabhū) saṁbhūḥ.
N4/4.56b, N8/4.97b, Ra/4.57b - vaṁśasya kāraṇāt tatra gato 'haṁ yatra padmabhūḥ.

104 N11 - namas kṛtyopaviṣyo 'haṁ tadā pṛṣṭaḥ svayambhuvā.

105 N1/4.53a - tan mayā kathitaṁ rājan putrasantāna h(s)etave.

106 N3/4.54b - tena coktam idaṁ vākyaṁ pūrvaṁ (N2/4.56a - rājan) putro bhaviṣyati.
Bo/4.57b - tenoktaṁ prathamaṁ putraḥ paścād bhāryā bhaviṣyati.

107 N4/4.59a, N8/4.200a, Ra/4.60a - paścād bhāryā bhavet kanyā (N7 - te vipra - short) raghuvaṁśasamudbhavā.
Bo/4.58a - tava bhāryā ca viprendra raghuvaṁśasamudbhavā.

108 N1/4.54b, N11 - evam ukt[v]ā tat(m)as tatra (N7 - tataḥ so 'pi, Bo/4.58b - tato brahmā) kṣ(t)aṇ(n)enāntaradhīyata.
N4/4.59b, N8/4.200b, Ra/4.60b - evam uktvaiva rājarṣe brahmā cāntaradhīyata.

109 N2/4.57b, N3/4.56a - tato 'ham āśramāyātas tatra cintāsamanvitaḥ.
N4/4.60a, N8/4.1a, Ra/4.61a - tato 'ham āśramaṁ svīyam āgataś cintayānvitaḥ.
N7 - tato 'ham āśrame sve tu (Bo/4.59a - rājan) āgataś cintayânvitaḥ.

kathaṁ me prathamaṁ putraḥ paścād bhāryā kathaṁ bhavet[110] [55]
tapasas tanmanaskasya vīryacyutir abhūt tadā[111]
tan mayā padmamadhye tu vīryaṁ kṣiptaṁ prayatnataḥ[112] [56]
kuśais tad veṣṭayitvā tu nikṣiptaṁ jāhnavījale[113]
tadā te kanyakā rājan gaṅgāṁ snānārthinī gatā[114] [57]
tayāghrātaṁ ca tat padmaṁ gaṅgāmadhye samāgataṁ[115]

how shall I first have a son, and a wife afterwards? [55]
Thinking while performing penance, my semen burst out.
With effort I cast that semen in the middle of a lotus flower, (and) [56]
having wrapped it with Kuśa grass, I threw it into the current of the Ganges.
Then your daughter, O king, came to the river to bathe. [57]
(Because) she smelled that lotus flower, coming in the midst of the river,

---

110 N2/4.58a - kathaṁ ca prathamaṁ putraḥ paścād bhāryā kathaṁ bhavet.
N4/4.60b, N8/4.1b, Ra/4.61b - kathaṁ me prathamaṁ putro bhāryā (Bo/4.59b - paścād bhaviṣyati) paścāt kathaṁ bhavet.
N7 - kathaṁ me prathamaṁ putro bhāryā kasmāt kathaṁ bhavet.

111 N1/4.56a, N11 - tapasas tanamaskasya (N3/4.57a - tapatas tanmanovīryaṁ) vīryacyutir abhūt tadā.
N4/4.61a, N8/4.2a, Ra/4.62a - tatas tad dhyānato reta udbhūtaṁ mama bhūtale.
N7 - tapyamānasya me tatra retotsargaṁ bhave mama.
Bo/4.60 - tapyamāne ca tapasi retotsargo vabhūva ha.

112 N1/4.56b - tan mayā padmamadhyaṁ tu vīryyaṁ (N11 - tiptaṁ ya prelataḥ) taptaṁ prayatnataḥ.
N4/4.61b, N8/4.2b, Ra/4.62b - tan mayā padmamadhye tu reto nikṣipya yatnataḥ.
Bo/4.61a - tan mayā padmapuṭake vīryaṁ kṣiptaṁ prayatnataḥ.

113 N3/4.58a - kuśais tad veṣṭayitvā tu nikṣiptaṁ jānhavītaṭe.
Half verse 4.57a is missing in N2.
N4/4.62a, N8/4.3a, Ra/4.63a - kuśaiś ca veṣṭayitvā tu (Bo/4.61b - gaṅgāmadhye visarjitaṁ) gaṅgāyāṁ sthāpitaṁ nṛpa.
N7 - kuśais tu veṣṭayitvā ca gaṅgāmadhye prayojitaṁ.

114 N1/4.57b, N2/4.59b, N3/4.58b, N11 - tadā te kanyakā rājan gaṅgāsnānārthinī gatā
N4/4.62b, N8/4.3b, Bo/4.62a, Ra/4.63b - tatas te kanyakā rājan gaṅgāsnānārtham āgatā.

115 N2/4.59b - tayāghrāṇāṁ [ca] tat padmaṁ gaṅgāmadhyasamāgataṁ.
N3/4.58a - tayā dṛṣṭaṁ ca tat padmaṁ gaṅgāmadhye samāgataṁ.
N4/4.63a, N8/4.4a, Ra/4.64a - tatrājighrac ca tat padmaṁ gaṅgāmadhyāt samāhṛtaṁ.
Bo/4.62b - tad āghrāya cyutaṁ samyak gaṅgāmadhye samāgataṁ.

tasyāsīd gārbhasaṁbhūtir mama vīryād asaṁśayaṁ[116] [58]
nāsāgreṇa viniṣkrānto nāsiketas tad ucyate[117] [59]
vaiśaṁpāyana uvāca
tato vismayam āpanno raghur antaḥpuraṁ gataḥ[118]
tad vṛttāntaṁ mahiṣyai sa yathāśrutaṁ nyavedayat[119] [60]
jñātasatyavṛtāntena prajāpatinivedanāt[120]

your own daughter, undoubtedly[(V)]*, became pregnant by my semen. [58]*
Since he came out of the nose, he is called Nāsiketa". [59]
Vaiśaṁpāyana said
Thus, filled with wonder, Raghu entered his inner chambers,
(and) told the queen that which he had just heard. [60]
(Now they both) knew how things had really happened, because of Prajāpati's prophesy,

---

116 N1/4.58b - tasyās(v)īd (N3/4.59b - tasyāś ca) gārbhasaṁbhūtir mama vīryād aśaṁsayaṁ.
N2/4.60b - tasyāś ca gārbhasaṁbhūtir mama vīryād asaṁmadaṁ.
N4/4.63b-64a, N8/4.4b-5a, Ra/4.64b-65a - tadā tatra sthītaṁ vīryaṁ nāsāgreṇodaraṁ gataṁ
tatas tasyāḥ samudbhūto garbho vīryyān mamaiva hi.
N7 - tasmāt gārbhasya saṁbhūto (Bo/4.63a - tenaiva gārbhasaṁbhūtir) mama vīryān na saṁśayaḥ.

117 N4/4.64b, N8/4.5b, Ra/4.65b - putraṁ ca nāsiketākhyaṁ nāsayā suṣuve tadā.
N7 - nās(ś)āgreṇai(ṇ)[va] niḥkrāntāṁ nāśiketaḥ prakathyate.
Bo/4.63b - nāsāgreṇa tu niṣkrānto nāsiketa iti śrutaḥ.

118 N1/4.60a - tato vismayam āpanno (N7 - raghur antaḥpuraṁ vrajet, Bo/4.64a - antaḥpure 'vrajat) raghus tasya puraṁ gataḥ.

119 N1/4.60b, N11 - tad vṛ(a)ttāntaṁ mahiṣyai (N3/4.61a - va yathāśruta[ṁ] tathābravīt) sa yathāśrutam avedayat.
N2/4.57b - tad vṛttāntaṁ (- - - - - - - -) tam avedayat.
N4/4.67a, N8/4.8a, Ra/4.68a - niveditaṁ ca tat sarvaṁ rājñā rājñyai yathāśrutaṁ.
N7 - tad vṛttāntaṁ kṛtaṁ sarvaṁ rājñī cāgre yathāśrutaṁ.
Bo/4.64b - tad vṛttāntaṁ tato rājā sva mahiṣyai nyavedayat.

120 N1/4.61a - j[ñ]ātam atyadbhutāṁ tābhyāṁ (N2/4.62a, N11 - prajāpatinivedite, N3/4.61b - prajāpatiniyojitaṁ) prajāpatiniveditaḥ.
N4/4.67b, N8/4.8b, Ra/4.68b - jātaṁ tad adbhutaṁ rājan prajāpatiniyojitaṁ.
N7 - jñātam atyadbhutaṁ ramyaṁ prajāpatiniyojitaṁ.

punaś caivāgato dvāri prahasya manaso 'ntare[121] [61]
bahubhaktisamāyuktaḥ sāṣṭāṅgaṁ praṇipatya taṁ[122]
baddhvā karāñjalipuṭaṁ vinayān munim abravīt[123] [62]
rājovāca[124]
kanyāṁ dadāmi te vipra śṛṇu me paramaṁ vacaḥ[125]
rathe suturage yukte samāruhyāśramaṁ vraja[126] [63]
tata ānaya tāṁ kanyāṁ yathāvṛtte dadāmy ahaṁ[127]

and then he reached the gate again, pleased at heart[(VI)]. *[61]*
Seized with much devotion, the king fell submissively, at the sage's feet, fully prostrated,
with bowl-shaped joined palms, (and) modestly he spoke to the sage. [62]
The king said
"I give you my daughter, O sage, listen to my important words.
Return to your hermitage, well disposed, in a chariot yoked to good horses, (and) [63]
then bring that girl. After that happens, I shall give (the princess to you)".

---

121 N1/4.61b, N11 - punaś caivāgato dvāre prahasya (N2/4.62b - bahuśat tadā, N7 - ca samaṁ tataḥ) manasotarā.
N3/4.62a - punaś caivāgato dvāri prahasya manaso 'ntare.
N4/4.68a, N8/4.9a, Ra/4.69a - punas tatrāgato rāja yatrāste munipuṅgavaḥ.

122 N2/4.63a - bahubhaktisamāyuktas (N3/4.62b - bahubhaktisamāyukto) sāṣṭāṅgaṁ (N11 - sāpyāṅgaṁ) praṇipatya ca.

123 N1/4.62b, N2/4.63b, N11 - ba[d]dhvā karāñjalipuṭaṁ vinayān (N3/4.63a - vinīyā) muni(r)m abravīt.
N4/4.68b, N8/4.9b, Ra/4.69b - bahubhaktisamayuktaḥ (N7 - bahubhaktisam ayukto) prahṛṣṭo munim abravīt.

124 N1, N2, N11 - munir uvāca.

125 N4/4.69a, N8/4.10a, Ra/4.70a - kanyā dattā mayā tubhyaṁ śṛṇu me paramaṁ vacaḥ.
N7 - kanyāṁ dadāmi te vipra śṛṇuṣvai para[ma]ṁ (Bo/4.65 - śṛṇu me paramaṁ) vacaḥ.

126 N2/4.64b - rathe suturagair (N3/4.64a - rathair aturagai(ḥ)r) yukte samāruhyāśramaṁ vraja.
N4/4.69b, N8/4.10b, Ra/4.70b - rathaṁ paramaśobhāḍhyaṁ vandhubhiḥ pariveṣṭitaṁ.
N7 - rathe surayate ramye mamājñākarasaṁyute.
Bo/4.66a - rathe śubhatare ramye sthitvā gaccha svamāśramaṁ.

127 N1/4.64a - ta[ta] (sāpy) ānaya tāṁ kanyāṁ yathādbhute dadāmy ahaṁ.
N3/4.64b - āśramād ayatāṁ (N11 - ta[ta] (so 'py) ānay(ā)a) kanyāṁ yathāvṛ(ra)tte dadāmy ahaṁ.
N7 - rathe 'py āruhya gama tvam ānayasva sutāṁ mama.
Bo/4.66b - mamānujīvibhir yukta ānayā svasutāṁ mama.

evam ukto munis tena rājñā santuṣṭamanasā[128] [64]
tato tām ānayāmāsa raghurājasya veśmani[129]
tā sānītā tadā kanyā saputrā kīrtivardhinī[130] [65]
vivāhavidhinā tasmai tatputraś ca niveditaḥ[131]
sutena nāsiketena candravatyā samarpaṇaṁ[132] [66]
uddālako mahiṣyāś ca samīpam anayat tataḥ[133]

The sage, as directed by the happy-minded king, [64]
then brought her to king Raghu's palace.
That girl was brought then with her son, she who increases (her family's) fame. [65]
At the marriage rituals, he (i.e. Uddālaka) handed his son over to him (i.e. the king).
He handed his son Nāsiketa over to him along with Candravatī. [66]
Uddālaka came with his beloved, to the queen.

---

[128] N1/4.64b - evam ukto (N2/4.65b - muniśreṣṭo) munis tena (N4/4.70, N8/4.11, Ra/4.71b - tathaivāśramam āgataḥ) rājñā santuṣṭamānasā.
N7 - evam uktā tatas tena tathaivānuṣito muni.
Bo/4.67a - evam uktas tatas tena tathaivā hi cakāra saḥ.

[129] N1/4.65a - taṁ tu tām (N2/4.66a, N3/4.65b, N11 - taṁ turṇām) ānayāmāsa raghurājasya veśmani.
N7 - tvaritāś cānayiṣyāmi raghunāthasya veśmani.

[130] N1/4.65b - tā sānītā tadā kanyā saputrā(ṁ) kīrtivardhinī.
N3/4.66a, N11 - tām ānītāṁ tadā kanyāṁ saputrāṁ kīrtivardhinīṁ.
N2/4.66b - sānītā tadā kanyā saputrī kulavardhinī.
N7 - ānītā sā tadā kanyā saputrā rathasaṁsthitā.
Bo/4.67b - ānītā ca tadā kanyā saputrarathasaṁsthitā.
Additional verse - N2/4.67:
āyātāyāṁ tu tasyāṁ ca sarveṣāṁ puravāsināṁ
vismayaṁ tu samutpannaṁ dṛṣṭvā tāṁ putrasaṁyutāṁ.
N7 - ānīyatāṁ tataḥ sarvā puraṁ ca sa ca tat tathā
vis(ś)mayaṁ ca samutpannaṁ sarveṣāṁ puravāsināṁ.

[131] N1/4.66a, N3/4.66b, N11 - vivāhavidhinā tasmai tatputraś ca niyojitaḥ.

[132] Emendation - NK. N1/4.66b - sutena nāsiketena candravatyā (N2/4.67a - subhāryayā, N3/4.67a - sabhāryayā) samarpayet.
N7 - vivāhaṁ ca kṛtaṁ sarvaṁ putraṁ tasya niveditaṁ.

[133] N1/4.67a - uddālako mahiṣyā sa priyā saha samāgataḥ.
N2/4.69a - uddālako mahiṣyāś ca priyā saha āgama (N3/4.67b - samīpam anayat) tataḥ.

dṛṣṭvā tāṁ mātaraṁ rājñī santuṣṭā hṛṣṭamanasā[134] [67]
kanyāṁ ca dharmaśīlāṁ tāṁ nāsiketaṁ viśeṣataḥ
dāsadāsīn dhanaṁ dhānyaṁ yuktābharaṇakuṇḍalaiḥ[135] [68]
mahākeyūraratnāni dadau nānāvidhāni sā[136]
gajāśvarathavastrāṇi mahiṣīr gām anekaśaḥ[137] [69]
jāmātre raghurājo 'pi dadau saṁhṛṣṭamānasaḥ[138]
uddālakas tadovāca rājānaṁ vinayānvitaḥ [70]
kiṁ kariṣyāmi rājendra rājavājirathadvipaiḥ[139]

The queen was filled with happiness, seeing her (daughter) a mother[(VII)], *[67]*
her daughter of pious conduct, and especially Nāsiketa.
She gave her slaves and slave-girls, food and grains, ornaments of pearls and earrings, (and) [68]
big jeweled bracelets, of various kinds.
The king (gave) many elephants, horses, chariots, cows and clothes. [69]
This is what King Raghu, glad at heart, gave his son-in-law.
Uddālaka then said to the king, full of modesty: [70]
"What am I going to do, O brave king, with royal horses, chariots, and elephants?

---

134 N1/4.67b - dṛṣṭvāyā (N2/4.69b - dṛṣṭvājñā) mātaraṁ rājñī santuṣṭā harṣama(ā)nasā.

135 N2/4.70b - dāsadāsīdhanaṁ dhānye muktābharaṇakuṇḍalaṁ.
N4/4.74, N8/4.15, Ra/4.75 - dāsadāsyo dhanaṁ dhānyaṁ mauktikābharaṇāni ca suvarṇābharaṇaṁ tadvat ratnābharaṇam eva ca.
N7 - dāsadāsīdhanaṁ dhānyaṁ muktābharaṇaṁ maṇḍale.
Bo/4.69a - dāsan dāsīr dhanaṁ dhānyaṁ muktābharaṇakuṇḍale.

136 N3/4.69b - hārakeyūraratnāni uddamavividhāni cā.
N7 - hārakeyūraratnādyai[ḥ] svarṇakeyūrasaṁyutaiḥ.
Bo/4.69b - hāragraiveyakeyūran nānāmāṇikyasamyutān.

137 N1/4.71b - gajāśvarathavastrāṇi (N3/4.70a - maharṣīṇām anekaśaḥ) mahiṣīr gām anekaśaḥ.
N7 - rathaṁ gajaṁ hy anvastraṁ mahiṣī[ś] cātigāṁ dadau.
Bo/4.70a - rathān gajān hy anvastra mahiṣī godhanāni ca.

138 N1/4.72a - yāmātre (N11- yāmoḥ) raghurājo 'pi dadau (N3/4.70b - saṁhṛṣṭamānasaḥ) santuṣṭamānasaḥ.
Additional half verse: Bo/4.70b - rājā raghur adāt sarvaṁ duhitre snehasaṁyutaḥ.

139 N2/4.73a - kiṁ kariṣyāmi rājendra (N3/4.71b - gajavājirathādibhiḥ) gajavājirathair dhanaiḥ.
N4/4.76b-77a, N8/4.17b-18a, Ra/4.77 - kanyāratnaṁ tvayā dattaṁ rājan mama sudurlabhaṁ

atraiva sarvam evaitad bhavān rakṣitum arhasi[140] [71]
atha sarvān pure tyaktvā mahiṣībhūpatidvijān[141] [72]
vijñāpya ratham āruhya jagāma strīsutānvitaḥ[142]

Let them all stay here, (under) your protection, O worthy one". [71]
He left all the goods with the king and queen(VIII)*, the twice-born. [72]*
Having cleared (the matter of the goods), he descended from the chariot, and left, accompanied by his wife and son.

---

kim anyair vastubhiḥ kāryyaṁ vayaṁ ya sma tapodhanāḥ.
N7 - kiṁ kariṣyāmi tenaiva drāveṇa vipulena hi.
BF/4.80b - kiṁ kariṣyāmi bho bhūpa gobhir dravyai rathair gajaiḥ.
Bo/4.72a - kiṁ karomy aham etena dhanena vipulena ca.

140 N1/4.71b, N11 - atraiva sarvam evaitad bhavān jvalitum arhasi.
N1/4.72b - atraiva sarvam evaitad bhavān bhuvi ra nāpya. (Additional redundant half verse).
N2/4.73b - nṛpa cātraiva mama caitad bhavān (- -) arhati.
Additional verses - N2/4.74-6:
atha sarvaṁ parityajya mahiṣībhūpatiṁ tadā
vadann idaṁ mahīpāla surājñā mama kāmanā
pūri tā hitva yā tasmāt pūrvāsyā tvāmalā tava
acalac calato rājñī vadati sma muner idaṁ
sukumārī cālpava yā(s)ḥ sukha dirghākṣudhāvati
rakṣanīyā - - - - - - - - - - - -.
N3/4.72a - atra sarvaṁ tavaitac ca bhavān dṛṣṭaṁ tu mamakaṁ.
Verse number 4.71 is skipped in N3.
BF/4.81 - tapodhanā vayaṁ nūnaṁ sukhārthāya dhanaṁ hi naḥ
tasmād ihaivāsmadīyaṁ dhanaṁ tiṣṭhatu bhupate.

141 Emendation - NK. N1/4.72, N11 - atha sarvāṁ dhuraṁ tyaktā mahiṣī bhūpati dvipaiḥ.
N2/4.77a - atha sarvāṁ dhuraṁ parityajya (N3/4.73a - tyaktā) mahiṣī bhūpati tathā.
Bo/4.72b-73a - tavaiva sarvathā rājan (N7 - tadārtha sarvatha caiva) gṛhe tiṣṭhatu suvrata
ity uktvā rājyam ākhilaṁ pratāryāgāt tapovanaṁ.

142 N1/4.73a - ratham āruhya jagāma rājastrīsasutānvitaḥ.
N4/4.76b, N8/4.17b, Ra/4.78b - rathena preṣayāmāsa muniṁ patnīsamanvitaṁ.
N7 - preṣyatāś ca pure sarve ratha[m] āruhya gacchati.

praviśya cāśramaṁ puṇyaṁ saputraḥ sakalatrakaḥ[143] [73]
uvāsa sukham āpannāḥ kurvan vedoditāḥ kriyāḥ[144]
itihāsakathāṁ viprāḥ puṇyāṁ pauraṇikīṁ śubhāṁ[145] [74]
śṛṇoti kathayed vāpi sarvapāpaiḥ pramucyate
brahmahā hemahārī vā surāpo gurutalpagaḥ[146] [75]
etasyāḥ śrutimātreṇa mucyate nātra saṁśayaḥ[147] [76]

He entered his beautiful hermitage, along with his son and wife, (and) [73]
dwelled there happily, performing the rituals prescribed in the Vedas.
This is the honourable, historical, inspiring, auspicious, ancient story. [74]
Whoever listens to it or tells it, is liberated from all his sins.
A killer of a Brahmin, or one who steals gold, or drinks wine, or lies with his guru's wife, [75]
just by listening to it, becomes liberated, there is no doubt. [76]

---

143 N2/4.78a, N11 - praviśya (N3/4.73b - praviṣṭa[ḥ]) āśrame puṇye saputraḥ sakalatrakaḥ.

N4/4.77, N8/4.18, Ra/4.79 - tato vai vāhikenātha praviṣṭaḥ svāśrame muniḥ saputraḥ sakalatro 'sau rājñā dattena tad yathā.

N7 - praviṣṭaḥ svāśrame vāpi (Bo/4.73b - vipraḥ) saputraḥ sakalatrakaḥ.

BF/4.83b - bhāryānvito munivaraḥ praviveśa nijāśramaṁ.

144 N4/4.79b-80a, N8/4.20b-21a, Ra/4.80 - candravatyā striyā sārddham ṛṣir uddālakas tataḥ
nāsiketena putreṇa gaṅgātīre sukhaṁ sthitaḥ.

N7 - sa eva candravatyā tu ṛṣir uddālakaḥ punaḥ
nāśiketas tata tatra gaṅgātīre sukhānvitaḥ.

145 N3/4.74b, N7 - itihāsakathāṁ ramyāṁ (N11 - itihāsapurākathāṁ viprā - vi) puṇyāṁ pauraṇikīṁ śubhāṁ.

N4/4.80b, N8/4.21b, Ra/4.82a - itihāsakathām etāṁ puṇyāṁ pauraṇikīṁ ca ye.

BF/4.84a - itihāsakathāṁ puṇyāṁ etāṁ pauraṇikīṁ śubhāṁ.

146 N1/4.75b - brahmehā hemahārī vā surālo gurutalpagaḥ.

N2/4.80b, N3/4.75b - brahmahā hemahārī cā surāpī gurutalpagaḥ.

147 N3/4.75c - anumodanamātreṇa mucyate nātra saṁśayaḥ.

N4/4.81, Ra/4.82b - kathayanti ca śṛṇvanti pāpair muktā bhavanti te.

BF/4.84b - yaḥ śṛṇoti naro bhaktyā mucyate sarvapātakaiḥ.

Bo/4.76b - kathayec chṛṇuyādyaś ca sarvapāpaiḥ pramucyate.

iti śrībrahmāṇḍapurāṇe nāsiketopākhyāne candravatyā vivāho nāma caturtho 'dhyāyaḥ

The fourth chapter of the Nāsiketa story, pertaining to the Brahmāṇḍa Purāṇa, called – Candravatī's marriage.

Translation Notes

I – According to other versions – "After finishing her work, O father, she went to the river to bathe".
II – According to other versions – "Go bring your mother".
III – Literally – "with concentrated mind".
IV – Nāsiketa is reciting his mother's words.
V – Or – unwillingly, without wishing.
VI – Literally – "laughing inside his mind".
VII – Or – seeing her mother, the queen, Candravatī was filled with happiness.
VIII – The whole scene alludes to KU/1.25-9 – Naciketas rejecting all the worldly temptations of Yama.

Chapter 5

Seeing Dharmarāja

janamejaya uvāca
śrutaṁ mayā purā putraḥ pitrā śāpenayojitaḥ[1]
aparāddhaṁ kim etena sutena janakasya hi [1]
yac chāpaṁ pradadau tasya sutāya munipuṅgavaḥ[2]
dṛṣṭavān narakaṁ ghoraṁ kathaṁ svargyasukhāvahaṁ[3] [2]
kathaṁ yamapurīṁ prāptaḥ kathaṁ caivāgamat punaḥ[4]

Janamejaya said
"I have once heard about that son, cursed by his father.
What was the offence done by that son against his father? [1]
O great sage, having cursed his son, sending him
to experience the horrible Hell, how can he go to the delightful Heaven? [2]
How did he reach Yama's city? How did he then come back?

---

[1] N4/5.1, N8/5.23, Ra/5.1 - etat pṛcchāmi viprendra kathayasva yathātathaṁ nāsiketa kathaṁ putraḥ pitrāśāpenayojitaḥ.
N7/5.1 - etat pṛcchāmi te vipra saṁś(s)ayaṁ kathaya suvrata durlabhaṁ putra nāmasya kathaṁ ś(s)āpenayojitaḥ.
Bo/5.1 - etat pṛcchāmy ahaṁ vipra saṁśayaṁ me hy apānuda durlabhaṁ putra nāmāpi manuṣyāṇāṁ taponidhe.

[2] N1/5.2a - yamāya pradadau (N10 - yac chāpaṁ pradadau) tasmai sutāya munipuṅgavaḥ.
N7/5.2a - kimarthaṁ tasya ś(s)āpo 'yaṁ sutāya ca pitā dadau.
BF/5.1b - kimarthaṁ pradattaṁ śāpaṁ pitrā putrasya dāruṇaṁ.
Bo/5.2a - kimarthaṁ dattavān śāpaṁ putram uddiśya suvrata.

[3] N2/52b, N3/5.2b - dṛṣṭavān narakaṁ ghoraṁ kathaṁ (N10 - svargasukhāvahe, N11 - svargasukhāvatve) svargasukhāvahaṁ.
N4/5.3a, N8/5.25a, Ra/5.3a - kathaṁ sa narakān svargaṁ dṛṣṭvā prāha munīn prati.
N7/5.3a - kathaṁ narakaṁ ghoraṁ kīdṛk svargasukhāvahaṁ.

[4] N4/5.2, N8/5.24, Ra/5.2 - hetunā kena ca mune kathaṁ prāpto 'tidustare kathaṁ yamapurīṁ prāptaḥ sa kathaṁ punar āgataḥ.
N7/5.2b - kathaṁ yamapurī gatvā katham evāgataḥ punaḥ.
BF/5.1a - kathaṁ sa pitur ādeśād yāto yamapurīṁ muniḥ.
Bo/5.2b - kathaṁ yamapurīṁ prāpto kathaṁ cāgatavān punaḥ.

etat kathaya viprendra vaiśaṁpāyana me 'grataḥ[5] [3]
vaiśaṁpāyana uvāca
śṛṇu rājan purāvṛttaṁ yathā śāpena yojitaḥ[6]
putraḥ pitrātiruṣṭena preṣito yamamandiraṁ[7] [4]
punar āgād yathānyāyaṁ narakāt kathayāmi te[8]
ekadoddālakaḥ putram uvāca munipuṅgavaḥ[9] [5]
gaccha putra vanaṁ yajñasamidhas tvaṁ samānaya[10]

(Please) tell me this, O venerable sage Vaiśaṁpāyana. [3]
Vaiśaṁpāyana said
Listen, O king, to the old story[(1)]*, how, burdened with a curse,*
the son was sent by his vexed father to Yama's palace. [4]
I shall tell you exactly (how) he returned again from Hell.
Once, the great sage Uddālaka said to his son: [5]
"Go son to the forest and bring (me) fuel for the (fire) sacrifice,

---

5 N4/5.3b, N8/5.25b, Ra/5.3b - etat sarvaṁ samācakṣva param asti kutūhalaṁ.
BF/5.2 - etan me saṁśayaṁ chinddhi vaiśaṁpāyana kautukāt
kathayasva mahāścaryaṁ mahāpātakanāśanaṁ.

6 N10 - śṛṇu etat purāvṛttaṁ yathā (Bo/5.3a - śāpo niyojitaḥ) śāpena yojitaḥ.
N4/5.4a, N8/5.26a, Ra/5.4a - śṛṇu rājan purāvṛttaṁ yathā kruddhaḥ pitā bhṛśaṁ.

7 N4/5.4b, N8/5.26b, Ra/5.4b - śāpe sutaṁ yojitavān dustare yamaśāsane.
Bo/5.3b - pitrā vai preṣito gatvā harṣito yamasādane.

8 N2/5.5a - purā rājyād yathā śāpaṁ tvat (Bo/5.4a - āgataḥ punar evātha tat) sarvaṁ kathayāmi te.
N3/5.5a - punar āgād yathā rājan (N4/5.5a, N8/5.27a, Ra/5.5a - āgataṁ tena ca yathā) tat sarvaṁ kathayāmy ahaṁ.

9 N4/5.5b, N8/5.27b, Ra/5.5b - kadācin muniśārdūlo nāsiketaṁ vaco 'bravīt.
BF/5.3-4a - evam uddālako muniḥ sabhāryas tapasi sthitaḥ
nāsiketuḥ sadaiva ca yogābhyāsarato 'bhavat
ekadā preṣitas tena pitrā so 'tha vanaṁ sutaḥ.
Bo/5.4b - uddālak(ā)o munivaraḥ suvrataṁ putram ekadā.

10 N4/5.6a, N8/5.28a, Ra/5.6a - gaccha putra vanaṁ śīghraṁ samidho 'dya samānaya.
N7 - gaccha putram idaṁ śīghraṁ samidhas tvam ihānaya.
No verse numbers from verse N7/5.3.
Bo/5.5a - uvāca putra gaccheti vanaṁ śīghram samānaya.

kuśapatraphalāny āśu mūlāni vividhāni ca[11] [6]
śīghram āgamyatāṁ putra agnihotrasya kāraṇāt[12]
vanāntare suto gatvā dṛṣṭavān śobhanaṁ saraḥ[13] [7]
suramyaṁ nirmalajalaṁ nānāpakṣiniṣevitaṁ[14]
nānāpuṣpasamakīrṇaṁ nānādrumasamākulaṁ[15] [8]
atīvaṁ śobhamānaṁ tat puṣpotpalakuśāśayaiḥ[16]

as well as Kuśa grass leaves, fruits and various root vegetables. [6]
You should return quickly, son, for the sake of the Agnihotra".
Going inside the forest, the son saw a beautiful lake, [7]
abundant with pure tasty water, inhabited by different kinds of birds,
spotted with various flowers, surrounded by a variety of trees. [8]
It was most beautiful, with heaps of lotus flowers and Kuśa grass.

---

11 N3/5.6a - kuśa[ṁ] putra phalāny āśu mūlāni vividhāni ca.
N4/5.6b, N8/5.28b, Ra/5.6b - kuśān puṣp(y)aṁ phalaṁ (N7 - kuśaṁ puṣp(y)aṁ phalaṁś) caiva mūlāni vividhāni ca.
Bo/5.5b - samitkuśaphalānīti hy agnihotraṁ yathā bhavet.

12 N4/5.7a, N8/5.29a, Ra/5.7a - sādhanāny agnihotrasya māvilanvaṁ kṛyā.
N7 - kṣipram āgamyatāṁ putra agnihotrasya kāraṇe.

13 N10 - vanāntare suto gatvā dṛṣṭavāñc chobhanaṁ s(ś)araḥ.
N4/5.7b, N8/5.29b, Ra/5.7b - evaṁ pitrā samājñapto vanāntaram āgat sutaḥ.
N7 - vanāntare sute prāpte atyantaṁ śobhanaṁ saraḥ.
Bo/5.6 - iti śrutvā pitur vākyaṁ nāsiketo vanaṁ prati
jagāma tatra sa munir yatrāste śobhanaṁ saraḥ.

14 N1/5.8a, N10 - sura(s)myaṁ nirmalajalaṁ (N11 - nānāpakṣiniṣedhitaṁ) nānāpakṣiniṣevitaṁ.
N4/5.8a, N8/5.30a, Ra/5.8a - tatra dṛṣṭaṁ saras tena ramyaṁ mānasasannibhaṁ.
N7 - dṛṣṭaṁ ramyaṁ sar(sut)aḥ (BF/5.5a - dṛṣṭvā manoramaṁ) sthānaṁ nānādrumasamākulaṁ.
Bo/5.7a - dṛṣṭvāraṇyaṁ śubhaṁ ramyaṁ nānādrumalatākulaṁ.

15 N4/5.8b, N8/5.30b, Ra/5.8b - nānāpuṣpaphalākīrṇaṁ latādrumalasattaṭaṁ.
N7 - nānāpuṣpasamākīrṇaṁ nānāvihaṅgasevitaṁ.
BF/5.5b - nānāvihaṅgamākīrṇaṁ nānāpuṣpopaśobhitaṁ.
Bo/5.7b - phalamūlayutaṁ caiva nānāpakṣiniṣevitaṁ.

16 N3/5.8b - atīva śobhamānaṁ taṁ (N10 - padmotpalakuśaiśayaiḥ) padmotpalakuśeśayaiḥ.
N4/5.9a, N8/5.31a, Ra/5.9a - nānāvihaṅgaṁ śobhāḍhyaṁ padmotpalasamākulaṁ.
N7 - nirjharair vividhais tasya padmotpalasamākulaṁ.

kṛtvā snānaṁ ca tatraiva vidhidṛṣṭena karmaṇā[17] [9]
devārcanaṁ kṛtaṁ tena divyaiḥ puṣpair manoharaiḥ[18]
naivedyaphalamūlādyais tarpitās tena devatāḥ[19] [10]
dhyānadhāraṇamārgeṇa yogābhyāsam asau 'bhyadhāt[20]
evaṁ prakurvatas tasya prahṛṣṭamanaso nṛpa[21] [11]
vyatītaṁ māsam ekaṁ tu dhyānayogasamādhinā[22]

Having bathed there, he performed the rituals according to the rule. [9]
He worshipped God with beautiful divine flowers,
with offerings of fruits and root vegetables he satisfied the gods. [10]
He practiced Yoga by (performing) Dhyāna and Dhāraṇa[(II)]*,*
thus, practicing these, he became very pleased, O king. [11]
At the end of one month[(III)]*, passed in deepest meditation*[(IV)]*,*

BF/5.6a - nirjharair vividhair yuktaṁ mahotpalavirājitaṁ,
Bo/5.8a - śubhe sarovare tatra vividhotpalamaṇḍite.

17 N4/5.9b, N8/5.31b, Ra/5.9b - snānaṁ kṛtvā tatas tatra vidhisṛṣṭena karmmaṇā.
N7 - sn(th)ānaṁ kṛtvā ca (Bo/5.8b - tu) tatraiva vidhidṛṣṭena karmaṇā.
BF/5.6b - snānaṁ samācaraṁs tatra śāstradṛṣṭena karmaṇā.

18 N3/5.9b - devārcanaṁ kṛtaṁ tena (N7 - divyapuṣpair manoharaiḥ) divyaiḥ (Bo/5.9a - puṣpaiś ca nīrajaiḥ) puṣpai[r] manoramaiḥ.
Verse 5.9b-10a is missing in N10.
N4/5.10, N8/5.32, Ra/5.10 - devatā ṛṣayaś cāpi tarpitās tena śāstrataḥ devārcanaṁ kṛtaṁ nānāpuṣpair api manoharaiḥ.

19 N1/5.10b, N2/5.10a, N3/5.10a - phalamūlādinair vedyai tarpitās tena devatāḥ.
N7 - naivedyaphalamūlāni devatāpitṛtarpitā.
Bo/5.9b - naivedyaphalamūlādyair devatāpitṛtarpaṇaiḥ.

20 N1/5.11a - dhyānadhāraṇamātreṇa (N2/5.10b, N3/5.10b, N10, N11 - dhyānadhāraṇayā tatra) yogābhyāsam asau 'bhyadhāt.
N4/5.12a, N8/5.34a, Ra/5.12a - yogadṛṣṭena mārgeṇa brahmadhyānaṁ cakāra saḥ.
N7 - yogam ārabhya tatraiva (Bo/5.10a - dhāraṇādhyānakarmaṇā) dhyānadhāraṇakarmaṇā.
Bo/5.10b - devārcanaṁ ca yogaṁ ca nityaṁ saṁpādya yatnataḥ.

21 N3/5.11a - evaṁ prakurvatas tasya saṇṭuṣṭamanaso (N2/5.11a - prahṛṣṭamanaso) nṛpa.
N7 - tadā tatraiva saṁlīnā atyadvai harṣiṭaṁ manaḥ.

22 N4/5.12b, N8/5.34b, Ra/5.12b - evaṁ saṁvatsarārddhaṁ tu nītaṁ tena mahātmanā.
BF/5.8a - samādhiniṣṭas tatrāsīt sārdhasaṁvatsaro gataḥ.

cyutaṁ samādhitas tasya mānasaṁ daivayogataḥ[23] [12]
acintayat tadā kiṁ me kṛtaṁ kiṁ vāsavarjitaḥ[24]
utthāya vāyuvegena samāgāt pitur antikaṁ[25] [13]
dṛṣṭvā pitāgataṁ putraṁ yajñavighnakaraṁ muniḥ[26]
uddālakaḥ prakupito vacanaṁ cedam abravīt[27] [14]
uddālaka uvāca
re putra phalamūlārthaṁ preṣito yajñakarmaṇi[28]

his mind abandoned meditation by his divine Yoga (power). [12]
He then thought – "What have I done? Why am I not at home[V]?"
He stood up, (and) by the speed of wind, arrived close to his father. [13]
The father sage saw the arrival of his son, the obstructionist of his sacrifice.
Uddālaka, being very angry, said the following words. [14]
Uddālaka said
"Where are the fruits and root vegetables of the sacrifice rite, you have been sent for?

---

23 N3/5.12a - cyutaḥ samādhitaś citraṁ kadācid daivayogataḥ.

24 N1/5.13a - acintayat tadā kiṁ me kṛtaṁ kiṁ vā sa (N2/5.12b, N3/5.12b - vakṣyati, N10 - vakṣati) varjati.
Bo/5.11a - pitur me vighnam utpannam agnihotre tu matkṛtaṁ.

25 N4/5.13, N8/5.35, Ra/5.13 - tataḥ pitur vacaḥ smṛtvā samitpuṣpaphalādikaṁ homasādhanam ādāya śīghram āśramam āgataḥ.
BF/5.8b - samādhivirataḥ paścād yāto nijapitur gṛhaṁ.
Bo/5.11b - iti niścitya(ṁ)manasā pitur āśramam āgamat.

26 N2/5.13b, N3/5.13b, N10, N11 - dṛṣṭvā cirāgataṁ putraṁ yajñavighnakaraṁ muniḥ.
N7 - uddālaka parikrudho dṛṣṭvā putraṁ samāgataṁ.
Bo/5.12a - tata uddālakaḥ kruddho dṛṣṭvā putraṁ cirāgataṁ.

27 N4/5.14a, N8/5.36a, Ra/5.14a - cirāgataṁ sutaṁ dṛṣṭvā pitā krodhād vacanam abravīt.
BF/5.10a - uddālako 'tikopito vidhilopāt tam abravīt.
Bo/5.12b - uvāca krodhatāmrākṣo hy agnihotra vighātakaṁ.

28 N1/5.15a, N2/5.14b, N10 - kutra te phalamūlārthaṁ preṣito yajñakarmaṇi.
N4/5.14b, N8/5.36b, Ra/5.14b - putrādya phalamūlāni samānītāni kiṁ tvayā.
N7 - kiṁ tvayā phalamūlāni ciraṁ gatvā vanāntaraṁ.
Bo/5.13a - kiṁ tatra phalamūlārthaṁ ciraṁ gatvā vanāntare.

tvam asthā agnihotraṁ ca sa mānādṛptalaṁpaṭaḥ[29] [15]
agnihotreṇa tṛpyanti brahmādidevatarṣayaḥ[30]
tathā pitṛgaṇāḥ sarve tṛpyanti satataṁ khalu
pitus tad vacanaṁ śrutvā nāsiketo vaco 'bravīt[31]
nāsiketa uvāca[32]
agnihotrādikaṁ tāta saṁsārasya nibandhanaṁ[33] [16]
mṛte janma punar mṛtyuḥ saṁsāragamanaṁ punaḥ[34]
yogābhyāsasamaṁ nāsti saṁsārārṇavatāraṇaṁ[35] [17]

You have obstructed my Agnihotra, and rendered it unsuccessful. [15]
Brahma and the rest of the gods are pleased with Agnihotra,
and so are always pleased all the ancestors".
Having heard his father's words, Nāsiketa said the following.
Nāsiketa said
"The Agnihotra and its like, father, bind one to Saṁsāra(VI)*. [16]*
The dead is born again to die, going again to Saṁsāra.
Nothing can be compared to repeated Yoga practice, for crossing the ocean of Saṁsāra. [17]

---

29 N2/5.15a - tvām asthā agnihotraṁ ca mām anāndaty alaṁpaṭaḥ.
N3/5.15b - tvam asya agnihotraṁ ca samānādṛptalaṁpaṭaḥ.
N4/5.15a, N8/5.37a, Ra/5.15a - saṁvatsarārddhaṁ durvuddhe hy agnihotraṁ gataṁ māma.
Bo/5.13b - sthitaṁ tvayā mandabhāgya yajñe vighnaḥ kṛto mama.

30 N1/5.16a - agnihotreṇa tṛpyanti (N10 - tuṣyanti) brahmādyādi (N2/5.15b - devatarpayaḥ, N3/5.15b - devatāś ca yaḥ) vaco 'bravīt.
N4/5.15c, N8/5.37b, Ra/5.15b - agnihotreṇa tṛpyanti brahmādyā (N7 - daivatā ṛṣayaḥ, Bo/5.14a - devatāgaṇā) devatā bhṛśaṁ.

31 Verse 5.16c-d is missing in N1, N10, N11.
N4/5.16b, N8/5.38b, Ra/5.16b - pitus tad vacanaṁ śrutvā praty uvāca sutas tadā.

32 Following N7, BF.

33 N4/5.17a, N8/5.39a, Ra/5.17a - agnihotrādikaṁ tāta karmab(v)andhanam ātmanaḥ.
N7 - agnihotram idaṁ tāta saṁsārasya (Bo/5.16a - tu bandhanaṁ) ca vardhanaṁ.
BF/5.13a - agnihotrādikaṁ karma sarvaṁ saṁsārabandhanaṁ.

34 N4/5.17b, N8/5.39b, Ra/5.17b - janmamṛtyujarāghore saṁsāre patanaṁ yataḥ.
N7 - janmamṛtyujarāghoraṁ (Bo/5.16a - mahāmohāḥ) saṁsāre patantaṁ dhruvaṁ.

35 N2/5.17b - yogābhyāsasamaṁ nāsti saṁsāragamanaṁ purā.
N4/5.18a, N8/5.40a, Ra/5.18a, BF/5.13b - yogābhyāsāt paraṁ (N7 - yogābhyāsaparaṁ) nāsti saṁsārārṇavatārakaṁ.

brahmādyā devatāś caiva śakrādyāś ca tathārṣayaḥ[36]
sarve yogavaśāt siddhiṁ prāptāḥ kiṁ na sa sevyate[37] [18]
yogena sadṛṣo nāsti upāyo munisattama[38]
kiṁ mahat te 'gnito yogaḥ sarvaśāstraviśārada[39] [19]
uddālaka uvāca
ṛṣayaś ca mahābhāga ye cānye tapasi sthitāḥ[40]
agnihotram upāsante munayaś ca mahāśayāḥ[41] [20]
agnihotrī sadāsnāto iti vedānuśāsanaṁ[42]

Brahma first and the gods, and Indra etc., as well as the seers,
they all attain super-powers from Yoga, why not resort to it? [18]
There is no means like Yoga, O great sage.
O expert in all branches of knowledge, don't you think that Yoga is superior to fire rites?" [19]
Uddālaka said
"Sages and highly virtuous persons, and others who stay in penance,
(as well as) wise and high minded ones – all perform[(VII)] *Agnihotra. [20]*
Whoever performs Agnihotra is always cleansed, according to the Vedas.

---

[36] N1/5.18a, N10 - brahmādyā daivataś caiva śakrādyāś ca tathā(a)rṣayaḥ.
N4/5.18b, N8/5.40b, Ra/5.18b - brahmādyā devataḥ sarve (N7 - indrādyā ye narā gaṇāḥ, Bo/5.17a - indrādyā kaśyapātmajāḥ) munayaḥ sanakādayaḥ.

[37] N2/5.19a, N11 - sarve yogavaśāt siddhiṁ prāptāḥ kin na (N10 - ki ca) sa (N3/5.19b - kiṁ tan na) sevyate.
N4/5.19a, N8/5.41a, Ra/5.19a - sarve te yogamārgeṇa siddhā jātā mahāmune.
Bo/5.17b - sarve yogavaśāt śiddhā gatās te paramāṁ gatiṁ.

[38] N1/5.19a, N11 - yogena s(ś)adṛṣo nāst(iḥ)y upāyo munisattama.

[39] Emendation - NK. N1/5.19b - kim ahaṁ te 'grato (N2/5.20a, N3/5.20b, N10, N11 - vacmi sarvaśāstraviśārada) vīryyasarvaśāstraviśārada.

[40] N4/5.20a, N8/5.42a, Ra/5.20a - ṛṣayaś ca mahābhāgā ye cānye (N7 - tapasaṁ sthitāḥ, BF/5.15a - yatātmānaś ca brāhmaṇāḥ) tapasisthitāḥ.
Bo/5.18a - sarvāśrameṣu bho putra ye cānye tapasi sthitāḥ.

[41] N1/5.20b - agnihotram upāsante munayaś ca mahāyaśāḥ.
N4/5.20b, N8/5.42b, Ra/5.20b - te sarve sarvadharma svam agnihotram upāsate.
N7 - agnihotram upāpānti tv agnihotraparāyaṇāḥ.
BF/5.15b - agnihotraratāḥ sarve yātās te tridaśālayaṁ.
Bo/5.18b - agnihotram upāsante svargalokāya suvrata.

[42] N2/5.21b, N11 - agnihotrī sadās (N3/5.21b - sadā) tāta iti vedānuśāsanaṁ.
N4/5.21a, N8/5.43a, Ra/5.21a - agnihotrī sadāsnāta ity eṣā vaidikī śrutiḥ.

agnihotraṁ vinā putra brahmajñānaṁ na vidyate[43] [21]
nāsiketa uvāca
svargaṁ gatvā punarjanma ghore saṁsārasāgare[44]
yogābhyāsaparo martyo na bhūyo bhuvi jāyate[45] [22]
agnihotreṇa nāpnoti pitṛyajñena tena ca[46]
na nānāvedayajñena yogābhyāsād yathāpnuyāt[47] [23]
ananyagatayo martyā bhogino 'pi parantapa[48]

Without Agnihotra, O son, there is no Brahman knowledge". [21]
Nāsiketa said
"Those who go to Heaven(VIII), are born again in the terrible ocean of Saṁsāra.
A man engaged in the practice of Yoga, is not born (again) in this world. [22]
It (i.e. the ultimate goal) will not be attained by Agnihotra, nor by the worship of ancestors,
nor by various Vedic sacrifices – by Yoga practice (alone) will it be attained. [23]
Mortals, performing the highest penance, have no other route.

N7 - agnihotraṁ sadāsnāti ity eṣā vaidikī smṛti.
BF/5.16a - vedābhyāsaratā ye syur agnihotraratāḥ sadā.

43 N2/5.22a - agnihotraṁ vinā putra (N3/5.22b - vatsa) brahmajñānaṁ na vidyate.

44 N1/5.22a, N11 - svargaṁ gatvā punarjanma (N10 - ghorasaṁsārasāgara) vīre saṁsārasāgare.
N4/5.22b, N8/5.44b, Ra/5.22b - svargaṁ bhuktvā punar yasmāj jāyante ghorasaṁsṛtau.
N7 - svargaṁ vāse punarjanmaṁ saṁsāre ghorasāgare.
Bo/5.19a - svargaṁ gatvā punar janma saṁsāre bhavati dhruvaṁ.

45 N7 - yogābhyāsaparaṁ tatvaṁ (Bo/5.19b - yogābhyāsāt paraṁ nāsti) na bhūto na bhaviṣyati.

46 N1/5.23a - agnihotreṇa (N11 - nāmoti) nāpnoti (N3/5.23a - pitur yajñena tan ca) pitṛpītena tena ca.

47 N11 - na nānā (N2/5.24a - na tātra, N10 - na tāta) devayajñena yogābhyāsād yathāpnuyāt.
N3/5.23a - na ca tad devayajñena yogābhyāsī yad āpnuyāt.
N4/5.23b, N8/5.45b, Ra/5.23b - na kuryād agnihotraṁ tat yogam eva samācaret.
Bo/5.20 - na kāryam agnihotraṁ tu yogābhyāsaṁ kuru prabho.

48 N1/5.24a - ananyagatayo martyā bhāgineyī parantapa.
N11 - ananyagatayau martyā bhogino 'pi parantapa.
Verses 5.24-36 are missing in N3.

jñānavairagyarahitāḥ brahmacaryādivarjitāḥ [24]
sarvadharmaratā viṣṇor nāmamātraikajalpakāḥ[49]
mukhena yāṁ gatiṁ yānti na tāṁ sarve 'pi dharmikāḥ[50] [25]
kiṁ tasya bahubhir mantraiḥ śāstraiḥ kiṁ bahuvistaraiḥ
vājapeyasahasrair vā bhaktir yasya janārdane[51] [26]
sarvatīrtham aho viṣṇuḥ sarvaśāstram atha prabhuḥ[52]
sarvakratur atho viṣṇuḥ satyaṁ satyaṁ vadāmy ahaṁ[53] [27]
ābrahmasārasarvasvaṁ sarvam etad mayoditaṁ[54]
āyur harati vai puṁsām
udyann astam ca yann asau[55] [28]
tasyarte yatkṣaṇo nīta uttamaślokavārtayā[56]

Without knowledge or detachment, without having taken the vow of celibacy etc., [24]
those adhering to all Dharma(IX) laws, do not attain the (ultimate) goal, that all the pious reach by means of reciting the name of Viṣṇu alone. [25]
What are the reciting of many Mantras, or knowledge of the Śāstras,
or thousands of Vājapeya sacrifices, (compared with) devotion to Janārdana(X)? [26]
Viṣṇu is equal to all pilgrimage sites (put together); he is like all the Śāstras.
Viṣṇu is equal to all the sacrifices, I am telling the truth, the (whole) truth. [27]
He is the essence of the whole existence of Brahman, I am telling all this.
He takes the life of people, from morning to evening. [28]
Without Him, gods become (like) common people.

---

49 N2/5.25b - sarvadharmostūtā viṣṇor nāmamātraikajalpakāḥ.

50 N1/5.25b - mukhena yā gatiṁ yānti(ṁ) (N11 - sukhena yāṁ gatiṁ yānti) tāṁ dharme 'pi na dharmikā[ḥ].
N2/5.26a, N10 - mukhena yāṁ gatiṁ yānti na tāṁ sarve vidyamikāḥ.

51 N1/5.26b - vājapeyasahasrair vā (N10 - bhaktiṁ yasya janārdanaṁ) bhaktir yasya janārdataiḥ.

52 N1/5.27a - sarvatīrtham aho (N10, N11 - sarvatīrthama(th)dho) viṣṇuḥ sarvaśāstram athaḥ (N10 - agra) prabhuḥ.

53 N1/5.27b, N10 - sarvaṛtum ayo viṣṇuḥ satyaṁ satyaṁ vadāmy ahaṁ.

54 N2/5.28b, N10 - ābrahmasārasarvasvaś ca satyam etan mayoditaṁ.

55 N1/5.28b - āyuś ca hara(ār)t(e)i (N10, N11 - āyur hara(ā)ti vai) puṁsām udyann astam ayānn asau.
The Stotra 5.28b-36, cited from the Bhāgavata Purāṇa - 2.3.17-24, is missing in N2 & N3.

56 N1/5.29a - tasyarte yat lajonīta uttamaṁ lokavārtayā.
N10, N11 - tasyarte yat(ta)kṣ[aṇ]o nīta amar(a)ā lokavārtayā.

taravaḥ kiṁ na jīvanti
bhastrāḥ kiṁ na śvasanty uta[57] [29]
na khādanti na mehanti
kim grāmapaśavo 'pare[58]
śvaviḍvarāhoṣṭrakharaiḥ
saṁstutaḥ puruṣaḥ paśuḥ[59] [30]
na yat karṇapathopeto
jātu nāma gadāgrajaḥ[60]
bile batorukrama vikramān ye
na śṛṇvataḥ karṇapuṭe narasya[61] [31]
jihvāsatī dārdurikeva sūta
na copagāyaty urugāyagāthāḥ[62]
bhāraḥ paraṁ paṭṭakirīṭajuṣṭam
apy uttamāṅgaṁ na namen mukundaṁ[63] [32]
śāvau karau no kurutaḥ saparyāṁ
harer lasatkāñcanakaṅkaṇau vā[64]

Don't trees live? And don't bellows "breathe"? [29]
Are village-animals inferior? Don't (they) eat and grow fat?
The human is an animal, along with bitches, pigs, buffaloes and donkeys. [30]
Whoever approaches (Viṣṇu) with ears at hearing range, will not suffer anxiety and disease.
Following Him is moving away from hearing the lamenting by others. [31]
A man's hearing organ will be like a frog's tongue,
when his son follows him(XI), singing hymn-songs,
if his head(XII) and upper part did not bow deeply to Mukunda(XIII). [32]
(Like) a corpse's hands are those that do not worship Hari(XIV), (even though) shining with gold bracelets.

---

57 N1/5.29b - taravaḥ kiṁ na jīvanti bhastraiḥ (N10 - aśvāḥ) kiṁ na śvasanty uta.

58 N1/5.30a, N11 - na (N10 - svādanti) khādanti na mehānti kim grāme paśavo 'pare.

59 N1/5.30b, N11 - śvavidvarāhoṣṭrakharaiḥ santuṣṭaḥ puruṣaḥ paśuḥ.

60 N1/5.31a - nāyakarṇapathopeto (N10 - nāyakarṇaya pathopeto (vi), N11 - nāsakarṇapathopeto) yā tu nāma gadāmṛtaḥ.

61 N1/5.31b, N10 - b(v)ile vato(n) anukramya vikramān ye na śṛṇvataḥ.

62 N1/5.32a, N10, N11 - karṇapuṭe narasyā jihvā satī dārdurikeva.

63 N1/5.32b - naraḥ paraṁ yasy(ṣṭ)a ki(a)rīṭapuṣṭam atho(ū)ttamāṅgaṁ na namen mukandaṁ.

64 N1/5.33a - śavau karau no kurutaḥ saparyā[ṁ] harer (N10 - lasatkāñcanakaṅkaṇe) lasatkāñcanakaṅkaṇau [vā].

barhāyite te nayane narāṇāṁ
    liṅgāni viṣṇor na nirīkṣato ye[65] [33]
pādau nṛṇāṁ tau drumajanmabhājau
    kṣetrāṇi nānuvrajato harer yau[66]
jīvañ chavo bhāgavatāṅghrireṇuṁ
    na jātu martyo 'bhilabheta yas tu[67] [34]
śrī viṣṇupadyā manujas tulasyāḥ
    svasañ chavo yas tu na veda gandhaṁ[68]
tad aśmasāraṁ hṛdayaṁ batedaṁ
    yad gṛhyamāṇair harināmadheyaiḥ[69] [35]

Eyes that do not see the signs of Viṣṇu, are like the "eye" on a peacock's tail. [33]
Those who please Viṣṇu are born again in Indra's paradise, those who do not pay homage to Hari, do not enjoy (heavenly) fields.
Even a minute particle[(XV)] of the Bhāgavatā is not coming out of a corpse, (only living) humans recite it with craving. [34]
Whoever smells the Tulasī leaves placed at Viṣṇu's feet, is like a worshipper who praises the Veda fragrance.
Paying obeisance to Hari makes the heart ready and strong, moving with compassion, and immortal. [35]

---

65 N1/5.33b - barhā(r)yite [te] (na) naye(a)n(o)a (N10, N11 - b(v)arhāyite te naye(a)n(e)a) narāṇāṁ liṅgāni viṣṇor na nirīkṣato ye.

66 N1/5.34a,N10, N11 - pādau n(v)ṛṇāṁ tau drumajanmabhājau kṣetrāṇi mānuvrajato hare(ṇ)r yau.

67 N1/5.34b - jīvaṇṣṭhavo bhāgavatāṁ hireṇuṁ vajā tu martye ābhilaṣena śastuḥ. N10 - jīvañ chav(au)o (N11 - jī(ā)vañ chavo) bhāgavatāṅgh(h)ireṇuṁ na jātu marty(e)o (N11 - 'bhilabh(ṣ)eta) 'bhilabh(kh)et(e)a ya[s] tu.

68 N1/5.35a - śrī viṣṇu(ṁ)p[ad]y(a)ā manuja(ḥ)s tulasyāḥ svasaṁ sarvo yas tu na veda gandhaṁ.

N10, N11 - śrī viṣṇuṁ priyayā manujas tulasyā svasa[ñ] chavo yas tu na veda gandhaṁ.

69 N1/5.35b - tadaśmasāraṁ hṛ(rū)dayaṁ bated(v)a[ṁ] ya[d] gṛhyamāṇ(e)air harināmadhey(t)aiḥ.

N10, N11 - tadaśmasāraṁ hṛdayaṁ b(c)ateda(ya)ṁ gṛhyamāṇ(au)ai[r] h[ar]i(re)nāmadhey(e)aiḥ.

nā vikriyetātha yadā vikāro
  netre jalaṁ gātraruheṣu harṣaḥ[70] [36]
vaiśampāyana uvāca
iti putravacaḥ śrutvā munir uddālakas tadā
ayuktavādī putras tvaṁ durātmā pitṛdūṣakaḥ[71] [37]
gaccha śīghraṁ yamapurīṁ paśya yajñavidūṣaka[72]
pituḥ śāpena raudreṇa patito dharaṇitale[73] [38]

He is pleased now with the work of Heaven, when the transformed body is being led[XVI] *". [36]*
Vaiśaṁpāyana said
When the sage Uddālaka heard his son's words, he then (said):
"What you have (just) said is illogical, O evil soul, father-offending. [37]
Go quickly to see Yama's city, (you) the slanderer of the sacrifice".
Because of his father's terrible curse, he fell to the ground. [38]

---

70 N1/5.36a, N10, N11 - nā [vi](ka)kriyetātha yadā vikāro netre jal(ā)aṁ gātr(e)a r(t)u[heṣu] harṣa[ḥ].

71 N1/5.37b - anenāyuktam uditaṁ durātmā (N3/5.25b - pitṛdūṣakaḥ) pitṛdūṣan(ā)aḥ.
N4/5.24-25a, N8/5.46, Ra/5.24-25a - uddālako vacaḥ srutvā sutasyāvirataṁ punaḥ
krodhena mahatāviṣṭo dadau śāpaṁ sudāruṇaṁ
ayuktavādī putras tvaṁ durātmā pitṛdūṣakaḥ.
Bo/5.21a - uddālakas tu tac chrutvā kruddhaḥ saṁs tanayaṁ prati.

72 N1/5.38a - gaccha śīghraṁ yamapurīṁ (N3/5.26a, N11 - paśya yajñavidūṣakan) yajñavidūṣakaṁ pituḥ.
N4/5.25b, N8/5.47a, Ra/5.25b - gaccha śīghraṁ yamaṁ paśya brahmadaṇḍo hi nānyathā.
N7 - [gaccha śīghraṁ yamaṁ] paśya brahmadaṇḍa[ṁ] yathārhatāṁ.
BF/5.18 - uddālakas tato 'jñātvā putram uttaradāyakaṁ
śaśāpa tanayaṁ kopād gaccha tvaṁ yamamandiraṁ.
Bo/5.21b - uvāca gaccha śīghraṁ tvaṁ yamaṁ paśya sutādhama.

73 N1/5.38b - śāpena rau deva gaṇāḥ patito dharaṇītale.
N4/5.26a, N8/5.47b, Ra/5.26a - pituḥ (N7 - tataḥ) śāpena raudreṇa patito dharaṇītale.
BF/5.19a - tatra śāpena ghoreṇa patito dharaṇītale.

praṇamya śirasā tātaṁ nāsiketo māhāmuniḥ[74]
vaivasvataḥ sthito yatra yāmi tatra tavājñayā[75] [39]
patitaṁ putrakaṁ dṛṣṭvā ṛṣir yāto 'tivihvalaḥ[76]
mahāśokena santapto bahudhā vilalāpa saḥ[77] [40]
hā putra hā vatsa kvāsi mahājñāṇi subuddhimān[78]
ahaṁ pāpo durācāro durātmā kroddhavān ahaṁ[79] [41]
yamāntike na gantavyaṁ dāruṇā yamayātanā[80]

Bowing his head to his father, Nāsiketa, the great sage (said):
"I am going to the place where Yama is staying, by your order". [39]
Seeing his son falling, the sage was filled with confusion.
He was seized with grief and wept a lot. [40]
"O son, O dear, there is nowhere a great knowledgeable, wise one (like you).
Being so full of anger, I am a sinner of bad behaviour, (and) evil soul. [41]
You do not have to approach Yama, the fierce torturer.

---

[74] N1/5.39a, N7 - praṇamya śirasā tāta[ṁ] nāsiket(ā)o (N3/5.31a - māhāmati) māhāmuniḥ.
N4/5.26b, N8/5.48a, Ra/5.26b - pramāṇam iti vādī hi nāsiketo māhāmanāḥ.
Bo/5.22b - pramāṇam iti pratyuktvā nāsiketo māhātmavān.

[75] N1/5.39b - vaivasvataḥ sthit(ā)o yatra (N3/5.27a, N4/5.27a, N8/5.48b, Ra/5.27a - tatra) yāmi (v)atra tavājñayā.
N7 - vaivasvataḥ sthito yatra yāsyāmi tava cājñayā.
Bo/5.23a - vaivasvatasthitir yatra paśyāmy eva tavājñayā.

[76] N4/5.28a, N8/5.49b, Ra/5.28a - uddālakaḥ sutaṁ dṛṣṭvā kṣaṇāj jāto 'tivihvalaḥ.
Bo/5.23b - patitaṁ putrakaṁ dṛṣṭvā ṛṣir jāto 'tivihvalaḥ.

[77] N4/5.28b, N8/5.50a, Ra/5.28b - mahāśokena santapto (N7 - vilāpa bahubhāṣayā, Bo/5.24a - vilalāpātiduḥkhitaḥ) b(v)ahuśovilalāya ca.

[78] N2/5.33b - ha putra hā vatsa kva yāsya vipra hā śubha (N10, N11 - kvāsi mahājñāniñcha) b(va)u[d]dhiman.
N3/5.29a - hā putra hā (Bo/5.24b - varaśiśo) vatsaśiśo (N4/5.29a, N8/5.50b, Ra/5.29a - kim idaṁ samupasthitaṁ) hā jñānin [hā] sub(v)uddhimān.

[79] N1/5.41b - ahaṁ pāpo durācāro durātmā (N4/5.29b, N8/5.51a, Ra/5.29b - krodhamohitaḥ) kruddhavān aha.
N7/5.24b - ahaṁ pāpo durācāraḥ krodhī caiva durātmikaḥ.
Bo/5.25a - ahaṁ pāpī durācārī ahaṁ krodhī dvijādhamaḥ.

[80] N4/5.30a, N7/5.25a, N8/5.51b, Bo/5.26b, Ra/5.30a - yatra vaivasvato rājā (BF/5.23a - naraka yatra saṁsthitāḥ) dāruṇā narakās tathā.

priyo 'si mama bho vatsa krodhān me nirgato mukhāt[81] [42]
raudraṁ yamapuraṁ tatra raudrāṇi narakāṇi ca[82]
tat putra te na gantavyaṁ tyaktvā tātaṁ ca mātaraṁ[83] [43]
tataḥ samāgataḥ sarve ṛṣayaś ca tapodhanāḥ
dṛṣṭvā taṁ mūrcchitaṁ te 'pi ruruduḥ susvaraṁ bhṛśaṁ [44]
atikolāhale vṛtte mūrcchā tyaktā sa hṛṣṭavān[84]
nāsiketa uvāca
mātar satyavatī mā śoca asatyās tena vā kvacit[85] [45]
kathaṁ putreṇa kartavyam asatyaṁ paitṛkaṁ vacaḥ

You are dear to me, O boy, being angry, (the curse) slipped out of my mouth. [42]
Fierce is Yama's city, and fierce are the quarters of Hell there.
Therefore son, you should not go there, leaving your father and mother". [43]
Then all the seers arrived, as well as the penance holders.
Seeing him (Nāsiketa) thus unconscious, they wept much and loudly. [44]
From the big noise he (Nāsiketa) regained consciousness, pleased at heart.
Nāsiketa said
"Don't cry, O truthful mother, one should (never be) even a bit untrue. [45]
How can a son render his father's words untrue?

---

81 N1/5.42b, N11 - priyo 'si mama bibhatsako vā(n)ṁ me nirgato mukhāt.
N4/5.30b, N8/5.52a, Ra/5.30b - na gantavyaṁ tvayā tatra (N7/5.25b - na g(s)antavyaṁ mahāmarge) priyo 'si mama putraka.
Bo/5.26a - tatra tvayā na gantavyaṁ prāyaścitaṁ vimarśaya,

82 N3/5.30a - raudraṁ yamapuraṁ tatra (N11 - raudrāpi narakāṇi ca) raudrāṇi narakāṁ pati.
N7/5.26a - raudrī yamapurī tatra narakās tatra bhīruṇā.

83 N7/5.26b - na gantavyaṁ tvayā tatra māṁ tyakt[v]ā caiva mātaraṁ.

84 N1/5.45a - agnikolāhale vṛtte mūrcchā (N2/5.37b - mūrcchāṁ, N3/5.33b - mūrcche) tyaktā sa hṛṣṭavān.
N10 - atikolāhale (N11 - kolohale) vṛtte mūrcchā tyaktā sa hṛṣṭavā[n] (ca).
Additional verse - N2/5.38b-39a:
mātaraṁ janakaṁ cāpi vilayaṁ (N3/5.32b - cātivilayaṁ) taṁ muhur muhuḥ
dṛṣṭvātikaruṇaṁ (N3/5. 33a - śrutvātikaruṇaṁ) snehāt nāsiketo 'bravīd vaca.

85 N1/5.45b, N10 - māta tā satyavat(ṇ)i ca asatyās tena vā kvacit.
N2/5.39a - mātāhatya ma (N3/5.34a - mātā tvaṁ satyavā) kva śocāsatyā [ca] tena vā (ka) kvacit.

ājñāṁ tava kariṣyāmi mā vikalpaṁ vada prabho[86] [46]
satyenārkaḥ pratāpati satyena pṛthivī sthitā[87]
jvalaty agniḥ svasatyena satye somādayo grahāḥ[88] [47]
aśvamedhasahasrāṇi satyaṁ ca tulayā dhṛtaṁ[89]
naramedhaśataṁ vāpi satyam evādhikaṁ tataḥ[90] [48]

I shall obey your uttered order, O great one, do not present other options to me. [46]
By Truth the sun heats, by Truth the earth stays (stable),
Agni[(XVII)] glows by his own Truth, by Truth the god Soma and his like, are supported. [47]
On a balance with a thousand Aśvamedha[(XVIII)] sacrifices, Truth weighs more.
Thus, it weighs even more than hundreds of man sacrifices. [48]

---

86 N1/5.46b - ājñāṁ vaca (N3/5.35a - tathā) kariṣyāmi mā vikalpaṁ vada prabho.
N4/5.33a, N8/5.54b, Ra/5.33a - avajñām akaraḥ putraḥ pitur dharmavivarddhanaḥ.
N7/5.28 - naivāsatyaṁ kariṣyāmi yadi satyo 'si māṁ pratiḥ
ājñāṁ tava kariṣyāmi (Bo/5.28a - maivaṁ vada mahāmate) mā kalpa ca vada prabho.
Bo/5.27b - tat satyaṁ ca kariṣyāmi nānyathā syāt kadā ca na.

87 N1/5.47a - satye(a)nārkaḥ pratāpa(e)ti (N4/5.33b, Ra/5.33b - satyenārko hi tapati, N7/5.29a - satyenārkas papratimā, BF/5.25b - satyena sūryas tapati, Bo/5.28b - satyena tapate sūryaḥ) satyena pṛthivī sthitā.
VP(Varāha Purāṇa)/191.34a - sūryas tapati satyena vāyuḥ satyena vāyati ca.

88 N1/5.47b, N11 - jvalaty agniḥ svasatyena satye somādayo grahī.
N4/5.34a, Ra/5.34a - satyena (N8/5.55b - cāgnijvalati) jvalate vahniḥ (vanhiḥ) (Bo/5.29a - sarvaṁ satyena pratiṣṭhitaṁ) satyenaiva grahāḥ sthitā[ḥ].
N7/5.29b - satyena jvalito vahniḥ (vanhiḥ) satye somagrahādayaḥ.
BF/5.26a - satyena meghā varṣanti satyenāgnir jvalaty api.
VP/191.34b - agnir dahati satyena satyena pṛthivī sthitā.

89 N10 - aśvamedhasahasrāṇi (N4/5.35a, Ra/5.35a - satyena (N7/5.30b - tulayā dhṛtīṁ) tulitāni ca) satyaṁ [ca] tulayādhataṁ.
Bo/5.29b - aśvamedhasahasraṁ (VP/191.45a - satyaṁ ca tulayā dhṛtaṁ) vai satyena tulayen na hi.
VP/191.45b - aśvamedhasahasrāddhi satyam eva viśiṣyate.

90 N1/5.48b, N11 - naramecaśataṁ vāpi (N3/5.37a - naramedhaśataṁ cāpi) satyam evādhikaṁ tataḥ.
N4/5.35b, Ra/5.35b - vājapeyaśatebhyo 'pi (N7/5.32a - naramedhaś(s)ataṁ samyak) satyam evādhikaṁ (N8/5.57a - mataṁ) phalaṁ.

satyena gamyate svarge satyena paramāgatiḥ[91]
satyadharmavihīnasya narake patanaṁ dhruvaṁ[92] [49]
tasmāt sarvaprayatnena śokaṁ tyaktvā sthiro bhava[93]
dṛṣṭvā yamapurīm āśu yamaṁ ca yamayātanāṁ[94] [50]
āgamiṣyāmy ahaṁ tāta tava pādasamīpataḥ[95]
vaiśaṁpāyana uvāca
pitaraṁ mātaraṁ cāpi namaskṛtya kṛtāñjaliḥ[96] [51]

By Truth Heaven is gained, by Truth the ultimate goal is attained.
Without adhering to Truth and Dharma[(XIX)]*, one certainly falls into Hell. [49]*
Therefore, by all efforts, you should abandon grief. Be strong.
Immediately after seeing Yama's city, Yama and Yama's tortures, [50]
I shall come back, O father, to the nearness of your feet".
Vaiśaṁpāyana said
Bowing to his father and mother with joined palms, [51]

---

91 N3/5.37b - satyāt saṅgamyate svarge satyena paramāgatiḥ.
N10 - satyena gamyate svarge satyena (N11 - paramā(ṁ)gatiḥ) yaṁ ramāpatiḥ.
N4/5.36b, N8/5.58a, Ra/5.36b - satyena gacchati svargaṁ (Bo/5.30a - gamyate svargaḥ) satyena paramāṁ gatiṁ.
VP/191.37b - satyaṁ svargaś ca dharmaś ca satyād anyan na vidyate.

92 N1/5.49b - satyadharmavihīnasya narake patitaṁ (N10, N4/5.37a, N8/5.58b, Bo/5.30b, Ra/5.37a - patanaṁ) dhruvaṁ.

93 N1/5.50a, N11, N7/5.33a - tasmāt sarvaprayatnena (N4/5.37b, N8/5.59a, Ra/5.37b - satyam evānupālaye) śok(e)aṁ tyaktvā sthiro (Bo/5.31b - 'bhavat) bhava.

94 N1/5.50b, N11 - dṛṣṭvā yamapurīm (N7/5.33b - samyak dharmarājasya veśmakaṁ) āśu yam(s)aṁ ca yamayātanāṁ.
N4/5.38a, N8/5.59b, Ra/5.38a - ahaṁ tu yamam ālokya bhagavān bhaktitas tvayi.
Bo/5.32a - dṛṣṭvā yamapuraṁ sadyo dharmarājasya mandiraṁ.

95 N10 - āgamiṣyāmy ahaṁ tāta (N4/5.38b, N8/5.60a, Ra/5.38b - satyam evāgamiṣyāmi, N7/5.34a - satvaraṁ cāgamiṣyāmi, Bo/5.32b - śīghraṁ caivāgamiṣyāmi) tav(dh)a (N11 - pādaṁ samīpataḥ) pādasamīpataḥ.

96 N1/5.51b - pitaraṁ m(bhr)ātaraṁ cāpi namaskṛtya kṛtāñjaliḥ.
N4/5.39a, N8/5.60b, Ra/5.39a - evam uktvā pituḥ pādau praṇamya ca kṛtāñjaliḥ.
N7/5.34b - pitaraṁ ca praṇamyadau namaskṛtya kṛtāñjaliḥ.
Bo/5.33a - pitṛpādau praṇamyādau namaskṛtvā svayaṁbhuve.

nāsiketo viśuddhātmā kṣaṇenāntaradhīyata[97]
divyamantraghanaś cāpi divyadṛṣṭis tathaiva ca[98] [52]
saṁprāpto vāyuvegena yatra rājā sthito yamaḥ[99]
dṛṣṭvā tu dharmarājānaṁ jvalantam iva pāvakaṁ[100] [53]
siṁhāsane samāsīnaṁ sūryaputraṁ mahābalaṁ
nāsiketas tam astauṣīd bhaktibhāvena saṁyutaḥ[101] [54]

iti śrībrahmāṇḍapurāṇe nāsiketopākhyāne dharmarājadarśanaṁ nāma pañcamo 'dhyāyaḥ

Nāsiketa, the pure soul, in a moment disappeared inside.
By a divine Mantra(XX) he went to see the (Death) god. [52]
By the speed of wind he reached the place of King Yama.
Seeing Dharmarāja (i.e. Yama), radiant like fire, [53]
seated on his lion-headed throne, that mighty son of the sun,
Nāsiketa praised him, being seized with devotion and emotion. [54]

This is the fifth chapter of the Nāsiketa story, pertaining to the Brahmāṇḍa Purāṇa, called – seeing Dharmarāja.

---

97 N4/5.39b, Ra/5.39b - nāsiketur vinītātmā kṣaṇenāntarabhūt tadā. N7/5.35 - nāśiketo vinītātmā (N8/5.61a - kṣaṇenāntardadhāt tadā) kṣaṇenāntaradhīyata.

98 N2/5.46a, N11 - dīvyamantradharaś (N1/5.52b - dīvyamantraghanaś) cāpi (N3/5.51a - cāsau) divyadṛṣṭis tathaiva ca. N4/5.40a, Ra/5.40a - divyamantraprabhāvena pitṛbhaktyāpy ananyayā.

99 N4/5.40b, Ra/5.40b - saṁprāptas (BF/5.34b - cātivegena) tatra vegena (N7/5.36a - saṁprāpto vāyuvegena) yatra (N8/5.62a - jaya) rājā svayaṁ yamaḥ.

100 N4/5.41a, N8/5.62b, Ra/5.41a - dharmarājan tato dṛṣṭvā (N7/5.36b - dṛṣṭvā ca (Bo/5.35a - dadarśa, BF/5.35a - dṛṣṭvā taṁ) dharmarājānaṁ) jvalantam iva pāvakaṁ.

101 N10 - nāsiketas (BF/5.35c - nāsiketus) tam astauṣ(t)īd bhaktibhāvena saṁyutaḥ. N4/5.41b, Ra/5.41b - siṁhāsanasamārūḍhaṁ (N7/5.37a, N8/5.63a - sīṁhāsanasamāsīnaṁ, BF/5.35b - siṁhāsane samāsīnaṁ) sūryaputraṁ mahāb(v)alaṁ.

Translation Notes

I – To what happened in the past.
II – High phases in Yoga practice.
III – In other versions the period may be longer, up to a year and a half (BF/5.8, for example).
IV – Dhyānayoga Samādhi - the highest phase of Yoga.
V – Either – "homeless", or – "without clothes".
VI – The circle of life and death.
VII – "Sit by", "worship".
VIII – After death.
IX – The common moral laws.
X – Viṣṇu.
XI – His death bed.
XII – Or – crown.
XIII – Viṣṇu.
XIV – Literally – "as a tree", or – "as a tree in Indra's paradise".
XV – Literally – "a grain of dust".
XVI – A more common translation for verses 5.35-6 follows the former negative form, for example – *http://www.srimadbhagavatam.org*:

> *"Certainly is that steel-framed heart which, in spite of being absorbed in chanting the name of the Lord, is not transformed with the emotional of having tears in the eyes and hairs standing on end therewith".*

XVII – Fire, the fire god.
XVIII – The horse sacrifice.
XIX – The moral law.
XX – Executing his mystic powers.

Chapter 6

Father and Son Dialogue

vaiśaṁpāyana uvāca
yamaṁ dṛṣṭvā sabhāmadhye vidvajjanavibhūṣite[1]
tena tasya kṛtaṁ stotraṁ śrūyatāṁ nṛpasattama[2] [1]
nāsiketa uvāca
namas te dharmarājāya dharmavardha namo 'stu te[3]
sarvalokaikaśāstas te namaḥ sarvadhṛtāya ca[4] [2]
namo mārtaṇḍatanaye dharmādharmavicāraka[5]

Vaiśaṁpāyana said
He saw Yama in the middle of his hall, surrounded by scholars.
Listen, O king, to the hymn of praise, he made to Yama. [1]
Nāsiketa said
"I salute you Dharmarāja, the increaser of the world's moral law, I bow to you.
Salutation to you, O punisher of all the worlds, who is bearing them all, [2]
I salute you, son of the sun who discerns between good and evil.

---

1 N1/6.1a - yamaṁ dṛṣṭvā (BF/6.1a - praviṣṭasya, Ra/6.1b - upaviṣṭaḥ) sabhāmadhye vidvajjanavibhūṣitaṁ.
BF/6.1b - praviṣṭas tu sabhāmadhye (Bo/6.1a - vidyāvinayabhūṣitaḥ) vidvadgirjanabhūṣite.
Ra/6.1a - athopacārair hṛṣṭātmā nāsiketo 'tidhīradhīḥ.

2 N7/6.2a - tena stot[r]aṁ samāra[b]dh(v)aṁ (Bo/6.1b - dharmmarājasya śobhanaṁ) śrūyatāṁ rājasattama.
BF/6.1b - divyastotram idaṁ tasya (Ra/6.2a - dharmmaṁ stotuṁ samārebhe) śrūyatāṁ rājasattama.

3 N1/6.2a, N2/6.2a, N3/6.2a - namas te dharmarājāya (Ra/6.2b - namas trailokyapāvana, N7/6.2b, Bo/6.2a - trailokasya (BF/6.2a - trilokasya) pitāmaha) j(ñ)agadvardha namo 'stu te.

4 Ra/6.3a - samhartre sarvalokānāṁ namaḥ sarvahitāya ca.
N7/6.3a - sarvalokasya trātā tvaṁ (Bo/6.2b - sarvalokasyat saṅgoptre) namaḥ sarvāśritāya ca.
BF/6.2b - sarvalokakṛtāntāya sadvṛttāya ca te namaḥ.

5 N3/6.3a - mārtaṇḍajanaye (N4/6.3b, N8/6.67b, Ra/6.3b - tvaṁ mārtaṇḍasutaḥ śreṣtho, N7/6.3b - mārtaṇḍasutatejase) dharmādharmavicāraka.

pitṝṇāṁ paramaśreṣṭha namas te surapūjite[6] [3]
sūryaprāyasvarūpāya namas te 'stu prajāpate[7]
nāsiketanamaskārāḥ kṛtās te bahurūpiṇe[8] [4]
namo dharmāya mahate namas te pāpaśāsaka[9]
jñānavijñānarūpāyadharmamūrte namo 'stu te[10] [5]

Salutations to you, O worshipped by the gods, superior of all the ancestors. [3]
You are radiant like the sun, salutations to you, O leader.
Nāsiketa offers salutations to you, O (god of) many forms. [4]
I salute you, great Dharma, salutations to you, punisher of sins.
I salute you, law incarnate, whose form is knowledge (both) worldly and ultimate. [5]

BF/6.3a - mārtaṇḍatejojātāya yamarāja vidhāraka.

Bo/6.3a - mārtaṇḍasūnave divyadehāyāmitatejase.

6 N4/6.4a, N8/6.68a, Ra/6.4a - pitṝṇāṁ paramo nāthaḥ (N7/6.3c - namas t(th)e surapūjita) surāsurasupūjitaḥ.

N4/6.4b, N8/6.68b, Ra/6.4b - namas te b(v)uddhivṛddhāya namas te nirmalāya ca.

BF/6.3b - namas te buddhirūpāya namas te vidurāya.

Bo/6.3b - namas te ravibhaktāya nirmalāya ca te namaḥ.

7 N1/6.4a - sūryaprāyasvarūpāya (N11 - suprabhāyasvarūpāya) namas te 'stu pratāyate.

N3/6.4a, N4/6.5a, N8/6.69a, Ra/6.5a - śubhāyaśubharūpāya (N2/6.3c - suprabhāya surūpāya, N10 - suprabhāyasvarūpāya, BF/6.4a - svayaṁbhūsamarūpāya) namas te 'stu prajāpate.

N7/6.4a - namas te buddhidhārāya namas te 'stu jagatpate.

8 N4/6.5b, N8/6.69b, Ra/6.5b, Bo/6.4b - dharmādhikāriṇe śrīmān (BF/6.4b - dharmādikāraṇadeva) namas te bahurūpiṇe.

N7/6.4b - dharmādhikāraṇaḥ śrīmān namas te surūpiṇe.

Bo/6.4a - sūprabhāṭyasvarūpāya namas te surapūjite.

9 N2/6.4b - namo dharmāya mahate (Bo/6.5a - namaḥ pāpāntakāya ca) namas te pāpanāsaka.

N3/6.5a - namo dharmāya vṛhate namas te pāpaśāsana.

BF/6.5a, Ra/6.6a - namo dharmmamahimne ca pāpasaṁśodhanāya ca.

10 N2/6.5a - jñānāyajñānarūpāyadharmamūrti (N10, N11 - dharmamūrte) namo 'stu te.

N3/6.5b - jñānāyajñānasūryāya (Bo/6.5b - jñānavijñānarūpāya) dharmamūrte namo 'stu te.

BF/6.5b, Ra/6.6b - jñānājñānasvarūpāya dharmmarūpa namo 'stu te.

nāsiketakṛtastotraṁ paramaṁ pāpanāśanaṁ[11]
ya idaṁ paṭhate stotraṁ tasyādharmo na dīyate[12] [6]
na tasya bhavati vyādhiḥ kapharogabhayaṁ kvacit[13]
yamaḥ santuṣyate tasya narakāṇi na paśyati[14] [7]
śrutvā viprakṛtaṁ stotraṁ dharmarājo vaco 'bravīt[15]
yama uvāca

The Nāsiketa praise-hymn is for you, supreme destroyer of sins.
Whoever recites this hymn, will never suffer Adharma[(l)]. *[6]*
He will never suffer from illness, (like) cough, nor any fear.
Yama will be pleased with him and he will not see Hell". [7]
Having heard the Brahmin's hymn of praise, Dharmarāja said the following:

---

11 N3/6.5b - nāsiketakṛtaṁ stotraṁ (N10, N11 - param(e)aṁ pāpan(t)āśana[ṁ], N4/6.6a, N8/6.70a, Ra/6.7a - puṇyaṁ pāpapraṇāśanaṁ, N7/6.6a, BF/6.6a, Bo/6.6a - pratyakṣaṁ pāpanāśanaṁ) dharmarājo vaco 'bravīt.

12 N2/6.5c, N3/6.6b, N10 - ya idaṁ paṭhate stotraṁ (N7/6.7b - samyak dharmasya kīrtanaṁ) tasyādharmo na hīyate.
N4/6.6, N8/6.70, Ra/6.7b - ye paṭhanti ca śṛṇvanti dharmarājasya dharmmiṇaḥ.
N7/6.6b - idaṁ stotraṁ madīye te brāhmaṇā kṣatriyā 'pi vā.
BF/6.6b - ya idaṁ paṭhate (Bo/6.6b - yaḥ paṭhet prayataḥ) samyag dharmarājasya kīrtanaṁ.

13 N2/6.6a - na tasya bhavati vyādhiḥ (N7/6.8a - na rogo na bhayaṁ kvacit) kvāpa (N10, BF/6.7a - kāye, N11 - kāpi) rogabhayaṁ kvacit.
N3/6.7a - na tasya bhavate vyādhiḥ kāye rogabhayaṁ kvacit,
N4/6.7a, N8/6.71a, Ra/6.8a - na teṣāṁ jāyate vyādhir matir dharmme ca jāyate.
Bo/6.7a - naiva tasya bhaved ādhiḥ kāye rogabhayaṁ na hi.

14 N1/6.7b, N10, N11 - yasya svatuṣyate tasya narakāṇi na paśyati.
N4/6.7b, N8/6.71b, Ra/6.8b - yamaś ca tuṣyatitarāṁ nekṣate narakāṁs tathā.
N7/6.8b - yamo na dṛśyate tena na ca [narakaṁ] paśyati.
BF/6.7b - yamaṁ na paśyate ghoraṁ (Bo/6.7b - yamas tuṣṭo bhavet tasya) narakaṁ ca na paśyati.

15 N2/6.7b - śrutvā viprakṛtaṁ stotraṁ ya(r)marājo vaco 'bravīt.
N11 - śrutvā viprakṛtastotraṁ (Bo/6.8a - vipreritaṁ stotraṁ, BF/6.8a - stutiṁ ca viprasya) dharmarājo vaco 'bravīt.
N4/6.8a, N8/6.72a, Ra/6.9a - evaṁ śrutvā stutiṁ vipraṁ dharmarājo vaco 'bravīt.
N7/6.9a - śrutvā stutiṁ ca [viprasya] dharmarājo 'pi 'bravīt.

toṣito 'haṁ ca viprendra brūhi kasmād ihāgataḥ[16] [8]
kena coktaṁ yamaṁ paśya kasmāc choko 'bhavat tava[17] [9]
kiṁ pṛcchasi mahāprājña vicāraṁ kathayāmy ahaṁ[18]
varaṁ brūhi prayacchāmi yat te manasi vartate[19] [10]
nāsiketa uvāca
yadi tuṣṭo 'si me deva evam etat prayaccha me[20]
paśyāmi te purīṁ sarvāṁ citraguptaṁ ca lekhakaṁ[21] [11]
duṣkṛtā yatra tapyante sukṛtāḥ sukhabhāgitaḥ[22]

"I am pleased, revered Brahmin, tell me, why have you come here? [8]
Who said that you should see Yama? Why has this sorrow come to you? [9]
What do you ask, O great knowledgeable one? Whatever you wish, I shall tell you.
What boon (you desire) tell me, and I shall grant you what is on your mind". [10]
Nāsiketa said
"If you are pleased with me, O god, grant me only this,
I (would like to) see your entire city, and also Citragupta, your secretary, (and) [11]
where the evildoers are roasted, and where the meritorious enjoy happiness.

---

16 N3/6.8a, N4/6.8b, N8/6.72b, Ra/6.9b - toṣito 'haṁ (BF/6.8b - stuto 'haṁ ca) tvayā (N2/6.7b - te) vipra brūhi kasmād ihāgataḥ.
Bo/6.8b - tuṣṭo 'haṁ tava viprendra brūhy āgamanakāraṇaṁ.
VP/196.21 - parituṣṭo 'smi bhadraṁ te mādhuryeṇa tavānagha.

17 N1/6.9, N2/6.8a, N10, N11 - ken(c)a coktaṁ yamaṁ paśya (N3/6.8b - kasmā(t)c ch(ś)oko 'bhavad bhava) ka[s]mā[c] chāpo 'bhavat tava.

18 N3/6.8c - kiṁ pracchāmi mahāprājña (N7 - vicarasva yathāsukhaṁ) vicāra kathayāhvalaṁ.
Verse numbers 6.11-4 are missing in N7.

19 N1/6.10b - varaṁ brūhi prayacchāmi ya tena (N11 - si vartate te) śiva vartate.
VP/196.22 - varaṁ varaya bhadraṁ te yaṁ varaṁ kaṅkṣase dvija śubhaṁ vā śreyyā yuktaṁ jīvitaṁ vā 'yanāmayaṁ.

20 N3/6.10b - yadi tuṣṭo 'si deveśa evam etat prayaccha me.
N4/6.12b, N8/6.76b, Ra/6.13b, BF/6.11a - yadi tuṣṭo 'si deveśa varam ekaṁ (Bo/6.11a - enaṁ) prayaccha me.
N7 - [yadi] tuṣṭo 'si me deva varam etat prayacchasi.

21 N10 - paśyāmi te purīṁ (N4/6.13a, N7, N8/6.77a, Ra/6.14a, BF/6.11b - tvatpurīṁ) sarvāṁ [citraguptaṁ] ca lekhakaṁ.
VP/196.24a - draṣṭum icchāmy ahaṁ deva tava deśaṁ yathātathaṁ.

22 N1/6.12a - duṣkṛtā yatra (yantapte) [tapyante] (N3/6.11b - tapyanti) sukṛtāḥ sukhabhāgataḥ.

draṣṭum etat prayaccha me prasādaṁ kuru sūryaja[23] [12]
vaiśaṁpāyana uvāca[24]
athāhūya dadāv ājñāṁ kiṅkarāṇāṁ yamaḥ svayaṁ[25]
citraguptālaye vipro nīyatāṁ susukhaṁ yathā[26] [13]
ayaṁ vipro mahāprājñaḥ satyadharmaparāyaṇaḥ[27]
pitṛśāpād ihāyātaḥ paśyatvaṁ yamasādanaṁ[28] [14]

Let me see this, grant (me your) grace, O son of the sun". [12]
Vaiśaṁpāyana said
Having called for his servants, Yama himself gave them the order:
"Lead this Brahmin to Citragupta's place, as pleases him. [13]
This Brahmin, great knowledgeable one, supreme adherent of Truth and moral laws,
has come here because of his father's curse to see Yama's abode". [14]

N10, N11 - duḥkṛtā yatra tapyante sukṛtāḥ sukhabhāgitaḥ.
N4/6.13b, N8/6.77b, Ra/6.14b - duḥkṛtā yatra pacyante sukṛtāḥ sukhasaṁsthitāḥ.
BF/6.12a - modante sukṛto yatra duḥkṛto yatra bādhyante.
Bo/6.12a - duṣkṛtī pacyate yatra sukṛtī sukham edhate.
VP/196.24b - pāpānāṁ ca śubhānāṁ ca yā gatis tv iha dṛśyate.

23 N1/6.12b, N11 - dra(tu)ṣṭum (N2/6.11b - etan mamecchāsti) i(e)cchāsti - - prasādaṁ kuru sūryaja.
N4/6.14a, N8/6.78a, Ra/6.15a - mahan me kautukaṁ tatra (Bo/6.12b - etad icchāmi sandraṣṭuṁ) prasādaṁ kuru sūryaja.
BF/6.12b - ahaṁ draṣṭuṁ tad icchāmi prasīda ravinandana.
VP/196.24c - sarvaṁ darśaya me rājan yadi tvaṁ varado mama.

24 Following Bo/6.13.

25 N3/6.12b - athā ha pradadāv ājñāṁ kiṅkarāṇāṁ yamaḥ svayaṁ.
N4/6.15a, N8/6.79a, Ra/6.16a - dharmma ājñāpayāmāsa kiṅkarānurataḥ sthitān.
Bo/6.13a - kiṅkarāṁs tatra cāhūya dharmarājena bhāṣitaṁ.
VP/196.26a - evam ukto mahātejā dvārasthaṁ sandideśa ha.

26 N1/6.13b, N11 - citraguptālaye vipro prītayetāṁ sukhaṁ yathā.
N3/6.13a - citraguptālayo vipro nīyatāṁ susukhaṁ yathā.
VP/196.26b - citraguptasakāśaṁ tu naya vipraṁ suyantritaṁ.

27 N1/6.14a - ayaṁ vipro mahāprājñaḥ (N4/6.15b, N7/6.15a, N8/6.79b, Ra/6.16b - satyadharmaparāyaṇaḥ) sarvadharmaparāyaṇaḥ.
Bo/6.13b - evaṁ vipraṁ mahāprājñaṁ satyavrataparāyaṇaṁ.

28 N3/6.13b - pitṛśāpād ihāyātaḥ paśyatvaṁ yamaśāsanaṁ.
N4/6.16a, N8/6.80a, Ra/6.17a - pitṛśāpād ihāyāto didṛkṣati purīṁ mama.

yamājñāṁ te tataḥ śrutvā dūtāḥ tvaritagāminaḥ[29]
sanāsiketāḥ saṁprāptāś citraguptasya veśmani[30] [15]
dvārapālam athocus te citraguptaṁ nivedaya[31]
preṣito dharmarājena brahmaṇo dvāri tiṣṭhati[32] [16]
darśaya svapurām enam uktam asti kṛte sthite[33]
teṣāṁ tad vacanaṁ śrutvā dvārapālo gato 'ntaraṁ[34] [17]

Having heard Yama's order, the swift-moving messengers,
arrived at Citragupta's abode, along with Nāsiketa. [15]
They said to the gatekeeper "Inform Citragupta
that the Brahmin sent by Dharmarāja, is standing at the gate. [16]
Show him your city – these are Yama's orders to you".
Having heard these words, the gatekeeper went inside. [17]

N7/6.15b - pitu(r)ḥ ś(s)āpād ihāyāto dadarśa mama ś(s)asānaṁ.
Bo/6.14 - pituḥ śāpād ihāyātaṁ darśayantu purīṁ mama.

29 N10 - yamoktaṁ te vacaḥ (N11 - yamākṣati taḥ, N7/6.16a - yamasyājñ(gy)ām imāṁ) śrutvā dūtās tvaritagāminaḥ.
N4/6.17b, N8/6.81b, Ra/6.18b - bhartturājñām iti jñātvā dūtās tvaritam āgatāḥ.

30 N4/6.18a, N8/6.82a, Ra/6.19a - nāsiketaṁ puraskṛtya (N7/6.16b - nāśiketasaha prāptā) citraguptasya veśmani.
Bo/6.15a-b - tadā te kiṅkarāḥ sarve citraguptasya veśmani
gatvā tadaiva sahitā nāsiketena bhārata.

31 N10 - dvārapālam atho(r)cus t(a)e citraguptaṁ nivedaya.
N4/6.18b, N8/6.82b, Ra/6.19b - dvārapālam idaṁ procur yamena preṣitā vayaṁ.
N7/6.17a - dvārapālasya brūta dūta idaṁ vacaḥ (short).
Bo/6.15c - citraguptasya te sarve dvārapālam athābruvan.

32 N4/6.19a, N8/6.83a, Ra/6.20a - b(v)rāhmaṇena samaṁ sarvam etad bhartre nivedaya.
N7/6.17b - yamena preṣitā nūnaṁ brāhmaṇena samanvitāḥ.
Bo/6.16a - yamena preṣito vipro nāsiketo mahātmavān.

33 N1/6.17a - darśaya(ḥ) svapurīm ena(ā)m uktam asti kṛt(o)e sthite.
N3/6.16b - darśayaś ca purīm etāṁ muktibhāgī bhaven naraḥ.
N7/6.18a - vacanaṁ cāsya śrotavyaṁ (Bo/6.16b - darśayadhvaṁ puraṁ mahat) darśanāya purīm imāṁ.

34 N1/6.17b - teṣāṁ tad vacanaṁ śrutvā dvārapāl(a)o (N4/6.19b, N8/6.83b, Ra/6.20b - 'ntaraṁ gataḥ, N7/6.18b - gata kṣaṇe) gato 'ntaraṁ.

uvāca śrūyatāṁ deva dharmeṇa preṣito dvijaḥ[35]
sahito yamadūtaiś ca dvāri tiṣṭhati vāritaḥ[36] [18]
tac chrutvā citraguptas tam ūce śīghraṁ praveśaya[37]
tac chrutvā dvārapālo 'pi punar āgatya vegataḥ[38] [19]
citragupta uvāca
praviśantu pratīhāra sarve te dvijasaṁyutāḥ[39]
athāgatān sa saṁvikṣya citragupto vaco 'bravīt[40] [20]

He said "Listen, O lord, a Brahmin sent by God Dharma,
along with Yama's messengers, is held waiting at the gate". [18]
Hearing it, Citragupta told him: "Bring him in quickly".
Having thus heard, the gatekeeper returned quickly again. [19]
Citragupta said
"Enter all, bringing the Brahmin with you".
Seeing them coming, Citragupta said the following: [20]

---

35 N1/6.18a - uvāca śrūyatāṁ deva (N7/6.19a - vacanaṁ śrūyatāṁ deva) dharmeṇāpreṣit(āṁ)o (N3/6.17b - sa dharmepreṣito) dvija[ḥ].
Bo/6.18a - vacanaṁ śrūyatāṁ deva yamenāpreṣito dvijaḥ.

36 N1/6.18b - sahito yamadūtaiś ca (N3/6.18a - sa dvāritiṣṭhavāritaḥ) dvāre tiṣṭhati vāritaḥ.
N4/6.20b, N8/6.84b, Ra/6.21b - sahito yamadūtaiś ca dvāre tiṣṭhati (N7/6.19b - 'sau dvijaḥ, Bo/6.18b - te 'nagha) dhārmikaḥ.

37 N1/6.19a, N2/6.18a - ta(t)c ch(ś)rutvā citraguptas t(e)am (N3/6.18b - citraguptasya) ūce śīghraṁ praveśaya.

38 N4/6.21b, N8/6.85b, Ra/6.22b - evaṁ bhartur vacaḥ prāpya dvārapālo b(v)ahir gataḥ.
N7/6.20b - citraguptavacaḥ ś(ch)rutvā dvārapālo 'ti vīsmitaḥ.

39 Following N4/6.21a, N8/6.85a, Ra/6.22a.
N1/6.20a, N2/6.19a, N10 - praveśayaṁ dūt(aṁ)āḥ sarve citraguptaniveśanaṁ.
N3/6.19b - pravīśantu dūt(aṁ)āḥ sarve citraguptasya veśmani.
N7/6.20a - praviṣṭās tvāritāḥ sarve sarve dūtā dvijena vai.
Bo/6.19-20a - vipraṁ tu tvari(a)tā dūta samānaya mamāntikaṁ citraguptavacaḥ śrutvā so 'pi sarvān samānayat.

40 N1/6.20b - āyātaṁ sannidhiṁ yāva[c] citragupto 'bravīd vacaḥ.
N10 - āyāntaṁ sannidhyā vā (N3/6.20a - sannidh(a)iṁ yāva(t)c) citragupto 'bravīd vacaḥ.
N4/6.22, N8/6.86, Ra/6.23 - ānināya ca tān sarvān citraguptasya sannidhau athāgatān sa saṁvikṣya citragupto vaco 'bravīt.

kimartham āgatas tvaṁ hi kiṅkāryaṁ brūhi tad vada[41]
kim āgatā yūyam iha kiṅkāryaṁ brūta sāṁpratam[42] [21]
dūtā ūcuḥ
preṣitaḥ sma mahābhāga dharmarājena dhīmatā[43]
eṣa vipro mahābhāgaḥ satyavrataparāyaṇaḥ[44] [22]
pitṛśāpād iha prāptas tavāgre preṣito mayā[45]
asya vāñchā prakartavyā dṛṣṭvā cainaṁ dvijottamaṁ[46] [23]

"What is the purpose of your arrival, O servants? This tell me.
Why have you come, O messengers? That let me hear". [21]
The messenger(s) said
"I am really sent here, Great one, by Dharmarāja, the wise one.
'This great Brahmin, adhering to Truth as a vow, [22]
has arrived because of his father's curse, and I have sent him to come before you.
Having seen this great Brahmin, we have to fulfill his wish'. [23]

N7/6.21b - āgāte sannidhau tatra citragupto vaco 'bravīt.

Bo/6.20b - uvāca citraguptas tān kiṅkāryaṁ brūta suvratāḥ.

41 N3/6.20b - kimartham āgatas tvaṁ bho kiṅkārya brūhi sattama.

42 N1/6.21b - kimartham āgatā dūtā bhavantaś ca (N3/6.21a - bruvantu tat) śruvantu tata.

N4/6.23a, N8/6.87a, Ra/6.24a - kim āgatā yūyam iha kiṅkāryyaṁ b(v)rūta sāṁpratam.

N7/6.22a - kim āgata iha tvaṁ bho kiṅkārya[ṁ] brūhi suvrataḥ.

43 N1/6.22a, N10, N11 - preṣit(o)aḥ (N3/6.21b - preṣitā[ḥ]) sm(y)a (N4/6.23b, N8/6.87b, Bo/6.21a, Ra/6.24b - preṣitāḥ smo) mahābhāgā dharmarājena dhīmatā.

44 N3/6.22a - eṣa vipro mahābhāga satyavāk tatparāyaṇaḥ.

N4/6.24b, N8/6.88b, Ra/6.25b - eṣa (N7/6.23a - eka) vipro mahāprājñaḥ satyadharmaparāyaṇaḥ.

N7/6.22b - pṛṣṭavāṁś ca mahābhāgo dharmarājaś ca dhīyutaḥ.

45 N2/6.22b - pitṛśāpād iha prāptas tavāgre preṣito (N3/6.22b - hy ayaṁ) yamaḥ.

N4/6.25a, N8/6.89a, Ra/6.26a - pituḥ śāpena kruddhasya prāpto yamamahāpure.

N7/6.23b - pituḥ sāpaniyojena prāpto yamaṁ mahāpurīṁ.

Bo/6.22a - pituḥ śāpāc ca yogena prāpto vaivasvata(ḥ)pure.

46 N1/6.23b - ṛṣy(a)ā (N2/6.23a, N10, N11 - asya) vāñchā prakartavyā pṛṣṭvā cainaṁ dvijottamaṁ.

N4/6.25b, N8/6.89b, Ra/6.26b - tvayāsya vāñcchitaṁ kartavyaṁ dvijasya mamājñayā.

dharmeṇedaṁ vacaḥ proktaṁ tad uktaṁ no 'gratas tava
dūtānāṁ vacanaṁ śrutvā citragupto vaco 'bravīt [24]
brūhi vipra mahāprājña kiṁ kariṣyāmy ahaṁ tava[47] [25]
nāsiketa uvāca
dṛṣṭas tvaṁ me mahāprājña sarvaśāstraviśārada[48]
yamatulyo mahātejā dharmādharmavicārakaḥ[49] [26]
tvaṁ cittaṁ sarvabhūtānāṁ kṛtaṁ karmaśubhāśubhaṁ[50]
mahāvīrya mahāprājña mahāyajña namo 'stu te[51] [27]
vaiśaṁpāyana uvāca[52]

These are the words of Dharmarāja as uttered, and we repeat them before you".
Having heard the messengers' words, Citragupta said the following: [24]
"Tell me, O Brahmin, great knowledgeable one, what I should do for you". [25]
Nāsiketa said
"I consider you, O great knowledgeable one, expert in all branches of knowledge,
as equal to the brilliant Yama, discerning between good and evil. [26]
You, who know all beings, and all their good and bad deeds,
I salute you great mighty one, great knowledgeable one, great sacrifice". [27]
Vaiśaṁpāyana said

N7/6.24a - asya vāñchā dhṛtiḥ kāry(aṁ)ā jñānavān sa dvijottamaḥ.
Bo/6.22b - asya vāñchā prakartavyā yad yad icchati vai dvijaḥ.

47 Bo/6.23a - brūhi vipra mahāprājña yat tvam icchasi tad vada.

48 N1/6.26a - dṛṣṭa(ṁ)s tvaṁ me mahāprājña (N3/6.25b - mahābhāga) sarvaśāstraviśārada.
N4/6.27b, N7/6.25b, N8/6.91a, Ra/6.28b - dṛṣṭo bhavān (BF/6.24a - dṛṣṭo 'si tvaṁ) mahābhāga sarvaśāstraviśārada.

49 Following N4/6.28a, N8/6.91b, Ra/6.29a.
N1/6.26b - yamatulyo mahātej(a)ā (N3/6.26a, BF/6.24b - mahātejo) dharmādharmavicāraka[ḥ].
N7/6.26a - yamatulyo mahātejā(ḥ) jñanavetā namo 'stu te.
Bo/6.24a - mahāvīryamahātejo dharmādharmavicāraka[ḥ].

50 N1/6.27a - tvaṁ ceṣṭh(sth)ya (N3/6.26b - praveśaḥ) sarvabhūtānāṁ kṛtaṁ karmaśubhāśubhaṁ.
N4/6.28b, N8/6.92a, Ra/6.29b, N7/6.27a, BF/6.25a - tvaṁ cittaṁ sarvabhūtānāṁ (Bo/6.24b - sarvaṁ vetsi śubhāśubhaṁ) jānāsi ca śubhāśubhaṁ.

51 N3/6.27a - mahāvīryya mahātejā jñānacitra namo 'stu te.
N4/6.29a, N8/6.92b, Ra/6.30a - citraguptaṁ mahāvīryaṁ tvāṁ namāmi punaḥ punaḥ.
BF/6.25b - mahāvīrya mahāprājña jñānaṁ citraṁ namo 'stu te.

52 Following N3/6.28.

evaṁ ca preṣitas tena citragupto mahātmanā[53]
īrṣitas tasya vākyena vacanaṁ cedam abravīt[54] [28]
citragupta uvāca
brūhi vipra kim iṣṭaṁ te jñānavijñānasaṁyutaḥ[55]
tuṣṭo 'haṁ tava viprendra dadāmi varam uttamaṁ[56] [29]
yat tubhyaṁ rocate 'tīva abhīṣṭaṁ manasas tava[57]
tad ahaṁ dvija dāsyāmi santuṣṭo vacanena te[58] [30]
nāsiketa uvāca
paśyāmy ahaṁ purīṁ sarvāṁ duḥkhāni ca sukhāni ca[59]
ājñāṁ dehi tvam apy ebhyaḥ kiṅkarebhyo mamājñayā[60] [31]

Since (Nāsiketa) was sent by him (Yama), the great soul Citragupta,
gladdened by his words, said the following: [28]
"Tell (me), Brahmin, full of worldly and ultimate knowledge, what is your wish?
I am pleased with you, venerable sage (and) I shall grant you the supreme wish. [29]
I shall give you whatever your mind craves for,
O twice born, since I am pleased with your words". [30]
Nāsiketa said
"(Please) show me the entire city, the suffering (sinners), and the happy (meritorious).
Give an order to your servants, this is my wish". [31]

---

53 N2/6.26b, N3/6.27b, N7/6.28a, N10, N11 - evaṁ ca toṣitas (N4/6.30b, N8/6.94a, Ra/6.31b - santoṣitas) tena citragupto (Bo/6.25a - mahātmavān) mahātmanā.

54 N1/6.28b, N11 - īrṣitas (N2/6.27a, N10 - harṣitas) tasya (N3/6.28a - tena) vākyena vacanaṁ cedam abravīt.
N7/6.28b - harṣitaś cārṣivākyena tv idaṁ vacanam abravīt.
Bo/6.25b - harṣito dvijavākyena punar evābravīd vac(j)aṁ.

55 N7/6.29a - brūhi vipra mahāprajñā jñānavijñānasaṁyutaṁ.

56 N7/6.29b - tuṣṭo 'haṁ tava viprarṣe dadāmi varam uttamaṁ.
Bo/6.26 - jñānavijñānasaṁyuktaḥ tuṣṭo 'haṁ te dvijottama
dadāmi tvāṁ varaṁ śīghraṁ ya te manasi vartate.

57 N2/6.28a - ya tubhyaṁ rocate vipra 'tīvrar bhaṣṭaṁ manas tava.

58 N1/6.30b, N11 - tad ahaṁ dvija dāsyāmi santuṣye vacanena te. End of N11.
N3/6.30a - tad ahaṁ dvija dāsyāmi santuṣṭo vacanaṁ (N10 - te (short)) śubhaṁ.
N7/6.30a - yo yaṁ yācayase bhāvaṁ rocase prārthī kiṁ tava.

59 N1/6.31a - darśayāmy (N7/6.30b - paśyāmy) ahaṁ (Bo/6.27a - vaḥ) purīṁ sarvāṁ duḥkhāni ca sukhāni ca.

60 N1/6.31b - ājñāṁ dehi tvam apy ebhya[ḥ] kiṅkarebhy(a)o mamākṣayāṁ.

uvāca tad aho dūtā yamavākyāt tathā mama[61]
etasya viṣamaṁ sarvaṁ darśayantu purīm imāṁ[62] [32]
yathā na pīḍyate vipro vidhibhir narakais tathā[63]
darśayitvā ca viprendraṁ punar ānīyatām iha[64] [33]
ājñāptāś citraguptena dūtāś cakrus tathaiva ca[65]

(Citragupta) spoke (and) said "O messengers, (it is) Yama's order and mine.
Show him the city, as well as whatever is unusual, [32]
in (such) a way that the Brahmin will not suffer, as is normal in the quarters of Hell.
After having shown him, bring the venerable Brahmin back here". [33]
And the messengers did exactly as ordered by Citragupta,

---

61 N1/6.32a, N10 - uvāca tad aho (N2/6.30b - āha) dūtā yamavākyā tathā (N3/6.31a - kṛthā) mama.
N4/6.31b, N8/6.95a, Ra/6.32b - prati re dūtā yamavākyena madvākyenāpi satvarāḥ.
Bo/6.28a - bho dūta y(m)amav(m)ākyena satvaraṁ dvijapuṅgavaṁ.
VP/196.31a - bho bho śṛṇuta me dūtā mama cittānuvarttakaḥ.

62 N1/6.32b - etasya viṣamaṁ sarvaṁ darśayantu purīm imāṁ.
N4/6.32a, N8/6.95b, Ra/6.33a - viṣamāviṣamāṁ sarvāṁ darśayadhvaṁ purīm imāṁ.
N7/6.32a - viṣamaṁ ca(m) idaṁ sarvaṁ darśāya(ya)[ntu] purīṁ punaḥ.
Bo/6.28b - viṣamaṁ ca śubhaṁ sarvaṁ darśayantu puraṁ mahat.

63 N3/6.32a - yathā na pīḍyate vipra (N2/6.31b - vyādhinā narakais tathā) vyādhibhi[r] narakais tadā.
N10 - yathā na prīyate vipro vyādhibhir narakais tathā.
N4/6.32b, N8/6.96a, Ra/6.33b - yathā na pīḍyate vipro narake duṣṭadarśanaiḥ.
N7/6.32b - yathā na pīḍyate vipro (Bo/6.29a - narakaiś caiva vyādhibhiḥ) narake vyādhibhis tathā.
VP/196.33a - naiva duḥkhena khedaḥ syān na coṣṇaṁ na ca śītalaṁ.

64 N1/6.33b - darśayitvā ca vipraṁ h(uḥ)i punar ānīyatām iha.
N4/6.33a, N8/6.96b, Ra/6.34a - darśayitvā punar vipram ānayadhvam iha cirāt.
N7/6.33a - darśayitvā ca viprendraṁ punar (Bo/6.29b - atrānayantuṁ ca) eva ihānaya.

65 N2/6.32b, N3/6.33a, N10 - ājñāptāś citraguptena dūtāś (N4/6.33b, N8/6.97a, Ra/6.34b - te yamaśāsanaṁ) cakrus tathaiva hi.
N7/6.33b - citraguptasya te ājñāṁ dūtā[ḥ] kurvanti nityaśaḥ.
Bo/6.30a - citraguptājñayā sarvair dūtais tvaritagāmibhiḥ.

darśayitvā purīṁ sarvāṁ bhūtvā tasyāgratas tathā[66] [34]
nāsiketaḥ samānītaś citraguptasya veśmani[67]
dūta uvāca[68]
asmābhir darśitaṁ sarvaṁ citraguptasya cājñayā[69] [35]
citragupta uvāca
nīyatāṁ sa dvijaḥ śīghraṁ dharmarājāsya sannidhiṁ[70]
vaiśaṁpāyana uvāca[71]
namaskṛtya gatā dūtā yatra vaivasvataḥ sthitaḥ[72] [36]

showing him the entire city, that was in front of him. [34]
Nāsiketa was then led to Citragupta's house.
The servant said
"We have shown (him) all according to Citragupta's order". [35]
Citragupta said
"Lead this Brahmin quickly to Dharmarāja's presence".
Vaiśaṁpāyana said
Having bowed to him, the messengers went to where Yama was staying. [36]

---

66 N3/6.33b - darśayitvā purīṁ [sar]vāṁ (Bo/6.30b - pṛthulāṁ dharmaśāsanāt) bhūtvā tasyāgratas tadā.

67 N10 - nāsiketaḥ samānītaś (N3/6.33c - nāśiketas tadānītaś) citraguptasya veśmani.
N4/6.34b, N8/6.98a, Ra/6.35b - ānītaś ca punar vipra(ā)ś (N7/6.34b - punas tasya) citraguptasya veśmani.
Bo/6.31a - ānītaṁ puratas tasya citraguptasya veśmani.

68 Following N7/6.36.

69 N1/6.34b - asmābhir darśi(a)taṁ (N10 - sadyaś) sarv(ā)aṁ (N3/6.34a - citragupta tavājñayā) citraguptasya cājñayā.
N7/6.35a - aśeṣaṁ darśayi(a)ṣyāmi viprasya ca tavājñayā.

70 N1/6.36a, N10 - nīyatāsau dvijaḥ śīghraṁ dharmarājāsya sannidhiṁ.
N2/6.34b - nīyatāṁ sa dvijaḥ(ś) (N3/6.34b - ca dvijaṁ) śīghraṁ dharmarājāsya sannidhi(ḥ)ṁ.
N4/6.36a, Ra/6.37a - nīyatām eṣa (N8/6.300a - nīyante tv eṣa) viprendro (N7/6.35b - citraguptaḥ nīyatāṁ ca, Bo/6.31b - nīyatāṁ vai dvijaḥ śīghraṁ) dharmarājāsya sannidhau.

71 Following Bo/6.32.

72 N1/6.36a, N10 - namaskṛtya gatā dūtā yatra (N2/6.34b - vai yamasaṁsthitaḥ) vaivasvataḥ sthitaḥ.
N4/6.36b, Ra/6.37b - ity uktaś citraguptena (N8/6.300b - dūtāḥ punar api dvijaṁ) gatās te yamamandiraṁ.

yamas tam āgataṁ dṛṣṭvā nāsiketaṁ dvijottamaṁ[73]
ardhāsanaṁ tato dattvā arghyapātreṇa pūjitaḥ[74] [37]
sukhāsīnasya viprasya vacanaṁ tena abravīt[75]
nāsiketa mahābhāga āgatas tvaṁ sukhena tu[76] [38]
dṛṣṭvā sthānāni sarvāṇi citraguptaṁ ca lekhakaṁ[77] [39]
nāsiketa uvāca

Seeing the great Brahmin Nāsiketa arriving, Yama
gave him half his seat, and honoured him with the worship pot. [37]
Yama then spoke, making the Brahmin happy by his words.
"Nāsiketa, O great one, have you arrived satisfied, [38]
having seen all the places and the secretary Citragupta as well?" [39]
Nāsiketa said

N7/6.36a - namaskṛtya (Bo/6.32a - taṁ praṇamya) gatās tatra yatra vaivasvataḥ sthitaḥ.

73 N4/6.37a, N8/6.1a, Ra/6.38a - yamasannidhim āninyur dūtāḥ punar api dvijaṁ.
N7/6.36b - yamenaivāgato dṛṣṭvā nāsiketo mahātapā.
Bo/6.32b - yamaś cāpy āgataṁ dṛṣṭvā nāsiketaṁ mahattamaṁ.

74 N2/6.36a, N7/6.37a - ardhās(ś)anaṁ tato dattvā arghyapātreṇa pūjitaḥ.
N4/6.38a, N8/6.2a, Ra/6.39a - ardhāsanaṁ dadau tasya madhuparkaṁ tathā punaḥ.
Bo/6.33a - arghyapādyāsanair enaṁ nāsiketam apūjayat.

75 N1/6.38a, N10 - sukhī narasya viprasya vacanaṁ tena(m) abravīt.
N3/6.35b, Bo/6.33b - sukhāsīnasya (N2/6.36b - sukhinasya ca, N7/6.37b - sthitāsanasya) viprasya (N4/6.38b, N8/6.2b, Ra/6.39b - sukhāsīnaṁ tato vipraṁ) yam(a)o vacanam abravīt.

76 N1/6.38b - nāsiketa mahābhāga āgatas tvaṁ (N2/6.37a - gatas tvaṁ ca) mukhena (N3/6.36a - ca) tu.
N4/6.39a, N8/6.3a, Ra/6.40a - nāsiketa tvayā kaccit sukhaṁ cātra samāgataṁ.
N7/6.38a - nāsiketa mahātmā ca āgatas tu sukhena ca.
Bo/6.34a - nāsiketa mahābhāga hy āgatas tvaṁ sukhena ca.

77 N3/6.36b - dṛṣṭvā sthānāni sarvāṇi citraguptaṁ tu lekhakaṁ.
N4/6.39b, N8/6.3b, Ra/6.40b - dṛṣṭaṁ kiṁ vividhaṁ sthānaṁ citraguptaś ca lekhakaḥ.
N7/6.38b, Bo/6.34b - dṛṣṭvā ca vividhaṁ sthānaṁ citraguptaṁ ca lekhakaṁ.

tvatprasādān mayā dṛṣṭaṁ vividhaṁ narakādikaṁ[78]
paraṁ tiṣṭhati me tāto duḥkhitaḥ śokamohitaḥ[79] [40]
tasya pādau ca paśyāmi svāmin ājñāṁ dadāsi cet[80]
yama uvāca
gaccha bho tvaṁ dvijaśreṣṭa tātas te yatra tiṣṭhati[81]
ajaraś cāmaraś caiva sarvadoṣavivarjitaḥ[82] [41]
vaiśaṁpāyana uvāca
evam uktas tadā tena nāsiketo yamāntikāt[83]

"By your grace, I have seen the various (quarters of) Hell.
Beyond (i.e. in the mortal world), my father is staying, unconscious because of grief. [40]
I shall come to his feet, if you give the order".
Yama said
"Go, you excellent Brahmin, to where your father is staying,
never to grow old, never to die, never to become ill"[(II)]*. [41]*
Vaiśaṁpāyana said
Nāsiketa, thus told by Yama,

---

78 N4/6.40a, N8/6.4a, Ra/6.41a - tvatprasādān mayā dṛṣṭaṁ (N7/6.39a - narakāni vividhāni ca, BF/6.36a - vividhaṁ narakādikaṁ) narakaṁ viṣamādikaṁ.
Bo/6.35a - tvatprasādān mayā dṛṣṭaḥ svargaś ca narakas tathā.

79 N4/6.40b, N8/6.4b, Ra/6.41b - pitaṁ me dharmarājādyanim agnaḥ śokasāgare.
N7/6.39b - pitā me duḥkhasantaptas tiṣṭhate ś(s)okamohitaḥ.
BF/6.36b - paraṁ tiṣṭh(ṭ)ati me tāto duḥkhita śokamohitaḥ.
Bo/6.35b - pitā me duḥkhato ghore vane tiṣṭhati mohitaḥ.

80 N2/6.39b, N3/6.38a, N10 - tasya padau ca paśyāmi (N7/6.40a - svām ājñām ādade hariḥ) svāminn ājñāṁ dadāsi cet.
N4/6.41a, N8/6.5a, Ra/6.42a - tasya padau ca paśyāmi (Bo/6.36a - prapaśyāmi) svāminn ājñā bhaved yadi.

81 N4/6.41b, N8/6.5b, Ra/6.42b - gaccha tatra dvijaśreṣṭa pitā te yatra tiṣṭhati.
N7/6.40b - gaccha dvijavaraśreṣṭha (Bo/6.36b - yatra tiṣṭhati te pitā) te tāto yatra gacchati.
BF/6.37b - gaccha dvijavarāśu tvaṁ yatrāste sa pitā tava.

82 N1/6.41b - antaraś cāmaraś caiva sarva eva vivarjitaḥ.
N10, N7/6.41a, BF/6.38a, Bo/6.37a - ajaraś cāmaraś caiva sarvad(r)oṣavivarjitaḥ.
N4/6.42a, N8/6.6a, Ra/6.43a - matprasādan mune bhūyād ajaraś cāmaro bhavān.

83 N4/6.43a, N8/6.7a, Ra/6.44a - evam uktas tu dharmmeṇa nāsiketo yamāntikāt.
BF/6.39a - evam uktas tatas tena nāsiketur yamena saḥ.
Bo/6.38b - evam ukto namaskṛtya dharmarājaṁ dvijottamaḥ.

dharmarājaṁ namaskṛtya vāyuvegena cāgamat [42]
yathā yena gatas tena pitur āśramam āgamat[84]
yatra sthitaḥ pitā tatra saṁprāpto nimiṣārddhataḥ[85] [43]
mātā rudantī putrasya vatsalyāt sadayaṁ bhṛśaṁ[86]
mahāśokena santaptau pitarau tāv ubhāv api[87] [44]
apaśyan nāsiketo 'sau satyavrataparāyaṇaḥ[88]
uddālakaṁ mahātmānaṁ putraṁ dṛṣṭvā samāgataṁ[89] [45]

bowing to him, left Yama's presence, by the speed of wind. [42]
By the same way he had gone, he returned to his father's hermitage.
In a moment, he arrived where his father(III) was standing. [43]
His mother was crying incessantly, because of her affection for her son.
Both parents were grief-stricken for their son. [44]
Seeing Nāsiketa, that excellent adherent of Truth,
Uddālaka, the great soul, came forward, having seen his son's arrival, [45]

---

84 N1/6.43a - yathā yena gatas tena pitur āśramam ārabhat.
Half verse 6.43a is missing in N3.
N4/6.43b, N8/6.7b, Ra/6.44b - yena mārgeṇa tu gatas tenaivāgat svamāśramaṁ.
N7/6.42b - yasmin mārgo gatas tena cāgataś cātmaveśmani.
BF/6.39b - mārgeṇa yena cāyāto yātas tenaiva mandiraṁ.
Bo/6.38b - gato 'sau yena mārgeṇa tenaiva punar āgataḥ.

85 N1/6.43b, N10 - yatra sthitaḥ pitā tatra (Bo/6.39a - saṁprāpto) santapto (BF/6.40a - saṁprāpto nimiṣena saḥ) nimiṣārddhata.
N3/6.41a - yatra sthitaḥ pitāmātā prāpto nimiṣārddhataḥ.
N4/6.44a, N8/6.8a, Ra/6.45a - yatra vas te pitā duḥkhī santaptas tatra satvaraṁ.
N7/6.43a - yatra sthitaḥ pitā tasya saṁprāpto nimiṣā(o)rddhataḥ.

86 N1/6.44a, N3/6.41b - sātānudantī putrasya vatsalyāt sadaya(d)ṁ (N2/6.42b - saday(e)aṁ) bhṛśaṁ.
N4/6.44b, N8/6.8b, Ra/6.45b - mātā ca putrasyavatsalyād rudatī janamejaya.
BF/6.40b - mātāpitṛbhyāṁ vatsalyāc chocyamānaḥ punaḥ punaḥ.

87 N1/6.44b - mahāśokena santapto (N10 - santaptau) putrāste tāv ubhāv api.
N7/6.44a - dṛṣṭaṁ ca pitaraṁ tatra rudataṁ śokavihvalaṁ.
BF/6.40b-41a - pitarau mahāśokena santaptau tāv ubhāv api.

88 N2/6.44a - āyāt(a)o nāsiketo 'sau satyavrataparāyaṇaḥ.

89 N2/6.44b - uddālako mahātmānaṁ (N3/6.43b - putraṁ dṛṣṭvā (Bo/6.39b - dṛṣṭvā putraṁ) samāgataṁ) putradṛṣṭā samāgamat.
N4/6.46a, N8/6.10a, Ra/6.47a - uddālakaś ca puṇyātmā (N7/6.44b - uddālako mahātmā ca) putraṁ dṛṣṭvā samāgataṁ.

upaviṣṭaṁ sutaṁ sarvam idaṁ vacanam abravīt[90] [46]
munir uvāca
adya me saphalaṁ janma adya me saphalāḥ kriyāḥ[91]
adya me saphalā pūjā yaj jātaṁ putradarśanaṁ[92] [47]
ahaṁ krodhī durācāro nirmitaḥ pāpakarmaṇā[93]
vināparādhaṁ te putra mayā śāpaṁ niyojitaṁ[94] [48]
dṛṣṭvā putraṁ samāyātaṁ mātā harṣād idaṁ jagau[95]
mātovāca

(and) said the following to his approaching son. [46]
The sage said
"Today my birth bears fruit, today my deeds bear fruit.
Today my worship bears fruit, seeing (the rebirth) of my son happening. [47]
Seized with anger, of bad conduct, committing sin,
I bound you, without blame of yours, son, with a curse". [48]
Seeing her son returning, the mother thus spoke, full of joy.
The mother said

---

90 N2/6.45a - upaviṣṭaṁ tanaṁ (N3/6.44a - janaṁ) sarvam (N10 - sardham) idaṁ vacanam abravīt.
N4/6.46b, N8/6.10b, Ra/6.47b - praharṣaṁ paramaṁ prāpyaṁ vacanaṁ cedam abravīt.
Bo/6.39c - uvāca taṁ pariṣvajya namantaṁ pādayor muhuḥ.

91 N3/6.44b, N4/6.47a, N8/6.11a, Ra/6.48a - adya me saphalaṁ janma adya me (N7/6.45b-46a - saphalī krīyā, Bo/6.40a - saphalāḥ kriyāḥ) saphalā kriyā.

92 N1/6.47b - adya me saphalā putra yaj jātaṁ putradarśanaṁ.
N4/6.47b, N8/6.11b, Ra/6.48b - adya me saphalā pūjā (Bo/6.40b - saphalaṁ sarvaṁ) yaj jātaṁ putradarśanaṁ.
N7/6.45b-46a - adya me saphalī pūjā sañjātaṁ putradarśanaṁ.

93 N3/6.45b - ahaṁ krodhī durācāro (N4/6.48a, N7/6.46b, N8/6.12a, Ra/6.49a, N10 - nirmitaḥ) nirmamaḥ (Bo/6.41a - nirdayaḥ pāpakarmakṛt) pāpakarmaṇā.

94 N1/6.48b, N10 - vināparādhaṁ te putra mayā śāpo niyo(vra)jitaḥ.
N4/6.48b, N8/6.12b, Ra/6.49b - vināparādhena mayā yamapāśe niyojitaḥ.
N7/6.47a - niraparādhakaḥ putro mayā ś(s)āpe niyojitaḥ.
Bo/6.41b - vināparādhaṁ putre tu mayā śāpo niyojitaḥ.

95 N1/6.49a - dṛṣṭvā putraṁ samāyātaṁ mātā (Bo/6.42 - provāca harṣitā) harṣaṁ didṛj jagau.
N7/6.47b - putraṁ dṛṣṭvā samāyātaṁ mātā ca ru(r)ṣasaṁyutā.

prabhāvaṁ mama putrasya bho paśyantu tapodhanāḥ[96] [49]
vaivasvatapuraṁ gatvā punar atra samāgataḥ[97]
tapoyogabalo yādṛk sutasya mama vidyate[98]
dṛṣṭo na tādṛk kutrāpi hy āgato yad yamālayāt[99] [50]
āgataṁ munayaḥ sarve dṛṣṭvā papracchur ādarāt[100]
uddālaka uvāca[101]

"O sages, behold the greatness of my son. [49]
Having gone to Yama's city, he has returned here again.
(Only) my son has such power of penance and Yoga.
The same has never been seen anywhere else – no one has come back from Yama's place". [50]
All the sages came to see him and ask him with respect.
Uddālaka said

---

96 N1/6.49b - prabhavaṁ mama putrasya nā (N10, BF/6.46a - bho) paśyantu tapodhanāḥ.
N4/6.49a, N8/6.13a, Ra/6.50a - puṇyaṁ mama prabhāvo 'pi putrasyāsya mahattaraḥ.
N7/6.48a - uddālakaḥ yasya prabhāvaṁ putrasya ca tapodhanaṁ.
Bo/6.43a - paśya paśya prabhāvaṁ vai matputrasya suśobhanaṁ.

97 N1/6.50a - vaivasvatadvaraṁ (N3/6.46d - vaivasvatapure, BF/6.46b - vaivasvatapuraṁ) gatvā (N4/6.49b, N8/6.13b, Ra/6.50b - yena vaivasvatapurāt) punar atra samāgataḥ.
N7/6.48b - vaivasvatapure prāpte punar eva ihāgataḥ.

98 N1/6.50b - tapayoge ca (N3/6.47a - tapoyoge vā) lo (BF/6.47a - tapoyogabalo) yādṛk sutasya (N10 - putrasya) mama vidyate.
N4/6.50a, N8/6.14a, Ra/6.51a - tapoyogab(v)alaṁ cāsya (N7/6.49a - prabhavaṁ me sutasya ca) nāsiketasya na kvacit.

99 N1/6.50c - dṛṣṭān tādṛk ca (N3/6.47b, N10 - dṛṣṭo na tādṛk) kutrāpi āgato (N2/6.49b - yamam ālayāt) yad yamālayāt.
N4/6.50b, N8/6.14b, Ra/6.51b - śrutaṁ naiva ca dṛṣṭaṁ me yadā yāto yamāntikāt.
N7/6.49b - śrutaś caiva na dṛṣṭaṁ me āgato yama ś(s)āsanāt.
BF/6.47b - dṛṣṭo na tādṛk kutracid āgato 'yaṁ yamālayāt.

100 N1/6.51a - āgataṁ munayaḥ sarve dṛṣṭvā ya (N2/6.50a - yat) pracchur ādarāt.
N4/6.51a, N8/6.15a, Ra/6.52a - papraccha ca pitā putraṁ yamaśāsanam ādarāt.
N7/6.50a - āgataṁ ṛṣayaḥ sarve dṛṣṭvā ca ṛṣim adbhutaṁ.

101 Following BF/6.48.

kathaṁ yamapurīṁ dṛṣṭvā kathaṁ śīghraṁ samāgataḥ[102] [51]
raghurājādayaḥ sarve bhūbhṛtaś ca mahābalāḥ[103]
uddālakāgṛhe jātāḥ nāsiketasya pṛcchayā [52]
kīdṛśas tasya mārgo 'sti yamaś caiva sa kīdṛśaḥ[104]
tatra kiñcic ca yal labdhaṁ pānabhojanakādikaṁ[105] [53]
yat kiñcid anyat te dṛṣṭaṁ yathāvat tad vadasva naḥ[106]
sukhaṁ vā yadi vā duḥkhaṁ svargaṁ narakam eva ca[107] [54]

"How have you seen Yama's city? How have you come back so quickly?" [51]
King Raghu, as well as other kings, all mighty and brave,
came to Uddālaka's abode, in order to pose questions to Nāsiketa. [52]
"Of what kind is the way to him? And Yama, what is he like?
Did you get anything to eat or drink there? [53]
(Please) tell us whatever else you have seen (there),
in the happy quarters (of the meritorious) or the suffering (of the sinners), Heaven and Hell. [54]

---

102 N3/6.48b - kathaṁ (N7/6.50b - yamapurīṁ) yamapurī (N4/6.51b, N8/6.15b, Ra/6.52b, Bo/6.44a - yamapurīṁ prāptaḥ) dṛṣṭvā kathaṁ śīghram ihāgataḥ.
BF/6.48 - kathaṁ yamapurīṁ yātaḥ panthāc caiva tu kīdṛśaḥ
kathaṁ yamapurī dṛṣṭā kathaṁ śīghram ihāgataḥ.

103 N10 - raghurājādaya(ā)ḥ sarve bhūbhṛtaś ca samāgataḥ.

104 N1/6.53a - kīdṛśas tasya mārgo 'sti (N4/6.52a, N8/6.16a, Ra/6.53a - kīdṛśas tatra pānthāś ca) yama(s)ś caiva sa kīdṛśaḥ.
N7/6.51a - panthā saḥ kīdṛś(s)aś caiva yamaś caiva tu kīdṛśaḥ.
BF/6.49a - kīdṛśo yamalokas tu yamaś cāpi sa kīdṛśaḥ.
Bo/6.44b - kīdṛśo yamalokasya panthāś caiva yamas tathā.

105 Emendation - DS. N1/6.53b - tatr(ā)a ki(a)ñci(āt)c [ca] ya[l] labdhaṁ pānabhojanakādikaṁ.
N4/6.52b, N8/6.16b, Ra/6.53b - ke ca tatra tvayā dṛṣṭās tasya dharmmādhikāriṇaḥ.
N7/6.51b - kiñci(at)l labdhaṁ tvayā putra bhojanaṁ jānam eva ca.
BF/6.49b - kiṁ tu labdhaṁ tvayā tatra pānabhojanam eva ca.
Bo/6.45a - kathaṁ labdhaṁ tvayā putra bhojanaṁ pānam eva ca.

106 N1/6.54a, N10 - ya kiñcid an(tva)y(ā)a[t te] dṛṣṭaṁ ya(r)th(y)āvat tad [v]adasva naḥ.
N7/6.52a - yat kiñcit tatra te dṛṣṭaṁ (Bo/6.45b - tat sarvaṁ brūhi me suta) kathayasva yathāvidhiḥ.
BF/6.50a - ya kiñcit tvayā dṛṣṭaṁ ca yathācāraṁ yathāsthitaṁ.

107 N1/6.54b - surā vā yadi vā duḥkhaṁ svargaṁ narakam eva ca.

brahmavaṁśe samutpanno vīryād uddālakasya ca
garbhāc ca candravatyās tvaṁ citraṁ kiṁ te balena hi[108] [55]
tan munīndra mahāprājña yamalokaḥ kīdṛśo vada[109] [56]
nāsiketa uvāca
tvatprasādena bho tāta saṁprāpto 'haṁ yamālaye[110]
buddhāś ca vividhā dṛṣṭvā yamaś ca bhagavān prabhuḥ[111] [57]
citragupto mayā dṛṣṭaḥ sarvalokānuśāsakaḥ[112]
kālo dṛṣṭaś ca lokānāṁ śāstā ca yamakiṅkarāḥ[113] [58]

Born in the lineage of Brahma, of Uddālaka's semen,
and Candravatī's womb, it is no wonder that you are so powerful. [55]
O divine sage, great knowledgeable one, tell (us) what is Yama's world like?" [56]
Nāsiketa said
"By your grace, O father, I arrived at Yama's place.
I saw various wise men, as well as the radiant Lord Yama. [57]
I saw Citragupta, the punisher of all the worlds.
I saw Kāla(IV), the destroyer of worlds, and the servants of Yama. [58]

---

108 N1/6.55b - garbhāc ca candravatyās tvaṁ (N3/6.52b - citra kiṁ te balasya hi) citraṁ kiṁ te balen(ā)a hā.

109 N1/6.56 - tan mu(a)nī[n]dra mahāprājñā yamaloka[ḥ] kīdṛśo (N3/6.53a - kathāṁ) vada (vi).

110 N1/6.57a - tvatprasādena bho tāta saṁprāpto ha yamālaye.
N4/6.53b, N8/6.18a, Ra/6.54b - tvatprasādād ahaṁ tāta (N7/6.52b - saṁprāpto (Bo/6.46a - yamasādanaṁ) yamaś(s)āsane, BF/6.51a - saṁprāptaṁ yamamandiraṁ) sukhaṁ prāpto yamālayaṁ.

111 N1/6.57b - budhāḥ sva vividhā dṛśy(a)ā (Bo/6.46b, BF/6.51b - devāś ca vividhā dṛṣṭā) yamaś ca bhagavān prabhuḥ.
N3/6.54b - yamaś ca vasati tatra mayā dṛśtaś ca vīryavān.
N4/6.54a, N8/6.18b, Ra/6.55a - yamaś ca bhagavān dṛṣṭo devāś ca vividhā mayā.
N7/6.53a - devāś ca vividhā dṛṣṭā yamo dṛṣṭaḥ svayaṁprabhuḥ.

112 N4/6.54b, N8/6.19a, Ra/6.55b - citraguptas tathā dṛṣṭaḥ sarvalokaikaśāsanaḥ.
N7/6.53b - citragupto mayā dṛṣṭaḥ (Bo/6.47a - sarvalokānuśāsanaḥ, BF/6.52b - sarvalokāntakas tathā) sarvalokasya ś(s)āsanaḥ.

113 N1/6.58b, N10 - kālo diṣṭaś ca lokānāṁ śāstāś ca yamakiṅkarāḥ.
N4/6.55a, N7/6.54a, N8/6.20a, Ra/6.56a - kālaś caiva kṛtāntaś ca (BF/6.52b - yamadūta(ā)u mahābala(ā)u) yamadūtā mahābalāḥ.

dharmarājaḥ sabhāmādhye stutibhis toṣito mayā[114]
tuṣṭena dharmarājena punar eva visarjitaḥ[115] [59]
dattas tena varo mahyam ajaraś cāmaro bhava[116]
gaccha tatra pitā prājña yatra tiṣṭhati te mune[117] [60]

iti śrībrahmāṇḍapurāṇe nāsiketopākhyāne pitṛputrasaṁvādo nāma ṣaṣṭho 'dhyāyaḥ

Dharmarāja became pleased when I praised him in the middle of his hall.
By Dharmarāja's contentment I was then released again. [59]
He granted me a boon – never to grow old or die, (saying)
'Go to where your father, the great knowledgeable one, is staying, O sage!'" [60]

This is the sixth chapter of the Nāsiketa story, pertaining to the Brahmāṇḍa Purāṇa, called – the father and son dialogue.

Translation Notes

I – Sin.
II – Or – free from all diseases.
III – In other versions – father and mother.
IV – Time.

---

114 N1/6.58b - dharmarājaḥ sabhāmādhye stutibhi(ḥ)s toṣito mama.
N4/6.56a, N8/6.20b, Ra/6.57a - tatra tāta mayā dharmmaḥ stutibhis toṣito bhṛśaṁ.
N7/6.54b - dṛṣṭo vai dharmarājaḥ ca (Bo/6.47b - dṛṣṭaś ca dharmarājo vai) stutibhis toṣito mayā.
BF/6.53a - dharmarājo mayā tatra stutyā ca toṣitas tathā.

115 N4/6.56b, N8/6.21a, Ra/6.57b - dharmarājena tuṣṭena preṣitas tava sannidhau.
N7/6.55a - dharmarājena tuṣṭena punar eva visarjitaḥ.

116 N10 - dattas tena varo makha hy amaraś cāmaro bhava.
N4/6.57a, N8/6.21b, Ra/6.58a - ādarāc ca varaṁ dattam ajarāmaratā mama.
N7/6.55b - tuṣṭena me varaṁ dattaṁ ajaraṁ cāmaraṁ ('bravīt) [tatha].
BF/6.53b - pradadau sa varaṁ mahyam amaratvaṁ surottamaḥ.
Bo/6.47b - tuṣṭena me varo datto ajaraś cāmaro bhava.

117 BF/6.54b - etad varaṁ mayā prāptaṁ tvatprabāvān muneśvara.

Chapter 7

Hell

vaiśaṁpāyana uvāca
ṛṣayaś ca tataḥ śrutvā sarve vismayam āgatāḥ[1]
yamasya bhavanaṁ gatvā nāsiketa ihāgataḥ[2] [1]
uddālakāśrame praṣṭum āgatās tapanaprabhāḥ[3]
māsopavāsatiratāḥ pañcalokāgnisādhakāḥ[4] [2]
ūrdhvapādasthitā kecid āgatās te mahotsukāḥ[5]

Vaiśaṁpāyana said
And the sages, thus hearing, were all filled with wonder (how),
Nāsiketa, having gone to Yama's abode, had (successfully) returned here. [1]
They arrived at Uddālaka's hermitage to ask, (all) penance-glowing.
(Some were after) one month fasting, performers of the 5 fires exercise(I)*. [2]*
Some had been standing with their feet up(II)*, coming very eager (to listen).*

---

1 N1/7.1a - ṛṣayaś ca tataḥ śrutvā sarvā vismayam āgatāḥ.
N3/7 starts with verse number 7.
N4/7.1a, N8/7.21a, BF/7.1a, Ra/7.1a - evaṁ śrutvā tu ṛṣayaḥ sarve vismitamānasāḥ.

2 N4/7.1b, N8/7.21b, Ra/7.1b - yamasya bhavanaṁ gatvā nāsiketa (BF/7.1b - nāsiketur) ihāgataḥ.
N7/7.1b - yamasya bhavane gatvā nās(ś)ike(a)ta ihāgataḥ.
Bo/7.1b - yamasya bhavanaṁ gatvā muniṁ punar ihāgataḥ.

3 N1/7.2a - uddālakāśubhe praṣṭu(r)m (N3/7.8a, N2/7.2a - uddālakāśrame pṛṣṭum) ā[ga]tās tapanaprabhāḥ.
N4/7.2, N8/7.22, Ra/7.2 - nāsiketam idaṁ sarvaṁ praṣṭuṁ vismitacetasaḥ āgatās te tataḥ śīghram uddālakatapovane.
N7/7.2 - pṛcchārthaṁ ca samāyātās tapino vratinas tathā
āgatā ṛṣayaḥ sarve uddālakāś ca samāśrame (vi).
BF/7.2a - pṛcchanto yamalokasya vṛttāntaṁ tātasannidhau.

4 N1/7.2b, N2/7.2b, N10 - māsopavāsatiratāḥ pañcakālāgnisādhakāḥ.
N4/7.3a, N8/7.23a, Ra/7.3a - anye ca b(v)ahavo rājan viprā māsopavāsinaḥ.
N7/7.3a - k(v)ālāgnisthā dvijā anye pūtā māsopavāsinaḥ.

5 Half verse 7.3a is missing in N3.

adhomukhāḥ sthitāś cānye ādityābhimukhāsthitāḥ[6] [3]
nirucchvāsāsthitāḥ cānye vāyubhakṣāḥ sthitāḥ pare[7]
pañcāgnisādhakāḥ kecin nirāhārās tapasvinaḥ[8] [4]
ekapādāsthitāḥ kecit pādāṅguṣṭena saṁsthitāḥ[9]
stuvanto bhāskaraṁ devaṁ kecit tatrāgatās tadā[10] [5]

Some had stood upside down(III)*, others had their faces turned towards the sun. [3]*
Some (practiced) deep breathing, and others had wind (only) for their food.
Some practiced the five fire-rites, others took the penance of no food. [4]
Some stood on one leg, others – on their tiptoes.
Some worshippers of the shining god (i.e. the sun), then came there. [5]

---

6 N1/7.3b - adhomukh(y)ā[ḥ] sthit(am)āś(vīn) [cān]ye (N10 - adhomukhā[ḥ]sthitaṁś cānye) ādityābhimukhāsthitāḥ.
N2/7.3b - adhomukhā[ḥ] sthitāś cānye vāyubhakṣāḥ sthitāḥ (N4/7.4b, N8/7.24b, Ra/7.4b - ādityābhimukhāḥ) pare.
N7/7.3b - pañcāgnisamādhyā ye ūrdhvapādasthitā pare.
Bo/7.3a - pakṣopavāsinaḥ kecid ye cānye jalavāsinaḥ.

7 N1/7.4a - tīvracchvāsāḥ sthitāḥ c(khy)ānye vāyubhejāḥ sthitāḥ pare.
N3/7.9b - nirucchvāsāsthitāḥ cānye vāmubhakṣyā sthitāḥ pare.
N4/7.5a, N8/7.25a, Ra/7.5a - prāṇāyāmaparāḥ pūtā vāyubhakṣaṇatatparāḥ.
N7/7.4b - [niruchvāsāsthitāḥ] cānye vāyubhakṣās tato pare.
BF/7.4a - adhomukhāḥ sthitāś cānye vāyubhakṣāḥ sthitāś cānye.
Bo/7.3b - adhomukhās tathaivānye vāyubhakṣās tathā pare.

8 N1/7.4b - pañcāgnisādhakāḥ kecit nirāhārās (N2/7.4b - tapasthitaḥ) tapasvin(ā)a[ḥ].
N4/7.4a, N8/7.24a, Ra/7.4a - pañcāgnisādhakāś cānye ūrdhvapādadhṛtās tathā.
N7/7.5a - pañcāgnitapasaṁyuktā nirāhāratayā(a)sthitāḥ.
BF/7.4b - ghore tapasi saṁsthitā (Bo/7.4 - ye cāgnisādhakāś cānye) nirāhārās tapasvinaḥ.

9 Verse 7.4b-5a is missing in N3.
N4/7.6a, N8/7.26a, Ra/7.6a - ekapādena tapyanti tapaḥ paramadāruṇaṁ.
N7/7.5b - ekapādena tiṣṭhanti nās(ś)iketa(s)papṛcchakāḥ.
BF/7.5a - ekapādena tiṣṭantas (Bo/7.5a - tapas taptuṁ sudāruṇaṁ) tapaḥ kurvanto dāruṇaṁ.

10 N1/7.5b - stuvanto bhāskaraṁ devaṁ (N2/7.5a - bhāskarair evaṁ) kecit tatrāgatās (N3/7.10a - kṛtvāgatās) tadā.
N4/7.6b, N8/7.26b, Ra/7.6b - bhāskarāstāvakā nityaṁ mahātejaḥ samanvitāḥ.
BF/7.5b - bhāskarārādhanaparā jvalantaś ca svatejasā.

nagnavratadharāś cānye agnihotraparāyaṇāḥ[11]
śuṣkaparṇāśanāś cānye cāndrāyaṇadharāḥ pare[12] [6]
āgatās tvaritāḥ sarve nāsiketasya pṛchakāḥ[13]
ṛṣaya ūcuḥ
uddālakātmaja prājña nāsiketamahāmune[14]
pitur ājñāniyogena dṛṣṭā saṁyamanī tvayā[15] [7]

Some used to walk naked, others were distinguished fire-worshippers[(IV)].
Some were dry-leaves-eaters, others took the Cāndrāyaṇa vow[(V)]. *[6]*
They all came crossing the river[(VI)], *to ask Nāsiketa.*
The sages said
"O Nāsiketa, great sage, Uddālaka's son, knowledgeable one,
by your father's order and by Yoga, you saw Yama's abode. [7]

---

11 N1/7.6a - nagnavratadharāś cānye (BF/7.6a - hy ūrdhvapādadhṛtāś ca ye) agninetraparāyaṇāḥ.
N4/7.7a, N8/7.27a, Ra/7.7a - agnivratadharāś cānye hy agnihotraparāyaṇāḥ.

12 N4/7.5b, N8/7.25b, Ra/7.5b - nirāhārās taponiṣṭhāḥ śuṣkaparṇāśinas tathā.
N4/7.8a, Ra/7.8a - parākakṛcchāniratāś (N8/7.28a - parākakṛbaniratā(ḥ)ś) cāndrāyaṇaparā api.
BF/7.7b - śuṣkaparṇāśinaś cānye cāndrāyaṇaparāyaṇāḥ.
Bo/7.7a - śuṣkaparṇāśanāḥ kecit tathā māsopavāsinaḥ.

13 N3/7.11b, N10 - āgatās tvaritā[ḥ] sarve nāsiketasya pṛchayā.
N4/7.8b, N8/7.28b, Ra/7.8b - āgatāḥ satvaraṁ sarve nāsiketasya pṛchakāḥ.
BF/7.8a - āgatāḥ pūjitāḥ sarve nāsiketuṁ ca pṛchakāḥ.
Bo/7.7b - papracchur militāḥ sarve nāsiketaṁ mahāmuniṁ.

14 N1/7.7b, N10 - uddālakātmanaḥ prājña nāsiketamahāmune.
N4/7.10a, N8/7.30a, Ra/7.10a - uddālakātmaja prājña nāsiketādbhutaṁ mahat.
N4/7.6a, Bo/7.8 - uddālakātmaja prājña dṛṣṭaṁ caiva tvayādbhutaṁ.
BF/7.9a - uddālakātmaja prājña nāsiketo mahāmune.

15 N1/7.7c, N10 - pitu(ā)r ājñāniyogena (N3/7.12b - ājñānirodhena) (taṁ) dṛṣṭvā saṁ[ya]manī tvayā.
N4/7.10b, N8/7.30b, Ra/7.10b - yat tvayā dharmarājasya purato 'tra samāgataṁ.
N7/7.6b - nās(ś)iketa mahātmā tvaṁ kīdṛśaṁ tatra te gate.
BF/7.9b - pitur ājñāpitena te dṛṣṭā saṁyamanī tvayā.

śrutaṁ yac ca tvayā dṛṣṭaṁ paraloke hi tad vada[16]
kīdṛśo yamalokaś ca panthās tatra ca kīdṛśāḥ[17] [8]
yamasya kīdṛśaṁ rūpaṁ yamadūtāś ca kīdṛśāḥ
kīdṛśī dharmasaṁpattis tasya yojanaṁ kīdṛśaṁ[18]
kīdṛśāḥ kālapāśāś ca kīdṛśaṁ narakāṇi ca[19]
kā sthitis tatra lokānām ācāras tatra kīdṛśaḥ[20]

Whatever you have heard, or seen, in the world yonder, that (please) tell.
What is Yama's world like? How is the road (leading) there? [8]
What is Yama's shape like? What are Yama's messengers like?
How is Yama's property? And how (many) Yojanas(VII) *is it?*
How are Kāla's(VIII) *nooses? And how are the (quarters) of Hell?*
Who are those who inhabit those places? How are there those who misbehave?

---

16 N3/7.13a - yac ca dṛṣṭaṁ tvayā dṛṣṭaṁ paraloke hi tad vada.
N4/7.11b, N8/7.31b, Ra/7.11b - śrutaṁ vā yadi vā dṛṣṭaṁ yamaloke tathā (N7/7.7a - varaloka kathaṁ) vada.
BF/7.10a - śrutaṁ ca tvayā dṛṣṭaṁ ca paraloke hitāhitaṁ.
Bo/7.9a - nāsiketa mahābhāga paralokakathāṁ vada.

17 N1/7.8b - kīdṛśo yamalokaś (N3/7.13b - 'yaṁ panthās) ca yathās tatra ca kīdṛśaḥ.
N4/7.12, N8/7.32, Ra/7.12 - kutas tatra gantaṁ kiṁ vā kiṁ ca prāptaṁ varaṁ paraṁ
kīdṛśo yamaloka(ṁ)sya panthā api sa kīdṛśaḥ.
N7/7.7b - kīdṛśaṁ yamalokaṁ tu panthās tatrāpi kīdṛśāḥ.
BF/7.10b - kīdṛśo yamalokaś (Bo/7.9b - tasya mārgaś) ca panthās tatra ca kīdṛśaḥ.

18 Additional half verse - following N10 - kīdṛśī dharmasaṁpattis ta[sya] yoj(ñ)ānaṁ (ca) kīdṛśa.
N7/7.9a - kīdṛś(s)a dharmasaṁyuktās tapojñāne hi kīdṛśaḥ.

19 Additional half verse - following N2/7.10, N3/7.14.
N4/7.13b, N8/7.33b, Ra/7.13b - kīdṛśās tasya te dūtāḥ kālaḥ prāptaś ca kīdṛśaḥ.
N4/7.15b, N8/7.35b, Ra/7.15b - kathaṁ te kālapāśāś ca yamadaṇḍāś ca mudgarāḥ.
N7/7.10a - kathaṁ tat kālapāśāṁ ca kathaṁ vā narakāṇi ca.

20 Additional half verse - following N2/7.9b, N3/7.15b, N10.
N4/7.14a, N8/7.34a, Ra/7.14a - kīdṛśas tatra vācāraḥ kā sthitiś ca dvijottama.
Bo/7.10a - kīdṛśā yamadūtāś ca kā sthitir varttate dvija.

iha yac ca kṛtaṁ karmapuṇyapāpādikaṁ naraiḥ[21] [9]
kathaṁ tal labhyate tatra vadasva muni puṅgava
sametya munayaḥ sarve pṛcchanti tvāṁ mahotsukāḥ[22] [10]
ete sarve mahābhāga yasyāmo yamaśāsanaṁ[23]
saṁsārārṇavabhītāś ca kālasya ca vaśe sthitāḥ[24] [11]
satyam ākhyāhi satyātman yathādṛṣṭaṁ yathāśrutaṁ[25]

People who do good deeds here, and those who commit sins, [9]
what do they get there? (Please) tell (us), O great sage.
Having gathered here, all sages ask you, and are very eager (to listen). [10]
All have to go from this world to Yama's kingdom, O great one,
greatly alarmed in the ocean of Saṁsāra, bound by Kāla's will. [11]
Tell the truth, O truth-soul, whatever you have seen, whatever you have heard".

---

21 N1/7.9b - iha yac ca (N2/7.11a - ya(ṣ)ḥ kva) kṛtaṁ karmapuṇyapāpādikaṁ naraiḥ.
N3/7.16a - iha(n) yat sukṛtaṁ karmapuṇyapāpātmakai(ḥ)r naraiḥ.
N4/7.13a, N8/7.33a, Ra/7.13a - yamasya kīdṛśaṁ rūpaṁ kāryyaṁ tasya ca kīdṛśaṁ.
N4/7.14b, N8/7.34b, Ra/7.14b - kīdṛśāś caiva lokāś ca krodhā vā priyavādinaḥ.
N7/7.9b - yamadaṇḍasya kiṁ rūpaṁ kiṁ vidhāvalibhujanaḥ.
N7/7.10b-11 - kathaṁ dṛṣṭvā tvayā tatra ṛṣayaḥ pūrvayoginaḥ
dānaṁ vāpy athavā puṇyavratāni niyamāni ca
ihaiva yat kṛtaṁ karma kathaṁ tatraiva labhyate.
Bo/7.10b-11a - kīdṛśas tatra lokaś ca krodhī vā priyavāg dvija
kīdṛśā narakās tatra kena pāpena ko bhavet.

22 N1/7.10b - same(a)tya munayaḥ sarve pṛcchanti tvā mahotsukāḥ.

23 N1/7.11a - itaḥ sarve mahābhāga gantavyaṁ yamaśāsane.
N4/7.19a, N8/7.39a, Ra/7.19a - ete sarve mahābhāga yāsyāmo yamaśāsanaṁ.
N7/7.12a - ete sarve mahābhāga paś(s)yanti yamaś(s)āsane.

24 N1/7.11b - saṁsārārṇavasaṁbhītā tasmāt kālācaro (N2/7.13a - kālavaśe) sthitān.
N3/7.28a - saṁsārārṇavasaṁbhūtān asmān kālavaśe sthitān. (Skipping verse numbers 16-27).
N4/7.19b, N8/7.39b, Ra/7.19b - saṁsārārṇavabhītāś ca kālasya ca vaśe sthitāḥ.
N7/7.12b - saṁsārārṇa[va]nītās te kālāsya ca vaś(s)aṁ sthitāḥ.

25 N1/7.12a, N10 - satyam ākhyāhi satyātmā yathādṛṣṭaṁ yathāśrutaṁ.
N4/7.18b, N8/7.38b, Ra/7.18b - satyaṁ brūhi yathādṛṣṭaṁ pṛcchāma ṛṣayo vayaṁ.
N7/7.13a - satyam brūhi yathāvṛtaṁ pṛcchanti tava suvrata.
Bo/7.11b - satyam brūhi mahāprājña ṛṣayaḥ praṣṭum āgatāḥ.

nāsiketa uvāca
śṛṇvantu munayaḥ sarve ye cānye 'tra tapasvinaḥ[26] [12]
yad dṛṣṭaṁ tat pravakṣyāmi paramaṁ lomaharṣaṇaṁ[27]
pitṛśāpādbhutaś cāhaṁ dharmarājo namaskṛtaḥ[28] [13]
stutibhis toṣito dharmo baddhvā yugakarāñjaliṁ[29]

Nāsiketa said
"Listen all the sages, and the other penance holders here. [12]
I shall tell what I have seen, which is most hair-bristling.
Because of my father's extraordinary curse, I bowed to Dharmarāja, [13]
having joined both palms, (and) he was pleased with my praise.

---

26 N1/7.12b - śṛṇvantu munayaḥ sarve ye cāny(n)e 'tra (N3/7.29a - cānye ca) tapasvinaḥ.
N4/7.20a, N8/7.40a, Ra/7.20a - śṛṇvantu (Bo/7.12a - śrūyatām) ṛṣayaḥ sarve (BF/7.16a - tathānye ca tapodhanāḥ) ye cānye (N7/7.13b - tapasaṁ sthitaḥ) tapasisthitāḥ.
VP/193.1a - kathyamānaṁ mayā viprāḥ śṛṇvantu tapasisthitāḥ.

27 N1/7.13a - yad dṛṣṭaṁ tat pravakṣyāmi paramaṁ lokam arṣaṇaṁ.
N4/7.20b-21a, N8/7.40b-41a, Ra/7.20b-21a - namaskṛtya mahātmānaṁ dharmarājaṁ mahādyutiṁ
dṛṣṭaṁ yat tat pravakṣyāmi romaharṣaṇam adbhutaṁ.
N7/7.14 - namaskṛtya mahātejaṁ (Bo/7.12b - mahādevaṁ) dharmarājaṁ mahāmatiṁ
dṛṣṭaṁ ca yat (Bo/7.12c - tatra dṛṣṭaṁ) pravakṣyāmi mahāntaṁ romaharṣaṇaṁ.
BF/7.16b-17a - namaskṛtya pravakṣyāmi dharmarājaṁ surottamaṁ
yad dṛṣṭaṁ tat pravakṣyāmi sarveṣāṁ lomaharṣaṇaṁ.

28 N1/7.13b - pitṛśāpādbhuta(s)ś c(v)āhaṁ dharmarājo namaskṛtaḥ.
N4/7.21b, N8/7.41b, Ra/7.21b - pitṛśāpād ahaṁ tatra gato yatra yamaḥ svayaṁ.
N7/7.15a - pitu(r)ḥ śāpād bhutaś cāhaṁ (BF/7.17b - śāpena yāto 'haṁ) yatra rājā svayaṁ yamaḥ.
Bo/7.13a - pituḥ śāpād ahaṁ prāpto viprāḥ saṁyamanīṁ purīṁ.

29 N1/7.14a - stutibhis toṣit(ā)o dharmo (N10 - vidhvā[yu]gakarāñjali(ḥ)ṁ, N4/7.22a, N8/7.42a, Ra/7.22a - namaskṛtya kṛtāñjaliḥ) badhvāyugakarāñjaliṁ.
N7/7.15b - stutibhis toṣito (BF/7.18a - devo mayā dṛṣṭo 'tisundaraḥ) dharmaprakṛtvā ca kṛśāñjaliṁ.
Bo/7.13b - tatra dṛṣṭo dharmarājaḥ stutibhis toṣito mayā.

tuṣṭo mahyaṁ dadau dharma āsanaṁ hṛṣṭamānasaḥ[30] [14]
devāś ca vividhā dṛṣṭā yamadūtā mahābalāḥ[31]
citragupto mayā dṛṣṭaḥ śubhāśubhanivedakaḥ[32] [15]
mayā tatra varo labdho vinayāviṣṭacetasā[33]
ajaratvaṁ cāmaratvaṁ ca vyādhiduḥkhavivarjitaṁ[34] [16]
āgato 'tra yutaś cāhaṁ prāsādāt pitur eva hi[35]
vistareṇa pravakṣyāmi śṛṇvantu yamaśāsanaṁ[36] [17]

(So), being pleased, Dharma(rāja) gave me a seat, happy at heart. [14]
I saw (there) various gods, (and) Yama's messengers, the great heroes.
I saw Citragupta(IX)*, the informer of good and evil (deeds). [15]*
I have received there a boon, from the pleased Yama –
not aging and not dying, not suffering from pain or disease. [16]
I have come here, along with these (boons), by the favour of the father.
Listen, I shall describe Yama's kingdom in detail. [17]

---

30 N4/7.22b, N8/7.42b, Ra/7.22b - tuṣṭas tato dadau dharmma āsanaṁ cārghyam uttamaṁ.
Bo/7.14a - tuṣṭe dharme mayā proktaṁ darśaya svapurīṁ tava.

31 N1/7.15a - devāś ca vi[vi]dh(va)ā dṛṣṭā yama hṛtātmā (BF/7.18b - yamadūtā) mahābalāḥ (vi).
N4/7.29a, N8/7.49a, Ra/7.29a - devāś ca divyarūpāḍhyāḥ siddhāḥ sādhyāḥ sayakṣakāḥ.

32 N7/7.17a - citragupto mayā dṛṣṭaḥ (Bo/7.15a - śubhāśubhavicārakaḥ) sarvalokāniś(s)āstikaḥ.
BF/7.19a - citragupto mayā dṛṣṭo lekhanīpustakāntikaḥ.

33 N3/7.33b - yamā tatra varo [labdh]o vinayāviṣṭacetasā.
N4/7.23a, N7/7.17b, N8/7.43a, Ra/7.23a - labdhaṁ varaṁ mayā tatra (Bo/7.15b - tato varaṁ mayā labdhaṁ) vinayāviṣṭacetasā.

34 N1/7.16b, N10 - anaratvā(ṁ)maratvaṁ vā (N7/7.18a - ajaraṁ cāmaraṁ caiva) vyādhiduḥkhavivarjitaḥ.
N4/7.23b, N8/7.43b, Ra/7.23b - ajarāmaratānām avyādhivarjanam eva ca.
Bo/7.15c - ajarāmaratā caiva vyādhiduḥkhavinaśanaṁ.

35 N2/7.18b - āgato 'tra punaś cāhaṁ prāsādāt pitur eva hi.
N4/7.24a, N8/7.44a, Ra/7.24a - āgato 'trāham ājñapto dharmeṇānugrahāt pituḥ.
N7/7.18b - āgato 'pi punaś cāhaṁ prāsādāc ca pitus tataḥ.
Bo/7.16a - āgato 'haṁ punaś caiva pitur mama prasādataḥ.

36 N7/7.19a - punaś cāhaṁ pravakṣyāmi (Bo/7.16b - yamalokasya vistṛtiṁ) yamaś(s)āsanaṁ vistarāt.

yojanānāṁ sahasraikaṁ nānāratnopaśobhitaṁ[37]
gītavāditrasaṁyuktaṁ nānāpuṣpopaśobhitaṁ[38] [18]
antar yamasya ca gṛhaṁ ṛṣīṇāṁ yogīnām api[39]
apsarogaṇagandharvavidyādharamahoragāḥ[40] [19]

It is a thousand Yojanas (long), all decorated with many jewels,
(full of) singing and instrumental music, adorned with various flowers. [18]
Yama's city, is the home of sages and hermits.
Apsarasas, Gandharvas, Vidyādharas, and mythological big serpents [19]

---

37 N2/7.19b, N3/7.35b, N10 - yojanānāṁ sahasraikaṁ vistīrṇaṁ tatparaṁ śubhaṁ.
Additional verses - N2/7.20, N10:
tatra durgapuraṁ (N3/7.36a - durgaparaṁ) ramya(ṁ)m ucchritaṁ pañcayojanaṁ
catuḥpanthāṁ caturdvāraṁ (N3/7.36b - caturcāraṁ) catuḥpretapurair yutaṁ.
N2/7.21a, N3/7.37a, N10, N4/7.26a, N7/7.21a, N8/7.46a, Ra/7.26a - nānājanapadākīrṇaṁ nānāratnopaśobhitaṁ.
N4/7.24b-25, N8/7.44b-45, Ra/7.24b-25 - sahasrayojanaṁ tāvad asti dharmapuraṁ śubhaṁ
tatra durgaṁ mahāyāmam ucchritaṁ pañcayojanaiḥ
puraṁ tac ca caturdvāraṁ catuḥpanthāṁ samanvitaṁ.
N7/7.20 - tatra durgā mahākāyaṁ pañcayojanamurdhakaṁ
catuḥpuraṁ caturdvāraṁ catu[ḥ]pretapure sthitaṁ.
Bo/7.17b - caturaś(s)raṁ caturdvāraṁ nānāratnopaśobhitaṁ.

38 N1/7.18b, N7/7.21b - gītavāditrasaṁyuktaṁ nānāpuṣpo(au)paśobhitaṁ.
N4/7.27a, N8/7.47b, Ra/7.27a - vāditrair vāditaiḥ saṁyak paramānandakāraṇaṁ.
N7/7.19b - sahasrayojanaṁ merus tat puraṁ caiva śobhanaṁ.
BF/7.22a - śatayojanavistīrṇaṁ puraṁ durgapariṣṭhitaṁ.
Bo/7.17a - śatāni daśā vistīrṇaṁ yojanānāṁ pramāṇataḥ.
Bo/7.18a - nānājanasamākīrṇaṁ gītavāditrasaṁyutaṁ.

39 N4/7.27b, N8/7.48a, Ra/7.27b - tatra santi mahātmāna ṛṣayo yoginas tathā.
N7/7.22b - yamaḥ sabhāntare caiva ṛṣayo [yo]gino 'pi saḥ.
BF/7.21a - yamo virājate madhye ṛṣīṇāṁ yoginām api.

40 N3/7.38b - apsarogaṇagandharvai[r] vidyādharamahoragaiḥ.
N10 - apsarogaṇagandharvyo vidyādharamahoragāḥ.
N4/7.29b, N8/7.50a, Ra/7.29b - apsarogaṇagandharvavidyādharamahoragāḥ.
N7/7.23a - apsarogaṇagandharvavividhādharamahoragāḥ (vi).
BF/7.21b - gaṇagandharvayakṣādividyādharamahoragāḥ.

pūrvadvāreṇa tiṣṭhanti śivabhaktiparāyaṇā[41]
grīṣme jalapradātāro māghe vahnipradāyakāḥ[42] [20]
viśrāmayanti śrāntān ye brahma svād atiśaṅkinaḥ[43]
satyadharmaratā ye ca krodhalobhavivarjitāḥ[44] [21]
devapūjāratā ye ca pitṛmatṛparāyaṇāḥ[45]

stand at the eastern gate, engaged in Śiva devotion.
Those who enrich the hot season with water, and the (cold) month Māgha with heat; [20]
Those who provide rest to the exhausted, who delight in Brahma;
Those engaged in Truth and Dharma, free from anger and greed; [21]
Those who are engaged in god worshipping, as well as (those who worship) their parents[(X)]*;*

---

41 N1/7.20a - pūrvadvāreṇa (N7/7.23b - praviśanti, BF/7.25a - ye yānti) tiṣṭhanti (N4/7.30b, N8/7.51a, Ra/7.30b - pūrvadvāre tu viśyeta, Bo/7.22b - praviśantiṁ dradigdvāre) śivabhaktiparāyaṇā.

42 N1/7.20b, N10, N4/7.31a, N8/7.51b, Ra/7.31a - grīṣm(o)e ja[la]pra(da)dātāro māghe vahn(nh)ipradāyakāḥ.
N7/7.24a - grīṣme toyaṁ (Bo/7.23a - grīṣmodaka) pradātāro māghe vahn(nh)ipradāyakāḥ.
BF/7.25b - grīṣme ye toyadātāro māghe ca vahnipradāyakāḥ.
Bo/7.19b - sarvaratnam ayaṁ vahn(nh)ividyud bālākar varcasaṁ.

43 N1/7.21a - viśrāmaṁ patitāṁ śrāṁmye (N3/7.40a - viśrāmayanti śrātānye) brahma svād atiśaṅkinaḥ.
N4/7.31b, N8/7.52, Ra/7.31b - viśrāmayanti ye śrāntān (N7/7.24b - vipra vyadhinnipīḍitan, Bo/7.23b - viprān adhvaprapīḍitān) vipraṁś cāpi namantiye.
BF/7.26a - śrāntaviśrāmadātāro viprā vyādhicikitsakāḥ.

44 N10, BF/7.27a - satyadharmaratā ye ca (N4/7.32b, N8/7.53b, Ra/7.32b - snānadānaparā nityaṁ, N7/7.25b - dānadharmaratāḥ satyāḥ, Bo/7.24a - dānadharmaratāś caiva) krodh(c)alobhavivarjjitāḥ.

45 N1/7.22a - devapūjāratā ye ca pitṛbhaktiparāyaṇāḥ.
N4/7.33, N8/7.54, Ra/7.33 - mātṛ(a)pitroḥ paraṁ bhaktā gurupūjāratās tathā atithīn pūjayed ye tu devayajñaratā narāḥ.
N7/7.26a - mātṛpitṛparabhaktā (Bo/7.24b - pitṛbhaktiratā ye ca) gurupūjār(v)atā[ḥ] sadā.
BF/7.27b-28 - pitṛdeveṣu ye bhaktā gurupūjāratāś ca ye
ete pūrveṇa dvāreṇa praviśanti uttamā narāḥ
atithīn arcayantīha sadā devārcane ratāḥ.
Bo/7.25 - te sarve pūrvadvāreṇa praviśanti cottare
atithīn pūjayeyur ye devadvijaprapūjakāḥ.

brahmeśaviṣṇubhaktāś ca tīrthasnānaparāyaṇāḥ[46] [22]
pravrajyāsādhakā ye ca mṛtā ye va vane sthitāḥ[47]
vārāṇasyāṁ mṛtā ye ca prayāgādau ca ye mṛtāḥ[48] [23]
purāṇaśravaṇe bhaktir yeṣāṁ pratidine smṛtāḥ[49]
tadvad bhaktiś ca yā bhaktiḥ kṛtā yaiḥ prativāsaraṁ[50] [24]
atra dāneparāyaṇāḥ vidhinaikādaśīkṛtāḥ[51]
śālagrāmasvadātāro ye ca bhūmipradā narāḥ [25]
harivaṁśapustakaṁ ca tathā bhāgavataṁ dvijāḥ[52]

Devotees of Brahma and Viṣṇu, and worshippers bathing (ritually) in holy places; [22]
Those worshippers of dead wandering (sages), or of those who are still in the forest;
Those who died in Varanasi, and those who died in water or fire; [23]
Those who are devoted to Purāṇa listening, who remember (to do it) daily,
(and) devotees of the speech rite, who practice daily; [24]
Those excellent in food donations here[(XI)], and those who fast twice a month[(XII)];
Those who donate a holy stone[(XIII)], and those who donate lands; [25]
Brahmins who donate the books Harivaṁśa and Bhāgavatta,

---

46 N4/7.34a, N8/7.55a, Ra/7.34a - brahmavādiṣu ye bhaktās tīrthasnānaratās tathā.
N7/7.26b - brahmaviṣṇoś ca ye bhaktā[s] (BF/7.29a - brahmaviṣṇvīśabhaktā ye, Bo/7.26a - brāhmaṇānāṁ ca ye bhaktās) tīrthas(ś)nānaratāś ca ye.

47 Emendation - DS. N1/7.23a - pravrajyāsādhakā ye ca m(s)ṛtā ye (N3/7.41b - naśane tathā) va v(ś)ane sthitāḥ.
N2/7.26a - pravakṣyāsādhakā ye ca mṛtā ye ca v(s)an(o)e sthitāḥ.
N4/7.34b, N8/7.56b, Ra/7.34b - pravrajyā niratāś cānye anāśakamṛtā narāḥ.
N7/7.27a - pravrajyāsādhitā yena anāsinenaṁ bhujite.

48 N1/7.23b - vārāṇasyāṁ mṛtā ye ca mṛtā vanhau jal(o)e 'thavā.
N3/7.42a - vārāṇasyāṁ gogṛheṣu mṛtā vanhau jale ca ye.
N4/7.35a, N8/7.57a, Ra/7.35a - vārāṇasigogṛheṣu prayāgādau ca ye mṛtāḥ.
N7/7.27b - vārāṇasyāṁ gogṛhe caiva jalamagnāś ca ye mṛtāḥ.
Bo/7.26b - vārāṇasyāṁ gograhe ca mṛtās te yānti cottare.

49 N1/7.24a - purāṇaśravaṇe bh(n)ak(r)tir yeṣ(s)āṁ pratidine smṛtāḥ.
Verses 7.24-6 are missing in N3

50 N2/7.27b - tadva[d bha]kt(ar)i[ś] ca yā bhaktiḥ kṛtā y(c)aiḥ prativāsaraṁ.

51 N1/7.25a, N10 - atra dānepraviṇā ye vidhinaikādaśīkṛtā.

52 N1/7.26a, N10 - harivaṁśapustakaṁ ye ca tathā bhāgavataṁ dvijāḥ (vi).

dadaty anyāny api tathā pustakāni viduṣe janāḥ[53] [26]
ete yānty uttaradvāraṁ vrajanty anye 'pi paścime[54]
paradravyaparastrīṣu paravādaparāṅmukhāḥ[55] [27]
ahiṁsakāś ca bhūteṣu viṣṇubhaktiparāyaṇāḥ[56]
yo vāpī nirjale deśe dadāti nirvane dine[57] [28]
prāṇināṁ yo 'bhayaṁ datte ye vārtāsu harer ratāḥ[58]

as well as those who are well versed in books, who donate other books; [26]
(All) those go to the northern gate (of Yama's city), while others go to the western.
Those who turn their backs upon other people's property and wives, and (those who abstain from) gossip; [27]
Those who do not kill animals, excellent devotees of Viṣṇu.
Those who donate land without forests, in the waterless regions of the East. [28]
Those who protect animals(XIV)*, (and) those who are content with the stories of Viṣṇu;*

---

53 N1/7.26b, N10 - dadaty anyās api tathā pustaka(ā)viduṣe janāḥ.
N2/7.29b - dadaty anyāny api tathā pustakāni viduṣe janāḥ (vi).

54 N1/7.27a - teṣāṁ punnarakaṁ dvāraṁ yajanty ante 'p(i)y āśrame.
N2/7.30a - te tu yānty uttaradvāraṁ vrajanty anye 'pi paścime.
N3/7.43a - ete yānty u[t]tare kāle vrajanty anyena paścime.
N4/7.35b-36a, N8/7.56b-57a, Ra/7.35b-36a - praviśanty uttaraṁ dvāram ete b(v)rāhmaṇapuṅgavāḥ
satyavādaikaniratāḥ sadā (BF/7.31a, Bo/7.27a - satyavratadharā ye ca nityaṁ) dharmmaparāyaṇāḥ.
N7/7.30b - ete ca uttare dvāre anye paścimasaṁsthitā.

55 N4/7.36b, N8/7.57b, Ra/7.36b - parāpavādavyavṛttāḥ parastrīṣu na puṁsakāḥ.
N7/7.29b - paradravyam ahiṁsātmā paravādaparāṅmukhāḥ.
Bo/7.27b - paradravyecchāvihīnāḥ (BF/7.32a - paradravyam ahiṁsantaḥ) paranindāparāṅmukhāḥ.

56 N1/7.28a - ahiṁsakāś cābhūteṣu viṣṇubhaktiparāyaṇā[ḥ].
N2/7.31a - ahiṁsakāś ca bhūteṣu me ca viṣṇuparāyaṇā[ḥ].
BF/7.32b, Bo/7.28a - viṣṇubhaktā mahātmānaḥ parastrīṣu na puṁsakāḥ.
Bo/7.28b - nityaṁ dharmakathāsaktāḥ parahiṁsāvivarjitāḥ.

57 N1/7.28b - prācāyī (N10 - yo vāpī) nirjale deśe yo dānaṁ nirvane dine.
Verse 7.28b-29a is missing in N2, N3.

58 N1/7.29a, N10 - prāṇināṁ yo 'bhayaṁ datte yo(r) vārtāsu hare[r] rataḥ.

vrajanti paścimadvāraṁ ye te parahite ratāḥ[59] [29]
durātmāno durācārā duḥśīlā raudrakarmiṇaḥ[60]
asatyavādinaś caiva gurudaivatadūṣaṇāḥ[61] [30]
dattvānutāpabhājo ye na svīkṛtya dadaty api[62]
śivaṁ prasaṅgato 'bhyarcya parārthena tu nātmanaḥ[63] [31]
purāṇavedamīmāṁsāmātāpitṛvinindakāḥ[64]

(All these) proceed to the western gate, as well as those who care for the welfare of others. [29]
Those evil souls, of bad behaviour and character, of terrible deeds,
tellers of lies, as well as those offending teachers and deities; [30]
Those who repent giving possessions, as well as those who do not give at all;
Those who worship Śiva with others' money, and not their own; [31]
Those who despise the Purāṇas, the Vedas, the Mimāṁsā, (as well as their) father and mother;

---

59 N1/7.29b - vrajanti paścimadvāraṁ ye te (N3/7.44b - paścime dvāre rate) parahite ratāḥ.
BF/7.33a - ete paścimadvāreṇa praviṣṭās tu śubhā narāḥ.
Bo/7.28a - ete vai paścime dvāre praviśanti sukhānvitāḥ.

60 N1/7.30a, N2/7.32a, N4/7.39a, N8/7.61a, Ra/7.39a - durātmāno durācāro (N10 - durācārā(ḥ)) duḥśīlā raudraukarmiṇaḥ.
N3/7.45a, N7/7.31a - durātmāno durācārā(ḥ) (BF/7.34b - durācārā durātmāno) duḥśīlā raudrakarmaṇaḥ.

61 N2/7.32b, N3/7.45b, N10 - asatyavādinaś caiva gurudaivatadūṣakāḥ.
N4/7.39b, N8/7.61b, Ra/7.39b - asatyavādino nityaṁ (BF/7.35a - gurudevaparāṅmukhāḥ) gurudevaikadūṣakāḥ.
N7/7.31b - sadācārā satyavacanā gurudevādidūṣakāḥ (vi).
Bo/7.30a - sadānṛtaparāḥ krūrā gurudevavidūṣakāḥ.

62 Emendation - NK. N1/7.31a, N2/7.33a - dattvānutāpa(ṁ)bhājo ye n(o)a [svī](tot)kṛty(vā)a dadaty api.
Verse 7.31 is missing in N3.

63 N1/7.31b - śivaṁ prasaṅgato 'bhyarcy(ā)a parārthena tu cātmanaḥ.

64 N4/7.40a, N8/7.62a, Ra/7.40a - purāṇavedamīmāṁsādharmmaśastraikadūṣakāḥ.
N7/7.32a - purāṇavedamīmāṁs(ś)āmātā(u)pitṛṣu nindakāḥ.
BF/7.35b - purāṇavedasacchāstramātāpitṛvinindakāḥ.
Bo/7.30b - purāṇavedamīmāṁsāmātāpitror vinindakāḥ.

vasanti dakṣiṇadvāre paradrohaparāyaṇāḥ[65] [32]
vedadātus tathā pitroḥ śuśrūṣāṁ na karoti yaḥ[66]
abhaktyā ye kathāṁ puṇyāṁ śṛṇvanti manujādhamāḥ[67] [33]
teṣāṁ puṇyaphalaṁ nāsti duḥkhaṁ syāj janmajanmani
purāṇaṁ ye tv asaṁpūjya tāṁbūlādyair upāyanaiḥ[68] [34]
śṛṇvanti ca kathāṁ bhaktyā daridrāḥ syuś ca pāpinaḥ[69]
kathāyāṁ kīrtyamānāyāṁ ye gacchanty anyato narāḥ[70] [35]
bhogāntare praṇaśyante teṣāṁ dattāś ca saṁpadaḥ[71]
tatra dvāre yathādṛṣṭaṁ tac chṛṇvantu munīśvarāḥ [36]

People extremely deceitful, (all those) dwell at the southern gate. [32]
Those who do not serve the Veda teachers, (nor their) parents,
foolish Manu's descendants[(XV)] *who listen to divine stories without devotion, [33]*
there is no good fruit for them – they will be reborn to suffer.
Those who listen to the Purāṇa divine stories without worshipping with betel nut mixture gifts, [34]
and without devotion, those sinners will be born again poor.
Those who go elsewhere while the stories are being told, [35]
they will perish in grief, along with their wealth.
This is what I saw in that gate, listen to it, O sages. [36]

---

65 N1/7.32b - vasanti dakṣiṇadvāre pare drohaparāyaṇāḥ.
N3/7.46b - viśanti dakṣaṇadvāre paradroharatā narāḥ.
N4/7.40b, N8/7.62b, Ra/7.40b - eteṣāṁ dakṣiṇe dvāre praveśaḥ pāpakarmmiṇāṁ.

66 Verses 7.33-36a are missing in N3.
N4/7.41a, N8/7.63a, Ra/7.41a - mātāpitroś ca ye nindāṁ kurvanty anyāyato 'pi ca.

67 N4/7.41b, N7/7.33a, N8/7.63b, Ra/7.41b - kathayāmi yathādṛṣṭaṁ śṛṇvantu dvijasattamāḥ.

68 N1/7.34b, N10 - purāṇa[ṁ] ye tv a(ṁ)saṁpūjya tāṁbūlādyair upāyanaiḥ.

69 N1/7.35a - śṛṇvanti ca kath(a)āṁ bhaktyā (N10 - bha[k]tavā) daridrāḥ syuś ca (N10 - pāpadaḥ) pāpinaḥ.

70 N1/7.35b - kathāṁ yāṁ kīrtyamānāyāṁ ye (N2/7.38a - tathā yā kīrtyamānāyāya) gacchanty anyato narāḥ.
Half verse 7.35b is missing in N10.

71 N1/7.36a - bhogāntare praṇaś(s)yante (N2/7.38b - praṇaśyanti) teṣāṁ dattā svasaṁpadaḥ.

kṛṣṇājinasamākārāḥ pāpino raudrarūpiṇaḥ[72]
asatyavādinaś caiva gurudaivatadūṣakāḥ[73] [37]
hāhākāraṁ prakurvanti tatra dvāre mayā śrutaṁ[74]
andhakāre mahāraudre kṛmikākaiś ca pīḍitāḥ[75] [38]
lohakaṇṭakatīkṣṇāgrair dvijihvāvyādhivṛścikaiḥ[76]
ṛkṣair vyāghraiś ca siṁhaiś ca dandaśūkādibhis tathā[77] [39]
yamadūtā mahāraudrāḥ pāpinaḥ pīḍayanti ca[78]

Sinners of fierce look, (having) the colour of black deerskin,
the tellers of lies, and those who disgrace teachers and deities[(XVI)]*, [37]*
I heard there at the gate, making wailing sounds.
They were tortured in very thick darkness, by worms and crows, [38]
by sharp-tipped iron thorns, by double-tongued serpents and by scorpions,
by bears, lions and tigers, as well as by snakes and their like. [39]
Yama's fierce-looking messengers also torture the sinners,

---

72 N1/7.37a - kṛṣṇāji(a)nasamākaśaḥ (BF/7.37a - kṛṣṇāji(a)nasamākārāḥ) pāpino raudrarūpiṇaḥ.
N4/7.42b, N8/7.64b, Ra/7.42b - kṛṣṇā(ṁ)ji(a)nasamākārā (N7/7.33b - duḥkhino ghorarūpiṇāḥ) durvṛttāghorarūpiṇaḥ.

73 Almost identical to 7.30b.

74 N4/7.43a, N8/7.65a, Ra/7.43a - hāhākārakarāḥ pāpādaṣṭās tatra sahasraśaḥ.
N7/7.34a - hahārava[ṁ] mahātyugraṁ tasmin dvāre ca viśrutaṁ.
Bo/7.31a - hāhākāro bhavaty ugras tasmin dvāre mayā śrutaḥ.

75 N1/7.38b - andha(ḥ)kāre mahāraudre (N1/7.48b - mahāghore) kṛmikākaiś ca pīḍitāḥ.
N7/7.34b - andha(ḥ)kārair mahāghoraiḥ ś(s)vabhiḥ kākaiḥ kṛmair api.
BF/7.38a - mahāndhakāragahanaṁ śvakākakṛmisaṅkulaṁ.
Bo/7.31 - andha(ḥ)kāram agraṁ ghoraṁ nānāroganiṣevitaṁ.

76 N1/7.39a - lohakaṇṭakatīkṣṇāgre dvijihvāvyādhikārikaiḥ.
N7/7.35a - kaṇṭakair lohatīkṣṇāgraiḥ vyādhisarpaiś ca vṛścikaiḥ.
BF/7.38b - kaṇṭakatīkṣṇajihvograir vyālaiḥ sarpaiś ca vṛścikaiḥ.

77 N1/7.39b, N2/7.42a, N3/7.49a, N10 - ṛkṣ(añj)air vyāghraiś ca siṁ(kṣi)haiś ca dandaśūkādibhis tathā.
N4/7.43b, N8/7.65b, Ra/7.43b - ṛkṣair vyāghrais tathā siṁhair gṛdhraiś cāpi mahāb(v)alaiḥ.
N7/7.35b - ṛcchai[r] vyāghraiś ca siṁhaiś ca gridhādibhir vahas(ś)evitaiḥ (vi).
BF/7.39a - vṛkair vyāghrais tathā siṁhair gṛdhrair nānāvidhair vanyaiḥ.

78 N1/7.40a - yamadūtā mahāraudrā pāpināṁ (N2/7.42b - pāvināṁ, N3/7.50a - pāpinaḥ) pīḍayanti ca.

mudgarair lohadaṇḍaiś ca tathānyair vividhāyudhaiḥ[79] [40]
karṣyanti mahāpāpās tāḍayanti punaḥ punaḥ[80]
tatra dṛṣṭāni ghorāṇi bahuśo narako mayā[81] [41]
yāni saṁkathyamānāni smṛtvā bhītiś ca jāyate[82]
tāny ahaṁ vaḥ pravakṣyāmi śṛṇvantu dvijasattamāḥ[83] [42]
bahusatvasamākīrṇanarakāṇi sahasraśaḥ
ghoraśabdāś ca gaṁbhīrās tatra hāheti sarvaśaḥ[84] [43]

by mallets, iron rods, as well as by other weapons. [40]
They drag the great sinners, whipping them again and again.
I saw there the many horrible quarters of Hell, [41]
that, recalling their stories told at night time, generate fear.
These I shall tell (you), listen, O excellent Twice-born. [42]
Thousands of quarters of Hell, full of many (tortured) beings,
where terrible, painful noises of wailing (are heard) everywhere. [43]

---

79 N4/7.44a, N8/7.66a, Bo/7.32b, BF/7.40a, Ra/7.44a - mudgarais tāḍyamānāś ca lohadaṇḍaiś ca dāruṇaiḥ.
N7/7.36a - tatraiva(i) pāpakarma(ā)ṇāṁ yamadūtā(ma)balāmahāḥ.

80 N1/7.40b - karṣayanti mahāpāpās (N2/7.43b, N10 - mahāpāpaṁs, N3/7.51b - mahāpāśāis) tāḍayanti punaḥ punaḥ.

81 N1/7.41b - tatra dṛṣṭvātighorāṇi b(v)ahuśo (N3/7.51b - narakāṇi me) narakā mayā.
N2/7.44a, N10 - tatra dṛṣṭāni ghorāṇi b(v)ahuśo narako mayā.
N4/7.44b, N8/7.66b, Ra/7.44b - praviśanto mayā dṛṣṭā (BF/7.40b - baddhāś ca yamakiṅkaraiḥ) narā narakasāgare.
N7/7.37a - praviṣṭanto mayā dṛṣṭāḥ kliṣṭatāpatakiṅkaraiḥ.
BF/7.43a - bahūni tatra dṛṣṭāni narakāṇ(n)i sahasraśaḥ.

82 N1/7.42a - yāni saṁkath[y]amānāni smṛtvā bhītiś ca (N10 - jāyata) jāyate.

83 N4/7.46a, N8/7.68a, Ra/7.46a - tān ahaṁ saṁpravakṣyāmi śṛṇvantu dvijasattamāḥ.

84 N1/7.43b - ghoraśaṣṭaś ca (N10 - ghoraśab(v)da(ṁ)ś(a) c(v)a) gaṁbhīrā(ṁ)s tatra hāheti sarvaśaḥ.
N2/7.46a - ghoraśaṣṭaś ca (N3/7.53b - gaṁbhīrās tatra) gaṁbhīrām atra hāheti sarvataḥ.
BF/7.43b - gaṁbhīro 'timahārāvo hāhāraveti dāruṇaḥ.

kuṁbhīpāko vīcimāṁś ca mahārauravarauravau[85]
duḥkhaghoro mahākīṭo mahāvīci sudāruṇaḥ[86] [44]
tāmiśram andhatāmiśraṁ nirucchvāso mahāravaḥ[87]
asipatravanaṁ ghoraṁ taptāṅgārakavālukaṁ[88] [45]
bhakṣyaṁ cakruḥ pate yatra pāpācāro narādhamaḥ[89]

The Kumbhīpāka and Vīcimāt(XVII) *hells, the Raurava and Mahāraurava hells, (hells of) terrible pain, big insects (and) very fierce big waves. [44]*
Tāmiśra and Andhatāmiśra Hells, Nirurucchvāsa and Mahārava.
There is the terrible Asipatra Forest (of sword-like leaves) Hell, and sand of burning coals. [45]
They (i.e. Yama's messengers) make the lowest sinners eat those fallen (sword-like leaves).

---

85 N1/7.44a, N2/7.46b, N10 - kuṁbhī(i)pāko (N4/7.47a, N8/7.69a, Ra/7.47a - mahāghoro) vivīmāṁś ca (N3/7.54 - mahārauravarauravāḥ) mahārauravarauravau.
N7/7.40b - kuṁbhīpāke pañcatīha mahāraudrasvarārave.
BF/7.44a - kuṁbhīpāko mahāghoro mahārauravo rauravaḥ.

86 N10 - duḥkhaghoro mahākīṭo (N3/7.55a - mahāvīrya sudāruṇaḥ) mahāvīci sudāracaṁ.
N4/7.47b, N8/7.69b, Ra/7.47b - duḥkhakārī mahājīrṇo mahādīrghaḥ sudāruṇaḥ.
N7/7.41a - duḥkhādhārī mahākīṭā mahādīrghasudāruṇā.
BF/7.44b - dṛṣṭaś cāpi mahākīṭaḥ atidīrghaś ca dāruṇaḥ

87 N4/7.48a, N8/7.70a, Ra/7.48a - vilocanāntako svaccho nirucchvāso mahāravaḥ.
BF/7.45a - nirapo narakaś caiva nirucchvāso mahārujaḥ.

88 N3/7.56a, N10 - asipatravanaṁ ghoraṁ (N2/7.48a - asipatravajraghoraṁ) taptāṅgārakavālukaṁ.
N4/7.48b, N8/7.70b, Ra/7.48b - asipatraṁ vanaṁ nāma asinādi mahārujaḥ.
N7/7.42a - asipatravane tatra atinādās tathaiva ca.
BF/7.45b - asipatravanaṁ tatra hy atiduḥkhaṁ tathaiva ca.
VP/198.18 - asipatravanaṁ cātra śṛṅgāṭakavanaṁ tathā
tatra śṛṅgāṭakāś caiva taptavālukamiśritāḥ.

89 N1/7.46a - dhānyaṁ cakruḥ pate (N3/7.56b, N10 - dhānyavad bharjate) yatra pāpacāro n(v)arādhamaḥ.
N2/7.48b - dhānyavad bharjate (- - - - -) ye narādhamaḥ.

viṣṭāpūyavahā vāpi kṛmikūpaṁ tathaiva ca[90] [46]
pūrṇā nadītaṭā tatra kūpāś ca kṛmipūritāḥ[91]
viṣṭāpūrṇās tathā kūpāḥ karṇanāsāvikartanaṁ[92] [47]
taptatailaṁ kaṭhāhaṁ ca taptājyasya kaṭhāhakaṁ[93]
aśmapātā mahāraudrāḥ tāmaśīlakaraṁ tathā[94] [48]

There is the Pūyavahā Hell, with a well full of excrement, (and) worms. [46]
There are riverbanks abundant with wells, full of worms (and) excrement, as well as wells full of cut noses and ears. [47]
(There are also) frying pans of boiling oil, as well as frying pans full of melted Ghi. Very fierce stones are falling there, as well as big rocks (and) pebbles. [48]

---

90 Emendation - DS. N1/7.46b - viṣṭāpūyavarāhāpi kṛmikūpaṁ tathaiva ca.
N3/7.57a - viṣṭāpūyadahāś cāpi kṛmicchāvās tathā paraḥ.
N10 - viṣṭāpūyavarāhavāpi kṛtikṛpas tathaiva ca.

91 N2/7.49a, N3/7.57a - pūyapūrṇānadī tatra (N10 - kṛpāś) kūpāś ca (N4/7.49a, N8/7.71a, Ra/7.49a - sakrośā) kṛmipūrītāḥ.
N7/7.42b - pūrṇā nadī tatra kūpātā sarvā kṛmipūrītāḥ.
BF/7.46a - pūyavahanadī tatra kṛmikīṭaprapūrītā.

92 N1/7.47b - viṣṭāpūrṇā[s] tathā kūpāḥ (N2/7.50a - karṇanāsāvikartṛṇaṁ, N3/7.58a, N10 - karṇanāsānikarttanaṁ, BF/7.46b - karṇanāsānirantarāḥ) karṇanāsāvikarcanaṁ.
N4/7.49b, N8/7.71b, Ra/7.49b - viṣṭāpūrṇo mahākūpaḥ (N7/7.43a - vṛṣṭipūrṇās tathā kūpāḥ) karṇanāsāvikartanaṁ.

93 N1/7.48a - taptatailaṁ kaṭhāhaṁ (N2/7.50b - taptatailakaṭhāhaṁ) ca taptāt pajyaka hāṭhakaṁ.
N4/7.50, N8/7.72, Ra/7.50 - mahad bhraṣṭraṁ mahāraudraṁ taptatailaghṛtaṁ tathā
mahātapto mahāśitaḥ kṛmisaṅkulam eva ca.

94 N1/7.48b - aśmapāt(a)ā mahāraudrāḥ mam(p)āśīlakaraṁ (N10 - tāpaśīlakaraṁ) tathā.
N2/7.51a - aśmapāt(a)e mahāraudre tāmaśīlakaraṁ tathā.
N3/7.59a - aś(s)mapātaṁ mahāraudrāṁ tāpasitākaraṁ tathā.
Additional verses - N2/7.51b-52, N3/7.59b-60:
parvatārohaṇaṁ caiva śūlārohaṇam eva ca
evamādīni ghorāṇi narakāṇi sahasraśaḥ
tīkṣṇā(ṁ)tuḍā mahākāyā vāyasāś ca bhayaṅkarāḥ.
N4/7.51a, N8/7.73a, Ra/7.51a - parvatārohaṇaṁ (N7/7.45b - caiva sūlārohaṇa) nāmaśīlārohaṇabhave ca.

siṁhavaktrair mahāraudraiḥ siṁhavyāghrabhayānakāḥ[95]
tatra pāpānṛtācārās tāḍyante vāyasādibhiḥ[96] [49]

iti śrībrahmāṇḍapurāṇe nāsiketopākhyāne narakavarṇano nāma saptamo 'dhyāyaḥ

Very fierce lion faced (animals), like fearful lions and tigers, bite those who behave sinfully and untruthfully. [49]

This is the seventh chapter of the Nāsiketa story, pertaining to the Brahmāṇḍa Purāṇa, called – Hell.

Translation Notes

I – Standing in the midst of 4 fires, facing the sun as fifth.
II – On their hands (?).
III – On their heads (?).
IV – Or – were distinguished by their fiery eyes.
V – Ate according to the moon.
VI – Swimming (?).
VII – Yojana – about 4-5 English miles.
VIII – Yama's name as Time, as well as the name of one of his main servants.
IX – Yama's secretary and account keeper.
X – Literally – "father and mother". In other versions – ancestors.
XI – In the material world.

N4/7.52b, N8/7.74b, Ra/7.51b - ete cānye ca b(v)ahavo narakaḥ santy anekaśaḥ.
N7/7.43b-44a - ataroṣaṁ mahāraudraṁ ghṛtatailo 'śnatā kṛtaṁ kutsavākyaṁ mahāraudratapasītakaraṁ tathā.

95 N1/7.49a - siṁhavaktrā mahāraudrāḥ (N3/7.61a - siṁhavyāghravinādinaḥ) siṁhavyāghrabhayānakā(a)ḥ.
N4/7.53a, N8/7.75a, Ra/7.52a - siṁhavaktrair mahāraudraiḥ siṁhagarjjitaduḥsahaiḥ.
N7/7.48a - siṁhavaktrās tathā raudrāḥ siṁhagarjita duḥsahāḥ.

96 N1/7.49a, N2/7.53b, N10 - tatra pāpānṛtācārās tāḍ(d)ya[n]te (N3/7.61b - vāyasād iti) v(c)āyasādibhiḥ.
N4/7.53b, N8/7.75b, Ra/7.52b - eṣu pāpānvitālokāḥ pātyyante yamakiṅkaraiḥ.
BF/7.52 - tatrāsau nīyate pāpās tāmisre duḥkhabhājane.

XII – On the eleventh day of each fortnight.
XIII – Worshipped by devotees of Viṣṇu. They come from a village (in Nepal), on the Gaṇḍaki riverbank (Monier-Williams).
XIV – Literally – "who make animals unafraid".
XV – The human beings.
XVI – Almost identical to 7.30b.
XVII – A hell of high waves.

Chapter 8

Forms of Sin

nāsiketa uvāca
punaś ca śrūyatām anyad dṛṣṭaṁ yal lomaharṣaṇaṁ[1]
brahmaghnāpi tatra dṛṣṭā goghnāś ca pitṛghātakāḥ[2] [1]
suhṛnmātṛsutaghnāś ca tathā viśvāsaghātinaḥ[3]
doṣaghrāhimahāpāpās tathaiva gurutalpagāḥ[4] [2]

Nāsiketa said
Again, listen to another hair-bristling (thing) that I have seen.
I saw Brahmin killers there, cow killers and father killers, [1]
killers of friend, mother and son, as well as deceitful (people).
Great sinners, susceptible to evil, and those who have sexual relations with the teacher's wife, [2]

---

1 N3/8.1a - punaś ca śrūyatām anyad v(a)ā dṛṣṭaṁ lomaharṣaṇaṁ.
N4/8.1b - śrutāḥ sarvetha dṛṣṭāś (N8/8.76b - sarve sudṛṣṭāś) ca tatra pāpāḥ sahasraśaḥ.
BF/8.1a - śrūyatāṁ mayā dṛṣṭaṁ yad adbutaṁ lomaharṣaṇaṁ.

2 N1/8.1b - brahmaghnāpi tatra dṛṣṭo goghnāś ca pitṛghātakā[ḥ].
N2/8.1b, N10, Bo/8.8a - brahmaghnās tatra me dṛṣṭa (N4/8.2a, N8/8.77a - brahmaghnā madyāniratā, BF/8.1b - brahmaghnāś ca mayā dṛṣṭā) goghnāś ca (N3/8.1b - te vighātakāḥ) pitṛghātakāḥ.

3 N1/8.2a - suhṛnmātṛsutaghnaś (N3/8.2a - suhṛnmātṛ(śca)strī(ṛ)ghnaś) ca tathā viśvāsaghātinaḥ.
N4/8.2b-3a, N8/8.77b-78a - mātṛghnāś ca suhṛdghnāś ca putraghnā (N7/8.2a - garbhapātanā) garbhaghātinaḥ
viśvāsaghātinaś cānye b(v)āladṛddhādighātakāḥ.
N7/8.2b - mitraviśvāsaghāti ca b(v)ālavṛddhās tathā striyaḥ.
BF/8.2a - mātṛghnāś ca suhṛdghnāś ca bālastrīvṛddhaghātakāḥ.
Bo/8.8b - mitraṁ viśvāsya mudyanti ye ca garbhanipātinaḥ.

4 N1/8.2b, N2/8.2b, N3/8.2b, N10 - doṣaghnā hī mahāpāpas tathaiva gurutalpagaḥ.
N4/8.3b, N8/8.78b - paradoṣapravaktāras (Bo/8.9a - strīṇāṁ doṣagṛhītāras) tathaiva gurutalpagāḥ.
N7/8.3a - doṣagrāhī mahāpāpā(ṁ)s tathā ca gurutalpagāḥ.
BF/8.2b - adoṣaghātinaḥ pāpāḥ kṛtaghnā gurutalpagāḥ.

svāmidrohā mayā dṛṣṭā narakeṣu prapīḍitāḥ[5]
vratabhaṅgakarāḥ pāpās tathā dattāpahāriṇaḥ[6] [3]
paradārāratā ye ca ete vai gotraghātinaḥ[7]
ye ca nindanti rājānam api dharmavinindakāḥ[8] [4]
mithyā santi pradātāro mithyā dharmaparāyaṇāḥ[9]

deceivers of master, (all those) I saw tortured in the (quarters of) Hell.
Sinners who break vows, and those who take back given presents; [3]
Those who enjoy others' wives, and destroy families;
Those who disgrace kings, and those who revile Dharma; [4]
False (persons), who adhere to false religions, (all) are taken away.

---

5 N1/8.3a - svāmidroho (N3/8.2b - svāmidrahī) mayā dṛṣṭ(v)ā narakeṣu prapīḍitāḥ.
N4/8.4a, N8/8.79a - svāminām ghātakā dṛṣṭā narā duḥkhena pīḍitāḥ.
N7/8.3b - svāmīghātī may(h)ā dṛṣṭā narā duḥkhena tāḍitā[ḥ].
BF/8.3a - svāmighātī mayā dṛṣṭaḥ paṇyastrīṣu rataḥ sadā.

6 N1/8.3b, N10 - vratabhaṅgakarāḥ pāpā(a)s tathā datāpahāriṇaḥ.
N4/8.4b, N8/8.79b - b(v)rahmabhaṅgakarāḥ pāpāḥ dattādattāpahāriṇaḥ.
N7/8.4a - vratabhaṅgakarāḥ pāpā hānadātṛ nivārakaḥ.
BF/8.3b - vratabhaṅgakarāḥ pāpī pradeyasya nivārakaḥ.

7 N1/8.4a - paradārāratā ye ca ete vai gotraghātinaḥ.
N2/8.4a, N4/8.5a, N7/8.4b, N8/8.80a, BF/8.4a - paradārāratā (Bo/8.9b - paranārīratā) ye ca (N3/8.4a - eva) paradravyābhilaṣiṇaḥ.
Additional verses:
N2/8.4b - tyajyanti (N3/8.4b - tyajanti) ye suvṛttiṁ hi striyaṁ vā b(v)rāhmaṇaṁ tathā.
N2/8.5a - agnidāha(-)tā ye ca ye ca vai gotraghatinaḥ.
N3/8.5a - agnidā garadāś caiva tathā gotrābhighatinaḥ.

8 N1/8.4b, N2/8.5b, N10 - ye ca nindanti rājānaṁ yati (N3/8.5b - dharmavinandakāḥ) dharmavinindakāḥ.
N4/87b, N8/8.82b - rājñāṁ ca nindakā nityaṁ yātī dharmasya nindakāḥ.
BF/8.5 - mitrahā mitraghātī ca vipradrohakaras tathā
rajñāṁ ca nindako nityaṁ yatīnāṁ dharmanindakaḥ.
Bo/8.10a - gobrāhmaṇaparityāgī sadhuvṛttāḥ striyas tathā.

9 N1/8.5a - mithyā santi (N2/8.6a - sakṣi) pradātāro mithyā dharmaparāyaṇāḥ.
N3/8.6a - kūṭa sā kṣipvadātāro kūṭa dharmaparāyaṇāḥ.
N4/8.6b, N8/8.81b - kūṭasākṣipradātāraḥ (BF/8.6b - kūṭasākṣyapradātāraḥ) kūṭakarmakarāś ca ye.
N7/8.7a - kūṭasākṣipradātā ye (Bo/8.11a - kūṭasākṣipradātāraḥ) kūṭakarmaratāś ca ye.

satyaśaucavihīnā ye ramante pāpakarmasu [5]
ruṣyanti duḥkhitaṁ dṛṣṭvā gotrāṇyenopajīvinaḥ[10]
bhūmigehapradātāro devadravyāpahārakāḥ[11] [6]
chedayanti mahāvṛkṣaṁ maṭhakṣetravibhañjakāḥ[12]
dayāhīnā durācāro ye ca dharmaparāṅmukhāḥ[13] [7]
madyapānenasaṁyuktā nityaṁ matsariṇaś ca ye[14]

Those devoid of Truth and purity, content with sinful deeds; [5]
Those who rejoice in seeing suffering, or live upon disgracing;
Those who take away land and houses, and those who steal gods' wealth; [6]
Those who cut down big trees, or destroy field huts;
Those who behave badly, without compassion, and those who turn their backs upon Dharma; [7]

---

[10] N1/8.6a - ruṣyanti duḥkhitā (N2/8.7a - hṛṣyanti duḥkhito) dṛṣṭā [gotra] (vākha)yenopajīvinaḥ.
N4/8.7a, N8/8.82a - anyasmin duḥkhite dūṣṭāḥ dūṣṭe duḥkhaṁ bhajanti ye.
N7/8.7b - duḥkhitāgre ca harṣā ca harṣite duḥkhadāyinaḥ.
BF/8.7a - paraduḥkhena santuṣṭāḥ saukhyaduḥkhākulāḥ sadā.
Bo/8.11b - duḥkhite harṣakārī ca sukhite duḥkhitaḥ sadā.

[11] N1/8.6b - bhūmigehaprahartāro (N2/8.7b - hemadravyāpahāriṇaḥ, N3/8.7b - devadravyāpahāriṇaḥ) devadravyā ca hāriṇaḥ.
N4/8.9b, N8/8.84b, Bo/8.13a - bhūharttā gṛhahartā (N7/8.9a - gṛhaharatā) ca devadravyāpahārakāḥ.

[12] N1/8.7a - bhedayanti mahāv(k)ṛkṣaṁ mahā(jaṁ)kṣe(do)travibhañjakāḥ.
N2/8.8a - chedayanti mahāvṛkṣaṁ maṭhakṣetravibhaṅgakāḥ.
N4/8.10a, N8/8.85a - chedayed yo mahāvṛkṣaṁ kṣetramaryādayā sthitaṁ.
N7/8.9b - vṛkṣān chedaya(ā)te nityaṁ kṣetram aṭha vibhuñjakāḥ.
BF/8.9a - chindanti ye mahāvṛkṣān rājamārgasya karṣakāḥ.

[13] N2/8.8b, N10 - dayāhīnā durācārā ye ca (N3/8.8b - dharme parāṅmukhāḥ) dharmaparāṅmukhāḥ.
N4/8.10b, N8/8.85b - dayāhīna durācārā (BF/8.9b - dharmakarmaparāṅmukhāḥ, Bo/8.14a - dānadharmavivarjitāḥ) duṣṭasaṅgatikarakā.

[14] N1/8.8a, N2/8.8b, N3/8.8b, N10 - madyapān(ṇ)ena saṁyuktā(ḥ) nityaṁ matsariṇaś ca ye.
N7/8.10b - mahāpāpena saṁyutā ceto(a)duṣṭasanātanāḥ.
BF/8.10a - mahāpāpena saṁyuktāś (Bo/8.14b - tathā ye vā kavṛttayaḥ) cetoduṣṭāś ca daṁbhikāḥ.

na śṛṇvanti guror vākyaṁ śāstravārtā na rocate[15] [8]
dānadharmavihīnāś ca paradrohaparāyaṇāḥ
ete cānye mayā dṛṣṭā narakeṣu sahasraśaḥ[16] [9]
viśanto dakṣiṇe dvāre gṛhītā yamakiṅkaraiḥ[17] [10]

iti śrībrahmāṇḍapurāṇe nāsiketopākhyāne pāpavarṇanaṁ nāma aṣṭamo 'dhyāyaḥ

Those who habitually drink wine, as well as those who are always jealous;
Those who do not listen to their teacher, and those who do not like theoretical religious discussions; [8]
Those who do not donate presents according to Dharma, as well as those who are engaged in deceiving others;
(All) those, and others, I saw by the thousands, in the quarters of Hell, [9]
entering the southern gate, seized by Yama's servants. [10]

This is the eighth chapter of the Nāsiketa story, pertaining to the Brahmāṇḍa Purāṇa, called – forms of sin.

---

15 N1/8.8b - tac chṛṇvanti guror vākyaṁ śāstravārtā na rocate.
N4/8.11a, N8/8.86a, Bo/8.15a - na śrutaṁ ca guror vākyaṁ śāstravārttā tathaiva ca.
N7/8.11a - na śṛṇvanti gu(rā)ror vācaṁ śāstrakārttās (BF/8.10b - pitur vākyaṁ śāstravādaṁ) tathaiva ca.

16 N4/8.11b, N8/8.86b - ete cānye ca bahavo narakeṣu vasanti hi.
N7/8.11b, BF/8.11a - hāhābhūtā durācārāḥ satyena ca vivarjitāḥ.
N7/8.12a - eṣāṁ caiva mahā(-)śo ghoraṁ dakṣiṇanirgamaṁ.
N7/8.12a - ete cānye ca b(v)ahavo mayā (BF/8.12a - dṛṣṭā (Bo/8.16a - hy anekaśaḥ) munīśvarāḥ) dṛṣṭāny anekaśaḥ.

17 N3/8.10c - viśanti dakṣi(a)ṇe dvāre gṛhītvā yamakiṅkaraiḥ.
BF/8.12b - atighoratare mārge dakṣiṇe te vyavasthitāḥ.

Chapter 9

The Destruction of Evil-souls

nāsiketa uvāca
ājñaptaiḥ kiṅkarair ghorair dharmarājena dhīmatā[1]
ānītaḥ puruṣaś caikaḥ pāśair baddhvāś ca śṛṅkhalaiḥ[2] [1]
dharmarājasabhāmadye samānītasya kiṅkaraiḥ[3]
śubhāśubhavicāraś ca sabhāsadbhir vidhīyate[4] [2]
dṛṣṭā ca munayas tatra mahātmāno mahātapāḥ[5]

Nāsiketa said
The terrible servants, ordered by Yama, the Wise One,
lead each man by the noose, bound by chains. [1]
The servants bring him to Dharmarāja's assembly hall,
(where) his good and bad (deeds) are discussed by the court judges. [2]
And I saw sages there, great souls, great ascetics,

---

1 N1/9.1a - ādyaiṣaḥ kiṅkarai[r] ghorai[r] dharmarājena dhīmatā.
N3/9.1a - ātaptaiḥ kiṅkarair ghorair dharmarājena ca dhīmatā.
N7/9.1a, BF/9.1a - ājñāpitāḥ kiṅkaras te dharmarājena dhīmatā.

2 BF/9.1b - ānītaḥ puruṣaḥ ko 'pi vicārāya tadagrataḥ.

3 N3/9.1a, N10 - dharmarājasabhāmadye samānītaś ca kiṅkaraiḥ.
N4/9.3a, N8/9.89a, Ra/8.3b - samānayanti bho viprā yamaloke yamāntikaṁ.

4 N4/9.3b, N8/9.89b, Ra/8.4a - tato vicārya te tasya śubhāśubhāmayaṁ kṛtaṁ.
N7/9.2a - teṣāṁ vicāraṁ me dṛṣṭaṁ śrūyatāṁ munisattamāḥ.
N7/9.2b - tatra sthitā mahāprājñā (BF/9.2b - adhitiṣṭhanti tatraiva) śubhāśubhāvicārakāḥ.
BF/9.2a - vicāras tasya me dṛṣṭaḥ śrūyatāṁ dvijasattamāḥ.

5 N1/9.3a - dṛṣṭvā svamunayas tatra hṛtātmāno paraṁ tayā.
N2/9.3a - dṛṣṭā ca munayas tatra (N3/9.3a - mahātmāno dhṛtavratāḥ) kṛṣṇātmāno mahātapāḥ.
N7/9.4a - tat sarvaṁ tatra (BF/9.4a - cāsthāne kathayanti samāsataḥ) saṁsthāne kathyate ca mahātmānaḥ.
Bo/9.3a - sabhāmadhye sthitā ye tu tāñ chṛṇudhvaṁ dvijottamāḥ.

maitreyaḥ sanako 'triś ca cyavano dhiṣaṇas tathā[6] [3]
kṛṣṇadvaipāyanaś caiva jātukarṇyo mahātapāḥ[7]
bharadvājo dadhīciś ca saṁvarto gautamas tathā[8] [4]
mahāmuniś ca durvāso marīcir bhṛgugālavau[9]
sanatkumāraḥ paramaḥ pulastyaḥ pulahaḥ kratuḥ[10] [5]
bhāsuraḥ suprasādas tu yājñavalkyo mahāmuniḥ[11]

Maitreya, Sanaka, Atri, Cyavana, as well as Dhiṣaṇa, [3]
Kṛṣṇadvaipāyana, and even the great Yogi Jātūkarṇya.
Bharadvāja and Dadhīci were gathered there, as well as Gautama, [4]
along with the great sages Durvāsa, Marīci, Bhṛgu (and) Gālava
the great[(1)] Sanatkumāra, Pulastya, Pulaha (and) Kratuh. [5]
(Among them), glowing, very calm, Yājñavalkya, the great sage,

---

6 N1/9.3b, N3/9.3b - maitreyaḥ sanakobhiś ca cyavano dhiṣaṇas tathā.
N2/9.3b - maitreyaḥ sanakotriś ca(ś) pravanadhiṣaṇas tathā.
N7/9.4b - atri ātreye maitreyasanakā ṛṣayas tathā.
BF/9.4b - atrigautamamaitreyā uśanā vākpatis tathā.

7 N2/9.4a, N10 - kṛṣṇadvaipāyanaś caiva jātakarṇo mahātapāḥ.
N4/9.4b, N8/9.90b - kṛṣṇanopāyano (Ra/8.5a - kṛṣṇadvaipāyano) nāma jātukarṇyo mahātapāḥ.
N7/9.5a - kṛṣṇadvaipāyanaś caiva (BF/9.5a - ahnukaṇvau) nāradaś ca mahātapāḥ.
Bo/9.3b - kṛṣṇadvaipāyanaḥ śṛṅgī bharadvājo mahā muniḥ.

8 N1/9.4b - bhāradvājo dadhītiś (N10 - marīciś, N4/9.5a, N8/9.91a, Ra/8.5b - dīdhitiś, N7/9.5b - dadhīcaś) ca saṁvarto gautamas tathā.
BF/9.5b - bharadvājo dadhiś caiva saṁvarto gobhilas tathā.

9 N3/9.5a - mahāmuniś ca durvāsā marīcir bhṛgu[r] gālavaḥ.
N4/9.5b, N8/9.91b, Ra/8.6a - durvāsaś ca mahātejāḥ marīcir bhṛgugālavau.
N7/9.6a - durvāsā[ś] ca ṛṣiḥ prokto (BF/9.6a - mahāśreṣṭho) marīcibhṛgugālavāḥ.
Bo/9.4a - durvāsagautamaś caiva marīcir bhṛgur eva ca.

10 N3/9.5b - sanatkumāraś ca ṛṣiḥ pulastyaḥ pulahaḥ kratuḥ.
N4/9.6a, N8/9.92a, Ra/8.6b - sanatkumārakaś caiva (BF/9.6b - ca tathā) pulastyaḥ kratur (N7/9.6b - pulastikratur) eva ca (vi).
Bo/9.4b - pippalādaḥ pulastyaś ca pulahaḥ sanakas tathā.

11 N2/9.6a - bhāsura(s)ḥ suprasādas tu yājñavalkyo (N10 - jājñavalkyo) mahāmuniḥ.
N3/9.6a - bhāsaś ca yājñavalkyotha (short - lacking a pāda).
N4/9.6b, N8/9.92b, Ra/8.7a - bhāsuraś ca prabhāsaś (N7/9.7a - bhāsuraḥ suraprabhāsaś) ca yājñavalkyo mahāmuniḥ.
BF/9.7a - bhāsuraś ca subhāsaś ca yājñavalkyo munīśvaraḥ.

viśvāmitraś ca māṇḍavyo hārimitrasumitrakau[12] [6]
ete ca ṛṣayaḥ sarve dharmādharmavicārakāḥ[13]
yamasyaiva sabhāmadhye mayā dṛṣṭāḥ sudarśanāḥ[14] [7]
vastrair āveṣṭitāḥ sūkṣmaiḥ padmarāgādibhūṣitāḥ[15]
dvādaśādityasaṅkāśā vedaśāstraviśāradāḥ[16] [8]
chandovyākaraṇādīni śāstrāṇi vividhāni ca[17]
udāharanti te dharme dharmādharma vinirbhayaṁ[18] [9]

Viśvāmitra, Māṇḍavya, Hārimitra and Sumitra. [6]
All these sages were judging the moral and immoral.
I really saw them, good looking, in the midst of Yama's assembly hall, [7]
clad in intangible clothes, adorned with red lotuses etc.,
brilliant like the twelve Ādityas, well versed in Veda and all the branches of knowledge, [8]
chanting treatises on metrics, grammar, and various other branches of knowledge.
Those Dharma experts declare what is right or wrong, without fear. [9]

---

[12] N1/9.6b - viśvāmitraś ca māṇḍavyo (N4/9.7a, N8/9.93a, Ra/8.7b - hārimitras tathā paraḥ) hāri mitrasumitrakau.
N4/9.7b, N8/9.93b, Ra/8.8a - yogeścaraḥ sumitraś ca mahāprabhur athāparaḥ.
N7/9.7b-8a - viś(s)vāmitraś ca māṇḍavyaḥ sarveṣāṁ ca matāntakaḥ hārimitra[ḥ] sumitraś ca yogeścaramahāprabhuḥ.
BF/9.7b - viśvāmitraś ca mārtaṇḍaḥ sarve tiṣṭhanti tatra te.
Bo/9.5 - surabhiḥ suradevaś ca vālmīkiś ca mahātapāḥ
viśvāmitro vasiśthaś ca kratur dakṣo haris tathā.

[13] N2/9.7a - ete ca (BF/9.8b - tatra te) ṛṣayaḥ (N7/9.9a - yamasya sahitā[ḥ]) sarve (N4/9.8a, N8/9.94a, Ra/8.8b - ete cānye ca b(v)ahavo) dharmādharmavicārakāḥ.
Bo/9.6b - yamena sahitāḥ sarve dharmādharmavicāraṇāṁ.

[14] N7/9.8b - ete ca ṛṣayaḥ sarve dṛṣṭā[ś] ca yamaś(s)āsane.
Bo/9.6a - ete cānye ca bahavo mayā dṛṣṭā hy anekaśaḥ.

[15] N7/9.9b - vastrair āveṣṭitā[ḥ] sūkṣmaiḥ padmarāgāvibhūṣitai[ḥ].
BF/9.9a - vastrair nānāvidhair dravyair bhūṣaṇaiś ca vibhūṣitāḥ.

[16] N4/9.8b, N8/9.94b, Ra/8.9a - dvādaśādityasaṅkāśā (N7/9.10a - chando(a)mīmāṁsapāṭhakāḥ, BF/9.9b - śrutimīmāṁsapāragāḥ) vedavedaṅgaparagāḥ.

[17] N7/9.10b - chando(a)vyākaraṇīyāni (BF/9.10a - sevante rājasaṅkīrṇāḥ) ś(s)āstrāṇi vividhāni ca.

[18] N2/9.9b - udāharanti te sarve (N10 - dharmādharmaviniścayaṁ, N7/9.11a - iha yatraiva yat kṛtaṁ) dharmādharmavinirlabhaṁ.
N3/9.9b - udāharanti te dharme (BF/9.10b - sarve) dharmādharmavinirṇaya(ḥ)ṁ.

vadanti saṁmatāḥ sarve dharmaśāstrasya nirṇayaṁ[19]
dharmarājā sa tejasvī teṣāṁ madhye vyāvasthitaḥ[20]
mukuṭena vicitreṇa tathā maṇivibhūṣito[21] [10]
dvādaśādityasaṅkāśo divyakuṇḍalamaṇḍitaḥ[22]
daṇḍahasto mahākayaḥ mahāmahiṣavāhanaḥ[23] [11]
vaivasvato narakeṣu kopasaṁraktalocanaḥ[24]
ājñāpayati pāpānāṁ śikṣārthaṁ ghorakiṅkarān[25] [12]

All together they issue their decision, according to the Dharmaśāstra.
The splendid Dharmarāja is situated in their midst,
wearing a colourful crown, adorned with jewel-ornaments. [10]
Brilliant like the twelve Ādityas, wearing divine earrings,
big-bodied, riding on his big buffalo, holding his stick. [11]
In the quarters of Hell, Yama, with fierce eyes, red from anger[II]*,*
gives orders to his terrible servants, to punish these sinners, [12]

N4/9.11b-12a, N8/9.97b-98a, Ra/8.12b-13a - udāharanti dharmajñā dharmarājāgratas tadā
tato dharmo mahāprajño dharmādharmavicārakaḥ.

19 N1/9.15a, N2/9.15a, N10 - vadanti saṁmatāḥ sarve (N3/9.15a - dharmaśāstra vinirṇayaṁ) dharmaśāstrasya nirṇ(y)ayaṁ.

20 Emendation - DS. N1/9.10a - dharmarāṣṭra labhejādyaḥ yeṣāṁ madhye vyāvasthit(ā)aḥ.
N2/9.10a - dharmarājan ahaṁ tatra samadrākṣ(j)yaṁ vyā[va]sthitaṁ.
N3/9.10a - dharmarāṭ tatra tejaś ca teṣāṁ madhye vyavasthit(ā)aḥ.
N7/9.11b - dharmarājaś ca tatraiva teṣāṁ madhye mahāmuniḥ.
BF/9.11a - dharmarājo 'pi tanmadhye tejorāśivirājitaḥ.

21 N4/9.12b, N8/9.98b, Ra/8.13b - mukuṭena vicitreṇa (N7/9.12a - mastakaṁ maṇibhūṣitaṁ, BF/9.11b - tathā bhāsureṇa virājitaḥ) sadā bhūṣitamastakaḥ.

22 Emendation - DS. N1/9.11a, N2/9.11a, N3/9.8b, N10 - dvādaśādityasaṅkāśo (N4/9.13a, N8/9.99a, Ra/8.14a - maṇikuṇḍalamaṇḍitaḥ, BF/9.12a - divyamaṇḍalamaṇḍitaḥ) divyakuṇḍaladhāriṇaḥ. (Compare with 9.8b).
N7/9.12b - dvādaś(s)ādityasaṅkāś(s)aṁ divyakuṇḍaladhāriṇaṁ.

23 N4/9.13b, N8/9.99b, BF/9.12b, Ra/8.14b - daṇḍahasto mahākayo mahiṣāsanasaṁsthitaḥ.

24 N1/9.13a, N10 - vaivasvato narakeṣu (N2/9.13a - pāryasaṁraktalocanaḥ) pāyasaṁraktalocanaḥ.
N3/9.13a - vivasvataś ca narake kopasaṁraktalocanaḥ.

25 Emendation - DS. N1/9.12a, N10 - ājñāpayan(taṁ) [pā]pānāṁ śā[s]tyarthaṁ d(dh)āruṇ(ony)akiṅkarā(au)n.

yamadūtāś ca tatraiva śāsanakāṅkṣiṇo vibhoḥ[26]
te nirdayās tāḍayanto bruvante pāpakāriṇaḥ[27] [13]
kimarthaṁ bho durācārāḥ pāpam īdṛg anuṣṭhitaṁ[28]
kathāpi na śrutā mūḍhā yamadūtograśāsanā[29] [14]
tatra dharmasabhāmadhye vratasthā bhāskaropamāḥ[30] [15]

and Yama's messengers carry out his orders.
(The servants) beat those sinners mercilessly, saying: [13]
"Why, O bad people, have you committed such a crime?
How come you have not heard of the punishment of Yama's fierce messengers, O fools?" [14]
There, in the midst of Yama's assembly hall, were those who have taken vows, self-restrained, radiant like the sun, [15]

N2/9.12a - ājñāpayantaṁ (N3/9.12a - ātnāpayanta) pāpānāṁ śāstyartha ghorakiṅkarān.
N4/9.14, N8/9.400, Ra/8.15 - yathā sabhyoditaṁ svargabhogārthaṁ dharmakarmiṇāṁ
ājñāpayati dūtāṁstān atisaumya sukhān śubhān.
N7/9.13b - ājñāpayanti pāpānāṁ ś(s)āsti caiva yathocitaṁ.
BF/9.13a - sūryaputro mahābāhuḥ pāpiṣṭhānāṁ bhayaṅkaraḥ.

26 N1/9.12b - yamadūtāś ca te sarve makareṣu (N2/9.12b, N10 - narakeṣu) kṣipanti tān.
N7/9.14a - yamadūtāś ca te sarve kṣayanti narake dhruvaṁ.
BF/9.13b - yamadūtāś ca tatraiva śāsanakāṅkṣiṇo vibhoḥ.

27 N1/9.13b - nird(y)ayāṁs tāḍayantas tān br(y)uvante pāpakarmaṇaḥ.
N2/9.13b - nirdayān pīḍyamānas tān bruvant(a)e pāpakarmaṇaḥ.
N3/9.13b - te nirdayās tāḍayanto bruvante pāpakāriṇaḥ.
N7/9.14b-15a - yamo vrūte 'ti teṣāṁ vai kopenottamalocanāḥ
tatas te nirdayā dūtā tāḍayanti vadanti ca.
BF/9.14-15a - mahogrā bhīmakarmaṇaḥ kopāruṇavilocanaḥ
tatra te nirdayā dūtā daṇḍahastā vadanti ca.

28 N1/9.14a - kimarthaṁ bho durācārāḥ pāpām idṛg anuṣṭhitaṁ.
N3/9.14a - kimarthaṁ te durācārāḥ pāpaṁ tava upārjitaṁ.
N4/9.16b, N8/9.2b, Ra/8.17b - kiṁ bhavadbhir idaṁ pāpāḥ pāpakarmma hy anuṣṭhitaṁ.
N7/9.15b - kiṁ tvayā pāpakarmaṇaḥ etat pāpām anuṣṭhitaṁ.

29 N1/9.14b, N2/9.14b, N3/9.14b - kathāpi na śrutā mūḍhā (yamahantāmaṇaṁ) yamadūtograśāsanāḥ.

30 N3/9.15b, N10 - tatra (N1/9.15b - tava, N2/9.15b - śrutvā) dharmasabhāmadhye vratasthā (BF/9.17a - vratastho bhāskaro yamāḥ) bhāskaropamāḥ.

surūpāḥ sphūṭavaktāro ṛṣayo dīptatejasaḥ[31]
tatas tair gaditaṁ vākyaṁ śrutvā te pāpinaṁ prati[32] [16]
yamājñayā bhṛśaṁ daṇḍair kuṁbhīpāke kṣipanti tān[33]
anye ca pāpinas tatra dṛṣṭāḥ śīghraṁ yathātathaṁ[34] [17]
gohatyā kṛtā yena pacyate vīciraurave[35]

good looking, frank-speaking sages, (shining) in bright luster,
listening to the words spoken to the sinners. [16]
Using sticks, (the messengers), according to Yama's order, throw them (i.e. the sinners) to the unbearable Kuṁbhīpāka (Hell).
I saw there other sinners, quickly (thrown) in exactly the same way. [17]
Those who kill cows are cooked in the (boiling) waves of the Raurava (River).

N4/9.17b, N8/9.3b, Ra/8.18b - evaṁ dharmasabhāmadhye dvijā dṛṣṭaṁ mayādbhutaṁ.
N7/9.17a - iti dharmasabhāṁ ramyāṁ varttate bhāskaro yamāṁ.

31 N1/9.16a - surūpāḥ (N10 - puruṣāḥ) sphuṭavaktā(o)ro ṛṣayo (N3/9.16a - saty(h)avaktāra cākṣuṣo) dīptatejasaḥ.
N7/9.17b - svadhāṁ ca sphūṭavaktā ca ṛṣayā dīptatejasaḥ.
BF/9.17b - surūpā sphūṭavaktāra ṛṣayaḥ sūryatejasaḥ.

32 BF/9.18a - tatas te cābruvan vākyaṁ dūtānītaṁ naraṁ prati.

33 N1/9.17a - yamājñayā tato dūtāḥ kuṁbhī(i)pāke (N10 - kṣipanti taṁ) suduḥ sahe.
Additional verses - N2/9.17b-18:
ha to yena (N3/9.17b - tena) dvijaḥ kopāt kuṁbhīpāke sa (N10 - na) pacyate yamājñayā bhṛśaṁ daṇḍair mudgarair (N3/9.18a - daṇḍamudgarair) abhihanyate nīt(o)aḥ so duḥkhab(v)ahule (N7/9.20b - kuṁbhīpākeṣu duḥsahe) kuṁbhīpāke suduḥsahe.
N4/9.22a, N8/9.8a, Ra/8.23a - yamājñām iti saṁprāpya dūtair daṇḍair nipiḍītāḥ.
N7/9.18b - dharmarājo mahāpāpī kuṁbhīpākeṣu nīyatāṁ.
N7/9.20a - athājñā ca yamasyeyaṁ dūte daṇḍena tāḍītāḥ.
BF/9.20 - athājñayā yamasyāpi dūtair daṇḍena tāḍitaḥ
nīto duḥkhātibahule kuṁbhīpāke durutsahe.

34 N1/9.17b, N2/9.19a - anye ca pāpinas tatra dṛṣṭvā vācā yathātathaṁ.

35 N1/9.18a - gohatyā kṛtā (N2/9.19b - gauhatyākṛtā) [ca] yena (N3/9.19b - gauhatyā ca kṛtā tena) pacyate (N10 - vīcaraurava) vīciraurave.
N4/9.23b, N8/9.9b - goghnāś cāpy atra kṣipyante (Ra/8.24b - tapyante) vīvitrai rauravai bhṛśaṁ.
N7/9.21b - gohatyā ca kṛtā yena avīcīrauravaṁ kṣipet.

strīghātī garbhapātī ca tailayantreṇa pīḍyate[36] [18]
kṣetradārāpahārī ca grāmasīmāvibhañjakāḥ[37]
svāmihantā guror hantā abhakṣyasya ca bhakṣakāḥ[38] [19]
paradravyāpahārī ca chidyate kṣuradhārayā[39]
viśvāsaghātako yaś ca kālasūtreṇa pīḍyate[40] [20]
pacyate gūḍhapākeṣu krakacaiś chidyate tathā[41]

Women killers and those who perform abortions, are tortured by an oil extracting machine, [18]
(as well as) those who steal other people's wives or fields, and those who extend (their fields) beyond the village boundaries,
teacher killers, master killers, as well as those who eat forbidden food. [19]
He who steals other people's property, is cut by a razor's edge[(III)].
Those who breach faith are tortured by black ropes. [20]
Those who hide their cooked food are thus torn apart again and again by crocodiles.

---

36 N4/9.24a, Ra/8.25a - strīghātī garbhapātī (N7/9.22a - parvapātī) ca tailayantreṇa pīḍyate.
BF/9.23 - kālasūtre prapaśyante bālavṛddhopaghātinaḥ
tailayantre prapaśyante krakaśair api daritaḥ.

37 N1/9.19a, N10 - kṣetre dārāpahārī ca grāmasīmāvibhañjakāḥ.
N4/9.26a, Ra/8.27a, N8/9.11a - kṣetradārāpahārī ca sīmā bhañjanakārakāḥ.
N7/9.23b - kṣetraṁ dārāpahārī ca sīmāṁ bhañjanadrohakāḥ.

38 N1/9.19b - svāmihantā guror hantā (N3/9.20b, N10 - abhakṣasya ca bhakṣakaḥ) abhakṣyasya ca bhakṣakāḥ.
N4/9.24b, Ra/8.25b - gurusvāmihato yena chidyate kṣuradhārayā.
N7/9.22b - gurusvāmihantā yena kṣudradhāreṇa chedayet.

39 N1/9.20a - paradravyāpahārī ca (N3/9.21a - grāmasīmāvibhañjakāḥ) cichidy(v)ante 'nusārayā.
N2/9.21b - paradravyāpahārī ca (N10 - [ci]chidyate jusvārayā) chidyate kṣuradhārayā.

40 N1/9.20b - viśvāsaghātake yac ce (N2/9.22a - viśvāsaghātako yaś ca) kālasūtreṇa pīḍyate.
Half verse 9.20b is missing in N3.
N10 - viśvāsaghātako yac ce kālasūtreṇa yāprate.
N4/9.25a, N8/9.10a, Ra/8.26a - viś(s)vāsaghātakā ye ca kālasūtraṁ viśanti te.
N7/9.23a - viśraṁbhaghātakā ye ca kālasūtreṇa pacyate.
Bo/9.14b - pacyate narake ghore kālasūtreṇa sa tu dvijaḥ.

41 N1/9.21a - pacyate gūḍhapākeṣu (N2/9.22b - guḍapākeṣu) krakac(i)[aiś] chidyate tathā.

bahavaḥ śṛṅkhalābaddhās tāḍyamānā nirīkṣitāḥ[42] [21]
dṛṣṭās te munayas tatra dharmādharmavicārakāḥ[43]
citragupto mahātejās taptakāñcanasannibhaḥ[44] [22]
dṛṣṭaś cākhilalokānāṁ puṇyapāpāni saṁlikhan[45]
agamyāgamanā ye ca abhakṣaṁ bhakṣayanti ye[46] [23]
samudravṛttis tenaiva kruddholūkena pīḍyate[47]
cauryopasevinaḥ kecid viṣayāsvādanecchayā[48] [24]

Many are seen properly beaten, fettered by chains. [21]
I saw the sages there, weighing up the right and wrong (deeds),
(and) the lustrous Citragupta, glowing like heated gold, [22]
taking account (of the deeds) of the righteous and the sinners in all the worlds.
Those who eat forbidden food, and (those who) make love with forbidden women, [23]
(as well as) those who take (forbidden) sea journeys, are tortured by angry owls.
Those who serve thieves, with a desire to taste the objects of enjoyment, [24]

N3/9.21b - pacyante guḍapākeṣu kṛkacai(ḥ)ś chidyate tathā.
N10 - pacyata gūḍhapākeṣu krakace chidyate tathā.
Bo/9.10b - guḍapākeṣu pacyante ye ca jīvavihiṁsakāḥ.

42 N1/9.21b - bahava śṛṅkhalā caddhās (N3/9.22a - bahavaḥ śṛṅkhalair b(v)addhvās) tāḍyamān(a)ā nirīkṣitāḥ.
N7/9.24b - b(v)ahavaḥ śṛ(sa)ṅkhalair b(v)addhvā yamasyāgreṇa saṁsthitāḥ.
Ra/9.5a - śṛṅkhalābhir dṛḍhaṁ b(v)addhā ānītā yamakiṅkaraiḥ.

43 N7/9.25a - dṛṣṭās te munivaktāro dharmādharmavicārakāḥ. (Compare with 9.7a).

44 N7/9.25b - citragupto mahātej(o)[ās] taptakāñcanasannibhaḥ.

45 N1/9.23a, N10 - dṛṣṭaṁ cākhilalokānāṁ puṇyapāpā(a)ni saṁlikhan.

46 N1/9.23b - agamyāsu gatau caiva (N2/9.25a - gato yo vai, N3/9.24a - gataṁ yena) tathābhakṣyaṁ ca bhakṣitaṁ. (Compare with 19b).
N10 - agamyāsu gato yo ghi ıathābhatryaṁ ca bhakṣetaṁ.
N4/9.27a, N8/9.12a, Ra/8.28a - agamyāgamanā (N7/9.26b - agamyāgamane) ye ca abhakṣaṁ bhakṣayanti ca.

47 Emendation - DS. N1/9.24a - samudvarta tu te (N2/9.25a - samudvṛtena tan) netre kruddholūkena pīḍyate.

48 Emendation - NK. N2/9.26a - cau(ā)ryyopajīvīka(ṣ)ḥ (N3/9.25a - caurye pāpajīvīn(y)aḥ) kaścid viṣayāsvādanecchayā.
N4/9.27b-28a, N8/9.12b-13a, Ra/8.28b-29a - te pāpās tu durācārāḥ pīḍyante krakacair api
cauryyopajīvīn(y)aḥ kaści(t)d aparan dveṣṭi nirarthakaṁ (vi).

anye ca pāpina eva anṛtāḥ paradūṣakāḥ[49]
nīyante te durācārā ghoreṣu narakeṣu ca[50] [25]
ekākṣarapradātāraṁ yo guruṁ naiva manyate[51]
sa yāti narakaṁ ghoraṁ yasmān na varttate kvacit[52] [26]
vastrāpahāri duṣṭātmā tāmrakāṁsyāpahārakaḥ[53]
kanyāpradāne mūḍhātmā yas tu vighnaṁ samācaret[54] [27]
narake ca sama ghore raurave dhāryate ciraṁ[55]

as well as other sinners, most corrupted cheaters –
these evil people are led to the terrible quarters of Hell. [25]
He who does not heed[(IV)] his spiritual teacher, who taught him the single syllable[(V)],
will reach the terrible Hell, never to return again. [26]
Those evil souls who steal clothes, as well as those who steal copper and brass, (and)
those fools, who obstruct the marriage-arrangements of a girl, [27]
will be upheld for a long time in the terrible Raurava Hell.

---

49 N1/9.25a - aye ca pāpinaḥ pāpādantā cānṛtayadrakāḥ.
N3/9.25b - aye ya pāpinaḥ pāpā (N2/9.26b - datvā vānṛtadūṣakāḥ) adattānṛtadūṣakāḥ.
N8/9.13b, Ra/8.29b - apeyapāyino (N4/9.28b - apeyapātino) eva anṛtāḥ paradūṣakāḥ.

50 N1/9.25b - nīyante te durācāro ghoreṣu narakeṣu ca.
N3/9.26a - nīyante te durācārā(ḥ) (N4/9.29a, N8/9.14a, Ra/8.30a - dūtaiḥ sthānaṁ bhayaṅkaraṁ, N7/9.28b - yatra sthānābhayaṅkarā) ghoreṣu narakeṣu hi.

51 N1/9.26a - ekākṣarapradātār(e)aṁ yoga[ṁ] n(u)a cai(ā)va manyate.
N2/9.27b - ekākṣaraṁ pradātāraṁ yo gurur na hi manyate.
N4/9.29b, Ra/8.30b - ekākṣarapradātāraṁ yo guru[ṁ] naiva manyate.
N7/9.29a - ekākṣaraguruṁ caiva yaḥ kaścin na vimanyate.

52 N1/9.26b - sa yāti (N3/9.26b - narake ghore) narakaṁ ghoraṁ (N7/9.29b - yasmin nāyā(a)ti kadācit) yasmān nāvartate (N4/9.30a, Ra/8.31a - nāyā(a)ti na) kvacit.

53 N4/9.30b, Ra/8.31b - vastrāpahārī duṣṭātmā tāmrakāṁs(ś)yāpahārakaḥ.

54 N1/9.27b, N4/9.31a, N7/9.30, N8/9.15a, Ra/8.32a - kanyāpradāne mūḍhātmā yas tu vighna[ṁ] samācaret.
BF/9.32a - kanyāpradānasamaye ye narā tu vighnakāriṇaḥ.

55 N1/9.28a - narake ca samā ghore raurave dhāryate ciraṁ.
Verse 9.28 is missing in N2.
N3/9.28a - narake ca mahārāve pacyate nātra saṁśayaḥ.
N4/9.31b, N8/9.15b, Ra/8.32b - raurave ca mahāghore narake pacyate ciraṁ.
N7/9.31a - mahārave mahāghore narake dhāryate ciraṁ.
BF/9.32b - mahārauravamadhye te pacyante suciraṁ narāḥ.

viprebhyo dīpadāneṣu yas tu vighnaṁ samācaret[56] [28]
prāṇināṁ ca vratasthānām api vighnaṁ samācaret[57]
śvabhiḥ sa bhakṣyate kṣipto hy asipatravane bhṛśaṁ[58] [29]
dīnāndhaghātino ye ca mitraghnāḥ kūṭacetasaḥ[59]
aṅgāreṣu pratapyante kṣipyante kakṣabhedane[60] [30]
bālānāṁ strījanānāṁ ca vṛddhānāṁ kleśakārakāḥ[61]

Whoever obstructs the donations of lamps to Brahmins, [28]
as well as those who block the space for (free) roaming of creatures,
are eaten by dogs, repeatedly thrown into the forest of sword-like leaves. [29]
Those who kill blind or poor people, as well as those who kill a friend, people of deceitful minds,
are thrown into heated coals, their armpits split. [30]
Torturers of children, women, or old people,

---

[56] N1/9.28b - vi(gh)prebhyo (N10 - dīyamāneṣu) dīpadāneṣu (N4/9.32a, N8/9.16a, Ra/8.33a - dāne ca dīyamāne tu, N7/9.31b - dānena dīyamānena, BF/9.33a - dāne dīyamāne hi) yas tu vighnaṁ samācaret.
N3/9.28b - viprebhyo dīyamāneṣu vighnaṁ yas tu samācaret.

[57] N3/9.29a - prāṇināṁ ca vratasthānām api vighnaṁ karot(u)i yaḥ.
N4/9.32b, N8/9.16b, Ra/8.33b - prāṇināṁ brahmacaryādi tapovighnakaraś ca yaḥ.
N7/9.32a - prāṇināṁ yamacāriṇāṁ upavighnaṅkarāś ca ye.

[58] N1/9.29b - ś(s)vabh(m)i[ḥ] sa bhakṣyate kṣiptau asipatravane (N10 - kṣipto (N3/9.29b - kṣipto hy) asipatraṁ vanaṁ) bhṛśaṁ.
N2/9.30a - śvabhi[ḥ] sa bhakṣite kṣipto asipatre vane bhṛśaṁ.
N4/9.34a - śvānaśva (N8/9.18a, Ra/8.35a - śvābhiś ca) bhakṣyate pūrvaṁ kṣipyate thāsipatrake.
N7/9.32b - [śv]abhi[ḥ sa] bhakṣ(ī)yate(t) so 'pi asipatre vinikṣipet.
BF/9.34b - asipattravane ghore pacyante puruṣādhamāḥ.

[59] N3/9.30a - dīnāndhāgh(y)ātino ye (N10 - ca mitraghnā[ḥ] kūṭacetasā) vai mitraghnā[ḥ] kūṭacedanā.
N4/9.34b, Ra/8.35b - dīnaś ca ghātino yena (N8/9.18b - dīni(n)ṁś ca ghātino ye ca) mitro vā mūḍhacetasā.

[60] N1/9.30b - aṅgāreṣu pratapyante (N10 - kṣipyant(a)e kakṣabhedane) kṣipyante (N2/9.31a - kakṣyaṁ bhedane) kakṣyabhedake.
Half verse 9.30b is missing in N3.

[61] N1/9.31a, N10 - bālānāṁ strījanānāṁ (N7/9.34b - b(v)ālākastrījanānāṁ) ca vṛddhānāṁ (N3/9.30b - vṛdvānāṁ) kleśakārakāḥ.
BF/9.37a - bālastrījanavṛddhānāṁ vañcakāḥ parinindakāḥ.

kūpanadīṣu sahasreṣu bhrāmyante pāpakāriṇāḥ[62] [31]
gurudravyāpahārī ca kṣipyate kṛmisaṅkule[63]
rājānaḥ pāpakarmāṇo yuktāyuktārthavarjjitāḥ[64] [32]
chidyante karapatreṇa prajārakṣāparāṅmukhāḥ[65]
adṛṣṭavārttavaktuś ca utkṛtye te 'kṣiṇī dhruvaṁ[66] [33]
aśrutādbhutavaktuś ca chidyante śravaṇadvayaṁ[67]
nityaṁ pāparatā martyāḥ kṣipyante vīciraurave[68] [34]

(those) sinners will be made to wander in the thousands pits and rivers (of Hell). [31]
Those who steal their teachers' property are thrown into piles of worms.
Sinner kings, who do not distinguish between good and bad, [32]
who neglect the protection of their people, are torn apart by the (sword-like) hand-leaves.
Those who describe anything not witnessed by themselves, their eyes are certainly taken out. [33]
(Likewise), those who describe something not heard by themselves, both their ears are cut off.
Mortals, who are constantly engaged in sin, are thrown into the waves of the Raurava (Hell). [34]

---

62 Emendation - NK. N1/9.31b, N10 - kūponīnāṁ sahasreṣu bhrāmyante pāpakāriṇāḥ.

63 N1/9.32a, N10 - gurudravyā(a)vināsā (N4/9.35b, N8/9.19b, Ra/8.36b - gurudravyā(a)pahārī, N7/9.35a - gurudravyā(a)vināsī) ca kṣipya[n]te kṛmisaṅkule.
BF/9.37b - gurudravyāpahāriṇaḥ paśyante kṛmisaṅkule.

64 N1/9.32b - etān naḥ pāpakarmāṇo yuktāyuktārthavarjitā[ḥ].
N4/9.36a, N8/9.20a, Ra/8.37a - rājakaḥ pāpamūḍhātmā yukto 'yuktaṁ na vedasaḥ.
BF/9.38a - ye cānye pāpakarmāṇaḥ kṛtyākṛtyāvicarakāḥ.

65 N2/9.33b - chidyante karapatreṇa prajārakṣyaparāṅmukhāḥ.
N10 - kṣipyante karapatreṇa prajārakṣaparāṅmukhā[ḥ].
BF/9.38b - bhidyante karapatreṇa prajārājaparāṅmukhāḥ.

66 N1/9.33b, N10 - adṛṣṭavā[r]tavaktuś ca utkṛtye te 'kṣiṇī dhruvaṁ.
N3/9.33a - adṛṣṭavārttavaktāś ca utkṛtye t(y)e kṣaṇī dhruvaṁ.
N4/9.37a, N8/9.21a, Ra/8.38a - adṛṣṭārthām avaktāro netrotpāṭanabhājanāḥ.

67 N1/9.34a - aśrutādbhutavaktaṁś cākṣipyate śravaṇadvayaṁ.
N4/9.37b, N8/9.21b, Ra/8.38b - aśrutaṁ śrāvayanto 'nye karṇachede vasanti ca.
N7/9.37a - aśrutādbhutavādi ca karṇair dvai chedyate api.

68 N1/9.34b, N10 - nityaṁ pāparato martyaḥ kṣipyate vīciraurave.
N7/9.37b - nityaṁ pāparatā ye ca (BF/9.40a - kumbhīṁ vā rauravaṁ gatāḥ) avīci(a)rauravaṁ kṣipet.
Bo/9.20a - sadā pāparatā ye tu kṣipyante raurave dhruvaṁ.

yo vai nakte kṛtasnāno vaiśvadevaṁ vinā dvijaḥ[69]
kṣipyate sa sakṛt kūpe pāvakāhutasaṁsrave[70] [35]
devasvaṁ caiva brahmasvaṁ ye harante narādhamāḥ[71]
sūcimukhe mahāghore pacyante te narādhamāḥ[72] [36]
paradārābhilāṣī ya eṣa brāhmaṇadūṣikaḥ
dūṣayed dharmaśāstrāṇi tīrthāni na ca manyate[73] [37]

A Brahmin who takes (a forbidden) bath at night, neglecting the all-gods rite,
is immediately thrown into a pit of burning oil. [35]
Those who steal something belonging to the gods or to Brahmins,
those lowest of people are roasted in the very terrible needle-mouth hell. [36]
Those who desire other people's wives and those who disgrace Brahmins,
degrading the Dharmaśāstras and not believing in holy places, [37]

---

69 N10 - yo vai nakte (N3/9.34b - mukte) kṛtasnāno vaiśvadevaṁ vinā dvij(t)aḥ.
N4/9.38a, N8/9.22a, Ra/8.39a - aś(s)nātā bhuñjate ye ca vinā ca ha vanakriyāṁ.
N7/9.38a - ye vai bhuñjati cāśnātā āhutī[ṁ] vinā dvijāḥ.
BF/9.20b - ye tu nirmantrabhoktāro vaiśvadevavivārjitāḥ.

70 N1/9.35b - kṣipya(n)te sa sakṛt kūpe (N3/9.35a - yāvad āhu(ū)tasaṁsravaṁ) pāvakāhutasaṁbhavaṁ.
N4/9.38b, N8/9.22b, Ra/8.39b - viṣṭākūpe sthitāste vai yāvad āhu(ū)tasaṁplavaṁ.
BF/9.21a - viṣṭakūpeṣu patitā mayā dṛṣṭā adhomukhāḥ.

71 N1/9.36a - daivas taṁ caiva brahmaghnaṁ (N2/9.36b - devaś ca brāhmaś ca[iva] ghnaṁ) ye haranti narādhamāḥ.
N4/9.39a, N8/9.23a, Ra/8.40a - ye narā brahmadevasvaṁ lobhamūḍhā haranti hi.
N7/9.39a - ye narā devabrahmasvamadhupā ya haranti ca.
BF/9.41b - ye vātha brahmadevasvaṁ dhanaṁ vāpi haranti ye.

72 N4/9.39b, N8/9.23b, Ra/8.40b - sūcimukhe mahāghore pacyante te (N7/9.39b - durātman(ā)aḥ) durāsade.
BF/9.42a - sū(u)cīmukhair mahāghorair bhujyante kṛmibhiś ca te.

73 N1/9.37b - dūṣayed dharmaśāstrāṇi tīrthādi (N3/9.36b - dharmaśāstrāṇi tīrthāni vṛddhāni) na ca manyate.
N4/9.40, N8/9.24, Ra/8.41 - paradārābhilāṣī ca (N7/9.40a, BF/9.42b - devabrāhmaṇadūṣakāḥ) vedabrāhmaṇadūṣakāḥ
dūṣayed dharmaśāstrāṇi tīrthāni (N7/9.40b - na vimanyate) ca na manyate.
BF/9.43a - dveṣṭi yo dharmaśāstrāṇi tīrthāni ca na manyate.
Bo/9.21b - dūṣayed dharmaśāstrāṇi tīrthānindāṁ karoti yaḥ.

śūlake ropyate pāpī śvabhiḥ kākaiś ca bhakṣyate[74]
ciraṁ bhuktvā ca yo nārīm iṣṭāṁ prāṇapriyāṁ śubhāṁ[75] [38]
tyajate yo durācāraḥ karapatreṇa chidyate[76]
pacyate narake ghore pāvakāhutasaṁbhave[77] [39]

iti śrībrahmāṇḍapurāṇe nāsiketopākhyāne
pāpātmanāṁ nāśanavarṇanaṁ nāma navamo 'dhyāyaḥ

those sinners are fixed on stakes, and eaten by dogs and crows.
He who enjoys a beloved beautiful woman for a long time, and [38]
then abandons her, that sinner is torn apart by (sword-like) leaf-hands,
(and) roasted in the fire of the terrible Hell. [39]

This is the ninth chapter of the Nāsiketa story, pertaining to the Brahmāṇḍa Purāṇa, called – the destruction of evil-souls.

Translation Notes

I – Literally – greatest, superior.
II – Originally – N1/9.13a.
III – The metaphor of KU/3.14b is here a realistic description. "The Razor's Edge" – the name of S. Maugham's book – is taken from the original metaphor.
IV – Or neglects, and thus insults him.
V – The sacred syllable "Om".

---

74 N1/9.38a, N10 - śūlake vyapyate pāpaḥ (N3/9.37a - śūlake ropyate pāpī, N4/9.41a, N8/9.25a, Ra/8.42a - śūle vyāropyate śīghraṁ) śvabhiḥ kākaiś ca bhakṣyate.
BF/9.43b - śūlapṛṣṭhair mahākākaiḥ śvabhir api sa bhakṣyate.

75 N1/9.38b, N3/9.37b - ciraṁ bhukt[v]ā ca (N4/9.41b, N8/9.25b, Ra/8.42b - cirabhuktāṁ tu) yo nārīm (N2/9.39a - dārām) iṣṭāṁ prāṇap[r]iyāṁ śubhāṁ.
BF/9.44a - ciraṁ bhaktāṁ caiva nārīm sadā prāṇādhikāṁ satīṁ.

76 N4/9.42a, N8/9.26a, Ra/8.43a - tyajet so 'pi durācāraḥ karapatreṇa pīḍyate.
N7/9.42 - tyajate vai durācārāḥ karapa(e)treṇa chedyate.
BF/9.44b - tyajate yo durācāraḥ karapattraiḥ sa bhidyate.

77 N1/9.39b, N3/9.38b, N10 - pacyate narake ghore pāvakāhutasaṁbhavaṁ.

Chapter 10

The Beautiful Story

nāsiketa uvāca
aparaṁ ca mayā dṛṣṭaṁ paramaṁ lomaharṣaṇaṁ[1]
śṛṇvantu munayaḥ sarve indrajālopamaṁ tv idaṁ[2] [1]
narakāś ca mayā dṛṣṭā jvalantas tīvratejasaḥ[3]
hriyante pāpinas teṣu virūpā dīnacetasaḥ[4] [2]

I saw there another hair-bristling thing,
listen, all sages, to what Indra's magic is like. [1]
I saw quarters of Hell, burning with intense heat.
Miserable-minded, deformed sinners were brought there, [2]

---

[1] N1/10.1a, N3/10.1a, N10, BF/10.1a - aparaṁ yan mayā dṛṣṭaṁ paramaṁ lomaharṣaṇaṁ.
N2/10.1a - aparaṁ ca mayā dṛṣṭaṁ (N4/10.1a, N8/10.39a, Ra/9.1a - romaharṣaṇam uttamaṁ) mahāntaṁ (N7/10.1a - romaharṣaṇaṁ) lomaharṣaṇaṁ.
Bo/10.1a - ataḥ paraṁ mayā dṛṣṭaṁ mahata(ā)ṁ romaharṣaṇaṁ.

[2] N2/10.1b - śṛṇvantu ṛṣayaḥ sarve (N4/10.1b, N8/10.39, Ra/9.1b - vakṣyāmy aham aśeṣataḥ, N7/10.1b - indrajālopa(i)maṁ tv idaṁ) mādṛśaṁ lomaharṣaṇaṁ.
BF/10.1b - śṛṇvantu munayaḥ sarve indrajālopamaṁ hi tat.
Bo/10.1b - adbhutaṁ tu śṛṇudhvaṁ bho munayo samāgatāḥ.

[3] N1/10.2a, BF/10.2a - narakā(a)ś ca mayā dṛṣṭā(aṁ) (Bo/10.2a - jvaladagnisamaprabhāḥ) jvalantas (N2/10.2a - taptatejasa(ṁ)ḥ, N3/10.2a, N10, N7/10.2a - tāmratejasaḥ) tīvratejasaḥ.
N4/10.2, N8/10.40, Ra/9.2 - kvacit atra mayā dṛṣṭā bhūmis tāmramayīpurā adhas tasyā mahān agniḥ jvalaty aviratam budhāḥ.

[4] N1/10.2b - h[r]iyante pāpinas teṣu virūpā dīnicetasaḥ.
N2/10.2b - pāpātmānaś ca dahyante (N7/10.2b - pāpātmānauha sthitās tatra) virūpā[ḥ] pāpākarmaṇaḥ.
N3/10.2b - hūyante pāpinas te hā virūpā dīnacetasaḥ.
BF/10.2b - dahyante pāpakarmāṇo virūpās tatra karmaṇā.
Bo/10.2b - pāpino yatra dahyante yamadūtair anekadhā.

ūrdhvakeśā mahākāyās tīkṣṇadaṁṣṭrā bhayāvahāḥ[5]
tīkṣṇāni nakhalomāni sūcivaktrā bhayaṅkarāḥ[6] [3]
dṛṣṭās te śṛṅkhalair baddhvā ānītā yamakiṅkaraiḥ[7]
daṇḍaiś ca tāḍyamānās te suvilāpāturā bhṛśaṁ[8] [4]
dūtaiś ca kleśitāḥ pāpāḥ patitā bhuvimaṇḍale[9]
dhāvantaś ca mayā dṛṣṭā gṛhītāś caiva nirdayaṁ[10] [5]

their bodies (very) big, their hair standing erect, fearsome, with sharp teeth,
having sharp hair and nails[(I)]*, pointed faces*[(II)]*, dreadful*[(III)]*. [3]*
I saw them bound with chains, led by Yama's servants,
beaten again and again by sticks, suffering heavily. [4]
Hurt by the messengers, the sinners fall on the ground.
I saw them running (away and) then caught mercilessly again. [5]

---

5 N1/10.3a, N4/10.4, N8/10.42, Ra/9.4a - ūrdhvakeśā mahākāyā[s] (N7/10.3a - tīkṣṇakeśā) tīkṣṇadaṁṣṭr(a)āḥ (N2/10.3a, N3/10.3a - bhayākarāḥ, N10 - mayāvahāḥ, BF/10.3a - bhayānakāḥ, Bo/10.3a - bhayaṅkarāḥ) bhayāvahāḥ.

6 N4/10.4, N8/10.42, Ra/9.4b - sutīkṣṇanakharomāṇaḥ sūcivaktrāḥ sahasraśaḥ.
N7/10.3b - tīkṣṇāni nakhalomāni sūcīvaktrā bhayaṅkarāḥ.
Bo/10.3b - vakratīkṣṇanakhāgrāś ca (BF/10.3b - dīrghāṅghriṇakharomāṇaḥ) sūcivaktrā bhayaṅkarāḥ.

7 N1/10.4a - dṛṣṭvās (N10 - dṛṣṭās) te (N2/10.4a - me) śṛṅkhalair (N3/10.4a - vaṅkhalair) baddhvā ānītā yamakiṅkar(ā)aiḥ.
N7/10.4a - dṛṣṭās te śṛ(sa)ṅkalair (N4/10.5, N8/10.43, Ra/9.5a - śṛṅkhalabhir dṛṭhaṁ) b(v)addhvā (BF/10.4a - baddhā) ānītā yamakiṅkaraiḥ.

8 N2/10.4b - daṇḍais tu hanyamānās te vipule (-)āturāvahā.
N4/10.5, N8/10.43, Ra/9.5b - yamadaṇḍais tāḍitās te patanti ca punaḥ punaḥ.
BF/10.4b - mudgarais tāḍyamānās te vilapantaḥ sudāruṇaṁ.

9 N1/10.5a - dūtaiś ca kleśitāḥ (N10 - dyāya) pāpā[ḥ] (BF/10.5a - patitāḥ punar utthitāḥ) patitā (N7/10.5a - dharamaṇḍale) bhuvimaṇḍale.
N2/10.5a - dūtaiś ca kleśitāḥ pāpā(aiṣ)ḥ patitā bhumīmaṇḍale.

10 N1/10.5b - dhāvantaś ca mayā dṛṣṭ(v)ā (N2/10.5b - gṛhītvā caiva nirdayaiḥ) gṛhītas te ca nirdayaṁ.
N3/10.5b - dhāvantaś ca mayā dṛṣṭā (BF/10.5b - gṛhītvā nigaḍitāpi) gṛhītas (N7/10.5 - tena nispṛhā) te va nirdayaiḥ.
N4/10.6a, N8/10.44a, Ra/9.6a - dhāvantī taṁ tataś cāpi vadyante ca punar dṛṭhaṁ.

tatra lohamayā rambhā surūpā ca subhūṣitā[11]
agninā jvālāvatī ca ānītā pāpino 'grataḥ[12] [6]
re re pāpa mahāmūḍha parastrīlampaṭo 'bhavaḥ[13]
iyaṁ sā yoṣid apy atra ānītā tava kāraṇāt[14] [7]
āliṅgaya yathāsnehaṁ satvaraṁ hṛṣṭacetasā[15]
etat saukhyaṁ tvayā pūrvam āhṛtaṁ svena karmaṇā[16] [8]

An iron-made beautiful courtesan, highly decorated,
and blazing with fire, was brought there before the sinner. [6]
"O sinner(IV)*, great fool, you used to chase other people's wives.*
Here is this woman, brought here for you, because of your (sinful) deeds. [7]
Embrace her with love, quickly, happy at heart, (since)
you used to steal this kind of comfort from others, in the past". [8]

---

11 N1/10.6a - tatra lohama(i)yā rambhā surūpā cakṣubhūṣitāḥ.
N2/10.6a - tatra lauhamayā[ḥ] stambhā(s)ḥ surūpāś ca sudhāṭikāḥ.
N3/10.6a - tatra mohamayā rambhā svarūpā ca subhūṣitā(ḥ).
N10, BF/10.6a - tatra lohamayī rambhā (N7/10.6a - svarūpā ca sughāṭikā) surūpā ca subhūṣitā.
N4/10.6b, N8/10.44b, Ra/9.6b - tatra madhye tāmrabhūmau stambho lohamayo mahān.

12 N1/10.6b, BF/10.6b - agni(ma)nā jvalavatī ca ānītā pāpino 'grataḥ.
N2/10.6b - agninā jvalitā madhye ānītāḥ pāpino narāḥ.
N4/10.7a, N8/10.45a, Ra/9.7a - jvālāmālā parīvṛto dāruṇo 'sti tapasvinaḥ.
N7/10.6b - agnimadhye jvalantī ca tv ānītā duṣṭacetasāṁ.

13 N1/10.7a, N10 - re re pāpa mahāmūḍha parastrīlampaṭo (N3/10.7a - 'bhavat) bhavaḥ.
N2/10.7a - re re pāpā[ḥ] t(mi)īvrā mūḍhāḥ parastrīlampaṭā bhuvi.
N4/10.8b, N8/10.46b, Ra/9.8b - re re pāpātmakā mūḍhāḥ parastrīlampaṭāḥ sadā.
BF/10.7a - re re pāpa mahāmūḍha parastrīlampaṭamanaḥ.

14 N1/10.7b - iyaṁ s(a)ā yoṣid apy atra ānītā bhavakāraṇāt.
N2/10.7b - imaṁ hi yoṣitā 'py atra svānītāḥ kāraṇāt tava.
N3/10.7b - iyaṁ sā yoṣitāpy atra ānītā tavakāraṇāt.
N4/10.9a, N8/10.47a, Ra/9.9a - eṣā sā parayoṣātra samānītā bhavatkṛte.
BF/10.7b - iyaṁ yoṣid atrānītā tava kāmaparāyaṇā.

15 N4/10.9b, Ra/9.9b - āliṅgyatāṁ yathā pūrvaṁstaṁ bho 'yaṁ (N8/10.47b - hrutamanase) drutamanasaiḥ.
BF/10.8a - āliṅgaya tāṁ snehena satvaraṁ hṛṣṭacetasā.

16 N1/10.8b, N10, BF/10.8b - etat saukhyaṁ tvayā̱ pūrvam āhṛtaṁ (N3/10.8b - sāhasaṁ) svena karmaṇā.
N2/10.8b - iti saukhyaṁ tvayā sarvaṁ ānītā(s)ḥ sarvakāraṇāt.

yadā nāliṅgate so 'pi tadā daṇḍena tāḍyate[17]
evaṁ dṛṣṭā mayā tatra narakeṣu sahasraśaḥ[18] [9]
hanyamānā nīyante vihvalā bhayavyākulāḥ[19]
tatra te yamadūtaiś ca śāsyante dharmavarjitāḥ[20] [10]
madyapānaratā ye ca abhakṣyasya ca bhakṣakāḥ[21]
pānārthaṁ tailamat piṣṭaṁ tebhyo dutaiḥ pradīyate[22] [11]

If he does not embrace her, then he is beaten by stick.
I really saw (such cases) by the thousands there, in the quarters of Hell. [9]
They are beaten while being led, confused and frightened,
those devoid of righteousness, punished by Yama's messengers. [10]
Those who drink alcohol, and those who eat forbidden food,
are given to drink (hot) oil mixed with ground flour, by the messengers, (that) [11]

---

17 N1/10.9a - yadā nā(ṁ)liṅgate tāṁ sa (N3/10.9a - yathā nāliṅgate 'tīva) tadā daṇḍena (N10 - daṇḍyate) tāḍyate.
N2/10.8c - yadā nāliṅgite so 'pi tadā daṇḍena (N7/10.7b - hanyate) tāḍyate.
N4/10.11a, N8/10.49a, Ra/9.11a - nāliṅganti tadā b(v)adhvā tāḍyante daṇḍamudgaraiḥ.
BF/10.9a - yadā nāliṅgate tāṁ sa tadā daṇḍena tapyate.

18 N1/10.9b - evaṁ dṛṣṭ(v)ā (BF/10.9b - dṛṣṭā) mayā tatra narakeṣu sahasraśaḥ.
N2/10.9a - sva dṛṣṭāś ca tadā tatra hy anekāś ca sahasraśaḥ.
N3/10.9b - evaṁ dṛṣṭā mayā tatra (N7/10.8a - anekāni sahasraś(s)aḥ) narake śatasahasraśaḥ (vi).

19 N2/10.9b - hanyamānāś ca niśśaṅkavikalā bhayavyākulā[ḥ].
N3/10.10a - hanyamānāś ca nīyate vihvalā[ḥ] subhayākulā[ḥ].
N7/10.8b - hanyamānāś ca nīyante (N10 - vihvalā(ḥ)s tu bhayākulā[ḥ]) vihvalā bhayahākulāḥ.

20 N1/10.10b, N10 - tatra te rājña dūtaiś ca śāsyante dharmavarjitā[ḥ].
N2/10.10a - tatra vai yamadūtais te (N7/10.8b-9a - yamadūtaiś ca) sādhyante dharmavarjitā[ḥ].

21 N1/10.11a - madyapānakṛte (N10 - madyapānakṛto) y(ā)e ca abhakṣasya ca bhakṣakāḥ. (Compare with 9/19b, 9/23b).
N2/10.10b - madyapānaratā ye cābhakṣyān bhakṣayanti yena.
N3/10.11a - madyapānakarā ye ca abhakṣasya ca bhakṣiṇaḥ.
N4/10.12b, N8/10.50b, Ra/9.12b - madyamāṁsaratā ye ca abhakṣyasyāpi bhakṣakā[ḥ].
BF/10.11a - madyapānakarā ye ca abhakṣyaṁ bhakṣayanti ye.

22 N1/10.11b, N10 - pānārthaṁ tailamat pi(a)ṣṭaṁ te(a)bhyo (N3/10.11b - dūtai(s)ḥ pr(t)adīyate) dūtair ha dīpyate.

pītamātreṇa tenaiva dagdhāṅgāni patanti te[23]
prārthayanti ca te chāyāṁ dāhadīnā bhayāturāḥ[24] [12]
nīyamānāś ca tair dūtair asipatravanāntare[25]
patanti tālapatrāṇi gātrachedo vidhīyate[26] [13]
pipāsāmūrcchāśokena vaktum api na śaknuyuḥ[27]
kathañcit te samutthāya pralapanti sudīnavat[28] [14]

by just drinking it, they really fall down, their limbs burning.
Miserably burning hot, and afraid, they beg for shade. [12]
They are brought by those messengers, into the iron-leaves forest.
The palm-like leaves fall and usually cut off their legs. [13]
Thirsty, powerless and faint with wretchedness, unable even to speak,
somehow, rising up, they lament, being very miserable. [14]

N2/10.10c - ha duṣṭaṁ tatas tailaṁ pācay(yac)anti vadanti (short).
N4/10.13a, N8/10.51a, Ra/9.13a - tailaṁ teṣāṁ mahātaptaṁ pātuṁ dadati kiṅkarāḥ.
BF/10.11b - pānārthaṁ tailam atyuṣṇaṁ tebhyo dutaiḥ pradīyate.

[23] N1/10.12a - pītamātreṇa (N3/10.12a, N10 - patanmātreṇa) tenaiva da[g]dh(v)āṅgāni patanti te.

[24] N1/10.12b - prāpayanti ca te chāyāṁ dagdhādīnāṁ bhayāturāḥ.
N3/10.12b - prārthayanti ca tvaritā dagdhādīnā bhayāturāḥ.
N10 - prārthayanti (BF/10.12b - prārthayante) ca te chāyāṁ dāh(dy)ādīnā bhayāturāḥ.

[25] N1/10.13a - nīyamānāś ca tair (N2/10.12a - nīyamānās tadā) dūtair asipatravanāntare.
N4/10.14b, N8/10.52b, Ra/9.14b - tadā nayanti tān dūtā asipatravanāntare.
BF/10.13a - nīyamānās tato dūtair dāruṇaiś ca vanāntaraṁ.

[26] N1/10.13b, N10 - patanti tāl(kṣ)avṛkṣais te (N2/10.12b - tālapatrāṇi) gātrach(v)edo 'bhidhīyate.
N3/10.13b - patanti tālavṛkṣais tai[r] gātrachedo vidhīyate.
N4/10.15a, N8/10.53a, Ra/9.15a - patanti tāni patrāṇi tīkṣṇāny asimayāni ca taiḥ.
BF/10.13b - patadbhis tālavṛkṣaiś ca gātrachedaḥ prajāyate.

[27] N2/10.13a - mṛtāś ca patitā bhūmau ś(s)vāsenocch[v]āsate tataḥ.
BF/10.14a - pipāsāmurcchāśokena vaktum api na śaknuyuḥ.

[28] N1/10.14b - kathañc(v)i[t] te samutthāya pralapanti (BF/10.14b - sudinatvaṁ) sadīna va.
N2/10.13b - tataḥ ūrdhvapraviṣṭāś ca utthitāḥ pralapanti ca.
N7/10.11b - tata(ḥ)ś cātmā praviśyanti cotthitā pralapanti ca.

evaṁ vai kliśyamānās te dṛṣṭās tatra sahasraśaḥ[29]
kūṭasākṣyapradātāraḥ kūṭadharmaratāś ca ye[30] [15]
nīyante narake ghore śiraś chitvā durātmanaḥ[31]
prāṇināṁ ghātako yas tu tailayantreṇa pīḍyate[32] [16]
duḥkhadāyī naro yas tu vyādhikūpe viniḥkṣipet[33]
ghṛtacoro ghṛte tapte taile tailasya hārakaḥ[34] [17]

Such distressed (sinners), I saw there by the thousands.
Those who bear false witness, as well as those engaged in deceitful deeds, [15]
those evil-souls are brought headless, to the horrible Hell.
Animal killers are tortured by an oil-extracting machine. [16]
Whoever inflicts pain is thrown into a well infected with disease.
One who steals Ghi, is burnt in Ghi, (and) one who steals oil – in oil. [17]

---

29 N1/10.15a - taś ca vai kliśyamānais te dṛṣṭ(v)ās tatra sahasraśaḥ.
N2/10.14a - evaṁ vai kliśyamānas te dṛṣṭā anye (N3/10.15a, N10 - dṛṣṭ(v)ās tatra) sahasraśaḥ.
N7/10.12a - evaṁ vai kliṣṭamānaś ca dṛṣṭāś ca va sahasraś(s)aḥ.
BF/10.15a - śvabhir vai kliśyamānās te dṛṣṭās tatra sahasraśaḥ.

30 N1/10.15b - kasmāt kṣiptā(a)ś ca dātāraḥ kūṭadharmaratāś ca ye.
N2/10.14b, N7/10.12b - kūṭasakṣipradātār(o)[aḥ] (BF/10.15b - kūṭasākṣyapradātāraḥ) kūṭakarmaratāś ca ye.
N3/10.15b - kūṭaśādipradātāra[ḥ] kūṭadharmaratāś ca ye.

31 N1/10.16a - nīyate makare (N3/10.16a - narake) ghore śira(i)ś chitvā mahātmanaḥ.
N2/10.15a - nīyate narake ghore (N10, N7/10.13a - śira(ḥ)ś chitvā (BF/10.16a - śiraścchinnā) durātmanaḥ) durātmanaḥ śiraśchidā.
N4/10.17b, N8/10.55b, Ra/9.17b - asipatreṣu nīyante śira(ḥ)ś chitvā punaḥ punaḥ.

32 N1/10.16b, N10 - prāṇināṁ (N4/10.18a, N7/10.13b, N8/10.56a, Ra/9.18a - ghātayed) ghātako (N3/10.16b - prāṇino ghātayed) yas tu tailayantreṇa (N2/10.15b - taḍyante) pīḍyate.
BF/10.16b - prāṇinaṁ ghātako yas tu mṛgādinaṁ tathaiva ca.

33 N1/10.17a - duḥkhadāyī narotpasya vyādhikuṣṭī (N3/10.17a - vyādhikūṭe) nipātyate.
N2/10.16a - duḥkhadāyī naro (N4/10.18b, N8/10.56b, Ra/9.18b - nūnaṁ kṣipyate vyādhikūpake) yas tu (BF/10.17a - vyādhikūṭe nipātyate) vyādhikūpe viniḥkṣipet.

34 N1/10.17b - ghṛtacoro ghṛte tapte (BF/10.17b - taile tailasya taskaraḥ) telatailasya hārakaḥ.

madhukṣīrājyahārī ca kṣipyate rudhirahrade[35]
devayātrāvināśī ca pūyaśoṇitamiśrite[36] [18]
kṣipyate pāpakarmā ca pāśair grīvāniyojitaḥ[37]
udyānavāṭikārāmadevatāyatanāni ca[38] [19]
chedayed yo dayāhīnas tv asthipūreṣu yujyate[39]

Whoever steals honey, milk, or butter, is thrown into a blood pond.
Whoever destroys vessels for Gods, is blended with pus and blood. [18]
Sinners are thrown (into Hell) with a bell attached (to their throat)[(V)] *by a noose.*
Those who destroy gardens, Banyan trees, farm houses, or temples, [19]
are yoked in a city of bones, mercilessly sliced to pieces.

N3/10.17b, N10 - ghṛtacauro ghṛte tapte (N2/10.16b - pacyate taile tailasya caurakaḥ) taile tailasya hārakaḥ.
N4/10.19a, N8/10.57a, Ra/9.19a - ghṛtacauro ghṛte pātyaḥ tailai tailasya caurakaḥ.
N7/10.14b - ghṛtacauraṁ ghṛte pacyas taile tailas tu caurakaṁ.

35 N1/10.18a - madhukṣīrājahārī ca kṣipyate ru(ū)dhire hṛde.
N2/10.17a - dadhikṣīramadhūnāṁ ca coras tatraiva pīḍyate.
N3/10.18a - madhukṣīrājyahārī ca kṣi(a)pyate (N10 - [ru]dhire h[r]ade) ru(ū)dhirahṛde.
N4/10.19b, N8/10.57b, Ra/9.19b - dadhikṣīrākṣaudrahāro hrade niḥkṣipyate dvijā.
N7/10.15a - dadhikṣīramadhudrohī te vai ru(o)dhir(a)e nikṣipet.
BF/10.18a - dadhi kṣiraṁ tathā takraṁ kṣ(s)audraṁ coranti ye narāḥ.

36 N1/10.18b - devayātrāvināśī ca kuṁbhīpāke ca (N2/10.17b - pūyaśoṇita, N10 - kuṁbhiṇeṇita) miśrate.
N3/10.18b - devayātrāvināśī b(v)ahūde śoṇitamiśrate.
N4/10.20a, N8/10.58a, Ra/9.20a - devayātrāvināśī ca (N7/10.15b - kūpe ś(s)oṇita ni(ḥ)kṣipet, BF/10.18b - śoṇite nikṣipanti tān) pūyaśoṇitamiśrate.

37 N1/10.19a - kṣipyate pāpakarme ca yāsau 'gnīvāsuyantritaḥ.
N3/10.19a - kṣipyate pāpakarmāsau (N10 - kṣipyati pāpakarmā sa) pāśai[r] grīvāsuyantritaḥ.
N4/10.20b, N8/10.58b, Ra/9.20b - kṣipyate narake pāpāḥ pāś(s)air b(v)andhā bhṛśaṁ gale.
N7/10.16a - kṣipyante pāpakarmāṇaḥ pāś(s)e grīvāniyojitāḥ.
BF/10.19a - pibanti pāpakarmāṇaḥ pāśai(ḥ)r grīvāsuyantritāḥ.

38 N2/10.18b, N7/10.16b - vāṭikodyānam ārāmadevatāyatanāni ca.
N4/10.21a, Ra/9.21a - vāṭikodyānakārāmadevatāyatanāni ca.

39 N1/10.20a, N10 - chedaye(c)d y(ch)o dayāhīna(o)s tv asthipūreṣu 'ṣṭa ca (short).
N2/10.19a - chedayed yo dayāhīno (N3/10.20a - hy asthipūreṣu yujyate) asthikarṇena pacyate.

bhojane vighnakārī ca pādatrāṇāpahārakaḥ[40] [20]
vastracaurāś ca ye mūḍhā lauhayantreṇa pīḍyante[41]
haranti annapānāni phalāni vividhāni ca[42] [21]
te 'pi tatra ca gacchanti yatra pīḍāḥ sudāruṇāḥ[43]
agnidagdhā mahāpāpā gṛhe vāpy athavā vane[44] [22]

One who obstructs food (supply), and one who steals footwear, [20]
and one who steals cloth, those fools are tortured in an iron machine.
Those who steal food, drinks and various fruits, [21]
go indeed to where there are dreadful tortures.
The great sinners are burnt by fire, either in the house, or in the forest, [22]

N4/10.21b, Ra/9.21b - nāśayed yo dayāhīnaḥ so 'sthicūrṇe sadā vaset.
N7/10.17a - chedayed yo dayāhīno hy āsthi bhūteṣu pacyate.
BF/10.20a - ārāmaṁ chedayed yas tu agnimadhye kṣipanti taṁ.

40 N1/10.20b, N10, N4/10.22a, BF/10.20b, Ra/9.22a - bhojane vighnakārī (N2/10.19b - vighnakāro) ca pādatrāṇāpahārakaḥ.
Additional half verse:
N2/10.20b - bhojane vighnakārtāro narāḥ pāpavimohitāḥ.

41 N1/10.21a, N3/10.21a, N10, BF/10.21a - vastracauraś ca (N7/10.18a - te) yo mūḍh(ā)o lohayantreṇa (N2/10.20a - tāḍitā[ḥ]) pīḍyate.
N4/10.22b, N8/10.60b, Ra/9.22b - vastracauras tathā mūḍh(au)o lohayantreṇa pīḍyate.

42 N1/10.21b, N10 - haranti (N3/10.21b - annapānāni) yen na pāpāni (N4/10.23a, N8/10.61a, Ra/9.23a - ye haranti ca puṣpāṇī) phalāni vividhāni ca.
N2/10.21a - haranṭi ye ca phalāni bhakṣyāni [vi]vahūni ca.
Additional half verse:
N2/10.21b - tāḍyante yamadūtais te vilapanti bahūnmathi.
BF/10.21b - haranti ye khānapānaṁ phalāni vividhāni ca.

43 N1/10.22a - te 'pi tatra ca (N10 - va) gacchanti ya(n)tra pīḍāḥ sudāruṇāḥ.
N2/10.22a - te 'pi tatraiva gacchanti (N3/10.22a -yatra pīḍā[ḥ] sudāruṇā[ḥ]) sañjñāprāptā 'tiduḥkhadā[ḥ].
N4/10.23b, N8/10.61b, Ra/9.23b - te 'pi tatraiva gacchanti (N7/10.19a - sthānayatrādiduḥsahāḥ, BF/10.22a - narakaṁ yatra duḥsahaṁ) sthānaṁ yatrātiduḥsah(e)aṁ.

44 N1/10.22b - agnidag(d)dhā(n) (N3/10.22b, N10 - agnidadyān, BF/10.22b - agnido hi) mahāpāpo gṛhe vā(tha)py a[tha]vā vane.
N2/10.22b - agnidā hī (N4/10.24a, N8/10.62a, Ra/9.24a - agnidandyān, N7/10.19b - agnidaś ca) mahāpāpī gṛhe vāpy athavā vane.

te nītā yamadūtaiś ca vahnikuṇḍeṣu pacyante[45]
bhartāraṁ dūṣayed yā tu paraṁ manasi dhārayet[46] [23]
nīyate śālmalīvṛkṣe tāḍyamānā ca mudgaraiḥ[47]
tatra rajvā gale baddhvā tasmin vṛkṣe 'valambite[48] [24]
bhartāraṁ tyajate yā tu tv anyasaṅgaṁ karoti yā[49]

led by Yama's messengers and roasted in fire-pits.
A woman who disgraces her husband, who betrays him in her mind, with others, [23]
is brought to a Śālmalī tree, and is beaten by mallets.
There she is hanged from that tree, tied with a rope to her neck. [24]
A woman that abandons her husband and embraces others,

---

45 N1/10.23a, N3/10.23a, N10 - sānītā (BF/10.23a - sa nīto) yamadūtaiś ca vahnikuṇḍeṣu pacyate.
N2/10.23a - te nītā yamadūtaiś ca (N7/10.20a - vahnikuṇḍeṣu pacya[n]te) pacyante 'gnikuṇḍare[ṣu].
N4/10.24b, N8/10.62b, Ra/9.24b - yaḥ sa b(v)addhvā dharmadūtair agnikuṇḍeṣu pātyate.

46 N1/10.23b - bhartāra[ṁ] dūṣayed yā tu (N3/10.23b - paraṁ manasi dhārayet, BF/10.23b - nityaṁ kalahakāriṇī) paramaṁ masi ṣārayet.
N2/10.23b - mātaraṁ dūṣaye(t)d astu paranindāṅkaras tu ya[ḥ].
N4/10.25a, N8/10.63a, Ra/9.25a - svāminaṁ dūṣayed yas tu paravāsaparāyaṇaḥ.

47 N10 - nīyate śīlmalīvṛkṣe tāḍyamānā ca mudgaraiḥ.
N2/10.24a - bādhyate (N4/10.25b, N8/10.63b, Ra/9.25b - nīyate) śālmalīvṛkṣe tāḍyamānās tu mudgaraiḥ.
N7/10.21a - nīya[n]te śālmalīvṛkṣaṁ tāḍyamānāś ca mudgaraiḥ.
BF/10.24a - nīyate śālmalīvṛkṣe tāḍyamānā tu mudgaraiḥ.
Bo/11.2b - ete śālmalīvṛkṣasthā mayā dṛṣṭā hy anekaśaḥ.

48 N1/10.24b - tatra rajvā gale b(v)addhvā(m) [t]atra vṛkṣ(ratr)e 'valaṁb(v)ate.
N2/10.24b - tatra rajvā dṛṣṭaṁ b(v)adhvā tasmin vṛkṣe 'valaṁb(v)itaḥ.
Additional half verse:
N2/10.25a - anyaṁ tu kāmayen nā(rga)sti sadṛśaṁ rūpayauvana[ṁ].
N3/10.24b, N10 - tatra rajvā gale b(v)addhvā tatra vṛkṣe 'valaṁb(v)ite.
N4/1026a, Ra/9.26a - tatra pāśair dṛḍhaṁ b(v)addhvo laṁb(v)ate 'dhomukhaś ciraṁ.
BF/10.24b - tatra sa rajjunā baddhā tasmin vṛkṣe pralaṁbate.

49 N1/10.25a - bhartāra[ṁ] yā(ṁ) parityajya param (N3/10.25a, N10 - āliṅgyaṁ cunvate) ā(a)liṅgyayaṁ ca te.

jvalantam agnisaṅkāśaṁ staṁbhaṁ lohamayaṁ tathā[50] [25]
taptam āliṅgayantyāś ca jihvāchedo vidhīyate[51]
yoginyāgamanaṁ kuryād agnikuṇḍe sa pacyate[52] [26]
krūracittāś ca ye pāpās tathaiva kalahapriyāḥ[53]
dvijaṁ jayanti vādena hy anṛte kūṭabhāṣakāḥ[54] [27]
bhrāmyante narake ghore hanyamānāś ca mudgaraiḥ[55]

is heated by (embracing) a pillar made of iron, burning like fire, [25]
and afterwards, her tongue is cut off, according to the rule.
A man, who has sexual intercourse with a Yogini, is roasted in a pit of fire. [26]
Merciless sinners, as well as people who love quarrelling,
those who defeat a Brahmin in debate, immoral, deceitful, telling lies, [27]
are made to wander in the terrible Hell, beaten by mallets.

---

50 N1/10.25b - jvalantam agnisaṅkāśaṁ (N2/10.26a - staṁbhalauhamayaṁ tathā, N7/10.22b - staṁbhālohāny anekaśaḥ) hyemaṁ (N3/10.25b, N10, BF/10.25b - staṁbhaṁ) lohamayaṁ tathā.
N4/10.27a, N8/10.64a, Ra/9.27a - jvalantam agnisadṛśaṁ staṁbhaṁ lohamayaṁ kṛtiṁ.
Bo/10.18a - prajvaladvahni saṁpūrṇe lohastaṁbhe pratāpanaṁ.

51 N1/10.26a - taptam āliṅgayatyā(a)ś ca jihvābhedo vidhīyate.
N2/10.26b - āliṅgayanti tā dūtā rasanād vedayanti te.
N3/10.26a - taptam āliṅgaṁyāt paśu (N4/10.27b, N8/10.65b, Ra/9.27b - āliṅgati punas tasyāḥ, BF/10.26a - taptam āliṅgayati sa) jihvāchedo vidhīyate.
N7/10.23a - tato hy āliṅgite teṣāṁ jihvāchedaṁ tathā kṛtaṁ.

52 N2/10.27a - agamyagāmī (N7/10.23b - āgamye gāmī) yaḥ kaścid (N3/10.26b - yo 'gamyāgamanaṁ kuryād) agnikuṇḍeṣu pacyate.
BF/10.26b - āgamyagāmī puruśo vahnikuṇḍena pacyate.
Bo/10.18b - agamyāgamanaṁ yena kṛtaṁ vai pāpakāriṇā.

53 N1/10.27a - krūraś cittāś (N3/10.27a - krūracittāś) ca ye pāpā(ḥ) ye narāḥ kalahapriyāḥ.
N4/10.28a, N8/10.66a, Ra/9.28a - krūracintā mahāpāpāḥ sarvadā kalahapriyāḥ.
BF/10.27a - krūracintā[s] tu ye pāpā dūṣiṇās tu kulastriyaṁ.

54 N1/10.27b, N3/10.27b, N10 - dvijaṁ jayanti vādena (N2/10.28a - hy anṛte kūṭabhāṣakāḥ, N4/10.28b, N8/10.66b, Ra/9.28b - dvijaś cānye 'pi ye tathā, N7/10.24b - te jātikleśabhājanā(a)[ḥ]) tat kṛtaṁ kleśabhāginaḥ.
BF/10.27b - dvijihvās te 'pi jayante kleśabhājo 'tiduḥkhitāḥ.

55 N1/10.28a, N3/10.28a, N10 - bhrāmyante narake ghore hanyamānāś ca (N2/10.28b - hanyamānās tu) mudgaraiḥ.

yo hared ratnamāṇikyaṁ suvarṇābharaṇāni ca[56] [28]
devastrībālavṛddhaṁ svaṁ harate yaś ca mūḍhadhīḥ[57]
kuṁbhīpākeṣu pacyeta khaṇḍakhaṇḍaṁ ca chidyate[58] [29]
duṣayed yaś ca śāstrāṇi dvijavedagurūṁs tathā[59]
jihvāchedo bhavet tasya pūyaśoṇitabhakṣiṇaḥ[60] [30]

Those who steal jewels, rubies, and gold ornaments, [28]
those fools who kill their own (house) god, wife, child, or elders,
are chopped to pieces, and roasted in Kumbhīpāka Hell. [29]
Those who blaspheme the Śāstra scriptures, and the Brahmin Veda-teachers,
will be made to consume blood and pus, and their tongue will be cut off. [30]

Additional verses - N2/10.29-30a:
parodveṣa paraklaśe dūṣṭātmā dharmadūṣakaḥ
adato 'nṛtavādī ca yāva[t] te ninditaṁ priyaṁ
mṛte sarve mayā dṛṣṭā vaṭavāvṛkṣeṣu ś(s)uṇḍaraiḥ.
N7/10.25a - bhrāmyate narakaiḥ sarvaiḥ (BF/10.28a - bhrāmyante narake ghore) hanyamānās tu mudgaraiḥ.

56 N2/10.30b - yo haren mārṇikaṁ raupyaṁ suvarṇasyābharaṇāni ca (vi).
N3/10.28b, N10, BF/10.30a - yo hared ratnamāṇikyaṁ (Bo/10.21b - ratnavastūni) suvarṇābharaṇāni (N7/10.27a - svarṇam ābharaṇāni) ca.
N4/10.29b, N8/10.67b, Ra/9.29b - yo hared ratnajātīyaṁ svarṇam ābharaṇaṁ tathā.

57 N1/10.29a - devastrībālavṛddhaṁ (N3/10.29a, N10 - devastrībālavṛdva) svaṁ harate yaś ca mūḍhadhīḥ.
N2/10.31a - puṣ(ukṣ)yarāg(u)aṁ hared vastu devatāya tād dhanaṁ (short).
N7/10.27b - puṣparāgaṁ hare[d] yas tu devatāpatinā dhanaṁ.

58 N1/10.29b, N10 - kuṁbhīpāke(śa)ṣu pacyante (N3/10.29b - kuṁbhīpāke sa pacyeta(ṁ) khaṇḍakhaṇḍaṁ ca chidya[n]te.
N2/10.31b - kuṁbhīpākeṣu pacyante (N7/10.28a - khaṇḍakhaṇḍaṁ ca chedyate) chidyante 'pi tile tile.
BF/10.31a - kuṁbhīpākeṣu pīḍyante pāpino duṣṭacāriṇaḥ.

59 N1/10.30a, N10 - hṛṣayed yaś ca śāstrāṇi dvijavedagurūṁs tathā.
N2/10.32a, N7/10.28b - dūṣayet sarvaśāstrāṇi (Bo/10.20.b - devatāṁ brahmaṇaṁ guruṁ) devatāgurubrahmaṇān.
N3/10.30a - dūṣayed yaś ca śāstrāṇi (N4/10.30b, N8/10.69a, Ra/9.30b - devatāḥ brahmaṇān gurūn) dvijadevagurūṁ[s] tathā.
BF/10.31b - dūṣakāḥ sarvaśāstrāṇāṁ brahmaṇānāṁ ca nindakāḥ.

60 N2/10.32b - jihvāchedo bhavet tasya (N4/10.31a, N8/10.69b, Ra/9.31a - bhakṣayet pūyaśoṇitaṁ, N7/10.29a - pūyaraktaṁ tu bhakṣayet, Bo/10.21a - mayā dṛṣṭo hy anekadhā) pūyaśoṇitabhakṣiṇaṁ.

miṣṭānnaṁ svayam aśnāti na dadāti dvijottame[61]
bāle naiva ca vṛddhe ca pitrarthe naiva homayet[62] [31]
tāḍito mudgarair dṛṣṭo bhakṣitaḥ siṁhaśūkaraiḥ[63]
sandhyāhīno vratabhraṣṭo nāstiko hantukaḥ śaṭhaḥ[64] [32]

One who eats sweet food by himself, without giving (of it) to excellent Brahmins,
nor even to a child, not to an elderly (person), nor to parental uncle, (and) he who does not sacrifice to the ancestors, [31]
I saw him beaten by mallets, eaten by lions and boars.
Whoever does not perform the morning and evening rites, breaches vows, does not believe in the Vedas, a killer, a shrewd, deceitful person, [32]

BF/10.32a - jihvāchedaḥ kṛtas teṣāṁ pūyaśoṇitabhojanaṁ.

61 N1/10.31a, N10, N4/10.31b, N8/10.70a, Ra/9.31b - miṣ(y)ṭā(a)nnaṁ svayam aśnāti na dadāti (N7/10.29b - dvijottamān) dvijottame.
BF/10.32b - kevalaṁ ye samaśnati miṣṭānnaṁ atithiṁ vinā.
Bo/10.22.b-23a - ekān te miṣṭam aśnāti bālakaṁ vañcayan khalaḥ svamāṁsaṁ bhakṣyamāṇaḥ sa mayā dṛṣṭo dvijottamāḥ.

62 N2/10.33b - bāle caiva tu vṛddhe ca na pītṛn manyate svakān.
N3/10.31b - bāle naiva pravṛddheṣu tanmukheṣu ca homayet.
N10 - b(v)āle naiva ca vṛdve ca pitrarthe naiva homayet.
N4/10.32a, N8/10.70b, Ra/9.32a - b(v)āle vṛddhāture vāpi yaḥ sa tṛṣṇā 'timohitaḥ.
N7/10.30a - bālebhyo na ca vṛddhebhyo na pītṛn havyaṁ homayet.
BF/10.33a - bālakaś ca tathā vṛddhā vipraś cāpi tu kanyakāḥ.

63 N1/10.32a - tāḍit(air)o mudgarair dṛṣṭo bharjitaḥ (N3/10.32a, N10 - bhakṣitaḥ) siṁhaśūkaraiḥ.
N2/10.34a - tāḍitā mudgarair ghorair (N7/10.30b - dṛṣṭā) bhakṣitā(s)ḥ siṁhaś(s)ūkaraiḥ.
Additional half verse:
N2/10.35a - mānabhaṅgaṁ kṛto yena brahmahā gaghate dhruvaṁ.
N4/10.32b, N8/10.70c, Ra/9.32b - tāḍyate mudgarair ghorair bhakṣyate siṁhaśūkaraiḥ.
BF/10.34 - khādyamānāḥ kṛmiśatair vṛkṣair vyāgraiś ca bhakṣitāḥ.

64 N1/10.32b - sandhyāhīno vratabhraṣṭo (N2/10.35b - nāstike hetuka) nāstiko hantuka (N10 - haitaka) śaṭh(t)aḥ.
N3/10.32b - sandhyāhīno bhravratabhraṣṭo nās(ś)iketaś ca dṛśtavān (vi).

pīḍitā mākṣikais tatra yamadūtaiḥ subhīṣaṇaiḥ[65] [33]

iti śrībrahmāṇḍapurāṇe nāsiketopākhyāne śubhopākhyāne nāma daśamo 'dhyāyaḥ

(all) are tortured there by bees, (and) by the very fierce messengers of Yama. [33]

This is the tenth chapter of the Nāsiketa story, pertaining to the Brahmāṇḍa Purāṇa, called – the beautiful story.

Translation Notes

I – Like animal claws.
II – Wolf-like faces.
III – The sinners' description resembles that of Yama's servants.
IV – The messengers said to the sinners.
V – Like domestic animals.

---

65 N2/10.36 - pīḍitā lākṣitās tatra (N3/10.33 - yamadūtaiḥ subhīṣaṇaiḥ) yamadūtaiś ca bhīṣaṇaiḥ.
N10 - pīḍitā bhākṣitās tatra yamadūtaiḥ samīṣaṇaiḥ.

Chapter 11

The Punishers

nāsiketa uvāca
bālasvavāsinīvṛddhāgurviṇyāturakanyakān[1]
saṁbhojyātithibhṛtyāṁś ca daṁpatyoḥ śeṣabhojanaṁ[2] [1]
pākāvaśiṣṭaṁ bhuñjānā yā kācit satyavādinī[3]
ātmārthena na kurvīta pākam etat kadā cana[4] [2]
anena vidhinā yoṣit kurvantī kālaparyāyaṁ[5]
kṣamāvatī satyaratā patibhaktā ca suvratā[6] [3]

After having fed the children, the married women, the elders, the pregnant women, the sick, the unmarried girls,
guests and servants, (only then) the husband and wife should eat the leftover. [1]
(The meritorious woman) speaks the Truth, eats the leftovers, (and) never cooks for herself alone. [2]
This woman (who) spends her time behaving in the following fashion –
full of mercy, adhering to Truth, devoted to her husband, and taking good vows – [3]

---

1 N7/11.1a - bālasvāmino vṛddhā guruputrās tu kanyakā.
BF/11.1a - bālopavāsivṛddhāṁś ca gurviṇīr yās tu kanyakāḥ.
Bo/11.1b - bālakaṁ svāminaṁ paṅguvṛddhaṁ vipraṁ ca kanyakāṁ.
Ra/9.32a - b(v)āle vṛddhātur evāpi yaḥ sa tṛṣṇāvimohitaḥ.

2 N1/11.1b, N10 - saṁbhojyātithibhṛtyāṁś (N3/11.1b - sa bhojyātithi bhṛtyāś) ca daṁpatyoḥ śeṣabhojanaṁ.
N2/11.1b - bhājaśeṣaṁ hy atithe [ca] dampatyoś ca va bhojanaṁ.
N7/11.1b - saṁbhojyātithibhṛtyānāṁ daṁpatyoḥ śeṣabhojanaṁ.
BF/11.1b - na saṁbhojyārthino bhṛtyān daṁpatī yau tu bhuñjānau.

3 Emendation - DS. N1/11.2a - pākāvaśiṣṭaṁ bhuñjānaḥ yat (N10 - ya) kiñcit satyavādinī.
Verses 11.2-11 are missing in N2.
N3/11.2a - pākāvariṣṭaṁ bhuñjānā ye kecit satyavādin(ā)aḥ.

4 Emendation - DS. N1/11.2b - ātmārthena n(c)a ku[r]vīta pākam et(c)a[t] kadā cana.
N3/11.2b - ātmānarthaṁ na (N10 - ātmārthena ca) kurvīta pākam anyat kapīś can(v)a(t).

5 N1/11.3a, N3/11.3a, N10 - anena vidhinā yoṣit kurvatī kālaparyāyaṁ.

6 N3/11.3b - yayāvatī satyaratā bhartṛśuśrūṣaṇe parā.

indraloke vased dhasya svatanuṁ yā parityajet[7]
sā vaset sūryaloke tu romakoṭyaṣṭasaṅkhyayā[8] [4]
vimāne sūryasaṅkāśe krīḍantī ramaṇena sā[9]
indrādyā devatāḥ sarvā namaskurvanti tāṁ satīṁ[10] [5]
nṛtyair gītaiś ca vāditraiḥ sevitā bhāskarair gaṇaiḥ[11]
martyaloke kṛtaṁ karma tatphalaṁ tatra bhujyate[12] [6]
dharmarājaḥ satīṁ dṛṣṭvā citraguptamunīśvaraiḥ[13]
sahito nāradenāpi mudā tām abhiṣaṁsati[14] [7]
dhanyāsi subhage sādhvī yat tvayā kṛtam īdṛśaṁ[15]
aśakyam anyair yat karma triṣu lokeṣu bhujyatāṁ[16] [8]
stutā svargaṁ samutsṛjya sūryaloke mahīyate

will live laughing in Indra's world. She who abandons her body(I)*,*
will dwell in Sūrya's world(II)*, as many long periods as the (number of) hair. [4]*
In a palace, brilliant like the sun, she plays with her husband.
Indra first, and all the other Gods, bow to that "satī", faithful woman. [5]
Groups of radiant suns serve her with dances, singing, and instrumental music.
The results of deeds performed in the mortal world are enjoyed there(III)*. [6]*
Seeing the faithful woman, Dharmarāja, along with Citragupta and the saintly sages, and with Nārada, praise her with joy. [7]
"You are praiseworthy, O fortunate, pious woman – having done such a deed, (so) difficult to perform by others. You may enjoy now the three worlds, [8]
leaving, Heaven-praised, to become great in Sūrya's world".

---

7 N3/11.4a - indraloke vā saṁdṛṣṭā tat tanuṁ kṣaṇam atyajet.

8 N1/11.4b - sā va te sūryaloke tu romakochabdasaṅkhyayā.
N3/11.4b, N10 - sā vaset sūryaloke tu romakoṭraṣṭasaṅkhyayā.

9 N1/11.5a - vimāne (N10 - sūryasaṅkāśe) sūryasaṅkāśo krīḍatā ramaṇena sā.

10 N1/11.5b, N10 - indrādyā devatāḥ sarvā (N3/11.5b - sarve) namaskurvanti tāṁ satīṁ.

11 N3/11.6a - nṛtyai[r] gītaiś ca vāditraiḥ sevitāṁ bhāskarair gaṇaiḥ.

12 N1/11.6b - martyaloke kṛtaṁ karma tatphalaṁ tatra (N10 - bhuñjyate) mucyate.

13 N1/11.7a - dharmarājaḥ satī dṛṣṭy(a)ā (N10 - citraguptamutaśvarai) citrarājamunīśvaraiḥ.

14 N10 - sahito nāradenāpi mudatām abhiṣiñcati.

15 N1/11.8a, N3/11.8a, N10 - dhanyāsi subhage sādhvī yat tvayā kṛtam īdṛśaṁ.

16 N1/11.8b - aśakyam abhyair yat karma triṣu [lokeṣu] bhujyatāṁ.
N3/11.8b - aśakyam anyayā karma triṣu lokeṣu [bhu]jitāṁ.

duḥśīlā yā mayā dṛṣṭā śrūyatāṁ tad vadāmi vaḥ[17] [9]
svapatiṁ yā parityajya duḥśīlā ramate paraṁ
raurave narake kṣiptā samās tiṣṭhati koṭiśaḥ[18] [10]
aṣṭadhātumayās taptāḥ puruṣā dīrghadānujāḥ
smarante tatra tāṁ duṣṭāṁ patyā sā dahyate tanuḥ[19] [11]
antaraṅgapraveśena dahyate nābhimaṇḍalaṁ[20]
antaḥpuraṁ mayā dṛṣṭaṁ paramaṁ lomaharṣaṇaṁ[21] [12]
śṛṇvantu munayaḥ sarve sthānam ekaṁ sudārūṇaṁ[22]
tatra vṛkṣo mayā dṛṣṭo jvaladagnisamaprabhaḥ[23] [13]

Listen to what I am telling about a woman of bad behaviour that I saw (there). [9]
She who abandons her husband, a bad woman, enjoying others,
is thrown into the Raurava Hell, remaining there for a million years. [10]
(She is embraced) by a tall heated man figure, made of eight metals,
remembering her disgrace there[(IV)]*, her body is burnt by her husband, [11]*
entering inside her, burning her navel.
I saw this hair-bristling (thing) in the hell inner-quarters. [12]
Listen all the sages! There is one very fierce place,
where I saw a tree, blazing like a flame of fire. [13]

---

17 N3/11.9b - duḥśīlā yādṛṣī dṛṣṭ(v)ā śr(st)ūyatāṁ tad vadāmi va.

18 N3/11.10b - raurave narake kṣiptvā samās tiṣṭhanti koṭiśa[ḥ].

19 N1/11.11b - smarante tatra tāṁ duṣṭāṁ patyā sā dahyate tanuḥ.
N3/11.11b - ramate tatra tāṁ duṣṭāṁ yatsparśā dahyate tanuḥ.

20 N2/11.2a - ete gṛhe pramodante svargagāḥ pathi nirbhayaḥ.

21 N3/11.12b - ataḥ paraṁ mayā dṛṣṭaṁ paramaṁ lomaharṣaṇaṁ.
N2/11.2b - aparaṁ ca mayā dṛṣṭaṁ mahāntaṁ lomaharṣaṇaṁ.
N7/11.2a - ata[ḥ] paraṁ mayā dṛṣṭaṁ mahāntaṁ romaharṣaṇaṁ.
N4/11.1a, Ra/9.33a - athānyat (N8/11.71a - anyathā) saṁpravakṣyāmi romaharṣaṇam adbhutaṁ.
BF/11.3a - ataḥ paraṁ pravakṣyāmi hy adbhutaṁ lomaharṣaṇaṁ.

22 N2/11.3a - śṛṇvantu ṛṣayaḥ sarve sthānam ekaṁ (N4/11.1b, N7/11.2b, N8/11.71b, Ra/9.33b, BF/11.3b - sudāruṇaṁ) tu dārūṇaṁ.

23 N1/11.13b, N10 - tatrāpy e(m)ka vṛkṣo jvaladag(jā)nisamaprabhaṁ (short).
N2/11.3b - tatra vṛkṣā mayā dṛṣṭā (N4/11.2a, N8/11.72a, Ra/9.34a - jvalanto vahn(nh)inā bhṛśaṁ) jvalante dīptatejasaḥ.
BF/11.4a - tatra vṛkṣo mayā dṛṣṭaḥ prajvalann agnitejasā.
Bo/11.3a - sa tu vṛkṣo mayā dṛsto jvaladagnisamaprabhaḥ.

pañcayojanavistīrṇa ekayojanam utthitaḥ[24]
atyugrabhayam ākrandaṁ tatra vṛkṣe śrutaṁ mayā[25] [14]
baddhāś ca śṛṅkhalaiḥ pāśair laṁbitā ekapāṇinaḥ[26]
tāḍitā lohadaṇḍaiś ca mudgarair musalarṣṭibhiḥ[27] [15]
anyat tatra mayā dṛṣṭaṁ narakaṁ taptavālukaṁ[28]

It spreads on five Yojanas, and is one Yojana tall.
I heard there, in the tree, very fierce, fearful cries. [14]
Fettered by chains and nooses, (the sinners) are made to hang by one hand,
beaten by iron rods, mallets, wooden clubs and spears. [15]
I saw another hell there with heated sand.

---

24 N1/11.14a - pañca(m)yojanavistīrṇam ekayojanam (N10 - ucchritaḥ) utthitaḥ.
N2/11.4a - pañcayojanavistīrṇā ucchāyāś (N4/11.3a, Ra/9.35a - ucchrāye) caikayojanaḥ.
N3/11.14a - pañcayojanavistīrṇo (Bo/11.3b - daśayojanam ucchritaḥ) ekayojanam utsavaḥ.
N7/11.3b - pañcayojanavistīrṇā (N8/11.73a - ucchāyekaikayojanaḥ) ucchrāyād daśayojanam.
BF/11.4b - pañcayojanavistīrṇa ekayojanam ucchritaḥ.

25 N1/11.14b - atyugrabhayam ākrandaṁ tatra vṛtte (N10 - vṛkṣe) śrutaṁ mayā.
N2/11.4b - hāhākāro mahān ugras tatra vṛkṣagaṇaiḥ śrutaḥ.
N3/11.14b - atyugra[ṁ] ha yam ākrandaṁ tatra vṛkṣo śruta[ṁ] mayā.
BF/11.5a - atyugrabhayam ākrandam atra vṛkṣe śrutaṁ mayā.

26 N2/11.5a - baddhvā saṅkulaiḥ pāśai(s)ḥ śāśava laṁbitapāpi va.
N4/11.4a, N8/11.74a - baddhvā pāśaiś ca vṛkṣeṣu lambyate tatra pāpinaḥ.
BF/11.5b - baddhāś ca śṛṅkhalaiḥ pāśair laṁbamānāś ca pāpinaḥ.
Bo/11.4a - tasmin baddhāḥ pāpinas te tāḍyante yamakiṅkaraiḥ.
Ra/9.36a - baddhāḥ pāśaiś ca vṛkṣeṣu laṁ(v)byante tatra pāpinaḥ.

27 N1/11.15b, N10 - tāḍitā lohadaṇḍaiś ca mudgarair muśala(ai)[r]ṣ[ṭ]ibhiḥ.
N2/11.5b - tāḍitā daṇḍapāśaiś ca mudgarair lauhayaṣṭibhiḥ.
N4/11.4b, N8/11.74b, Ra/9.36b - tāḍyante duḥsahair daṇḍai[r] mudgarair lohayaṣṭibhiḥ.
N7/11.5a - tāḍitā b(v)ahu daṇḍaiś ca mudgarai[r] lohadaṇḍabhiḥ.
BF/11.6a - tāḍitās tatra daṇḍaiś ca mudgarair lohaya(ā)ṣṭibhiḥ.
Bo/11.4b - tāḍitā vajradaṇḍaiś ca mudgarair bhinnamastakāḥ.

28 N1/11.16a - anya[t] tatra (N2/11.6a, BF/11.6b - aparaṁ ca) mayā dṛṣṭaṁ narakaṁ (N3/11.16a - prāptavān bhṛśaṁ) taptavālukaṁ.

jvaladagnipratīkārā bhajyante tatra pāpinaḥ[29] [16]
kṣutpipāsāpariśrāntā yamadūtaiś ca pīḍitāḥ[30]
rudanti pāpinas tatra kṛtāñjalipuṭās tathā[31] [17]
vijñāpayanti dūtebhyaḥ pāpiṣṭās te nirāśrayāḥ[32]
punaḥ punaś ca te dūtair hanyante lauhayaṣṭibhiḥ[33] [18]

The sinners are engaged there in fighting against the fire flames. [16]
Tortured by Yama's messengers, exhausted by hunger and thirst,
the sinners there (plead) crying with joined palms. [17]
The messengers inform these sinners that there is no refuge for them.
The messengers beat them (i.e. the sinners) again and again, with iron rods. [18]

N7/11.6b - aparaṁ ca mayā dṛṣṭaṁ narakaṁ tatra dūtaiś ca tāḍitāḥ (vi).
N4/11.5a, N8/11.75a, Ra/9.37a - aparaṁ tat samīpe 'sti narakaṁ taptavālukaṁ.
Bo/11.5a - punas tatra mayā dṛṣṭo narakas taptavālukaḥ.

29 N3/11.16b - jvaladagnipratīkāśaṁ bhajyante tatra pāpinaḥ.
N2/11.6b - jvalantam agnisaṅkāśaṁ tatra dahy atipāpinaḥ.
N10 - jvaladagnipratīśo bharjyante tatra pāpinaḥ.
N4/11.5b, N8/11.75b, Ra/9.37b - jvaladagnisamākāraṁ (Bo/11.5b - prajvaladvahnisadṛśo) dahyante tatra pāpinaḥ.
BF/11.6c - prajvaladvahnisaṅkāśaṁ pacyante tatra pāpinaḥ.

30 N4/11.6a, N8/11.76a - kṣutpipāsāpariklāntā (Ra/9.38a - kṣutpipāsāpariśrāntā) yamadūtaiś ca pīḍitāḥ.
BF/11.7a - kṣutpipāsārditāḥ sarve tāḍyamānāś ca kiṅkaraiḥ.
Bo/11.6a - kṣudhayā tatra pīḍyante baddhahastapado narāḥ.

31 N1/11.17b - rudanti pāpinas tatra (N3/11.17b - kṛtāñjalipuṭāmukhe) kṛtāñjalipuṭās (N4/11.6b, N8/11.76b - tadā, Ra/9.38b - tathā) va te.
N2/11.7b - rudanti pātitā bhūmau (N7/11.7a - kṛtāñjalim upasthitā[ḥ]) kṛtāñjalipuṭās tathā.
BF/11.7b - tāḍitāḥ patitā bhūmau baddhāñjalipuṭās tathā.

32 N1/11.18a, N10 - vijñāpayaṁś ca dūtebhyaḥ pāpiṣṭās te nirāśramāḥ.
N4/11.7a, N8/11.77a - vijñāpayanti tānṛtā (Ra/9.39a - tān dūtān) bhūyo bhūyo nirāśrayāḥ.
N7/11.6b - vijñāpayanti dūtebhyaḥ pāpiṣṭāś ca (BF/11.8a - pāpiṣṭās te) nirāśrayāḥ.

33 N1/11.18b, N10 - punaḥ punas te dūtais te (N3/11.18b - punaś ca tair (N7/11.7a, BF/11.8b - te) dūtair) hanyante lohaya(ā)ṣṭibhiḥ. End of BF/11.
N4/11.7, N8/11.77, Ra/9.39b - vijñāptas te punar ghnanti nirdayā lohayaṣṭibhiḥ.

mudgarais tomaraiḥ kuntaiḥ gadābhiḥ pātitā bhṛśaṁ[34]
tāḍitāś caiva niśceṣṭās teṣāṁ trātā na vidyate[35] [19]
tathā niśceṣṭitān dṛṣṭvā kiṅkarās tān vadanti hi[36]
bho bho pāpā durācārāḥ kim kṛtaṁ duṣṭacetasaḥ[37] [20]
sulābhāni na dattāni pānīyaṁ nānnaṁ eva ca[38]
grāsād ardhaṁ na te dattaṁ na deve na dvijottame[39] [21]

They are knocked down repeatedly by javelins, mallets, spears and maces,
(so) tortured until they cannot even move, (and) there is no one to protect them. [19]
When the servants see them motionless, they say so:
"O sinners of bad conduct, what have you done, you evil minded. [20]
Though easily obtained, you have not given (even) a little food, or water,
not even half a bite to the Gods, nor to excellent Brahmins. [21]

---

[34] N2/11.9a, N3/11.19a - mudgarais tomaraiḥ (N4/11.8a, N8/11.78a, Ra/9.40a - kuntair anyaiś ca vividhāyudhaiḥ) kuntais tāḍitā (N7/11.8b - daṇḍaraudrakaiḥ) daṇḍayaṣṭibhiḥ.

[35] N1/11.19b, N3/11.19b, N10 - tāḍitāś caiva n(ī)i[ś]ceṣṭās teṣāṁ trātā na vidyate.
N2/11.9b - pātitāś caiva (N7/11.9a - ca va) niścaṣṭās (N4/11.8b, N8/11.78b, Ra/9.40b - tataḥ patanti niśceṣṭaṁ) trātā teṣu na vidyate.

[36] N1/11.20a, N3/11.20a, N10 - tathā niceṣṭitā[n] dṛṣṭvā kiṅkarās tān vadanti hi.
N2/11.10a - dṛṣṭā[s] tu pātitā bhūmau dūtās tatra vadanti tān.
N4/11.9a, N8/11.79a - dṛṣṭvā tu pātitān pāpān dūtāḥ duṣṭāḥ hasanti vai.
N7/11.9b - dṛṣṭāś ca pātitā bhūmau dūtās teṣāṁ vaded idaṁ.

[37] N1/11.20b - bho bho pādyā durācārāḥ kim (N10 - ete duṣṭacetasaḥ) evaṁ caṇḍaś ca veṣṭaḥ.
N2/11.10b - aho pāpā durācārāḥ karmata(-)tacetasaḥ.
N4/11.9b, N8/11.79b - vadaty api ca re pāpā(ḥ) durācārā (Ra/9.41b - durātmikāḥ) durātmakāḥ.
N7/11.10a - bho bho pāpā durācārāḥ kukarmāyuṣṭacetasaḥ.

[38] N1/11.21a, N10 - sul(ṭ)ābhān(t)i na dattāni (N7/11.10b - pāpābhiś cānnam eva ca) jal(ā)am annāni (N3/11.21a - jalānanyāni) vaḥ kvacit.
N4/11.10a, N8/11.80a, Ra/9.42a - api dattaṁ na sulābham annaṁ pānīyam eva ca.

[39] N2/11.11b - grāsam ardha[ṁ] (N3/11.21b - grāsād arthaṁ) na te dattaṁ na deve na dvijottame.
N4/11.10b, N8/11.80b, Ra/9.42b - grāsārddham api no dattaṁ bhavadbhir b(v)rāhmaṇāya vai.
N7/11.11a - grāsamātraṁ na(n) tair dattaṁ na devā[n] na dvijottamān.

na hutaṁ homakāle 'pi na datto vāyase baliḥ[40]
āgatasya namaskāro na kṛtaṁ pitṛtarpaṇaṁ[41] [22]
na śrutaṁ kīrtitaṁ te vai caritaṁ harer uttamaṁ[42]
śrutvā kiñcit na te dattaṁ hiraṇyādy annam eva ca[43] [23]
na kiñcit te kṛtaṁ tīrthaṁ sthāpitā naiva devatāḥ[44]
gṛhāśramasthito mūḍha pañcayajña bahiḥkṛtaḥ[45] [24]
ekākī miṣṭam aśnāti kiṁ pāpā na śrutā vayaṁ[46]

Not even in any time of sacrifice, have you offered to the crows.
You have not welcomed a guest, nor have you satisfied your ancestors. [22]
You have not even listened to the story of Lord Kṛṣṇa, nor have you behaved accordingly.
Having listened (so) little, you have not given gold etc. nor even food. [23]
You have established neither sacred bathing ponds, nor even (shrines for) Gods.
You have a house shrine, fools(VII)*, but you have not performed the five compulsory fire-(rites). [24]*
You took sweet food all by yourselves, haven't you heard of us, O sinners?

---

40 N1/11.22a - na hutaṁ homakāle 'pi na śvadhāṁ puś[p]ayor (N3/11.22a, N10 - naś ca vāyasayor) baliḥ.
N2/11.12a - na hutaṁ vipravadane na cātno hutam asti hi.
N4/11.11a, N8/11.81a, Ra/9.43a - na hutaṁ naiva japtaṁ ca na datto vāyase b(v)aliḥ.

41 N1/11.22b - namaskṛtyāvatithye yo na kṛtaṁ pitṛtarpaṇaṁ.
N2/11.12b - āgatasya namaskāro na (N4/11.11b, N8/11.81b, Ra/9.43b - kṛto vidhipūrvakaṁ, N7/11.12a - kṛtaṁ pitṛtarpaṇaṁ) dhātaḥ pitṛkarmaṇa.

42 N1/11.23a - na śrutaṁ kīrtitaṁ te vai caritaṁ har(im)er uttamaṁ.
Verse 11.23 is missing in N2, N3.

43 N10 - śrutvā kiñcit na te dattaṁ hiraṇyādhanam eva ca.

44 N2/11.13a, N3/11.23a, N7/11.12b - na kiñcit te kṛtaṁ tīrthaṁ toṣitā naiva devatāḥ.
N4/11.12a, N8/11.82a - na tarpitāś ca pitaras toṣitā naiva devatāḥ.

45 N4/11.12b, N8/11.82b - gṛhasthale na (Ra/9.44b - gṛhasthatve na) vihitaḥ pañcayajñāḥ śubhāvahāḥ.
N7/11.13a - gṛhasthāś ca sthitau mūḍhaiḥ pañcayajñā na tarpitāḥ.
Bo/11.9a - gṛhe sthitā ye puruṣāḥ pañcayajñavivarjitāḥ.

46 N3/11.24a - ekākī miṣṭam aśn(r)āti (N10 - ekākinā dhṛtā miṣṭaṁ) pāpā te na śrutā vayaṁ.
N7/11.13b - ekākī miṣṭaṁ aśnāti kiṁ tvayā na śrutā vayaṁ.

vāsaro 'pi harasya tu nākāri vidhinā svayaṁ[47] [25]
prasaṅgenāpi te mūḍha na kṛtaṁ harikīrtanaṁ[48]
ity uktvā tāḍayanty etān kiṅkarā ghorarūpiṇaḥ[49] [26]
amedhyakūpapūyeṣu tapyante pāpakarmiṇaḥ[50]
kṛmiyoniṣu jāyante mriyante tu punaḥ punaḥ[51] [27]
tasmin sthāne mayā dṛṣṭā marditāḥ pāpā riṣṭhibhiḥ[52]
āpo hy agnis tathā vāyuḥ pṛthvī ca vanadevatāḥ[53] [28]

You did not perform the various rites of an adherent on the day of Hara(V). *[25]*
You have not recited the praises for Hari(VI) *in the right context, even occasionally, you fools".*
While thus speaking, those horrible-looking servants were beating them. [26]
The sinners are heated in impure pits of pus, (and)
they are reborn and die as worms, again and again. [27]
At that place I saw those sinners crushed by spears.
"Water, fire, as well as air (wind), earth and forest goddesses(VIII)*; [28]*

---

47 N1/11.25b - vāsaro 'pi haraḥ sakto nākiriṁ vividhā tvayā.
Verse 11.25b-26a is missing in N2, N3.
N10 - vāsaro 'pi ḥarasya(nto) [tu] nākāri vidhinā svayāṁ.

48 N1/11.26a, N10 - prasaṅgenāpi te mūḍha na kṛtaṁ harikīrtanaṁ.

49 N2/11.15a - tato vadanti dūtāś ca kiṅkarān ghorarūpiṇaḥ.
N7/11.14a - tato bhakṣanti bhūtāni kiṅkarā ghorarūpiṇaḥ.

50 N2/11.15b - kṣipyantāṁ kūpamadhye tu tāḍyantāṁ pāpakarmā(a)ṇaḥ.
N3/11.25a - amedhyapūyakūpeṣu tapyante pāpakarmā(a)ṇaḥ.
N7/11.15a - kṣipya[n]te 'medhyakūpena daṇḍyās tu pāpakarmā(a)ṇaḥ.

51 N2/11.16b, N7/11.14a - kṛmiyoniṣu nīyante jāyante ca mriyanti ca.
N3/11.25b - kṛmiyoniṣu jāyante mriyante ca punaḥ punaḥ.
Bo/11.10a - kṛmiyoniṣu jāyante narāḥ svenaiva karmaṇā.

52 N1/11.28a - tasmin sthāne mayā dṛṣṭ(v)ā (N2/11.16a - mṛtā jātās tathā (N7/11.15b - janmamṛtyusthitā) pare, N3/11.26a - marditā[ḥ] pāṇipādābhiḥ, Bo/11.9b - punar dehāntaraṁ bhavet) uditāḥ pāpā riṣṭibhiḥ.

53 Additional half verse:
N2/11.17a - sādhyante kūṭavadī cātithyā dānaṁ vadanti ye.
N2/11.17b, N10 - āpo tv (N7/11.17a - 'stv) agnis (N4/11.13b, N8/11.83b, Ra/9.45b - nilas) tathā vāyuḥ pṛthvī ca vanadevatāḥ.
Bo/11.11a - so 'mutra svakṛte naiva dahyate vāyuḥ vahninā.

brāhmaṇāś caiva rājāno pitā vidyāgurus tathā[54]
ete sarve mahābhāgā viṣṇuvrataparāyaṇāḥ[55] [29]
kathaṁ na pūjito mūḍha bhuṅkṣva pāpaphalaṁ svakaṁ[56]
yato dharmavihīno 'si tataḥ santāḍyase bhṛśaṁ[57] [30]
evaṁ vadantas te dūtā nirdayās tāḍayanti tān[58]
daṇḍahastair mahākāyair bhrāmyante yamaśāsanāt[59] [31]

Even Brahmins, kings, ancestors, as well as teachers of knowledge;
All these great persons are engaged in Viṣṇu's worship. [29]
Why have you not worshipped (Viṣṇu), O fool? 'Enjoy' (now) the fruits of your own sins.
Since you are devoid of righteousness, you are beaten so hard". [30]
Just saying that, those merciless messengers beat them (again).
Big bodied, holding sticks, they make them wander, by Yama's order, (and) [31]

---

54 N1/11.29a, N10 - brahmāṇāś caiva bho rājan pitā vidyāgurus tathā.
N2/11.18a, Ra/9.46a - brahmāṇāś caiva rājāno (N4/11.14a, N8/11.84a - vaiṣṇavaś ca gurus) gurur (N3/11.27a - rājānaḥ pitā) vidyāgurus (N7/11.17b - vidyāyatis) tathā.
Bo/11.11b - viprāṁś ca devatāś caiva gaṅgādisaritas tathā.

55 Emendation - NK. N1/11.29b - ete sarve mahābhāgā (N3/11.27b - vidyante pāpahāriṇaḥ) viṣṇuvatyāpavariṇaḥ.
N2/11.18b - ete sarve mayā dṛṣṭā(s) sarvakarmasusākṣiṇaḥ.
N4/11.14b, N8/11.84b - ete sarve (Ra/9.46b - mahākhyātā) samākhyātā viṣṇutulyā viśeṣataḥ.
N7/11.18a - ete sarve mayā khyātā viṣṇutulyāni pāpahāḥ.

56 N2/11.19a - viṣṇutulyamahātmānaḥ kathaṁ mūḍha na pūjitāḥ.
N3/11.28a - kathaṁ na pūjit(ā)o mūḍha(ḥ) bhuṅkṣ[v]a pāpaphalaṁ svakaṁ.
N4/11.15a, N8/11.85a, Ra/9.47a - ete 'pi devatātmānaḥ kathaṁ mūḍhair na pūjitāḥ.
N7/11.18b - īdṛśo devatā[ḥ] sākṣāt kathaṁ mūḍhair na pūjyate.

57 N1/11.30b - yato dharmavihīno 'si tataḥ santāḍyate bhṛśaṁ.
N2/11.19b - parityaktvā tvayā mūḍha vinā dharmātam u hy asi.
Bo/11.12a - na manyate naro yas tu narake pīḍyate bhṛśaṁ.

58 N1/11.31a - evaṁ vadantas (N2/11.20a - vadanti) te (N4/11.15b, N8/11.85b, Ra/9.47b - tatra niraye taptavāluke) dūtā nirdayās tāḍayanti (N2/11.20a - ca) tān.
N7/11.19b - evaṁ vadanti te dūtā nirdayās tāḍayanti te.

59 N1/11.31b, N3/11.29b, N10 - daṇḍahastair mahākāyair bhrāmyante yamaśāsanāt.

kuṁbhīpākādighoreṣu pacyante te muhur muhuḥ[60] [32]

iti śrībrahmāṇḍapurāṇe nāsiketopākhyāne śāstikaraṇaṁ nāmaikādaśamo 'dhyāyaḥ

they are roasted in the terrible Kuṁbhīpāka (Hell), again and again. [32]

This is the eleventh chapter of the Nāsiketa story, pertaining to the Brahmāṇḍa Purāṇa, called – the punishers.

Translation Notes

I – Satī – a faithful woman who burns herself on her dead husband's pyre.
II – The Sun-world – Heaven.
III – In the hereafter.
IV – In the mortal world.
V – Śiva.
VI – Viiṣṇu.
VII – In the text there is a mixture of singular and plural in the messengers' speech. Though sometimes in the singular, the narrator's words indicate that the address is to a group of sinners.
VIII – All these represent Viṣṇu.

N2/11.20b - daṇḍahastā mahākāyā (N7/11.20a - bhrāmya[n]te yamaś(s)ās(ś)anaṁ) bhrāme te yamaśāsanāt.
Bo/11.14a - daṇḍahastair mahāghorair vadhabandhādibhis tathā.

60 N2/11.21 - pāpināṁ śāsanāsyārthe dharmiṇāṁ bhaktikāraṇe.
N7/11.20b - kuṁbhīpākādinarake pacyante muhur muhuḥ.

Chapter 12

Kāla and the Demons

nāsiketa uvāca
śrūyatāṁ tan mayā dṛṣṭaṁ rūpaṁ teṣāṁ bhayaṅkaraṁ[1]
nānāprahāraṇā raudrā nānāvarṇadharā gaṇāḥ[2] [1]
tasmins tu dakṣiṇe dvāre kleśayanti narādhamān[3]
dūtāś ca vānarārūḍhā dṛṣṭā nānāvidhā mayā[4] [2]
kokilāṁś ca samārūḍhā mahiṣaskandhasaṁsthitāḥ[5]

Nāsiketa said
Listen to what I saw – the frightening form of those
troops carrying various fierce weapons, of various kinds, [1]
at that southern door, torturing the lowest of persons.
I saw various messengers, of various kinds, mounted on monkeys, [2]
as well as (others) mounted on buffalo backs, (or) riding on cuckoos.

---

1 N2/12.1a - śrūyatāṁ tan (N7/12.1a - ca) mayā dṛṣṭaṁ bhayaṁ saṁsārasāgare.
N4/12.1, N8/12.87, Ra/10.1 - idānīṁ yamadūtānāṁ svarūpaṁ vāhanādikaṁ tathā kālasya vṛttāntaṁ pravakṣyāmi tapasvinaḥ.

2 N1/12.1b - nānāpraharaṇā raudrā nānāvarṇā (N3/12.1b, N7/12.1b - dharā gaṇā) bhayaṅgaṇāḥ.
N2/12.1b - nānāprahāriṇā raudrā nānāvarṇā vibhagiṇāḥ.

3 N1/12.2a, N10 - tasmins tu dakṣiṇe dvāre kleśayanti (N2/12.2a - ca pāpinaḥ) nara(n)dhamān.
N4/12.2a, N8/12.88a, Ra/10.2a - tasmiṅś ca dakṣiṇadvāre pīḍyante cātipāpinaḥ.
N7/12.2a - tasmiṅś ca dakṣi(a)ṇe dvāre nityaṁ kliṣyanti te 'dhamāḥ.
Bo/12.1 - athātaḥ saṁpravakṣyāmi yad dṛṣṭaṁ yamaśāsanaṁ
tasmin vai dakṣiṇe dvāre kliśyante pāpino janāḥ.

4 N1/12.2b - dūtāś ca vānarārūḍhā (N2/12.2b - dṛṣṭā nānāvidhā, N3/12.2b - dṛṣṭāś ca vivi(a)dhā) dṛṣyakharva(i)vidhā mayā.
N4/12.2b, N8/12.88b, Ra/10.2b - dūtāḥ svavāhanārūḍhā (N7/12.2b - dūtāś ca vāhanārūḍhā) dṛṣṭā nānāvidhā mayā.
Bo/12.2a - tatra nānāvidhā dṛṣṭā dūtā ye vai vibhīṣaṇāḥ.

5 N1/12.3a - kokilāsvāṁ[s] samārūḍhā (N7/12.3a - kokilāś ca samārūḍhā) mahiṣaskandhasaṁsthitāḥ.

dṛṣṭā ca kecid apare gṛdhrasārasavāhanāḥ[6] [3]
mahendreṣu samārūḍhāḥ śṛgāleṣu ca hastiṣu[7]
mṛgādhirūḍhā dṛṣyante dhāvanto yamakiṅkarāḥ[8] [4]
dṛśyante ca mahāghorāḥ ūrdhvakeśabhayānakāḥ[9]
netrānte ca śikhījvālāḥ kṛṣṇavarṇā mahodarāḥ[10] [5]

And I saw some others (having) vultures and cranes for their mount. [3]
(Others) were riding on lions[(1)], as well as on jackals and elephants.
I saw (other) Yama's servants running, riding on deer. [4]
I also saw (others), very fierce, frightening, with their hair standing erect,
with fire flames in their eyeballs, black coloured, big bellied, [5]

N2/12.3a - kokilāś ca samārūḍhā (N3/12.3a - śṛgāleṣu ca vā(s)śvasu) mahiṣāsanasaṁsthitāḥ.

N4/12.3a, N8/12.89a - kecit tu kokilārūḍhā (Ra/10.3a - balākāskandhasaṁsthitāḥ) mahiṣāskandhasaṁsthitāḥ.

6 N1/12.3b - dṛṣṭ(v)ā c(sv)a kecid apare (N2/12.3b - apare ca mahākecit) gṛdhrasārasavāhavāḥ.

Verse 12.3b-4a is missing in N3.

N4/12.3b, N8/12.89b, Ra/10.3b - apare gradhram āruḍhā kecit sārasavāhanāḥ.

N7/12.3b - apare dṛśyate kecit gṛdhasārasavāhanāḥ.

7 N1/12.4a - mahendreṣu (N10 - maheṣṭriṣu) samārūḍhāḥ śṛgāleṣu tathāśvasu.

N2/12.4a - vānareṣṭhasamārūḍhāḥ śṛgāleṣu ca hastiṣu.

N4/12.4a, N8/12.90a, Ra/10.4a - śṛgālavāhanāś cānye kesarīvāhanāḥ pare.

N7/12.4a - vānareṣu samārūḍhāḥ śṛgāle keśarīṣu ca.

8 N1/12.4b, N3/12.3b, N10 - mṛgādhirūḍhā (N2/12.4b - mṛgādirūḍhā) dṛśyante (N4/12.4b, N8/12.90b, Ra/10.4b - dhāvantaḥ kecanāpare) dhāvanto yamakiṅkarāḥ.

N7/12.4b - mṛgādhīruḍhā eke ca ūrdvakeṣā bhayānakāḥ.

9 N1/12.5a - dṛśyante ca mah(vit)āgh(k)orā (N2/12.5a - mahānto lomaharṣaṇāḥ) ūrdhvakeṣabhayānakāḥ.

N2/12.5b - dṛśyante vikṛttārūpā (N4/12.5a, N8/12.91a, Ra/10.5a - evaṁ ca kṛtavāhāste, Bo/12.2b - dīrghadeśāś ca laṁboṣṭā) ūrdhvakeṣā bhayāṅkarāḥ.

N3/12.4a - dṛśyante vikṛtā kāre ūrdhvakeṣā bhayānakā.

10 N1/12.5b - netrā ne ca śikhījvālāḥ kṛṣṇavarṇā mahodayaḥ.

N3/12.4b - netrānte ca śikhījvālā[ḥ] (N4/12.5b, N8/12.91b, Ra/10.5b - vahnijvālā jvalanetrāḥ) kṛṣṇavarṇā (N10 - kṛṣṇavarṇau (short)) mahodarāḥ.

dīrghā mahāvirūpāṅgāḥ karālakaṭhināntarāḥ[11]
kecid dīrghās tathā hrasvā mahāsthūlās tathāpare[12] [6]
vānarāṇām iva mukhād dṛśyante cetare pare[13]
kecit siṁhānanās tatra vyāghrāsyā rāsabhānanāḥ[14] [7]
mārjāravadanāḥ śvāsyāḥ bhīṣaṇā vikṛtānanāḥ[15]

very tall men, with abnormally big limbs, (having) cruel gaping mouths.
Some were tall, some short, as well as others being fat. [6]
And I saw others there, having monkey-like faces.
Some had lion faces, (others) had tiger or donkey faces, [7]
cat faces, dog faces – fierce, abnormal faces,

---

[11] N1/12.6a - dīrghā mahāvirūpāṅgāḥ (N10, N7/12.5b - kāralāḥ kaṭhināntarāḥ) karāla(ā)kaṭhinā (N3/12.5a - karāla(ā)kaṭhinī) narā.
N2/12.6b - mahādīrghā virūpāś ca karāla(ā)kaṭhinā(ṁ) n(v)arāḥ.
N4/12.6a, N8/12.92a, Ra/10.6a - mahāvirūpasarvāṅgāḥ karālakaṭhināntarāḥ.

[12] N2/12.7a, BF/12.7a - kecid dīrghās tathā (N7/12.6a - tato) hrasvā mahāśūlās tathāpare.
N4/12.6b, N8/12.92b, Ra/10.6b - kecid dīrghāḥ pare hrasvāḥ sthūlāḥ kecit kṛśāḥ pare.

[13] N2/12.7b - mukhaṁ vānarasaṅkāśaṁ (N7/12.6b - vā janasaṅkāśaṁ) dūtānāṁ (BF/12.7b - tatra dṛśyate) dṛśyate tataḥ.
N4/12.7a, N8/12.93a - kecid vānaramukhāś caiva (Ra/10.7a - kecic ca vānaramukhās) tathā siṁhamukhāḥ pare (vi).

[14] N1/12.7b, N10 - kecit siṁhānānās tatra vyāghrās(ś)yā (N3/12.6b - rāsabhānanāḥ) vāsabhānanāḥ.
N2/12.8a - apare sṛṅginaḥ kecit vyāghrarūpā bhayaṅkarāḥ.
N4/12.7b, N8/12.93b - vyāghrānanā (Ra/10.7b - vyāptānanā) rāsabhāsyāḥ mārjjārāsyās tathāpare.
N7/12.7a - anye siṁhānanā kecit vyāghrarāsabhasannibhāḥ.
BF/12.8a - siṁhāsyā hy apare tatra vyāghrarāsabhasannibhāḥ.
Bo/12.3b - apare siṁhapādāś ca vyāghrarūpās tathāpare.

[15] N1/12.8a - mārjjāravadanāḥ svāsyāḥ (N3/12.7a - śvasyā) bhīṣaṇā (N10 - māṣaṇā) vikṛtānanāḥ.
N2/12.8b - kharoṣṭragajavaktrāś ca bhīruṇavikṛtānanāḥ.
N7/12.7b - ś(s)vānamārjārasadṛśāḥ bhīṣaṇā v(b)igatānanāḥ.
BF/12.8b - śvānamārjārasaṅkāśāḥ kutsitā vikṛtānanāḥ.
Bo/12.4a - mārjārarūpiṇaś cānye tan netrās tu tathāpare.

raktanetrā mahādaṁṣṭrā rudhirārdrakarāḥ sadā[16] [8]
raudrā bharaṇasaṁyuktāḥ sarpavṛścikabhūṣaṇāḥ[17]
nīlapītapaṭābaddhāḥ kṛṣṇāṁbaradharāḥ pare[18] [9]
pāpinas tatra paśyantaḥ śūlahastāś ca kiṅkaraiḥ[19]
śaktidaṇḍadharāś cānye gadāmudgaradhāriṇaḥ[20] [10]
khadirāṅgārakāḥ kecid yaṣṭihastās tathāpare[21]

with red eyes, big teeth, their hands always blood-stained. [8]
(They were) fierce, adorned with serpents (and) scorpions (as) ornaments.
Some were wrapped in yellow-blue cloth, others wore black clothes. [9]
Sinners are bound there by spear-bearing servants.
(Some) hold śakti "missiles", others carry mallets and maces. [10]
(Some hold) acacia tree coals, while others hold sticks.

---

16 N1/12.8b, N10 - raktanetr(a)ā mahādaṁṣṭrā (N2/12.9a, N4/12.9a, N8/12.96a, Ra/10.9a - rudhirārdrakarāḥ sadā, N3/12.7b - rudhirākṣā virūpiṇaḥ, N7/12.8a - rūdhirārdr(a)ā sad(gh)ā karāḥ) rudhirāktā virūpiṇaḥ.
BF/12.9a - raktanetrā mahāraudrāḥ kṛṣṇavaktrā vigandhinaḥ.

17 N1/12.9a, N3/12.8a, N10 - raudrā bharaṇasaṁyuktāḥ (N2/12.9b - raudram ābhāṣaṇaṁ (N7/12.8b - raudrā bharaṇās) teṣāṁ) sarppavṛścikabhūṣaṇāḥ.
Bo/12.4b - sarpavṛścikarūpāś ca raudrā bharaṇabhūṣitāḥ.

18 N1/12.9b - nīlapītapaṭābaddhāḥ kṛṣṇāb(v)aradharāḥ (N3/12.8b, N10 - kṛṣṇāṁb(v)aradharā[ḥ]) pare.
N2/12.10a - kaṭinīlapaṭāb(v)addhā (N7/12.9a - kṛṣṇavāsāsugu[ṇ]ṭhitāḥ) kṛṣṇavāsāvalaṁb(v)inaḥ.

19 N1/12.10a - pāpātmānaś ca (N2/12.10b - paśyantaḥ) majjantiṁ (N3/12.9a - tatra kṣantiṁ, N7/12.9b - pāpātmānas te rakṣanti, BF/12.9b - pāpiṣṭhāṁs tu tudanty ete) śūlahastāś ca kiṅkarāḥ.
N4/12.9b, N8/12.96b, Ra/10.9b - tathā śastradharāḥ sarve śūlahastā(a)ś ca kecana.

20 N4/12.10a, N8/12.95a, Ra/10.10a, N7/12.10a, BF/12.10a - śaktidaṇḍadharāś cānye gadāmudgaradhāriṇaḥ.
Bo/12.5a - triśūladhāriṇaḥ kecid daṇḍamudgaradhāraṇaḥ.

21 N1/12.11a - khadirāṁ gārakāḥ kecid aṣṭihastās tathāpare.
N2/12.11b - mūrasādhariṇaḥ kecit pāśahastās tathaiva ca.
N3/12.10a - khaḍgair ghatadharāḥ kecit yaṣṭihastās tathāpare.
N4/12.10b, Ra/10.10b - paraśughotitāḥ kecit pāśahastās tathāpare.
N7/12.10b - karasāghatanaḥ kecit kecit yaṣṭiparāyaṇāḥ.
BF/12.10b - dhṛtvā tu paraśuṁ kecid yaṣṭipāśāṁs tathāpare.
Bo/12.5b - khaḍgakheṭadharāḥ kecid bhuśuṇḍīparighāyudhāḥ.

lohadaṇḍadharāḥ kecit kecit paraśupāṇayaḥ[22] [11]
musalā dhāriṇaḥ sarve bhiṇḍipālādidhāriṇaḥ[23]
bhūṣitāś ca mayā dṛṣṭāḥ kiṅkarās te sahasrāśaḥ[24] [12]
niyuktā dharmarājena pāpanigrahakāriṇaḥ[25]
dharmarājavacaḥ śrutvā tathā kurvanti kiṅkarāḥ[26] [13]

(Some) carry iron rods, while others have axes in their hands. [11]
All carry heavy wooden clubs, javelins, etc.
I saw those adorned servants, by the thousands, [12]
appointed by Dharmarāja, as fighters against sin.
Hearing Yama's orders, the servants act accordingly. [13]

---

22 N2/12.12a, N4/12.11a, Ra/10.11a - khaḍgahastāś ca saṁnaddhā lauhadaṇḍadharās tathā.
N7/12.11a - khaḍgapharasasannaddhā lohadaṇḍadharās tathā.
BF/12.11a - parighakhaḍgahastāś ca lohadaṇḍadharāś cānye.
Bo/12.6b - karālāsyāḥ śaktidharāḥ kecit paraśupāṇayaḥ.

23 N1/12.12a - musalā dhāriṇaḥ sarve(ā) (N3/12.11a - bhiṇḍaṁ pālādidhāriṇaḥ) bhiṇḍipālādidhāriṇaḥ.
N2/12.12b - mus(ś)alān dhārayanti sma bhiṇḍipālān sadā yudhān.
N4/12.11b, N8/12.97b, Ra/10.11b - bhiṇḍipālayudhāḥ kecit kecin musa(u)ladhāriṇaḥ.
N7/12.11b - mus(ś)alodhāraṇā sarve bhiṇḍipālādi cāyudhāḥ.
BF/12.11b - tomarair bhiṇḍipālais tu musalais tu vibhiṣaṇaiḥ.
Bo/12.6a - bhindipāladharāḥ kecit kecin mus(ś)alapāṇayaḥ.

24 N1/12.12b - bhūṣitāś ca mayā dṛṣṭ(v)ā[ḥ] (N3/12.11b, N10 - dṛṣṭāḥ) kiṅkarās te sahasraśaḥ.
Verse 12.12b-13a is missing in N2.
N7/12.12a - bhūṣitāś ca mayā dṛṣṭā asaṅkhyāś ca sahasraś(s)aḥ.
BF/12.12a - bhūṣitās te mayā dṛṣṭā asaṅkhyātāḥ sahasraśaḥ.

25 N1/12.13a, N3/12.12a - niyuktā dharmarājena pāpan(v)igrahakāriṇe.
N10, BF/12.12b - niyuktā (N4/12.12a, N8/12.98a, Ra/10.12a - nirmitā) dharmarājena pāpanigrahakāriṇaḥ.
N7/12.12b, Bo/12.7a - nirmitā yamarājena pāpānugrahakāriṇa[ḥ].

26 N1/12.13b, N10 - nāsiketavacaḥ śrutvā tathā kurvanti kiṅkaraḥ.
N2/12.13a - yamadi(ṛ)ṣṭaṁ ca kurvanti sarve te ghorarūpiṇaḥ.
N4/12.12b, N8/12.98b, Ra/10.12b - dharmarājavacaḥ śrutvā (BF/12.13a - tathā kurvanti kiṅkarāḥ) kurvate ghoradarśanaṁ.

pāpināṁ te ca kurvanti nāḍīchedaṁ ca bandhanaṁ[27]
krandante bahudhā pāpās trātā teṣāṁ na vidyate[28] [14]
anyad vanaṁ mayā dṛṣṭam asipatrasamanvitaṁ[29]
tatra vai yamadūtāś ca ghorā durdarśanā api[30] [15]
dīrghadaṁṣṭrā laṁbakarṇā ūrdhvakeśāgnilocanāḥ[31]
tadvṛkṣe yatra khaṭvāṅgaṁ pṛthulaṁ saghanaṁ vanaṁ[32] [16]

They tear out the sinners' veins and then (use them to) tie them up.
The sinners shout loudly a great deal, (but) there is no one to protect them. [14]
I also saw a forest there, full of sword-like leaves.
And there were really Yama's terrible messengers, very hard to look at, [15]
having long teeth, elongated ears, erect hair and fiery eyes.
At that tree in the thick forest, was a skull-headed club. [16]

---

27 N1/12.14a - pāpināṁ te ca kurvanti (N3/12.13a - nāḍīchedaṁ (BF/12.13b - pīḍaṁ chedaṁ) ca b(v)andhanaṁ, N10 - jīvakṣedaṁ va b(v)andhanaṁ) tāḍite daṇḍabandhanaṁ.
N2/12.13b - dhāvantaś ca mayā dṛṣṭā śirasichedi te vane.

28 N2/12.14a - karuṇayā krandante pāpo trātā tasya na vidyate.
N3/12.13b, N10 - krandante b(v)ahudhā(ṁ) pāpā[s] trātā teṣāṁ na vidyate.
N7/12.14a - karuṇā krandate pāpā[s] trātā teṣū na vidyate.
BF/12.13c - krandante karuṇaṁ pāpās trāṇaṁ teṣāṁ na vidyate.

29 N1/12.15a, N10 - anyad van(t)a mayā dṛṣṭa(m) asipatrasamānvitaḥ.
N2/12.14b - anyat kaṣṭaṁ mayā dṛṣṭam asipatravane (N7/12.14b - dvijāḥ, BF/12.14a - tathā) mahut.
N4/12.13b, N8/12.99b, Ra/10.13b - idānīṁ śrūyatām anyad asipatram ayaṁ vanaṁ.

30 N1/12.15b, N2/12.15a, N10 - tatra vai yamadūtāś ca (N3/12.14a - duḥsah(o)ā ghoradarśanāḥ) ghorā durdarśanā api.
N7/12.15a - tatra vai yamadūtās te ghorāś ca durdinā api.
BF/12.14b - tatraiva yamadūtāś ca ghorā durdarśanāpi ca.
Bo/12.11b - raudrarūpair mahāghorair yamadūtair itas tataḥ.

31 N1/12.16a - dīrghadaṁṣṭrā laṁbakarṇā (N7/12.15b, BF/12.15b - ūrdhvakeśāgnilocanāḥ) durdasāke 'gnilocanāḥ.

32 N2/12.16a - tad vṛkṣā khaṭu yatrābhāḥ pṛthulaṁ sarvato vane.
N3/12.15b - tad vṛkṣapatraṣaḍgāntaṁ (N7/12.16a - vṛkṣapatraṁ ṣaḍgaṁ) pṛthulaṁ saghanaṁ vanaṁ.
N4/12.14b, N8/12.1ą, Ra/10.14b - vṛkṣās tatrāpi patrāḍhyāḥ pṛthulāś ca mahocchritāḥ.
BF/12.15b - tad vṛkṣapattradurgamyaṁ pṛthulaṁ saṁhataṁ vanaṁ.

pāpakarmā durācāro dūṣakaḥ kalahapriyaḥ[33]
kṣipyate yamadūtaiś ca asipatravanāntare[34] [17]
patitais tālapatraiś ca gātrachedo hi pāpināṁ[35]
pralāpaṁ kurvate tatra hāhākāraṁ ca duḥkhitāḥ[36] [18]
evaṁ vai kliśyamānās te mayā dṛṣṭā hy anekaśaḥ[37]

The evil doer of bad conduct, wicked, who loves quarrelling,
is thrown by Yama's messengers into the forest of sharp sword-like leaves. [17]
The fallen down leaves cut off the sinners' limbs.
Those miserable ones cry there, uttering wailing sounds. [18]
I really saw many of those tortured souls,

---

33 N1/12.17a, N10 - pāpakarmā durācāro (BF/12.16a - lohamohavaśaṁ gataḥ) dūṣakaḥ (N3/12.16a - kalahaḥ priyaḥ) kalaha(ā)priyaḥ.
N2/12.16b, N7/12.16b - pāpakarmā (N4/12.15a, N8/12.1b, Ra/10.15a - pāpātmāno) durācār(ā)o dūṣakaḥ kalahapriyaḥ.
Bo/12.8a - pāpakarmaratān krurāṁs tathaiva kalahapriyān.

34 N1/12.17b - kṣipyate yamadūtaiś ca as(p)ip(s)atravanāntare.
N2/12.17a, N7/12.17a - kṣipyante yamadūtaiś ca asitālavanāntare.
N4/12.15b, N8/12.2a, Ra/10.15b - kṣipyante tādṛśair dūtair (BF/12.16b - yamadūtais tv) asipatravanāntare.
Bo/12.8b - kṣipanti yamadūtās te hy asipatravanāntare.

35 N1/12.18a - patanā tena patreṇa gātrakṣedo (N3/12.17a - gātrachedo) vidhīyate.
N4/12.16, N8/12.2b-3a, Ra/10.16 - patanti yatra patrāṇi mahānty asimayāni ca
taiḥ patraiḥ patitais teṣāṁ gātracchedo 'bhijāyate.
N7/12.17b - patitās tatra patrāṇi gātr(v)acchedo hi pāpināṁ.
BF/12.17a - patitais tālapattrais tu gātracchedo vidhīyate.
Bo/12.9a - patitāḥ kālasūtreṣu mayā dṛṣṭāś ca kecana.

36 Additional verse - N2/12.18b-19a:
sṛṣṭamātre tato dehevahadhā tat praśasyate
jarāmṛtyur na vai tatra kleśa eva (N7/12.19a - kleśam ekaṁ) ca pāpināṁ.
N7/12.18 - pralāpaṁ kurvatas tatra cheditāḥ khaṇḍakhaṇḍitāḥ
sṛṣṭamātraṁ punar dehaṁ vāyus teṣāṁ na paśyati.
BF/12.17b - pralāpaṁ kurvate tatra ccheditāḥ khaṇḍaśaḥ kṛtāḥ.

37 N3/12.18a - evaṁ vai kliś(s)yamānās te mayā dṛṣṭe sv anekaśaḥ.
BF/12.19a - evaṁ vai kleśitās tatra mayā dṛṣṭāḥ sahasraśaḥ.
Bo/12.11a - tatra sthāne mayā dṛṣṭā manuṣyā bahupīḍitāḥ.

kūṭasākṣipradātāraḥ kūṭadharmaparāyaṇāḥ[38] [19]
nānājanasamāsaktāś cauryavṛttyā ca jīvinaḥ[39]
nikṣepahāriṇaś cānye viśvāsabrahmaghātakāḥ[40] [20]
ete sarve mayā dṛṣṭāḥ saṁsthitāḥ kaṇṭhaśṛṅkhalāḥ[41]
laṁbante teṣu vṛkṣeṣu duḥkhena pralapanti ca[42] [21]

bearers of false witness, practicing dishonest, deceitful ways, [19]
having (deceitful) relations with many people, living the life of a thief.
Others, stealing entrusted items, breaching faith, Brahmin killers – [20]
I saw all of those, standing (there), their necks tied with chains,
hanging from those trees, crying because of their misery. [21]

---

38 N1/12.19b - kūṭasākṣipradātāraṁ (N10 - kūṭadharmaparāyasa) kuṭadharmapa(ṇacchale)rāyaṇāḥ.
N2/12.20a - kūṭisākṣipradātāraḥ kūpaḥ pāpebhapīḍitāḥ.
N3/12.18b - kūṭ(r)aḥ sākṣipradātāro kūṭadharmaparāyaṇaḥ.
BF/12.19b - kūṭasākṣyapradātāraḥ kūṭadharmeṇa jīvinaḥ.

39 N1/12.20a - nānājanasamaṁ saktaś coravṛtyāc ca jīvati.
N2/12.20b - chalenopārjate yas tu caurapāpena jīvati.
N3/12.19a - chalenārjena saṁsaktaś cauryyavṛttyā (N10 - corakṛtyā) ca jīvati.
N4/12.18b, N8/12.5a, Ra/10.18b - ye jayanti chalenāpi ye ca cauryyopajīvinaḥ.
BF/12.20a - chalena jīvate yas tu jīved yaś caurakarmaṇā.
Bo/12.9b - jīvanti mlecchavṛttyā ye caurakarmopajīvinaḥ.

40 N1/12.20b - nikṣipyahārakā(r) ye (N3/12.19b, N7/12.21a - vai) ca (BF/12.20b - nikṣepaṁ ca hared yas tu) viśvāsabrahmaghātakāḥ.
N2/12.21a - ye ca vichedya hartma(-) ye ca viśvāsaghātinaḥ.
N4/12.19a, N8/12.5b, Ra/10.19a - nikṣepahāriṇaś cānye pare vikhyātaghātakāḥ.

41 N1/12.21a, N3/12.21a - ete sarve mayā dṛṣṭā(aṁ)ḥ (N2/12.21b - śṛṅkhalaiḥ kaṇṭhasaṁsthitaiḥ, N4/12.19b, N8/12.6a, Ra/10.19b, BF/12.21a - kaṇṭhasaṁsthitaśṛṅkhalāḥ, N7/12.21b - kaṇṭhasaṅkalasaṁsthitāḥ) saṁsthitāḥ kaṇṭhaśṛṅkhalāḥ.

42 N1/12.21b, N3/12.21b, N10 - l(k)aṁb(v)ate teṣu vṛkṣ(t)eṣu duḥkhitā[ḥ] pralapanti ca.
N2/12.22a - avalaṁb(v)itāś ca vṛkṣeṣu duḥkhena pralapanti ca (vi).
N4/12.20a, N8/12.6b, Ra/10.20a - asipatreṣu pātyante vṛkṣeṣu yamakiṅkaraiḥ.
N7/12.22a - avalamb(v)itatā vṛkṣe tasmin duḥkhena duḥkhināḥ.
BF/12.21b - lambamānā mahāvṛkṣe dūṣitā kākapakṣibhiḥ.

pātyante te mahāraudre kūpe kṛmiṣu pūrite[43]
tasya pārśve mahāśvāno dīrghadantā mahānanāḥ[44] [22]
anena vidhinā dṛṣṭās tatra vṛkṣasamīpataḥ[45]
teṣāṁ saṁsmaraṇād eva romaharṣaś ca jāyate [23]
tāḍyante mudgaraiḥ kecid badhyamānāś ca kiṅkaraiḥ[46]
nīyante kliśyamānāś ca kaṇṭhabaddhāś ca yāyinaḥ[47] [24]

They are thrown into those very fierce wells, filled with worms.
At his (Yama's) side there are big dogs, with big mouths and long teeth. [22]
In this way I did see (things) there, near that tree,
that the mere memory of them causes hair-bristling. [23]
Some (sinners) are tied up and beaten with mallets by (Yama's) servants.
They are tormented while moving, being led (away) tied by their necks. [24]

---

43 N1/12.22a, N3/12.21a, N10 - pātyante te mahāraudre kūpe kṛ(ta)miṣ(s)u pūrite.
N2/12.22b - śākhānte ca mahāraudre kṛmikūpāśu pūrite.
N4/12.20b, N8/12.7a, Ra/10.20b - teṣāṁ madhye mahāraudraḥ kṛmipūyasupūritaḥ.
N7/12.22b - pralapanti patanti te mahāraudrāḥ kṛmipūritāḥ.

44 N1/12.22b, N3/12.22b, N10 - tatra yāyāt mahāśvāno bhakṣyanti muhur muhuḥ.
N2/12.23a - tasya pārśve mahāśvāno dīrghadantā mahanmukhāḥ.
N4/12.21b, N8/12.8a, Ra/10.21b - tasya tīre mahāśvāno mahādaṁṣṭrā bhayaṅkarāḥ.
N7/12.23a - tasya pārśve mahāś(s)vān(ā)o dīrghadaṁṣṭrā mahānanāḥ.

45 N1/12.23a, N3/12.22a, N10 - anena (N7/12.25b - vividhā) vidhinā dṛṣṭās tatra vṛkṣasamīpataḥ.
Verses 12.23-25 are missing in N2. Additional verses - N2/12.23b-24:
bhakṣyanti ca pāpiṣṭān māṁsam ādāya bhūriśaḥ
chinnāḥ chinnāḥ patanty ete tālavṛkṣaphul[l](a)ā yathā
dehe ca patite tatra bhakṣitāḥ kṛmisaṅkulaiḥ.
N7/12.23b-24a - śīrṣaṁ grīvāpatanty eva tālavṛkṣaphalaṁ yathā
dehe tatra patanty eva bhakṣ[y]a[n]te kṛmiksaṅkulaiḥ.

46 N1/12.24a, N3/12.23a, N10 - tāḍyante mudgaraiḥ keci[d] b(v)adhyamānāś ca kiṅkaraiḥ.
N7/12.26b - mudgarais tāḍya[n]te kecit b(v)addhamānāś ca saṅku(a)laiḥ.

47 N2/12.25a - nīyante kaṇṭhabaddhās tu kliśyamānās (N7/12.27a - te samānāhitā[ḥ] - vi) tu pāpinaḥ.
N3/12.23b - nīyante kliśyamānāś ca kaṇṭha (N10 - kaṇṭhe) b(v)adhvāś ca pāpinaḥ.

nikṣipyante mahāraudre dustare narake narāḥ[48]
na nistaranti te ghoraṁ mānuṣaṁ prāpyamohitāḥ[49] [25]
mahārauravavikhyātaṁ dusthānaṁ ca bhayaṅkaraṁ[50] [26]
anyathā ca mayā dṛṣṭaṁ bhīṣaṇaṁ śāsanaṁ mahat[51]
ete kṛtāś ca dūtāś ca mahābalaparākramāḥ[52] [27]
kālaś ca kālapāśaś ca mahāpāśadharaḥ sudhīḥ[53]

People are thrown into the hard-to-cross quarters of the fierce Hell,
unconscious, unable to cross that terrible, inaccessible to humans, [25]
a bad and frightening place, which is called the Mahāraurava. [26]
I also saw there the great terrifying punisher,
(with) his abysses and his mighty and aggressive messengers – [27]
Kāla[(II)]*, and his noose. And the Wise one (Yama), holding the big noose*[(III)]*,*

---

48 N1/12.26b - nikṣipyante mahāraudre dustare (N10 - narake(na) narāḥ) narakena ca.
N2/12.25b, N7/12.27b - niḥkṣipyante mahāghore (N3/12.24a - mānuṣaṁ prāpyamohitāḥ) dustare narak(ās)e sarve.

49 N1/12.27a - na nistaranti te ghorān mānuṣaṁ śakyamohitāḥ.
N2/12.26a - kathaṁ nistarate ghore (N7/12.28a - ghoraṁ) mānuṣatve vimohitāḥ.

50 N2/12.28a, N3/12.26a - mahārauravavikhyātaṁ (N7/12.30a - dusthānaṁ bhayaṅkariṇaṁ) tat sthānaṁ [ca] bhayaṅkaraṁ.

51 N2/12.26b - anyat sthānaṁ (N7/12.28b - athānya ca) mayā dṛṣṭaṁ bhīṣaṇaṁ mānasaṁ mahat.
N3/12.24b - athānyac (N1/12.24b - tatra ca) ca mayā dṛṣṭaṁ bhīṣaṇaṁ śāsanaṁ mahat.
N4/12.26b, N8/12.13a, Ra/10.26b - tatra tāvan mayā dṛṣṭaṁ kālasthānaṁ mahādbhutaṁ.
Bo/12.12a - ekasmin samaye dṛṣṭo mayā vaivasvato yamaḥ.

52 N3/12.26b, N7/12.30b - dūtās tasya (N10 - dūtāś ca te, N4/12.29b, N8/12.16b, Ra/10.29b - tasya dūtā) mahākāyā mahāb(v)alaparākramāḥ.

53 N1/12.25a - kālaś ca kālapāśaś ca mahāpāśadharā sudhīḥ.
N2/12.27a - kālasthānaṁ ca kālaś ca (N3/12.25a - tat kṛte saṁyamatsudhīḥ) ye manuśyā[ṁ]ś ca tāḍayet.
N10 - kālaś ca kālapāśadharaḥ sudhīḥ (short).
N4/12.27a, N8/12.13b, Ra/10.27a - tatra kālo mahābhīmo mahākṛṣṇatanur dvijāḥ.
N7/12.29a - kālasthānaṁ ca kālāntaṁ mānuṣasya ca sādhayet.

mahāraudro mahākṛṣṇaḥ svarṇābharaṇabhūṣitaḥ[54] [28]
daṇḍaś ca dakṣiṇe haste pāśaś caivottare kare[55]
mahiṣāsanam ārūḍho rudhirāraktalocanaḥ[56] [29]
parivāraśataṁ teṣāṁ duṣṭākṛtibhayaṅkaraṁ[57]
kṛtāntadūtās te khyātāḥ kiṅkarās tu mahāyudhāḥ[58] [30]
yamena preṣitās te vai kiṅkarā cāgrataḥ sthitāḥ[59]

very fierce, very black, decorated with gold ornaments, [28]
holding the stick in his right hand, and the noose in the other,
riding on his buffalo, his eyes blood-red. [29]
Surrounded by hundreds of those wicked, fierce, frightening (creatures),
called the Destroyer's[(IV)] *messengers, those heavily armed servants. [30]*
They were ordered by Yama to perform their special task:

---

54 N7/12.29b - mahāraudraṁ mahākṛṣṇaṁ mukuṭaṁ svarṇābhūṣitaṁ.

55 N1/12.29a, N10 - daṇḍaś ca (N3/12.27a - daṇḍas tu) dakṣiṇe haste (N2/12.29a - pāśaṁ vāmakare tathā, N4/12.28a, N8/12.14b, Ra/10.28a - pāśaṁ vāme śubhaṁ dadhat) pāśaś (N7/12.31a - pāśaṁ) caivottare kare.
Bo/12.13a - kuṇḍalālaṅkṛtaḥ śrīmān daṇḍapāśadharo dvijāḥ.

56 Half verse 12.29b is missing in N2.
N10 - mahiṣāsanam ārūḍho (N4/12.28b, N8/12.15a, Ra/10.28b - rudhirārdravilocanaḥ, N7/12.31b - rudhirārdra[ś] ca vilocanaḥ (vi), Bo/12.12b - mahābalaparākramaḥ) [rudhi]rāraktalocana[ḥ].

57 N1/12.30a - parivāraśataṁ teṣāṁ (N3/12.28a - duṣṭākṛtibhayaṅkarāḥ, N10 - duṣṭākṛtabhayaṅkaraṁ, N7/12.32a - kālapāś(s)asya kiṅkaraiḥ) duṣṭāt krūrabhayaṅkaraṁ.

58 N2/12.30b - kṛtānta iva vikhyāt(a)āḥ kiṅkarair api dāruṇaiḥ.
N3/12.28b - kṛtāntadūtās te khyātāḥ kiṅkarās tu (N10 - ta) mahāyudhā[ḥ].
N4/12.27b, N8/12.14a, Ra/10.27b - kṛtānta iti cākhyato rājā cāsuraśāsanaḥ.
N7/12.32b - kṛtāntadūtatare khyātāḥ kiṅkarā mah(ad)āyudhāḥ.
BF/12.32a - kṛtāntadūtās te khyātāḥ kiṅkarāḥ prasthitās tathā.
Bo/12.13b - buddhiśālī mahākāyo dūtaiś ca parivāritaḥ.

59 N1/12.31a - yamena preṣitās te(ś) ca kiṅkarā[ḥ] svayataḥ (N3/12.29a - vai kiṅkarāś cāgrata[ḥ]) sthitāḥ.
N2/12.31a - yamena preṣitā dūtāḥ (N10 - kiṅkarās(ś)vayataḥ sthitāḥ, N4/12.31b, N8/12.18b - rākṣasārthaṁ kadā cana, N7/12.33a - kiṅkarāś cāgrasaṁsthitāḥ) kiṅkarāś cāgr(a)e saṁsthitāḥ.
Ra/10.32a - ekadājñāpayāmāsa yamo hi nijakiṅkarān.

ānaya asurādhyakṣaṁ bhūtale parvate sthitaṁ[60] [31]
athavaite gatās tatra dūtā daityārthinas tathā[61]
āsurās te mahāśūrā yudhyante yamakiṅkaraiḥ[62] [32]
mahābalais tair asurair yamadūtā vinirjitāḥ[63]
bhagnā yamapuraṁ prāptā dharmarājasamīpataḥ[64] [33]

"Bring (here) the demons' king, who is staying on a mountain, on Earth". [31]
The messengers then departed quickly, searching the demons.
The demons fought very bravely with Yama's servants(V)*, (and) [32]*
Yama's messengers were defeated by the demons with great force.
Broken, they reached Yama's city and Dharmarāja's presence, [33]

---

60 N1/12.31b - ānaryasv asurā bhṛtya (N7/12.33b - ānaye (BF/12.32b - ānayan) daityarājānaṁ) bhūtale parvate sthitaṁ.
Half verse 12.31b is missing in N2.
N3/12.29b, N10 - ānaya asurādhyakṣaṁ bhūtale parvataṁ sthitā.
N4/12.32a, N8/12.19a - te ca tatra gatā yatra rākṣasā santy anekaśaḥ.
Ra/10.32b - gatāyuṣo 'surān dūtā ānayadhvam ihācirāt.

61 N1/12.32a - atha te vegatās tatra (N7/12.34a - gatās tatraiva) dūtā daityārthinas tadā.
N3/12.30 - atha te vai haṭhāt tatra dūtaiś ca prārthitas tataḥ.
BF/12.33a - atha te vai gatās tatra dūtās taddaityasya tadā.
Ra/10.33a - ity ājñaptā gatās tatra dūtā daityārthinas tathā.

62 N1/12.32b, N3/12.31a, N10 - āsurās te (N7/12.34b - ca) mahāśūrā yudhyante yamakiṅkaraiḥ.
Verses 12.32b-33 are missing in N2.
N4/12.32b-33a, N8/12.19b-20a - tato 'surās tu vijñāya tān sarvān yamakiṅkarān ayudyanta mahāśūrās taiḥ samaṁ tatra (Ra/10.34a - vedinaḥ) vaidinaḥ.
BF/12.33b - āsurāś ca mahāśūrā yuyudhur yamakiṅkaraiḥ.
Ra/10.33b - gṛhītum udyatāḥ kruddhāḥ śāstrāṇy udyamya sarvataḥ.

63 N1/12.33a - mahābalair varaṁsurai(ḥ)r (N3/12.31b - mahāb(v)alais tair asurai[r], N4/12.33b, N8/12.20b - tato 'surair (Ra/10.34b - mahāvīryyair) mahāghorair) yamadūtā vinirjitāḥ.
N7/12.35a - śastrair (BF/12.34a - astrair) mahāb(v)alais teṣāṁ yamadūtāś ca nirjitāḥ.

64 N3/12.32a, N10 - bhagnā yamapuraṁ (N7/12.35b - yamapurīṁ) prāptā(ḥ) dharmarājasamīpataḥ.
N4/12.34a, N8/12.21a - khinnā yamapurīṁ prāptā dharmarājasya (Ra/10.35a - veśmani) vai tataḥ.
BF/12.34b - bhagnāyudhāḥ samāyātā dharmarājasamīpagāḥ.

vijñāpayanti sma ca te dānavair nirjitā vayaṁ[65]
dharmarājā vacaḥ śrutvā kālam āhuya vai tataḥ[66] [34]
aho kāla kṛtānta tvam ātmīyabalasaṁyutaḥ[67]
gaccha śīghraṁ mahābāho baddhvā dānavam ānaya[68] [35]
jayaśabdaṁ tataḥ kṛtvā niḥsṛtā yamasādanāt[69]
sannaddhās tatkṣaṇāt sarve śastrāyudhakaroddhatāḥ[70]

and informed him of their defeat by the demons.
Having heard their words, Dharmarāja thus summoned Kāla, (and said): [34]
"O Kāla, you, the destroyer, by your own power,
go quickly, O mighty one, and bring the demon(s' king) chained". [35]
Shouting "Victory!", with fastened armour, he (i.e. Kāla) left Yama's abode,
immediately, along with all the other terrible (servants), their weapons ready.

---

65 N2/12.32a, N7/12.36a - vijñāpayanti dharmasya dānavena jitā vayaṁ.
N4/12.34b, N8/12.21b, Ra/10.35b - jñāpayanti sma tat sarvam asurair nirjitā vayaṁ.
BF/12.35a - vināśakāle dharmas te dānavais tair jitā vayaṁ.

66 N1/12.34b, N10 - dharmarājo vaca (BF/12.35b - dharmarājā vacaḥ) śrutvā kālam āhuya vai tataḥ.
N2/12.32b - dharmarājavacaḥ śrutvā kālam (N3/12.33a - āhur yamai tataḥ) vijñāpayanti te.
N4/12.35a, N8/12.22a, Ra/10.36a - dharmas tu tad vacaḥ śrutvā svadūtānāṁ parājayaṁ.

67 N1/12.35a, N10 - aho kāla(ḥ) (N2/12.33a - kṛtāntaś ca) kṛtānta tvam (N3/12.33b - ātmano b(v)alasaṁyutaḥ, N4/12.37a, N8/12.24a, Ra/10.38a - ajeyab(v)alasaṁyutaḥ) ātmīyabalasaṁyutaṁ.
BF/12.36a - aho kāla jayas tena vihito rākṣasena ca.

68 N1/12.35b - gaccha śīghraṁ maho gatvā (N10 - dāvena manayajaya) dāna yajñajayaṁ tataḥ.
N7/12.37b - gaccha śīghraṁ mahāb(v)āho (N4/12.37b, N8/12.24b, Ra/10.38b - deśaṁ rākṣasāsevitaṁ, BF/12.36b - tatra dānavamāraṇe) b(v)addhvā (N3/12.34a - gatvā) dānavam ānaya.

69 N1/12.36a - kṛtvā tiṣṭhatoya praṇasanāt (incomplete).
N3/12.34b - jayaśabd(ṣṭ)aṁ tataḥ kṛtvā niḥsṛto (N10 - nisṛto) yamaśāsanāt.
N4/12.38b, N8/12.25b, Ra/10.39b - evaṁ yamājñāṁ saṁprāpya nirgato deśam asuraṁ.
N7/12.38a - jayaḥ ś(s)abdaṁ tataḥ kṛtvā nisṛtā yamaś(s)āsanāt.
BF/12.37a - jayāśiṣas tataḥ kṛtvā nirgato yamaśāsanāt.

70 N1/12.36a - sannad(t)dhās ta[t]kṣaṇaṁ sarve ghore śastrakṛtoddhataḥ.
N3/12.35a - sannaddhā tu kṣaṇaṁ (N10 - sannaddhās tatkṣaṇaṁ) sarve ghoraśastrakaroddhṛ(a)tāḥ.

yuddhārthaṁ nirgatā ghorāḥ kālas teṣāṁ ca nāyakaḥ[71] [36]
candrahāraṁ kare khaḍgaṁ pāśaṁ vāmakare tathā[72]
asuraiḥ kiṅkarāṇāṁ ca yuddhaṁ jātaṁ sudāruṇaṁ[73] [37]
sāyakair niśitaiḥ khaḍgair vajramudgarayaṣṭibhiḥ[74]
kuntaiś ca musalair daṇḍair yaṣṭilohamayais tathā[75] [38]

Those terrible (servants) went to fight, with Kāla as their leader, [36]
holding a crescent-like saber in one hand, and a noose in the other.
The demons and the servants had a very fierce battle, [37]
with sharp arrows, swords, Vajra(VI)*, mallets and sticks,*
with spears, heavy wooden clubs, rods, and iron sticks, [38]

N4/12.39a, N8/12.26a, Ra/10.40a - sannaddhāḥ śastrasaṁyuktāḥ sarve samarakovidāḥ.
N7/12.38b - sannaddhās ta[t]kṣaṇā(ḥ)t sarve śastraś(s)ubhrakaroddhatāḥ.

71 N1/12.36b - yuddhārthaṁ nirgatā dhārāḥ (N2/12.35a, N7/12.39a - yuddhārthe nirgatā(s)ḥ, (N3/12.35b, N10 - ghorāḥ, N4/12.39b, N8/12.26b, Ra/10.40b - śīghraṁ) sarve) kālas teṣāṁ ca nāyakaḥ.
BF/12.37b-38a - nānāyudhadharāḥ daṇḍapāśakarās tathā
jvalanto nirgatāḥ sarve kālas teṣāṁ ca nāyakaḥ.

72 N2/12.35b - candrahāsakaraṁ khaḍgaṁ (N3/12.36a - candrahāraṁ kare ṣaḍgaṁ) pāśaṁ vāmakare tathā.
N7/12.39b - candrahāsaṁ kare ṣaḍgaṁ pāś(s)aṁ vāmakare sthitaṁ.
BF/12.38b - candrahāsaḥ kare khaḍgaḥ pāśo vāmakare tathā.

73 N1/12.37b - asuraiḥ kinnarāṇāṁ (N3/12.36b, N10 - kiṅkarāṇāṁ) ca yuddhaṁ (N7/12.40a - yānta mahāgho(gu)ra(ū)ṁ) jātaṁ sudāruṇaṁ.
N2/12.36a - asuraiḥ kinnarāṇāṁ tu (N4/12.40a, N8/12.27a, Ra/10.41a - tato 'suraiḥ kiṅkarāṇāṁ) yuddho 'bhūd atidāruṇaḥ.
BF/12.39a - asurakiṅkarāṇāṁ tu yuddhaṁ jātaṁ mahābalaṁ.
Bo/12.17b - tatra tair abhavad yuddhaṁ prāsamudgaratomaraiḥ.

74 N1/12.38a, N10, N4/12.40b, N8/12.27b, Ra/10.41b - sāyakair niśitaiḥ (BF/12.39b - tac cāpi saṁhataiḥ) khaḍgair vaj[r]amudgarayaṣṭibhiḥ.
N2/12.36b - s(ś)āyakair asitaiḥ khaḍgavajramudgarayaṣṭibhiḥ.
Bo/12.18a - sāyakair lohadaṇḍaiś ca khaḍgaiḥ śūlair bhuśuṇḍibhiḥ.

75 N1/12.38b - kuntaiś ca kuśale pāśai[r] daṇḍalohamayais tathā.
N2/12.37a - kuntais tu mus(ś)alair (N3/12.37b - pāśai(ḥ)r daṇḍai[r] lohamayais tathā) daṇḍair yaṣṭilohamayai(ḥ)r varaiḥ.
N10 - ku[n]taiś ca ku[śa]lai[ḥ] pāśair daṇḍair lohamayais tathā.
N4/12.41a, N8/12.28a, Ra/10.42a - kuntaiś ca musa(u)laiḥ pāśair daṇḍair (BF/12.40a - lohamayais tathā) lohamayair varaiḥ.

śilākhaṇḍaiś ca pāśaiś ca dhanubhir bahubhis tathā[76]
hastihastair nakhair dantair bahubhir muṣṭibhis tathā[77] [39]
evaṁ pravṛddhaḥ saṅgrāmaḥ sughoro lomaharṣaṇaḥ[78]
kālo 'pi nirjitas tena cāsureṇa balīyasā[79] [40]
tadā gato mahākālo sarvasaṁhārakaṁ vibhuṁ[80]

with pieces of rocks, nooses and bows – many of those.
Using elephant trunks, nails, teeth (and) fists, [39]
the fighting developed, becoming stronger, very fierce, (and) hair-bristling,
(and) even Kāla was defeated by the mighty demon. [40]
Then great Kāla, the destroyer of all, went to the All-pervading (and)

---

76 N1/12.39a - śilākhaṇḍaiś ca pāśāṇo [dhanubhir] bahubhis tathā.
N2/12.37b - śilākhaḍgaiś ca pāśāiś ca dhanubhiś ca dvidhā vidhaiḥ.
N3/12.38a - śilāṣaṇḍaiś ca pāśāṇaiḥ dhanubhir b(v)ahubhis tathā.
N10 - śilākhaṇḍaiś ca pāṣ(m)āṇair dh(dv)anu(kṣa)[bhir bahu]bhis tathā.
N7/12.41b, BF/12.40b - śilākhaṇḍaiś ca pāṣāṇair dhanubhir bahu yudhyate.

77 N1/12.39b - hastihastanakhair (N2/12.38a - hastair hastair nakhair, N3/12.38b - hastā hastanakhair) dantair bahubhir muṣṭibhis tathā.
N10 - tastihastanakhair dantair dyaḍubhir muṣṭibhis tathā.
N4/12.42a, N8/12.29a, Ra/10.43a - śilākhaṇḍair nakhair dantair muṣṭibhir vajrarṣṭibhiḥ.
N7/12.42a - hastahastair nakhair dantair yudhyate b(v)ahu muṣṭibhiḥ.
BF/12.41a - hastanakhair yudhyate ca ghaṭṭabhir muṣṭibhis tathā.

78 N1/12.40a - evaṁ pravṛddhaḥ (N3/12.39a - pravṛtta) saṅgrama[ḥ] sughoro lomaharṣaṇaḥ.
N2/12.38b - evaṁ pravartate ghore nirjitā dānavās tadā.
N10 - evaṁ pravṛtte saṅgrāme sughore romaharṣaṇe.
N7/12.42b - evaṁ pravarttate ghoraṁ saṅgrāmaṁ lomaharṣaṇaṁ.
N4/12.42b, N8/12.29b - evaṁ pravarttamāne tu saṅgrāme romaharṣaṇe.
BF/12.41b - evaṁ pravartito ghoraḥ saṅgrāmo romaharṣaṇaḥ.
Bo/12.18b - evaṁ teṣā(ṁ)m [a]bhūd yuddhaṁ mahad vai romaharṣaṇaṁ.

79 N1/12.40b, N10 - kālo 'pi nirjitas tena cāsureṇa balīyasā.
Verses 12.40b-43b are missing in N2, N3.
N4/12.43a, N8/12.30a - kāladūtair (Ra/10.43a - yamadūtair) mahābhīmair asurās te parājitāḥ.
Bo/12.19a - kiṅkaraiḥ kālapāśena jitās te rākṣasā raṇe.

80 N1/12.41a - tadā gato mahākālaṁ sarvasaṁhārakaṁ (N10 - vibhuṁ) vibhuḥ.

upatasthe mahāviṣṇuṁ devaṁ devajagadguruṁ [41]
tvayaiva sthāpitaḥ pūrve sarveṣām ādyakāriṇā[81]
śāntyarthaṁ kim ahaṁ nātha śāsitas te kṛpāyitaḥ[82] [42]
iti kālavacaḥ śrutvā viṣṇuḥ kopaṁ jagāma ha
kopāj jāto mahākālaḥ preṣito dānavaṁ prati[83] [43]
kiṅkarais tair mahāghorair nirjitās tena dānavāḥ[84]
viṣṇukṣiptena pāśena baddhā daityā mahābalāḥ[85] [44]
daṇḍamudgaraghātena kṛtās te tatkṣaṇād vaśe[86]

prayed to the great god Viṣṇu, the teacher of gods and of the universe: [41]
"In the past you have posted me above all beings.
Wretched (as I am now), order me what I should do for (achieving) peace." [42]
Having heard Kāla's words, Viṣṇu became very angry, (and)
out of his anger, he sent great Kāla (again) against the demons. [43]
With the very terrible servants, he (Kāla) defeated the demons,
tying the mighty demons up with the noose, obtained from Viṣṇu. [44]
They subjugated them in a moment, (and) beating them with sticks and mallets,

---

81 N1/12.42a, N10 - tvayaiva sthāpitaḥ pūrva[ṁ] sarveṣām adyakāriṇā.

82 Emendation - DS. N1/12.42b - śāntyarthaṁ kim ahaṁ nātha śāsita(e)s te kṛpāya vā.
N10 - śāstyarthaṁ kiṁ so(a) 'haṁ nātha śās(ś)itas tena yā(-)nā.

83 N10 - kopāj jāto mahākālaḥ preṣito va dānavaṁ prati (vi).

84 N2/12.39a - kiṅkaraiś ca mahāghorais taṁ grāme lomaharṣaṇe.
N3/12.39b - kiṅkarais tair mahāghorai(ḥ)r nirjitā dānavās tadā.
N7/12.43a - kiṅkarais tu mahāghorair nirjitā (BF/12.42a - dānavādhipāḥ) dānavā api.

85 N1/12.44b - viṣṇur jitena (N3/12.40a - kālakṣiptena) pāśena b(v)adhvā daityā mahābalā[ḥ].
N2/12.39b - kālākhyena ca pāśena badhvā daityaṁ mahāb(v)alaṁ.
N4/12.43b, N8/12.30b, Ra/10.44b - tataḥ kālo mahāpāśair b(v)adhvā daityāṁś ca dānavān.
N7/12.43b - kālena nikṣiptaṁ pāśaṁ b(v)addhā daityā mahāb(v)alā[ḥ].
BF/12.42b - kālākṣipati tān pāśair baddhā daityā mahābalāḥ.

86 N2/12.40a - daṇḍamudgaraghātena (N10 - kṛtās tena kṣaṇād vaśe, N7/12.44a - vaśīkṛtvā ca tatkṣaṇāt, BF/12.43a - vaśīkṛtās tataḥ kṣaṇāt) vaśaṁ kṛtvā ca tatkṣaṇāṁ.
N4/12.43a (repeated verse number 43), N8/12.31a, Ra/10.45a - gatāyuṣo vaśībhūtān daṇḍaghātaiḥ pramardya ca.

pāśair baddhāḥ samānītā dharmarājasya cāgrataḥ[87] [45]
tāṁs ca dṛṣṭvā yamaḥ kṛṣṇaḥ kruddhaḥ teṣāṁ vaco 'bravīt[88]
atha dūtais tato nītāś citraguptasya vartmani[89] [46]
vicārya citraguptena dūtebhyas te samarpitāḥ[90]
kākagṛdhrāgrataḥ kṣiptā bhakṣaṇāya paśūnāṁ ca[91] [47]

brought them tied together by the noose, before Dharmarāja. [45]
Seeing them, the angry black Yama said his word to them.
Then the messengers led them by the road to Citragupta. [46]
Having settled (the matter) with Citragupta, the messengers delivered them to him.
They were thrown before crows (and) vultures, to be eaten by the wild beasts, [47]

---

87 N1/12.45b - pāśair baddh(v)ā[ḥ] sa(ṁ)m[ān]itā (N2/12.40b - ānīto b(v)adhyamānās tu) dharmarājasya cāgrataḥ.
N3/12.41a - pāśair (N10 - pāśais (ta)) b(v)addh(v)ā[ḥ] samānītā (N7/12.44b - ānītā b(v)addhamānās te) dharmarājasya cāgrataḥ.
N4/12.43b, N8/12.31b, Ra/10.45b - ānītavān mahāb(v)āhur dharmmarājasya sannidhau.
BF/12.43b - atas taiḥ kiṅkarair nītā dharmarājāgratas tataḥ.
Bo/12.19b - pāśair baddhān mahādaityān āninyu(ḥ)s te yamāntikaṁ.

88 N1/12.46a - tāṁs ca dṛṣṭvā yamaḥ (N10 - kruddhaḥ) kṛṣṇaḥ (N3/12.41b - tīkṣṇadṛṣṭir yamaḥ kruddho) sāstyai teṣā[ṁ] vaco 'bravīt.
N2/12.41a - tena dṛṣṭo yamaḥ kruddhaḥ kālaśāsti karoti ca.
Bo/12.20a - dharmarājaś ca tān dṛṣṭvā mahāghorataro 'bhavat.

89 N2/12.41b - atha nīto rasaḥ śīghraṁ (N3/12.42a, N10 - atha dūtais tato nītāś) citraguptasya veśmani.
N4/12.44b, N8/12.32b - evaṁ śrutvāsurā (Ra/10.46b - rāvaṁ jñātvāsurā) dūtair nītā lekhakamandiraṁ.
N7/12.45b - atha nītā asurāḥ ś(s)īghraṁ citraguptasya veśmani (vi).
BF/12.44 - te ca dṛṣṭā mayā krūrāḥ krūraśastradharās tathā
citraguptaṁ nītāḥ sarve tadgehe samupāgatāḥ.
Bo/12.20b - svān dūtān praty uvācātha nīyantāṁ citraveśmani.

90 N2/12.42a - vicārayitvā mahāpāpaṁ dūtair bhavena dhārgate (vi).
N3/12.42b - vicāryyāṁ (N10 - vicārya) citraguptena (BF/12.45a - vicāritā mahāpāpā) dūtebhyas te samarpitā[ḥ].
N4/12.45a, N8/12.33a, Ra/10.47a - citraguptavicāreṇa tān śrutvā cātatāyinaḥ.

91 Emendation - DS. N1/12.47b - kākagṛdhrāgrataḥ prakṣipad bhakṣaṇāya śunāṁ dhuraḥ (vi).
N2/12.42b - kālasyāgre viniḥkṣipte svāgre tatkṣaṇam eva ca.

yamadūtaiḥ punaḥ kṣiptā mahārauravaraurave[92]
punas te duḥsahair ghorair vahnikuṇḍe ca dānavāḥ[93] [48]
kṛmiyoniṣu nītās te pāpinaś ca pṛthak pṛthak[94]
anena vidhinā sarve te daityā duḥkhasaṁsthitāḥ[95] [49]
ato 'haṁ ṛṣibhir manye saṁsāraṁ svapnasannibhaṁ[96]
atra tiṣṭhen na balavān na dhanī na ca nirdhanaḥ[97] [50]

(and) thrown again by Yama's messengers, into the Raurava River, in Mahāraurava.
Again, those demons, were (thrown) into fire pits by the terrible, hard-to-resist (messengers). [48]
Those demons[(VII)] *were led, one by one, to be reborn as worms*[(VIII)].
In this way all those demons were afflicted with misery. [49]
Therefore I, together with the sages, consider Saṁsāra to be like a dream.
No one survives there, not the strong, neither the wealthy, not the penniless, [50]

N3/12.43a - kākagṛdhrāgrataḥ sthitvā(t) tatkṣaṇ(ā)e paśū(u)nāṁ puraḥ.
N10 - kākagṛ(ra)dhrāgrataḥ kṣipta bhakṣaṇāya śunāṁ puraḥ.
N4/12.46a, N8/12.34a, Ra/10.48a - kākagṛdhraśunām agre 'cikṣipan bhakṣaṇāya tān.
BF/12.45b - kākagṛdhrādibhir ghorair bhakṣitās te 'pi pāpinaḥ.
Bo/12.21a - citraguptas tu tān sarvān kṛmikuṇḍeṣu nyakṣipat.

92 N2/12.43a - pātito yamadūtena (N7/12.47a - sādhitā [ya]madūtaiś ca, BF/12.46a - sāditā yamadūtais te) mahārauravaraurave.

93 N1/12.48b, N10 - punas te duḥsahair ghorai[r] vāh[n]ikuṇḍe ca dānavāḥ.
N2/12.43b - niḥkṣipto duḥsahe agnikuṇḍe ca dānavas tadā.
N3/12.44a - punas te duḥsahe ghore vahnikuṇḍe ca dānavāḥ.
N7/12.47b - nikṣiptā duḥsahe ghore agnikuṇḍeṣu (BF/12.46b - hy agnikuṇḍe ca) dānavāḥ.

94 N1/12.49a - kṛmiyoniṣu nītās te pāpinarā(a)ḥ (N2/12.44a - nīto vai pāpayoni[ṁ], N3/12.44b - nītāś ca (N7/12.48a - pāpayoniṁ, BF/12.47a - pāpayonau) pāpinas te) pṛthak pṛthak.

95 N1/12.49b - anena vidhinā sarve (BF/12.47b - daityā yātā ya(ā)mālayaṁ) te dantyā (N2/12.44b - daitvā, N7/12.48b - daityā) duḥkhasaṁsthitā(a)ḥ.

96 N1/12.50a - ato 'ha(m)ṁ ṛṣi(a)bh(a)ir many(o)e saṁsāre s[v]apnasannibhe.
N2/12.45a - maharṣayo hy ahaṁ manye sahāraṁ svapnasaṁsthitaṁ.
N10 - ato 'ha(m)ṁ ṛṣayo manye saṁsāre sadmasannibhe.
N7/12.49a - bho ṛṣayaś ca manye 'haṁ saṁsāraṁ svapnasannibhaṁ.
BF/12.48a - tasmād asāraṁ saṁsāraṁ svapnavaicittyasannibhaṁ.

97 N1/12.50b - atra tiṣṭhe[n] na balavān na dh(c)anī na ca nirdhanaḥ.
N2/12.45b - balavāns tiṣṭhate nātra na yuvāsthavirasthitāḥ.

na kṣīṇo bālo vṛddho 'pi kālo grasati sarvathā[98]
bālāṁś ca yauvanasthāṁś ca vṛddhān garbhagatān api[99] [51]
sarvāṁś ca grasate kāla evaṁbhūtam idaṁ jagat[100]
evaṁbhūteṣu sarveṣu ye ca svalpāyuṣo narāḥ[101] [52]
purīṣa iva bindujāḥ harivārtānabhijñāś ca na tīrthaṁ paripanthinaḥ[102]

nor the weak, the young, or even the old people – time devours all.
Children and youth become aged, (die and) become embryo again. [51]
Time devours everything – that is really the nature of this world.
This being the nature of all things, short-lived men [52]
(are like) dung-born small creatures – the ignorant people, not interested in

---

N3/12.46a - atra tiṣṭhan na va b(v)alavān garbhagatān api.
BF/12.48b - nādhāni tiṣṭhate tatra na dhanī nāpi taskaraḥ.

98 N1/12.51a, N3/12.46b, N10 - yuvā bālo 'thavā vṛddh(o)aḥ [kā]l(a)o grasati cākhilān.
N7/12.50a - kṣa(e)ṇena b(v)ālavṛddhaś ca kālo grasati sarvasaḥ.
BF/12.49a - na kṣīṇo bālo vṛddho vā kālo grasati sarvadā.

99 N1/12.51b, N10 - bālāś ca yauvanasthāṁś ca (N2/12.46b - vṛddhān garbhagatām api) vṛddhā(a)[ṁs] tā bhagavān api.
N4/12.51a, N8/12.38b, Ra/10.52b - b(v)ālaṁ yuvānam athavā vṛddhaṁ garbhagataṁ tathā.
N7/12.50b - b(v)ālāś ca yauvanasthāś ca vṛddhagarbhagatās tv api.
BF/12.49b - bālaṁ vā yauvanākrāntaṁ vṛddhaṁ vā jarasā tathā.
Bo/12.22a - yuvāno bālakāḥ kecid vṛddhāś ca garbhagāḥ pare.

100 N3/12.47b, N10 - s(ś)arvān āviśate kāla (N7/12.51a - sarveṣv āviś(s)ate kāle) evaṁbhūtam idaṁ jagat.
N4/12.53a, N8/12.40b, Ra/10.54b - kālo grasati sarvāṁs tān tadānityam idaṁ jagat.
BF/12.50a - sarvatra vidyate kālo na kālena vinā jagat.
Bo/12.22b - evaṁbhūtāni sarvāṇi kālasya vaśavarttinaḥ.

101 N1/12.52b - evaṁbhūteṣu sarvasthā ye ca svelāyuṣo (N10 - svalpāyuṣo) narāḥ.
N2/12.47b - evaṁbhūteṣu bhūtāni sarvāvasthā susarvadā.
N7/12.51b - evaṁbhūteṣu bhūteṣu sarvavasthāvināśiṣu.

102 N1/12.53a - purīṣām iva bindu(ū)jāḥ harivārtānabhijñāś ca na tīrthaṁ paripanthinaḥ.
Half verse 12.53a is missing in N2, N3, N10. Additional verse - N2/12.48:
ko na duḥkhe na jāteṣu ko nu śocati vāmate
ye narāḥ pāpayonisthā atmāyuṣa tathā para.

sadā vyādhiparigrastās te jñeyā narakāgatāḥ[103]
divaś cyutānāṁ cihnāni śṛṇutātyādhṛtā dvijāḥ [53]
vijñānabhāvā nīrujāḥ suvaṁśyā dīrghajīvinaḥ[104]
pāpakarma nivṛtāś ca prajātā harisevane[105] [54]
śrotāraś ca kathāṁ viṣṇor dhadhirāḥ piśunoniṣu[106]
yathā ha pathikaḥ kaścic chāyām āśritya tiṣṭhati[107] [55]
viśrāmya ca punar yāti tadvad bhūtasamāgamaḥ[108]
ataḥ saṁprāpya mānuṣyaṁ kathañcid api bhārata[109] [56]
nityaṁ yateta dharmāya yataḥ sarvatra modate[110] [57]

Hari-knowledge, or in going on pilgrimage to holy places.
Always devoured by disease, it should be known that they go to Hell.
Brahmins, listen attentively to the signs of those coming from Heaven: [53]
They are knowledgeable, healthy, born in good lineage, long-lived,
devoid of evil deeds, and born for the service of Hari. [54]
They listen to the story of Viṣṇu, ignoring the tales of bad people.
Like a traveler who stands in the shade for a while, [55]
takes rest and then goes on again, so is it with all the creatures.
So, when born as human beings, however (shortly) even, O Bhārata(IX)*, [56]*
one should always strive for Dharma, and thus find joy. [57]

---

103 N2/12.49a - vyadhigrastās tathā tiṣṭhaṁ te jñeyā narakagatāḥ.
Half verse 12.53b is missing in N1, N10.

104 N2/12.49b - vijñānabhavāniratā dīrghāyur bhavyavaṁśājāḥ.
N4/12.56b, N8/12.44a, Ra/10.58a - jñānino nīrujo dīrghayuṣa uttamavaṁśajāḥ.
N7/12.53b - sajñāna bhāvo virajo dīrghāyur bhavyavaṁśājaḥ.

105 N4/12.57a, N8/12.44b, Ra/10.58b - pāpakarmā nivṛttāś ca jñeyāḥ svargagatā narāḥ.
N7/12.54a - pāpakarm(a)ā nivṛtātmā te jñeyāś ca gatā diviḥ.

106 Half verse 12.55a is missing in N2, N3.

107 N1/12.55b - yathā ha (N2/12.51a, N10 - hi) pathika(ā)ḥ kaścic chāyām āśritya tiṣṭhati.
N3/12.51a, N4/12.57b, N8/12.45b, Ra/10.59a, N7/12.55a, BF/12.54a - yathā hi pathikaḥ kaścic chāyām āśritya viśramet.

108 N2/12.51b, BF/12.54b - viśrāmya ca punar gacchet tadvad (N7/12.55b - bhūtaṁ samāgam(e)aḥ) bhūtasamāgamaḥ.
N4/12.58a, Ra/10.59b - sa viśramya gṛhaṁ gacched evaṁ jagad idaṁ dvijāḥ.

109 Verses 12.56b-57 are missing in N2.
N10 - attaḥ sa prāpya mānuṣyaṁ kathañcid api bhārata.
N4/12.58b, N8/12.46a, Ra/10.60a - iha kṣaṇaṁ tu viśramya svargaṁ narakam eva ca.

110 N1/12.57, N10 - nityaṁ yate t(n)a dharmāya yataḥ sarva namo 'stu te.

iti śrībrahmāṇḍapurāṇe nāsiketopākhyāne kālāsurayuddhavarṇano nāma dvādaśo 'dhyāyaḥ

This is the twelfth chapter of the Nāsiketa story, pertaining to the Brahmāṇḍa Purāṇa, called – Kāla and the demons.

Translation Notes

I – Literally – "The great Indra".
II – "Time", and sometimes – Yama himself.
III – Another description of both Kāla and Yama, as well as their titles.
IV – Yama.
V – In Varāha Purāṇa the battle occurs between the rebellious servants and the summoned Rākṣasas.
VI – The thunderbolt weapon.
VII – Originally – "sinful people". The similar descriptions of the fates of the demons and the sinners, may cause confusion.
VIII – Or – insects.
IX – "Bhārata" seems to be misplaced. The phrase is part of Nāsiketa's words to the Brahmins and not Vaiśaṁpāyāna's words to Janamejaya.

Chapter 13

The Forms of Dharma

nāsiketa uvāca
dharmiṣṭhānāṁ pravakṣyāmi śrūyatāṁ dvijasattamaḥ[1]
ghṛtakṣīrā mahānadyo madhvājyaṁ udakāni ca[2] [1]
peyaṁ tu vividhaṁ svādu dadhi dugdhasya rāśayaḥ[3]
sarvaṁ cottamamadhyasthaṁ kautukāni hy anekaśaḥ[4] [2]

Nāsiketa said
Listen, O excellent Brahmins, I shall describe the place of the meritorious.
There are large rivers of milk and Ghi there, and rivers of honey-like water. [1]
There is a variety of drinks, as well as heaps of cooked rice with milk.
All that is inside (there) is the best – many wonderful objects. [2]

---

1 N1/13.1a, N3/13.1a, N10, N7/13.1a, BF/13.1a - dharmiṣṭhānāṁ pravakṣyāmi śrūyatāṁ (N2/13.1a - munipuṅgava) dvijasattamāḥ.
N4/13.1a, N8/13.47a, Ra/11.1a - idānīṁ saṁpravakṣyāmi dharmikāṇāṁ gatiṁ śubhāṁ.

2 N1/13.1b, N10 - vratakṣīrā mahānadyo madhvājyaṁ udakāni ca.
N2/13.1b - ghṛtakṣīrā mahānadyo madhūni ca sarāṁsi ca.
N3/13.1b - ghṛtakṣīravahānadyo miṣṭādyā udakāni ca.
N4/13.3a, N8/13.49a, Ra/11.3a - tatra kṣīramahānady(aḥ)o madhvājyasaritas tathā.
N7/13.1b - ghṛtakṣīramahānadyo madhvādyā udakāni ca.
BF/13.1b - ghṛtakṣīrāṇi miṣṭānnaṁ kṣaudrakhaṇḍodakāni ca.
Bo/13.2a - tatra sthāne mahānadyo mayā dṛṣṭā manoharāḥ.

3 N3/13.2a - peyaṁ ca vividhaṁ svādu dādhi dugdhasya rāśayaḥ.
N10 - ye yantu vividhaṁ svādu (N4/13.3b, N8/13.49b, Ra/11.3b - peyaś ca vividhākārāḥ, N7/13.2a - gajāsvā vividhākārā) dadhibhaktasya rāśayaḥ.
BF/13.2a - pakvānnarāśayas tatra yatheṣṭāś cānnarāśayaḥ.

4 N1/13.2b, N3/13.2b, N10 - sarvaṁ cottamamadhya(ā)sthaṁ kautukāni hy anekaśaḥ.
Half verse 13.2b is missing in N2.
N7/13.2b - sarvaṁ uttaramadhyāsthanānārūpaś ca kautukaṁ.

hemakuṇḍalasaṁyuktāḥ śubharatnaiś ca bhūṣitāḥ[5]
annadharmaprabhāvena krīḍante ca varāṅgaṇaiḥ[6] [3]
uccāsanasamārūḍhā vījyante cāmarottamaiḥ[7]
sugandhalepaliptāṅgāḥ sudhūpair dhūpitā bhṛśaṁ[8] [4]
sevakasevitāḥ saumyā nānābhogaiḥ samanvitāḥ[9]
divyarūpadharāḥ strībhiḥ krīḍante dharmaniratā[10] [5]

(The righteous) are adorned with golden earrings, and decorated with beautiful jewels.
Because of their previous food donations according to Dharma, they are playing now with the best of women, [3]
who are waving excellent fans (over them), while seated on high seats.
Their limbs are fragrantly anointed, perfumed with strong scent. [4]
They are served by servants, O dear friends, enjoying various enjoyments.
The righteous people are playing with women of divine forms – [5]

---

5 N2/13.2b - hemakuṇḍalakarṇā vai vividhā ratnabhūṣitāḥ.
N4/13.5a, N8/13.51a, Ra/11.5a - hemakuṇḍaladhāriṇyaḥ kanyāḥ kanakabhūṣaṇāḥ.
N7/13.4a - hemakuṇḍalasaṁyuktā vividhai ratnabhūṣitaiḥ.
BF/13.3b - hemakuṇḍalakeyūramuktāharāvirājitāḥ.
Bo/13.4a - hemakuṇḍalaśobhāḍhyā hārakeyūradhāriṇaḥ.

6 N1/13.3b, N10 - annadharmaprabhāvena krīḍante ca varāṅgaṇaiḥ.
N2/13.3a - tatra dharmaprabhāvena (BF/13.4a - krīḍanto 'psarasāṁ gaṇaiḥ) krīḍayanti varāṅgaṇāḥ.
Additional verse - N2/13.3b-4a:
tasmin sthāne ca bhu(a)ñjanti dānāni vividhāni ca
taptakāñcana(ṁ)varṇābhā(s)ḥ sarūpā dharmikāḥ.
N7/13.4b - t(a)e ca dharmaprabhāvena krīḍante ca varāṅganāṁ.

7 N2/13.4b - uccāsanasamārūḍhāś (N7/13.6a - cāmarais te hi vījyante) cāmaraś ca va jīvitāḥ.
N10 - uccāsanasamārūḍhā (N4/13.9a, N8/13.54a, Ra/11.8a - vījyamānāś cāmaraiḥ, Bo/13.5a - hy apsarobhir upāsitāḥ) vījyante cāmarottamaiḥ.

8 N2/13.5a - sugandhalepaliptāṅgāḥ (N4/13.9b, N8/13.54b, Ra/11.8b - parito dhūpadhūpitā) vividhair dhūpitās tathā.
N7/13.6b - sugandhair lepya[li]ptāṅgā vividhair dhūpadhūpitāḥ.
Bo/13.5b - divyasraggandhaliptāṅgā vividhair utsavair vṛtāḥ.

9 N2/13.5b, N7/13.7a - sevakair bhūṣitā(s)ḥ saumyair (N4/13.10a, N8/13.55a, Ra/11.9a - nānābhūṣālasaddehā) nānābhogasamanvitā[ḥ].
N3/13.5a, N10 - sevakaiḥ sevitāḥ saumyā nānābhogaiḥ samanvitāḥ.

10 N2/13.6a, N3/13.5b - divyarūpadharāḥ strībhiḥ krīḍante (N10 - dharmaśīlatā, N7/13.7b - dharmaśīlayā) dharmalīlayā.

vāpikūpataḍāgādi pravāhe śītavāriṇaḥ[11]
nirmalāṇi sudānāni dattāni brāhmaṇeṣu yaiḥ[12] [6]
annavastrādyābharaṇaṁ kartavyaṁ puṇyasañcayaṁ[13]
dvijānāṁ ca namaskāraṁ vṛddhaveśmaniveśanaṁ[14] [7]

those who donate ponds, wells, pools, canals (and)
good donations of cool, pure water, to Brahmins. [6]
(People) should collect merits (by donating) food, clothes (and) ornaments,
by bowing to Brahmins, and by providing shelter for the elderly. [7]

N4/13.10b, N8/13.55b, Ra/11.9b - divyarūpābhir aniśaṁ strībhiḥ krīḍanti dharmmataḥ.

BF/13.5a - krīḍamānāḥ surastrībhiḥ kāmātmabhiḥ sadevatāḥ.

11 N1/13.6a, N3/13.6a, N10 - vāpikūpataḍāgādi pravāhe ś(s)ītavāriṇa(ā)[ḥ].

N2/13.6b - vāpikūpataḍāgāni pānāni vividhāni ca.

N4/13.11a, N8/13.56a, Ra/11.10a - vāpikūpataḍāgādyāḥ kāritā yaiḥ prapās tathā.

BF/13.5b - vāpīkūpataḍāgānāṁ ārāmāṇāṁ ca sevakaḥ.

12 N1/13.6b - nirmalāṇ(n)i sudānāni dattāni (N3/13.6b, N10 - brāhmaṇeṣu yaiḥ) brāhmaṇaiḥ svayaiḥ.

N2/13.7a - nirmalāṇi ca dānāni dattāni brāhmaṇādiṣu.

N4/13.11b, N8/13.56b, Ra/11.10b - mahādānāni dattāni tulādīni dvijanmasu.

13 N2/13.7b - annādivastrābharaṇaṁ bhakṣaṁ bhojyaṁ tathāpare.

Additional verses - N2/13.8-9a:

bhūmir gāvo hiraṇyāni (N4/13.12b, N8/13.57b, Ra/11.11b - te tasmin bhuñjate sukhaṁ) dātā bhuñja[n]ti saukhyatāṁ

dharmarājaprasādena (N4/13.13a, N8/13.58a, Ra/11.12a - svargasthāne 'tiśobhane, N3/13.8a - datvā bhuñjanti tat phalaṁ) sukhasya teṣu sarvadā

bhogātmā vittastariṇā kartavyaṁ vittasañcayaṁ.

Additional half verse: N3/13.7b - dātāras tatra bhuñjanti svakṛtaḥ karmaṇaḥ phalaṁ.

N3/13.8b - bho bh(ā)o ātmānusāreṇa karttavyaṁ (N7/13.10a - dharmasañcayaṁ) puṇyasañcayaṁ.

N4/13.12a, N8/13.57a, Ra/11.11a - dattam annaṁ śubhaṁ vastraṁ bhakṣyaṁ bhojyaṁ tathottamaṁ.

N7/13.8b - annāni vastrābharaṇā bhakṣa bhojyās tathāpare.

Bo/13.7b - annadānāni vastrāṇi hiraṇyaṁ bhakṣyabhojanaṁ.

14 N2/13.9b - dvijāya ca namaskāraṁ ye ca veśmani cāgataṁ.

N3/13.9a - dvijānāṁ ca namaskāraṁ vṛddhānāṁ (N10 - veśmanaṁ - short) veśmani veśanaṁ.

N7/13.10b - dvijāgata namaskāraṁ vṛddhav(b)eśmani ye sthitāḥ.

āyatam atithiṁ dṛṣṭvā puṇyadaṁ pāpanāśanaṁ[15]
āsanaṁ bhaktito deyaṁ viśrāmya miṣṭavāg yathā[16] [8]
bhojanaṁ ca yathāśakti kandamūlaphalair api[17]
atithiḥ pūjito yena pūjitāḥ sarvadevatāḥ[18] [9]
yasmāt sa vimukho yāti atithiḥ puṇyo yāti vai[19]
dvijānām uttamo dharma agnihotraṁ śrutaṁ mayā[20] [10]

Seeing a guest arriving, is a promise of merit and an end to sin –
one should provide him devotedly with a seat, rest and sweet words. [8]
Food (should be given) according to means, bulb roots (and) fruits as well.
By worshipping a guest, all Gods are worshiped. [9]
Whoever lets a guest leave unsatisfied, all his previous merit leaves him.
I heard that Brahmins' best merit is the Agnihotra. [10]

---

15 N2/13.10a - āgataṁ ca yadā dṛṣṭam atithiṁ (N7/13.11a - puṇyapāvanaṁ) purāpayācanaṁ.
N4/13.15b, N8/13.60b, Ra/11.14b - āgatān atithīn dṛṣṭvā pṛcchanti madhuraṁ purā.
BF/13.8b - āgataṁ tu yadā dṛṣṭvā gṛhasthair atithiṁ gṛhaṁ.

16 N1/13.10a - āsanaṁ bhaktito deyaṁ viśrāmāṁ (N3/13.10a - viśrāmo) miṣṭavācayā.
N2/13.10b - āsanaṁ bhaktim ā(a)dāya viśrāmya miṣṭavāg yathā.
N4/13.16a, N8/13.61a, Ra/11.15a - āsanaṁ bhaktiyogena datvā viśrāmayanty atha.
BF/13.9a - āsanaṁ madhuraṁ vākyaṁ pūrvaṁ deyaṁ yathāvidhi.

17 N2/13.11a - bhojanaṁ ca yathāśaktiṁ [kan]damūlai(ṣ)ḥ phalair api.
Half verse 13.11b is missing in N2. Additional half verse:
N2/13.12a - bhuñjate vividhān bhogān kāmukaś ca (N7/13.13a - kāmikas tu) yathesthitān.
N3/13.10b - bhojanaṁ ca (N10 - yathāśāstaṁ) yathāśaktyā (BF/13.9b, N7/13.12a - bhojayitvā yathāśakti) kandamūlaphalair api.
N4/13.16b, N8/13.61b, Ra/11.15b - bhojyanti yathāśakti kandamūlādibhis tu ye.

18 N4/13.17a, N8/13.62a, Ra/11.16a - evaṁ yaiḥ pūjitāḥ sarve 'tithayo gṛham āgatāḥ.
N7/13.12b - atithi(ṁ)ḥ pūjito yena pūjitāḥ (BF/13.10a - pitṛdevatāḥ) sarvadevatāḥ.
Bo/13.9b - āgatān vaiśvadevāṁ te hy atithīn pūjayanti ye.

19 N3/13.11b - yasmāt sa vimukho yāti tataḥ puṇyaṁ vrajāni (N10 - puṇya[ḥ] prayāti) vai.

20 N1/13.10b, N10 - dvijānāṁ uttamo dharma agnihotraṁ (N3/13.12a - dharmas tv agnihotraṁ) [śr](s)utaṁ mayā.
N4/13.18a, N8/13.63a, Ra/11.17a - yo brāhmaṇottamo dhīmān agnihotraṁ karoti vai.
N7/13.13b - dvijānāṁ dharma[ṁ] me śrūt(v)ā agnihotraṁ ca kārayet.

ṛtukālābhigamanaṁ sarvabhūtahite ratāḥ[21]
dāyasaṁyamaśīlāś ca nityaṁ dharmaparāyaṇāḥ[22] [11]
te dvijāḥ svargagāmīti māviṣīdan munīśvarāḥ[23]
kṣatriyasya vivekatvaṁ śastrapāṇiḥ kṛpāparāḥ[24] [12]
satyaśīlaratāḥ samyak prajānāṁ pālane ratāḥ[25]
viṣṇubhaktimayasevās tatkathāsumahotsukāḥ[26] [13]

Those committed to the welfare of all creatures and have sexual relations in the fertile period,
who are excellent in Dharma and good conduct, tend to donations (and) restraint, [11]
those Twice-born go quickly to Heaven, O godly sages.
Kṣatriyas are distinguished by their weapons in hand (and) their compassion for others. [12]
They are properly satisfied with protecting people, and truthful conduct,
devoted to the worship of Viṣṇu, very eager to listen to his stories. [13]

---

21 N1/13.11a - kratukālābhigamanaṁ (N2/13.13a, N4/13.18b, N8/13.63b, Ra/11.17b, BF/13.11b - ṛtukālābhigāmī ca) sarvabhūtahite ratāḥ.

22 N1/13.11b - dānasaṁyamaśīlāś (N2/13.13b, N4/13.19a, N8/13.64a, BF/13.12a, Ra/11.18a - dayāsaṁyamaśīlaś) ca (N3/13.13a - dānasaṁyamaśālāgne, N7/13.14b - dayāsaṁyamaśīlena) nityaṁ dharmaparāyaṇāḥ.

23 N1/13.12a, N3/13.13b, N10 - te dvijāḥ svargagā(ṁbhā)[mī]ti māviṣīdan munīśvarāḥ.
N2/13.14a - dvija(s)ḥ svargam avāpnoti mā vilāpaṁ manā (- -).
N4/13.19b, N8/13.64b, Ra/11.18b - sa satyaṁ svargam āpnoti māvikalpayatānaghā.
N7/13.15a - sa dvijaḥ svargam āpnoti māvikalpaṁ kṛpā hṛdi.
BF/13.12b - brā(a)hmaṇas tu divaṁ yāti yāvad ābhūmisamplavaṁ.

24 N1/13.12b, N3/13.14a, N10 - kṣatriyasya vivekatvaṁ (N7/13.15b - kṣatriyo dhyāyate ś(s)ūraḥ) śastrapāṇi[ḥ] kṛpāḥ parāḥ.
N4/13.20a, N8/13.65a, Ra/11.19a - kṣatriyaḥ samareśur ādīneṣu ca kṛpānvitāḥ.
BF/13.13a - kṣatriyas tu dhanurdhārī śastrapāṇiḥ kriyāparaḥ.

25 N1/13.13a - satyaśīlo yataḥ samyak yajñānāṁ (N10 - prajānāṁ) pālane ratiḥ.
N4/13.20b, N7/13.16a, N8/13.65b, Ra/11.19b, BF/13.13b - satyaśīlaratāḥ (N3/13.14b - satyaśīlo yataḥ) samyak prajānāṁ pālane ratāḥ.

26 Emendation - DS. N1/13.13b, N10 - viṣṇubhaktimaya(ṁ)s(ś)evā[s] tatkathāsumahotsukā(a)ḥ.
Half verse 13.13b is missing in N2, N3.

vaiśyaḥ sadā vinītas tu paśupālanatatparaḥ[27]
dātā vai svalpabhāṣī ca paraloke sukhī bhavet[28] [14]
devārcaṇeṣu saṁyukto dvijānāṁ karmakārakaḥ[29]
satyātmā ca dayāluś ca sa śūdro dharmavittamaḥ[30] [15]
divyaṁ vimānam ārūhya sa yāti paramāṁ gatiṁ[31]
brāhmaṇakṣatriyavaiśyaśūdrā varṇaparāś ca ye[32] [16]

Vaiśyas (should be) always modest, dutiful in protecting cattle.
Those who donate and speak a little become happy in the world yonder. [14]
That Śūdra who is engaged in the worship of gods, serving Brahmins in their work,
who knows Dharma best, truthful and compassionate(II)*, [15]*
will reach the supreme goal, having mounted an air-vehicle.
Brahmins, Kṣatriyas, Vaiśyas, Śūdras, and those of other categories, [16]

---

27 N1/13.14a - vaiśyaiḥ sadā vinīt(y)as tu (N2/13.15b - vinītātmā, N4/13.21a, N8/13.66a, Ra/11.20a - prabhītaś ca, N7/13.16b - vinītajñaḥ) paśupālanatatparaḥ. BF/13.14a - vaiśyaḥ sadā vinītātmā devabrāhmaṇapūjakaḥ.

28 N1/13.14b - dātā vai k(kh)alyabhikṣa(o)ś ca paraṁ loke sukhī bhavet. N2/13.16a - dānaṁ svalpaṁ va satyaṁ ca paraloke sukhaṁ bhavet. N4/13.21b, N8/13.66b, Ra/11.20b - dātāraś ca susatyaś ca vāṇijyai karatās tathā. N7/13.17a - dānavān satyavādī ca paraloke sukhī bhavet.

29 N1/13.15a - devārcaṇeṣu saṁyukto dvijānāṁ karmakeśavaḥ. N2/13.16b - devavargasadāsa(śā)kto dvijānāṁ dharmatatparaḥ. N3/13.16a - devārcaṇeṣu saṁs(ś)aktaḥ (N10 - saṁyukto) dvijānāṁ karmakārakaḥ. N4/13.22a, N8/13.67a, Ra/11.21a - nivṛttāvedavārttāto dvijaśuṣrūṣaṇe ratāḥ. N7/13.17b - devavārttā sadās(ś)akto dvijānāṁ karma kārayet.

30 N2/13.17a - satyavādī (N7/13.18a - satyātmāno) dayāluś ca ś(s)ūdro dānena ś(s)udhyati. N4/13.22b, N8/13.67b, Ra/11.21b - satyātmāno dayāyuktāḥ śūdrā dānaikasadhanāḥ.

31 N2/13.17b - divaṁ vimānam (N3/13.17a - ārūhya) ārūḍhā (BF/13.16a - dṛṣṭā devapuraṁ gatāḥ) yās(ś)yanti paramāṁ gatiṁ. N4/13.23a, N8/13.68a, Ra/11.22a - ete vimānam ārūhya prayānti paramāṁ gatiṁ.

32 N1/13.16b, N10 - brāhmaṇakṣatriyaṁ vaiśyāḥ (N7/13.19a - brāhmaṇaḥ kṣatriyo vaiśyāḥ) śūdrā varṇaparāś ca ye. N2/13.18a - brāhmaṇakṣatriyavaiśyāś(s)ūdrā dharmaparāś ca ye. N4/13.23b, N8/13.68b, Ra/11.22b - brāhmaṇāḥ kṣatriyavaiśyāḥ śūdrāś cānye ca ye bhuvi.

ātmadharmaparityaktās te janāḥ patitā bhuvi[33]
sādhayanti mahātmānaḥ pañcāgnīnāṁ samāsthitāḥ[34] [17]
pañcayajñaratāḥ śāntāḥ krodhalobhavivarjitāḥ[35]
dīnaduḥkhitaviprebhyo bhikṣubhikṣāpradāś ca ye[36] [18]
kāmabhogapradasthāne krīḍante tatra dharmikāḥ[37]
gṛhaṁ dadāti yaś cānnaṁ śuddhabhāvena dharmavit[38] [19]

who abandon their own Dharma(III)*, those people fall to the ground.*
The great souls(IV) *who perform the five fire vows, [17]*
those who are engaged in the five rites, who are serene (and) free from anger and lust,
those who give alms to the poor, to the suffering, to the Brahmins and to the mendicants, [18]
those righteous play there, enjoying the desired enjoyments that they have donated on Earth.
He who knows Dharma, and donates a house or food, with pure intention, [19]

---

33 N1/13.17a, N3/13.18a - āśādharmaparibhraṣṭās (N2/13.18b, N7/13.19b - ātmadharmaparityaktā[s], N10 - ātmadharmaparibhraṣṭās) te janāḥ patitā bhuvi. N4/13.24a, N8/13.69a, Ra/11.23a - ātmadharmaparityāgaṁ kurvanti patitā(ḥ) hi te.

34 N1/13.17b, N10 - sādhayanti mahātmānaḥ (N2/13.19a - pañcagniś ca hutāś(s)anaṁ) pañcāgnītāsanasthitāḥ.
N3/13.18b - y(o)e sādhyaṁ mahātmāna[ḥ] pañcāgnīnāṁ samāsthitā[ḥ] (short).
N4/13.24b, N8/13.69b, Ra/11.23b - sādhayanti mahātmāno ye pañcāgnivrataṁ mahat.

35 N10 - pañcaprītāsanāḥ (N4/13.25b, N7/13.21a, N8/13.70b, Ra/11.24b - pañcayajñaratāḥ) śāntāḥ (BF/13.18a - pañcāgnisevino viprāḥ, Bo/13.12b - pañcāgnisādhakāḥ ye tu) krodhalobhavivarjitāḥ.

36 N1/13.18b - dīnaduḥkhitaviprebhyo (N3/13.19b - bhikṣyo bhikṣyapradāś ca ye) bhikṣubhikṣāpr(m)adāś ca ye.
N4/13.26a, N8/13.71a, Ra/11.25a - pañcabhikṣā[ṁ] pradātāro dīnaduḥkhitarakṣakāḥ.
N7/13.21b - dīnaduḥkhadayāyuktā[ḥ] pañcabhikṣā dada(n)ti.
BF/13.18b - sadācāraratā nityaṁ sadāvabhinnabhojanāḥ.

37 N2/13.21a, N3/13.20a - kāmabhogakarasthāne (N7/13.22a - kāmabhogakasthāneṣu) krīḍante tatra dharmikāḥ.
N4/13.26b, N8/13.71b, Ra/11.25b - kāmabhogāśraye sthāne tatra krīḍanti dharmmikāḥ.

38 N1/13.19b, N3/13.20b, N10 - gṛhaṁ dadāti yaḥ sānnaṁ śuddhabhāvena dharmavit.

sa yāti paramaṁ sthānaṁ sa yāti paramāṁ gatiṁ[39]
bahuśo bhogān bhuñjate tatra te kalpavāsinaḥ[40] [20]
suvelām avelāṁ vāpy annadāś caiva ye narāḥ[41]
svarge krīḍanti te tṛptāḥ yuvānaḥ kanyakā vṛtāḥ[42] [21]
dadhikṣīrapradātāraḥ surabhīlokamātaraṁ[43]
purāṇapustakaṁ caiva vāso ye rūpasundaraṁ[44] [22]

will go to the highest place, he will reach the supreme goal.
They enjoy many delights, staying there for one Kalpa(VI). *[20]*
Those who donate food, in proper or improper time, those people,
play satisfied in Heaven, holding young maidens. [21]
Donors of curd(V) *and milk are like Surabhi*(VII), *mother of the world.*
He who donates Purāṇa books, or clothes of beautiful form, [22]

N2/13.21b - gṛhaṁ dadāti yaḥ kaścic chuddhabhāvena dhārmikaḥ.
N4/13.27a, N8/13.72a, Ra/11.26a - gṛhaṁ dadati ye sānnaṁ śuddhabhāvā dvijanmane.
BF/13.19b - gṛhaṁ dadāti yo bhaktyā viprāya gṛhamedhine.

39 N2/13.22a, N7/13.23a - te yānti (N3/13.21a - sa yāti) paramaṁ sthānaṁ yatra (N4/13.27b, N8/13.72b, Ra/11.26b - himamayā gṛhāḥ) hemamayaṁ gṛhaṁ.
BF/13.20a - sa yāti paramaṁ sthānaṁ yatra hemamayā gṛhāḥ.

40 N2/13.22b - bhuñjate ca varān (N3/13.21b - b(v)ahūśo (N10, BF/13.20b - bhuñjate) bhujyate) bhogā[ṁ]s tatra te kalpavāsinaḥ.
N4/13.28a, N8/13.73a, Ra/11.27a - bhuñjate ca b(v)ahūn bhogān tatra kalpāntavāsinaḥ.
N7/13.23b - b(v)ahavo bhuñjate teṣāṁ bhogaṁ kevalavāsinaḥ.

41 N2/13.23a - suvelāṁ ca avelāṁ vā annadānaṁ prakurvate.
N3/13.22a - suvelāyām avelāyāṁ vā annadāś caiva ye narāḥ.
N4/13.28b, N8/13.73b, Ra/11.27b - akāle 'py athavā kāle hy annaṁ dadati ye narāḥ.

42 N1/13.21b, N3/13.22b - svarge (N10 - sarve) krīḍanti te tṛptā(ḥ) yuvānaḥ kanyakā (N7/13.24b - yutāḥ) vṛtāḥ.
N2/13.23b - svarge krīḍanti te viprāḥ yuvatibhi(s)ḥ sadā (N4/13.29a, N8/13.74a, Ra/11.28a - nityaṁ paritaḥ kanyakā) vṛtāḥ.

43 N1/13.22a, N2/13.24a, N3/13.23a, N10 - dadhikṣīrapradātāraḥ surabhīlokamātaraṁ.
N4/13.29b, N8/13.74b, Ra/11.28b - dadhikṣīrapradātāraḥ surabhīṁ ca payasvinīṁ.
N7/13.25a - dadhikṣīra(ḥ)ṁ pradātāraḥ surabhīlokamātaraṁ.

44 Verse 13.22b is missing in N2, N3.

grāsādardham api grāsaṁ yo dadāti suniścitaṁ[45]
sarvabhūtadayānvitaḥ śaraṇāgatapālanaḥ[46] [23]
svarge manorame sthāne krīḍante tatra nityaśaḥ[47]
svarṇādidhātuyuktāni vastrāṇi vividhāni ca[48] [24]
maṇipravāladātāraḥ krīḍante devayoniṣu[49]

who donates whole-heartedly even half a bite[(VIII)], *or the whole bite,*
who is compassionate towards all creatures, maintaining those seeking shelter, [23]
will always play there, in the beautiful place – in Heaven.
(Donors of) various clothes, adorned with gold and other metals, [24]
donors of jewels and corals, (all) play (in Heaven), having been reborn as Gods.

---

45 N1/13.23a - grāsārdhena vā grāsa (N3/13.23b, N10 - grāsādayyarddha grāsa vā) yo dadāti suniścitaṁ.
N2/13.24b - grāsam ardhe api grāsaṁ ye praya (- -) niścitaṁ.
N4/13.30a, N8/13.75a, Ra/11.29a - grāṣārdham api ye dadyur brāhmaṇāya mahātmane.
N7/13.25b - vāsagrāsam api grāmaṁ ye dada(an)ti suniścitā.
BF/13.21a - grāsād api ca yo grāsaṁ dadāti kṣudhite sadā.

46 N1/13.23b - sarvabhūtadayāyu(a)k(n)taḥ śaraṇāgatap(m)ālakāḥ.
N2/13.25a - sarvabhūtadayānvi(a)taḥ (N3/13.24a, N10 - śaraṇāgatapālakāḥ, N7/13.26a - śaraṇāgatapālinaḥ) śaraṇāgatapālanaḥ.
N4/13.30b, N8/13.75b, Ra/11.29b - śaraṇāgatarakṣāṁ ca ye kurvanti dvijottamāḥ.
BF/13.21b - sadā bhūtadayāyuktaḥ śaraṇāgatapālakaḥ.

47 N2/13.25b - svarge manoharasthāne krīḍante tatra (N3/13.24b - niścitaḥ) niścaya[ṁ].
N4/13.31a, N8/13.76a, Ra/11.30a - svarge manorame sthāne (N7/13.26b - krīḍante tatra nityaśaḥ, BF/13.22a - krīḍaty apsarasāṁ gaṇaiḥ) krīḍantīti suniścitaṁ.

48 N2/13.26a - svarṇadānamauktikaś ca (N10 - svarṇādidhā(ī)tuyuktāni, N4/13.31b, N8/13.76b, Ra/11.30b - svarṇaṁ dadati muktāś (N7/13.27a - svarṇādi dhātumuktaś) ca) vastrāṇi vividhāni ca.
Bo/13.14b - hemante vastrādātāro vahnidāś ca tathaiva ca.

49 N2/13.26b - maṇipravāladātāraḥ krīḍante (N10, BF/13.22b - devayoniṣu) saha devataiḥ.
N4/13.32a, N8/13.77a, Ra/11.31a - maṇīn pravālān yacchanti krīḍanti saha daivataiḥ.

kṣetraṁ ca vipulaṁ ramyaṁ sarvadhānyaprarohitaṁ[50] [25]
dadāti yo vai viprebhyo nīyate svargakāmikaṁ[51]
upānahau tathā kṣetraṁ śītatoyaṁ ca bhojanaṁ[52] [26]
aśvayuktavimānena nīyante hy amarāvatīṁ[53]
uṣṭrāśvarathadānena gavāṁ vā hastināṁ tathā[54] [27]

(Donors of) a vast, beautiful field, bearing crops of all sprouts, [25]
those[(IX)] *who thus give to Brahmins, are certainly led to the desired Heaven.*
(Donors of) a pair of footwear, as well as a field, cold water and food, [26]
are led to the city of Gods by a celestial vehicle harnessed to horses.
Those who donate horses, camels and chariots, as well as cows and elephants, [27]

---

50 N2/13.27a - kṣetraṁ ca vipulaṁ ramya(ā)ṁ (N4/13.32b, N8/13.77b, Ra/11.31b - sarvasasyasamanvitaṁ) sarvadhānyasamanvitaṁ.
N3/13.26a - kṣetre ca vipulaṁ ramyaṁ sarvadhānyaprarohitaṁ.
BF/13.23a - yo dadāti mahākṣetraṁ dhānyaśāliprapūritaṁ.

51 N3/13.26b - yaṣṭanti ye vai viprebhyo bhavanti svargagāminaḥ.
N10 - dadāti yo vai viprebhyo nī(a)yant(i)e svargagāminaḥ.
N4/13.33a, N8/13.78a, Ra/11.32a - ye prayacchanti viprebhyo nīyante svargabhūmiṣu.
N7/13.28b - dadati te vai viprebhyo nīyante svargakāmikaṁ.
BF/13.23b - sa yāti paramaṁ sthānaṁ vimānaiḥ svargagāmibhiḥ.

52 N2/13.28a - upānahau (ca) tathā kṣe(a)traṁ (N3/13.27a, N10, N7/13.29a, BF/13.24a - chattraṁ) śītatoyaṁ ca bhojanaṁ.
N4/13.33b, N8/13.78b, Ra/11.32b - upānahau tathā chatraṁ śītaṁ toyaṁ ca bhojanaṁ.

53 N2/13.28b, N10 - aśvayuktavimānena (N1/13.27a - aśvaguptavimānena) krīḍante (N3/13.27b - krīḍate) hy amarāvatīṁ.
N4/13.34b, N8/13.79b, Ra/11.33b - vimānair atha saṁyuktair gaccheyur amarāvatīṁ.
N7/13.29b - aś(s)vayuktavimānena krīḍante ye 'marāvatīṁ.
BF/13.24b - aśvāruḍhaḥ sa ca yāti nagarīm amarāvatīṁ.

54 N1/13.27b - aśvān uṣṭ[r]āś ca dātāro gavāṁ hī tāṁ (N10 - hastīn) tathaiva ca.
N3/13.28a - aśvā rathāś ca dātāro gav(ī)āṁ hasti[n] tathaiva ca.
N4/13.35a, N8/13.80a, Ra/11.34a - uṣṭrāśvarathagohastidātāro bhuvi mānavāḥ.
N7/13.30a - ikṣvāś ca rathadā aśvagogajāṁś ca dada(n)ti ye.
BF/13.25a - uṣṭrasya ca dātāro ye yo hastituragapradaḥ.

nīyante paramaṁ sthānaṁ gandharvaiḥ saha moditāḥ[55]
yena mānuṣyabhāvena ropitaṁ dharmavṛkṣakaṁ[56] [28]
tasya janma kṛtārthaṁ hi śepaś codarapūrakaḥ[57]
kanyādānakṛtaṁ yena ropitaṁ dharmavṛkṣakaṁ[58] [29]
yena sā duhitā dattā prāṇāj jātā garīyasī[59]
tena dattaṁ jagat sarvaṁ trailokyaṁ sa carācaraṁ [30]
sa vaset svargaloke tu kalpam ekaṁ na saṁśayaḥ[60]

are brought to the highest place, (where) they rejoice with Gandharvas.
Those who plant a Dharma tree and treat it as human, [28]
their birth is meaningful, as the male penis filling the woman's womb.
Whoever gives away a girl nursed as a Dharma tree – [29]
the daughter born to him, dearer than life itself – is praiseworthy.
It is (as if) he gave the whole universe, the three worlds along with live and inanimate[X] *(beings). [30]*
He will live in Heaven for one Kalpa, there is no doubt.

---

55 N1/13.28a - nīyante paramaṁ sthānaṁ (N4/13.35b, N8/13.80b, Ra/11.34b - yakṣagandharvarājitaṁ) gandharvaiḥ saha moditā(a)ḥ.
N3/13.28b - nīyate (N2/13.29b - nīyante) paramaṁ sthānaṁ (N7/13.30b - [parame] sthāne) gandharvai[ḥ] saha modate.
BF/13.25b - nīyante paramasthāne gandharvair gaṇais tatparaiḥ.

56 N2/13.30a - yo dadāti gṛhaṁ ramyaṁ satyātmā dharmasañcitaḥ.

57 N1/13.29a - tasya janma kṛtārtha(ā)ṁ hi śepa(ā)ś (N3/13.29b - ca śeṣāś) co darapūrakāḥ.
N2/13.30b - sadyā to martyaloke vai śepa(ā)ś codarapūrakāḥ.
N4/13.36b, N8/13.81b, Ra/11.35b - sa jātyā manyate cātra śeṣāḥ svodarapūrakāḥ.
N7/13.31b - sa jāto manyate loke śevāś ca bhayapūrikāḥ.

58 N2/13.31a, Bo/13.13a - kanyādānaṁ kṛtaṁ yena (N3/13.30a - ropitaṁ dharmamaṇḍapaṁ, BF/13.27a - raupyakāñcanasaṁyutaṁ) ropitā dharmato (N4/13.37a, N8/13.82a, Ra/11.36a - yena ca ropitā) drumāḥ.
N7/13.32a - kanyādānakṛtaṁ yena ropitaṁ dharmato drumāḥ.

59 N1/13.30a, N3/13.30b, N10 - yena s(r)ā duhitā dattā (N7/13.32b - prāṇādhikagarīyasī) prāṇā[j] jātā garīyasī.

60 N2/13.32b - krīḍante (N7/13.33b - krīḍate) svargavāsena (N10 - sa vaset (BF/13.28b - vaseta) sarvaloke tu, N4/13.38a, N8/13.83a, Ra/11.37a - krīḍante tridive viprāḥ) kalpam ekaṁ na saṁśayaḥ.
Additional half verse:
N2/13.33a - vinādānāt kathaṁ prāptiḥ svargasyāc ca dharmarāmarāḥ.

yasya dharmavihīnasya dināny āyānti yānti vai[61] [31]
sa lohakārabhastreva śvasann api na jīvati[62] [32]

iti śrībrahmāṇḍapurāṇe nāsiketopākhyāne
dharmavarṇanaṁ nāma trayodaśo 'dhyāyaḥ

One who is devoid of Dharma, his days are passing in vain(XI), [31]
he is not alive, though breathing, like a blacksmith's bellows. [32]

This is the thirteenth chapter of the Nāsiketa story, pertaining to the Brahmāṇḍa Purāṇa, called – the forms of Dharma.

Translation Notes

I – Between good and bad.
II – The verse in the text is in the singular.
III – A different reading in other versions – "People endorsing false Dharma".
IV – The sages in Yama's court.
V – "An era" – the period of time between the appearance of the world and its dissolution.
VI – Yogurt.
VII – The cow of bounty.
VIII – Half of his food.
IX – Originally – in the singular.
X – Moving and unmoving (beings).
XI – Literally – "coming & going".

---

61 N1/13.31b - yasya dharmavihīnasya dināny (N2/13.33b - āyānti yānti (BF/13.29a - vai) ca) anyādi yanti (N10 - ca) vai.
N3/13.32a - yasya dharmavihīnāni (N4/13.38b, N8/13.83b, Ra/11.37b - dināni ha gatāni ha) dinān anyāni yāti ca.

62 N2/13.34 - sa lauhakāraṅkucīva ś(s)vasann api sa jīvati
yathādyaṭī dyaṭās tad vat tathā dharmārtha hī nakāḥ.
N3/13.32b - sadvyarthaṁ vimukho mūḍho (N4/13.39a, N8/13.83b, BF/13.29b, Ra/11.38a - sa lohakārabhastre 'va) ś(s)vasann api na jīvati.
N10 - sa lohakārabhastre 'va sa sutrapita j(o)īvati.

Chapter 14

Dharma Behaviour

nāsiketa uvāca
aparaṁ ca mayā dṛṣṭam īśānyāṁ diśi saṁsthitaṁ[1]
ramaṇīyaṁ mahāsthānaṁ dharmarājena bhāṣitaṁ[2] [1]
dharmarāja uvāca[3]
aho dūtāś ca ye kecid dhārmikā vasudhātale[4]
na te baddhā bhavanty atra īśānyāṁ nīyante dhruvaṁ[5] [2]

Nāsiketa said
Standing in the North Eastern direction, I saw up there
a great beautiful place, mentioned by Dharmarāja. [1]
Dharmarāja said
"O messengers, those who were somewhat righteous on the surface of Earth, should not be bound by you here. They should certainly be led to the Northeast". [2]

---

1 N1/14.1a, N2/14.1a. N3/14.1a - aparaṁ (N10 - jatra) tatra me (N4/14.1a, N8/14.84a, Ra/11.39a - aparaṁ ca mayā) dṛṣṭam īśānyāṁ diśi (N7/14.1a - īśānadiśi) saṁsthitaṁ.
BF/14.1a - ataḥ paraṁ pravakṣyāmi yathādṛṣṭaṁ yathāśrutaṁ.

2 N1/14.1b. N2/14.1b, N7/14.1b - ramaṇīyaṁ (N3/14.2b, N10 - mahat sthānaṁ) mahāsthānaṁ (N4/14.1b, N8/14.84b, Ra/11.39b - yatraivaṁ dharmavāk sadā) dharmarājena bhāṣitaṁ.
BF/14.1b - ramaṇīyaṁ mahat sthānaṁ dharmabhūpālapālitaṁ.
Bo/14.1a - punaḥ sthānaṁ mayā dṛṣṭaṁ dharmātmā yatra tiṣṭhati.

3 Following N2.14.2.

4 N1/14.2a, N10 - aho dūtāś ca ye keci(t)d (N2/14.2a - dharmaśāstraratā narāḥ) dhārmikā vasudhātale.
N4/14.2a, N8/14.85a, Ra/11.40a - aho dūtā mahātmānaḥ śāstrato dharmmakārakāḥ.
BF/14.2a - tatra dūtāḥ sthitāḥ kecid dharmasthānasya dhāriṇaḥ.

5 N1/14.2b - tān mṛtān naiva pūrvasyām īśānyāṁ cādi nīyatāṁ.
N2/14.2b - na te b(v)addhā bhavanty atra īśānyāṁ nīyate dhruvaṁ.
N3/14.2b - tān mṛtān puruṣān pūrvam īśānyāṁ diśi nīyate.
N4/14.2b, N8/14.85b, Ra/11.40b - yena rāstān idaṁ sthānam ānayadhvaṁ tvarānvitāḥ.
BF/14.2b - pūrvadvāreṇa nīyante puṇyātmāno 'marāvatiṁ.

āśvine kārtike cānnam indhanaṁ pauṣamāghayo[6]
jyeṣṭhāṣāḍhe tu pānīyaṁ yo dadāti vased divi[7] [3]
meṣakarkaṭayor madhye yadā tapati bhāskaraḥ[8]
pānīyasya pradānaṁ tu suvarṇasadṛśaṁ smṛtaṁ[9] [4]
vasante phaladātāraḥ sthāne sthāne suśobhanaṁ[10]
te narās tatra gacchanti yatra sūryo mahārathaḥ[11] [5]
durbhikṣe annadātāraḥ subhikṣe ca hiraṇyadāḥ[12]

(Righteous are) those who give food in the months of Aśvina and Kārtika, and firewood in the months Paṣa and Māgha[(I)].
Whoever gives drinking water in the month of Aṣāḍha[(II)], *is most excellent, and will reside in Heaven. [3]*
When the sun gives its heat, between Aries and Cancer (of the Zodiac)[(III)], *a donation of water is regarded as a donation of gold. [4]*
Whoever donates fruit in springtime, engaged in decorating places (i.e. temples), these people go there, where the Sun reigns[(IV)]. *[5]*
Those who supply food in (times of) famine, gold when there is an abundance of food,

---

6 N2/14.3a - āśvine kārtike cānnaṁ (BF/14.3a - indhanaṁ pauśamāghayoḥ) pauṣe (N4/14.3a, N8/14.86a, Ra/11.41a - māghe tathendhanaṁ) māghye ca indhanaṁ.

7 N1/14.3b, N10 - jyeṣṭhāṣāḍh(d)e (BF/14.3b - jyaiṣṭhāṣādhe) tu pānīyaṁ yo dadāti vased divi.
N2/14.3b - jyeṣṭāṣāḍhe ca pānīya(ṁ)m (N3/14.3b - yo dadāti vased iti) īśānyāṁ nīy[at]e tadā.

8 N1/14.4a, N10, N4/14.3b, N8/14.86b, BF/14.4a, Ra/11.41b - meṣakarkaṭayor madhye yadā tapati (N7/14.3 - madhe yadā krama(n)ti) bhāskaraḥ.

9 N1/14.4b, N10, BF/14.4b - pānīyasya pradānaṁ tu (N3/14.4b - pradānena) suvarṇasadṛśaṁ smṛtaṁ.
N2/14.4b - pānīvayalam ekaṁ tu suvarṇaphalam ucyate.

10 N1/14.5a - vasante phaladātāraḥ sthāne (N2/14.5a - sthāne ca saṁbhava) sthāneṣu (N3/14.5a - saṁbhava, N10 - sosanaṁ) śobhanaṁ.
N4/14.5a, N8/14.88a, Ra/11.43a - phalāni ye prayacchanti vasanti vividhāni ca.
N7/14.4a - vasante pha[la]dātāraḥ sthānasthāneṣu saṁbhavā(a)t.
BF/14.5a - vasante tu ye dātāraḥ phalānāṁ ca tathaiva hi.

11 N10, N7/14.4b - te narās tatra gacchanti yatra (BF/14.5b - sūryarathaḥ sthitaḥ) sūryo (N4/14.5b, N8/14.88b, Ra/11.43b - mahārathā[ḥ]) yamārathāḥ.

12 N1/14.6a - durbhikṣe annaṁ dātāraḥ (N2/14.6a, N10, N4/14.6a, N8/14.89a, Ra/11.44a - cānnadātāraḥ, N3/14.6a - annadātā ca, (BF/14.6a - hy, N7/14.5a - 'py) annadātāraḥ) subhikṣe ca hiraṇyadaḥ.

svarge ca bhuñjate bhogān vahnidātā himālaye[13] [6]
ālaye tatra ye divi gacchanti tapasā narāḥ[14]
jalado viṣṇubhaktaś ca brāhmaṇānāṁ cikitsakaḥ[15] [7]
sarve te ratham ārūḍhāḥ śobhante divi devavat[16]
haṁsayuktarathā ramyāś cakravākopaśobhitāḥ[17] [8]
aśvair gajair vicitraiś ca mayūraiḥ sārasair api[18]

(and) fire in the snowy areas, will enjoy pleasures in Heaven. [6]
Those people who perform penance, go there, to the divine place in Heaven.
Donors of water, Viṣṇu's devotees, and healers of Brahmins, [7]
all those are like Gods, mounted on chariots in beautiful Heaven.
The beautiful chariots harnessed to swans, are decorated with Cakravāka birds, [8]
wonderful horses and elephants, peacocks, and even lakes.

---

13 N1/14.6b - svarge ca bhuñjate bhogān (N3/14.6b - nanadātā himāgame) vahn(nh)i[dā]t(a)ā dadāti hi.
N2/14.6b, N7/14.5b, BF/14.6b - svarge ca bhuñjate bhogān vahnidātā himālaye.
N4/14.6b, N8/14.89b, Ra/11.44b - bhogāṁś ca bhuñjate svarge yāvad āhūtasaṁplavaṁ.
Bo/14.8a - vasanto vividhān bhogān bhuñjante pūrvakarmaṇā.

14 N1/14.7a - ālaye y(g)atra ye devi gacchanti tapasā narāḥ.
N2/14.7a - jayas te svargam āpnuyuḥ svalpena tapasā narāḥ.
N3/14.7a - tatra ye divi gacchanti hy alpena (N10 - svalpena) tapasā narāḥ.

15 N1/14.7b, N10 - jalado viṣṇubhaktaś ca (N3/14.7b - brāhmaṇā vicikitsakaḥ) brāhmaṇaṁ ca (N4/14.7a, N7/14.6b, N8/14.90a, Ra/11.45a - brāhmaṇānāṁ) cikitsakaḥ.
Bo/14.11b - viṣṇubhaktiratā ye tu viṣṇudhyānaparāyaṇāḥ.

16 N2/14.8a, N7/14.7a - sarve te rathamārūḍhāḥ (N3/14.8a, N10 - tasya samārūḍhāḥ) śobhante divi devavat.
N4/14.8a, N8/14.91a, Ra/11.46a - vimānāni vicitrāṇi yānāni svargagāmināṁ.

17 N1/14.8b - daśacakrarathā (N10 - haṁsacakrarathā) ramyāś (N2/14.8b - haṁsayuktās tathā yānti, N3/14.8b - haṁsayuktarathā (N7/14.7b - haṁsayuktā rathā) ramyā[ś]) cakravākopaśobhitāḥ.
N4/14.8b, N8/14.91b, Ra/11.46b - kānicinddhaṁ sa yuktāni cakravākayutāni ca.

18 N1/14.9a - aśvair vanair vicitraiś (N2/14.9a - gajavicitraiś, N3/14.9a, N10, N7/14.8a - gajair vicitraiś) ca mayūraiḥ sārasair (N3/14.9a - iva) api.
N4/14.9b, N8/14.92b, Ra/11.47b - mayūrayuktāni tathā sārasālaṅkṛtāni ca.

tatra dharmānusāreṇa krīḍante devarūpiṇaḥ[19] [9]
śuklāṁbaradharā ramyā aneke 'pi sahasraśaḥ[20]
taptakāñcanavarṇābhāḥ śuddhasphaṭikanirmalāḥ[21] [10]
mahārūpadharās tatra divyapuṣpair alaṅkṛtāḥ[22]
sindūrasadṛśāḥ kecin nīlameghasamaprabhāḥ[23] [11]
nānāratnavicitraiś ca kaṇṭhābharaṇabhūṣitāḥ[24]
dhvajachatraiś ca saṁyuktā ardhacandreṇa śobhitāḥ[25] [12]

(Thus) the Dharma followers are playing there in God-like shapes. [9]
There are thousands of them, wearing white, beautiful clothes,
having the luster and colour of melted gold, pure and crystal clear. [10]
Mighty in form, decorated with divine flowers,
some are like vermilion powder, having the luster of black clouds. [11]
They are adorned with necklaces of various colourful jewels.
They have flags and umbrellas, adorned with half-crescent (ornaments), [12]

---

19 N3/14.9b - tatra dharmānusāreṇa krīḍante (N7/14.8b - div[y]arūpiṇaḥ) divirūpiṇaḥ.

20 N1/14.10a, N10 - śuklāṁbaradharā ramyā anekāś ca (N2/14.10a - aneke 'pi, N7/14.9a - anekāni) sahasraśaḥ.
N3/14.10a - śuklāṁb(v)aradhara ramyāś c(v)ā(a)nekāś ca sahasraśaḥ.

21 N4/14.10, N8/14.93, Ra/11.48 - taptakāñcanavarṇāni vimānāni tu kānicit śuddhasphaṭikaṁ varṇāni sindūravarṇāni ca.
N7/14.9b - taptakāñcanavarṇābhāḥ ś(s)uddhasphaṭikanirmalā.

22 N2/14.11a - mahārūpadharā ramyā(ḥ) devakanyā manoramāḥ.
N2/14.11b - sidhyate nararakṣabhir (N7/14.10a - mahārūpadharā[ḥ] kanyā) divyapuṣpair alaṅkṛtāḥ.

23 N4/14.11, N8/14.94, Ra/11.49 - nīlameghasamānāni citrāṇi dvijapuṅgavāḥ sarvāṇy api mahāmuktā ratnahārair manoharaiḥ.
N7/14.10b - sindūrasadṛśāḥ kaści(t)d nīlameghasamaprabhāḥ.

24 N2/14.12b - nānāvarṇavicitrābhā (N7/14.11a - nānāvarṇavicitrāṇi) kaṇṭhābharaṇabhūṣitāḥ.
N10 - nānāratnavicitrāś ca kaṁpabharaṇabhūṣitāḥ.
N4/14.12b, N8/14.96a, Ra/11.51a - nānāvarṇapatākaughair vātair mandaiḥ suśītalaiḥ.

25 N2/14.13a - patālā dhvajasaṁyuktā ardhacandravibhūṣitāḥ.
N3/14.12b - dhvajachatraiś (N10 - dhvajai(a)ś chatraiś) ca saṁyuktā arddhacandreṇa śobhitāḥ.

ratnamālāpralambaiś ca jyotirdīpamukhopamāḥ[26]
apsarogītasaṁyuktā divyakaṇṭhāsamākulāḥ[27] [13]
nṛtyavāditrasaṁyuktā vasante tatra dhārmikāḥ[28]
sthāpitā dharmarājena puṇyānāṁ karmaṇātmanāṁ[29] [14]
ārohanti vimānena yena yena kṛtaṁ śubhaṁ[30]
dharmasya kāraṇaṁ vakṣye dharmacinhakṛtaṁ dvijāḥ[31] [15]

and with hanging jewel garlands(V)*, their faces shining like lamp flames.*
Accompanied by the singing of Apsarasas, endowed with divine voices, [13]
and by dances and instrumental music, the righteous live there,
posted by Dharmarāja, those meritorious, (as a result of) their own good deeds. [14]
Performers of good deeds, are mounted on celestial vehicles,
(their) righteous deeds, performed with Dharma consciousness, are increased, O Twice-born. [15]

---

26 N2/14.13b - ratnamālāpralamb(v)ais te jyotir dīpamu(śi)khopamāḥ.
N7/14.11b - ratnamālāpralamb(v)aiś ca jyotidīpā(a)[r]c(ś)iṣopamā.

27 N3/14.13b - apsarāgītasaṁyuktā (N7/14.12a - divyakanyā manoramāḥ) divyakanyāsamāvṛ[t]tā.
N2/14.14a - tatra te gītasaṁyuktā divyakanyā manoramāḥ.
N10 - divi apsarāgītasaṁyuktādi dhvajac chatraiś ca.
N4/14.14a, N8/14.97a, Ra/11.52a - apsarobhis tathā divyakanyābhiḥ kalitāni vai.

28 N1/14.14a, N3/14.14a, N10 - nṛtyavādyasamāyuktā vasante tatra (N2/14.14b - nivasante (N7/14.12b - upāsante) ca) dhārmikāḥ.
N10 - Additional pāda - [di]vyakanyā sa ṣākulāḥ.
N4/14.14b, N8/14.97b, Ra/11.52b - nṛtyair gītais tathā vādyaiḥ pūritāni samaṁ tataḥ.

29 N2/14.15a - sthāpitā dharmarājena (N7/14.13a - yai[ḥ] puṇyāni kṛtāni ca) puṇyānāṁ (N10 - pāpākarmaṇāṁ) kāraṇe nṛpaḥ.
N4/14.15a, N8/14.98a, Ra/11.53a - kṛtāni dharmarājena dhārmikāṇāṁ sukhāya ca.

30 N1/14.15a, N10 - ā(a)ro(nu)hanti (N2/14.15b - ārūḍhās te, N7/14.13b - ārohaṁ tv iti) vim(j)ānena yena(yaṁ na) [yena] (N3/14.15a - yaṁ yaṁ yena) kṛtaṁ śubhaṁ.
N4/14.15b-16a, N8/14.98b-(?), Ra/11.53b-54a - evaṁ vidhāni divyāni vimānāni sahasraśaḥ
āruhya dhārmikāḥ svarga[ṁ] yānti dharmānusārataḥ.

31 N1/14.15b, N3/14.15b - dharmasya kāraṇaṁ vakṣye (N10 - vacm(e)i) dharmād ant(o)e kṛtaṁ (N2/14.16a - dharmavārttā stut(e)ā) dvijāḥ.
N4/14.16b, Ra/11.54b - bhuñjate kāmitān bhogān ākalpaṁ sahadaivataiḥ.
N7/14.14a - dharmasya kāraṇaṁ vakṣe dharmacinhakṛtaṁ dvijāḥ.

paramaṁ lokaṁ gopradāḥ prāpnuvanti
datto 'nnaddhān sūryaloke vasanti[32]
vāsodānāir candraloke cāmṛtatve hiraṇyadāḥ[33] [16]

iti śrībrahmāṇḍapurāṇe nāsiketopākhyāne
dharmāvicāraṇo nāma caturdaśo 'dhyāyaḥ

Cow-donors attain the highest world, while food-donors reside in the sun-world. Donors of clothes (reach) the moon-world, and gold-donors (attain) immortality. [16]

This is the fourteenth chapter of the Nāsiketa story, pertaining to the Brahmāṇḍa Purāṇa, called – Dharma behaviour.

Translation Notes

I – 4 cold months.
II – A hot summer month.
III – In summer time.
IV – Literally – where Sūrya, the Sun-god, is the great charioteer.
V – Necklaces.

---

32 N1/14.16a - paramaṁ gavāṁ golokaṁ gopradā[ḥ] prāpnuvanti stānnadānāḥ (N10 - dattānnadānāḥ) sūryaloke vasanti.
N2/14.16b - anadvāhas tu yair dattā(s)ḥ sūryyaloke vasanti te.

33 N1/14.16b - vāsodānair yāti sūryasya lokaṁ da(p)tte svarṇ[e cā](a)mṛtatva[ṁ] (N10 - prayānti) yā[n]ti.
N2/14.17a - vāsodātā candraloke cāmṛtattve hiraṇyadāḥ.
Compare - ṚgVeda/10.107.4 - hiraṇyadā amṛtatvaṁ bhajante vāsodāḥ soma pratranta āyuḥ.
Additional verse - N2/14.17b-18:
śivabhaktaśivasthāne yatrasthā pārvatī priyā
tasyā(a)m ukti(ṣ)ḥ kathaṁ samyak dānaṁ yo na dadāti ca.
N3/14.16b - vāsodānaiḥ yāti candrasya loke suvarṇe datte cāmṛtatvaṁ pra(i)yānti.
N7/14.14b-15 - te yānti paramaṁ lokaṁ gopradāḥ prāpnuvanti te
dat[t]vā natvā sūryaloke vrajanti vāsaṁ dattaṁ candraloke samaś ca
loke svarge gopradātā vrajanti dat[t]vā hiraṇyam amṛtatvam eti.
BF/14.17 - dattvā svarṇaṁ sūryalokaṁ prayānti dattvā vāsaś ca
indraloke śrayante te annaṁ dattvā hy amṛtatvaṁ
bhajante ca tasmāl lokaiḥ sarvair dānaṁ pradīyatāṁ.

Chapter 15

The Water Offering Ceremony of the Dead Person

nāsiketa uvāca
dṛṣṭvā tu narakaṁ ghoraṁ mahāntaṁ romaharṣaṇaṁ[1]
pāpino yatra pacyante yamadūtaiś ca yantritāḥ[2] [1]
dharmasthānaṁ tato dṛṣṭaṁ tiṣṭhante yatra dhārmikāḥ[3]
nadī puṣpodakā nāmnī puṇyatoyā sukhāvahā[4] [2]
suvarṇā vālukās tatra sadhanāḥ saralā drumāḥ[5]

Nāsiketa said
I also saw the great, horrible, hair-bristling Hell,
where sinners are cooked, controlled by Yama's messengers. [1]
I saw the place of Dharma as well, where the meritorious are staying,
(and) the river called Puṣpodakā(I), its pure water carrying happiness. [2]
The sand there (on the riverbank) is golden and the trees thick and straight,

---

1 N3/15.1a, N7/15.1a - dṛṣṭvā ca narakaṁ ghoraṁ mahāntaṁ romaharṣaṇaṁ.

2 N1/15.1b, N10, N7/15.1b - pāpakarmāś ca pacyante yamadūtaiś (N3/15.1b - yamadūtāś) ca yantritāḥ.

3 N2/15.2a - dharmasthānaṁ (BF/15.1a - mayā) punar (Bo/14.1a - punaḥ sthānaṁ mayā) dṛṣṭaṁ (N7/15.2a - dharmasthānā punar dṛṣṭā) dharmātmā yatra tiṣṭhati.

N3/15.2a - dharmasthānaṁ tato dṛṣṭ(v)aṁ tiṣṭha[n]te yatra dhārmikāḥ.

N4/15.1a, N8/15.99a, Ra/12.1a - svargasthānaṁ mayā dṛṣṭaṁ paramaṁ yatra tiṣṭhati.

4 N4/15.1b, N8/15.99b, Ra/12.1b - nadī puṣpodakā nāma (Bo/14.1b - jalaṁ vahati śītalaṁ) dhārmiṣṭhānāṁ (N7/15.2b, BF/15.1b - puṇyatoyā) sukhāvahā.

5 N1/15.3a, N2/15.3a - suvarṇā vālukās tatra sadhanāḥ saralā (N3/15.3a - saralāsadhanāḥ) dhumāḥ.

N4/15.2b, N8/15.600b, Ra/12.2b - sauvarṇā sikatā tatra mṛdusparśā samaṁ tataḥ.

N7/15.3a - svavarṇā vālukā[s] tatra sadhanā[ḥ] saralā drumāḥ.

BF/15.2a - suvarṇā v(b)ālukās tatra śaṅkhapadmasuradrumāḥ.

Bo/14.2a - suvarṇā vālukās tasyāṁ tīre nānāvidhā drumāḥ.

supuṣpaiḥ śobhitā vṛkṣāḥ siddhagandharvasevitāḥ[6] [3]
madhye kṣīropamaṁ toyaṁ vahate vāmṛtopamaṁ[7]
tasyās tīre mayā dṛṣṭaṁ vanaṁ cātyantaśobhanaṁ[8] [4]
tasmin manorame sthāne krīḍante dharmacāriṇaḥ[9]
krīḍante vālukāloke dharmātmāno mahājanāḥ[10] [5]

adorned with beautiful flowers, surrounded by Yogis and Gandharvas[(II)]. *[3]*
The water in midstream is like milk, flowing like nectar[(III)].
I also saw a most beautiful forest on its bank. [4]
The meritorious people play in that beautiful place,
the righteous souls, the great people, they play there in that sandy place. [5]

---

6 N1/15.3b, N7/15.3b - supuṣpaiḥ (N2/15.3b - puṣpaiś ca, N3/15.3b, N10 - sa puṣpaiḥ) śobhitā (BF/15.2b - supuṣpaśobhitā) vṛkṣāḥ (N4/15.3b, N8/15.1b, Ra/12.3b - tatra vṛkṣā mahāchāyāḥ) siddhagandharvasevitāḥ.
Bo/14.2b - puṣpāṇi ca sugandhī nidhārayanti ca te drumāḥ.

7 N3/15.3b, N10 - madhye kṣīropamaṁ toyaṁ vahate cāmṛtopamāḥ.
N2/15.4a - kṣīropamāni toyāni (N7/15.4a - kṣīropama[ṁ] tv idaṁ toyaṁ) vahate sāmṛtodaka.
N4/15.2a, N8/15.600a, Ra/12.2a - kṣīropamajalaṁ tasyāḥ pravahaty aniśaṁ dvijāḥ.
BF/15.3a - kṣīropamaṁ payas tatra vartate cāmṛtopamaṁ.

8 N2/15.4b, N7/15.4b - tasyās tīre mayā dṛṣṭ(v)ā (N10 - vanaṁ cātyanta(i)śobhanaṁ, BF/15.3b - maṇayo raśmibhiḥ śubhāḥ) bhuvanātyantaśobhanāḥ.
N4/15.3a, N8/15.1a, Ra/12.3a - tasyās tīre mahodyānam asti sarvatra śobhanaṁ.
Bo/14.3a - nadyās tīre hy ahaṁ viprā dṛṣṭavān mandirāṇi ca.

9 N1/15.5a, N3/15.5a, N10 - tasmin manorame sthāne krīḍante (N7/15.3a - dharmapālanāḥ, BF/15.4a - dharmaśālinaḥ) dharmasevinaḥ.
N4/15.4b, N8/15.2b, Ra/12.4b - tasmin sthāne mahāpuṇyāḥ krīḍanti sukhinojanāḥ.

10 N1/15.5b, N10 - krīḍante vālukālokā (N3/15.5b - vāluko lokāḥ) dharmātmāno mahājanāḥ.
N2/15.5b - sevyate ca sadā devair dharmātmā ca mahātapā[ḥ].
No more verse numbers in N3 after 15.5.
N7/15.3b - vālukā sutaṭe loko dharmātmāno mahātapāḥ.
BF/15.4b - krīḍante v(b)ālukāmadhye jale krīḍāṁ ca kurvante.
Bo/14.3b - teṣu krīḍanti manujāḥ sadā dharmasya pālakāḥ.

mahāsaukhyākaraṁ tatra udyānaṁ saritas taṭe[11]
sugandhasahito vāyur atyantena suśītalaḥ[12] [6]
siddhagandharvakānyābhir apsarobhiś ca ceṣṭitā[13]
padmaiś ca vividhākāraiḥ sevitā sā mahānadī[14] [7]
strīyaś ca divyarūpāś ca tasya tīre vasanti tāḥ[15]

That garden there, on the riverbank, gives great pleasure.
It is fragrant, along with a very cool wind. [6]
It is full of the activity of Yogis and Gandharvas, young girls and Apsarasas[(IV)].
That great river is full of lotuses of various shapes, [7]
and women of divine forms are living on its banks,

---

[11] N1/15.6a - mahāsaukhyākaraṁ tatra dhāmaṁ sarasa te (N3/15.6a - udyāna saritas) taṭe.
N2/15.6a - mahāsaumyākaraṁ (N7/15.6a - mahāsauṣyākaraṁ) sthāna(ṁ)m (BF/15.5a - mahāsaukhyākaraṁ tatra) udyānaṁ saritas (N10 - tatrāghānaṁ sarasas) taṭe.

[12] N2/15.6b - sugandhavasitā sarve mārūrtoś ca mṛtopamāḥ.
N3/15.6b - sugandhasahito vāyuvahatiś ca suśītalaḥ.
N10 - sugandhasahito vāyu(ḥ)r atyantasuśīt(l)al(tā)aḥ.
N7/15.6b - sugandhavāsitaṁ tatra mārutam amṛtopamaṁ.
BF/15.5b - sugandho vāyur vahati sukhadaḥ puṇyakarmaṇāṁ.

[13] N1/15.7a - siddhagandharvavāṇ(ij)yā ye apsarābhiś ca ceṣṭitā(ḥ).
N2/15.7a - siddhagandharvanilapā apsarāgīta vahinī.
N3/15.7a - siddhagandharvaviṣaye apsarobhiḥ suceṣṭitaṁ.
N10 - siddhagandharvāṇī ca vai 'psarībhi[ḥ] suceṣṭitāḥ.
N7/15.7a - siddhagandharva nilayaṁ apsarāgītavādyabhiḥ.
BF/15.6a - siddhagandharvakanyābhir apsarobhiḥ samantataḥ.
Bo/14.5a - siddhagandharvaṁ vṛdaiś ca kinnraiś copasevitāḥ.

[14] N2/15.7b - yakṣaiś ca b(v)ahubhir (N7/15.7b - yakṣair b(v)ahu(a)bhir (short)) lokai(s)ḥ sevyate (N3/15.7b - vivadhākāraiḥ (N10, BF/15.6b - vividhākaraiḥ) sevitā) sā mahānadī.

[15] N1/15.8a, N10 - strīyaś ca divyarūpā[ś] ca tasya tīre (N3/15.8a - va saṁsthitāḥ) ca santi tāḥ.
N4/15.7a, N8/15.5a, Ra/12.7a - strīyaś ca divyarūpāṭhyā divyavastrair alaṅkṛtāḥ.
N7/15.8a - strīyaś ca sarvarūpāś ca tasya tīre vasanti tāḥ.
Bo/14.4b - divyarūpādharā nāryaḥ krīḍānti narapuṅgavaiḥ.
Additional verses:
N2/15.8b, N7/15.8b - nānāvastradharā(s)ḥ sarvā (N3/15.8b - nānābhūṣaṇabhūtā) nānāratnavibhūṣitāḥ.

saṁpūrṇāś candravaktreṇa ākarṇāyatalocanāḥ[16] [8]
nirmitā dharmarājena krīḍārthaṁ dharmiṇāṁ sadā[17]
nṛtyagītamanoramyaṁ tat sthānaṁ dṛśyate śubhaṁ[18] [9]
devārcaneṣu tiṣṭhanti ye ratā gurupūjane[19]
sarvabhūtadayāyuktāḥ sarvaśāstraviśāradāḥ[20] [10]

with full moon faces, their (big) eyes reaching up to their ears. [8]
They have been created by Dharmarāja for the constant play of the righteous.
(By) their pleasing dancing and singing, the place looks wonderful. [9]
Those who persist in Gods' rites, those who are pleased with teacher-worship,
those who have compassion for all creatures, well versed in all branches of knowledge, [10]

N2/15.9a - garvitāś cograrūpaś ca manoharṣakarā(s)ḥ sadā.
N3/15.9a - garvitā rūpasaṁpatyā mano vai harṣakāriṇī.
N7/15.9a - garvitārūpa nilayāmana[ḥ] sāharṣakāriṇāḥ.
Bo/14.5b-6a - nānāvastraparidhānā nānāratnopaśobhitāḥ rūpalāvaṇyasaṁyuktā dṛṣṭa mātrā manoharāḥ.

16 N1/15.8b - saṁpūrṇāṁ candravaktreṇa ākarṇāyatalocanāḥ.
N2/15.9b, N3/15.9b, N10, N4/15.8b, N7/15.9b, N8/15.6b, Ra/12.8b - saṁpūrṇacandravadanā ākarṇāyatalocanāḥ.
Bo/14.6b - saṁpūrṇacandravadanāḥ karṇāntāyatalocanāḥ.

17 N2/15.10a - nirmitā dharmarājena krīḍārthe dharmiṇāṁ (N3/15.10a - dharmiṇī) ca tāḥ.
N4/15.9b, N8/15.7b, Ra/12.9b - nirmitā dharmarājena krīḍārthaṁ (N7/15.10a - dharmalālāsāḥ) dharmacāriṇāṁ.

18 N1/15.9b, N10 - nṛtyagītamanoramyaṁ sthānaṁ ta[d] dṛśyate (N3/15.10b - prabhe) śubhaṁ.
N2/15.10b - gītanṛtyamanoramyaṁ tat sthānaṁ dṛśyate śubhaṁ.
N4/15.10a, N8/15.8a, Ra/12.10a - raṁbhā ghṛtācīmenādyā nṛtyagītādi tat parāḥ.
N7/15.10b - nṛtyagītamanoramyaṁ tat sthānaṁ dṛśyate dhruvaṁ.

19 Emendation - DS. N1/15.10a - devārcaṇasadṛkṣā ye ye hatā gurupūjane.
N2/15.11a - devārcaneṣu tiṣṭhā ye ye ratā gurubrāhmaṇaṁ.
N3/15.11a - devārcane sadīna (N10 - sadakṣā) ye ye ratā gurupūjane.
N4/15.10b, N8/15.8b, Ra/12.10b - devārcanaparā nityaṁ paretā brāhmaṇe gurau.
N7/15.11a - devārcaṇena tiṣṭhā ye ye ratā gurubrāhmaṇāḥ.

20 N2/15.11b - sarvadharmaviśāradāḥ sarvaśāstraviśāradāḥ.
N4/15.11a, N8/15.9a, Ra/12.11a - sarvabhūtadayāyuktāḥ (N7/15.11b - sarvaś(s)āstraviśāradāḥ) sarvaśāstravicārakāḥ.

sarvakāmapradātāro dṛśyante bahavo jaṇāḥ[21]
teṣāṁ vikrīḍanārthe vai ramyāpuṣpodakā nadī[22] [11]
trailokye ye ca vikhyātā dharmarājasya veśmani[23]
dṛṣṭās te bahavas tatra te vasanti sārittaṭe[24] [12]
na teṣāṁ kṣutpipāsa ca na tāpaṁ śītalaṁ na hi[25]
ajarābhayaduḥśokaṁ duḥkhabhārādikaṁ na hi[26] [13]

donors of objects desired by all – many (such) people I have seen there.
That beautiful Puṣpodakā River is (there) for the sake of their playing. [11]
They are all well known in the three worlds, and at Dharmarāja's abode.
I saw many of them, living on the riverbank. [12]
They never suffer from hunger or thirst, nor from heat or cold,
not from fear and sorrow, nor from painful burden, etc., and they do not grow old. [13]

---

21 N3/15.12a, N10 - sarvakāmapradātāro (N4/15.11b, N8/15.9b, Ra/12.11b - ye svadharmasupālakāḥ, N7/15.12a - dṛṣṭā tatra mahātapāḥ) dṛśyante b(v)ahavo janāḥ.
Verse 15.11 is missing in N2.

22 N3/15.12b, N7/15.12b - teṣāṁ vai krīḍanārthe ca ramyāpuṣpodakā nadī.
N4/15.12a, N8/15.10a, Ra/12.12a - teṣāṁ bhogāya vidhinā kṛtā puṣpodakā nadī.

23 N2/15.12a - trailokye caiva (N10 - eva, N7/15.13a - cāpi) vikhyātā (BF/15.13a - cātivikhyāte) dharmarājasya veśmani.
N4/15.12b, N8/15.10b, Ra/12.12b - evaṁ trailokya vikhyātā dharmarājapure kvacit.
Bo/14.8b - narās trailokyavikhyātā dharmarājapure sthitāḥ.

24 N3/15.13b, N10 - dṛṣṭās te (N2/15.12b - ca) b(v)ahavas tatra krīḍante saritas taṭe.
N4/15.13a, N8/15.11a, Ra/12.13a - mayā dṛṣṭā hi b(v)ahavaḥ krīḍantas tatsarittaṭe.
N7/15.13b - dṛṣṭāś ca b(v)ahavas (BF/15.13b - tatra vilāsās tatsarittaṭe) ta krīḍantaḥ saritas taṭe.

25 N1/15.13a, N3/15.14a, N10 - na teṣāṁ kṣutpipāse ca na tāpaṁ śītalaṁ na hi.
N2/15.13a - na kṣudhā na pipāsā na kācid dhānir na nidrikā.
N4/15.13b, N8/15.11b, Ra/12.13b - na kṣudhā na pipāsā ca na (N7/15.14a - tāpāṁ ca na śītalaṁ, BF/15.14a - tapto nāpi vedanā, Bo/14.9a - tāpaśītajaṁbhayaṁ) tāpo na ca śītatā.

26 N2/15.13b - na jarā vighate tatra dṛṣṭa bhāvādikaṁ na hi.
Half verse 15.13b is missing in N3.
N10 - na jarā na śokaṁ duḥkhabhārādikaṁ na hi (short).

priyaṁ vadanti te sarve manaprahlādakāriṇaḥ[27]
iha janmani ye kaṣṭān paśyanti tapasi sthitāḥ[28] [14]
na te duḥkhena dahyante paralokagatā api[29]
yama uvāca
re re mūḍha durācāra mānuṣaṁ janma durlabhaṁ[30] [15]

They all speak pleasantly, making the mind happy.
In life here(V) they had experienced great stress, performing penance, [14]
(now), having reached the highest Heaven, they are not scorched by sorrow.
Yama said
"O fool sinner, having been born as human, which is hard to achieve, [15]

N4/15.14a, N8/15.12a, Ra/12.14a - na jarā na ca b(v)ālatvaṁ vidyate tatra tāpasāḥ.
N7/15.14b - narās tāsyā hitīrasthā duḥkha bhāvādikaṁ na hi(ḥ).
BF/15.14b - duḥkhaleśo 'tha nāsty atra mānuṣāṇāṁ kriyāvatāṁ.
Bo/14.9b - na jarā naiva mṛtyuś ca na duḥkhaṁ palitāni ca.

27 N1/15.14a - priyaṁ vadanti te sarve (N2/15.14 - manaḥ prahlādakāriṇaḥ, BF/15.15a - na teṣām apriyaṁ kvacit) mama āhlāda kārakaṁ.
N3/15.14b - priyaṁ vadanti sarve te mana āhlāda kāriṇaḥ.
N7/15.15a - sarve priyanti b(v)ruvanti manaḥ prāhrādakārakaṁ.

28 N1/15.14b - iha janmani ye (N2/15.15a - kaṣṭaṁ tapyanti tapārava hi, N10 - kaṣṭāt parayanti (N4/15.14b, N8/15.12b, Ra/12.14b - kaṣṭaṁ kurvanti) tapasi sthitāḥ) kaṣṭān (N7/15.15b - tapyante tapasi sthitāḥ) paramaṁ 'bhitapasthitāḥ.
BF/15.15b - bhūmau yais tu kṛtaṁ kaṣṭaṁ tapaś ca gātraśoṣaṇaṁ.

29 N1/15.15a - na te duḥkhe ca dagdhāś ca paramaṁ yasya saṁsthitāḥ.
N2/15.15b - na te duḥkhena dahyante paraloke (N4/15.15a, N8/15.13a, Ra/12.15a - 'tiduḥkhitāḥ) na 'thaiva ca.
N10 - na te duḥkhena dagdhāś ca paralokagatām api.
N7/15.16a - na te duḥkhaiś ca dahyante paramalokagati(a)r api.
BF/15.16a - na te duḥkhair vidahyante na bhayaṁ teṣu kutracit.

30 N1/15.15b - re re mūḍha durācāra (BF/15.18a - mānuṣyaṁ prāpya durlabhaṁ) mānuṣa (N4/15.17a, N8/15.15a, Ra/12.17a - mānuṣya) tv eti durlabhe.
N2/15.16a - pāpātmano durācārā (N3/15.16a - māṇuṣa tv eti dur(l)labhe) nityaṁ kalahakāriṇaḥ.
N7/15.16b - pāpātmā durācārā mānuṣye sāṣyi durlabho (short).
Additional half verse:
N2/15.16b, N3/15.16b - doṣagrāhādi yuktāś ca bhayaṁ tatrāpnuvanti va.

kathaṁ pāpādikaṁ kṛtaṁ paralokaviruddhakaṁ[31]
iha janma sukhārthāya kalpānte narakāya vai[32] [16]
ciraṁ tiṣṭhate kāyaḥ kim arthaṁ pāpam ācaret[33]
mayā śrutaṁ yamaproktaṁ śṛṇudhvaṁ dvijasattamāḥ[34] [17]
kiṅkarebhyo yamas tatra yatnena kathitaṁ ciraṁ[35]
naivānayata narake naraṁ kṛṣṇasya vallabhaṁ[36] [18]

why have you committed sin, (a deed) obstructive to (achieving) the other world?
This (human) birth (you spent) chasing pleasures, which certainly lead to Hell. [16]
The body stays (only) a short time, what is the point of behaving sinfully?"
Listen O excellent Brahmins, to Yama's words that I have heard. [17]
What Yama said to his servants there, has long-term consequences.
"Do not bring to Hell a man most beloved by Kṛṣṇa". [18]

---

31 N1/15.16a, N10 - katham āyadikaṁ cepsaṁ (N3/15.16b - pāpādikaṁ rakṣan) paralokaviruddhaye.
N2/15.17b - kathaṁ pāpādikaṁ kuryyu(ṣ)ḥ paralokaviruddhakaṁ.
N4/15.17b, N8/15.15b, Ra/12.17b - katham pāpaṁ kṛtaṁ karmaparalokavināśanaṁ.
N7/15.17a - katham pāpādikaṁ tv īpset paralokaṁ virūddhayet.
BF/15.18b - kasmāt pāparatā yūyaṁ lobhopahatabuddhayaḥ.

32 N1/15.16b, N3/15.17a, N10 - iha janma sukhārthāya kalpānte narakāya (N2/15.18a - ca) vai.
N4/15.18a, Ra/12.18a - atrāyātāḥ suduḥkhāyāniśaṁ (N8/15.16a - tatrāyata sukhāyātrāniśaṁ) narakabhukta ye.
N7/15.17b - mekajanma sukhārthāya kalpānte narakaṁ yayau.
BF/15.19a - kṣaṇaṁ ekaṁ sukhārthāya kalpāntaṁ narakāya ca.

33 N2/15.18b - aciraṁ tiṣṭha(k)ti (N7/15.18a - tiṣṭhate, BF/15.19b - na ciraṁ tiṣṭhate) kāyaḥ kim arthaṁ pāpam ācaret.
N4/15.18b, N8/15.16b, Ra/12.18b - bhavanto duṣṭasaṅgena kim arthaṁ pāpam ācaran.

34 N2/15.19a - śrutaṁ mayā yamaproktaṁ śṛṇvantu dvijapuṅgavāḥ.
N4/15.19a, N8/15.17a, Ra/12.19a - evaṁ yamamukhāt tatra śrutaṁ brāhmaṇapuṅgavāḥ.
N7/15.18b - yama proktaṁ mayā śrutvā śṛṇudhvaṁ dvijapuṅgavāḥ.

35 N1/15.18a - kiṅkarebhyo yamas tatra phalena (N3/15.18b, N10 - yatnena) kathitaṁ ciraṁ.
N2/15.19b - āhū(-)ḥ kiṅkarās tena bhakti yatnena vai tathā.
N7/15.19a - kiṅkarā hy ānitā tena yatnena vada te idaṁ.

36 N2/15.20a - na nīyatāṁ ca narake yo naraḥ kṛṣṇasya (N3/15.19a - vatsalaṁ) vallabhaḥ.

svapuruṣam abhivīkṣya pāśahastaṁ
  vadati yamaḥ kila tasya karṇamūle[37] [19]
parihara madhusūdana prapannān
  prabhur aham asmi nṛṇāṁ na vaiṣṇavānāṁ[38]
aham amaragaṇārcitena dhātrā
  yama iti lokahitāhite niyuktaḥ [20]
hariguruvaśago 'smi na svatantraḥ
  prabhavati saṁyamane mamāpi viṣṇuḥ[39]
kaṭakamukuṭakarṇikādibhedaiḥ
  kanakam abhedam apīṣyate yathaikaṁ[40] [21]

Seeing his man holding his noose, Yama spoke, whispering in his ears: [19]
"Keep clear of worshippers of Madhusūdana[(VI)]*,*
I am the lord of men, (but) not of Viṣṇu's devotees.
I, Yama, have been appointed by the creator, (to sit in) the assembly of immortals, for the benefit of the world. [20]
I am going according to Viṣṇu's will, not my own free will, (so)
Viṣṇu can prevail even in my Yama-city.
Though gold appears in diverse forms as bracelet, crown and earrings, etc. it is just one substance, thus, [21]

N10 - naivānayeta narake naraṁ kṛṣṇasya vallabhaṁ.

N7/15.19b - naivānayātra narake ye narā viṣṇu niṣcalāḥ.

37 Verses 15.19-40 are extracted from Viṣṇupurāṇa 3.7.14-34, omitting ViṣP/3.7.17-18a + one pāda.

N1/15.19a, N10 - svapuruṣam abhi(ī)vīkṣya pāś(s)ahastaṁ (N4/15.21a, N8/15.19a, Ra/12.21a - pāśahasto) vada(n)t[i] yamaḥ kila(ṁ) tasya karṇa(bh)mūle.

N2/15.20b - iti [yama]vacanāni [ni]śamy(āth)a yamaḥ kila tasya karṇa(bh)mūle.

N3/15.19b - svapuruṣam api vīkṣya pāśahastaṁ va[da] te yamaḥ kiṁ na tasya karṇamūle.

38 N4/15.21c-d, N8/15.19c-d, Ra/12.21c-d - parihara madhusūdana prapannān prabhur aham atra nṛṇāṁ na vaiṣṇavānāṁ.

39 N1/15.21a, N10 – hariguruvaśago 'smi na svatantraḥ prabhavati saṁyamane mamāpi viṣṇuḥ.

40 N1/15.21b-22a, N10 - kaṭakamukuṭakarṇikādibhedaiḥ kanakam abhedam apīṣyate yathaikaḥ.

surapaśumanujādikalpanābhir
  harir akhilābhir udīryate tathaikaḥ[41] [22]
parihṛtya yathāgnim ājyasiktaṁ[42]
iti yamavacanaṁ niśamya pāśī
  yamapuruṣas tam uvāca dharmarājaṁ[43]
kathaya mama vibhoḥ samastadhātur
  bhavati hareḥ khalu yādṛśo 'sya bhaktaḥ[44] [23]
yama uvāca
na calati nijavarṇadharmato yaḥ
  samamatir ātmasuhṛdvipakṣapakṣe[45]
na harati na ca hanti kiñcid uccaiḥ
  sthiramanasaṁ tam avehi viṣṇubhaktaṁ[46] [24]
kalikaluṣamalena yasya nātmā
  vimalamater malinīkṛto 'stamohaḥ[47] [25]

Hari is one and the same, though modified as gods, animals, and people, etc. [22]
They, (Viṣṇu's devotees) should be avoided, as (one avoids) oil-fed fire".
Having heard Yama's words, Yama's man, the noose holder, said to Dharmarāja:
"Tell me, master, (how to identify) such a devotee of Viṣṇu – the creator". [23]
Yama said
"He who never deviates from the duties prescribed to his own caste,
who looks with equal indifference upon his own friend or foe(VII)*,*
who does not take anything, nor hurt anyone with violence,
know him, the strong-minded, to be a Viṣṇu-devotee. [24]
He, whose limpid soul is unstained by the dirt of the Kali age,
who has thrown (i.e. abandoned) old confusion, [25]

---

41 N1/15.22b, N10 - surapaśumanujādikalpanābhir harir adibalābhit udīryate tathaikaḥ.

42 N1/15.23a - p(h)arihṛtya (N10 - nimījyaśiktam) yathā[g]nim ājyaśiktam.

43 N1/15.23b - iti yamavacanaṁ niśamya pāṇi (N10 - pārṇa) yamapuruṣas tam uvāca dharmarājaṁ.

44 N1/15.23c, N10 - kathaya mam(bh)a vibh(ā)o[ḥ] samastadhātur bhavati hare khalu yādṛśo 'sya bhaktaḥ.

45 N1/15.24, N10 - na calati nijavarṇadharmato yaḥ samamatir ātma suhṛdvipakṣapakṣe na hara(n)ti na ca hanti.

46 N1/15.25a, N10 - kiñcid ucchaiḥ sthiramanasaṁ tam ave(au)hi viṣṇubhaktaṁ.

47 N1/15.25b - kalikaluṣamalena yasya n(t)ātmā vim(pr)alamater (N10 - vipulamater) malinīkṛto 'stamo(au)ha[ḥ].

manasikṛtajanārdanaṁ manuṣyaṁ
satatam avehi harer atīva bhaktaṁ[48] [26]
kanakam api rahasy avekṣya buddhyā
tṛṇam iva yaḥ samavaiti vai parasvaṁ[49]
bhavati ca bhagavaty ananyacetāḥ
puruṣavaraṁ tam avehi viṣṇubhaktaṁ[50] [27]
sphaṭikagiriśilāmalaḥ kva viṣṇur
manasi nṛṇāṁ kva ca matsarādidoṣaḥ[51] [28]
na hi tuhinamayūkharaśmipūñje
bhavati hutāśanadīptijaḥ pratāpaḥ [29]
vimalamati vimatsaraḥ praśāntaḥ
śucicarito 'khilasattvamitrabhūtaḥ[52]
priyahitavacano 'stamānamāyo

who constantly holds Janārdana(VIII) *in his mind,*
is Hari's worshipper, of great devotion. [26]
Even when he sees gold in secret, he considers it (as useless) as grass,
if it is someone else's property.
All his thoughts are devoted to the lord, not to anyone else.
Consider that excellent man to be a real Viṣṇu-devotee. [27]
(Look at) the difference between Viṣṇu, pure as a mountain of clear crystal,
and people's minds, (full of) greed, wickedness, etc. [28]
A glow born out of fire, does not survive in the cool rays of the moon. [29]
The pure hearted, unselfish, calm, virtuous (person),
who treats all living creatures as friends,
he who speaks kindly and wisely, who has cast off pride and delusion(IX)*,*

---

48 N1/15.26, N10 - manasikṛtajanārdanaṁ puruṣaṁ satatam ave(ai)hi [h]rare(d)r atīva bhaktaṁ.

49 N1/15.27a - kanyakām api rahasy avekṣya buddhyā kṣaṇam (N10 - tṛṇam) iva yaḥ samavaiti vai parasvaṁ.

50 N1/15.27b - bhavati ca bhagavaty a(ā)nanyacetāḥ puruṣavaraṁ tam ave(ai)hi viṣṇubhaktaṁ.

51 N1/15.28b, N10 - sphaṭikagiriśi(a)lāmalaḥ kva viṣṇur manasi nṛṇāṁ kva matsarādidoṣaḥ.

52 N1/15.29b - vimalamatir amatsaraḥ prayā(n)taḥ suvicari(e)to 'khilaṁ sattvamitrabhūtaḥ.

vasati sadā hṛdi tasya vāsudevaḥ[53] [30]
vasati hṛdi sanātane ca tasmin
bhavati pumāñ jagato 'sya saumyarūpaḥ[54]
kṣitirasam atiramyam ātmano 'ntaḥ
kathayati cārutayaiva śālapotaḥ[55] [31]
yamaniyamavidhūtakalmaṣānām
anudinam acyutasaktamānasānāṁ[56]
apagatamadamānamatsarāṇāṁ
vraja bhaṭa dūratareṇa mānavānāṁ[57] [32]
hṛdi yadi bhagavān anādir āste
harir asiśaṅkhagadādharo 'vyayātmā[58]
tad agham aghavighātakartṛbhinnaṁ

Vāsudeva dwells always in his heart. [30]
When the eternal Viṣṇu dwells in the heart of a human being,
that man appears lovely to the world,
like a young Śal tree (showing by) its loveliness, that it is full of juice inside – the essence of the earth. [31]
People whose unmentionable sins are removed by Yama and Niyama(X)*, (and) whose minds cling all the time to Acyuta*(XI)*,*
their greed, conceit and desire for enjoyment vanished – keep far away from these people. [32]
If in (one's) heart is Viṣṇu Anādi, Hari of the unchanging self,
carrying a sword, conch and mace,
how can sin exist in the presence of one who dispels it?

---

53 N1/15.30 - priyahitavacano 'stamān(a)o yo vas(ṁś)ati (N10 -mānaso vasati) sadā hṛdi tasya vāsudevaḥ.

54 N1/15.31a, N10 - vasati hṛdi sanāt(n)ane ca tasmin bhavati pumān ajagato 'sya sau[mya]('nu)rūpaḥ.

55 N1/15.31b, N10 - kṣitirasam atirasyam ātmano 'ntaḥ kathayati [cāru](rā)tayaiva śā(ī)lapotaḥ.

56 N1/15.32a - yamaniyamavidhṛtakalmaṣānām (N10 - yam(t)aniyamavibhūta kalmaṣānām) anuditam acyutasaktamānasānāṁ.

57 N1/15.32c - apagatamadamānamatsarāṇāṁ vraja bhaṭa dū(u)ratareṇa sānavānāṁ.

58 N1/15.33a - hṛdi yadi bhagavān anādir āste harihara śaṅkhagadāvaro (N10 - harir as(r)iśaṅkhagadāvaro) 'tmayātmā(ḥ).

bhavati kathaṁ sati vāndhakāram arke[59] [33]
harati paradhanaṁ nihanti jantūn
vadati tathānṛtaniṣṭhurāṇi yaś ca[60]
aśubhajanitadurmadasya puṁsaḥ
kaluṣamater hṛdi tasya nāsty anantaḥ[61] [34]
na sahati parasaṁpadaṁ vinindāṁ
kaluṣamatiḥ kurute satām asādhuḥ[62]
na yajati na dadāti yaś ca martyo
manasi na tasya janārdano 'dhamasya[63] [35]
paramasuhṛdi bāndhave kalatre
sutatanayā pitṛmātṛbhṛtyavarge
śaṭham atirūpayati yo 'rthatṛṣṇāṁ
tam adhamaceṣṭam avehi nāsya bhaktaṁ[64] [36]

How can darkness exist in the light of the sun? [33]
He who steals other people's property, who injures living creatures,
who speaks harshly and untruthfully,
whose mind is evil and who is proud of his born viciousness,
Viṣṇu, the Eternal, does not dwell in his heart. [34]
He who envies others' success, who acts wickedly towards the righteous,
who neither sacrifices, nor gives gifts to the pious,
Janārdana (Viṣṇu) does not prevail in the mind of that lowest. [35]
He who out of avarice is unkind to his closest friend and relatives,
to his children and parents, to his wife and dependants,
that vile wretch is no devotee of Viṣṇu(XII)*. [36]*

---

59 N1/15.33b - t(n)ad agham aghavighātakartṛbhinnaṁ bhavati kathaṁ sati v(c)āndhakāram arke.

60 N1/15.34a, N10 - harati paradhanaṁ niha(ā)nti jantūn vad(r)ati tathānṛtaniṣṭurāṇi yaś ca.

61 N1/15.34b - aśubhajanitadurmarasya puṁsaḥ kaluṣaṁ mate hṛdi (N10 - kalikaluṣaṁ hradi) tasya nāsty anantaḥ.

62 N1/15.35a - na sahati paraṁ saṁpadaṁ vinindi (N10 - parasaṁpadaṁ vin(t)i[n]d(o)āṁ) kaluṣamatiḥ kurute satām asādhuḥ.

63 N1/15.35b, N10 - na yajati na dadāti yaś ca martyo manasi na tasya janārdano 'dhamasya.

64 Verse 36c-d is added to the text following ViṣP/3.7.30.

aśubhamatir asatpravṛttisaktaḥ
satatam anāryaviśālasaṅgamattaḥ[65]
anudinakṛtapāpabandhayatnaḥ
puruṣapaśur na hi vāsudevabhaktaḥ[66] [37]
sakalam idam ahaṁ ca vāsudevaḥ
paramapumān parameśvaraḥ sa ekaḥ[67]
iti matir amalā bhavaty anante
hṛdayagate vraja tān vihāya dūrāt[68] [38]
kamalanayanavāsudeva viṣṇo
dharaṇidharācyuta śaṅkhacakrapāṇe[69]
bhavaśaraṇam itīrayanti ye vai
tyaja bhaṭa dūratareṇa tān apāpān[70] [39]

He who has evil thoughts, who is always engaged in unrighteous behaviour, (and) clings to vile people,
who makes daily efforts to be bound to crime, a brute-like person, is no devotee of Vāsudeva. [37]
Those who know that Vāsudeva, the supreme Man and supreme God,
is one and the same with their individual self and the entire material world(XIII)*,*
those who think of Ananta(XIV) *and have him in their hearts – keep away from them. [38]*
The lotus eyed Vāsudeva, Viṣṇu, the upholder of the Earth, conch and discus in hand,
those who follow him – leave them (alone) O servant, keep a distance from those sinless. [39]

---

65 N1/15.37a - aśubhamatir asatpr(m)avṛttiśaktaḥ satatam anāryāviśilasaṅgamātraḥ.

66 N1/15.37b, N10 - anudinakṛtapāpabandhayatnaḥ puruṣapaśu[r] na hi vāsudevabhaktaḥ.

67 N1/15.39a, N10 - sakalam idam aha[ṁ] ca vāsudevaḥ paramapumān parameśvaraḥ s(y)aśaṅkaḥ.

68 N1/15.39b, N10 - iti matir amalā bhavaty anante hṛdayegate v[r]aja vihāya tān [d]ūrāt.

69 N1/15.40a, N3/15.21a, N10, N4/15.22a, N7/15.21a, N8/15.19c, Ra/12.22a - kamalanayana vāsudeva viṣṇo dharaṇidharācyuta (N2/15.21a - śaṅkhacakrapāṇau) śaṅkhacakrapāṇe.

70 N1/15.40b, N2/15.21b, N4/15.22b, N8/15.19d, Ra/12.22b - bhavaśa(ā)raṇam itīrayanti (N3/15.21b, N7/15.21b - udīrayanti) ye vai t(j)yaja bhaṭa dū(u)ra(n)tareṇa tān apāpān. End of N2/15, N3/15.

vasati manasi yasya so 'vyayātmā
  puruṣavarasya na tasya dṛṣṭipāte[71]
tava gatir athavā mamāsti cakra
  pratihata vīrya balasya so 'nyalokyaḥ[72] [40]
kalikalmaṣam atyugraṁ narakārtipradaṁ nṛṇāṁ[73]
prayāti vilayaṁ sadyaḥ sakṛd dhātranusaṁsmṛte[74] [41]
yatra matkīrtitaṁ bhaktyā vilāpanam anuttamaṁ[75]
maitreyāśeṣapāpānāṁ dhātūnām iva pāvakaḥ[76] [42]

iti śrībrahmāṇḍapurāṇe nāsiketopākhyāne puruṣodakavarṇanaṁ nāma pañcadaśo 'dhyāyaḥ

Those worthy persons, in whose minds dwells the Imperishable soul[(XV)]*, (and) (Viṣṇu) is their refuge, neither you*[(XVI)] *can enter their field of vision, nor I*[(XVII)] *– my power is dispelled by the power of Viṣṇu's discus. [40]*
The most terrible Kali age, that brings suffering to people, in Kalmaṣa Hell, is overcome by thinking even once on the Creator[(XVIII)]*. [41]*
There, (in the world of Kali age), uttering my name[(XIX)] *in devotion is like fire, burning up sins, like the burning of other elements". [42]*

This is the fifteenth chapter of the Nāsiketa story, pertaining to the Brahmāṇḍa Purāṇa, called – the water-offering ceremony of the (dead) person.

Translation Notes

I – "The Flower-water River".
II – Celestial female music players.
III – Amṛta – the immortality elixir.
IV – Celestial female dancers.

---

71 N1/15.38a, N10 - vasati manasi yasya so 'vyayātmā puruṣavarasya [na tasya dṛṣṭipāte].

72 N1/15.38b, N10 - (vatsya dṛṣṭi pāte) na va (N10 - tava) gatir athavā mamāsti cakrapratidattavīryya balasya (N10 - so 'nyalokyaḥ) sānyalokāḥ.

73 N1/15.40c, N10 - kalikalmaṣam atyugraṁ narakārtipradaṁ nṛṇāṁ.

74 N1/15.41a - prayāyi (N10 - prayāti) vilayaṁ sadyaḥ sakṛd dhātra(ā)nusaṁsmṛte.

75 N1/15.41b, N10 - yatra matkīrtitaṁ bhaktyā vilāpanam anuttamaṁ.

76 N1/15.42, N10 - maitreyāśeṣapāpānāṁ dhātūnām iva pāvakaḥ.

V – On Earth.
VI – Viṣṇu. Following H. H. Wilson's translation.
VII – Following H. H. Wilson's translation.
VIII – Viṣṇu.
IX – "Humble and sincere" – following H. H. Wilson's translation.
X – Practices of moral behaviour and self control, the first steps of Yoga.
XI – "Firm" – one of Viṣṇu's 1000 names.
XII – Following H. H. Wilson's translation.
XIII – Literally – the world which is conceived as comprised of many parts.
XIV – "Endless, Eternal, Infinite" – one of Viṣṇu's 1000 names.
XV – Viṣṇu.
XVI – Yama's messenger.
XVII – Yama.
XVIII – Brahma/Viṣṇu.
XIX – It should be "Viṣṇu's name", since the speaker is Yama.

Chapter 16

The Dimensions of the Road

nāsiketa uvāca[1]
athātaḥ saṁpravakṣyāmi yamalokaṁ sudāruṇaṁ[2]
yathāsaṅkhyāṁ pravakṣyāmi śṛṇudhvaṁ dvijasattamāḥ[3] [1]
ṣaḍaśītisahasrāṇi yojanānāṁ pramāṇataḥ[4]
yamalokasya cādhvānaṁ yena gacchanti mānavāḥ[5] [2]

Nāsiketa said
I shall now describe the very fierce world of Yama.
Listen, excellent Twice-born(I), I shall describe its dimensions. [1]
Eighty six thousand Yojanas (long) is the
road by which people go to Yama's world. [2]

---

1 N1/16 - maitreya uvāca.
N2/16.1-2 - Additional unidentified and undeciphered Stotra.

2 N2/16.3a - athātaḥ saṁpravakṣyāmi (N3 - yamalokaṁ sudāruṇaṁ) yamalokasya (N4/16.1a, N8/16.20a, Ra/13.1a, BF/16.1a - dāruṇaṁ) kāraṇaṁ.
No verse numbers in N3.
Bo/15.1a - athāhaṁ saṁpravakṣyāmi yamamārgasya vistaraṁ.

3 N1/16.1b - yama(ḥ)sakhyāṁ ca vachyāmi śṛṇudhvaṁ dvijasattamāḥ.
Additional half verse: N3 - raudrākāraṁ mahāghoraṁ tathānyataptavalukaṁ.
N4/16.1b, N8/16.20b, Ra/13.1b - mārgaṁ svarūpamānābhyāṁ śṛṇvantu dvijasattamāḥ.
BF/16.1b - mārgasaṅkhyāṁ samāsena śṛṇudhvaṁ munipuṅgavāḥ.

4 N1/16.2a - ṣadaśītisahasrāṇi yojanānāṁ (N7/16.2a, BF/16.2a, Bo/15.1b - pramāṇataḥ) pramāṇatiḥ.
N4/16.2a, N8/16.21a, Ra/13.2a - ṣaḍaśītisahasrāṇāṁ yojanānāṁ pramāṇataḥ.

5 N1/16.2b - yamaloka sa (N7/16.2b - yamalokasya) cādhvānaṁ yena gacchanti mānavāḥ.
N10 - yamalokasya cādyānaṁ (BF/16.2b - cādhvāno) yena gacchanti mānavāḥ.
N2/16.4b - yamalokasya cādhvānaṁ (Bo/15.2 - āhur mānuṣalokataḥ) yatra gacchanti pāpinaḥ.
N4/16.2b, N8/16.21b, Ra/13.2b - yamalokasya mārge 'sti yena gacchanti mānuṣāḥ.

tasmin mārge mahāraudre jvalantaṁ cāgnitejasa[6]
saṅkīrṇaṁ kaṇṭakais tīkṣṇaiḥ sūcivaktraṁ ca dāruṇaṁ[7] [3]
raudrākāraṁ mahāghoraṁ tathā taptapravālukaṁ[8]
pīḍitāḥ kṣutpipāsābhyāṁ pāpiṣṭhās tatra durgame[9] [4]
nīyante te bhayārtā hi sarve te pretarūpiṇaḥ[10]
vinā dharmeṇa pāpiṣṭhā mārgaṁ paśyanti cedṛśaṁ[11] [5]

On that very fierce road – blazing like fire,
full of sharp, fierce, needle-tipped thorns, [3]
terrible, very fierce, with heated sand,
impassable – are the sinners, tortured by hunger and thirst. [4]
They are brought there frightened, all in the form of dead souls.
Being devoid of Dharma, those sinners see that same road. [5]

---

6 N1/16.2a - tasmin mārge mahāraudre g(v)irayaḥ parvatā(ai)ḥ kvacit.
N2/16.5a - tasmin mārge mahāghore (N3 -jvalantaṁ cāgnitejasaṁ) jvalantaś cāgnitejasā.
Additional verses:
N2/16.5b-6a - tasmin mārge mayā dṛṣṭā bhramya(ḥ)mānāś ca tathā (ca) te kvacin mārge hi raudrāṁ taṁ vikāraṁ parvataṁ kvacit.
N3 - kvacit kṛmibhir aspantaṁ andhakāraṁ kvacid vanaṁ
kvacid vanaṁ mahāraudraṁ vikaṭaḥ parvataiḥ kvacit.

7 N1/16.3b, N3 - saṅkīrṇaṁ kaṇṭakais tīkṣṇaiḥ (N7/16.4b - kaṇṭakais tīkṣṇaiḥ saṅkīrṇa[ṁ]) sūcivaktraṁ (N2/16.6b, N10 - sudāruṇaṁ) ca dārūṇaṁ.
N4/16.5a, N8/16.24a, Ra/13.5a - āyasaiḥ kaṇṭakais tīkṣṇaiḥ saṅkirṇaś ca samaṁ tataḥ.

8 N1/16.4a - raudrākāram athānyaṁ [tapta]pr(tas)avālukaṁ pipās(a)ā (ha).
N3 - tathānyataptavālukaṁ tathā taptapravālukaṁ.
N7/16.5a - raudrakāraṁ mahājñātaṁ tathānyaṁ taptavālukaṁ.

9 N4/16.6a, N8/16.25a, Ra/13.6a - pīḍitāḥ kṣutpipāsābhyāṁ (N7/16.5b - pipāsā himasītaṁ ca) pāpiṣṭhās tatra durgame.
BF/16.7a - patanti tatra te mārge pāpiṣṭhāś cātidurgame.

10 N2/16.8a - nīyante te bhayārt(t)ā hi (N7/16.6a - pretāḥ sarve narādayaḥ) pretai(s)ḥ sarve na śadayaḥ.
N4/16.6b, N8/16.25b, Ra/13.6b - nīyante bhayam āpannāḥ pretāḥ sarve 'pi mānuṣāḥ.
BF/16.7b - nīyante tena mārgeṇa pretāḥ sarve durātmakāḥ.

11 N1/16.5b, N10, N3 - vinā dharmeṇa pāpiṣṭhā(ḥ) (BF/16.8a - durgamārgapravartinaḥ) mārgaṁ paśyanti cedṛśaṁ.

krūraiś ca kiṅkaraiḥ sarvair baddhā dṛṣṭāś ca śṛṅkhalaiḥ[12]
tāḍitā lohadaṇḍaiś ca patanti dharaṇītale[13] [6]
utthāpayanti tān dūtā ākṛṣyante ca śṛṅkhalaiḥ[14]
grīvāvāhaprayatnena badhvā pṛṣṭhaprayatnataḥ[15] [7]
anekāś ca mayā dṛṣṭās tasmin mārge ca pāpinaḥ[16]

I saw (the sinners) bound with fetters, by all the cruel servants,
falling to the ground, beaten by iron rods. [6]
Those messengers make them rise up, dragged by their chains,
bearing bells on the neck, bound, their backs (exhausted) with efforts. [7]
I saw many sinners on that road,

N2/16.8b - vinā dharmeṇa te pāpā durgāṇi prāpnuvanti hi.
N4/16.7a, N8/16.26a, Ra/13.7a - vinā dharmeṇa te durgaṁ mārgaṁ paśyanti tāpasāḥ.

12 N2/16.9a - krūrais tai(ś)ḥ kiṅkarai(s)ḥ sarvair b(v)addhā dṛṣṭāś ca śṛṅkhalaiḥ.
N10 - krūraiś ca kiṅkaraiḥ sarvair b(v)a[d]dhvā (N7/16.7a - dṛṣṭāś ca saṅkulaiḥ) dūṣṭāś ca śṛṅkhalaiḥ.
N4/16.7b, N8/16.26b, Ra/13.7b - krūraiś ca yamadūtais te b(v)addhāḥ śṛṅkhalayā bhṛśaṁ.
BF/16.8b - krūrais tu kiṅkaraiḥ sarvair baddhās te lohaśṛṅkhalaiḥ.
Bo/15.6a - krūrās te kiṅkarāḥ sarve pāpiṣṭhāṁs tāḍayanti hi.

13 N2/16.9b - śāsitā lauhadaṇḍaiś (N7/16.7b - dakṣiṇā lohadaṇḍaiś) ca (BF/16.9a - tāḍitā lohadaṇḍais te) patitā dharaṇītale.
Verses 16.6b-8a are missing in N3.
N4/16.8a, N8/16.27a, Ra/13.8a - tāḍitā āyasair daṇḍaiḥ patanti dharaṇītale.

14 N1/16.7a, N10 - utthāpayanti tān dūtā(n) ākṛṣyante ca śṛṅkhalaiḥ.
N2/16.10a - utthāpayanti te dūtā ākṛṣyante ca saṅkulaiḥ.
N4/16.8b, N8/16.27b, Ra/13.8b - utthāpayanti tān dūtā (BF/16.9b - daṇḍaghātaiḥ sudāruṇaiḥ) nayanti ca punaḥ punaḥ.

15 N1/16.7b, N10 - grīvāb(v)āhuprayatnena baddhakṛṣyaḥ prayatnataḥ.
N2/16.10b - grīvāvāhaprayatnena b(v)adhvā pṛṣṭhaprayatnataḥ.
N4/16.9a, N8/16.28a, Ra/13.9a - grīvāb(v)āhuprakāreṇa b(v)addhā yatnena bhūyasā.
BF/16.9b - grīvābāhuprahāreṇa baddhāḥ pṛṣṭhe prayatnataḥ.

16 N1/16.8a, N10 - aneke ca mayā dṛṣṭās tena mārgeṇa pāpinaḥ.
N7/16.9a - anekaś ca mayā dṛṣṭās (BF/16.10b - anītās te durācārās) tena mārgeṇa pāpinaḥ.

yamadūtair mahāghorais tāḍyante nirdayair bhṛśaṁ[17] [8]
daṇḍamudgarahastaiś ca tāḍyante pralapanti ca[18]
mūrcchitāḥ kṣaṇabhūmiṣṭhā utthitā bhayaśaṅkitāḥ[19] [9]
yāvat pāpena smaranti tāvat te tāḍyante bhṛśaṁ[20]
rudanti karuṇās te vai trātā teṣāṁ na vidyate[21] [10]
dūtās teṣāṁ vadanty evaṁ śṛṇudhvaṁ dvijasattamāḥ[22]

beaten very hard, mercilessly, by Yama's very fierce messengers. [8]
They are beaten by sticks, mallets and fists, and they cry.
As soon as they fall faint to the ground, they are pulled up, frightened and weak. [9]
While beaten (so) hard, they recall their sins, (and)
they cry, exhausted, (but) there are no protectors for them. [10]
Listen, O excellent Twice-born, to what the messengers said to them:

---

17 N3 - yamadūtair mahāghorais tāḍyante (BF/16.11a - nirdayair bhṛśaṁ) pralapanti ca.
Verse 16.8b-9b is missing in N2.
N4/16.9b, N8/16.28b, Ra/13.9b - tato nirdayabhāvena tāḍayanti punar bhṛśaṁ.
N7/16.9b - yamadūtair mahāghorair nirdayais tāḍite bhṛśaṁ.

18 Half verse 16.9a is missing in N3.
N7/16.10a - daṇḍamudgarahastaiś ca tāḍitā[ḥ] prayatanti ca.

19 N1/16.9b - mūrcchit(o)aḥ kṣaṇabhūmiṣṭh(sth)o utthito bhayaśaṅkitaḥ.
N3, N7/16.10b - mūrcchitā[ḥ] kṣaṇabhūmiṣṭh(sth)ā utthitā bhayaśaṅkitāḥ.
N4/16.10a, N8/16.29a, Ra/13.10a - tāḍitās tais tadā pāpā mūrcchanti ca tataḥ paraṁ.
Bo/15.6b - mūrcchitān kṣaṇamātreṇa patitān punar utthitān.
BF/16.11b - mūrcchitāḥ kṣiṇadehās tu socchvāsā bhayasaṅkulāḥ.

20 N2/16.11b - smaranti pāpaṁ yāvac ca tāvat tāḍyant(i)e mudgaraiḥ.
N4/16.10b, N8/16.29b, Ra/13.10b - mānuṣatve kṛtaṁ karmma saṁsmaranti dvijottamāḥ.

21 N1/16.10b, N10 - rudanti karuṇās te vai(ḥ) trātā teṣāṁ na vidyate.
N2/16.12a - rudanti karuṇā vācā trātā teṣāṁ na vartate.
N4/16.11a, N8/16.30a, Ra/13.11a - rudanti karuṇaṁ yeṣāṁ trātā tatra na vidyate.
N7/16.11b - rudanti karuṇā yuktās trātā teṣu na vidyate.
BF/16.14a - rudanti karuṇaṁ pāpā dharmajñānavivarjitāḥ.

22 N1/16.11a, N7/16.12a - dūtās teṣāṁ vada[n]ty evaṁ (N2/16.12b - śrūyataṁ munipuṅgavāḥ) śṛṇuddhvaṁ dvijasattamāḥ.
N4/16.11b, N8/16.30b, Ra/13.11b - tāṁś cedaṁ kiṅkarāḥ prāhuḥ śrūyatām avadhānataḥ.
BF/16.22a - dūtās teṣu vadante vai śṛṇudhvaṁ pāpakāriṇaḥ.

pāpakarmaratāḥ sadā sarvadharmabahiḥkṛtāḥ[23] [11]
bho bho pāpā durācārā mānuṣatve niyojitāḥ[24]
sulabhāni na dattāni indhanāny udakāni ca[25] [12]
lakṣmyā tu garvitā mūḍhā gataṁ janma nirarthakaṁ[26]
na kasmins tv āgatas tīrthe pūjitā na tvayā dvijāḥ[27] [13]
mūḍha kiñcin na te dattaṁ panthānaṁ tarase kathaṁ[28]

"You have always been engaged in sin, and have done what is forbidden by all moral laws[(II)]. *[11]*
O sinners of bad behaviour, (though) born as humans,
you have not given (even of) the readily available, neither fuel nor water. [12]
You fools, conceited because of (your) wealth, you have wasted this birth.
You have not gone on pilgrimages, nor have you worshipped the twice-born. [13]
O fools, you have not donated anything of yours, how will you cross this road?

---

23 N1/16.11b - re re pāpāḥ sadāḥkūṭāḥ (N2/16.13a - pāpākarmasadāra(k)tā(s)ḥ, N4/16.12a, N8/16.31a, Ra/13.12a - pāpakarmmaratā nityaṁ, N7/16.12b - pāpakarma sadā kuryuḥ, BF/16.22b - bho pāpino durācārāḥ) sarvadharmab(v)ahi[ḥ]kṛtāḥ.

24 N2/16.15a - bho bho pāpā durācārā (N3 - mānuṣatve (N10, N7/16.13a - na yoj(t)itāḥ) niyojitāḥ) mānuṣyatve ca yojitāḥ.
Verse numbers 13, 14 are skipped in N2.
N4/16.12b, N8/16.31b, Ra/13.12b - re mānuṣyā bhavadbhis tu mānuṣatve viyojitaiḥ.

25 N2/16.15b - sulabhāni na dattāni dadhanāny (N3 - cendhanān, N4/16.13a, N7/16.13b, N8/16.32a, Ra/13.13a - indhanāny) udakāni ca.
N10 - s(ś)ulabhān na nikṣi(ā)tāni indhanāny udakāni ca.
BF/16.23b - sulabhāni ca dānāni toyapānatṛṇāni ca.

26 N1/16.13a - lakṣmīnigarvitā mūḍhā gatajanmā nirarthakaḥ.
N2/16.15a - lakṣmyā ca garvitā mūḍhā(ḥ) evaṁ janmā nirarthakaṁ.
N3 - lakṣyanti garvitā (N4/16.13b, N8/16.32b, Ra/13.13b - vyarthā lakṣmīr gatā, N7/16.14a - lakṣmī sugarvitā) mūḍhā gataṁ janma nirarthakaṁ.
N10 - lakṣmyā tu garvitā mūḍha gatajanma nirarthake.
BF/16.24a - kuto naiva pradattāni janma syād yan nirarthakaṁ.

27 N2/16.16b - gatā na tīrthaṁ rājendra pūjito naiva brāhmaṇaḥ.
N3, N10 - na kasmins tvaṁ gat(o)as tīrthe pūjitā na tvayā dvijā[ḥ].
N4/16.14a, N8/16.33a, Ra/13.14a - na kadācid gataṁ tīrthaṁ (BF/16.24b - na kaścid āgatas tīrthe) pūjitā na dvijottamāḥ.

28 N1/16.14a, N10 - mūḍha kiñci(t)n na te dattaṁ (N3 - vadantantye) kathaṁ nistarase pathaḥ.

na śruto yamaloko 'yaṁ yamamārgo 'pi na śrutaḥ[29] [14]
maithunavyasane saktaḥ sarvakāle na śaṅkitaḥ[30]
kāmabhogeṣu saṁsakto yuktāyuktaṁ na cintitaṁ[31] [15]
na bhūr dattā hiraṇyaṁ ca gāvo naiva tathā tilāḥ[32]

Have you not heard of Yama's world, or even of Yama's road? [14]
You have been engaged all the time in the habit of sexual intercourse, without being apprehensive.
You have adhered to satisfying passion, heedless of right and wrong. [15]
You have not donated any land, nor gold, neither cows, nor oil.

N2/16.17a - mūḍha kiñcin na dattaṁ te pathānaṁ tarase kathaṁ.
N4/16.14b, N8/16.33b, Ra/13.14b - na dattaṁ na hutaṁ tasmāt tapyate mārga[ir] īdṛśaiḥ.
BF/16.25a - muḍhāḥ kathaṁ nistaranti ghoraṁ narakapātanaṁ.

29 N2/16.17b - na śruto yamalokās te mahāpathā na hi śrutaḥ.
N3 - na śrutaṁ yamaloko 'yaṁ yamamārgo 'pi na(ḥ) śrutaḥ.
N4/16.15a, N8/16.34a, Ra/13.15a - na śruto yamaloko 'yaṁ tasya pathāś ca na śrutaḥ.
N7/16.16b - na śrutaṁ yamalokaṁ te mahā(ṁ)pathā ca na śrutaḥ.
BF/16.25b - na śrutaṁ yamalokasya dāruṇaṁ vartma durgamaṁ.

30 N1/16.15a - maithunavyasane śaktiḥ (N10 - sarvakāle na śaṅkitaḥ) parvakāle na saṁsthitaḥ.
N2/16.18a - maithunair vyasatā śakta(s)ḥ (N7/16.15a - maithunavyasanāsaktaḥ) sarvakāle na śaṅkitaḥ.
N3 - maithune vyasane śaktiḥ sarvaloke na śaṅkitaḥ.
N4/16.15b, N8/16.34b, Ra/13.15b - maithunavyasanāsaktaiḥ parvakāle 'py aśaṅkitaiḥ.
BF/16.26a - maithunavyasanāsaktās tathā pāpātmakāḥ sadā.

31 N2/16.18b - kāmabhogeṣu saṁyukto yuktāyukto na cintitaḥ.
N3 - kāmabhogeṣu saṁśakto yuktāyuktaṁ na cintayan.
N4/16.16a, N8/16.35a, Ra/13.16a - manobhuvaśamāpannair yuktāyuktavivarjjitaiḥ.
N7/16.15b - kāmabhoge na saṁyukto yuktāyuktaṁ na cintitaṁ.
BF/16.26b - kāmalobharatā nityaṁ dharmācārabahiḥkṛtāḥ.

32 N1/16.16a - na bhūhiraṇyadattena na gāvo na tatha tilāḥ.
N2/16.19a, N3, N10 - na bhūhiraṇyadattaṁ te na gāvo vā tatha tilāḥ.
N4/16.16b, N8/16.35b, Ra/13.16b - na bhūr dattā hiraṇyaṁ ca gāvo naiva tathā tilāḥ.

candrasūryoparāge tu suptaḥ śayyāṁ sukhena tu[33] [16]
na hutaṁ na tvayā japtaṁ naratvaṁ niḥphalaṁ gataṁ[34]
dustaraṁ tarase kena yamalokaṁ sudāruṇaṁ[35] [17]
satvaraṁ gaccha pāpātman dharmajñānavivarjita[36]
sarvaśāstraparibhraṣṭo na bhakto brāhmaṇeṣu ca[37] [18]
guruvākyaṁ na sañjñātaṁ mūḍha garveṇa cātmanā[38]

At the time of sun or moon eclipse, you enjoyed sleeping in bed[III)]. *[16]*
Since you have not sacrificed, nor recited (hymns), your human birth has been wasted.
By which (means) will you cross the fierce, so-hard-to-cross world of Yama? [17]
Go quickly, O sinner, devoid of knowledge and Dharma,
not devoted to any form of all the Śāstras, nor to Brahmins. [18]
You have not heeded teachers' instructions, O fool, because of your own conceit".

N7/16.17a - na bhūhiraṇyaṁ dattaṁ te (BF/16.27a - na hiraṇyaṁ na va bhūmir) na gāvo na tathā tilāḥ.

33 N2/16.19b - grahaṇe candrasūryo tvaṁ supto 'si sukhe (- - -).
N3 - candrasūryoparāge ca suptaśayyāṁ sukhena ca.
N4/16.16b, N8/16.35b, Ra/13.16b - suptaṁ śayyādiṣu tathā grahaṇe candrasūryyayoḥ.
N7/16.17b - grahaṇe candrasūryasya suptasajyāṁ sukhena ca.
BF/16.27b - grahaṇe sūryaśaśinor na dattāni dvijottame.

34 N1/16.17a - nāhutaṁ tvat tathā japtaṁ naratv(y)aṁ niḥphalaṁ gataṁ.
N2/16.20a - na hutaṁ na va tathā japtaṁ narābhyo madhusudanaṁ.
N3, N10 - na hutaṁ na tvayā japtaṁ (N7/16.18a - naras tvaṁ vihvalāṁ gataḥ) naratv(y)aṁ niḥphalaṁ gataṁ.
N4/16.17b, N8/16.36b, Ra/13.17b - na dattaṁ na hutaṁ japtaṁ naratvaṁ viphalīkṛtaṁ.
BF/16.28a - na hutaṁ na tapas taptaṁ sarvaiḥ pāpibhir dustaraṁ.

35 N1/16.17b - dustaraṁ tarase kenas yamalokaṁ ca dāruṇaṁ.
N2/16.20b - dustaraṁ kena taras(s)e yamamārgasudāruṇaṁ.
N7/16.18b - dustaraṁ tarase kena yamalokaṁ tu dāruṇaṁ.
BF/16.28b - tīryate kena dānena dāruṇaṁ narakārṇavaṁ.

36 N7/16.19a - satvaraṁ gaccha pāpiṣṭha dharmajñānavivarjitaḥ.
BF/16.29a - satvaraṁ yātāḥ pāpiṣṭhā yamalokaṁ sudāruṇaṁ.

37 N2/16.21b - sarvakarmaparibhraṣṭo na bhaktir dvijadaivato.
N7/16.19b - sarvaś(s)āstraparibhraṣṭo na bhaktadvijadevatāḥ.
BF/16.29b - dharmaśāstraparibhraṣṭā gurubhaktiparāṅmukhāḥ.

38 N1/16.19a - guruvākya na vā (N10 - guruvākyaṁ na ca) jñātaṁ mūḍha garveṇa cātmanaḥ.
N2/16.22a - guruvākyaṁ na sañjñātaṁ mūḍha garvitam ātmanā.

vidhinā tena nīyante mayā dṛṣṭā anekaśaḥ[39] [19]
brahmaghnāś ca surāpāś ca goghnāś ca svāmighātakāḥ[40]
strīghātī garbhapātī ca gṛhakṣetraharāś ca ye[41] [20]
saktā ye paradāreṣu nityo mattāś ca ye narāḥ[42]
vyasane madyamāṁse tu parvakāle ca maithune[43] [21]

I saw many (sinners) taken away in this manner by them[(IV)] *– [19]*
killers of Brahmins and spiritual masters, wine drinkers, cow killers,
woman killers, abortion performers, and those who steal houses and fields. [20]
(I saw also) those who covet others' wives, and people who are always intoxicated,
those who habitually have sex in forbidden lunar times, take alcohol and meat, [21]

N3 - guror vākyam avajñātaṁ mūḍha garveṇa cātmanā.
N7/16.20a - guror vākyam api 'jñātaṁ mūḍha garvitamānavāḥ.
BF/16.30a - vṛddhavākyaṁ na śṛṇvanti mūḍhā garvitamānasāḥ.

39 N1/16.19b - vidhinā tena nīyante mayā (N10, N7/16.20b - dṛṣṭā anekaśaḥ) dṛṣṭādy anekaśaḥ.
N2/16.22b - anena vidhinā yānti mayā dṛṣṭās tv anekaśaḥ.
N3 - vidhibhāvena nīyante mayā dṛṣṭāny anekaśaḥ.
BF/16.30b - anena vidhinā dṛṣṭā nīyamānā yamālayaṁ.

40 N2/16.23a, N3, BF/16.31a - brahmaghnaś ca surāpaś ca (N7/16.21a - surāpā ye) goghnaś ca svāmighātakaḥ.
BF/16.15a - brahmaghnaś ca paśughnaś ca nindākṛd gurusvāminoḥ.
Bo/15.9b - brahmahatyā surāpānaṁ steyaṁ gurvaṅganāgamaḥ.

41 N2/16.23b, N10, N7/16.21b - strīghātī garbhapātī ca (N3 - gṛhakṣetraharas tathā) gṛhakṣetraharāś ca ye.
BF/16.32a - strīghātino dayāhīnā gṛhakṣetraharāś ca ye.

42 N2/16.24a - s(ś)aktā ye paradāreṣu nityaṁ (N10 - yūtāś ca ye narāḥ) yūtaratāś (N7/16.22a - dūtaratāś) ca ye.
Verses 16.21-3 are missing in N3.
BF/16.31b - ye saktāḥ paradāreṣu paradroharatāś ca ye.

43 N1/16.21b - vyasane madyamāṁse tu parvakāle ca maithunāḥ.
N2/16.24b - vyasanaṁ madyamāṁseṣu avarṇā pāpasya maithunaṁ.
N7/16.22b - vyasanaṁ madyamāṁsena tv avarṇai yas tu maithunaṁ.
BF/16.32b - vyasanī madyamāṁsānām avarṇyavarṇabhāṣakaḥ.

agamyāgāmino ye ca abhakṣyābhakṣaṇe ratāḥ[44]
ye haranti gurudravyaṁ devadravyaṁ viśeṣataḥ[45] [22]
strīdravyahāriṇaḥ pāpā bāladravyaṁ haranti ye[46]
paṅgvandhavṛddhaklībānāṁ mūkānāṁ ca tathaiva ca[47] [23]
vṛttighnā ṛṇahantāraḥ kṣetradārāpahārakāḥ[48]
pracchannapāpaghnā mūḍhā ye saroṣā dvijottamāḥ[49] [24]

those who have sexual relations with forbidden women, and
those who ignore (the rules of) permitted and forbidden food,
those who steal teacher's property, (and) especially – Gods' wealth. [22]
Sinners who steal women's property, and those who steal children's property,
those who steal the property of the lame, blind, old people, and that of the mute or impotent, [23]
those who breach moral conduct, who kill because of debt, steal fields and wives,
those angry fools, sinners who kill in secret, O excellent Brahmins. [24]

---

44 N2/16.25a - agamyāgāmane ye ca (N7/16.23a - agamyāgāmano yena) abhakṣyābhakṣ(y)aṇe ratāḥ.
BF/16.33a - agamyāgāmino ye ca ye cābhakṣyāsya bhakṣakāḥ.

45 N1/16.22b, N10, BF/16.33b - ye haranti (N7/16.23b - cauranti) guror dravyaṁ (N2/16.25b - corayanti gurudravyaṁ) devadravyaṁ viśeṣataḥ.

46 N1/16.23a - strīdravyaṁ hāriṇaḥ (N10, BF/16.15b - strīdravyahāriṇaḥ) pāpā bāladravyaṁ haranti ye.
N2/16.26a - strīdravyaṁ harate [ya]s tu b(v)āladravyaharec ca yaḥ.
N7/16.24a - strīdravyaṁ harate (b(v)āla) [pāpā] b(v)āladravyaṁ haranti ca.

47 N1/16.23b - paṇḍuvandhavṛddhaklībānāṁ (N3 - vikalāndhakaklīb(v)ānāṁ) mūkānāṁ ca tathaiva ca.
N2/16.26b - vadhirāndhamūkavikalaḥ klīb(v)adravyaharāś ca ye (vi).
N10 - paṅkhāndhavṛddhaklīb(v)ānāṁ mūkānāṁ tu tathaiva ca.
N7/16.24b - va(n)dhirāndhamūkavikaklīb(v)adravyaharāś ca ye.
N4/16.27a, N8/16.46b, Ra/13.27a - vadhirāndhakamū(u)kārttaklīb(v)adravyaharāś ca ye.
BF/16.16a - paṅgvandhavṛddhaklībānāṁ mūkānāṁ caiva vittaghnāḥ.

48 N1/16.24a, N10 - vittaghnā (N7/16.25a - svar(ṛ)ṇahārī ca) ṛṇahantāraḥ (N2/16.27a - vṛttighnāś cā(- - -) ca, N3 - kṛttighnās tṛṇahantāraḥ, BF/16.34b - rājavittaprahārī ca) kṣetradārāpahārakāḥ.
BF/16.16b - vṛttikāntāhariṇaś ca tathā kṣetrahārāś ca ye.

49 N1/16.24b - praccha[nna]pāpaghna (ye) mūḍhā ye saroṣā dvijātayaḥ.
N2/16.27b - pracchannapāpaṁ ye kuryyuḥ (N7/16.25b - pracchannāpāpā ye mūḍhāḥ) surāpā yo dvijottamāḥ.

ghātino garbhabālānāṁ viṣāgnyor dānakārakāḥ[50]
nīcācārāratā nityaṁ adharmaṁ cintayanti ye[51] [25]
pāpakarmamahāraudrāḥ śaucācāravivarjitāḥ[52]
jvālite cāgnisaṅkāśe tat pathi duratikrame[53] [26]
nīyante pāpakarmāṇo durācārā adhārmikāḥ[54]
kṣuttṛṣṇāśramataptāṅgāḥ praṇiyante ca kiṅkaraiḥ[55] [27]

Children-killers and abortion-performers, those who supply poison or ignite fire,
always engaged in low conduct, and thinking about doing wrong, [25]
very fierce sinners, devoid of pure conduct,
(all those) – blazing like fire on that hard-to-traverse road, [26]
unrighteous sinners of bad conduct – are taken away.
Hungry and thirsty, exhausted, with heated limbs, they are carried away by the servants. [27]

Verse 24b-25a is missing in N3.
BF/16.35a - pracchannāpāpā ye mūḍhāḥ surāpāne ratā dvijāḥ.

50 N2/16.28a - garbha hā bālaghātī vā viṣādānamarās tathā.
N10 - ghātino ye ca b(v)ālānāṁ viṣāgnyor dānakārakāḥ.
N7/16.26a - garbha ha b(v)ālaghātī ca viṣādānamahārakāḥ.
BF/16.35b - garbhaghātī bālāghātī viṣadātāro nirghṛṇāḥ.

51 N1/16.25b - nītācārar(t)atā ni(e)[tyaṁ] (mā) (N3 - aghā(a)n(ī)i (N10 - [a]dharma) cintayanti ye) dharmādharmaṁ vicinti te.
N7/16.26b - nīcācārāratā nityam adharmaṁ cintayanti ye.
BF/16.36a - nīcācāragato nityam adharmasya ca cintakāḥ.

52 N1/16.26a - pāpakarmamahāraudrāḥ śaucācīravivarjitāḥ.
N2/16.29a - pāpakarmaratā y(m)e ca (N7/16.27a - pāpakarmaharā[ś] caṇḍāḥ, N3 - pāpakarma mahācaṇḍā[ḥ]) satyaśaucavivarjitāḥ.
Additional half verse:
N2/16.29b - yamamārge (N7/16.27b - mahāpath(i)e) mayā dṛṣṭā rodamānā vṛhatsvaraiḥ.

53 N1/16.26b, N3, N10 - jvālite cāgnisaṅkāśe tat pathe duratikrame.
N2/16.30a - jvālantam agnisaṅkāśaṁ tat pathyaṁ duratikrame.
N7/16.28a - jvalantam agnisaṅkāśaṁ tat pathaṁ duratikramaṁ.

54 N1/16.27a, N3, N7/16.28b - nīya[n]te pāpakarmāṇo (BF/16.20a - gatās te kṣutpipāsitāḥ) durācārā adhārmikāḥ.

55 N7/16.29a - kṣuttṛṣṇāśramataptāṅgāṁ vinayant(i)e yamakiṅkar(ān)aiḥ (vi).

vadanto dīnavākyāni mayā dṛṣṭās tv anekaśaḥ[56]
ākṛṣyante balātkārād vamantaḥ śoṇitaṁ mukhāt[57] [28]
dūtā ūcuḥ
saṁsāre tu kṛtaṁ karma iha sthāne phalapradaṁ[58]
kṛṣṇā gaur na tvayā dattā vaitaraṇyās tu tāraṇe[59] [29]
pathi śrānte gṛhāyāte na kṛtaṁ tava gauravaṁ[60]

I saw many (sinners) uttering words of misery,
dragged forcibly, blood pouring out of their mouths. [28]
The messengers said
"The deeds done in Saṁsāra (i.e. the mortal world), bear fruit in this place.
You have not donated a black cow, for crossing the Vaitarṇī (River). [29]
You have not shown respect to him, who came to your home wearied by the road –

---

56 N1/16.28a - vadato (N10 - vadanto) dīnavākyāni mayā dṛṣṭās t(s)v anekaśaḥ.
N2/16.31a - vadanti kṛpaṇaṁ vākyaṁ (BF/16.20b - bruvantaḥ kṛpaṇāṁ vācaṁ) mayā (N7/16.29b - dṛṣṭās tv) dṛṣṭā (BF/16.20b - sahasraśaḥ) anekaśaḥ.
Additional verses - N2/16.32-33a:
asti kutraiva śalilaṁ mahātṛṣṇāprapīḍitā
evaṁ vadanti pretoktān nīyamānās tu kiṅkaraiḥ
tatas te kupitā dūtā(ḥ) (N3 - hanyamānās tu mudgaraiḥ) ghna[n]titā(ṁ)n lauhamudgaraiḥ.
BF/16.40b - tatas te kupitair dūtais tāḍyante lohamudgaraiḥ.

57 N1/16.28b - ākṛṣyate (N3 - ākṛṣyati, BF/16.41a - ākṛṣyante) balātkārād (N2/16.33b - ākṛṣya mānavāḥ pāpāḥ) vamantaḥ śoṇitaṁ mukhāt.

58 N1/16.29a - saṁsāre durmathaṁ (N10, N7/16.32a - durlabhaṁ) dharmam (N3 - durllabhadhana(ṁ)m) iha loke (N7/16.32a - sthāne) phalapradaṁ.
BF/16.41b - saṁsāre durlabho dharmo yamaloko bhayāvahaḥ.

59 N1/16.29b, N10 - kṛṣṇā gaur na (N2/16.34b - na gāvas tu, N7/16.32b - na gāvaḥ kṛṣṇā[s]) tvayā dattā vaitaraṇyās tu (N3 - tāraṇāḥ) tāraṇe.
N8/16.37a, Ra/13.18a - na gauḥ śrcṣṭhā (N4/16.18a - kṛṣṇā) dvije dattā vaitariṇyāś ca tāriṇī.
BF/16.42b - na gāvo na tilā dattā na viprebhyo 'pi bhojanaṁ.

60 N1/16.30a, N10 - pathi śrāntaṁ gṛ(ra)hāyāntaṁ (N3 - pathi āntagṛhāyātaṁ) n(j)a kṛtaṁ [ta]sy(v)a gaurava[ṁ].
Verses 16.30-2 are missing in N2.
N4/16.18b, N8/16.37b, Ra/13.18b - pathiśrānte gṛhāyāte na kṛtaṁ śramanodanaṁ.

dṛṣṭvā na katham asya na saṁskāravacanais tathā[61] [30]
tṛṇaprastaraṇaṁ śayyā pādaśaucaṁ tathāsanaṁ[62]
sulabhaitāni dattāni sarvāṇi haritaṁ malaṁ[63] [31]
mārgaṁ ca dāruṇaṁ ghoraṁ kathaṁ mūḍha gamiṣyasi[64]
kṣuttṛṣṇārto 'tra saṁbhūtas tvaṁ mārge kiṁ kariṣyasi[65] [32]
evaṁ vadanti pratyekaṁ baddhaṁ dūtaiś ca śṛṅkhalaiḥ[66]

having seen his condition, you have not adopted (the right) speech and good manners(V). *[30]*
A bed strewn of grass, a seat for foot cleaning,
and other cheap(VI)*, dispensable, straw-(articles), are all that you have donated. [31]*
O fool, how will you go (now) on this dreadful, difficult road?
What will you do here on the road, (wearied by) hunger and thirst?" [32]
This was said to each (sinner) shackled by the messengers.

---

61 N1/16.30b, N10 - dṛṣṭvā na katham utth(sy)ā(a)nasaṁskāraṁ vacanais (N3 - utthānasatkāravacanais) tathā.
N7/16.33b - darśanaṁ pathikaṁ panthaṁ satkāravacanās tathā.

62 N1/16.31a, N3, N10 - tṛṇaprastaraṇaṁ śayyā (N7/16.34a - tṛṇaiḥ prastaraṇaṁ śayyāṁ) pādaśaucaṁ tathāsanaṁ.
N4/16.19a, N8/16.38a, Ra/13.19a - mahāsanaṁ tṛṇam ayaṁ madhurāṇi vacāṁsi ca.

63 N1/16.31b - sulabhyāny (N10 - sulabhāny) e(ca)[tāni] dātāni sarvāṇi haritaṁ (N10 - palaṁ) malaṁ (vi).
N3 - sulabhaitāni dātāni sarvāṇi haritān palaṁ.
N4/16.20a, N8/16.39a, Ra/13.20a - atithibhy(ā)o na dāttāni etāni sulabhāny api.
N7/16.34b - etāni sulabhyā[ni] mūḍhā [p]alaṁ vargeṇa hāritaḥ.

64 N3 - mārgaṁ ca dāruṇaṁ ghoraṁ kathaṁ (N7/16.35a - mūḍha gamiṣyasi) yūyaṁ gamiṣya(ti)tha.

65 N1/16.32b, N10 - kṣuttṛṣṇārto 'tra (N3 - kṣuttṛṣṇātreti) saṁbhūtas tvaṁ mārge kiṁ kariṣyasi.
N4/16.20b, N8/16.39b, Ra/13.20b - kṣutpipāsābhramadbhūmau dadur na katham agrataḥ.
N7/16.35b - kṣuttṛṣṇādha[n] saṁbhūtā agrataḥ kiṁ kariṣyas(t)i.

66 N1/16.33a, N10 - evaṁ vadati (N3 - vadanti) pratyekaṁ baddhaṁ dūtaiś ca śṛṅkhalaiḥ.
N2/16.35a - evaṁ vadanti te dūtā b(v)addhvā [pāpān ca] śṛṅkhalai(r)ḥ (gala).
N4/16.22b, N8/16.42a, Ra/13.22b - evam uktā b(v)ahuvidhaṁ dūtair b(v)addhāś ca pāśakaiḥ.
N7/16.36a - evaṁ vada[n]ti dūtāś ca b(v)addhā[n] ca yamasaṅkulaiḥ.

durgame tan mahāmārge mayā dṛṣṭā hy anekaśaḥ[67] [33]
tatra pāpā durācārā vikalāḥ śāstravarjitāḥ[68]
katham nistīryate samyak bho bho tad dvijasattamāḥ[69] [34]
ṛṣaya ūcuḥ
kathaṁ mṛtyupatho vipra katisaṅkhyāta eva ca[70]
kathaṁ vā śāsanaṁ tatra kena dānena mucyate[71]

I saw on that impassable road many [33]
exhausted sinners of bad conduct, devoid of learning.
How can they come out safely, O excellent Twice-born? [34]
The sages said
"O venerable one, how is the path to Death, and how many (paths) are there?
How is (Yama's) punishment there, and by what donations can one be saved (from it)"?

---

67 N1/16.33b, N10 - durgame tan mahāmārge mayā (N7/16.36b - dṛṣṭāny anekaśāḥ) dṛṣṭās tv anekadhā.
N2/16.35b - durgame tan mahāmārgaṁ mayā dṛṣṭāny (N3 - dṛṣṭā hy) anekaśāḥ.
N4/16.22c, N8/16.42b, Ra/13.23a - pāpātmāno yamapathe mayā dṛṣṭāḥ sahasraśaḥ.

68 N2/16.36a - tatra pāpā mayā dṛṣṭā vikalā (N7/16.37a - vikale) dharmasaṅgrahe.
N3 - tatra pāpā durācārāk(a)ā vināśāstravarjjitāḥ.

69 Emendation - DS. N1/16.34b - katham et(at)e samarthās (N3 - taṁ tat u vai bho dvijottamāḥ) tata[s] t(v)aṁ bho dvijasattamā.
N7/16.37b - kathaṁ nistarate śakyaṁ bho bho tad dvijasattamāḥ.

70 N1/16.35a - kathaṁ carāmy (N3, N7/16.40a, N10 - vadāmy) ahaṁ vipr(ā)a mṛtyusaṁsārasāgare.
N3 - katham ity utpathe vipr(āḥ)a katisaṅkhyāś ca te śubhāḥ.
N4/16.31a, N8/16.50a, Ra/13.31a - kiṁ pramāṇo mṛtyupathaḥ kena dānena tīryyate.
N7/16.39a - kathaṁ mṛtyupathaṁ vipra katisaṅkhyā ca te kathaṁ.
BF/17.1a - kīdṛṅ mṛtyupatho vipra katisaṅkhyāta eva ca.

71 Following N10, missing in N1.
N2/16.37b - kathaṁ vā śobhave tatra kena dāneṣu mucyate.
N3 - kathaṁ vā śāsanā vipra (N7/16.39b - [śā]sānaṁ, BF/17.1b - cāsanaṁ) kena dānena mucyate.
Verse number N7/16.38 is skipped.
N4/16.31b, N8/16.50b, Ra/13.31b - kathaṁ vā [śā]sānaṁ tatra viśeṣād brūhi tatvattaḥ.

nāsiketa uvāca
sūryasūnurathasyādho yāsyante mṛtyugocaraṁ[72] [35]
vimukhā bāndhavā yānti dharmas tam anugacchati[73]
śmaśānāc ca nivartante suhṛdaḥ svajanā narāḥ[74] [36]
na sakhāyaḥ pitā mātā bhāryā putrās tathaiva ca[75]
bhrātaro bhaginī mitrā na ceṣṭā na vā bāndhavāḥ[76] [37]

Nāsiketa said
Those who go to the pasture-grounds of Death, under the chariot of the Sun's son[(VII)], *[35]*
go bound and depressed, and Dharma[(VIII)] *follows them.*
The close friends and relatives return from the cremation ground. [36]
Not a father, mother, wife, nor sons and friends,
not a brother, sister, friend, nor the beloved, nor relatives (go with the dead man). [37]

---

72 N2/16.38 - alaṁ vadāmi bho viprā(ḥ) mṛtyusaṁsārasāgare
sarve ['pi] tarasā nūnaṁ mṛtyor gocaram āgatāḥ.
N3 - sarvaṁ sūryasthā ced ye pāyāsyante mṛtyugocaraṁ.
N4/16.32, N8/16.51-52a, Ra/13.32 - kathyamānaṁ mayā viprāḥ śrūyatāṁ mahad adbhutaṁ
asmin sarve varttamānāḥ prāṇino mṛtyugocarāḥ.
BF/17.2-3 - sthānāni devahārmyāṇi lokaṁś caiva bhayānakān
yatra pretaśarīrāṇi nirjīvāni sahasraśaḥ
vṛthā vadāmy ahaṁ viprā mṛtyusaṁsārasāgare
sarve te pretarūpeṇa mṛtyugocaratāṁ gatāḥ.

73 N4/16.33a, N8/16.52b, Ra/13.33a - vimukhā bāndhavā sarve yānti (N7/16.41a - apradharme 'nugacchati, BF/17.4a - dharma eko 'nugacchati) dharmas tam anugacchati.

74 N2/16.39b - śmaśānena nivartante ye kecit svajanā narāḥ.
N3 - śmaśānāc ca nivart(t)ante (N4/16.33b, N8/16.53a, Ra/13.33b - mṛtaṁ tyaktvā tu kāṣṭavat) suhṛd(ā)a[ḥ] svajanā janāḥ.
BF/17.5a - śiśavaś ca nivartante sarve svajanabāndhavāḥ.

75 N2/16.40a - na tadā vai (N3 - sakhā na) pitā mātā bhāryyā putrās tathaiva ca.
N4/16.34a, N8/16.53b, Ra/13.34a - pitā mātā sakhāyo vā bhāryyā putrās tathaiva ca.
BF/17.6a - na bhāryā na pitā tatra na mātā bhaginī tathā.

76 N2/16.40b - bhaginyau bhrātaraś ca va ye cāmī dṛṣṭab(v)āndhavāḥ.
N3 - bhrātaro bhaginī putrā na j[y]eṣṭh(ā)a na ca vai(ī)ṣṇavā[ḥ].
N10 - bhrātaro bhaginī mitrā na ceṣṭā na ca b(v)āndhavāḥ.
N4/16.34b, N8/16.54a, Ra/13.34b - bhrātaro bhāginī caiva bhāgine yādayaḥ pare.
BF/17.6b - na suto na sutā bhrātā pitṛvyo mātulas tathā.

hiraṇyādi dhanaṁ caiva mahiṣī goś ca dantinaḥ[77]
parityajyante sarvaṁ hi puṇyapāpaiḥ sahāyanaiḥ[78] [38]
pathi tasmin mahāghore bhairave bhayakāriṇi[79]
nīyante pāpakarmāṇas tasmin mārge bhāyavahe[80] [39]
asatyā ye narā duṣṭāḥ krodhalobhavimohitāḥ[81]
tāṁś ca sarvān pathānītān samyag jānāti dharmarāṭ [40]
teṣāṁ ca tādṛśaṁ bhogaṁ sūryaputraḥ prayacchati[82]

Gold etc. and wealth, buffalos, cows and elephants,
all have to be left behind, by the righteous and sinners equally. [38]
That terrible road is (leading to) the frightening Bhairava Hell.
The sinners are led on that terrifying road, [39]
those untruthful, corrupted people, deluded by anger and greed.
Dharmarāja knows all about those led together on that road, [40]
and (he), the Sun's son, gives each of them what he deserves.

---

77 N2/16.41a - hiraṇyādi dhanaś caiva gomahiṣyādika[s] tathā.
N3 - hiraṇyādi dhanaṁ caiva mahiṣī (N10 - go 'śvadantinaḥ) goś ca hastinaḥ.
N7/16.43a - hiraṇyādi dhanaṁ caiva gomahiṣyā gajāś(s)va ye.
BF/17.7a - hiraṇyādīni dravyāṇi dhanaṁ godhanam eva ca.
N4/16.35a, N8/16.54b, Ra/13.35a - hiraṇyādīni bastūni gomahiṣyādikaṁ tathā.

78 N1/16.38b - parityajyanti sarvau (N10 - sarve) hi puṇyapāpaiḥ sahāyanaiḥ.
N2/16.41b - parityajya idaṁ sarvaṁ puṇyapāpai(s)ḥ samanvitaḥ.
N3 - parityajyanti hi sarve puṇyapāpau mahāvanau.
N4/16.35b, N8/16.55a, Ra/13.35b - sarvaṁ vas tu parityajya puṇyapāpe paraṁ naraḥ.
BF/17.7b - samastaṁ tat parityajya pāpapuṇyaiḥ samaṁ sthitāḥ.

79 N1/16.39a - pathi ti(a)ṣṭh(sth)et mahāvīro raurave bhayakāriṇī.
N7/16.44a - pathi tasmin mahāghore bhairave bhayakāriṇī.

80 N1/16.39b, N10 - nīyante pāpakarmāṇaḥ (N3 - pāpakarmāṇi) savikalpam anekadhā.
N7/16.44b - nīyante pāpakarmāṇo māvikalpamanāḥ kṛthā.
BF/17.8 - nīyante tena mārgeṇa kiṅkarair yamaśāsanāt
svargaṁ ca nirapaṁ ghoraṁ sarve svenaiva karmaṇā.

81 N1/16.40a, N10 - asatyā(ṁ) ye narā duṣṭāḥ (N2/16.43a - krodhalobhanamohitāḥ) krodhalobhavimohitāḥ.

82 N1/16.41a - teṣāṁ ca tādṛśaṁ bhogaṁ (N3 - candraṁ ca saṁbhogaṁ, N7/16.46a - tādṛś(s)as tena bhāvena) sūryaputraḥ prayacchati.
Verse 16.40b-41a is missing in N2.
N10 - teṣāṁ ca tādṛś(s)aṁ bhīmaṁ sarpaputraḥ papraccha[ti].

atha vākyaṁ mahāghoraṁ yamamārgasya nirṇayaṁ[83] [41]
kṣuradhāraṁ ca saṅkīrṇaṁ sūcīvaktraṁ sudāruṇaṁ[84]
kālarātrisamāyuktaṁ saṅkāśaṁ ghorarūpiṇaṁ[85] [42]
yatra vaivasvato dharmaḥ prajvalann agnitejasā[86]
tat purasya pradeśe tu devakāryaṁ nirantakaṁ[87] [43]
ekataḥ pretakāyās te 'saṅkhyā jīvavivarjitāḥ[88]
dharma to devakāyāś ca pāpā ye pretarūpiṇaḥ[89] [44]
yamalokeṣu nikṣiptā bhuñjanti te śubhāśubhaṁ[90]

Now begins the most terrible description of Yama's road. [41]
It is very fierce, strewn with sharp razors[(IX)] and pointed needles.
Having a terrible shape, it seems connected to Kālarātri[(X)]. [42]
There, Dharma[(XI)], the Sun's son, is blazing, having the luster of fire.
In that eastern land, Gods' worshipping goes on incessantly. [43]
On one side there are innumerable Preta[(XII)] bodies, devoid of life –
the sinners are in Preta shape – while the righteous receive divine bodies. [44]
(All) are thrown into Yama's world, getting good or bad (treatment).

---

83 N2/16.43b, N7/16.46b - atha vakṣyāmy ahaṁ ghoraṁ yamamārgasya nirṇayaṁ.

84 N1/16.42a - kṣ(s)uradh(th)āraṁ ca saṅkīrṇe s(ś)ūcīvakt[r]aṁ ca dāruṇaṁ.
N2/16.44a - kṣuradhārā tu saṅkīrṇaṁ s(ś)ūcīvaktraṁ sudāruṇaṁ.
N3 - kṣuradhāraṁ ca saṅkīrṇaṁ śrūtvā vaktre (N10 - s(ś)ūcīvaktraṁ) ca (N7/16.47a - sūcīvaktraṁ tu) dāruṇaṁ.
Cf. KU/3.14b - kṣurasya dhārā niśitā duratyayā durgaṁ pathas tat kavayo vadanti.

85 N1/16.42b, N3, N10 - kālaratrisamāyuktam (N2/16.44b - kālaratrisahāyuktam, N7/16.47b - kālaratrir mahāyuktam) ākāśaṁ ghorarūpiṇaṁ.

86 N1/16.43a, N3 - yatra vaivasvato dharmaḥ prajvala(ṁ)nn agnitejasā.
N2/16.45a - yatra vaivasvato dharmo jvalantaṁ prāgnitejasā.

87 N1/16.43b - tat purasyati deśe tu devakāryā (N10 - devakāyā) nirātmakā[ḥ].
N2/16.45b - dharmātmā devakāryyeṣu pāpātmā ghorarūpiṣu.

88 N1/16.44a - ekataḥ pretakāyā rato 'saṅkhyā jīvavivarjitāḥ (vi).
Verse 16.44 is missing in N2.
N7/16.49a - ekataḥ pretakāyāyām asa[ṅ]khyā jīvavivarjitāḥ (vi).

89 N1/16.44b, N10 - dharma yo devakā(r)yās te pāp(p)ād vai pāparūpiṇaḥ.
N7/16.49b - dharmātmā devakāyāś ca pāpātmā daityakāyyā.
BF/17.10a - dharmātmā devakāyeṣu pāpātma pretavigrahe.

90 N1/16.45a, N10 - nikṣiptā yamaloke te bhuñjante te (N3 - svaṁ, BF/17.10b - vai) śubhāśubhaṁ.
N7/16.50a - nikṣipya yamaloke ca bhuñjanti te śubhāśubhaṁ.

eṣa dharmo mayā dṛṣṭas tatra sthāne dvijottamāḥ[91] [45]
pāpiṣṭhānāṁ mahākāyā dharmiṣṭhānāṁ nirātmakāḥ[92]
dvayor mūrtir mayā dṛṣṭā taṭasthā kautukaṁ mahat[93] [46]
dharmarājapurī ramyā nirmitā dhārmiṇāṁ purā[94]
ṛṣayo nāradādyāś ca brahmakarmaṇi ye sthitāḥ[95] [47]
te tatra sukhasaṁsthāś ca pāpino duḥkhabhāginaḥ[96]

I saw Dharma[(XIII)] *there, in that place, O Brahmins, (as well as) [45]*
the great sinners having big bodies, (and) the very righteous, devoid of individuality.
I saw in great wonder, both (forms of) manifestation standing (there) on the banks. [46]
The beautiful, spotlessly clean, city of Yama, is the city of the righteous.
Those who perform the rites, Nārada and other sages like him, stay there [47]
in happiness, while the sinners' lot is suffering.

---

91 N2/16.46b - eṣa dharmo mayā dṛṣṭ(as)o yamasthāne (N3, N10 - dṛṣṭa(ḥ)s tatra sthāne) dvijottamāḥ.
N7/16.50b - eṣa dharm(a)o mayā dṛṣṭa[s] tatsthāne dvijasattamāḥ.
BF/17.11a - evaṁvidhā mayā dṛṣṭas tasmin sthāne dvijottamāḥ.

92 N1/16.46a - pāpiṣṭhānāṁ mahākāyā dharmiṣṭhānāṁ n(bh)irātmak(n)ā[ḥ].
N2/16.47a - pāpātmānaṁ tathā kāryye dharmātmānaṁ tu (- -)thā.
N7/16.51a - pāpātmanāṁ tu yā kāyā dharmiṣṭhānāṁ tu yā punaḥ.
BF/17.11b - pāpātmāno 'pi pretatvaṁ gatā dharmyaś ca devatāṁ.

93 Emendation - DS. N1/16.46b - dvayo[r] mūrtir mayā dṛṣṭās (N3, N10 - tatrāste) tatāste (N2/16.47b - tatra sthāne tu (N7/16.51 - kautakaṁ) kautukā) kautukaṁ mahat.
BF/17.12a - dvayī mūrtir mayā dṛṣṭā[s] tasmin sthāne tu kautukāt.

94 N1/16.47a - dharmarāja(ā)purī ramyā nirmitā (N2/16.48a - b(v)rahmaṇā[ṁ] purā, N7/16.52a - brahmaṇā[m] api, BF/17.12b - sā svayaṁbhuvā) dhārmiṇāṁ purā(ṁ).

95 N2/16.48b - vratāni yamasthitāya (ca) brahmacaryyam akalmaṣāḥ.
N3 - ṛṣayo nāradādyāś ca brahmakarmaṇi saṁsthitaṁ.
N7/16.52b - nāradādyā ṛṣayaḥ sarve brahmacaryeṇa ye sthitāḥ.
BF/17.13a - nāradādyāś ca ṛṣayaḥ sarve tatra sukhaṁ sthitāḥ.

96 N1/16.48a - te tatra sukh(r)asaṁsthāś ca (N2/16.49a, N7/16.53a - duḥkhitā pāpakarmāṇaḥ) pāpino (N3 - duḥkhabhājinaḥ) duḥkhabhāginaḥ.
BF/17.13b - pāpātmāno 'pi tatraiva duḥkhāni pratibhuñjate.

tatra dānāni dattāni hemaraupyaṁ ca bhūmigāḥ[97] [48]
upatiṣṭhanti divyāni turaṅgādīni yāni ca[98]
tatra mārge labhante te yānāni vividhāni ca[99] [49]
hastyaśvarathadānāni bhojanācchādānāni ca[100]
pūrvam eva yathādattam upatiṣṭhanti tat pathi[101] [50]
aṣṭau sthānāni raudrāṇi mahāmārge dvijottamāḥ[102]

Those who give donations of gold, silver, cows and land, [48]
are placed on divine vehicles with horses, (and)
receive various chariots, (for crossing) that road. [49]
Donators of elephants, horses, chariots, food, and crystals,
whatever they have donated, is at their disposal on that road. [50]
O excellent Twice-born, there are eight horrible places on that road,

---

[97] N1/16.48b, N10 - tatra dānāni dattāni (N2/16.49b - hemaraupyaṁ bhuvaṁ ca gāṁ, N3 - hemarūpyanta bhūmy agāḥ, N7/16.53b - hemaraupyaṁ ca bhūmigau, BF/17.14a - hemarūpyatra ca) hemarūpyatra bhūmigāḥ.

N4/16.39b, N8/16.59a, Ra/13.38b - mahādānāni dattāni hemaraupyaṁ tathaiva ca.

[98] N1/16.49a - upatiṣṭha[n]ti diṣṭyāni tṛṇāni vividhāni ca.

N2/16.50a - upatiṣṭhanti divyāni turaṅgādīni yāni (N3, N10 - turagā vividhāni) ca.

[99] N1/16.49b, N7/16.54b - tatra mārg(a)e labhante te yānāni vividhāni ca.

BF/17.15a - turagādīni dattāni tatra mārge labhanti te.

[100] N1/16.50a, N10 - hastyaśv(c)aratham ārūḍho (N7/16.55a - hastyaś(s)varathadattāni, BF/17.15b - hastyaśvarathadānāni) bhojanācchādānāni ca.

N4/16.40a, N8/16.59b, Ra/13.39a - hastyaśv(c)aratharūpāṇi yānāni vividhāny api.

[101] N1/16.50b, N7/16.55b - pūrvam eva yathā datta(u)m (N2/16.51b - yair dattam, N3 - ca yair dattā) upatiṣṭhanti tat pathi.

N4/16.40b, N8/16.60a, Ra/13.39b - bhojanācchādanādīni pūrvadattāni tāpasāḥ.

BF/17.16a - pūrvam eva yad dattam ca tat tatraivopatiṣṭhati.

[102] N2/16.52a - aṣṭau dānāni divyāni dattāni bhuvimair naraḥ.

N3, N10, BF/17.16b - aṣṭau sthānāni ghorāṇi (N4/16.41b, N8/16.61a, Ra/13.40b - santi tatra mahāpathe) mahāmārge (N7/16.57a - mahāpathi) dvijottamāḥ.

yojanānāṁ sahasraikaṁ hāhākāraṁ mahāpathi[103] [51]
raudraṁ bhayānakaṁ mārgaṁ vipulataptavālukaṁ[104]
sthānaṁ tac ca mayā dṛṣṭaṁ kathaṁ puṇyaṁ sukhāvahāḥ[105] [52]
tataḥ pañcasahasrāṇi yojanānāṁ pramāṇataḥ[106]
kaṇṭakaiś ca bhayākīrṇaṁ sutīkṣṇaiś cātidurgamaṁ[107] [53]
kathañcid vrajate tasmāt tathāgnes taptavālukāḥ[108]

that great road – a thousand Yojanas of wailing cries. [51]
The terrible, dreadful road, full of heated sand,
that very place which I saw, how can it bring good and happiness? [52]
It measures five thousand Yojanas.
It is frightening, (full of) very sharp thorns, and very hard to pass, [53]
since its sand is heated by fire, wherever one goes.

---

103 N2/16.52b - yojanānāṁ sahasraikaṁ (N4/16.42a, N8/16.61b, Ra/13.41a - hāhākāraḥ pravartate, N7/16.57b - ihākāraṁ mahāpathaṁ, BF/17.17a - raudrarāvaṁ sudāruṇaṁ) siṁhākāraṁ bhayāvahaṁ.
N3 - yojanāni (N10 - yādavānāṁ) sahasraikaṁ hāhākāraṁ mahāpathi.

104 N1/16.52a - pṛthumāyā kṣ(k)itaiḥ (N7/16.57a - raudraṁ tat sahitaḥ) pāpaiḥ pṛthulaṁ daśa dāruṇaṁ.
N2/16.53a - raudraṁ bhayānakaṁ mārga[ṁ] vipulataptavālukaṁ.
N3, N10 - [pṛthumāyā kṣitaiḥ pāpaiḥ] pṛthulaṁ śabdadāruṇaṁ.

105 N1/16.52b, N10 - sthānaṁ tac ca (N3 - sthānam etat) mayā dṛṣṭaṁ (N7/16.57b - kathitaṁ bhayaṁ saṁsthitaṁ) kathaṁ puṇyaṁ sukhāvahāḥ.
N2/16.53b - tan (- - -) mayā dṛṣṭa[ṁ] vadato jāyate bhayaṁ.

106 N10 - tataḥ pañcasahasrāṇi (N4/16.43a, N7/16.58a, N8/16.63a, Ra/13.43a - pañcasahasrāṇaṁ, Bo/15.1b - aṣṭāśītisahasrāṇi) yojanānāṁ pramāṇataḥ.
BF/17.18b - sahasram ekaṁ tan mārgaṁ yojanānāṁ prakīrtitaṁ.

107 N1/16.53b - kaṇṭakaiś ca bh(m)ayākīrṇaṁ (N10 - bhayākīrṇe) sutīkṣṇaiś caiva (N3 - durgamaiḥ, N10 - durgamaṁ) durlabhaṁ.
N2/16.54b - saṅkīrṇaṁ kaṇṭakakulais tīkṣṇāgraṁ cātidurgamaṁ.
N4/16.43b, N8/16.63b, Ra/13.43b - kaṇṭakaiḥ saṅkulaṁ sthānam asti tīkṣṇāgrabhīṣaṇaiḥ.
N7/16.58b - kaṇṭakaṁ drumasaṅkīrṇaṁ tīkṣṇāgraṁ ca durgamaṁ (short).
BF/17.19a - kaṇṭakīdrumasaṅkīrṇaṁ mahāśvabhraiś ca durgamaṁ.

108 N1/16.54a - kathañcid vijate tasmāt athāgne[s] taptavālukāḥ.
N2/16.55a - tat kṛcchrān mucyate so 'pi (BF/17.19b - kathañcid gamyate tasmāt) tad agne[s] taptavālukaṁ.

yojanānāṁ sahasre dve tatroṣṇā vālukā bahu[109] [54]
upānahapradātāro yānti tatra yathāsukhaṁ[110]
tato daśasahasrāṇi yojanānāṁ pramāṇataḥ[111] [55]
gantavyaṁ viṣamaṁ durgaṁ kṣurāṇāṁ ca mahāpathaṁ[112]
kṣuradhārāsamabhūmi na gantuṁ tatra śakyate[113] [56]
tatra śayyāpradātāraḥ sukhaṁ yānti mahāpathi[114]

There are two thousand Yojanas of many burning sands. [54]
Those who donate shoes go happily there, (on that road),
which measures ten thousand Yojanas. [55]
(The sinners) have to walk on that rough, cutting, hard-to-walk, great road,
impossible to walk on, the whole ground as sharp as a razor's edge[(XIV)]*. [56]*
Those who donate beds go happily there, on that great road,

N3, N10 - kathañcid vrajate tasmāt tathāgne[s] taptavālukā[ḥ].
N7/16.59a - kathañcit tyaj[y]ate tasmāt [ta]thā taptavālukā.

109 N1/16.54b - yojanānāṁ sahasre dve (N4/16.44, N8/16.64a, Ra/13.44a - tad agne[s] taptavālukaṁ) tatroṣṇ(ṭ)ā vālukā bahu.
N2/16.55b - dve sahasre mahā coṣṇavālukaṁ yojanāni ca.
BF/17.20a - sahasraṁ yojanānāṁ mārgaṁ syāt taptav(b)ālukaṁ.

110 N1/16.55a - upānahapradātāro pānthi tatra yathāsukhaṁ.
N2/16.56a - upāna[ha](t)pradātāra(s)ḥ (N7/ 16. 60a - upānahau pradātāraḥ) sukhaṁ yānti (BF/17.20b - mahāpathe) mahāpathi.
N4/16.46a, N8/16.65b, Ra/13.45b - upānahaḥ pradātāraḥ sukhaṁ gacchanti mānavā.

111 N4/16.46, N7/16.60b, N8/16.66a, Ra/13.46a - tato daśasahasrāṇāṁ yojanānāṁ pramāṇataḥ.
Half verse 16.55b is missing in N2.
BF/17.22a - śataṁ cāṣṭasahasrāṇi yojanānāṁ pramāṇataḥ.

112 N1/16.56a - gantavyaṁ vimalaṁ durgaṁ kṣurāṇāṁ ca mahāpathaṁ.
N2/16.57a - gacchanti (N7/16.61a - gacchate) viṣame durge kṣurādhāre (BF/17.21b - mahāpathe) mahāpathiḥ.

113 N1/16.56b - kṣuradhārāsamā bhūmir (N2/16.57b - na gantu(r)ṁ śakyate (N7/16.61b - kvacit) tadā) gantuṁ tatra na ś(y)akyate.
N10 - kṣuradhārātaptabhūmiṁ tatra gantuṁ na śakyate.
N4/16.47a, N8/16.66b, Ra/13.46b - viṣamaḥ kṣuradhārābhir durgamo 'sti mahāpathaḥ.

114 N3 - tatra śayyapradātāraḥ sukhaṁ yānti mahāpathiḥ.
Ra/13.47a - tatra śayyāpradātāraḥ sukhaṁ (BF/17.23a - yānti mahāpathe) gacchanti (N4/16.47b, N8/16.67a - dharmikāḥ) mānavāḥ.

tatra cāṣṭasahasrāṇi yojanānāṁ pramāṇataḥ[115] [57]
agnibhir dahyate tatra jvalantaś ca diśo daśa[116]
vāpīkūpataḍāgāni pathi viśrāmamandiraṁ[117] [58]
vaṭādikaṁ ropayante devānāṁ yājanaṁ tathā[118]
tatra te sukhino yānti vāyunā śītalena ca[119] [59]
yojanānāṁ sahasrāṇi daśapañcāśikāni ca[120]

a distance of eight thousand Yojanas. [57]
(The road) burns with fire, blazing in all[XV] directions.
Ponds, wells and pools on the road, are (like) a temple of tranquility. [58]
A Banyan tree and other trees of its like, grow and promote sacrifice to the Gods there,
where the happy ones go, cooled by the wind. [59]
Measuring fifty one thousand Yojanas, (is the)

Ra/13.47b - ataḥ śayyā pradātavyā satā tatra sukhepsunā.
N7/16. 62a - tatrāpy annapradātāraḥ sukhaṁ yānti mahāpathi.

115 N1/16.57b - tatra (N2/16.58b, N7/16. 62b - tataś) cāṣṭausahasrāṇi yojanānāṁ pramāṇ(n)ataḥ.
N4/16.48a, N8/16.67b, Ra/13.48a - tad agre 'ṣṭasahasrāṇāṁ yojanānāṁ pramāṇ(n)ataḥ.

116 N10, BF/17.23b - agnibhir dahyate tatra jvalantyaś ca diśo daśa.
N4/16.48b, N8/16.68a, Ra/13.48b - agninā mahatā mārge jvalann asti diśo daśa.

117 N1/16.58b - vāpīkūpataḍāgādi pathi viśrāmya mandiraṁ.
N2/16.61a - vāpīkūpetaḍāgādi prāyo dattāś ca yair naraiḥ.
N3 - vāpīkūpataḍāgāni (N7/16. 63b - prapā dattāś ca yair naraiḥ, BF/17.24a - devatāyatanāni ca) prajāviśrāmamandiraṁ.
N4/16.49a, N8/16.68b, Ra/13.49a - vāpīkūpataḍāgānāṁ ye prapānāṁ ca dāyakāḥ.

118 N1/16.59a - vaṭādikaṁ ropa(r)yate (N10 - ropa(r)yante) devānāṁ yajanaṁ (N3 - ropayante devātā yajanaṁ) tathā.
N2/16.61b - vaṭikāropaṇaṁ mārge devātābhavanaṁ tathā.
N4/16.49b, N8/16.69a, Ra/13.49b - vaṭikāropakāś cānye devāyatanapālakāḥ.
N7/16.64a - vaṭādiropakā mārge devānā[ṁ] bhavanaṁ tathā.

119 N1/16.59b - tatra te sukhino yānti(r) (N3 - vāyunā śītalo (N10 - śītale) yathā, N4/16.50a, N8/16.69b, Ra/13.50a - dustare jvaladāgnike, N7/16.64b - vāruṇaṁ jvalanaṁ sthitaṁ) vāyunā śītalaṁ yathā.

120 N3 - yojanānāṁ sahasrāṇi (N4/16.50b, N8/16.70a, Ra/13.50b - daśadvādaśapañca ca, N7/16.65a - daśapañcādhikāgrataḥ) daśapañcāśakāni ca.
Half verse 16.60a is missing in N2.
BF/17.25a - yojanānāṁ sahasrikaṁ daśabhiś cādhikaṁ tathā.

kṛṣṇaghoraṁ mahāsthānaṁ kālarātrir nivedyatāṁ[121] [60]
timireṇa samākīrṇaṁ tatra bhīṣyanti mānavāḥ[122]
narā dīpapradātāro sukhaṁ yānti mahāpathi[123] [61]
tasmāt pradeyaṁ dīpaṁ vai mṛtapṛṣṭhe ha mānavaiḥ[124]

dreadful, dark place, (as if) presented by the powers of darkness, [60]
very gloomy, where people get terrified.
People who donate a lamp, go happily on (that) road – [61]
this is the reason why people should give lamps (to put) on the back of the dead.

---

[121] N2/16.62b - kṛṣṇaṁ ghoraṁ mahārātrikālaratri[r] nivedyatāṁ.
N3 - uṣṇaghoraṁ mahāsthānaṁ kālaratri[ḥ] śivoditā.
N4/16.51a, N8/16.70b, Ra/13.51a - kṛṣṇaṁ ghoraṁ mahāraudraṁ kālarātrim ivoditaṁ.
BF/17.25b - kṛṣṇaṁ ghoraṁ mahāsthānaṁ kālarātrī tu kathyate.

[122] N1/16.61a, N3, N10 - timireṇa samākīrṇaṁ (N2/16.63a - gantu[ṁ] tatra na śakyate, N4/16.51b, N8/16.71a, Ra/13.51b - sthānam ekaṁ mahādbhutaṁ) tatra bh(r)īṣ[y]anti mānavāḥ.
BF/17.26a - mahāraṇyaṁ samākīrṇaṁ tatra vindanti mānavāḥ.

[123] N1/16.61b - narā dīpapradātāro gaccha[n]ty udyotate vane.
N2/16.63b - dīpadānapradātāraḥ sukhaṁ yānti mahāpathi.
Additional verses - N2/16.64-5:
kārtike mā[gh](v)amāse tu vaiśāṣe viṣṇusannidhau
jvalantaṁ dīpakaṁ tatra mahoratreṇa ye narāḥ
te dyotamānā gacchanti yamamārge yamālayaṁ.
Verses N2/16.66-7 - see footnote for verse 98b.
N4/16.52a, N8/16.71b, Ra/13.52a - narā dīpapradātāras tatra dyotasamākule.
N7/16.66b - narā dīpapradātāra udyotena hi yānti te.
BF/17.26b - tac ca dīpapradātāras tarītuṁ śaknuvanti vai.

[124] N2/16.68 - te narā(s)ḥ sukhino yānti dvijā ghore mahāpathe
tasmāc ca dīyate dīpo mṛtapṛṣṭhe va sarvadā.
Additional verses - N2/16.69-70a:
agne[r] dīpāḥ pracalanti preto gacchanti pṛṣṭhataḥ
tatra vaitaraṇī durgā garjamānā mahāravāḥ
tatra dhenupradātaras tarante hi mahānadī[ṁ].
N3 - tasmāt pradeyaṁ dīpaṁ vai mṛtyupṛṣṭhe hi (N10 - ha) mānavaiḥ.
N7/16.67a - tasmāt pr(t)a(n)dīyate dīpaṁ mṛtaḥ pṛṣṭhena mānavaiḥ.
BF/17.27a - tasmins tu dīyate dīpo mṛtapṛṣṭhe tu mānavaiḥ.

mahāniśā mahāmeghair mahākṛṣṇaṁ bhayāvahaṁ[125] [62]
tatra tat sthānam atulaṁ kṛṣṇameghasamaprabhaṁ[126]
dṛśyate tatra pāpānāṁ darśanādarśanaṁ kvacit[127] [63]
caturbhujasamākārāḥ sragmālābhir alaṅkṛtāḥ[128]
taranti te mahādurgaṁ gopradānena mānavāḥ[129] [64]
aśvadānena divyena gajadānena cāpare[130]
tīrthasnānakṛtadehāḥ pitṛdevādipūjakāḥ[131] [65]

Very black and frightening, by midnight great clouds, [62]
he (i.e. Yama) is standing there, unequalled, glowing like a black cloud,
witnessed by sinners there, a sight (better) not to be seen, [63]
built with four arms, adorned with garlands.
People who donate cows, cross that very-hard-to-cross road, [64]
(as well as those) who donate divine horses, elephants, etc.
Those bathing their bodies in Tīrthas[(XVI)], who worship Gods and ancestors, [65]

---

[125] N3 - mahāniśā yath(aiḥ)ā meghai(ḥ)r (N7/16.67b - meghaṁ) mahā(at)kṛṣṇaṁ bhayāvahaṁ.
Verses 16.62b-64 are missing in N2.
BF/17.27b - mahāniśā tathā meghair andhakāro bhayāvahaḥ.

[126] N1/16.63a - tatra tasya namasthūla (N3 - tathā (N10, N4/16.56b, BF/17.28a - tatra) tat sthānam atulaṁ) kṛṣṇameghasamaprabhaṁ.
N8/16.73a - kṛṣṇameghasamākāratimireṇa bhayāvahe.

[127] N1/16.63b, N3, N10, BF/17.28b - dṛśya(n)te tatra pāpānāṁ darśanād(v)arśanaṁ kvacit.

[128] N1/16.64a - caturbhujasamākāśaḥ (BF/17.29a, N3 - caturbhujasamākārāḥ) sragmālābhir (N3 - sṛgmālābhir) alaṅkṛtā[ḥ].

[129] N10 - taranti me (N7/16.69b - tarante te) mahādu(a)rg(j)aṁ gopradānena mānavāḥ.
N4/16.55b, N8/16.75a, Ra/13.53b - tarānti tan mahādurgaṁ godānenāpi mānavāḥ.
BF/17.29b - santaranti mahāghoraṁ godānena ca mānavāḥ.

[130] N1/16.65a - aśvadānena divyena (N7/16.70a - gajadāne tathā pare) gajadāne[na] (N2/16.70b - mānuṣāḥ, N3 - vā pare) cāpare.
Additional half verse: N2/16.71a - antarikṣe ca gacchanti tasmin mārge bhayāvahe.
N4/16.56a, N8/16.75b, Ra/13.54a - aśvadānena bho viprā gajadānena vā punaḥ.
BF/17.30a - aśvadānaprabhāvena gajadānena ca tathā.

[131] N2/16.71b - yai(ṣ)ḥ pūjito vāsudevas toṣitāḥ pitṛdevatāḥ.
N4/16.56b, N8/16.76a, Ra/13.54b - puṇyatīrtheṣu yaiḥ snānaṁ toṣitāḥ pitṛdevātāḥ.
N7/16.70b - tīrthe 'pi sthāpitā devās toṣitā[ḥ] pitṛdevātāḥ.
BF/17.30b - tīrthasnānakṛtadehāḥ pitṛdevādipūjakāḥ.

dānāni tatra dattāni copatiṣṭhanti tat pathe[132]
yojanānāṁ sahasrāṣṭau jalākīrṇaṁ mahāpathaṁ[133] [66]
tatra bhūmipradātāras taranti pathi dustare[134]
yojanānāṁ sahasraṁ tu pañcaviṁśati kīrtitaṁ[135] [67]
doṣodadhiṁ ca taṁ prāhur dīrghādyāsuradustaraḥ[136]
tasmin pathe mahāraudre narā dṛśyante vākulāḥ[137] [68]

who make donations there[(XVII)]*, get served with them on that road –*
the great road of water, measuring eight thousand Yojanas. [66]
Those who donate land there, cross that hard-to-be-crossed road,
measuring twenty five thousand Yojanas. [67]
It is told that it is a dark ocean, long, demoniacal, unbearable,
(with) multitudes of people seen on that fierce road. [68]

---

132 N2/16.72a, N7/ 16.71a - dānāni tatra dattāni sukhaṁ yānti mahāpathi. N4/16.57a, N8/16.76b, Ra/13.55a - dānāni cātra dattāni te 'pi yānti sukhaṁ pathi. BF/17.31a - evaṁ puṇyakṛto lokāḥ sukhaṁ yānti mahāpathaṁ.

133 N1/16.66b - yojanānāṁ sahasrāṣṭau jalākīrṇaṁ mahāpatho. N4/16.57b, N8/16.77a, Ra/13.55b - tad agre 'ṣṭasahasrāṇāṁ yojanānāṁ pramāṇataḥ. N7/ 16.71b - yojanāni sahasrāṣṭau (BF/17.31b - yojanāṣṭasahasrāṇi) jalāk(t)īrṇaṁ mahāpathaṁ.

134 N1/16.67a, N3 - tatra (N10 - bhūmipradātāras) bhūmipradātāro (N4/16.58b, N8/16.78a, Ra/13.56b - dustare yānti dharmikāḥ, N7/ 16.72a - dustaraṁ tarate pathaṁ, BF/17.32a - dustaraṁ saṁtaranti tat) taranti pathi dustare. Half verse 16.67a is missing in N2.

135 N1/16.67b, N3, N10 - yojanānāṁ sahasraṁ tu (N7/16.72b - pañcaviṁśati kīrtitaṁ) pañcavistīrṇakīrtita(ḥ)ṁ. Additional half verse: N2/16.73b - atikaṣṭataraṁ tatra mayā dṛṣṭaṁ hi tathaṁ (short). N4/16.59a, N8/16.78b, Ra/13.57a - yojanānāṁ sahasrāṇi (BF/17.32b - pañcaiva tu prakīrtitaṁ) pañcaviṁśatir asti hi.

136 N1/16.68a - doṣodadhiṁ ca taṁ prāhu[r] (N3 - dīrghakārī durutsukaḥ, N10 - dīrghākāsuri duḥsahaḥ) di(ī)rgha(ā)dy āsuradustaraḥ. Half verse 16.68a is missing in N2. N10 - dīrghākāsuri (N7/16.73a - dadhikārī ca) duḥsahaḥ) dīrghādyāsuradustaraḥ.

137 N1/16.68b, N3 - tasmin (N7/16.73b - tatra) pathi mahāraudre (N4/16.60b, N8/16.80a, Ra/13.58b - dṛśyante vyākulā narāḥ) narā dṛśyanti (N10 - vākulāḥ) cākulāḥ. N2/16.74a - tasmin mārge mahāghore (Bo/15.5a - taptavālukasaṁyute) nā(a)śaṁ tiṣṭhanti vākulāḥ. BF/17.33b - tatra mārge mahāraudre naro gacchati saṅkulaḥ.

majjanti pāpākarmāṇaḥ kṣutpīpāsā prapīḍitā[138]
pāraṁ gacchati tatraiva dānaiś ca vividhottamaiḥ[139] [69]
tatra pāṇīpradānena gacchanti manujā mṛtāḥ[140]
ṣaḍaśītisahasrāṇi yojanānāṁ pramāṇataḥ [70]
yamalokasya cāgreṇa vaitariṇyā vinā dvijāḥ[141]
atha krameṇa gacchanti prāptāś caiva nadītaṭe[142] [71]

Tormented by hunger and thirst, the sinners sink (in that ocean-path).
By donating various excellent donations, one crosses over to the other shore. [69]
By keeping promises there, the dead people go
the length of eighty six thousand Yojanas. [70]
This is the entrance to Yama's world, excluding the Vaitaraṇī, O Twice-born.
Thus going in this course, they eventually reach the riverbank. [71]

---

138 N2/16.74b - taptā kṣudhāpipāsābhyāṁ (N7/16.74a - kṣutpīpāsāmahātaptā) tāḍyante tatra bhīṣaṇāḥ.
N10 - majjanti(r) [p]āpakarmāṇaḥ kṣutpīpāsāprapīḍitāḥ.
N4/16.61a, N8/16.80b, Ra/13.59a - pīḍitāḥ kṣutpipāsābhyāṁ mahāpātakakāriṇaḥ.
BF/17.34a - kṣipyante pāpākarmaṇas tāḍyante tatra bhīṣaṇaṁ.

139 N2/16.75a - pāraṁ gacchanti te brahma(- -) dāne jalena (-).
N3, N10 - pāraṁ gacchanti (BF/17.34b - tasyāpi) tasyaiva (N7/16.74b - gacchati tasyaitat) dānaiś ca (BF/17.34b - vividhair narāḥ) vividhottamaiḥ.
N4/16.61b, N8/16.81a, Ra/13.59b - pāraṁ tasyā hi gacchanti dānair atra kṛtaiḥ śubhaiḥ.

140 N1/16.70a - tatra pāṇīpradānena gacchanti manujāḥ (N3 - mṛtāḥ) smṛtāḥ.
Verses 16.70-71a are missing in N2.
N4/16.62, N8/16.81b-82a, Ra/13.60 - tathā pānīyadānena ghṛtadānena (N7/16.75a - tva(ṁ)m annadānena) mānavāḥ
gacchanti kṣaṇamātreṇa tatra dānaprabhāvataḥ.
N7/16.75b - gacchate kṣaṇamātreṇa prabhāvaṁ dānam arpitaṁ.
BF/17.36a - anena kramayogena gacchanti mānavā mṛtāḥ.

141 N1/16.71a - yamalokasya cāgreṇa (N3, N10 - cāgre ca) vaitariṇyā vinā nṛpa.
N4/16.63b, N8/16.83a, Ra/13.61b - evaṁ yamapathaḥ prokto vinā vaitaraṇīṁ dvijāḥ.

142 N2/16.75b - kṣaṇamātreṇa (N7/16.77b - atha krameṇa) gacchanti prataptāś (N7/16.77b - saṁprāptāś) ca nadītaṭe.
BF/17.37b - krameṇaiva prayānty ete vaitaraṇīnadītaṭe.

yamalokasya madhye vai tatra vaitaraṇī nadī[143]
mārgaṁ cātikramaṁ gatvā punaḥ paśyanti tāṁ nadīṁ[144] [72]
dṛṣṭvā jalpanti seyaṁ vai yasyā vārtā bhayāvahā[145]
śatayojanavistīrṇā mahāpārā sudustarā[146] [73]
pūyaśoṇitapūrṇā sā sarpākīrṇā bhayaṅkarā[147]
pakṣiṇaś ca mahāduṣṭā bhakṣayanti hi pāpināṁ[148] [74]
dustarā durgapathā sā saviśeṣaṁ ca karmiṇāṁ[149]

In the middle of Yama's world is the Vaitaraṇī River.
Having traveled that very long way, they see that river. [72]
Seeing it they murmur: "This is a frightful river".
The other bank is at a distance of a hundred Yojanas, very hard-to-traverse. [73]
That (river) is frightening, full of pus and blood, and abundant with snakes.
Very evil birds eat the sinners (there). [74]
That road is hard-to-go, and hard-to-traverse, especially for those burdened by (evil) deeds.

---

143 N3 - yamalokasya gacched vai tatra vaitaraṇīnadī.
Verses 16.72-73a are missing in N2.

144 N1/16.72b - majjanti kramaṇaṁ (N10 - mārgaṁ cātikrame) gatvā puraḥ paśyanti tāṁ nadīṁ.
N4/16.65b, N8/16.85a, Ra/13.63b - dṛṣṭā pratyakṣam anena nadī vaitaraṇī mayā.
N7/16.78a - dṛṣṭā tatra mahāvārttā nadī vaitaraṇī mahat.
BF/17.38a - dṛṣṭā tatra mahāvarte mahāvaitaraṇī nadī.

145 N1/16.73a - dṛṣṭ(v)ā jalpanti śaiveyaṁ (N3, N10 - seyaṁ vai) yasyā vārttā bhayāvahā(ḥ).

146 N10 - śatayojanavistīrṇe mahāpār(p)ā sudustarā.
N2/16.76a - śatayojanavistīrṇā (N7/16.78b - mahāpārā mahānadī, N4/16.66a, N8/16.85b, Ra/13.64a - mahāb(v)ālamahoragā) sarvavṛścikadūṣitā.

147 N1/16.74a - pūyaśoṇitapūrṇā(ṁ) s(a)ā (BF/17.39a - sarpakīṭabhayaṅkarā) sūryakīrṇā (N10, N7/ 16.79a - sarpākīrṇā) bhayaṅkarā.
N2/16.76b - bahulaṁ tatra durgandhi śatāvartā bhayaṅkarā.
N4/16.66b, N8/16.86a, Ra/13.64b - pūyaśoṇitasaṅkīrṇā sarvato 'tibhayaṅkarā.

148 Emendation - DS. N1/16.74b - durgasaṁsāravistīrṇā mahāpāpā sudustarā.
N2/16.77a - pakṣuvaś ca mahāduṣṭā bhakṣayanti hi pāpināṁ.
Half verse 16.74b is missing in N3, N10.

149 N1/16.75a - dustarā durgasarvā sā saviśeṣāś ca pāpināṁ.
N2/16.77b - dustarāṁ durgamāṁ ca v(a)ā viśeṣātyātmā (ma) karmiṇāṁ.

yamagṛhāgre vartate nirmitā viśvakarmaṇā[150] [75]
tasyās tu taraṇārthāya kṛṣṇā dhenuḥ pradīyate[151]
annadānaṁ ca yair dattaṁ te pāraṁ yānti satvaraṁ[152] [76]

It flows in front of Yama's house, as created by Viśvakarman[(XVIII)]*. [75]*
For crossing (that river) a black cow should be given.
Those who have donated food, go quickly to the other bank. [76]

---

150 Emendation - NK. N1/16.75b - yamagṛhāgre varta(eti)te nirmitā viśvakarmaṇā. Half verse 16.75b is missing in N2. Additional verses - N2/16.78-87a:
tatraiva tāḍyante dūtair sarvair lohayaṣṭibhiḥ (short)
praviṣyantāṁ praviṣyantāṁ dūtāś ca bruvanti hi (short).
na tvayā brahmaṇe dattaṁ na hutaṁ havyakavyayoḥ
ātithyan na (- -)yāmin sadā svabhavane rataḥ
(- - - - - - - - - - - - -) sūryyayoḥ
abhāyāṁ (- - - - -) ca na datta pitṛtarppaṇaṁ
til(a)o dhenur gajo vājī annāni vividhāni ca
rasāni pānibhūr loke svayam utpādha bhakṣitaṁ
idānīṁ hi mahāmārge kathaṁ nistarate janaḥ
na yam(aṁ)o yamaloka[ś] ca na dūtā na ca kiṅkarāḥ
na śrutāś ca tvayā māyi na kathyamānā mahāśayaiḥ
tatra sādhuḥ sthitā (- - -) kathāṁ paurāṇi(r)kīṁ śubhāṁ
jāto 'si mahāpāpa kathaṁ nistarate 'dhunā
adhunā gatab(v)uddhis tvaṁ dhāvase ca mṛto yathā
bhāryyā me (- - -) nityaṁ putra(s)ḥ suhṛc ca b(v)āndhavāḥ
iti bruvanti pāpāḥ paśudravye ca nityadā (short)
N3 - dusvarā durgapanthā so saviśeṣā ca pāpinī.
N3 - yamagrahāgre (N10 - vartatī) varttanti (N4/16.67b, N8/16.87a, Ra/13.65b - dharmarājapurasyāgne) nirmitā viśvakarmaṇā.
N10 - dustarā durgam(s)arg(hy)ā sā saviśe(ro)ṣā[ṁ] ca pāpināṁ.
N7/16.80a - yamagṛhāgr(n)e varttante nirmitā pāpakarmaṇāṁ.
N4/16.67a, N8/16.86b, Ra/13.65a - dustarā sarvalokānāṁ (N7/16.79b, BF/17.39b - durgamā caiva) viśeṣāt pāpakarmaṇāṁ.

151 N1/16.76a, N10, N7/16.80b - tasyās tu taraṇārthāya kṛṣṇā[ṁ] dhenuṁ (N2/16.87b - pradīyate) ca dāpayet.
N4/16.68a, N8/16.87b, Ra/13.66a - tasyās tu taraṇārthāya (BF/17.40a - tasyāḥ santaraṇārthāya) kṛṣṇā dhenuḥ pradīyate.

152 N2/16.88a - annadānaṁ ca y(e)[air] dattaṁ (N3, BF/17.40b - te pāraṁ yānti satvaraṁ) te taranti mahānadīṁ.

deyāny anyāni dānāni param icchanti ye dvijāḥ[153]
tīrthasnānaratā nityaṁ gaṅgāsāgarasaṅgame[154] [77]
śāstraṁ vedāṁś ca manyante nityaṁ caiva dṛḍhavratāḥ[155]
satyaṁ caiva mahotsāhaṁ dānaṁ caiva pradakṣiṇaṁ[156] [78]
te 'pi mārge mahāghore vaitaraṇyāṁ ca nirbhayāḥ[157]
yāsau vaitaraṇī nāma yamadvāre mahāsarit[158] [79]
yatpramāṇā ca sā devī śṛṇvatāṁ vai bhayāvahā

They have to give (many) food donations, wanting (to attain) the highest (goal), O Brahmins.
Those who always perform the ritual bathing where the Ganges meets the ocean, [77]
thinking on the Śāstra and Veda, their minds always really fixed on them,
those who adhere firmly to Truth, and give respectfully, [78]
for them, the terrible road and the Vaitaraṇī River, are not frightening.
That great river, called the Vaitaraṇī, is the door to Yama('s world)[(XIX)]. *[79]*
Listen to the size of that frightening goddess[(XX)] –

N4/16.68b, N8/16.88a, Ra/13.66b - anyāny api ca dānāni yair dattāni dvijottamāḥ.
N7/16.81a - anye dānāś ca yair dattās te pāraṁ satvaraṁ gatāḥ.

153 N3 - deyān anyāni dānāni param icchanti ye dvijāḥ.
Half verse 16.77a is missing in N2.

154 N2/16.88b - tīrthasnāne ca ye satyā gaṅgāsāgarasaṅgame.
N4/16.69a, N8/16.88b - tīrthasnānaratā ye ca (Ra/13.67a - ye ca gaṅgādh(v)isaṅgame) snāta gaṅgādhisaṅgame.
BF/17.41a - tīrthasnānaratā nityaṁ (N7/16.81b - tīrthasnāne narāḥ satyāḥ) gaṅgāsāgarasaṅgame.

155 N2/16.89a - śāstravedā[s] tadadhītā yair (N10 - ś(ṇ)āstraṁ vedāś ca (N7/16.82a - śāstravedādi) manyante) nityaṁ caiva dṛḍhavratāḥ (vi).
N3 - śāstravedāś ca manyante nityaṁ caiva yadṛcchayā.
N4/16.70a, N8/16.89b, Ra/13.68a - nityaṁ dṛḍhavratā ye ca vedaśāstrādimānakāḥ.

156 Half verse 16.78b is missing in N2.
N7/16.82b - satyaṁ taṁ ca manotsāhaṁ dānadharme mahītale.

157 N1/16.79a - ye tu (N2/16.90a, N3 - te 'pi) mārge (N2/16.90a - mārgaṁ) mahāghore vaitariṇyāṁ ca nirbhayāḥ.
N4/16.71a, N8/16.90b, Ra/13.69a - te 'pi mārge mahāraudre (N7/16.83a - vaitaraṇyāś ca nirbhayāḥ) tatra vaitaraṇīṁ dvijāḥ.

158 N1/16.79b - yās(o)au vaitaraṇī nāma yamadvāre (N10 - yamadvāra mahāsarit) mahāsasi.
Verses 16.79b-98a are missing in N2, N3.

śatayojanavistīrṇā pṛthutve sā mahāsarit [80]
pūyaśoṇitatoyādyā māṁsasaṅkulakardamā[159]
patanti tatra vai martyāḥ krandamānās tu pāpinaḥ[160] [81]
hā bhrātar putra māteti vilapante muhur muhuḥ[161]
vitarante nimajjanti glāniṁ gacchanti jantavaḥ[162] [82]
caturvidhaiḥ prāṇigaṇair draṣṭavyā sā mahānadī[163]
taranti tasyāṁ dānena anyathā ca patanti vai [83]
mātaraṁ ye ca manyante ācāryaṁ gurum eva ca[164]
avamanyanti ye mūḍhās teṣāṁ vāso 'stu santataṁ[165] [84]
viśvāsapratipannānāṁ svāmimitratapasvināṁ
strībālavikalānāṁ ca chidram anveṣayanti ye [85]
pacyante tatra madhye tu krandamānas tu pāpinaḥ
agnido garadaś caiva kūṭasākṣipradāyinaḥ[166] [86]

it is a hundred Yojanas wide, that great river. [80]
Pus and blood are its water, rising up full of meat and slime.
The dead sinners fall there, calling out (loudly): [81]
"O brother, O son, O mother" – so they cry now and again.
They go exhausted, these people, (and) while traversing they drown. [82]
Four kinds of groups of living creatures must see that great river:
Those who have not donated – fall, and those who have – cross, [83]
as well as those who have honoured their mother, master or teacher.
Those fools, who have not honoured them, stay there (in Hell) forever. [84]
The sinners who harm those who trust them – teachers, friends and ascetics,
the maimed, mutilated, women or children – [85]
are roasted there in the middle, crying out (loudly).
He who is an incendiary, and also a poison giver, his forehead and eyes will be dried. [86]

---

159 N1/16.81a - pūyaśoṇita y(o)aḥ pādyamāṁsasaṅkulakardamā.
N10 - pūyaśoṇitatoya(u)dya māṁsasaṅkulakardamā.

160 N1/16.81b - patanti tatra vai martyā krandamānā supāpinaḥ.

161 Emendation - DS. N1/16.82a - aprāptaputramāteti (N10 - hā bhr(t)ātṛputramāteti) vilapantc muhur muhuḥ.

162 N10 - vitaranti vimajjanti glāniṁ gacchanti tantavaḥ.

163 N1/16.83a - caturvidhaiḥ prāṇigaṇair draṣṭavyā sā mahānadī.

164 N10 - mātaraṁ ye ca manyante ācāryaṁ gurum eva ca.

165 N1/16.84b - avamanyeti ye mūḍhās teṣāṁ vāso 'stu santataṁ.

166 Emendation - NK. N1/16.86b - agnicoraga[ra]daś ca(iva) kaṇṭhasākṣiṣupadyayaḥ.
N10 - agnido garadaś caiva kūṭasākṣiprado hi yaḥ.

yajñavidūṣakaś caiva rājñīgāmī ca paiśunī[167]
kathābhaṅgakaraś caiva svayaṁvṛttyāpahārakaḥ[168] [87]
kṣetrasetuvibhedaś ca paradārāpradharṣakaḥ[169]
dvijo rasena vikretā tathā yo vṛṣalīpatiḥ[170] [88]
godhanasya tṛṣārtasya pāṇibhedaṁ karoti yaḥ[171]
kanyāvidūṣakaś caiva dānaṁ dattvā tu nāyakaḥ[172] [89]
no yacchati kathāṁ śrutvā hy anyān api niṣevati[173]
dattvānutāpabhājo ye na svīkṛtyā dadaty api[174] [90]
śūdras tu kuṭilaḥ pāpī brāhmaṇāmāṁsabhojanaiḥ[175]
etair vasanti satataṁ mā vicāraṁ kṛthāḥ kvacit[176] [91]
sadā dveṣī sadā krodhī nijavākyāpramāṇakṛt[177]

He who defiles a sacrifice, those wicked who abuse the queen,
he who interrupts a conversation, as well as he who steals one's livelihood, [87]
he who breaks the dike boundaries in the fields, or violates another's wife,
a Brahmin who sells mercury drugs, or has a low caste woman as concubine, [88]
he who denies water to the thirsty cattle – (all these, their) hands are cut off.
He who defiles a young girl, must give her a gem as a gift. [89]
He, who goes away and serves others, while hearing the story,
those who give and then repent, and those who don't give at all, [90]
a Śūdra and a crooked sinner, who eat Brahmins' food,
stay forever (in Hell) – have not the slightest doubt about it. [91]
Always hating, always angry, not keeping his own words,

---

167 Emendation - DS. N1/16.87a, N10 - yajñavindasakaś caiva rājñāgāmī ca paiśun(ṇ)ī.

168 N1/16.87b - kathābhaṅgakarāś caiva svaya[ṁ]vṛtyāpahārakaḥ.

169 Emendation - NK. N1/16.88a - kṣetre (N10 - kṣaitre) setuvibhede ca paradārāpradharṣakaḥ.

170 N1/16.88b - dvijai rasena vikretā tathā (N10 - dvijo rasavikretājñathā) yo vṛṣalīpatiḥ.

171 N10 - godhanasya tṛṣārtasya pāṇibhede karoti yaḥ.

172 N10 - kanyābhidūṣakaś caiva dānaṁ datvā tu nāyaka[ḥ].

173 N1/16.90a, N10 - no yaccha(i)ti kathāṁ śrutvā hy [any]ān api niṣevati.

174 Emendation - NK. N1/16.90b - da(ṛk)tt[v]ānutāpa(ā)bhājo ye n(o)a svī(no)kṛty(v)ā dadaty api.
Identical to 7.31a.

175 Emendation - NK. N10 - ś(s)ūdras tu kapilā pāpī brāhmaṇā māṁsabhojanāīḥ.

176 N1/16.91b - etair vasanti satataṁ m(a)ā vicāraṁ kathāḥ kvacit.

177 N10 - sadā dve(i)ṣī sadā kro(ī)dhī dvijavākyāpramāṇakṛt.

yas tv ahaṅkāravān pāpī svavikatthanakārakaḥ[178] [92]
kṛtaghno garvasantāpī vaitaraṇyāṁ vasec cīraṁ[179]
kadāpi bhāgyayogena raṇe rakṣā bhaved yadi [93]
sānukūlo bhaved yena tad ākarṇaya kāśyapaḥ
yaḥ saṁsārārṇavaṁ tartum udyogaṁ kurute naraḥ [94]
śṛṇuyād yaḥ purāṇāni iti śāstreṣu niścitaṁ
purāṇasaṁhitāvaktā harir ity abhidhīyate [95]
tadbhaktiṁ kurvatāṁ nṛṇāṁ gaṅgāsnānaṁ dine dine[180]
purāṇaśravaṇe bhaktir gaṅgāsnānopamā smṛtā[181] [96]
tadvaktari ca yā bhaktiḥ sā prayāgopamā smṛtā[182]
purāṇadharmakathane yaḥ samuddharate janaḥ[183] [97]

the sinner who is egocentric and does not care for others, [92]
boastful, ungrateful people, with burning arrogance, (all of them) will stay long in the Vaitaraṇī Hell.
(Listen) how by fortune one becomes protected in battle, [93]
(and) becomes favourable, listening to Kāśyapa[(XXI)].
He who continually strives to cross the ocean of Saṁsāra, [94]
who listens to ancient stories, to what is stated in the Śāstras,
who recites the Purāṇas and Saṁhitā – should be called Hari. [95]
Those who bathe in the Ganges everyday are his devotees.
Listening to the Purāṇas with devotion is considered like bathing in the Ganges. [96]
Devotion to whoever recites this is considered like going to Prayāga[(XXII)].
Whoever saves, by reciting Dharma and Purāṇa, [97]

---

178 Emendation - NK. N1/16.92b - vaitariṇyāṁ vasec ciraṁ yas tv ahaṅkāravān payaḥ.
N10 - vācako nitya[ṁ] vaitariṇyāṁ vasec ciraṁ yas tv ahaṅkāravān pāpī svavikatthanakārakāḥ.

179 N1/16.93a - savikalpanarāḥ krūrāḥ kṛtagnī garvasantāpī vaitaraṇyāṁ vasec ciraṁ.
N10 - kṛtaghno garvasantāpī vaitaraṇyāṁ vasec cīraṁ.

180 Emendation - NK. N1/16.96a - na ṣuktiṁ kurva(i)tāṁ (N10 - ta(ā)d [bh]aktiṁ kurvatāṁ) nṛṇāṁ gaṅgāsnānaṁ dine dine.

181 N1/16.96b - purāṇaśravaṇe bhaktir gaṅgāsnānopamā [s]mṛtā.

182 Emendation - NK. N1/16.97a - tadvaktari ca yā bhakti[ḥ] sā puryāgopamā smṛtā.

183 Emendation - DS. N1/16.97b, N10 - purāṇe dharmakathane yaḥ samuddharate jana[ḥ].

saṁsārasāgare magnaṁ sa harir nātra saṁśayaḥ
tulasīkānanaṁ yatra yatra padmavanāni ca[184] [98]
purāṇapaṭhanaṁ yatra tatra sannihito hariḥ[185]
pibanti ye bhagavata ātmanaḥ satāṁ
 kathāmṛtaṁ śravaṇapuṭeṣu sambhṛtaṁ[186] [99]
punanti te viṣayavidūṣitāsayaṁ
 vrajanti taccaraṇasaroruhāntikaṁ[187]
manujānāṁ hitaṁ dānam ante vaitaraṇī smṛtā [100]
dattā pāpaṁ dahet sarvaṁ viṣṇulokaṁ ca sā nayet
na dattā ced dvijaḥ krūraṁ prāpya duḥkhaṁ samajjati[188] [101]

people immersed in the ocean of Saṁsāra, is Hari, no doubt.
Where there are forests of lotuses, a forest of holy basil, [98]
where the study of the Purāṇas is taking place, there Hari is present.
Those who drink with their ears the elixir of the stories of Viṣṇu, the beloved by the devotees, [99]
purify themselves of sense imperfections, and reach Viṣṇu's lotus-feet.
Giving donations is best for human beings, considering the Vaitaraṇī Hell in the end. [100]
That (cow) which is offered burns all sins, and leads (the giver) to the world of Viṣṇu.
He who does not give to Brahmins, sinks into cruel suffering. [101]

---

184 N1/16.98b - tulasīkānanaṁ yatra padmapatravanāni ca.
N2/16.66a - tulasīkānane dīyaṁ tathā viṣṇoś ca mandire.
Additional verses - N2/16.66b-67:
bhavānyā cālaye brahmaṁs tathā mā(a)heśvare maṭhe
gaṅgāyā(a)munayoḥ sthāne tathā sārasvatītaṭe
nityaṁ brahmālaye sthāne kurute ca ahan nityaṁ.
Half verse 16.98b is missing in N3.

185 N1/16.99a - purāṇapaṭhanaṁ yatra sati hito hariḥ.
Verses 16.99-101 are missing in N2, N3.

186 N1/16.99b, N10 - pibanti ye bhagavata ātmanaḥ santā kathāmṛtaṁ śravaṇapuṭa(puṁ)sam[bh]ṛtaṁ.
Verse 99b-100a is extracted from Bhāgavatta Purāṇa 2.2.37.

187 N1/16.100a - punanti te viṣayavidū(u)ṣitā svayaṁ vraja[n]ti taccaraṇasaroruhā(a)ṁsikaṁ.
N10 - punanti te viṣayavidūṣitā svayaṁ vraja[n]ti taccaraṇasaroruhāntikaṁ.

188 Emendation - NK. N1/16.101b, N10 - na dattā ce[d] dvijāḥ krūraṁ prāpya duḥkhāt samajjati.

kṣaṇenaite sukhaṁ yānti lagnā dhenoś ca pucchake[189]
vikramanto mayā dṛṣṭāḥ praviśantaḥ sahasraśaḥ[190] [102]
tatrāgre dharmaśīlāś ca dṛśyante hemasannibhāḥ[191]
rathārūḍhā mahāśubhrāḥ śuddhasphaṭikasannibhāḥ[192] [103]
pāpātmānaś ca dṛśyante niṣkāśā dāruṇāḥ punaḥ[193]
kṛmikūpeṣu raudreṣu agnikuṇḍeṣu bhakṣitāḥ[194] [104]

(Those who have given) immediately go to Happiness, clinging to a cow's tail.
I saw thousands of such departed (souls) entering. [102]
First I saw there the pious, (glowing) like gold,
mounted on chariots, very radiant, like pure crystal. [103]
And again, I saw the sinners, dark and terrible,
being consumed in fire pits, and in dreadful wells full of worms. [104]

---

189 N2/16.90b - kṣaṇena lagnā dheno(ya)ś ca pucchake tatra te sukhaṁ.
N4/16.72a, N8/16.91b, Ra/13.70a - dattā yā martya loke 'smin lagnā dhenos tu pucchake.
N7/16.83b - kṣaṇena tarasaṁ sarvalagnā dhenoś ca pu(ñ)cchake.
BF/17.42a - kṣaṇena tāritāḥ sarve dhenupucchavilambinaḥ.

190 N1/16.102b - nikramanto mayā dṛṣṭ(v)ā āviśantaḥ sahasraśaḥ.
N2/16.91a - mayā dṛṣṭ(v)ā[ḥ] [pra]viś(y)anto vaitaraṇyāṁ sahasraśaḥ.
N3 - nikṛmanto (BF/17.42b - nirgacchanto) mayā (N7/16.84a - nikramitayā [tu]) dṛṣṭā[ḥ] praviśantaḥ (N10 - āviśa[n]taḥ) sahasraśaḥ.
N4/16.72b, N8/16.92a, Ra/13.70b - vikramanto mayā dṛṣṭāḥ praviśanti sahasraśaḥ.

191 N1/16.103a, N10 - tatrāgre varmaśīlāś (N3 - tatrāgni dharmaśīlāś) ca dṛśyante hemasannibhāḥ.
N2/16.91b - tatrāgre dharmaśīlāś ca paśyanto hemasannibhāḥ.
N4/16.73a, N8/16.92b, Ra/13.71a - tadāgre dharmaśīlās tu vimānān āruhya vai rathān.
N7/16.84b - tatrāgne dharmaśīlāś ca paśyanti haimasa[n]nibhāḥ.

192 N2/16.92a - yathā ha yās tathā śubhrāḥ (N3 - rathārūḍhā mahāśubhrā[ḥ]) ś(s)uddhasphaṭikasannibhāḥ.

193 N1/16.103b - pāpātmānaś ca dṛśyante niṣkāśā dāruṇā[ḥ] punaḥ.
N2/16.92b - pāpātmānas tatra duḥkhā na paśyante dāruṇās tathā.
N3 - pāpātmāna(i)[ḥ] svaniṣkāśā dṛśyante dāruṇā[ḥ] punaḥ.

194 Emendation - DS. N1/16.104b - kṛmikūpe(ś)ṣv a[g]ni(ḥ)kuṇḍe[ṣu] raudreṣ(ś)u ca (miś ca mannik) [bhakṣi]tāḥ.
N2/16.93a - agnikuṇḍe kṛm(e)ikūpaṁ tatra dūtāḥ sukhāvahāḥ.

śubhāśubhaṁ cātmanā yat tasmin mārge prayujyate[195]
kiṅkarāś ca mayā dṛṣṭā yathāyogyaṁ ca kurvate[196] [105]
aho dvijā mayā dṛṣṭāḥ śubhā vai dhārmikā narāḥ[197]
tatrasthā dharmasaṅkāśā vṛddhadharmāś ca niścalāḥ[198] [106]
vastrādikaṁ ca kauśeyaṁ dhātuhemādikaṁ tathā[199]

Righteous and evildoers are in effect on that same road, (and)
I saw the servants (of Yama) thus doing what was proper. [105]
O Twice-born, I saw (there) pure, righteous people,
as well as people of great piety, as radiant as Dharma. [106]
Silky garments etc., gold and other minerals,

N10 - kṛm(bh)ikūpeṣv a(ā)[g]nikuṇḍe raudre (śa) ca miśr(c)abhakṣitāḥ.
N4/16.74a, N8/16. 94b, Ra/13.73b - kṛmikūpān agnikuṇḍān raudrākārān mahāśunaḥ.
N7/16.86a - agnikuṇḍā[ḥ] kṛmikūpāḥ raudrasthānāś ca kiṅkarāḥ.

195 N1/16.105a - śubhāśubhaṁ cātmanā ya[s] tasmin mārge prayujyate.
N2/16.93b - śubhaṁ vācāśubhaṁ tatra gṛhītvā tatra yujyate.
N10 - śubhāśubhaṁ vātmanā yutāsmin mārge pra(ju)yujyate.
N4/16.77a, N8/16.97, Ra/13.76b - śubhāśubham id(ay)aṁ karma tat tat sthāneṣu bhuñjate.
N7/16.86b - śubhaṁ vāpy aśubhaṁ kiñcit atra sthāne 'pi bhuñjati.

196 N1/16.105b, N2/16.94a, N7/16.87a - kiṅkārāś (N10 - vikārāś) ca mahāduṣṭā yathāyogyaṁ ca kurvate.
N4/16.77b, N8/16.98a, Ra/13.77a - kiṅkārāś ca tathānyāyaṁ prasādapiḍanaṁ tathā.

197 N1/16.106a - aho dvijā (ya)ma[yā] dṛṣṭāḥ śubhā vai dhārmikā narāḥ.
N2/16.94b - bho bho dvijā mayā dṛṣṭāḥ śrutaṁ ca (N7/16.87b - b(v)ahutaraṁ mayā) b(v)ahudhā mama.
N3 - aho dvijā mayā dṛṣṭā[ḥ] śrutā vai dhārmikā narāḥ.
N10 - aho dvi[jā] ('trā yā)m[ay]ā dṛṣṭāḥ (- - -) dhārm(n)ikā(ṁ) narāḥ.

198 N2/16.95a - dharmasthā tatra tiṣṭhanti vidhidharmeṇa niścayāḥ.
N4/16.78b, N8/16.99a, Ra/13.78a - b(v)ahavo dhārmasaṅkāśās tatra santi maharṣayaḥ.

199 N1/16.107a, N10 - vastrādike ca yat krośeyaṁ he(a)mādir dhātur eva ca.
N2/1695b - vastrādikaṁ ca kaunteya dhātuhemādikaṁ tathā.
N3 - vastrādikaṁ ca kauśeyaṁ (N7/16.88b - dhātuhe(a)mādi sarvathā) hemādir dhātur eva hi.
N4/16.79b, N8/16.700a - kauśeyaṁ vastram anyac ca hemarūpyādikaṁ tathā.
Ra/13.80b - yadi dattam ihānnādi vastrādy apy upayogataḥ.

svalpaṁ vai hy annadānaṁ ca yad dattaṁ tatra labhyate[200] [107]
iha loke bhavet kīrtiḥ paraloke sukhāvahā[201]
dharmaḥ śarma dadāti tatra ca nṛṇāṁ
dharmo 'ndhakāre raviḥ[202] [108]
dharmo bandhur abāndhave
yamapathe dharmaḥ suhṛn niścalaḥ[203]

even a small portion of food, whatever has been given (here) is obtained there. [107]
The (good) deeds done in this world bring happiness in the world yonder.
Dharma gives bliss in the hereafter. Dharma is a sun in darkness. [108]
Dharma is a friend to the friendless, a companion on the path of Yama[(XXIII)].

---

200 N1/16.107b - svalpaṁ vai brahmadattā ca ya[d] dattaṁ t(n)a[t] tu labhyate.
N2/16.96a - śayyādir ātmāṇikyaṁ [ca] yad dattaṁ (yad dattaṁ) tatra labhyate.
N10 - svalpaṁ vai brāhmaṇadānaṁ ca yad dattaṁ tal labhyate.
N4/16.80a, N8/16.700b - nānāvidhāni cānyāni yad ajñaṁ (Ra/13.80a - cānnani yad dattaṁ) tatra labhyate.
N7/16.89a - śilādir annam ākhyānaṁ ya[d] dattaṁ tatra labhyate.
Ra/13.80a - svalpaṁ dattaṁ sukāle 'pi b(v)ahuśas tatra labhyate.

201 N2/16.96b - iha loke bhavet kīrti(ṣ)ḥ paraloke (N3, N7/16.89b - sukhāvahaṁ) sukhāni ca.
Additional verse (skipping verse numbers N2/16.97-9) - N2/16.100:
dharmapavitram akhilaṁ dharmo hi mahatāṁ dhanaṁ
vaisatā dharme(-)ta vināśane na ca vihito darmo hīmātāmitā.

202 N1/16.108b - dharmaḥ svargaparatraṁ ca ha nṛṇāṁ dharmādhikāriṇaḥ.
N2/16.101 - dharmāt svargā (-)vargam evam akhilaṁ satyaṁ mayā noditaṁ dāyāsundaratā kulaṁ vibhūti nicayo dharmaḥ kuṇḍuvādikaḥ.
N10 - dharmaḥ svargaparatra ca ha nṛṇāṁ dharmādhikārī ravi[ḥ].
N4/16.78b, N8/16.101a - dharmaparan (Ra/13.81a - dharmaḥ śarma) dadāti tatra ca nṛṇāṁ dharmo 'ndhakāre raviḥ.
N7/16.(89b) - dharmaḥ sarvaṁ paratraṁ ca. No verse number; missing a pāda; end of N7/16.

203 N1/16.109a-b - pāpavināśanaḥ sumanasā dhanau nidhāno vidhiḥ
dharmo bandhur abāndhavaiḥ
surapath(ai)e dharmastuti[r] niścalā(ṁ).
Verses 16.109-10 are missing in N2.
N3 - dharma[ḥ] pāpavināśa(e)na sumanasā dharmābhidhāno nidhiḥ dharmo b(v)andhurab(v)āndhave (N4/16.80b, N8/16.101b, Ra/13.81b - yamapathe dharmmaḥ suhṛn niścalaḥ) surartha (N10 - surapathe) dharmastuti(ḥ)r niścalā.
BF/17.50a - dharmo bandhur abāndhūnāṁ dharmaḥ pāpanivā(a)rakaḥ.

saṁsāre 'tra mahārṇave suratarur
  nāsty eva dharmāt paraḥ[204] [109]
yāvat svastham idaṁ śarīraṁ mānujaṁ
  yāvaj jarā dūrato[205]
yāvac cendriyaśaktir apratihatā
  yāvaj jayo nā 'puḥ[206]
ātmaśreyasi tavād eva viduṣā
  kāryaḥ prayatno mahān[207]
sandīptir bhavane ca kūpakhananaṁ
  praty udyamaḥ kīdṛśaḥ[208] [110]

iti śrībrahmāṇḍapurāṇe nāsiketopākhyāne mārgasaṅkhyāvarṇanaṁ nāma ṣodaśo 'dhyāyaḥ

It is the wish-giving tree in the ocean of Saṁsāra,
there is nothing greater than Dharma. [109]
As long as a man self-abides in this body (i.e. is healthy), and aging is still far,
as long as the strength of physical organs is not destroyed, and there is victory, not impotence,
the wise man must constantly make a great effort for his own good.
What is the sense in starting to dig a well, when the house is already on fire? [110]

This is the sixteenth chapter of the Nāsiketa story, pertaining to Brahmāṇḍa Purāṇa, called – the dimensions of the road.

Translation Notes

I – Brahmins.
II – Literally – "outside of all Dharma".

---

204 N1/16.109c, N3, N10 - saṁsār(a)e tu mahāstha jalā(a)ś(m)aye (N4/16.81b, N8/16.1d, Ra/13.81d - 'tra mahārṇave suratarur) nāsty eva dharmāt paraḥ.

205 N1/16.110a, N10 - yāvat svastham idaṁ śarīraṁ mā(a)nujo yāvaj jarā dūrato. Verse 16.110 is mising in N3.

206 Emendation - NK. N1/16.110b - yāvac cendriyaśaktir a(ma)pratihatā yāva(kṣ)j j(y)ayo nā purayaḥ.
N10 - yāvac candrimaśaktir apratihatā yāvaj jayo nā apuya.

207 N1/16.110c - ātmaśreyasi tāvad eva viduṣā kārya[ḥ] praya(s)t[n]o mahān.

208 N1/16.110d - sandīp[t]e bhavane ca kūpakhananaṁ (N10 - v(a)ā kayasvananaṁ) praty udyamaḥ kīdṛśaḥ.

III – Rather than remaining awake and fasting.
IV – The messengers.
V – Translation suggested by Dr. N. Kulkarni.
VI – Literally – easy to obtain.
VII – A metaphoric description of the dead as falling under Yama's chariot.
VIII – Death – Dharmarāja – Yama.
IX – The metaphor of KU/3.14b is here once again a realistic description – see also 9.20a and in this chapter 56b.
X – The night of destruction at the end of the world; The night of a man's death; One of Kāli's names; The combination of Time and Night – see a modern version of their marriage in R. Zelazny's book – "Lord of Light".
XI – Yama – see note VIII.
XII – "*preta*" – "he who goes on" – Filippi (1996), p. 130, note 3. The form of the souls on their way to Yama's world.
XIII – Yama – see notes VIII, XI.
XIV – See above note **IX.**
XV – Literally – ten directions, which represent the whole compass.
XVI – Bathing pools at pilgrimage sites and temples.
XVII – In the material world.
XVIII – Viṣṇu as the "All-Creator" – identified with Prajāpati/Brahma, or with Brahma's son, or with Tvaṣṭṛ.
XIX – The entrance to the realm of the dead – like the river Styx in Greek mythology.
XX – The Vaitaraṇī River.
XXI – One of Viṣṇu's names.
XXII – A site of pilgrimage at the confluence of the Ganges and the Yamuna rivers, near Allahabad.
XXIII – Translation suggested by Prof. D. Shulman.

Chapter 17

The Yama-Nārada Dialogue

nāsiketa uvāca
dharmiṣṭhānāṁ pravakṣyāmi śṛṇvantu dvijasattamāḥ[1]
niṣkaṇṭhakaṁ śuciṁ mārgaṁ ramaṇīyaṁ ca dharmiṇāṁ[2] [1]
mahāvṛkṣā vanacchāyā utthitā gandhavāsinaḥ[3]
ghṛtakṣīramahānadyo madhumastuvahās tathā[4] [2]

Nāsiketa said
Listen excellent Twice-born, I shall tell (now) of the most righteous.
The road of the righteous is free of thorns, clean and pleasant. [1]
A forest of big, fragrant, shady trees, is standing there,
as well as big rivers with sweet flows of honey and cream. [2]

---

1 N1/17.1a - dharmabhog(n)ām avakṣyāmi śṛṇvantu munisattamā(a)ḥ.
N3/17.1a - dharmabhogān pravakṣyāmi śṛṇudh(t)va[ṁ] dvijasattamāḥ.
N4/17.1a, N8/17.2a, Ra/14.1a - dharmiṣṭhānāṁ pravakṣyāmi (N7/17.1a - śṛṇu bho (BF/18.1a - śṛṇudhvaṁ) dvijasattamāḥ) sāṁprataṁ svargatiṁ dvijāḥ.

2 N1/17.1b, N3/17.1b - niḥkaṇṭhakaḥ śuciḥ (N10 - panthā) dharma (N4/17.1b, N8/17.2b, Ra/14.1b - sa eva sugamaḥ pānthāḥ) ramaṇīyaś ca dharmiṇāṁ.
N2/17.1b - nirmalaṁ komalaṁ mārge (BF/18.1b - mārgaṁ) ramaṇīyaṁ ca [dharmiṇaṁ].
N7/17.1b - nirmalaṁ komalamārgaṁ ramaṇīyaṁ ca dharmikaṁ.
BF/18.2a - nirmalaḥ komalaḥ panthā vyomākāro hy akaṇṭakaḥ.

3 N1/17.2a - mahāvṛkṣaś ca yacchāyā uṣitā gandhavāsitaḥ.
N2/17.2a - mahāvṛkṣavanacchāyām uṣitāṁ gandhavāsitaḥ.
N3 - mahāvṛkṣ(y)ā dhanacchāyā utthitā gandhavāsinaḥ.
No verse numbers after N3/17.1.
N4/17.2a, N8/17.3a, Ra/14.2a - mahāvṛkṣaghanacchāyaḥ puṣpagandhasamākulaḥ.
BF/18.2b - vṛkṣā nānāphalaiś channāḥ puṣpitā bhramarākulāḥ.

4 N1/17.2b, N10, N3 - ghṛtakṣīravahā nadyo madhumat suvahās (BF/18.3b - madhumastuvahās) tathā.
N2/173a - dadhikṣīramahānadyo bhakṣyabhojyamūlānvitāḥ.
N4/17.3a, N8/17.4a, Ra/14.3a - dadhikṣīrāpagās tatra rāśayo bhakṣyabhojyayoḥ.
N7/17.3a - dadhikṣīraghṛta(ā)nadyo bhakṣabhojyaphalāni ca.

vividhaṁ ca tathā peyaṁ dadhi bhakṣyasya rāśayaḥ[5]
vāpīkūpataḍāgāś ca prapā vai tatra vāriṇāṁ[6] [3]
vimānāni samāruhya tat pathaṁ yānti dharmiṇaḥ[7]
sudīrgham api panthānam alpakālaṁ vrajanti te[8] [4]
labhante tatra dānāni pūrvadattāni mānavaiḥ[9]
dharmarājasabhāmadhye dṛṣṭaṁ yat kautukaṁ mayā[10] [5]
tad ahaṁ vaḥ pravakṣyāmi śṛṇudhvaṁ munisattamāḥ[11]

They have a variety of drinks, as well as milk and heaps of food.
Ponds, wells and water tanks of drinking water are there. [3]
The righteous cross that road mounted on celestial chariots, (and)
though the way is so long, they make it in a very short time. [4]
They get there things previously donated by (them as living) humans.
I was surprised by what I saw in the midst of Yama's hall – [5]
I am going to tell (you) about it, listen, O excellent sages.

---

5 N1/17.3a - vividhaṁ ca tathā peyaṁ dadhi bhaktā y(a)ā (N3 - dadhibhakṣ[y]asya) rāśayaḥ.
Half verse 17.3a is missing in N2.

6 N3 - vāpīkūpataḍāgāś ca prapā vai taptavāriṇāṁ.
N4/17.2b, N8/17.3b, Ra/14.2b - vāpīkūpataḍāgaiś ca prapābhiś ca manoharaḥ.
N7/17.2b - vāpīkūpataḍāgāni (BF/18.3a - pūrāṇi śītavāriṇā) prapā vīsitavāriṇaḥ.

7 N1/17.4a - vimānāni samā(a)ruhya tat pathaṁ yānti varṇinaḥ.
N2/17.3b - vimāneṣu tam āruhya (N7/17.3b - vimānenaivam āruhya) tat pathaṁ yānti dharmik(aṁ)āḥ.
N4/17.3b, N8/17.4b, Ra/14.3b - vimānāni samārūḍhas tat padaṁ yānti dharmikāḥ.
BF/18.4a - vimānāni samāruhya taṁ pathaṁ yānti dharmiṇaḥ.

8 N1/17.4b - sudīrgham api panthāś ca (N3 - panthānam) alpakālaṁ vrajanti te.
N2/17.4a - dīrghamārgeṇa gacchanti bhogena vividhena (N7/17.4a - ś(s)ubhe svalpe vrajanti) te.

9 N2/17.4b - ihaiva yena dattāni yamaloke hi bhujyate.
N3 - labhyate (N4/17.4a, N7/17.4b, N8/17.5a, Ra/14.4a - labhante) tatra dānāni pūrvadattāni (BF/18.4b - te narāḥ) mānavaiḥ.

10 N2/17.5a - athānyaṁ saṁpravakṣyāmi (N7/17.5a - dṛṣṭamānaṁ tu kautukaṁ) yamadṛṣṭaṁ kautukaṁ mayā (vi).
N4/17.4b, N8/17.5b, Ra/14.4b - athānyat saṁpravakṣyāmi śrūyatāṁ kautukaṁ mahat.
BF/18.5b - atyadbhutaṁ pravākṣyāmi yad dṛṣṭaṁ tatra kautukaṁ.

11 N2/17.5b - saṁstuto 'ḥaṁ (N7/17.5b - saṁsthitas tu) sabhāmadhye dharmarājasya veśmani.

nāradaḥ paryaṭaṁl lokāṁs tatrāgād brahmanandanaḥ[12] [6]
tam āgataṁ muniṁ dṛṣṭvā dharmarājaḥ samutthitaḥ[13]
tataḥ svāgatam ābhāṣya dattvāsanam apūjayat[14] [7]
saṁpūjya vidhivat pādāv idaṁ vacanam abravīt[15] [8]
yama uvāca

Nārada, Brahma's son, who traveled over those places, arrived there. [6]
Seeing the sage coming, Dharmarāja stood up,
thus greeting him, (and) reverenced him by giving him a seat. [7]
Bowing to his feet according to law, he said the following. [8]
Yama said

N7/17.6a - ś(s)obhite muni madhyaṁstha tārāmadhye ca candramā.
BF/18.6 - saṁsthitaś ca sabhāmadhye dharmarājaḥ svaveśmāni.

12 N1/17.6b, N10, BF/18.7a - nāradaḥ paryaṭaṁ[l] lokaṁs tatr[āgād](eṇa) brahmanandanaḥ.
N2/17.6a - tasmin sthāne (N4/17.6a, N8/17.7a, Ra/14.6a - tadā tatra) rathārūḍho dvādaśādityasannibha[ḥ].
N3 - nāradaḥ paryaṭa(n)ṁl loke tatrāgād brahmavādinaḥ.
N4/17.6b, N8/17.7b, Ra/14.6b - nārado nāma bhagavān āgato munipuṅgavaḥ.
VP/205.4 - ahaṁ tatra mahātejā nārado munisattamaḥ
dharmarājasabhāṁ prāptas tapasā dyotitaprabhaḥ.

13 N1/17.7a - tam āgataṁ muniṁ dṛṣṭvā dharmarāja (BF/18.7b - samutthitaḥ) munisthitaḥ.
N2/17.6b - āgato nārado devo yamena paripūjitaḥ.
N4/17.7a, N8/17.8a, Ra/14.7a - athāgataṁ muniṁ dṛṣṭvā pratyutthāya yamo dadau.
VP/205.5a - tatra rājātha vegena taṁ dṛṣṭvā svayam āgataṁ.

14 N1/17.7b - tata[ḥ] svāgatamānāś ca dattvāsanam apūjayat.
N2/17.7a - divyāsanaṁ pradattaṁ ca manaḥsantoṣakārakaṁ.
N4/17.7b, N8/17.8b, Ra/14.7b - tasmai divyāsanam atho hy arghyeṇāpy abhyapūjayat.
N7/17.7b - divyāsanaṁ pradattaṁ ca arghapādādipūjita[ḥ].
BF/18.8a - tataḥ svāgatam ābhāṣya dattvāsanam apūjayat.
VP/205.5b - arcayi(e)tvā yathānyāyaṁ kṛtvā caiva pradakṣiṇaṁ.

15 N1/17.8, BF/18.8b - saṁpūjya vidhivat pādāv (N3 - pādyair) idaṁ vacanam abravīt.
Verse 17.8 is missing in N2.
VP/205.6a - uvāca ca mahātejāḥ sūryaputraḥ pratāpavan.

adya me saphalaṁ janma adya me saphalā kriyāḥ[16]
adya me saphalā pūjā yad bhavān dṛṣṭigo 'bhavat[17] [9]
bhagavan vada tat kāryaṁ yadarthaṁ tvam ihāgataḥ[18]
yamasya vacanaṁ śrutvā nārado vākyam abravīt[19] [10]
nārada uvāca

"Today my birth bears fruit, today my deeds bear fruits,
today my worship bears fruits, when I see you. [9]
Tell me, your honour, the purpose of your coming here, (and) it should be fulfilled."
Hearing Yama's words, Nārada said the following. [10]
Nārada said

---

16 N1/17.9a, N4/17.9a, N8/17.10a, Ra/14.9a - adya me saphalaṁ janma adya (N2/17.8a, BF/18.9b - cādya) me (N7/17.8b - saphalī) saph(r)alā (N3 - saphalā me 'dya ca) kriyāḥ.

Additional half verse:

N2/17.7b, N4/17.8b, N8/17.9b, Ra/14.8b - svāgataṁ (N7/17.8a - svāgate) te dvijaśreṣṭha (VP/205.6b - diṣṭyā prāpto 'si nārada) b(v)rahmaputra mahāmune.

BF/18.9a - svāgataṁ te mahāprājña brahmaputra muneśvara.

17 Emendation - NK. N1/17.9b, N10 - adya me saphalā pūjā (N4/17.9b, N8/17.10b, Ra/14.9b - yaj jātaṁ tava darśanaṁ, N7/17.9a - tvayā y(ai)ad darśanaṁ kṛtaṁ) yad (N2/17.8b - bhavaddarśanaṁ śubhaṁ) bhavān dṛṣṭigo (N3 - dṛṣṭigocaraḥ) 'bravīt.

BF/18.10a - tuṣto 'dya me jagannātho mahārṣe tava darśanāt.

VP/205.7 - sarvajñaḥ sarvadarśī ca sarvadharmavidāṁ varaḥ
gāndharvasyetihāsasya vijñātā tvaṁ mahāmune.

18 N1/17.10a - adya me bhagavan (N3 - bhagavan vada tat) kṛtyaṁ yadarthaṁ tvam ihāgataḥ.

Half verse 17.10a is missing in N2.

N4/17.10a, N8/17.11a, Ra/14.10a - ācakṣva sāṁprataṁ kasmād āgato 'si prayojanāt.

VP/205.8 - yatkāryaṁ yena vā kāryaṁ yad vai manasi vartate
prabrūhi bhagavānn āśu yac chānyat kiñcid uttamaṁ.

19 N3, N7/17.9b - yamasya vacanaṁ śrutvā nārado vākyam abravīt.

N4/17.10b, N8/17.11b, Ra/14.10b - evaṁ dharmmaṁ vacaḥ śrutvā nāradaḥ pratyuvāca ha.

BF/18.10b - nārado vacanaṁ śrutvā dharmarājasya sādaraṁ.

dharmarājaḥ śruto me tvaṁ bahuśo lokaviśrutaḥ[20]
tataḥ prabhṛti me ceto darśanāya tavotsukaṁ[21] [11]
yathāśrutaṁ tathā dṛṣṭo dharmarāṭ yamo bhavān[22]
bhavatā sadṛśo nānyo dharmādharmavinirṇaye[23] [12]
dharmarāja mama brūhi viśeṣaṁ puṇyapāpayoḥ[24]
bhavān bhagavatā bhūtakarmasākṣyaṁ niveśitaḥ [13]

"I have heard about you, Dharmarāja, famous in many worlds, (and)
since then, my heart has been eager to see you. [11]
You are exactly as I have heard, O Dharmarāja, honourable Yama.
There is no other being like you to determine what is right or wrong. [12]
(Please) tell me Dharmarāja the difference between virtue and sin, (since)
the Creator made you the witness to the working of Karma among all creatures". [13]

---

[20] N2/17.9b - tvā(a)m āgato 'haṁ mahābhāga tava darśanaṁ lālasaḥ (vi).
N3 - dharmarāja śruto me tvaṁ b(v)ahuṣo [hy e]ka(sa)saṁstutaḥ
dharmarājas tathā dṛṣṭo dharmarājādya me bhavān.
N4/17.11a, N8/17.12a, Ra/14.11a - tvat prasādāt suraśreṣṭha sarvataḥ kuśalaṁ mama.
N4/17.11b, Ra/14.11b - darśanārthaṁ ca bhavata āgato 'haṁ (N8/17.12b - mahāmate) mahāmune.
N7/17.10 - darśanārthaṁ paraṁ ramyaṁ mahārājasya darśanaṁ
dharmātmā darśanārthaṁ ca āgato 'haṁ mahāmate.
BF/18.11 - dharmarāja vicārāya sthāpito hariṇā svayaṁ
dharmasandarśanārthāya samāyāto bhavadgṛhaṁ.

[21] N3 - tataḥ prabhṛti mac ceto t(a)e darśanāya utsakaṁ.
N10 - tataḥ prabhṛti me ceto darśaṇāya tavotsuk(e)aṁ.
N2/17.10a - kīdṛśas tava loka hi vicāras tava kīdṛśaḥ.

[22] N1/17.12a - yathāśrutaṁ (N10 - yathāśrute) tathā dṛṣṭo dharmarāṭ yamo bhavān (short).
Half verse 17.12a is missing in N2.

[23] N1/17.12b - bhavatāṁ s(ś)adṛśo nāny(au)o dharmādharmavinirṇaye.
N2/17.10b - pretānāṁ kriyate samyak dharmādharmavicāraṇaṁ.
N3 - bhava tvasadṛśo nānyo dharmādharmavinirṇayaḥ.
N4/17.13, N8/17.14, Ra/14.13 - dṛṣṭas tvaṁ pūrvapuṇyena b(v)ahunā dharmikottama
dharmādharmavicāro 'pi tvayā samyag vidhīyate.
BF/18.12a - dharmādharmavicāraṁ ca sarvaṁ brūhi mamāgrataḥ.

[24] Verse 17.13 is missing in N2.

nāsiketa uvāca
evaṁ kathayatas tatra nāradasya yamena hi[25]
tatra devāḥ samāyātā vimānāni sahasraśaḥ[26] [14]
meghagaṁbhīranirghoṣair lakṣitāni vidūrataḥ[27]
hastighaṇṭāninādaiś ca srajair mālākulāni ca[28] [15]
muktājālavicitrāṇi bhūṣitāny apsarogaṇaiḥ[29]

Nāsiketa said
When Nārada was talking there to Yama,
the gods came over (in) thousands of celestial vehicles, [14]
making noise like the deep rumbling of clouds visible from afar,
and the sound of elephants' bells, decorated with garlands. [15]
(The gods came accompanied) by groups of Apsarasas, decorated with various pearl ornaments,

---

25 N1/17.14a - yamaṁ katha(ṁ)yatas tatra nāradasya yamena hi.
N2/17.11a - evam ābhā(ī)ṣya vākyāni nārado dharmasatkathaḥ.
N3 - evaṁ kathayatas tatra nāradasya yamena (BF/18.13a - hi) ha.
N4/17.14a, N8/17.15a, Ra/14.14a - vadator evam anyonyaṁ yamanāradayos tadā.

26 N1/17.14b, N3, N10, BF/18.13b - āgacchanti vimānāni dṛśyante sma sahasraśaḥ.
N4/17.14b, N8/17.15b, Ra/14.14b - tatrāgatāni parato vimānāni sahasraśaḥ.

27 N1/17.15a - meghagaṁbhīranirghoṣai[r] lakṣyetāny avidustaraḥ.
N2/17.12b, N7/17.13b - meghadundubhinirghoṣair (N3 - lakṣi(a)tāni vidūrataḥ, N4/17.15a, N8/17.16a, Ra/14.15a - apsarogaṇagītakaiḥ) aparair [gītavādibhiḥ].

28 N1/17.15b - hastir ghaṇṭāninādaiś ca srajair mālākulāni ca.
N2/17.13a - ghaṇṭahastāninādaiś ca dhvajamālākulā ku(-).
N10 - hastighaṭāninādaiś ca gajair mālākulāni (N3 - dhvajamālākulāni) ca.
N4/17.15b, N8/17.16b, Ra/14.15b - yaṁ yaṁ ghoṣair hastinīnāṁ jayamālābhir eva ca.
N7/17.14a - ghanṭhā hastān(ebh)ināda is tu dh(u)vajamālākulaṁ mahat.
BF/18.14b - hastyaśvarathasaṁghānāṁ nādair bhūrinadīkalpaiḥ.

29 N1/17.16a, N10 - muktājālavicitrāṇi (N3 - muktādāmavicitrāṇi) bhūṣaṇāny apsarogaṇaiḥ.
N2/17.13b - muktābharaṇavividhair bhūṣitāś cāmarair (N7/17.14b - cāpsaro) gaṇaiḥ.
N4/17.16a, N8/17.17a, Ra/14.16a - muktāguccaiś ca vividhaiḥ śobhitāni samaṁ tataḥ.

nānāvidhāni vādyante yatra nādaviśeṣakaiḥ[30] [16]
airāvatasamārūḍho devarājas tad agrataḥ[31]
nirgato vāyuvegena yama utthāya tatkṣaṇāt[32] [17]
dharmarājo mahātejāḥ satvaraṁ ca svaveśmani[33]
praviṣṭo bhayasantrastas te dūtāś ca diśo daśa[34] [18]

playing various musical instruments. [16]
In front, riding on his elephant Airāvata, was the Gods' king (i.e. Indra).
With the speed of wind, Yama got up and came forth – [17]
brilliant Dharmarāja, immediately withdrew to his abode,
(and) his messengers entered terrified (and ran off) in all directions. [18]

BF/18.14a - mahādundubhinirghoṣair apsarobhiḥ samāvṛtaḥ,
BF/18.15a - muktābharaṇavāsobhir dhvajacchattrair vibhūṣitaḥ.

30 N2/17.14a - vāditravividhās tatra (N7/17.15a - vaṁśavīṇā manoramāḥ) vīnāvaṁśamanoramā[ḥ].
N3, N10 - nānāvidhāni vādyāni vādyante yatra vādakaiḥ.
N4/17.16b, N8/17.17b, Ra/14.16b - vāditrair vividhair vīṇāvaṁśādibhir api dvijāḥ.
BF/18.15b - vāditrair vividhais tatra vīṇāveṇumanoramaiḥ.

31 N1/17.17a, N10 - airāvatasamārūḍho (N2/17.14b - devarājapuraprati, N4/17.17a, N8/17.18a, Ra/14.17a - devarājas tadagrataḥ, BF/18.16a - devarājaḥ puraḥsthitaḥ) devarājamunisthitaḥ.
N7/17.16a - airāv(p)atisamārūḍho devarājapure sthitaḥ.

32 N1/17.17b - nirgato vāyuyogena mama utthāyamaṁ nṛṇāt.
N2/17.15a - nirgatā vāyuvegena yama kruddhena (N3 - mayarutthāpya) tat kṣaṇāt.
N4/17.17b, N8/17.18b, Ra/14.17b - nirgato vāyuvegena (BF/18.16b - yamo muniganair vṛtaḥ) yamagehasya copari.

33 N1/17.18a - dharmarājo mahātejāḥ (N10, N7/17.15b - sa(ra)tvaraṁ ca svaveśmani) susvaraṁ paśya veśmani.
N2/17.15b - dharmarāja mahā(a)rājaḥ satvaraṁ cāsya veśmani.
N4/17.18a, N8/17.19a, Ra/14.18a - dharmarājo 'pi tejasvī tatkṣaṇād eva veśmani.
BF/18.17a - dharmarājo mahātejā sa veśmani praviṣṭaḥ.

34 N1/17.18b, N7/17.16a, N10 - praviṣṭo bhayasantrastas te dūtāś ca diśo daśa.
N4/17.18b, Ra/14.18b - praviṣṭo bhayam āpanno dūtā api diśo (N8/17.19b - diśa) daśa.
BF/18.17b - dūtās te bhayasantrastāḥ sarve naṣṭā diśo diśa.

kṣaṇād gatā bhayāviṣṭās te sarve dhārmiṇas tathā[35]
aham ekaḥ sthitas tatra vismayāviṣṭamānasaḥ [19]
yat kiñcit kāraṇaṁ yena dharmarājo bibheti tat[36]
māyeyaṁ muniśārdūla vicintyaṁ jagataḥ pateḥ[37] [20]
paśyatas tasya ca munes āgatās te rathāyutāḥ[38]
tejomayā visphuliṅgair jvalanta iva vahnayaḥ[39] [21]

In a moment, all the righteous[(I)] *there became terrified.*
I was standing there alone, my mind full of wonder. [19]
As for the reason for Dharmarāja's fear,
that is a mystery devised by the Lord of the World, O great sage[(II)]. *[20]*
Before the sage's eyes, (the gods arrived) on chariots,
glowing with sparks, blazing like fire. [21]

---

35 N1/17.19a - tatkṣaṇā[t] (N10 - kṣaṇād gatā (vi)) bhayā(a)viṣṭās te sarve kiṅkaradhārmiṇaḥ.
N2/17.16b - gatāḥ kṣaṇena pāpiṣṭhā nirghṛṇā (N4/17.19a, N8/17.20a, Ra/14.19a - santrastā niḥkriyāḥ) krūrakarmiṇaḥ.
Additional half verse:
N2/17.17a - pretās tatraiva mārgeṇa sarve cādhvani varttitāḥ.
N7/17.17b-18a - gaṇā kṣaṇe bhayāviṣṭā nirghaṇāḥ krūrakarmiṇaḥ.
tenaiva tatra mārgeṇa pretāḥ sādhvani varttitāḥ.

36 N1/17.20a, N10 - kiñcit tat (N3 - kim etat) kāraṇaṁ yena dharmarājo b(v)ibhe(ī)t(a)i yat.
N2/17.18a - brahmaputro vilakṣyo 'bhūd vada tenaiva kiñcana.

37 N1/17.20b - māyeyaṁ muni(e)śārdūlo vicintyaṁ jagataḥ pateḥ.
Half verse 17.20b is missing in N2.
N7/17.19a - anye ca muniś(s)ārdūl(a)ā[s] tiṣṭhanti ca yathāsthitaṁ.

38 N1/17.21a - parayas tasya (N10 - tava) ca munes te vai rathavarā gatāḥ.
N2/17.18b - tatkṣaṇ(ā)e tena mārgeṇa āgatās te (N7/17.20a - rathā punaḥ) rathāyutāḥ.
N3 - paśyatas tasya ca mune(ḥ)s te vai rathavarāṁ gatāḥ.
N4/17.21a, N8/17.22a, Ra/14.21a - tatas tenaiva mārgeṇa nivṛttās te vimānagāḥ.

39 N1/17.21b, N10 - tejomayā visphuliṅge jvalanta iva va(n)hna(u)yaḥ.
N2/17.19a - jvalatam agnisaṅkāśaṁ gatās te ca diśo daśa.
N4/17.21b, N8/17.22b, Ra/14.21b - jvaladagnisamudbhūtā sphuliṅgā iva tejasā.
N7/17.20b - jvalanto 'py agnisaṅkāśaḥ sphuliṅgāni daśo diśa.

punas tatrāgato dharmo bhayabhītena cetasā[40]
tathā dṛṣṭvā dharmarājaṁ provāca munipuṅgavaḥ[41] [22]
nārada uvāca
satyaṁ brūhi mahāprājña brahmatulyaparākrama[42]
asurāḥ rākṣasāḥ ghorāḥ sarve te balasaṁsthitāḥ[43] [23]
trailokyam akhilaṁ caiva tava śāsane āsthitaṁ[44]
mamedaṁ kautukaṁ jātaṁ tad vadasva yathātathaṁ[45] [24]

Dharma(rāja) arrived there again, his mind full of fear.
Thus seeing Dharmarāja, the high sage spoke. [22]
Nārada said
"Please tell me the truth, O great knower, O hero[(III)] equal to Brahma,
all the terrible demons and Rakṣasas are at your power (and) [23]
the entire three worlds are also in your control.
(Please) tell everything exactly as it is, (quelling) my aroused curiosity. [24]

---

40 N1/17.22a, N10 - punas tatra gato dharmo bhayabhītena cetasā.
N2/17.19b - kṣaṇena vāgato dharmo bhayārtto naṣṭacetanaḥ.
N7/17.21a - kṣaṇenaivāgato dharmo bhayārtto bhraṣṭacetasaḥ.

41 N1/17.22b, N10 - tayā dṛṣṭvā dharmarājaṁ provāca munipuṅgavaḥ.
Half verse 17.22b is missing in N2.
N3 - tathā dṛṣṭ[v]ā dharmarājam uvāca munipuṅgava[ḥ].
N4/17.22b, N8/17.23b, Ra/14.22b - āgacchantam imaṁ viprāḥ papraccha tvaritaṁ muniḥ.

42 N1/17.23a, N3, N10, BF/18.20a - satyaṁ brūhi mah(m)ārāja (N7/17.21b, Bo/18.5a - viṣṇutulyaparākrama) brahmatulyaparākrama(ḥ).
N2/17.20a - satyaṁ brūhi mahāprājña (N4/17.23a, N8/17.24a, Ra/14.23a - dharmeśātulyavikrama) viṣṇutulyaparākrama(ḥ).

43 N1/17.23b - asurā rākṣasā ghorāḥ sarve te (N2/17.20b, N7/17.21b - b(v)alasaṁsthitāḥ, N3, BF/18.20b - vaśavarttinaḥ, N10 - vaṁśavarddhinaḥ, Bo/18.5b - vaśasaṁsthitāḥ) vaśavarjitaḥ.
N4/17.24a, N8/17.25, Ra/14.24a - dānavā devatā daityāḥ sarve tava vaśe sthitāḥ.

44 N1/17.24a - trailokyam akhilaṁ ca vai (N3 - caiva) tava śāsanam āsthitaṁ.
N2/17.21a - trailokyam akhilaṁ sarvaṁ tv abhitiṣṭhati dharmataḥ.
N4/17.24b, N8/17.26a, Ra/14.24b - trailokyam api deveśa tava śāsanasaṁsthitaṁ.
BF/18.21a - trailokyam akhilaṁ caiva tava śāsane saṁsthitaṁ.

45 N2/17.21b - mama kautukam utpannaṁ kathayasva (N7/17.23a - yathāsthitaṁ, BF/18.21b - mamāgrataḥ) yathātathaṁ.
N4/17.25a, N8/17.26b, Ra/14.25a - kautukaṁ ca mamāsty atra tan me brūhi yathārthavat.

kasmāt tvaṁ bhayasaṁyukto vāyuvegena nirgataḥ[46]
nāradasya vacaḥ śrutvā pratyuvāca yamas tadā[47] [25]
yama uvāca[48]
atiguhyaṁ muniśreṣṭha vacmi pāpapraṇāśanaṁ[49]
śrotavyaṁ te prayatnena dharmapuṇyapravardhanaṁ[50] [26]
martyaloke mahātejāḥ satyavāk nṛpasattamaḥ[51]

Why have you gone away by the speed of wind, seized with fear?"
Having heard Nārada's words, Yama told him so. [25]
Yama said
"The great secret of the sinners' punishment, I tell you, O excellent sage.
One should listen to it attentively, (in order to) increase good and righteousness. [26]
In the mortal world, there was a great hero, excellent king, a man of truth,

---

46 N1/17.25a - kasmāt tvaṁ bhayasaṁyukto (N10 - vāyuvegena nirmita(ā)ḥ) vāyuvege vinirmita(ā)ḥ.
N3 - kasmāt tvaṁ jayasaṁyukto (N7/17.23b, Bo/18.5c - bhayasantrast(a)o, BF/18.22a - bhayasaṁyukto) vāyuvegena nirgataḥ.

47 N1/17.25b - nāradasya vacaḥ śrutvā pratyuvāca (N2/17.22b - kṛtāñjaliḥ, N7/17.24a - yathāsthitaṁ, BF/18.22b - tadā yamaḥ) yama[s t](kṣ)adā.
N4/17.25b, N8/17.27a, Ra/14.25b - evaṁ munivacaḥ śrutvā pratyuvāca yamo 'khilaṁ.

48 Bo/18.6 - dharmarāja uvāca.

49 N1/17.26a - atiguhya[ṁ] muniśreṣṭha (N2/17.23a - kathitaṁ pāpanāśanaṁ) vacmi pāpapraśāsanaṁ.
N4/17.26a, N8/17.27b, Ra/14.26a - asti guhyaṁ muniśreṣṭha (N7/17.24b - kathyate pāpanāśanaṁ) vadāmi mahad adbhutaṁ.
BF/18.23 - kathayāmi muniśreṣṭha sarvam etat tavāgrataḥ
asti guhyaṁ dvijaśreṣṭha tv ahaṁ vakṣyāmi te rahaḥ.
BF/19.3a - atiguhyaṁ muniśreṣṭha (Bo/18.6a - kathāṁ pāpapraṇaśinīṁ) kathayāmi tavāgrataḥ.

50 N1/17.26b, N2/17.23b - śrotavyaṁ te (N10 - śrīma(-) te) prayatnena (N3, N7/17.25a - dharmapuṇyavivarddhanaḥ) dharmapuṇyapravarddhanaṁ.
N4/17.26b, N8/17.28a, Ra/14.26b - śrūyatāṁ matprayatnena puṇyaṁ pāpapraṇāśanaṁ.
BF/19.3b - sarvapāpapraśamanaṁ dharmapuṇyavivardhanaṁ
Bo/18.6b - bravīmi sakalāṁ vidvan punar dharmavivardhanāṁ.

51 N1/17.27a - martyaloke mahātejāḥ (N10 - śrīmān nṛpatisattamaḥ) satyayā munipuṅgava.
N2/17.24a - martyaloke mahārāja (N3 - satyavāk munipuṅgava) śrīmān satyavān [tu] naraḥ.

janako nāma vikhyātaś cāśvamedhaṁ purākarot[52] [27]
satyadharmaparo nityaṁ suśānto vijitendriyaḥ[53]
prajānāṁ vatsalo rājā bhayārtābhayadas tathā[54] [28]

whose name was Janaka, and he had performed the horse sacrifice in the past. [27] Following truth and justice, (he was) always very calm, controlling the senses, a king loved by his people, giving security to those afraid and distressed. [28]

N4/17.27a, N8/17.28b, Ra/14.27a - martyaloke mahārājaḥ (N7/17.25b - janako satyavādinaḥ) kaścid atyantadharmikaḥ.
BF/19.4 - upakhyānam idaṁ divyaṁ narāṇāṁ pāpanāśanaṁ
purāṇe tretāyuge vai rājā hy āsīn mahātapāḥ.
Bo/18.7a - mṛtya(u)loke mahāprājñaḥ satyavrataparāyaṇaḥ.
VP/206.26 - purā kṛtayuge tāta nimir nāma mahāyaśāḥ
āsid rājā mahātejāḥ satyasandheti viśrutaḥ.

52 N1/17.27b, N3 - janako nāma vikhyātaḥ śrīmān nṛpatisattamaḥ.
The first pāda of 17.27b is missing in N10, the other appears in 17.27a.
N4/17.27b, N8/17.29a, Ra/14.27b - janakaś ceti vikhyāto hayamedhaṁ purākarot.
N7/17.26a - janako nāma vikhyāto (BF/19.5a - hy aśvamedhakaraḥ sadā) aśvamedha[ṁ] cakāra saḥ.
Bo/18.7b - janako nāma vikhyātaḥ prajānāṁ paripālakaḥ.
VP/206.27a - tasya putro mithir nāma jananāj janako 'bhavat.

53 N1/17.28a - satyadharmaparo nityaṁ śuddhato (N3, N10 - suśānto) vijite[n]driyaḥ.
N2/17.25 - tasya rājyaṁ pravakṣyāmi śrūyatāṁ munipuṅgava
satyadharmaparo rājā nityaṁ kṣāntau jitendriyaḥ.
N4/17.28b-29a, N8/17.30, Ra/14.28b-29a - satyadharmmarato nityaṁ rājā janaka sañjñakaḥ
śānto jitendriyaḥ śrīmān prajānāṁ rakṣakaḥ paraḥ.
N7/17.27a - satyadharmarato rājā nityaṁ kṣāntijitendriyaḥ.
BF/19.6a - mahāvratadharo rājā nityaṁ kṣānto jitendriyaḥ.

54 N1/17.28b, N3 - prajārakṣāparo (N10 - prajārakṣākar(āṁ)o) nityaṁ bhayārtābhayadas tathā.
N2/17.26a - prajānāṁ vatsalo rājā prabhītānāṁ ca pālakaḥ.
N2/17.27a - prajānāṁ rakṣako dakṣo devapūjanatatparaḥ.
N7/17.27b - prajānāṁ pālanārthāya sadā rājā hi tatparaḥ.
BF/19.6b - prajānāṁ vatsalaś caiva pṛthivīpālakas tathā.

karoti jātu na krodhaṁ prajānāṁ sa narādhipaḥ[55]
rāmasyeva hi tadrājye lokadharmaparāyaṇaḥ[56] [29]
bahupuṣpaphalā vṛkṣā bahukṣīrāś ca dhenavaḥ[57]
dīrghāyuṣaḥ prajāḥ sarvās tejasatyātidhārmiṇaḥ[58] [30]
evaṁvidhaṁ mahārājyaṁ janakasya mahātmanaḥ[59]
tasya bhāryā samākhyātā nāmnā satyavatī śubhā[60] [31]

He never made his people angry with him, that king,
excellent in worldly Dharma. In his kingdom which was like Rāma's, there were [29]
many trees bearing flowers and fruits, as well as cows yielding plenty of milk.
All the people were long-lived, very righteous, brilliant, truth-telling. [30]
This is the nature of the great kingdom of the high-souled Janaka.
His wife was called the beautiful Satyavatī[(IV)]*. [31]*

---

55 N1/17.29a, N3 - karoti jātu na krodhaṁ (N2/17.26b - na krodhaṁ ca prakurvāṇaḥ) prajānāṁ sa narādhipaḥ.
BF/19.7a - naivodvegaṁ karoti sa prajānāṁ ca narādhipaḥ.

56 Half verse 17.29b is missing in N2.
N3, N10 - ramasyaiva (BF/19.8a - ramaṇīye) hi tadrājye lokā dharmaparāyaṇāḥ.

57 N1/17.30a, N3 - bahupuṣpaphalā vṛkṣā (BF/19.8b - bahupuṣpāḥ kālavṛkṣā) bahukṣīrāś (N10 - b(v)ahudhārāś) ca dhenavaḥ.
N2/17.28a - gāvaś ca b(v)ahudhākṣīrā[ś] cāmṛtaṁ praphullā drumāḥ.
N4/17.29b, N8/17.31a, Ra/14.29b - bahukṣīrapradā gāvo drumāḥ puṣpaphalānvitāḥ.
N7/17.29b - gāṅg(a)ā dadāti bahukṣīrām amṛtāṁś ca phalādrumān.

58 N1/17.30b, N3, N10 - dīrghāyuṣaḥ prajāḥ sarvās (N4/17.30a, N8/17.31b, Ra/14.30a - tejasvinyaś ca dhārmikāḥ. N7/17.30a - tejasvinaś ca dhārmiṇaḥ) tejaḥsatyātidhārmiṇaḥ.
N2/17.28b - dhanavanto janāḥ sarve tejovantaś ca dhārmikāḥ.
BF/19.9a - dīrghāyuṣaḥ prajāḥ sarvā rogavyādhivivarjitāḥ.

59 Following N2/17.29a, N4/17.30b, N7/17.30b, N8/17.32a, Ra/14.30b.
N1/17.31a - evaṁvidhā (BF/19.9b - evaṁvidhaṁ) hi tad rāj(av)yaṁ nareś(s)asya (BF/19.9b - janakasya) mahātmanaḥ.
VP/206.31a - evaṁ bahuguṇopetaṁ tasya rājyaṁ mahātmanaḥ.

60 N1/17.31b, N3, N10, BF/19.10a - tasya (N2/17.29b - yasya) bhāryā (N2/17.29b,N4/17.31a, N7/17.31a, N8/17.32b, Ra/14.31a - 'ti vikhyātā) samākhyātā (Bo/18.8a - patnī surūpāsīn) nāmnā satyavatī śubhā.
VP/206.27b - tasya rūpavatī nāma patnī priyahite ratā.

sarvalakṣaṇasaṁpannā sarvadharmaparāyaṇā[61]
bhārtṛdevamatiḥ sādhvī nityaṁ dharme dṛḍhavratā[62] [32]
pativratā patiprāṇā bhartṛvākye sadā ratā[63]
hṛṣṭe svāmini saṁhṛṣṭā duḥkhite caiva duḥkhitā[64] [33]
parivāre samaste sā bhukte bhartari bhojitā[65]

She was endowed with all the good signs, totally devoted to all Dharma (laws).
She was devoted to her husband, as if he were God, always well disposed, firm in Dharma. [32]
(She was) loyal to her husband, whom she considered as dear as her life, and was always pleased with his words.
She rejoiced in her lord's joy and grieved in his sorrow. [33]
She would eat only after her entire retinue and her husband had taken food.

---

61 N1/17.32a, N3, N10 - sarvalakṣaṇasaṁpannā (N4/17.31b, N8/17.33a, Ra/14.31b - sadā dharmaparāyaṇā) sarvadharmaparāyaṇā(ḥ).
N2/17.30a, N7/17.31b, Bo/18.8b - sarvalakṣaṇasaṁpūrṇā (BF/19.10b - satyavrataparāyaṇā) sarvadharmaparāyaṇā.

62 N1/17.32b, N10 - mātṛdevamatī (N3 - bhartṛdevamatī) sādhvī (N7/17.32a - bhartuś ca devabhaktiś ca) nityaṁ dh(v)arme dṛḍhavratā.
Verse 17.32b-33a is missing in N2.
N4/17.32a, N8/17.33b, Ra/14.32a - gurubhaktā devabhaktā dvijabhaktā dṛḍhavratā.

63 N3, Bo/18.9a -pativratā patiprāṇā (BF/19.11a - bhartṛvākye (N7/17.3b - bharttuḥ vākye) sadā ratā.
N4/17.32b, N8/17.34a, Ra/14.32b - pativratā patimānī pativākye sadā sthitā.
VP/206.28 - sā cāpi śubhasarvāṅgī patibhaktā pativratā
prityā paramayā yuktā bhartur vacanakāriṇī.

64 N1/17.33b, N10 - hṛṣṭasvāmini sā hṛṣṭā duḥkhite caiva duḥkhitā.
N2/17.30b-31a - sukhito bhavati sukhitā duḥkhite cātiduḥkhitā
tuṣṭe ca tuṣṭi(a)saṁyuktā hy atuṣṭe priyavādinī.
N4/17.33a, N8/17.34b, Ra/14.33a - sukhini svāmini sukhā bhartṛduḥkhena duḥkhitā.
N7/17.33a - sukhit(o)e svāmi s(m)ukhitā duḥkhitena ca duḥkhitā(s).
BF/19.12a - bhartuḥ saukhyena sukhitā bhartur duḥkhena duḥkhitā.
Bo/18.9b - sukhite sukhitā nityaṁ duḥkhite duḥkhitā ca yā.

65 N1/17.34a, N10 - parivāre samaste ca bhukte (N2/17.31b - sā bhuṅkte) bhartari (N3 - bhojitā, N2/17.31b - bhuñjate) bhojati.
N4/17.33b-34a, N8/17.35, Ra/14.33b-34a - tuṣṭe tuṣṭimatī tasmin kruddhe ca priyavādinī

evaṁ bahuguṇair yuktā patnī janakabhūpateḥ[66] [34]
janakasya priyātīva dharmādiṣu sahāyinī[67]
idaṁ vimānam āruhya prayātā sāmarāvatīṁ[68] [35]
śakrādidevataiḥ sarvair vanditā sā mahātmabhiḥ[69]

Really endowed with many virtues, was king Janaka's wife, [34]
a helpmate to Janaka in Dharma, etc., very beloved by him.
Riding on a celestial car, she arrived in Amarāvatī[(V)]*. [35]*
Indra and all the gods, those high-souled, praised her.

---

bhukte bhartari yā(ṁ) bhukte parivārasamanvitā.
BF/19.12b - hṛṣṭā bhartari santuṣṭe kruddhe 'pi parivādinī.

66 Additional half verse:
N2/17.32b, N7/17.34b - pativratā mahāpuṇyā sarvabhūtahite ratā.
N4/17.34b, N8/17.36a, Ra/14.34b - etair etādṛśair anyaiḥ strīguṇaiḥ samalaṅkṛtā.
N7/17.35a - evaṁ b(v)ahugaṇair yuktā patnī janakabhūpateḥ.
BF/19.14b - evaṁ guṇaiḥ samāyuktā rājapa(u)tn(r)ī manoharā.

67 N1/17.35a, N3, N10 - janakasya priyātīva dharmā(a)diṣu sahāyinī.
N2/17.33a, N7/17.35b - janakasya priyā bhāryyā (BF/19.16a - dharmakāmārthamokṣakā, Bo/18.11a - dharmakārye sadā ratā) dharmakāmādisaukhyadā.
N4/17.35, N8/17.36b-37a, Ra/14.35 - nāmnā satyavatī vipra patnī janakabhūpateḥ
sā cāyuṣi gate nāśaṁ kāladharmmam upāgatā.

68 N1/17.35b, N10 - idaṁ (BF/19.16b - divyaṁ) vimānam āruhya (N2/17.33b - ārūḍhā) [pra]yātā (N3 - sā sabhūpate) sāmarāvatī[ṁ].
N4/17.36a, N8/17.37a, Ra/14.36a - varaṁ vimānam ārūḍhā prayātā cāmarāvatīṁ.
N7/17.36a - pitāmahena sā rājñī iyaṁ vimānam ārūḍhā prayātā sāmarāvatīṁ.
Bo/18.11b - sā yāti brahmaṇo lokaṁ vimānavaram āsthitā.

69 N2/17.34a - śakrādyā devatā(s)ḥ sarvās tasyā[ḥ] sammukham āgatāḥ.
N3 - śakrādidevataiḥ sarve vanditā sā mahātmabhiḥ.
N4/17.36b, N8/17.38a, Ra/14.36b - śakro devagaṇaiḥ sārddhaṁ tadagre nirgato dvija.
N7/17.36b - ś(s)akrādidevatā[ḥ] sarvās tasyāḥ sammukhanirgatāḥ.
BF/19.17a - sarve śakrādayo devā nirgatās tatra sammukhaṁ.
Bo/18.12a - śakrādayo devagaṇās tasyāḥ sammukham āgatāḥ.

stutiṁ karoti satataṁ svayaṁ tasyāḥ prajāpatiḥ[70] [36]
sāgatā ratham āruhya nṛtyagītādiśobhitaṁ[71]
aham ugreṇa rūpeṇa sthitas tena bhayākulaḥ[72] [37]
gṛhāntare gatā dūtā mayā te ca nivartitāḥ[73] [38]
nāsiketa uvāca
evaṁ hi kathayāmāsa nāradasya yamo hi vai[74]
tatas te cāgatā dūtā dharmājñākāriṇo 'khilāḥ[75] [39]

Prajāpati himself continually praised her, [36]
when she arrived riding in a chariot, accompanied by beautiful songs and dances, etc.
I was standing there in my terrible form, frightened by her, (and) [37]
the messengers went into another house, sent by me". [38]
Nāsiketa said
This is what Yama told Nārada there.
The messengers arrived, performing Dharmarāja's orders, [39]

---

70 N2/17.34b, N7/17.37a - pitāmahena sā rājñī praṇipatya (BF/19.17b - samarcitā) stuti(ṣ)ḥ kṛtā(ḥ).
N3 - stutiṁ karoti satataṁ svayaṁ yasyā prajāpatiḥ.
Bo/18.12b - pitāmahaś ca tasyā vai praṇatiṁ kṛtavān vibho.

71 N2/17.35a - vimāne ropitā sā vai gītanṛtyādiśobhitā(ḥ).
N7/17.37b - vimānāruhya satyātmā gītanṛtyādiś(s)obhitā.
BF/19.18a - sā vimānasamārūḍhā gītavāditraśobhitā.

72 N2/17.35b-37a - āgatā śāsane cāsya (N7/17.38a - cāsmin) mahādīptā pativratā.
rūpeṇogreṇa dagdho 'haṁ tena vai (N7/17.38b - tenāhaṁ) bhayamāgataḥ.
Verse number N2/17.36 is skipped.
BF/19.18b - tasyā darśanamātreṇa pāpāś copahatā bhayāt.

73 N2/17.37b - tato gṛhāṁ tasmin dūtās tasya nivarjitāḥ.
Additional half verse: N2/17.38a - mahāsatyamahāprājñī kathitā sā tapasvinī.
N7/17.39a - gatī gṛhāntare svasya dūtās tasmān nivarttitāḥ.

74 N1/17.39a, N3 - evaṁ kathayatas tatra nāradasya yamasya ca.
N2/17.38b - evaṁ hi kathayāmāsa nā[radas]ya (N7/17.40a - yamasya ca) yamo hi vai.
N4/17.39b, N8/17.41a, Ra/14.39b - evaṁ vadati tat sarvaṁ nāradāya yame tadā.

75 N2/17.39a - tatas te āgatā dūtā dharmasvājñā[ṁ] (N7/17.40b - kṛtā narāḥ) tu kārakāḥ.
N3 - tatas te cāgatās tatra dharmājñākāriṇo 'khilā[ḥ].
N4/17.40a, Ra/14.40a - tat kṣaṇād āgatā dūtā (N8/17.41b - dharmasyājñavarākarāḥ) dharmasyājñakarāvarāḥ.
BF/18.25a - sabhāṁ praviṣṭās te dūtā yamasya vaśavartinaḥ.

praṇipatyāstuvan sarve dharmarājāgrataḥ sthitāḥ[76] [40]
dūtā ūcuḥ
kathayasva kathaṁ śāstiṁ vaivasvata vidadhmahe[77]
pāpakarmasu duṣṭeṣu viruddhācārakāriṣu[78] [41]
atha dharmo 'bravīd vākyaṁ dūtānāṁ śāstikāraṇaṁ[79]
māvilaṁbaṁ kurudhvaṁ bho pāpānāṁ tāḍane punaḥ[80] [42]
mamājñākārā ye dūtāḥ śaṅkārahitakiṅkarāḥ[81]

all prostrating, full of praise, in front of Dharmarāja. [40]
The messengers said
"Tell us, O Vaivasvata[(VI)]*, what punishment we should execute on evil doers, the wicked, (and) on those who misbehave?" [41]*
Then Yama[(VII)] *told the punishing messengers:*
"Without delay, do the work of punishing the sinners. [42]
You messengers, fearless servants, who carry out my orders".

---

76 N1/17.40, N10 - praṇipaty(a)āstuvan sa(ā)rve dharmrājāgrataḥ sthitā[ḥ].
Verse 17.40 is missing in N2.
N3 - praṇipatyāb(v)ruvan vākyaṁ dharmarājāgrata[ḥ] sthitāḥ.

77 N3 - kathayasva kathaṁ śāstaṁ vaivasvata vidadhmahe.
N2/17.39b - kathaṁ śaktiṁ kariṣyāmaḥ kathaṁ (-)pānu tāḍanaṁ.

78 N1/17.41b - pāpakarmasu duṣṭeṣu virūḍhācārakārm(ar)eṣu.
Half verse 17.41b is missing in N2.

79 N10 - atha dharmo 'bravīd vākyaṁ dūtān āśāstikāraṇaṁ.
N2/17.40 - etad dharma mahā(i)rāja duḥkhaṁ dattaṁ tvayā 'dhunā
atha dharmo 'vadad vākyaṁ dūtānāṁ śast(r)adhāriṇāṁ.
N3 - atha dharmo 'bravīd vākyaṁ (dharmarājāgratasthitaḥ - misplaced) dūtānāṁ śāstikāraṇaṁ.
N4/17.42a, N8/17.43b, Ra/14.42a - iti dūtavacaḥ śrutvā yamo 'py āhānuyāyinaḥ.

80 N1/17.42b, N10 - māv(c)ilaṁbaṁ ca kurute pāpināṁ (N3 - tāḍayantu ca) tāḍayanti te.
N2/17.41a, N4/17.42b, N8/17.44a, Ra/14.42b - māv(c)ilaṁbaṁ kurudhvaṁ bho pāpānāṁ tāḍane pun(tr)a[ḥ].

81 Additional verse - N2/17.41b-42a:
yathā yogyaṁ tathā kāryyaṁ (N3 - śrutvedaṁ nirgatas tataḥ) śrutvā dūtā vi[ni]rgatāḥ
satvarākrodhasaṁyuktā(ḥ) (N3 - b(v)rahmadaṇḍodyataiḥ karaiḥ) b(v)rahmadaṇḍakaroddhatāḥ.
N2/17.42b - tāḍayanti ca pāpiṣṭhān (N3 - sma te pāpā[n]) niḥśaṅkās te ca kiṅkarā(n)ḥ.

mudgarair niśitair daṇḍaiḥ śaktikuntaiś ca yaṣṭibhiḥ[82] [43]
vikṛṣyante ca te pāpā yamadūtair mahābalaiḥ[83]
dhāryante pāpino bhārā dakṣiṇasyān tato diśi[84] [44]
evaṁ dṛṣṭā mayā tatra baddhāś ca svāmighātakāḥ[85]
yānti vaitaraṇīṁ ghorām apārām atidurgamāṁ[86] [45]
tatra te tāḍitāḥ pāpāḥ pibanti kila śoṇitaṁ[87]

With mallets, sharpened sticks, powerful spears, and maces, [43]
the mighty messengers of Yama, drag those sinners,
loaded with burdens, towards the Southern region. [44]
And I also saw there bound master-killers,
going on the terrible, very hard-to-cross Vaitaraṇī, with no other bank (in sight). [45]
The sinners are tortured there, drinking blood, indeed.

N4/17.44b, N8/17.46a, Ra/14.44b - tāḍayanti ca tān pāpān niḥśaṅkaṁ brāhmaṇottamāḥ.

N7/17.44a - tāḍayanti ca pāpānāṁ niḥś(s)aṅkās te 'pi kiṅkarāḥ.

82 N1/17.43b - mudgarair niśitair daṇḍai[ḥ] śaktikuntaiś ca (N3, N7/17.44 - yaṣṭibhiḥ) yādṛśaiḥ.

N2/17.43a - mudgarair niśitaiḥ khaṅgai(ś)ḥ (N4/17.45a, N8/17.46b, Ra/14.45a - khaḍgaiḥ) śaktibhir yaṣṭibhis tathā.

83 N1/17.44a - vikṛṣyanti ca [tān] pāpān yamadūtamahābalāḥ.

N2/17.43b - hanyamānāś ca (N4/17.46a, N8/17.47b, Ra/14.46a - dūyamānās tu, N7/17.45a - hanyamānās tu) nīyante yamadūtair mahāb(v)alaiḥ.

N3 - vikṛṣyanti ca t(e)ān pāpā[n] yamadūtā mahāb(v)alāḥ.

84 N2/17.44a, N7/17.45b - [dhā]vanto bhayasantrastā diśaṁ durddharadakṣiṇāṁ.

N3 - dhāvanto pāpino bhīt(o)ā dakṣiṇasyāṁ (N10 - tato diśi) diśi tataḥ.

85 N1/17.45a - evaṁ dṛṣṭ(v)ā mayā tatra (N2/17.44b - b(v)rahmaghnāḥ svāmighātināḥ) baddhāś ca (N3, N10, N4/17.46b, N7/17.46a, N8/17.47c, Ra/14.46b - brahmaghnāḥ) svāmighātakāḥ.

86 N1/17.45b, N3, N10 - yānti vaitaraṇī[ṁ] ghorām (N2/17.45a - śīrṇayā[ṁ] s(śma)ā durātmanaḥ) apārām atidurgamāṁ.

N4/17.47a, N8/17.47d, Ra/14.47a - dṛṣṭā vaitariṇī ghorā mahāpāpadurāsadā.

87 N1/17.46a - tatra nityapitāḥ (N3 - tatrātitṛṣitāḥ) pāpā[ḥ] pibanti kila śoṇitaṁ.

N2/17.45b - tatra te tāḍitāḥ pāpāḥ pibanti hy atiśoṇitaṁ.

N4/17.47b, N8/17.48a, Ra/14.47b - pūyaśoṇitasaṁpūrṇā śāsane pāpakārmiṇāṁ.

sā sarid rudhirāpūrṇā vahantī pāpakarmaṇāṁ[88] [46]
mahāghorā nigarjantī durnirīkṣyā bhayaṅkarī[89]
kṛmikoṭisamākīrṇā bahuvyādhiprapūritā[90] [47]
mahāghorātivipulā sevitā kṛṣṇapannagaiḥ[91]
tanmadhye patitāḥ pāpās teṣāṁ trātā na vidyate[92] [48]
duṣṭamārge yamadvāre durnirīkṣye bhayaṅkare[93]
tasya darśanamātreṇa pāpāḥ syur gatacetanāḥ[94] [49]
na pāraṁ dṛśyate tasyā dustarātibhayaṅkarā[95]

That blood-red stream carries the evildoers, [46]
roaring, terrible, hard-to-look-at, frightening,
full of millions of worms, infested with many diseases, [47]
very terrible, very wide, frequented by black serpent-demons –
there is no rescue for the sinners who fall into it. [48]
(That) bad road at Yama's door, hard-to-look-at, frightening,
just by looking at it[(VIII)]*, the sinners may lose their minds. [49]*
It is terrifying, most difficult-to-traverse, (and) its other shore cannot be seen.

---

88 N1/17.46b - saṁsāre rudhirāpūraṁ vahantī pāpakaryaṇāṁ.
N2/17.46a - duṣkarmaṇāṁ śvāsa (-) ca (N7/17.47b - ś(s)āsanaṁ pāpakarmāṇāṁ) vahanti pāpanirdayāḥ.
N3 - sā sarid rudhirāpūrṇā vahantī pāpakarmaṇā[ṁ].

89 N1/17.47a, N10 - mahāghorā nigarjanti durnirīkṣy(a)ā bhayāvahā(ḥ).
N2/17.46b - garja(n)tī ca mahāghorā(ṁ) (N7/17.48a - garjatīti mahāghorā) durn(n)irīkṣ[y]ā bhayaṅkarī.
Verse 17.47 is missing in N3.
N4/17.48a, N8/17.48b, Ra/14.48a - garjatīva mahāghorā durn(n)irīkṣyā bhayaṅkarā.

90 N4/17.48b, N8/17.49a, Ra/14.48b - kṛmikoṭisamākīrṇā b(v)ahuv(b)ṛścikapūritā.

91 N1/17.48a - mahāghorātivipulā (N4/17.49a, N8/17.49b, Ra/14.49a - mahāyāmātivistārā) sevitā kṛṣṇapa[nnag]aiḥ.
N2/17.47b - mahāghorātibahulā mahālolasamanvitā.

92 N2/17.48b - tanmadhye prālapan (N3 - patitā[ḥ]) pāpās (N4/17.50a, N8/17.50b, Ra/14.50a - tatra santāḍyamānānāṁ) trātā teṣāṁ na vidyate.

93 N1/17.49a - durgamārge yamadvāre durnirīkṣyabhayaṅkare.
Verses 17.49-55 are missing in N2.
N3 - duṣṭamārge yamadvāre durnirīkṣ[y]e bhayaṅkare.

94 N1/17.49b, N10 - tasya darśanamātreṇa pāpāḥ syur (N3 - gatacetasaḥ) gatacetanāḥ.

95 N1/17.50a - nāparaṁ dṛśyate tatra dustarāntabhayaṅkarā(ḥ).

āvartaśatasahasraiḥ pātāle yānti pāpinaḥ[96] [50]
kṣaṇaṁ tiṣṭhanti pātāle kṣaṇaṁ duḥparivartinaḥ[97]
pāpināṁ kāraṇāyaiva pūyaśoṇitavāhinī[98] [51]
puṇyātmānaś ca paśyanti madhusarpirvahāṁ hi tāṁ[99]
godānena ca kurvanti pāraṁ gacchanti tatkṣaṇāt[100] [52]
ye cānnam atithibhyaś ca bhayārtābhayadās tathā[101]
dānān paṇyāni yacchanti ullaṅghante mahānadīṁ[102] [53]
parastrīgāmino ye ca paradravyāpahārakāḥ
te nadīmadhyagāḥ pāpā bhakṣyante sarpavṛścikaiḥ[103] [54]
tyaktadārasutā duṣṭā raudrāś ca priyavādinaḥ[104]

Revolving, hundreds of thousands of sinners go to the crowded Pātāla(IX)*. [50]*
The moment they arrive at Pātāla, immediately they (start) rotating miserably.
For the sinners, the river flows with pus and blood, (while) [51]
the righteous see that river flowing with honey and butter.
Those who donate cows go to the other shore right away. [52]
Those who (give) food to guests, and soothe (people) full of fear,
those who donate commodities, leap over that great river. [53]
Those who have sexual intercourse with others' wives, as well as those who steal others' property,
those sinners go to the midst of the river, to be eaten by serpents and scorpions. [54]
Those appalling flatterers, and those wicked who abandon wife and children,

---

96 N1/17.50b - āvartarājasahasraiḥ pātāle (N3, N10 - āvartaśatasāhasraiḥ pātālaṁ) yānti pāpinaḥ.

97 N3, N10 - kṣaṇaṁ tiṣṭha[n]ti pātāle kṣ(l)aṇ(ā)[aṁ] du[ḥ]parivartina[ḥ].

98 N3 - pāpināṁ kāraṇāyaiva pūyaśoṇita(r)vāhinī.

99 N1/17.52a - puṇyātmānaś ca paśyanti madhusarpir va vāhinī(ā)ṁ.

100 N3 - godānaṁ ye ca gacchanti bhayārttābhayadās tathā.
N10 - godānaṁ ye t(p)u k(v)urv(dh)anti pāraṁ gaccha[n]ti tatkṣaṇāt.

101 N1/17.53a - ye cānnam atithibhyaś ca bhayārtābhayadā(a)s tathā.
First pāda of 17.53a is combined with the second pāda of 17.52b in N3.

102 N1/17.53b - dānān(ty) [p]a[ṇy](n)āni gacchanti calanty ete (N10 - laṅgha(e)nte te) mahānadī.
N3 - dānān paṇ(n)yāni(ī) yacchanti ullaṅghante mahānadīṁ.

103 N3 - tān nadīmadhyagāḥ pāpā bhakṣyante sarpavṛścikaiḥ.

104 N1/17.55a - tyaktā dārasutā duṣṭā raudrāś ca priyavādinaḥ.
N2/17.49a - tyajanti putrān dārān ye adha[mā]satyavādinaḥ.
N3 - tyaktadārasutā dṛṣṭā raudrā apriyavādinaḥ.

dāṁbhikā lobhasaṁyuktās tathā mithyābhilāṣiṇaḥ[105] [55]
viśvāsaghnāḥ kṛtaghnāś ca apakāraparāyaṇāḥ[106]
ātmadharmaṁ parityajya paradharmaparāyaṇāḥ[107] [56]
klībavṛttiratā mūḍhāḥ paradāraratāḥ sadā[108]
vratabhaṅgakarā ye ca ātmāṅge liṅgadhāriṇaḥ[109] [57]
vaitariṇyāṁ ciraṁ kālaṁ dhāryante pāpino narāḥ[110] [58]

lustful hypocrites, and those seized with improper desire, [55]
those who breach faith, killers, and those who are engaged in inflicting injury,
those who abandon their own Dharma and adhere to others' Dharma(X)*, [56]*
those fools who live as impotents, attached to others' wives,
those who break their vows, and those who wear liṅga(XI) *on their limbs, [57]*
(all those) sinful people are held for a long time in the Vaitaraṇī Hell. [58]

---

105 N1/17.55b, N10 - dām[bh]ikā lobhasaṁyuktās tathā (N3 - mithyābhibhāṣiṇaḥ) mithyābhilāṣiṇaḥ.

106 N1/17.56a - viśvāsaghnāḥ kṛtaghnāś ca (N2/17.48a - any(v)e[du]ṣṭo ya[ś] cāriṇaḥ) a(u)pakāraparāyaṇā[ḥ].
N4/17.51b, N8/17.52a, Ra/14.51b - viśvāsaghnāḥ suhṛdghnāś ca durācārās tathaiva ca.

107 N2/17.49b - ātmadharmaparityāgī (N7/17.50a - ātmadharmaṁ parityāgī) durbhikṣye ca palātinaḥ.
N2/17.50b - ātmadharmaparityajya paradharmaparāyaṇaḥ.
N4/17.52a, N8/17.52b, Ra/14.52a - parityaktātmadharmāś ca durbhikṣe svāṁs tyajānti ye.

108 Emendation - DS. N1/17.57a, N10 - klīb(v)avṛttiratā (N3 - klīb(v)avṛttikarā) mūḍhāḥ (N4/17.52b, N8/17.53a, Ra/14.52b - paravāde sadā ratāḥ) parivāraratāḥ (N2/17.50a - paradāra[ra]tāḥ) sadā.

109 Emendation - NK. N1/17.57b - vratabhaṅgakarā ye ca (N2/17.51a - [a]liṅge liṅgadhā[riṇ]āḥ) ātmaṁ cā(o)liṅgadhāriṇaḥ.
N4/17.53a, N8/17.53b, Ra/14.53a - vratabhaṅgakarā pāpās tathānucitāliṅginaḥ.
N7/17.51a - vratabhaṅgaśramāṇāṁ ca aliṅgā liṅgadhāriṇaḥ.

110 N2/17.51b - dhāryante suciraṁ kālaṁ te vai (N7/17.51b - vaitaraṇī nadī) vaitaraṇīnadīṁ.
N10 - vaitaraṇyāṁ [ci]ra(tā)ṁ kālaṁ dhāryyante pātito narāḥ.
N4/17.53b, N8/17.53c, Ra/14.53b - vadhyante suciraṁ kālaṁ vaitariṇyāṁ tu pāpinaḥ.

iti śrībrahmāṇḍapurāṇe nāsiketopākhyāne yamanāradasaṁvāde saptadaśo 'dhyāyaḥ

This is the seventeenth chapter of the Nāsiketa story, pertaining to the Brahmāṇḍa Purāṇa, called – the dialogue between Yama and Nārada.

Translation Notes

I – In other versions – the righteous messengers.
II – Here Nāsiketa is addressing his father.
III – Literally – "striding beyond", one of Viṣṇu's names.
IV – Identical to Candravatī's mother name (3.20a).
V – Indra's capital. According to other versions she came along with her husband, the king.
VI – Yama.
VII – In the text – "Dharma", for Dharmarāja.
VIII – The Vaitaraṇī River.
IX – The lower regions of Hell.
X – Probably – those who quit their own caste and pretend belonging to another.
XI – False marks.

Chapter 18

The Holy Examination of Dharma

nāsiketa uvāca
punaś cāhaṁ pravakṣyāmi janma yena śubhāśubhaṁ[1]
yatpuṇyam adhikaṁ karma sadā satyarataḥ śuciḥ[2] [1]
satyam evānyajanmani mānuṣatve bhavet punaḥ[3]
caturāśītilakṣāṇi jīvānām api saṅkhyayā[4] [2]
yoniḥ sarvāḥ paribhramya tato yāti manuṣyatāṁ[5]

Again I am going to tell (you) of the birth taken by the virtuous and non-virtuous.
He whose acts are always aimed at purity, who is clean (and) adheres to truth, [1]
will indeed be born again in human form, of truthful nature,
(to lead) a life characterized by eighty four (good) signs. [2]
Having wandered in all (kinds of) wombs, he will thus be born as human.

---

1 N1/18.1a, N3/18.1a - punaś cāhaṁ pravakṣyāmi (N7/18.1a - janma yena kṛtaṁ śubhaṁ) janme yena śubhāśubhaṁ.
N4/18.1a, N8/18.1a, Ra/15.1a - punaś cedaṁ pravakṣyāmi yena pāpena yad bhavet.

2 N1/18.1b, N10 - tatpuṇyam adhikaṁ karmaṁ sadā satyarataḥ śuciḥ.
N2/18.1b - yatpuṇyam saṁyutaṁ karma kṛtaṁ vai śubhajantubhiḥ.
N4/18.1b, N8/18.1b, Ra/15.1b - janma puṁsāṁ tathā strīṇāṁ śruyatām avadhānataḥ.
N7/18.1b - yaḥ puṇyavān mahāprājñaḥ sa(n)dā satyarataḥ śuciḥ.

3 N2/18.2a - sampa(-)ānu yaj janma mānuṣatve bhavat punaḥ.
N3/18.2a - satyatvaṁ nijajanmāni mānuṣatve bhavet punaḥ.
N4/18.2, N8/18.2, Ra/15.2 - janmany ekatra yat puṇyaṁ pāpaṁ vā vihitaṁ purā
janmāntaro 'pi tatraiva naraḥ saṁsaktacetasaḥ.

4 N2/18.2b, N3/18.2b, N10 - caturāśītilakṣ(y)āṇi jīvān(j)ām api saṅkhyayā.
No more verse numbers after N3/18.2.
N4/18.3a, N8/18.3a, Ra/15.3a - caturāśītilakṣeṣu bhrāmaṁ bhrāmaṁ hi yoniṣu.

5 N2/18.3a - sarvayonau (N10 - yoniḥ sardhā) paribh[rām]ya tato yāti manuṣyatāṁ.
The right edge of page 61 in N2 is cut, and a few verses are fragmented.
N7/18.3a - yonī[ḥ] sarvā[ḥ] paribhramya tataḥ pāpī pramucyatāṁ.

atha pāpī naro yāti kadācin mānuṣīṁ tanuṁ[6] [3]
nīcanirdayavaṁśeṣu sthitvā āyuḥ samāpayet[7]
punas tenaiva pāpena pīḍyate so 'nyajanmani[8] [4]
goghnaś caiva bhavet pūrvaṁ cāṇḍālatve bhaved bahiḥ[9]
duṣṭayoniṣu cānyeṣu vyādhirogeṇa pīḍyate[10] [5]
gurutalpagatā ye ca gurubhāryāṁ bhajanti ye[11]

But the sinful man will never be born (again) as human, [3]
(and) his stay as a human being will be consumed in an excessively short lineage.
He who sins again, will be tortured in other births. [4]
He who has once killed a cow, will be reborn many times as a Cāṇḍāla[(l)]*,*
to unchaste women, tortured by sickness and disease. [5]
Those who defile their Guru's bed and enjoy their Guru's wife,

---

[6] N1/18.3b, N10, N3 - atha pāpī naro (N4/18.3b, N8/18.3b, Ra/15.3b - pāpātmā tu tato) yāti kathañcin mānuṣīṁ (N7/18.3b - mānuṣaṁ) tanuṁ.

[7] N2/18.4a - nīcanirdayavaṁśeṣu sthitvā (-)āyuṣakṣayaḥ (short).
N3 - nīcanirddhanavaṁśeṣu sthitvā āyuḥ sama(ā)rthayet.

[8] N1/18.4b - punas tenaiva duṣkṛtye pīḍyate (N7/18.4b - naiva janmani) so 'nyajanmani.
N2/18.4b - punas tenaiva pāpena tāḍyate janmajanmani.
N3 - naratve naiva duḥkṛtve pīḍyate te 'nyajanmani.
N10 - puna(ḥ)s tenaiva duḥkṛtve (N4/18.4b, N8/18.4b, Ra/15.4b - tatas tenaiva pāpena) pīḍyate so 'nyajanmani.

[9] N1/18.5a, N3, N10 - goghnā(c)ś caiva bhavet pūrvaṁ cāṇḍālatve bhaved b(v)ahi[ḥ].
N2/18.5a - gohatyā ye prakurvante te cāṇḍā bhavanti hi.
N4/18.6a, N8/18.6a, Ra/15.6a - goghno janmāntaro pāpāc cāṇḍālo jāyate dhruvaṁ.
N7/18.5a - goghnāś ca ye pravartante cāṇḍālatve bhavantu te.

[10] N1/18.5b - duṣṭayoniṣu cā(dh)nyeṣu nirogeṇa ca pīḍyate.
N2/18.5b - [mārga]grāhī pareṣāṁ yo rogeṇa paripīḍyate.
N10 - duṣṭayoniṣu vānyādhirogeṇa [ca] pīḍyate.
N4/18.6b, N8/18.6b, Ra/15.6b - mārgagrahī tathā rogaiḥ pīḍyate 'nyatra janmani.
N7/18.5b - mārg(m)agrahī janmavyādhirogeṣu jāyate naraḥ.

[11] N1/18.6a - gurutalpakarā ye ca (N3 - gurubhāryāṁ dharanti y(ai)e) gurubhāryā[ṁ] bhajanti te.
N2/18.6-7a - garado 'nṛtavādī ca duṣkarmā gurutalpagaḥ

icchayā bhajate pāpaḥ sarvayoniṣu jāyate[12] [6]
strīghātī garbhaghātī ca pulindo jāyate bhuvi[13]
gurulopy anyajāteṣu jāyate śubhayoniṣu[14] [7]
parastrīratisantoṣī śūkaratve bhavet punaḥ[15]
brāhmaṇo vedavikretā śūdrayoniṣu jāyate[16] [8]
viśvāsamitraghātī ca pāpayoniṣu jāyate[17]
bhāṣate bhaginīṁ yas tu kāmakrīḍāṁ karoti yaḥ[18] [9]

the sinners who follows their desires, are reborn in the source of all[(II)]. *[6]*
Woman-killers and abortion-performers are born again on earth as barbarians.
Whoever takes Indra as Guru, is born in another life in a fine family. [7]
Whoever enjoys other people's wives is born again as a pig.
A Brahmin who transforms the Vedas, is born again as a Śūdra[(III)]. *[8]*
Whoever breaches a vow to a friend, will be (re)born in a sinner's womb.
It is said that whoever sleeps with his sister, [9]

(- - - - - - -) ca mūkaś caiva tathā tṛtī
gurutalpagās tu ye 'nye gurubhāryyā[ṁ] bhajanti ye.
N10 - gurutalpakarād ye va gurubhā[r]yāṁ bha(ñ)janti ye.
N7/18.6a - gurutalākarā ye ca gurunāryā bhajanti te.

12 N2/18.7b - bhajante svecchayā pāpāḥ jā[ya]ta[ḥ] sar(p)payoniṣu.
N3 - icchayā bhajate pāpa sar(p)payoniṣu jāyate.
N7/18.6b - svecchayā ramate pāpī sarvayoniṣu jāyate.

13 N10, N4/18.9a, N8/18.9a, Ra/15.9a - strīghātī garbhaghātī ca pulindo jāyate bhuvi.
Verse 18.7 is missing in N2, N3.

14 N1/18.7b, N10 - gurulopy anyajanmāni śubhāṁ yoniṣu jāyate.
N4/18.9b, N8/18.9b, Ra/15.9b - gurulopy anyajāteṣu jāyate ś(s)vānayoniṣu.

15 N1/18.8a - parastrīratisantoṣī śūkaratve (N7/18.7a - bhaved api) bhave(a)t punaḥ.
N2/18.12b - parastrīrata[ḥ] santāryā śukare (- -) jāyate.
N4/18.10a, N8/18.10a, Ra/15.10a - māṁsāhārībhaved vipraḥ sṛgālo jāyate dhruvaṁ.

16 N2/18.8a - b(v)rāhmaṇo vedavikrīta(ś)ḥ (N3 - vedavikrītā, N10 - vedavikrīti, N4/18.10b, N7/18.7b, N8/18.10b, Ra/15.10b - vedavikretā) śūdrayoniṣu jāyate.

17 Additional half verse: N3 - ye ca yoniṣu jāyante svakarmāpīḍyate ratā[ḥ].
N3, N4/18.11a, N8/18.11a, Ra/15.11a - viśvāse mitraghātī ca pāpayoniṣu jāyate.
Verse 18.9a is missing in N2.

18 N1/18.9b, N3 - bhāṣ(s)ate bhaginī[ṁ] (N10 - bhāṣate mārganī) yas tu kāmakrīḍāṁ karoti yaḥ.

paṇḍurogī bhaven mūko jvaradagdhaḥ sadā bhavet[19]
kanyāghātī mahāpāpaḥ sarvayoniṣu jāyate[20] [10]
tasmin pāpe kṣayaṁ yāti punar janmāntare bhavet[21]
pūrvadoṣaprabhāvena dāridryaṁ ca kurūpatā[22] [11]
śūdrāgāmī bhaved yas tu caṭakatve bhavet sa hi[23]

becomes ignorant and dumb, always burning with fever.
The great sinner who kills a girl, is born again in the source of all[IV]. *[10]*
He who goes towards the destruction of sins, will be reborn again as human,
deformed and poor (because of) the power of previous sins. [11]
He[V] *who has sexual intercourse with a Śūdra, is reborn as a sparrow.*

N2/18.8b - bhāṣate bhaginīṁ bhrātā kāmakrī[ḍāṁ] karoti ca.
N4/18.11b, N8/18.11b, Ra/15.11b - bhāvitvā garbhiṇa(ā)ṁ nārīṁ saṅkrīḍayati yo naraḥ.

19 N2/18.9a - paṇḍurogī bhaven mūko (N4/18.12a, N8/18.12a, Ra/15.12a - jvaladāsyaḥ sadā ca saḥ) vai jvarādha(s)ḥ sa hā (N3 - jvaradādhaḥ (N10, N7/18.8b - jvara[dag]dha[ḥ]) sadā) bhavet.

20 N2/18.9b - kanyāghātī mahāpāpī sarppa[yo]niṣu (N3, N4/18.12b, N8/18.12b, Ra/15.12b - śavareṣu (N7/18.9a - samareṣu) ca) jāyate.
N10 - kanyāghātī mahāpāpaḥ sarvayoniṣu jāyate.

21 N1/18.11a, N3, N7/18.9b, N10 - tataḥ pāpakṣayaṁ yāti ekam anyat karoti ca.
Verse 18.11 is missing in N2. Additional verses - N2/18.10-12a:
kharo vai b(v)ahudhābhū(t)d vā . . . . yoniṣu jāyate
avidyāṁ (-)praya(-)ec ca vṛṣa(-) jāyate naraḥ
vipro 'parokṣabhogī ca śūkaro vijane vane
jyāṁsāhāro bhaved yas tu sṛgālann abhijāyate
nirbhayaḥ pāpakarmabhyo vyādh(u)iyoniṣu jāyate.
N4/18.13a, N8/18.13a, Ra/15.13a - tasmin pāpe kṣayaṁ yāte punar janmāntare bhavet.

22 N3 - pūrvadoṣaprabhāvena (N7/18.10a - daridraś ca kurūpatā) daridraṁ ca kurūpatāṁ.
N4/18.13b, N8/18.13b, Ra/15.13b - pūrvajanmaprabhāvena daridraś ca kurūpadhṛk.

23 N2/18.14b - sadākāmī bhaved (N3 - yasva) yas tu (N10 - caṭakatve bhavet sa hi, N7/18.10b - ciṭakatve bhaved iti) kaṭukatvam avāpnuyāt.
N4/18.14a, N8/18.14a, Ra/15.14a - sadākāmī ca puruṣaḥ vaṭako jāyate dhruvaṁ.

pakṣacchedī bhaved yas tu kṛmiyoniṣu jāyate[24] [12]
vastracauraḥ paradveṣī rajakaḥ so 'pi jāyate[25]
ratnahārī ca vai duṣṭaḥ phale kaṭakahā kṛmiḥ[26] [13]
svāmighātī mahāpāpaḥ pāṣāṇe kīṭako bhavet[27]
dhanahārī bhaved andho janmāndhaḥ pustakaṁ haret[28] [14]
gṛdhro mṛtyuvaśaṁ yāti mārjāraś ca bhavet punaḥ[29]

Whoever cuts (birds) wings is reborn as a worm. [12]
People who hate others, who steal clothes, will be reborn as washmen(VI).
The bad man, who steals jewels, will end up as an insect worm in fruit. [13]
A great sinner, who kills his master, is reborn as an insect in a stone.
Whoever steals a gift will become blind; whoever steals a book will be reborn blind. [14]
The greedy person comes into Death's power and will be reborn as a cat.

---

24 N2/18.15a, N7/18.11a - pakṣacchede (N3 - pakṣacchedī, Ra/15.15a - vṛkṣacchede) bhaven (N4/18.14b - paṭhācchede (N8/18.14b - padacchede) bhaved) mṛtyu[ḥ] kṛmiyoniṣu jāyate.
N10 - pakṣakṣedī bhaved yas tu kṛmiyoniṣu jāyate.
N4/18.15b, N8/18.15b, Ra/15.14b - phalahārī ca duṣṭātmā phale tasmin bhavet kṛmiḥ.

25 N1/18.13a - vastracauro (N10 - vastracoro, N7/18.11b - vastracaura[ḥ]) paradveṣī rajako bhavate naraḥ.
N4/18.14a, N8/18.14a, Ra/15.15b - śāstrācāraiḥ paradveṣī rajako jāyate bhūvi.

26 N1/18.13b - ratnahārī (N10 - strīhārī) ca vai duṣṭaḥ phale kaṭukahā kṛmi.
N2/18.16a - ratnahārī ca duṣṭātmā mauktikānāṁ prahāraka[ḥ].
N3 - ratnahārī bhaved duṣṭo phale kaṭakahā kṛmiḥ.
N7/18.12a - ratnahārī ca duṣṭātmāka phale kaṭukike kṛmaḥ.

27 N2/18.16b - svāmighātī mahāpāpī (N3, N4/18.16a, N7/18.12b, N8/18.16a, Ra/15.16a - mahāpāpa) pāṣāṇe (N10 - mahāpāpaḥ pāpāṇaṁ) kīṭako bhavet.
Additional verses - N2/18.17-18a:
pratiśrutya dvijebhyo 'the madatvā jaṭuko bhavet
avikrayaṁ vikrayaghas tu vikaṭākṣo bhaven naraḥ (vi)
vivādayed dvijebhyaś ca kacchapo jāyate naraḥ.

28 N1/18.14b, N2/18.18b, N10, N7/18.13a - dhanahārī ca vadhiraḥ (N3 - vandhira(ṁ)[ḥ]) śmaśāne gṛdhratāṁ vrajet.
N4/18.16b, N8/18.16b, Ra/15.16b - dhanaharttāndhavadhiraḥ śmaśāne gṛdhrako bhavet.

29 N1/18.15a - gṛdhro mṛtyuvaṁśa (N10 - mṛtyuśaṁ) yāti mārjāro bhavate naraḥ.
N2/18.19a - gṛdhrān mṛtyuvaṁśajāto mārjāraś ca bhavet punaḥ.

prajāhīnakaro martyaḥ kṛkalāso 'pi nikṣipet[30] [15]
sūtragrāhī amedhyeṣu kīṭako bhavate punaḥ[31]
karpāsamaṇikāṁsyāni brahmavastuharāś ca ye[32] [16]
upānatkarapātraṁ ca matsyas te jalavāsinaḥ[33]
ghṛtahārī bhavet kuṣṭhī tasmin naṣṭe kṛmir bhavet[34] [17]

A man who kills (his) offspring, will be thrown (i.e. reborn) as a lizard. [15]
A (Brahmin), carrying the sacred thread, who becomes unfit to perform a sacrifice (i.e. impure), will be reborn as an insect,
as well as he who covets cotton cloth, and steals Brahmins' property. [16]
(Those who steal) shoes and leather cups for drinking, will be (reborn as) fish in water.
He who steals Ghee of any colour, perishes there, becoming a worm. [17]

N3 - gṛdhro mṛtyuvaśaṁ yāti mārjjāraṁ tu bhavet punaḥ.
N4/18.17a, Ra/15.17a - b(v)adhān mṛtyuvaśo (N8/18.17a - mṛtyuvase) yāti mārjjāro jāyate punaḥ.
N7/18.13b - gṛdhe mṛtyuvaṁśaṁ yāti mārjāro jāyate punaḥ.

30 N1/18.15b - prajāhīna martya[ḥ] karau kṛkalā(o)so 'pi nikṣipet.
N2/18.19b - prajāhīnākaro yas tu kṛkalāso 'bhıjāyate.
N3 - prajāhīnakaro martya[ḥ] kṛkalās(ś)o vinikṣipet.
N4/18.17b, Ra/15.17b - prajāpīḍanako rājā bhavet (N8/18.17b - kurkaṭayoniṣu) kukkuṭayoniṣu.
N7/18.14a - prajāhīnakaro mṛtyuḥ kṛkilāyoni nikṣipet.

31 N2/18.20a - hastigrāhī ca puruṣa kīṭakatve bhavec ciraṁ.
N4/18.18a, N8/18.18a, Ra/15.18a - sūtrahārī mahīmadhye kīṭo bhavati pīḍitaḥ.
N7/18.14b - sūtragrāhī amedhyena kīṭako bhavate hy api.

32 N2/18.20b - karppāsamaṇikāṁsyāni b(v)rahmasvaṁ ca haranti ye.
N3 - karpāsasanakīśaś ca b(v)rahmasvasyaharāś ca ye.
N4/18.18b, N8/18.18b, Ra/15.18b - karpāsaśaṇahārī ca b(v)rahmavastuharāś ca yaḥ.
N7/18.15a - karpāsāsaṇakāsaś ca b(v)rahmaviṣṇuharāś ca ye.

33 N1/18.17a - upānatkarapātraṁ ca matsy(cch)o 'pi jalavāsinaḥ.
N2/18.21a - upānahau hemacchatra[ḥ] matsyās te jalavāsinaḥ.
N4/18.19a, N8/18.19a, Ra/15.19a - upānahoś ca yaś cauraḥ sa matsyo jāyate jale.
N7/18.15b - upānahau karapatraṁ mṛto 'pi jalavāsinaḥ.

34 N2/18.30a - ghṛtahārī bhavet kuṣṭhī tasmān naṣṭa[ḥ] (N3 - tasmin naṣṭe, N4/18.19b, N8/18.19b, Ra/15.19b - tasmād (N7/18.16a - bhṛṣṭe) bhraṣṭaḥ) kṛmir bhavet.

māṁsahārī piśācaś ca annahārī cātṛptakaḥ[35]
tailahārī bhavet tailī tilahārī ca gardabhaḥ[36] [18]
gandhapuṣpopahārī ca mukhadurgandhir jāyate[37]
dugdhahārī ca kūrmatve jāyate jalavāsinaḥ[38] [19]
yasya śāstrakṛte pāpaṁ saptajanmāndhako bhavet[39]
tataḥ pāpāt paribhraṣṭo lomaśo bhavate punaḥ[40] [20]

He who steals meat (becomes) a monster, and he who steals food (is reborn) never satisfied. Whoever steals oil becomes an oil-monger, and he who steals sesame, becomes a donkey. [18]
Whoever steals offerings of fragrant flowers is reborn with a bad-smelling mouth. He, who steals milk, is reborn as a turtle living in water. [19]
He, who according to Śāstric rule is a sinner, is reborn seven times as a blind man, thus fallen because of sin, he is born again as a ram. [20]

---

35 N1/18.18a - māṁsahārī piśācāś ca muṇḍahārī(ś) (N10 - piśāco 'bhūd annahārī(ś)) cā(a)tṛptakaḥ.
N2/18.31a - agniṁ harati yaḥ śīte paṅgu[r] janmatrayaṁ bhavet.
N3 - māṁs(ś)aṁ hārī piśāco 'bhūt atṛpto cānnahārakaḥ.
N4/18.20a, N8/18.20a, Ra/15.20a - māṁsahārī piśācaḥ syat sūcīvaktro 'nnahārakaḥ.

36 N1/18.18b - tailahārī bhavet telī tilahārī (N2/18.30b - tailīlilahārī) ca gardabhaḥ.
N3, N7/18.17a - tailahārī bhavet tailī tilahārī (N4/18.20b,N8/18.20b - tu) ca (Ra/15.20b - madhuhārī tu) gardabhaḥ.

37 N2/18.31b - gandhapuṣpopahārī ca mukhe (N7/18.17b - durgandhi jāyate) durgandhatām iyāt.
N4/18.21a, N8/18.21a, Ra/15.21a - gandhapuṣpādihārī ca durgandho jāyate mukhe.

38 N1/18.19b - durgahārī ca karmatve (N3 - dugdhahārī ca kūrmatve) jāyate jalavāsinaḥ.
N2/18.32a - aṁb(v)uhārī bhavet kūrma utpattir jāyate jale.
N4/18.21b, N8/18.21b, Ra/15.21b - dugdhahārī tu kūrmmaḥ syāj jalavāsī jitendriyāḥ.
N7/18.18a - aṁb(v)uhārī karmatve ca jāyate (ca) jalavāsinaḥ.

39 Emendation - NK. N1/18.20a - ta sa śāstrakṛte (N2/18.32b, N3, N10 - pracchannaṁ kurute) pāpaṁ saptajanmāndhako bhavet.
N4/18.22a, N8/18.22a, Ra/15.22a - pracchannapāpakarttus tu saptajanmāndhatā bhavet.

40 N2/18.33a - tasmāc ca hi paribhraṣṭo duḥkhaśokaparo bhavet.
N3 - tataḥ pāpaparitiṣṭho lomaśo bhavate punaḥ.

nityaṁ ca krūracitto yo nakulo bhavate kila[41]
paradveṣakaraḥ krodhī jalaukā jāyate ciraṁ[42] [21]
akṛte vaiśvadeve ca bhuñjate ye dvijātayaḥ[43]
vṛthā caitena pākena kākayoniṣu jāyate[44] [22]
paścāttāpī kṛte dāne kokilo jāyate vane[45]
pitṛmātṛsuhṛd drohī bako ākāśago bhavet[46] [23]

He who is always cruel minded, is reborn as a mongoose.
An angry person, hating others, will be reborn for a long time as a leech. [21]
Brahmins who eat without performing the Vaiśvadeva rites,
(thus eating) a vainly prepared food, are reborn as crows. [22]
He, who donates and then regrets, is reborn as a cuckoo in the forest.
Whoever injures his father, mother, or his friend, is reborn as a heron. [23]

---

41 N2/18.33b - krūracittas tu nityaṁ vai nakulaś ca bhavet kila.
N3 - nityaṁ ca krūracitto yo nakulo bhavate (N7/18.19b - kila) punaḥ.
N4/18.23a, N8/18.23a, Ra/15.23a - nityaṁ krūro vikārī yo nakulo jāyate naraḥ.

42 N1/18.21b - paradveṣakarī (N10 - paradveṣakaro) randhrī jalaukā jāyate ciraṁ.
N2/18.34a - paradveṣakarī (N7/18.20a - paradveṣakaraḥ) krodhī (N4/18.23b, N8/18.23b, Ra/15.23b - paradveṣī paraṅkrodhī) jalaukā jāyate ciraṁ.

43 N2/18.34b - akṛttvā vaiśvadevaṁ vai ye bhuñjanti dvijāttayaḥ.
N4/18.24, N8/18.24a, Ra/15.24a - akṛtvā vaiśvadevaṁ tu bhuñjate ye dvijātayaḥ.
N7/18.20b - akṛte vai svadehe 'pi bhuñjanti te dvijātayaḥ.

44 N1/18.22b - vṛthā caitena pākena (N2/18.35a, N10 - kākayoniṣu jāyate) kākayoni[ḥ] prajāyate.
N3 - vṛthā (te) [cai]tena pākena kīṭayoniṣu jāyate.
N4/18.24b, Ra/15.24b - te vṛthā pāpinaḥ sarve jāyante (N8/18.24b - jāyeran) pāpayoniṣu.
N7/18.21a - vṛthā vaitena pākena kākayoniṣu jāyate.

45 N1/18.23a - paścāttāpī kṛte dāne kokilo tāpate (N3 - bhavate) vane.
N2/18.35b - paścāttāpakṛtaṁ dānaṁ kokilā jāyate vane.
N4/18.25a, N8/18.25a, Ra/15.25a - paścāttāpakaro (N7/18.21b - paścāttāpaṁ kṛte) dāne kokilo jāyate vane.

46 N1/18.23b - svapitāmātaradrohī taka (N3 - bakī) ākāś(s)ago bhavet.
N2/18.36a - svamitrasya baved ghatī baka yo (- - -)mate.
N4/18.25, N8/18.25, Ra/15.25 - pitṛmātṛsu(a)hṛd drohī b(v)ako bhavati khecaraḥ.
N7/18.22a - svapitṛmātaro drohī b(v)aka ākāsinī bhavet.

nityaṁ sakalahā nārī bhavate vanamakṣikā[47]
bhartāraṁ vañcayed yā tu jalaukā jāyate vadhūḥ[48] [24]
āhūtā cāpi śayane yā strī yauvanagarvitā[49]
bhartṛsaṅkāśaṁ na yāti sā kṣayaṁ narakaṁ vrajet[50] [25]
tataḥ karmakṣayenānte bhavate grāmaśūkari
yoṣitāṁ jārasaktānāṁ narake yamakiṅkarāḥ[51] [26]
satataṁ lohaparidhaṁ kṣipanti smaramandire
striyāḥ kāmena naśyanti brāhmaṇā nīcasevayā[52] [27]
rājāno brahmadaṇḍena yatayo bhogasaṅgrahāt[53]
yas tu raudropajīvī ca bhramate sañcaran vane[54] [28]

A woman who is always quarrelsome, is reborn as a forest fly.
A wife, who deceives her husband, is reborn as a water-creature(VII). [24]
A young wife, proud of her youth, who, when summoned to her husband's bed, does not appear, proceeds to destruction in Hell. [25]
Then, when her Karma is worn away, she becomes a village sow.
Adulterous women, always engaged in love-making, Yama's servants in Hell [26] put metal objects into their "abode of love" (i.e. vagina).
Brahmins who have sexual relations with low (women) are lost by their desire for women. [27]
Kings, who are immersed in enjoyment, are restrained by Brahma's stick.
He who lives by fierce means thus amassing wealth, is made to wander in the forest(VIII). [28]

---

47 N1/18.24a - nityaṁ ca kalahā (N3 - nārī) nāma (N10 - kalahāṁ (hā) nā[rī], N7/18.22b - kalahakārī) bhavate vanamakṣikā.
N4/18.26a, N8/18.26a, Ra/15.26a - nityaṁ sakalahā nārī jāyate vanamakṣikā.

48 N1/18.24b, N3, N10 - bhartāraṁ vañcayed yā tu jalaukā (N4/18.26b, N8/18.26b, Ra/15.26b - jāyate vadhūḥ) bhavate (N7/18.23a - ca sā) striyaḥ.

49 Verses 18.25-28a are missing in N2, N3.

50 N1/18.25b - bha(ṛ)rtṛśaṅkā na meyānti sā kṣayaṁ narakaṁ vrajet.

51 N10 - yoṣ(dh)itāṁ jārasaktāṁ no narake yamakiṅkarāḥ.

52 N1/18.27b, N10 - striyā(a)ḥ kāmena naśyanti brā(a)hmaṇo nīcasevayā.

53 N1/18.28a - rājāno brahmadaṇḍena yati no bhogasaṅgrahāt.

54 Emendation - DS. N1/18.28b - yas tu raudropajīvī (N10 - raudrau pā(pra)jīvī) ca bhramate sañcayo vane.

devabrahmasvahārī ca kṛṣṇasarpo girau bhavet[55]
tāmrakāṁsyāpahārī ca meṣayoniṣu jāyate[56] [29]
phalahārī bhaved vindhye kuñjaraḥ sa ca jāyate[57]
ghaṇṭāvāditrahārī ca ghaṇṭāvādako jāyate[58] [30]
śāstracauro naro yas tu śunāṁ yoniṣu jāyate[59]
padenāgnidvijasparśī paṅgur janmatrayaṁ bhavet[60] [31]

He who steals what belongs to Gods or Brahmins, will become a black serpent in the mountain.
Whoever steals copper and brass is reborn in a sheep's womb. [29]
He who steals fruit, will be reborn as an elephant in the Vindhya (Mountains)[(IX)].
Whoever steals a bell and musical instruments, will be reborn as a bell-sound. [30]
He, who steals a knife, will be reborn as a dog.
Whoever touches the legs of a Brahmin engaged in ritual performance is thrice reborn lame. [31]

---

55 N3 - devānnahāsvahārī ca (N2/18.38a - devabrahmasvahārīnaḥ) kṛṣṇasarppo girau bhavet.
N4/18.27b, N8/18.27b, Ra/15.27b - devabrahmasvahārī ca kṛṣṇasarpo (N7/18.24a - girau bhavet) bhaved vane.

56 N4/18.28a, N7/18.24b, N8/18.28a, Ra/15.28a - tāmrakāṁsyāpahārī ca meṣayoniṣu jāyate.

57 N2/18.21b - phalahārī ca vindheṣu kuñjaraś caiva jāyate.
N3 - phalahārī c(r)a vindhe(na)ṣu kuñjaro bhavate sa ca.
N10 - phalahārī bhaved vipro kuñjaraḥ sa ca jāyate.
N4/18.28b, N8/18.28b, Ra/15.28b - phalahārī ca vindhyādrau kuñjaro jāyate vane.

58 N3 - gha[ṇ]ṭāhārī bhaved yas tu pradyā ghā[ṇ]ṭak(a)o jāyate.
Verse 18.30b-31a is missing in N2.
N4/18.29a, N8/18.29a, Ra/15.29a - ghaṇṭāvāditrahārī ca ghaṇṭāghaṇṭo 'pi jāyate.

59 N1/18.31a - śāstracauro nayo yas tu śunīyoniṣu jāyate.
N4/18.29b, N8/18.29b, Ra/15.29b - śāstracauro naro nityaṁ śunāṁ yoniṣu (N7/18.25a - yo ca ś(s)vānayoniṣu) jāyate.

60 N3 - agnicaraṇena spṛśati paṅguyoniṣu jāyate (vi).
Verse 18.31b-32a is missing in N10.
N4/18.30a, N8/18.30a, Ra/15.30a - padenāgnidvijasparśī (N7/18.25b - agnidvijau spṛś(s)et yādau) paṅgur janmatrayaṁ bhavet.

surāpānakaro vipraḥ śunāṁ yoniṣu jāyate[61]
paravastuharā ye ca sarvabhakṣyāś ca ye narāḥ[62] [32]
śṛgālayonau gaccheyuḥ kākayonim anekadhā[63]
mantrahīnā dvijāḥ kecid dīkṣāṁ dadyur dvijottamāḥ[64] [33]
tena doṣeṇa te viprā mārjāratvaṁ niyojitāḥ[65]
vācā yad yad pratijñātaṁ karmaṇā nopapāditaṁ[66] [34]
ṛṇāntadharmasaṁyukto ihaloke paratra ca

A Brahmin who drinks alcoholic drinks, will be reborn as a dog.
Those who steal others' clothes and all their food, those people [32]
will be reborn in many jackal-wombs, and crow-wombs.
Brahmins devoid of any Mantras, who give initiation, O venerable Twice-born, [33]
those Brahmins will be reborn as cats, because of that sin.
Whoever fails to act according to what he has promised, [34]
remains indebted in this world, as well as in the hereafter.

---

61 N1/18.32a - surāpānakaro vipraḥ (N3 - śunāṁ yoniśataṁ bhavet) śunīyoniṣu jāyate.
N4/18.30b, N8/18.30b, Ra/15. 30b - surāpānakaro vipraḥ (N7/18.26a - ś(s)vānayoniṣu jāyate) śvayoniṁ samavāpnuyāt.

62 N1/18.32b - paraṁ vastuharā ye ca sarvabhakṣyāś ca ye narāḥ.
N2/18.23a - ye vai parānnaha[r]tār(au)o jā[n]yate sarppayoniṣu.
N10 - paravastuharā ye ca saṅghabh(m)akṣ[y]āś (N4/18.31a, N8/18.31a, Ra/15.31a - sarvabhakṣyāś, N7/18.26b - sarvabhakṣāś) ca ye narāḥ.

63 N1/18.33a - śṛgālayonir gaccheyuḥ (N3 - śṛgālayoni te gacchet, N7/18.27a - śṛgālayoni te yānti) kākayonim anekadhā.
N2/18.23b - mṛgāyoniṣu gaccheti pāpayoniṣv anekadhā.
N4/18.31b, N8/18.31b, Ra/15.31b - śṛgālayoniṁ gatvātha kākayonim vrajanti te.

64 N1/18.33b - mantraṁ hīnā dvijāḥ kecid (N2/18.24a - bhaved yas tu, N4/18.32a, N8/18.32a, Ra/15.32a - mantradīkṣāvihīnā ye) dīkṣāṁ dadyur dvijottamāḥ.
N3 - mantrahīnā yadā (N10 - narāḥ) kecid [d]ikṣāṁ dādyu[r] dvijottamāḥ.

65 N2/18.24b - tena doṣeṇa te viprā mārjāratvaṁ (N3 - niyojayet) viśanti ca.
N4/18.32b, N8/18.32b, Ra/15.32b - tena doṣeṇa viprās te mārj(j)āratvaṁ vrajanti hi.
N7/18.28a - tena doṣeṇa tān viprān mārjāratvaṁ niyojayet.

66 N10 - vācā yad ya[d] pratijñātaṁ karmaṇā nopapādite.
Verse 18.34b-35a is missing in N2, N3.

chedayed yas tu vṛkṣāṇi puṣpitāni phalitāni ca[67] [35]
grāhako bhavitā samyak paścād bhavati kukkuṭaḥ[68]
svagotre yo 'paghātī ca svagotrāṁ ramate striyaṁ[69] [36]
te śvayoniṣu jāyante pitṛcchedaṁ kurvanti ye[70]
mātṛpitṛgurudveṣī dharmaśāstravinindakaḥ[71] [37]

Whoever cuts trees bearing plenty of flowers and fruits, [35]
becomes a demon, (and) then a hen.
He who ruins his family, and sleeps with a woman from his own clan, [36]
(and) those who cut off the ancestors, are reborn in a bitch's womb.
Those who hate their parents and Guru, and who abuse the Dharmaśāstra, [37]

---

67 N1/18.35b, N3 - chedayed ya(u)s tu vṛkṣāṇi pu[ṣpi]t(i)āni(ṣ) phalitāni ca.
N2/18.25a - ch(dv)edayed yas tu vṛkṣāś ca sapuṣpān saphalān api.
N4/18.33a, N8/18.33a, Ra/15.33a - chedayed yo mahāvṛkṣaṁ puṣpitaṁ phalitaṁ tathā.
N7/18.29a - chedayed yas tu vṛkṣāṁś ca puṣpitān phalitāṁś ca yaiḥ.

68 N2/18.25b - vātakaś ca bhavet so 'pi (N3 - jāhako bhavitā samyak) paścād bhavati kurk(v)uraḥ.
N4/18.33b, N8/18.33b, Ra/15.33b - jāhakaḥ sa bhavet samyak paścād bhavati kukkuṭaḥ.
N7/18.29b - grāhako bhavati samyak paścād bhavati kurkuṭaḥ.

69 N1/18.36b - svagotre yo 'paghātā ca svagotrāṁ (N2/18.26a - 'bhighātā vai svagotre) ramate striyaḥ.
N3 - svagotra yo 'paghātī ca svagotrāṁ ramate striyaṁ.
N10 - svagotre yo 'paghātī ca (N7/18.30a - svagotre ramate strīyaḥ) svagotrābhatastriyaḥ.
N4/18.34a, N8/18.34a, Ra/15.34a - svagotra ghātino ye ca svagotrīṣu ca laṁpaṭāḥ.

70 N1/18.37a - te śvayoniṣu jāyante pitṛcchedaṁ karoti yaḥ.
N2/18.26b, N3, N7/18.30b - ṛkṣayoniṣu jāyante yāvac candrārkamedinī.
Additional half verse:
N2/18.27a - kaścid dadāti dānāni (N7/18.31a - dānaṁ bhaṅgaṁ karoti yaḥ) dānabhaṅga[ṁ] (N3 - dāttabhaṅgaṁ) karoti ca.
N4/18.36a, N8/18.36a, Ra/15.36a - cakravāko bhavet so 'pi snehacchedaṁ karoti yaḥ.

71 N1/18.37b - mātṛpitṛgurudveṣī (N4/18.36b, N8/18.36b, Ra/15.36b - dharmaśāstrasya nindakaḥ) dharmaśāstrakathaṁ (N10 - dharmaśāstrakathā) punaḥ.
N2/18.27b - mātṛpitror guro[r] dveṣī dharmaśāstravinindakaḥ.
N7/18.31b - mātāpitāgurudrohī dharmaś(s)āstra tathā punaḥ.

te ca garbhād vinaśyanti yāvad yonisahasraśaḥ[72]
ekākī miṣṭam aśnāti parivāraṁ vinā naraḥ[73] [38]
marudeśe bhavet sarpaḥ śuṣkakoṭare jāyate[74]
nārādhitaṁ ca yaiḥ śaivaṁ liṅgaṁ viṣṇus tathātmabhūḥ[75] [39]
na devīṁ pūjayed durgāṁ na tīrthāgamanaṁ kṛtaṁ[76]

they will be totally lost from thousands of wombs.
He who eats sweets all by himself, without his family, [38]
will become a serpent in the desert, living in a dry cave.
Those who do not worship the Śivaliṅga, nor Viṣṇu the self-generator, [39]
he who has not worshipped Durgā, nor gone on a pilgrimage,

---

72 N10, N7/18.32a - te ca garbhād vinaśyanti yāvad yonīḥ sahasraśaḥ.
N4/18.37a, N8/18.37a, Ra/15.37a - ete garbhe vinaśyanti yāvajjanma sahasrakaṁ.

73 N1/18.38b - ekākī miṣṭam aśnāti (N2/18.28b - putrabhāryyāvivarjita[ḥ], N4/18.37b, N8/18.37b, Ra/15.37b - parivāraṁ vinā (N7/18.32b - n(m)araḥ) tu yaḥ) parivāra vinī n(t)araḥ.

74 N1/18.39a - manudeśe bhavet (N1/18.40a - sarpa[ḥ] śukakoṭar(a)e jāyate) sādhyo śukakoṭaravāsinaḥ.
N2/18.29a - ma(u)rudeśe bhavet sarppas ta(u)rau ś(bh)uṣke ca koṭa(e)re.
Additional half verse:
N2/18.29b - dharmaghnā hī pare pāpo rogeṇa paripīḍyate.
N3, N10 - marudeśe bhavet sarppo śuṣkakoṣṭhāṣṭhavāsinaḥ.
N3 - andhakūpe bhavet sarppo dīnanetra na saṁśayaḥ.
N4/18.38a, N8/18.38a, Ra/15.38a - marudeśe bhavet sarpaḥ (N7/18.33a - śuśkakoṭaravāsinaḥ) śuṣkakoṭarago mahān.

75 N1/18.39b - nārādhyaṁ śivaliṅge tu tena brahmavinā naraḥ.
N2/18.38 - devabrahmasvahārī yaḥ kṛṣṇasarppo girā bhavet nārā[dhyaṁ] śiveliṅge [tu] b(v)rahmāviṣṇudvijottamaiḥ.
Verse N1/18.40 is almost identical to N1/18.39, missing in N2, N3, N10.
N10, N1/18.40b - nārādhyaṁ śivaliṅgaṁ (N7/18.33b - ca viṣṇub(v)rahmadvijotta māḥ) tu brahmaviṣṇudvijottamāḥ.
N4/18.38b, N8/18.38b, Ra/15.38b - nārādhitaṁ ca yaiḥ śaivaṁ liṅga[ṁ] viṣṇus tathātmabhūḥ.

76 N1/18.41a - na devī (N10 - devā) pūjaye[d] durgāṁ na tīrthaṁ gamanaṁ kṛtaṁ.
N2/18.39a - na tvayā pūjitā (N4/18.39a, N8/18.39a, Ra/15.39a - na pūjitā tathā) durgā na tīrthagamanaṁ kṛtaṁ.
N7/18.33c - na divyāṁ pūjayet saṅgī na tīrthe gamanaṁ kṛtaṁ.

na hutaṁ naiva dattaṁ ca narake patanaṁ dhruvaṁ[77] [40]
devārcanaratā ye ca tīrthasnānaratāś ca ye[78]
satyadharmaratāḥ śūrās tapaḥsaṁyamasaṁyutāḥ[79] [41]
te narāḥ saptajanmeṣu sukhaṁ krīḍanty amarāvatīṁ[80]
evaṁ dṛṣṭaṁ mayā tatra gatena dvijasattamāḥ[81] [42]
mamātīva samutpannaṁ citraguptasya kautukaṁ[82]

neither sacrificed, nor donated, will definitely fall into Hell. [40]
Those devoted to the rites of Gods and those devoted to bathing in pilgrimage sites,
heroes adhering to Truth and Dharma, engaged in penance and restraint, [41]
these people will play happily in the Amarāvatī Heaven for seven births.
I really saw (all this), when I went there, O excellent Brahmins. [42]
My utmost astonishment occurred (at seeing) Citragupta,

---

[77] N2/18.39b, N7/18.34a - na hutaṁ naiva japtaṁ ca na dattaṁ (N4/18.39b, N8/18.39b, Ra/15.39b - b(v)rahmaṇe gurau) gurub(v)rāḥmaṇe.
N3, N10 - na hutaṁ naiva taptaṁ ca na dattaṁ gurub(v)rāhmaṇaṁ.
Additional half verses:
N2/18.40a - ālasyena gataṁ janma narakapatanaṁ (N10 - narake patanaṁ) dhruvaṁ.
N3 - ālasyena gatā jānā narake patanaṁ dhruvaṁ.

[78] N1/18.42a - devārcane rat(j)ā ye ca tīrthasnānarat(j)ā[ś] c(y)a y(t)e.
N2/18.40b - devārcananarā ye ca prāta[ḥ]snānaratāś ca ye.
N3 - devārcanaṁ ratā ye ca tīrtharatā narāś ca ye.
N4/18.40b, N8/18.40b, Ra/15.40b - devārcanaratā ye ca tīrthasnānaparāś (N7/18.35a - tīrthasnānaratāś) ca ye.

[79] N2/18.41a, N7/18.35b - dānadharmaratā(s)ḥ satyās (N3, N4/18.41a, N8/18.41a, Ra/15.41a, N10 - satyadharmaratāḥ śūrās) tapa(s)ḥsaṁyamasaṁyutāḥ.

[80] N1/18.43a, N10 - te narā[ḥ] saptajanmeṣu sukhaṁ krīḍanty a[ma]rav(c)atī[ṁ].
N2/18.41b - iha janmani dhanyās te sukhaṁ yāty amarāvatīṁ.
N4/18.41b, N8/18.41b, Ra/15.41b - te tu janmāny anekāni krīḍanty amaramandire.
N7/18.36a - teṣāṁ janmani janme ca te krīḍante 'marāvatīṁ.

[81] N1/18.43b, N3, N10, N7/18.36b - evaṁ dṛṣṭaṁ mayā tatra gate caiva (N4/18.42a, N8/18.42a, Ra/15.42a - yamaloke) dvijottamāḥ.

[82] N2/18.42a - mayīṣṭahastam utpannaṁ citraguptasya veśmani.
N3 - mayā gṛhasamutpannaṁ citraguptasya kautukaṁ.
N4/18.42b, N8/18.42b, Ra/15.42b - anyac ca saṁpravakṣyāmi citraguptasya kautukaṁ.

likhitāni pūrvakarmāṇi martyaloke kṛtāni ca[83] [43]
anyac chṛṇvantu bho viprā dharmarājasabhāntare[84]
nārada uvāca
pṛcchāmi tvāṁ mahātejāḥ sūryaputra mahābala[85] [44]
mārtaṇḍatejasaṅkāśāc charīram atiśobhanaṁ[86] [45]
hemādhikatanus tvaṁ hi rūpavāṁś ca mahādyutiḥ[87]

writing down (all) previous actions performed in the mortal world. [43]
Listen, O Brahmins, to what else happened in Yama's hall:
Nārada said
"I ask you, O great hero, the mighty son of Sūrya(X)*, [44]*
your very beautiful body shines with luster like the sun. [45]
Your very radiant body is more fine-looking than gold.

---

83 N1/18.44b, N10 - likhitaṁ pūrvakarmāṇi (N3 - pūrvakarmabhiḥ) martyalokeṣu jāyate.
Additional verses:
N2/18.43 - śubhāśubhaṁ ca sak(k)ala(n)m iha loke t(va)u yat kṛtaṁ
tāni karmāṇi sarvāṇi jñātvā likhitav(ai)ān tataḥ.
N3 - śubhaṁ ca sakalaṁ teṣ(y)āṁ (yam) iha loke ca yat kṛtaṁ
tat sukarmma sukarmmaṁ ca aparaṁ śṛṇvantu me dvijāḥ (vi).
N4/18.43a, N8/18.43a, Ra/15.43a - sadā likhati karmāṇi martyaloke kṛtāni ca.

84 N1/18.45a, N3 - anyac chṛ(a)ṇu(a)ta bho viprā dharmarājasabhāntare.
N2/18.44a - śṛṇudhvam aparaṁ viprāḥ kathitaṁ y(k)amanāradaiḥ.

85 N1/18.46a - pṛcchāmi tvāṁ (N3, N7/18.39a - te) mahātejāḥ (N2/18.44b - mahāprājñāḥ) sūryaputra (N10 - yadā b(v)alaṁ) mahāb(v)alaṁ.
N4/18.44a, N8/18.44b, Ra/15.45a - pṛcchāmi tvaṁ mahāprājñāsūryyaputramahābala.

86 N2/18.45a - mārtaṇḍatejasaṅkāśaṁ śarīratva[ṁ] (N7/18.39b - atiśobhate) va śobhanaṁ.
N3 - mārttaṇḍatanasaṅkāśaṁ śarīram atiśobhanaṁ.
N4/18.44b, N8/18.45a, Ra/15.45b - mārttaṇḍamaṇḍalodyoti śarīraṁ te 'tiśobhanaṁ.

87 N3 - hemādhikatanus tvaṁ hi rūpavāṁś ca mahāmatiḥ.
N4/18.45a, Ra/15.46a - hemādhikojjvalan (N8/18.45b - himādhikojjvalaṁ dehaṁ) deh(a)o dṛśyate lokaṁ sundaraṁ.
N7/18.40 - hemāyakatanus tvaṁ hi rūpavāṁś ca atipriyaḥ.

kimarthaṁ te mahābāho mukhaṁ kṛṣṇājinaprabhaṁ[88] [46]
nāradena tadā pṛṣṭho dharmarājo 'yam abravīt[89]
yamadharma uvāca
mahāvratakarā viprā jitakrodhā jitendriyāḥ[90]
śivabhaktās tathā kecic chivamantreṇa dīkṣitāḥ[91] [47]
atithiṁ nityaṁ pūjanti mahāsatyamahāvratāḥ[92]
viṣṇudhyānayutāḥ kecid dvijabhaktāś ca dharmikāḥ[93]

Why, O hero, is your face as black as an antelope skin?" [46]
Thus asked by Nārada, the King of Righteousness (i. e. Yama), spoke.
Yamadharma said
"Brahmins who perform great vows, of restrained senses, who have overcome anger,
those devotees of Śiva, initiated into the rites of Śiva, [47]
always paying reverence to a guest, great adherents of Truth, (keeping their) vows,
engaged in meditation on Viṣṇu, righteous devotees of Brahmins,

---

88 N4/18.46a, Ra/15.46b - kathaṁ tava mahāb(v)āho (N8/18.46a - mahābhāga) mukhaṁ kṛṣṇāṁ janaprabhaṁ.
N7/18.40 - kimarthaṁ te mahātejā mukhaṁ kṛṣṇājanaprabhaṁ.

89 N1/18.45b - nāradena tadā pṛṣṭhe dharmarājo 'yam abravīt.
Verse 18.45b is missing in N2.
N3 - nāradena tadā pṛccha (N10 - pṛṣṭho) dharmarājo yad abravīt.

90 N1/18.48a - mahāvratak(v)arā (N2/18.46b, N3 - mahāvratadharā) viprā jitakrodh(o)ā jitendriyā(a)ḥ.
N4/18.46a, N8/18.46b, Ra/15.47a - mahāvratamahāprājñajitakrodhajitendriyāḥ.
N7/18.41a - mahāvratadharā viprā jitakrodhajitendriyāḥ.

91 N1/18.48b - śivabhaktās tathā kṛṣṇa śivamantreṇa dīkṣitāḥ.
N3 - śivabhaktā(a)s tathā te ca śivamantreṇa dīkṣitāḥ.
N4/18.46b, N8/18.47a, Ra/15.47b - viṣṇubhaktās tathā viprā(a)ḥ śivamantreṣu dīkṣitā(a)ḥ.
N7/18.41b - śivabhaktās tathā kṛṣṇe śivamantreṇa vīkṣitāḥ.

92 N2/18.47b - (a)pūjayann atithīn nityaṁ mahāsatyā mahāvratāḥ.
N3 - atithi[ṁ] nitya[ṁ] pūjyanti mahāsatyā mahātapāḥ.
N4/18.47a, N8/18.47b, Ra/15.48a - mahāsatyo mahotsāho nityaṁ cātithipūjakaḥ.

93 N3 - viṣṇusmaraṇaśaktāś ca dvijabhaktātidharmikāḥ.
N4/18.47b, N8/18.48a, Ra/15.48b - rāmanāma smaranto 'ny(o)ā dvijabhaktās tathā pare.

teṣāṁ tejaḥ mahātīvraṁ dagdhaṁ caiva tu manmukhaṁ[94] [48]
tena nārada kṛṣṇāsyaṁ tanuḥ kavacarakṣitā[95]
te asādhyā mayā samyak ramante viṣṇusadmani[96] [49]
itthaṁ śrutaṁ mayā tatra saṁsthitena sabhāntare[97]
nāradena saha dharmo vācyamānaḥ punaḥ punaḥ[98] [50]

their very strong luster indeed scorches my face. [48]
That is the reason for my blackness, Nārada, (and) for protecting my body by armour.
They rejoice in Viṣṇu's abode and cannot be mastered by me". [49]
That is what I (Nāsiketa) heard, standing there in the court,
what Dharma conversed over and over again with Nārada. [50]

---

94 N1/18.50a - brahmaghnāṁ caitan mukhyaṁ. Distorted half verse - second part identical to 18.49a.
Additional verse - N2/18.48b-49:
pañcayajñasya kartāra[ḥ] pañcāgni vrata sādhakāḥ
yānti te paramaṁ sthānaṁ vimānasthā dvijāttamaḥ
. . . (tayo) jāta tejasā teṣāṁ dagdhaṁ mukhavidaṁ mamaḥ.
N3 - teṣāṁ tejogataṁ tīvraṁ (N10 - tejā mahātīvraṁ) dagdhaṁ caiva tu manmukhaṁ.
N7/18.43-44a - yajñānte b(v)ahudhānyāni pañcāgnivratasādhakāḥ
yānti te paramaṁ sthānaṁ vimānasthā dvijottamāḥ
teṣāṁ tejo mahātīvraṁ dagdhaṁ caiva hi me mukhaṁ.

95 N1/18.50a - tena nārada kṛṣṇāsyaṁ tanuḥ (N3 - kavacarakṣitā) kavacarakṣitaḥ.
N2/18.50a - tena nāra[da] kṛṣṇābha[ṁ] śarīraṁ vakarakṣitaṁ.
N4/18.49, N8/18.49b, Ra/15.50 - tena nārada kṛṣṇās(bh)yaṁ tanuś ca kavacavratā.
N7/18.44b - tena nārada kṛṣṇābh(y)aṁ tanuṁ kavacarakṣatāṁ.

96 N2/18.50b - dharmātmānaḥ kratubhā(a)jo narā yānty amarāvatīṁ.
N3 - te asādhyā mayā samyak samane hitasaṁsthitā[ḥ].
N4/18.50, N8/18.51a, Ra/15.51 - ete 'sādhyā mama mune dhārmikā vaiṣṇavā janāḥ.

97 N1/18.51a, N10 - nāradasahito dharmaṁ bhāṣyamāṇo mayā saha.
N3 - itthaṁ mayā śrutaṁ tatra saṁsthitasya yamagrahaṁ
nāradasya hite dharma bhāṣyamāṇo mayā saha.

98 N1/18.51b - dharmarājan bharadvājo rāja(ā)siṁhāsane sthitaḥ.
N3 - dharmarājā naradvāre tatra (N10 - dharmarājan bharadvāre rāj(ā)a) siṁhāsane sthitaḥ.

vaiśaṁpāyana uvāca
janamejaya nṛpaśreṣṭha iti pūrvamuniśrutaṁ[99]
idaṁ te kathitaṁ guhyaṁ nāsiketaṁ kathānakaṁ[100] [51]
yaḥ śṛṇoti mahābāho prayatne bhaktimān naraḥ[101]
sarveṣv api ca pāpeṣu mucyate nātra saṁśayaḥ[102] [52]

Vaiśaṁpāyana said
Janamejaya, the best of kings, you have just heard about the ancient sage,
this little mysterious tale of Nāsiketa, that I have told you. [51]
Whoever listens to it attentively, full of devotion, O hero,
is liberated from all his sins, there is no doubt about it. [52]

---

99 N1/18.52a - jan[a]mejaya naraśreṣṭha iti (N10 - pūrvam anuṣṭhitaṁ) pūrvamunisthitaṁ.
N2/18.52b - janamejaya nṛpaśreṣṭha iti pūrvair (N7/18.47b - anuṣitaṁ) anuṣṭhitaḥ.
N4/18.52a, N8/18.51b, Ra/15.53a - yamalokakathām etāṁ dṛṣṭvā tu janamejaya.
Bo/18.16a - janamejaya mahārāja pūrvakalpāśritāṁ kathāṁ.

100 N2/18.54b - idaṁ te kathitaṁ guhyaṁ (N3 - nās(ś)iketaṁ kathānakaṁ, N7/18.49b, N10 - nās(ś)iketakathānakaṁ) nās(ś)iketakathāmṛtaṁ.
Additional verses - N2/18.53-54a:
nās(ś)iketena sakalaṁ bhāṣitaṁ dvijai(s)ḥ saha
punaś caiva yathāṣṭhāna(ṁ)m (N3 - yathānyāya(ṁ)m) abhivādāmatāṁś ca ye
nās(ś)iketas tato (N3 - tadā) jñānaṁ (N3 - abhyāsaṁ mokṣagāminaḥ) gṛhītvā muktim āpnuyāt.
Additional half verse:
N3 - kathaṁ purāyaṁ caritaṁ sakalaṁ śṛṇu(m) adbhutaṁ.
N4/18.54b, N8/18.55a, Ra/15.56a - idaṁ tu kathitaṁ guhyaṁ nāsiketasya bhūpate.
N7/18.48a - nās(ś)iketasya sakalaṁ vadanti śṛṇvanti dvijāḥ.

101 N2/18.55a - yaḥ śṛṇoti mahāb(v)āho (N3, N7/18.50a - prayatne (N10 - prayatnair) bhaktimān naraḥ) prayatnena sa mānavaḥ.

102 N2/18.55b, N3 - kṛtebhyaḥ sarvepāpebhyo (N4/18.54b, N8/18.55a, Ra/15.56a - sasarvebhyo 'pi (N7/18.50 - āśu sarvebhya(o)[ḥ]) pāpebhyo) mucyate nātra saṁśayaḥ. End of N4, N7, N8, Ra.
Bo/18.16b - śṛṇoti śraddhayā yuktaḥ sarvapāpaiḥ pramucyate.

prāyaścittasahasreṣu pūto bhavati tatkṣanāt[103]
saṁvatsaraśataṁ sāgraṁ pāpaṁ ca bahudhā kṛtaṁ[104] [53]
mucyate nātra sandeho nāsiketakathāśrutāṁ[105]
śrutvā divi gamiṣyati yamaṁ caiva na paśyati[106] [54]
uddālakasutavākyaṁ pāpahṛt puṇyapravardhanaṁ[107]

A man becomes cleansed immediately (as by) thousands of penances, (even if)
for a hundred years of life, he committed many sins. [53]
He who hears the Nāsiketa story becomes liberated, there is no doubt.
He goes to Heaven, and never sees Yama, having heard [54]
the sin-removing, good-increasing words of Uddāllaka's son.

---

103 N1/18.54a, N3 - prāyaścittasahasreṣu pūto bhavati tajjanāt.
N10 - prāyaścittapradas teṣu pūto bhavati tatkṣanāt.
Verses 18.54-8, (as well as 18.59-127 in appendix I) are missing in N2.
Additional verses N2/18.56–64:
N2/18.56 - . . . . undeciphered.
N2/18.57 - karyyāsaṁlab(v)aṇaṁ caiva ghṛtaṁ tailantaḥ gā paraṁ
yad yad dānaṁ yair dattaṁ labhante kāñcanīṁ purīṁ.
N2/18.58 - sarvadeveṣu yat purāṁ (ya) sarva tīrtheṣu yat phalaṁ
tat phalaṁ labhate vidvā(ś)ḥ śṛṇuyādyaḥ kathām imāṁ.
N2/18.59 - gosahasrakṛtaṁ dānaṁ suvarṇābharaṇabhūṣitaṁ
tat phalaṁ labhate martya[ḥ] śrutvā paurāṇikīm imāṁ.
N2/18.60 - . . . ca pāpāni b(v)rahmahatyāsamāni ca
nās(ś)iketakathāṁ śrutvā vilayaṁ yānti kṛtāny api.
N2/18.61 - aputro labhate putrān vandho mucyeta badhanāt
dharmārthī vyāpnuyād bhadra dhanārthī dhanam āpnuyāt.
N2/18.62 - vidyārthī labhate vi[dyā] (- -)kṣārthī labhate gatiṁ
bhūmyarthī labhate bhūmiṁ sarva . . . na saṁśayaḥ.
N2/18.63 - bhāryyārthī labhate bhāryyaṁ kanyārth[ī la]bhate sūtāṁ
ratnārthī prāpnuyād ratnam annārthī cānnavān bhavet.
N2/18.64 - nās(ś)iketasya ma(ā)hātmyaṁ ye śṛṇvanti (-) yānti vai
sarvapāpaviniryuktāḥ yānti viṣṇoḥ paraṁ padaṁ. End of N2.

104 N3, N10 - saṁvatsaraśataṁ sāgraṁ pāpaṁ ca b(v)ahudhā kṛtaṁ.

105 N3 - mucyate nātra san[deho nāsiketakathāśrutaṁ]. End of N3 - incomplete.

106 N10 - śrutvā divi gamiṣyanti yamaṁ caiva na paśya[n]ti.
Bo/18.17 - nāsiketena kathitam ākhyānaṁ pāvanaṁ mahat.

107 N1/18.56a - uddālake suto jāto vākyaṁ puṇyapravardhanaṁ.

śrutvā gantā raver lokaṁ vadan mokṣam avāpnuyāt[108] [55]
yaḥ śṛṇoti naro nityaṁ śraddhayā vinayānvitaḥ[109]
sa gacchet paramaṁ sthānaṁ yatra gatvā na śocati[110] [56]
śṛṇvan caiva kathāṁ divyāṁ satyāṁ paurāṇakīṁ śubhāṁ[111]
jñānavijñānasaṁpannaḥ santatiṁ ciraṁ ca jīvet[112] [57]
iyaṁ kathā tu saṁpūrṇā kṛṣṇadvaipāyanakṛtā[113]
janamejayāya kathitā kuśalaṁ sarvaśāstravit[114] [58]

iti śrībrahmāṇḍapurāṇe nāsiketopākhyāne
bhāgavatadharmanirūpaṇaṁ nāma aṣṭādaśo 'dhyāya[115]

Having heard them, one goes to the sun, reciting them he attains liberation. [55]
Whoever hears it with attention and discipline,
goes to the highest place, where he feels no sorrow. [56]
Hearing the divine, true, ancient, beautiful story,
he lives long, having progeny, full of wisdom and knowledge. [57]
This rich story by Kṛṣṇadvaipāyana(XI)*, is completed,*
properly told to Janamejaya, the knower of all law-books. [58]

This is the eighteenth chapter of the Nāsiketa story, pertaining to the Brahmāṇḍa Purāṇa, called the holy examination of Dharma.

Translation Notes

I – An outcast, the lowest social status.
II – "Starts all over again". The original verse is in the singular.
III – The lowest of the four castes.
IV – See verse 18.6b.
V – One of an upper caste.

---

108 N1/18.56b - śrutvā gantā rave lokaṁ padan mokṣam avāpnuyāt.

109 N10 - yaḥ śṛṇoti naro nityaṁ [śr](dv)ad[dh]ayā(d) vinayānvitaḥ.

110 N10 - sa gacchet paramaṁ sthānaṁ pannagatvān na śocati.

111 N10 - śṛṇvantau va kathāṁ divyāṁ satyāṁ paurāṇakīṁ śubhāṁ.

112 Emendation - DS. N1/18.58b - jñānavijñānasaṁpannaḥ santatiṁ (N10 - santatiś) ciram āyuṣaṁ.

113 N10 - iyaṁ kathā tu saṁpūrṇā kṛṣṇadvaipāyanaiḥ kṛtā.

114 N1/18.59b - jan[a]mejayāya kathitaṁ kuśalaṁ sadya śāstrakṛt.

115 There is a later addition to N1 and N10 - see appendix I.

VI – A low caste.
VII – See verse 18.21b.
VIII – Following the translation suggested by Dr. N. Kulkarni.
IX – The Vindhya Range is a low mountain range of central India.
X – Yama, the Sun's son.
XI – "The Black Islander" – the sage Vyāsa.

Appendix I

Chapter 18 – Additional Verses

pituḥ śāpānusāreṇa gato 'sau dharmaveśmani
kṣaṇenaivāgamat yatra sthāpitau pitṛmātarau[1] [60]
candravatyai namaskāraṁ kṛtvā coddālako muniḥ[2]
gaṅgāyai ca namaskṛtya tadā tat kathyate vacaḥ [61]
nāsiketa uvāca
yamalokaḥ mayā dṛṣṭaḥ caturdvāreṣu nirṇayaṁ[3]
tat sarvaṁ varṇayiṣyāmi śṛṇvantu brahmavādinaḥ[4] [62]
uddālako mahāprājñaś candrāvatyāś ca mātaraṁ[5]
sthirā bhava tu me mātā raghūṇāṁ dyotakāriṇī[6] [63]
tava prasādād gacchati martyaloke tv iyaṁ kathā[7]

---

1 Emendation - NK. N1/18.60b - janenaivāgamaṁ tatra sthāpitā pitṛmātaraḥ. N10 - jan(ṇ)enaivāgamat tatra tatrasthāḥ pitṛmātaraḥ.

2 N10 - vaḍāvatyai namaskāraṁ kṛtvā coddālako muniḥ.

3 N10 - yamalokaṁ mayā dṛṣṭaṁ caturdvāreṣu nirṇ(n)ayaṁ.

4 N10 - tat sarvaṁ cūrṇayiṣyāmi śṛṇvantu b(v)rahmavādinaḥ.

5 Emendation - NK. N1/18.63a - uddālako mahāprājñaś (N10 - mahāprājñaṁś) candrāvatyāś ca mātaraḥ.

6 N10 - sthirā bhava tu me mātā raghūṇo dyotakāriṇī.

7 Emendation - DS. N1/18.64a - tava prasādā[d] gaccha(n)ti (me) martyaloke tv iyaṁ kathā.
Verse 18.64 is missing in N10. Additional verses - N10:
tava . . . (tramāṣṇo) dhenuṁ ca dāpayet (short)
annadānaṁ ca yai[r] datta[ṁ] te pāraṁ yānti sa[t]varaṁ
deyāny any(n)āni dānāni pāram icchanti 'pi hitāḥ
tīrth(gh)āsnānaratāni gaṅgāsāgarasaṅgame
śāstraṁ vedāṁś ca manyante nityaṁ caiva dṛṭavratāḥ
satyaṁ caiva mahā(ī)tmān(h)aṁ dānaṁ caiva . . .
ye tu mārge mahāghore vaitaraṇyāṁ ca nirbhayāḥ
(yā so vai(e) bhayāvahā śatayojana vistīrṇāṣṭathutve sāma
[vai]taraṇī nāma ya dvāre mahāsarit yat pramāṇā ca
sā devī śṛṇv aṅgaṁ ve - - - hā sarit apūyaśoṇitāṁ
patanti tatra vai martyā krandamānās tu pāpinaḥ

na mucyate tu pāpebhyo na teṣāṁ puṇyavardhanaṁ [64]
nāsiketapurāṇaṁ vai na śrutvā śraddhayānvitaḥ[8]
sa pāpātmā durācāro raurave vasate ciraṁ [65]
sa brahmajño mahānantaḥ sa puṇyātmā sa buddhimān[9]
yaḥ śṛṇoti naro bhaktyā labhate svargam uttamaṁ [66]
bālo yuvā vā vṛddho 'pi daridro durbalo 'pi vā[10]
nīcabuddhir na kurvīta purāṇaśravaṇe ca yaḥ[11] [67]
bhavakoṭisahasreṣu bhūtvābhūtvāvasīdati[12]
teṣām api ca sarveṣāṁ purāṇajñaḥ paro guruḥ [68]
purāṇajñaḥ sadā vandyaḥ pūjyo 'tha sukṛtārthibhiḥ[13]
yo dadāty anyāṁ vṛttiṁ ko 'nyas tasmāt paro guruḥ[14] [69]
purāṇajñaḥ kṛpodāttaḥ śānto vigatamatsaraḥ[15]
sādhuḥ sakaruṇo vāgmī vadet puṇyakathāṁ sudhīḥ[16] [70]
vyāsāsane samārūḍho yadā pauraṇiko dvijaḥ
āsamāpteḥ prasaṅgasya namaskuryān na kasyacit [71]
abhaktyā ye kathāṁ puṇyāṁ śṛṇvanti manujādhamāḥ[17]

. . . . (5 undeciphered verses)
taranti tasyāṁ dānena anyathā ca patanti vai
mātaraṁ ye ca manyante ācāryaṁ gurum eva ca
avamanyanti ye mūḍhās teṣāṁ vāsos tu satataṁ
. . . . (4 undeciphered verses)
viśvāsapratipannānāṁ svāmimitratayas svi[nā]ṁ
strīb(v)ālavikalānāṁ ca kṣidram anveṣayanti ye
pacyante tatra madhye tu krandamānās tu pāpinaḥ
agnido garadaś caiva kūṭasākṣim upadyā eṣa varddhetaṁ.

8 Emendation - DS. N10 - nāsiketapurāṇaṁ va(u)i na śrutaṁ śraddhayānvitaiḥ.

9 N1/18.66a, N10 - sa brahmajño mahānantaḥ sa[ḥ] puṇyāsa[ḥ] sa buddhimān.

10 N10 - b(v)ālo yuv(s)ā vo vādaddho 'pi daridro durghelo 'pi vā.

11 N1/18.68a - nīcabuddhi[r] na ku[r]vīta (N10 - purāṇataś ca [śravaṇe]) purāṇaśravaṇeś ca ye.

12 N1/18.69a - tava koṭisahasreṣu bhūtvābhūtvāvasīdati.

13 N10 - purāṇajñaḥ sadā b(v)andhaḥ pūjyotha sukṛtārthibhiḥ.

14 Emendation - DS. N1/18.69b, N10 - yo dadāty apunar vṛtti[ṁ] ko 'nyas tasmāt paro guruḥ.

15 N1/18.70a - purāṇajña kṛpīdātaḥ śāntāvigatamatsaraḥ.

16 N1/18.70b - sādhuḥ sakaruṇācāram avadet puṇyayā sudhīḥ.

17 N1/18.72a, N10 - abhaktyā ye kathāṁ puṇyā(a)ṁ śṛṇvanti manujādhamāḥ.

teṣāṁ puṇyaphalaṁ nāsti duḥkhaṁ syāj janmajanmani[18] [72]
purāṇaṁ ye na saṁpūjya tāṁbulādyair upāyanaiḥ[19]
śṛṇvanti manujādhamāḥ daridrāḥ syuś ca pāpinaḥ[20] [73]
kathāyāṁ kīrtyamānāyāṁ ye gacchanty anyato narāḥ[21]
bhogāntare praṇaśyanti teṣāṁ dattāś ca saṁpadaḥ[22] [74]
soṣṇīṣamastakā ye ca kathāṁ śṛṇvanti pāvanīṁ[23]
vālukāyāṁ pratapyante pāpino manujādhamāḥ[24] [75]
tāṁbūlaṁ bhakṣayanto ye kathāṁ śṛṇvanti pāvanīṁ[25]
śvaviṣṭhāṁ svādayanty enāṁ narake yamakiṅkarāḥ [76]
ye ca tuṅgāsamārūḍhāḥ kathāṁ śṛṇvanti dāṁbhikāḥ
akṣayān narakān bhuktvā te bhavanty eva vāyasāḥ[26] [77]
ye ca nīcāsanārūḍhā ye cāpy āyanasaṅgatāḥ[27]
śṛṇvanti satkathāṁ te vai bhavanty arjunapādapāḥ [78]
asaṁpraṇamya śṛṇvanto viṣavṛkṣā bhavanti te
kathāṁ śayānā śṛṇvanto bhavanty ajagarā narāḥ [79]
yaḥ śṛṇoti kathāṁ vaktuḥ samānāsanam āsthitaḥ[28]
gurutalpasamaṁ pāpaṁ saṁprāpya narakaṁ vrajet [80]
nindanti ye purāṇajñaṁ kathāṁ vā pāpāhāriṇīṁ[29]
te vai janmaśatair mārtyā śunakāḥ saṁbhavanti ca[30] [81]
kathāyāṁ vartamānāyāṁ ye vadanti tadanantaraṁ[31]

---

18 N10 - teṣāṁ puṇyam aphalaṁ nāsti duḥkha[ṁ] syāj janmajanmani.

19 N10 - purāṇaṁ ye tu saṁpūjya tāṁb(v)ulādyair upāyanaiḥ.

20 N10 - śṛṇvanti ca kathāṁ puṇyā[ṁ] daridrāḥ syuś ca pāpinaḥ.

21 N10 - kathāyāṁ kīrtyamānāyāṁ ye gacchanty anyato janāḥ.

22 N1/18.74b - bhogāntare praṇaś(s)yanti teṣāṁ dattāś ca saṁpada(ā)ḥ.

23 N10 - soṣṇīs(ṣ)amastakā ye ca kathāṁ śṛṇvanti pāv(c)anīṁ.

24 Emendation - DS. N1/18.75b - te vālukāḥ pratap(ja)yante (N10 -pratapante) pāpino manujādhamāḥ.

25 N10 - tāndalaṁ bhakṣayanto ye kathāṁ śṛṇvanti pāvanīṁ.

26 N10 - akṣayān narakān bhuṅkt[v]ā te bhavanty eva vāyasāḥ.

27 N10 - ye ca nīcāsanārūḍhā ye ca dhyāmanasaṅgatāḥ.

28 Emendation - NK. N1/18.80a, N10 - yaḥ śṛṇoti kathāṁ vaktuḥ samānāsa[na]m āsthitaḥ.

29 Emendation - DS. N1/18.81a - na ve nindati purāṇajñaḥ kathāṁ vā pāpā(a)hāriṇīṁ (vi).

30 Emendation - NK. N1/18.81b - te vai janmaśatair mārtyā (N10 - śucakāḥ saṁbha[van]ti ca) śunakāḥ samatīti ca.

31 Emendation - NK. N1/18.82a - kathāyāṁ vartamānāyāṁ ye vadanti (N10 - tadanuttaraṁ) na dustaraṁ.

te gardabhāḥ prajāyante kṛkalāsās tataḥ paraṁ[32] [82]
kadācid api te puṇyā na śṛṇvanti kathāṁ narāḥ[33]
te bhuktvā narakān ghorān bhavanti vanaśūkarāḥ[34] [83]
ye kathām anumodante kīrtyamānaṁ narottamāḥ
na śṛṇvanto 'pi te yānti śāśvataṁ paramaṁ padaṁ [84]
kathāyāṁ kīrtyamānayāṁ vighnaṁ kurvanti ye sadā[35]
kīṭakā narakān bhuktvā bhavanti grāmaśūkarāḥ[36] [85]
ye śrāvayanti manujāḥ puṇyāṁ paurāṇakīṁ kathāṁ[37]
kalpakoṭiśataṁ sāgraṁ tiṣṭhanti brahmaṇaḥ pade[38] [86]
āsanārthaṁ prayacchanti purāṇajñasya ye narāḥ
kaṁbalājinavāsāṁsi mañcaṁ phalakam eva ca [87]
svargalokaṁ samāsādya bhuktvā bhogān yathepsitān[39]
sthitvā brahmādilokeṣu padaṁ yānti nirāmayaṁ[40] [88]
purāṇasya prayacchanti ye sūtraṁ vasanaṁ navaṁ[41]
bhogino jñānasaṁpannās te bhavanti bhaved yadi[42] [89]
ye mahāpātakair yuktā upapātakinaś ca ye[43]
purāṇaśravaṇād eva te yānti paramaṁ padaṁ [90]
satyaṁ bravīmi paralokahitaṁ bravīmi
sāraṁ bravīmy upaniṣad dhṛdayaṁ bravīmi[44] [91]

---

32 N1/18.82b - te gardabhāḥ prajāyante kṛkalāsāsamaṁ tataḥ.

33 N1/18.83a - kadāpi dayite puṇyaṁ na (N10 - kathācid api ye puṇyā te) śṛṇvanti kathā[ṁ] narāḥ.

34 N1/18.83b - te bhuktvā narakān ghorān śṛṇvanti vanaśūkarāḥ.

35 Emendation - NK. N1/18.85a - kathā(ṁ)yāṁ kīrtyamānā(am)yāṁ vipra kurvanti ye sadaḥ.
N10 - kathāyāṁ kīrtyamānayāṁ vighnaṁ kurvanti ye saṣaḥ.

36 Emendation - DS. N1/18.85b - kīṭake narakān bhuṅktvā bhavanti grāmaśūkarāḥ.

37 N1/18.86a - ye śrāvayanti tanujāḥ kathāṁ paurāṇakīṁ śubhāṁ.
N10 - ye śrāvayanti manujān puṇyāṁ paurāṇakīṁ kathāṁ.

38 N1/18.86b - kalpakoṭiśataṁ sāgraṁ tiṣṭhan[ti] brahmaṇaḥ pade.

39 N1/18.88a - svargalokaṁ samāsādya bhuktvā bhogān yathepsitāḥ.

40 N1/18.88b - sthitvā brahmādilokeṣu padaṁ yā[n]ti nirāmayaṁ.

41 N1/18.89a - purāṇasya prayacchanti ye sūtrā vacanaṁ navaṁ.

42 Emendation - NK. N1/18.89a - bhogino jñānasaṁpannās te bhavanti (N10 - bha(- -) ve) bhaved yadi.

43 N1/18.90a - mahāpātakakair yuktau upapatakinaś ca ye.

44 N1/18.91b-c - sāraṁ bravīmy upan(r)īṣa(u)d vadayaṁ (N1/18.91d - dhṛdayaṁ) bravīmi saṁsāram na vācya jantoḥ . . . bravīmi.

saṁsāram ulbaṇam asāram avāpya jantoḥ[45]
sāro 'yam īśvarapadāṁbujayoś ca sevā [92]
viprāya dīyamāne tu yo vighnaṁ kurute naraḥ[46]
sa yāti brahmahatyānāṁ sahasrāṇaṁ śatāyutaṁ [93]
apahṛtyā parasyārthaṁ yaḥ parebhyaḥ prayacchati[47]
sa yāti narakaṁ ghoraṁ yasyārthas tasya vai phalaṁ [94]
anyāyāsādhitaṁ dravyaṁ yas tv anyasmai prayacchati[48]
sa dātā narakaṁ yāti narakān koṭikoṭiśaḥ[49] [95]
devadravyāpahartāro gurudravyāpahārakāḥ
brahmahatyāyutaṁ pāpaṁ duṣkṛtaṁ bhuñjate narāḥ[50] [96]
viṣṇoḥ kathāṁ tu yaḥ śrutvā no dadāti narādhamaḥ
tasya karṇeṣu pātyante taptāyaḥkīlasañcayāḥ[51] [97]
tataḥ śateṣu chidreṣu tailam atyuṣṇam ulbaṇaṁ[52]
pūryate ca tataś cāpi kuṁbhīpākaṁ prapadyate[53] [98]
adātāṁ kopaparyantaṁ lavaṇaṁ bhuñjate hi te
tataś ca kalpaparyantaṁ purīṣaṁ bhuñjate dvijāḥ[54] [99]
yugaṁ tu rauravaṁ paścāt taptatailena bhojanaṁ[55]
brāhmaṇān ye nirīkṣyante kopadṛṣṭyā narādhamāḥ[56] [100]
tam aśucisahasraṁ tu teṣāṁ cakṣuṣi yujyate[57]
upavāsadine prāptau dantadhāvanakaṁ naraḥ[58] [101]
sughoraṁ narakaṁ yānti vyāghrajanma caturyugaṁ[59]

---

45 N10 - saṁsāram ulb(v)aṇam [asāram] avāpya janto.

46 N10 - viprāya dīyamāne tu yo vipraṁ kurute naraḥ.

47 N1/18.94a - apahṛtyā parasyārtha[ṁ] yaḥ parebhyaḥ prayacchati.

48 N1/18.95a - anyāyā(a)sādhitaṁ dravyaṁ prakhyānyasmai prayacchati.

49 N1/18.95b - sa dātā narakaṁ ghoraṁ narakān koṭikoṭiśaḥ.

50 N10 - brahmahatyāyutaśataṁ duṣ(ḥ)kṛtaṁ bhuñjate narāḥ.

51 N1/18.97b - tasya karṇeṣu pātyante t(n)apt(s)āyaḥkīlasañcayā(a)ḥ.

52 N10 - tataś ca teṣu chidreṣu tailam atyuṣṇam ulb(v)aṇaṁ.

53 Emendation - NK. N1/18.98b, N10 - pūry(j)ate ca tataś cāpi kuṁbhīpāk(y)aṁ prapadyate.

54 N10 - tataś ca kalpaparyantaṁ purīṣaṁ bhuñjate dvitāḥ.

55 N10 - y(m)u(r)gaṁ tu rauravaṁ paścāt taptasaikatabhojanaṁ.

56 N10 - brāhmaṇān ye nirīkṣante kopadṛṣṭā narādhamāḥ.

57 N1/18.101a, N10 - tam aś(s)uci(ī)sahasraṁ tu teṣāṁ cakṣuṣi yu(ū)jyate.

58 N1/18.101b - upavāsadine prāptau(e) dantadhāvanaka(i)ṁ naraḥ.

59 Emendation - DS. N1/18.101a - sughoraṁ narakaṁ yānti (N10 - vyāghrabhakṣ(j)a[ṁ] catury(ṣ)ugaṁ) vyāghraṁ bhurjacaturbhujaṁ.

ayonau ca viyonau ca paśuyonau ca ye naraḥ [102]
siktaretā mahāpāpī retobhañjanam āpnuyāt[60]
brahmahatyādipāpānāṁ kathañcin niṣkṛtir bhavet[61] [103]
brāhmaṇaṁ dveṣṭi yas tasya niṣkṛtir nāsti kutracit[62]
viśvāsaghātakānāṁ ca kṛtaghnānāṁ nareśvara[63] [104]
śūdrastrīsaṅgino caiva niṣkṛtir nāsti kutracit[64]
śūdrānnapuṣṭadehānāṁ vedanindāratātmanāṁ [105]
gurunindāparāṇāṁ vai niṣkṛtir naiva vidyate[65]
śivanindāparāṇāṁ ca viṣṇunindāparātmanāṁ [106]
satkathānindakānāṁ ca nehāmutra ca vidyate[66]
vṛttito jñānato vāpi dvijo bauddhālayaṁ viśet[67] [107]
jñātvā vai niṣkṛtir nāsti śāstrāṇām eṣa nirṇayaḥ
bauddhā pākhaṇḍinaḥ proktā yato vai vedanindakāḥ[68] [108]
kramukasyāpi haraṇaṁ yat peśaṁ candanasya ca[69]
kārpāsasya ca haraṇaṁ svarṇasteyasamaṁ smṛtaṁ [109]
tāmrapātrayutaṁ kāṁsyam ājyasya ca madhos tathā[70]
steyaṁ sugandhadravyāṇāṁ hemasteyasamaṁ smṛtaṁ [110]
rasadravyāpaharaṇaṁ dhānyānāṁ haraṇaṁ tathā[71]
rūdrākṣaharaṇaṁ caiva svarṇasteyasamaṁ smṛtaṁ [111]
bhaginīgamanaṁ caiva putrastrīgamanaṁ tathā
rajasvalābhigamanaṁ gurutalpasamaṁ smṛtaṁ [112]
akālakarmakaraṇaṁ parastrīgamanam eva[72]

---

60 N1/18.103a - sikta(ā)reto mahāpāpī retobhojanam āpnuyāt.

61 N1/18.103b, N10 - brahmahatyādipāpānāṁ kathañcin na kṛtir bhavet.

62 N1/18.104a - brāhmaṇaṁ dveṣṭitas (N10 - dveṣṭinyas) tasya niḥkṛti(ḥ)r nāsti kutracit.

63 N10 - viśvāsaghātakānāṁ ca kṛtaghnānāṁ nareśv(c)ara(ḥ).

64 N10 - śūdrastrīsaṅginā caiv(dyai)a ni[ṣ]kṛti(ḥ)r nāsti kutracit.

65 N10 - (pu)gurunindāparāṇaṁ ca niḥkṛtir naiva vidyate.

66 N1/18.107a - satkathānindakānāṁ ca nehāmutra ca nirvṛtiḥ.

67 Emendation - NK. N1/18.107b - jñānato 'jñānato vāpi dvijo (N10 - vṛtti[to] jñānato vāpi dvijair) b(v)auddhālayaṁ viśet.

68 N10 - b(v)auddhapāṣaṇḍinaḥ proktā yato vai vedanindakāḥ.

69 N10 - kramukasyāpi ha[ra]ṇaṁ ya[t] yasaś candanasya vā.

70 Emendation - DS. N1/18.110a - tāmrapātrayutaṁ kāṁsyaṁ nimajyasya madhos tathā. Verse 18.110a is missing in N10.

71 N10 - rasadravyā[pa]haraṇaṁ dhānyānāṁ haraṇaṁ tathā.

72 N1/113a, N10 - akālakarmakaraṇaṁ purīgamanam eva ca.

vedaśraddhāvihīnatvaṁ gurutalpāgamaṁ smṛtaṁ[73] [113]
paropakāraniratāḥ paradravyaparāṅmukhāḥ
napuṁsakāḥ parastrīṣu te vai bhāgavatāḥ smṛtāḥ[74] [114]
tulasyupāsanaratāḥ sadā nīraparāyaṇaḥ[75]
gorakṣaṇaratā ye ca te vai bhāgavatāḥ smṛtāḥ [115]
pratimānavihīnā ye parānnavimukhās tathā[76]
annodakapradātāras te vai bhāgavatāḥ smṛtāḥ [116]
puṇyatīrtharatā nityaṁ satsaṅgatiratās tathā
lokānugrahaśīlā ye te vai bhāgavatāḥ smṛtāḥ [117]
paropatāpavimukhāḥ śivārcanaparāyaṇāḥ
satkathāśravaṇāsaktās te vai bhāgavatāḥ smṛtāḥ [118]
sarvabhūteṣu yaḥ paśyed bhagavadbhāvam ātmanaḥ
bhūtāni bhagavaty ātmany eṣa bhāgavatottamaḥ [119]
īśvare tadadhīneṣu bāliśeṣu dviṣatsu ca
prema maitrī kṛpopekṣā yaḥ karoti sa madhyamaḥ[77] [120]
arcāyaṁ eva haraye pūjāṁ yaḥ śraddhayehate[78]
na tadbhakteṣu tnyeṣu sa bhaktaḥ prākṛtaḥ smṛtaḥ [121]
gṛhītvā 'pīndriyair arthān yo na dveṣṭi na hṛṣyati[79]
viṣṇor māyām idaṁ paśyan sa vai bhāgavatottamaḥ[80] [122]
dehendriyaprāṇamano 'dhiyāṁ
  yo janmāpya yakṣudraya tarṣa kṛcchraiḥ[81]
saṁsāradharmair ravimuhyamānaḥ smṛtyā
  harer bhāgavatapradhānaḥ [123]
na yasyaḥ janmakarmabhyāṁ
  na varṇāśramajātibhiḥ[82]

---

73 N10 - [ve]d(r)aśraddhāvihīnatvaṁ gurutalpāga(ḥ)[maṁ smṛtaṁ].

74 N10 - napuṁsakāḥ parastrīṣu tai vai bhāgavatā[ḥ] smṛtāḥ.

75 Emendation - DS. N1/18.115a, N10 - tulasyupāsanaratāḥ sadā nīpaparāyaṇaḥ.

76 Emendation - DS. N1/18.116b, N10 - pratimāhavihīnā ye parānnavimukhās tathā.

77 N10 - premamaitrīkṛpā(o)p(dy)ekṣā[ṁ] yaḥ karoti sa madhyamaḥ.

78 N1/18.121a - ārghyāyām eva haraye[t] pūjāṁ yaḥ (N10 - arghāyām eva haraye pūjāyaḥ) śraddha ye hate.

79 N10 - gṛhītvā pāndriyair arthān yo na dveṣṭi na hṛṣyati.

80 N10 - viṣṇo moyām idaṁ paśyan sa vai bhāgavatottamaḥ.

81 Verses 18.119-127 are extracted from Bhāgavata Purāṇa XI.2.49, 45-55. N10 - dehendriyaprāṇamano 'dhiyāṁ yo janmāpya yakṣudbhaya tarṣa kṛcchraiḥ.

82 N1/18.124a - na yaḥ svajanmakarmabhyāṁ (N10 - ca yasya janmakarmābhyāṁ) na varṇāśramajātibhiḥ.

sajjate 'smin nahaṁ bhāvo dehe vai
  sa hareḥ priyaḥ[83] [124]
na yasya svaḥ para iti
  vitteṣvātmani vā bhidā[84]
sarva bhūtasamaḥ śāntaḥ
  sa vai bhāgavatottamaḥ[85]
tribhuvanavibhava hetave 'py akuṇṭha smṛtir
  ajitātma surādibhir vimṛgyāt[86] [125]
na calati bhagavatpadāra vindāllavani
  miṣārdham api yaḥ sa vaiṣṇavāgryaḥ[87]
bhagavata uru vikramāṅghri śākhānākhamaṇi
  candrikayā nirastatāpe[88] [126]
hṛdi katham upasīdatāṁ punaḥ sa prabhavati
  candra ivodite 'kartāpaḥ[89]
visṛjati hṛdayaṁ na yasya sākṣād dharir
  avaśābhihito 'py aghau ghanāśaḥ[90]
praṇayaraśanayā dhṛtāṅghripadmaḥ sa bhavati
  bhāgavata pradhāna uktaḥ[91] [127]

---

83 N1/18.124b - sajje (N10 - sakṣe) tasmin nahaṁ bhāvo de[he] vai sa(ha) (N10 - hareḥ priyaḥ) haripriyaḥ.

84 N1/18.125a - ta yasya sva paradravya vitteṣṭātmani vā bhidā.
N10 - na yasyasvaḥ para iti vitteṣṭyātmani vā bhidā.

85 N1/18.125b - sarva bhūta sa mat śāṁsaḥ sa vai bhāgavato mepteḥ.
N10 - sarvva bhūgayāta na calati bhagavat pidāravindāṁ llavatamasaḥ śāntaḥ sa vai bhāgavatottamaḥ.

86 N1/18.125c - tribhuvanavibhava hetave 'py akuṇṭha smṛtim ātmasurādibhir (N10 - ātmasurādir) vimṛgyāt.

87 N1/18.126a, N10 - na yalati bhagavatyadāra vindāllavani miṣārdham api sa vaiṣṇavāgraḥ.

88 N1/18.126b - bhava hetaven (N10 - bhagavata) uru vikramāṅgri śāsānakhamaṇi candrika (N10 - yā nirastatā ye) yān nirastatāpe.

89 N1/18.127a - hṛdi katham upasīda yā (N10 - upasīdatāṁ) punaḥ sa prabhavati candraka ivodito 'kantā (N10 - candra ivoditerkatā) yaḥ.

90 N1/18.127b - visṛjati hṛdayaṁ nayasya sākṣād dharirayasābhi ha so 'py adhau ghanāśaḥ.
N10 - visṛjati hṛdaya nayasya sāc chariravas(ś)ābhi hitau 'py adhauc ca nārāḥ.

91 N1/18.127c, N10 - praṇayarasanayā dhṛtāṅghripadmaḥ sa bhavati bhāgavata pradhāna uktaḥ.

Appendix II

The Nāsiketa Story Manuscripts

A. Collected MSS copies

Nāśiketopākhyāna,	No. BD255/3, Town Hall Library Asiatic Society, Mumbai.
"	No. 3094, Mumbai University Library, G.S. Nirantar Collection.
"	No. 3988, " " ".
"	No. C100(4), Oxford University MSS Collection.
"	No. C108(4), " " " ".
"	No. C127(2), " " " ".
"	No. 147, The Bhandarkar Institute, Pune.
"	No. 377, " " " ".
"	No. 3713, Pune University Library.
"	No. 3955, The Oriental Institute, Vadodara
"	No. 14859, MSS Government Collection Sanskrit University, Varanasi.
"	No. 14456, " " " " ".
"	No. 14777, " " " " "
"	No. 14956, " " " " ".
Nāciketopākhyāna,	No. 15784, " " " " ".
Nāciketopākhyānaṁ,	No. 72302, " " " " ".
"	No. MS. San. Sham. 109, Göttingen University, Germany.
Nāsiketopākhyānaṁ,	No. 11639, Oriental Research Institute, Jodhpur.
"	No. 12479, " " " ".
"	No. 12646, " " " ".
"	No. 13892, " " " ".
"	No. 15226, " " " ".
"	No. 15528, " " " ".
"	No. 16437, " " " ".
"	No. 17093, " " " ".
"	No. 115761, Punjab University Library, Patiala.
"	No. 1707, " " " ".
"	No. 3551, Raghunatha Temple, Jammu.

B. Other viewed MSS

Nāsiketopākhyānaṁ, No. 233, Scindhiya Oriental Institute, Ujjain.
" No. 4326, " " " ".
" No. 4422, " " " ".
" No. 4610, " " " ".
" No. 14919, " " " ".
" No. 3855, Raghunatha Temple, Jammu.
" No. 15491, MSS Government Collection Sanskrit University, Varanasi.
" No. 15661, " " " " ".
" No. 15662, " " " " ".
" No. 15835, " " " " ".
Nāsiketupākhyāna, No. 11688, The Oriental Institute, Vadodara.
" No. 17, Sri Dwarkadhis Sanskrit Academy, Dwarka.
" No. 5511/677, The Oriental Research Institute, Kotah.
Nāśiketopākhyāna, No. 8476.93, " " " " ".
Nāsiketopākhyāna, No. 1690, Leipzig University Library, Germany.
Itihāsa Samuccaya Nāsiketopākhyāna, No. 7192, Leipzig University Library.

Appendix III

Methodological Notes

1. The text

This text aims at providing a comprehensive critical edition of the Nāsiketa story in Sanskrit, accompanied by an English translation[1]. It is based on N1 which is longer, and richer than most of the other texts, representing a specific late developmental branch of the story, probably North-Western. An effort has been made to adhere as much as possible to the original N1 MS, reconstructing it with the aid of other texts of the same developmental branch – the "family"[2]. It has also been compared to other typical MSS, and to the printed versions of the story. Scriptures of the Viṣṇu lore, when used by N1, have been quoted from their sources.

2. The "family"

N1 – No. BD255/3 in the MSS collection of the Town Hall Library in Mumbai[3], formerly at the Bhau Daji collection in the city. It has probably been copied from another source, in small, beautiful, generally clear handwriting, with many Sandhi irregularities and other mistakes. Some paragraphs and verses are misplaced, and some are meaningless, as copied.

N2 – No. 72302 in the Government MSS collection of the Sanskrit University at Varanasi. It suffers from fewer mistakes than N1, but is very blurred in large parts and is hard to read. Some of the pages are damaged at the edge, cutting off parts of the verses.

N3 – No. 3713 in the Pune University MSS collection, is written in clear handwriting and reasonable Sanskrit in most parts. The last page, with the concluding verses, is missing[4].

---

1 It is the first translation of a Sanskrit version into English. The other English translations are Nāsiket Ākhyan (1892) translated from Hindi and Krause's English translation from Rājasthāni (Krause 1924).

2 Karte (1954), p. 39.

3 Mumbai Town Hall Library is the Asiatic Society of Bombay Library.

4 Ends in a verse parallel to 18.55a in our text.

N7 – No. 145 in the MSS collection of the Bhaṇdarkar Institute, at Pune, is written in big and quite clear handwriting, with a great affinity to N2. Since there is an abundance of mistakes and meaningless verses, as well as missing verses, it has not been fully reconstructed and its verses are cited sporadically.

N10 – No. 14777 in the Government MSS collection of the Sanskrit University at Varanasi, is most similar to N1, written in a clear handwriting.

N11 – No. C127(2) in the Oxford Chandra Shum Shere MSS collection, is very similar to N1 and seems to be copied from the same source, but less carefully. It is incomplete, ending at chapter 6.

3. Printed texts

BF – Belloni-Filippi's work[5] is the only previous critical edition of **Nāsiketopākhyāna**, based on two almost identical MSS of the British Museum Library collection[6]. It has been the only translation of a Sanskrit version of the story into a European language – Italian. The text is very reliable, but incomplete, since the editor has omitted many paragraphs.

Ra – The Nāsiketagrantha (1930) is a printed form of the annotated text No. 3855 in the MSS collection of the Raghunātha temple in Jammu, which is identical to the not annotated MS No. 3551 in the same collection. Great similarity has been found between this text and N4 and N8.

Bo – Nāsiketopākhyāna (1945) shows almost no linguistic similarity to the present text, but is referred to since it is one of the few published texts.

VP – Varāha Purāṇa, being the base for the descriptions of Nāsiketa's visit in Hell, has been referred to in several cases.

Bhāgavata Purāṇa (BP) and **Viṣṇu Purāṇa (ViṣP)** have been quoted either in the text itself or in the apparatus, in cases where Stotras from them have been inserted into N1.

---

5 Belloni-Filippi (1902-4).

6 Another almost identical MS is No. 377 in the MSS collection of the Bhandarkar Institute, Pune.

4. "External" MSS

N4 – No.1489 in the Government MSS collection of the Sanskrit University at Varanasi, has been found to be almost identical to N8 and Ra. It has been chosen for the apparatus because of its antiquity – though not dated, there are many external signs identifying it as a very old MS.

N8 – No. 11639 in the Rājasthān MSS collection of the Oriental Research Institute at Jodhpur, is almost identical to N4 and Ra. It has been chosen as representing a large number of MSS collected in Rājasthān[7]. It is unique in its numbering system – a change every hundred verses, in most cases, regardless of the changing chapters.

5. The apparatus

Examining the "family" – all the found texts of this textual tradition – the apparatus fully conserves meaningful variations of the verses according to critical philology, and ignores others, like copying mistakes, grammatical mistakes, etc. Phonological variations, lexical and morphological variations, are fully preserved, as well as dialectical forms – local linguistic developments. For example "*mapūṣam*" replacing the original "*mañjūṣam*"[8] in N1, and the derivations of "*mapūṣam*" in the later N10, N11 texts.

Identical verses of the "family" are not quoted separately, unlike identical verses from external sources, which are fully cited in order to show their affinity to the text.

Half verses have been compared, and not *pāda*s as usual, since it seems to be more meaningful, considering the great variations among the texts.

In most cases only parallel verses have been quoted. Unparalleled verses from external sources were brought only for the sake of reconstructing the text, and in special cases, as a meaningful addition to the N1 text.

When a word is wrongly written in the source, the wrong letter is preserved in parentheses ( ).

---

7 Appendix II.

8 Verses 3.31, 3.37, 3.39.

When a syllable, word, or paragraph, are missing or wrong, the proposed alternative appears in square brackets [ ].

Blurred or missing syllables and words are brought as hyphens in parentheses (- -).

When missing parts are cited as missing in the source itself, they are brought as hyphens without parentheses - - -.

Clearly written but unintelligible and undecipherable words or paragraphs are brought as consecutive dots – . . . .

Redundancy in a verse – *vipuḷa* – is pointed out as (vi), whereas an unconventionally short verse is pointed out as (short).

Appendix IV

Scheme of Transliteration

अ a	आ ā	इ i	ई ī	
उ u	ऊ ū	ऋ ṛ	ॠ ṝ	
ऌ ḷ	ॡ ḹ	ए e	ऐ ai	
ओ o	औ au	अं aṁ	अः aḥ	
क ka	ख kha	ग ga	घ gha	ङ ṅa
च ca	छ cha	ज ja	झ jha	ञ ña
ट ṭa	ठ ṭha	ड ḍa	ढ ḍha	ण ṇa
त ta	थ tha	द da	ध dha	न na
प pa	फ pha	ब ba	भ bha	म ma
य ya	र ra	ल la	व va	
श śa	ष ṣa	स sa	ह ha	

References

Agni Purāṇa. (N. Gangadharan, trans.)
Ancient Indian Traditions & Mythology. (G. P. Bhatt, ed.) Vol. 40.
Delhi: Motilal Banarsidass, 1987.

Agnipurāṇaṁ.
Poona: Anandasrama Sanskrit Series, 1957. Vol 41.

Belloni-Filippi, F. – "Nāsiketopākhyānam".
Giornalle della Societa Asiatica Italiana. Vols.: XV, (1902), pp. 27-77; XVI, (1903), pp. 33-88, 229-255; XVII, (1904), pp. 113-153, 273-294.

Biardeau, M. et Malmoud, C. – **Le Sacrifice dans l'Inde Ancienne.**
Section de Sciences Religieuses. Vol. LXXIX.
Paris: Presse Universitaire de Hautes Etudes, 1976.

Brahma Purāṇa.
Ancient Indian Traditions & Mythology. (G. P. Bhatt, ed.). Vol. 36.
Delhi: Motilal Banarsidass, 1986.

Coomaraswamy, A.K. – "Notes on the Katha Upanishad".
New Indian Antiquary. No. 1, (1938), pp. 43-56.

Dowson, J. – **A Classical Dictionary of Hindu Mythology & Religion, Geography, History & Literature.**
London: Routledge & Kegan Paul Ltd., 1961.

Easwaran, E. – **The Upanishads**.
London: Arkana, 1987.

Eliade, M. – "Mythology of Death: An Introduction".
in: Reynolds, F.E. & Waugh, E.H. (ed.) – **Religious Encounters with Death.**
The Pennsylvania State University Press, 1977, pp. 13-23.

Eliade, M. – **Yoga – Immortality and Freedom.**
London: Routledge & Kegan Paul, 1958.

Filippi, G.G. – **Dialogo di Naciketas con la Morte**.
Venezia: Libreria Editrice Cafoscarina, 2001.

Filippi, G.G. – **Mṛtyu - Concept of Death in Indian Traditions.**
New Delhi: D. K. Print World (P) Ltd., 1996.

Ghimire, K.P.S. – **Naciketasam.**
Varanasi: Shrikrishna Granthamala Prakashana, 1975.

Grinshpon, Y. – **Crisis and Knowledge: The Upanishadic Experience and Storytelling.**
New Delhi: Oxford University Press, 2003.

Gupta, A.S. (ed. & trans.) – **The Varāha Purāṇa.**
Varanasi: All-India Kashiraj Trust, 1981.

Helfer, J.S. – "The Initiatory Structure of the Kaṭhopaniṣad".
History of Religions. Vol. 7, (1967-8), pp. 348-67.

Iyer, V. S. M. – **Brahmarishi Nachiketas.**
Translation from Tamil – Subramanian, K. N.
Krishnapuram: Sri Vembaiyer Sasvatha Dhama Sasanam, 1981.

Kaelber, W. O. – "The 'Dramatic' Element in Brahmanic Initiation: Symbols of Death, Danger & Difficult Passage".
History of Religions. Vol. 18, No. 1, (1978), pp. 54-76.

Karte, S.M. – **Introduction to Indian Textual Criticism.**
Poona: Deccan College, 1954.

Kaṭha Upaniṣad. (R. H. Pelly, trans.)
Calcutta: Association Press, 1924.

Kaṭhakopaniṣad. (M. Hiriyanna, trans.)
(With the commentary of Śaṅkarācarya).
Srirangam: Sri Vani Vilas Press, 1915.

Kaṭhopaniṣad. (Śarvānanda, Swami, trans.)
Mylapore & Madras: Sri Ramakrishna Math, 1962.

Kaṭhopaniṣad. (S. C. Vasu, trans.)
Allahabad: Allahabad Press, 1905.

Krause, C. – "Nāsaketari Katha, an Old Rajasthani Tale".
Asia Major. Vol. 1, (1924), pp. 347-427.

Lévi-Strauss, C. – **Structural Anthropology II.**
Chicago: The University of Chicago Press, 1983.

The Mahābhārata. (SR – Southern Recension)
Madras: V. Ramaswamy Satrulu & Sons, 1935.

Merh, K. P. – **Yama – The Glorious Lord of the Other World.**
Reconstructing Indian History & Culture. No. 12.
New Delhi: D. K. Print World (P) Ltd., 1996.

Monier-Williams, M. – **Sanskrit-English Dictionary.**
Delhi: Motilal Banarsidas, 1993.

The Nāsiket Ākhyan or The Journey of Nāsiket to the Realms of the Dead.
(trans. – Raghunathaji, K.)
Bombay: 1892.

Nāsiketagrantha.
Gaṅgārāma Jīne, 1930.

Nāsiketopākhyāna.
Mumbai: Śrī Veṅkaṭeśvara Press, 1945.

Nevo, A. – **The Boy who Returned from Death: The Naciketa Story in Sanskrit Literature.**
Jerusalem: 2003. Ph.D. dissertation (Hebrew).

Nevo, A – "Naciketas the 'Good Boy' – Is He?"
Purāṇa. Vol. XLVII, 1, (2005), pp. 4-18.

Oldenberg, H. – **Ṛgveda.**
Berlin: Weiđmanche Buchhandlung, 1912.

Panda, G. – "Bhāratīya Ākhyāna Paraṁparā Aura Naciketopākhyāna". (Hindi).
Madhya Bharati, Research Journal of Dr. Harisingh Gour University. No. 45, (1998), pp. 5-8.

Raja, K. K. (ed.) – **The New Catalogus Catalogorum.**
Madras: University of Madras, 1997/8. Vols. 10, 11.

Ramaswami, S. – "Naciketas".
The Adyar Library Bulletin. Vol. 60, (1966), pp. 261–65.

Rawson, J.N. – **The Kaṭha Upaniṣad.**
London: Oxford University Press, 1934.

Sahi, J. – **The Child and the Serpent.**
London: Routledge & Kegan Paul, 1980.

Shankaracharya – **The Upanishadbhashya.**
Works of Shankaracharya in Original Sanskrit. (H. R. Bhagavat, ed.). Poona: Ashtekar & Co., 1927. Vol. II, part I.

Sharma, S.S.P. – **Amṛta Manthanaṁ Mahākāvyaṁ.**
Sarvodaya press.

Shulman, D. – **The Hungry God – Hindu Tales of Filicide & Devotion.**
Chicago: University of Chicago Press, 1993.

Śivaram, M. – **Death and Nachiketas.**
Bangalore: Vikas Publishing House. PVT Ltd., 1981.

Śrīmadbhāgavata.
Bombay: Pandurang Jawaji, 1929.

Toporov, V. – "The Episteme of Knowledge and the Myth about Immortality".
Elementa. Vol. 1, (1994), pp. 331-52.

Upadhyaya, B. – "Nāsiketopākhyānamulasya Naciketopakhyānasya Vedetihāsa Purāṇeṣu Vikasa".
Purāṇa. Vol. 6 (1964), No. 2, pp. 391-410.

Varāha Purāṇa. (V.S. Iyer, trans.)
Ancient Indian Traditions & Mythology. (G. P. Bhatt, ed.). Vol. 32. Delhi: Motilal Banarsidas, 1985.

Wadhawani, Y.K. – "A Semantic Study of the Term 'Naciketas'".

Journal of the University of Poona. Humanistic Section, No. 37, (1972), pp. 33-6.

Wadhawani, Y.K. – "Implications of the Vedic Term Naciketas". *Vishveshvarananda Indological Journal.* No. 11, (1973), pp. 19-23.

Wilson, H.H. – **Works – The Viṣṇu Purāṇa.** (Vol. 1). London: Trubner & Co., 1864.

Zaehner, R.C. – **Hinduism.** London: Oxford University Press, 1962.